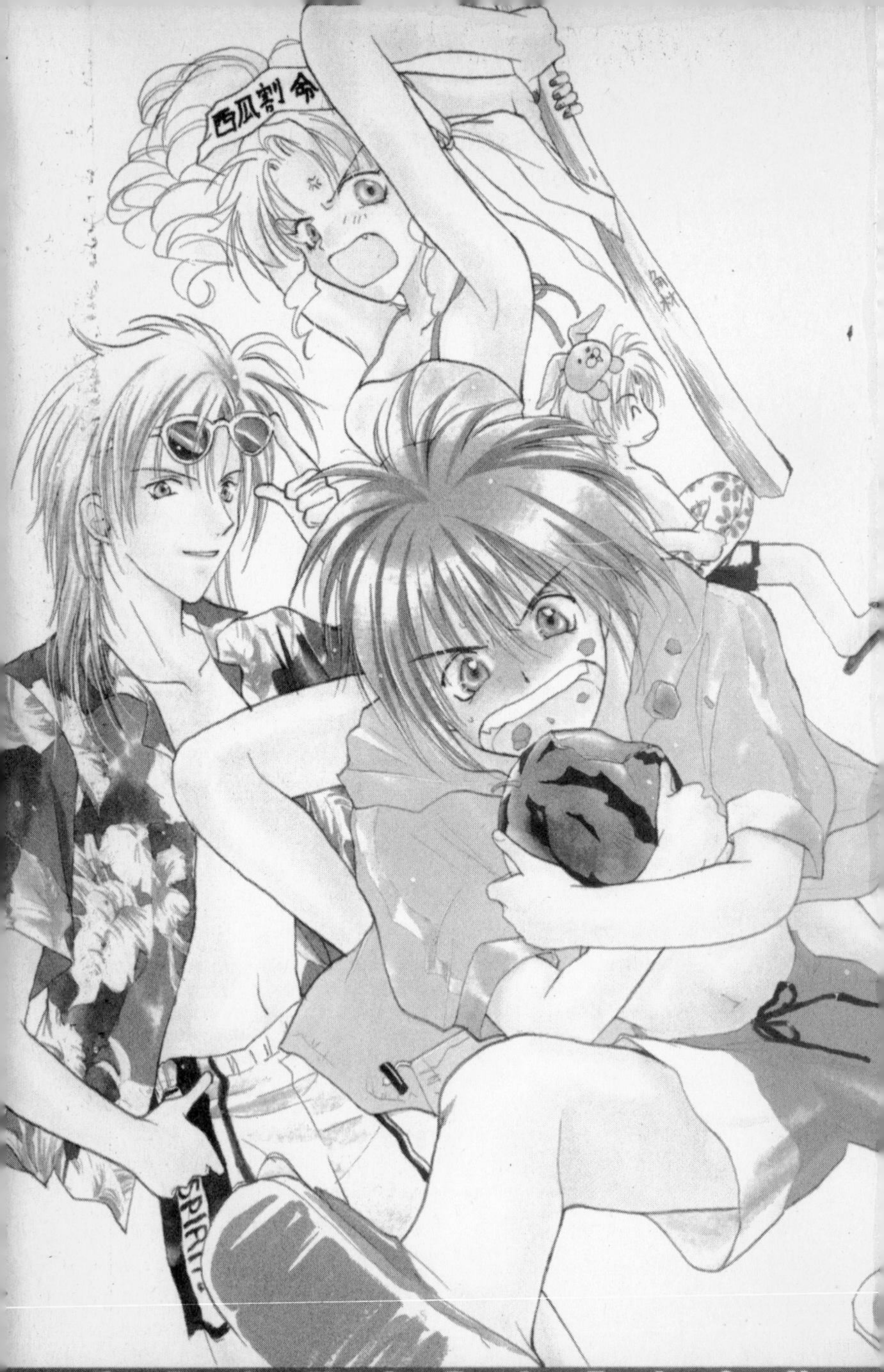
西瓜割命
SPIRIT

GRAVITATION

Gravitation Vol. 7
Created by Maki Murakami

Translation - Ray Yoshimoto
English Adaptation - Jamie S. Rich
Copy Editor - Carrisa Knight
Retouch and Lettering - Riho Sakai
Production Artists - James Lee and Vicente Rivera, Jr.
Cover Design - Raymond Makowski

Editor - Paul Morrissey
Digital Imaging Manager - Chris Buford
Pre-Press Manager - Antonio DePietro
Production Managers - Jennifer Miller and Mutsumi Miyazaki
Art Director - Matt Alford
Managing Editor - Jill Freshney
VP of Production - Ron Klamert
President and C.O.O. - John Parker
Publisher and C.E.O. - Stuart Levy

A 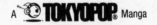 Manga

TOKYOPOP Inc.
5900 Wilshire Blvd. Suite 2000
Los Angeles, CA 90036

E-mail: info@TOKYOPOP.com
Come visit us online at www.TOKYOPOP.com

ISBN: 1-59182-339-0

First TOKYOPOP printing: August 2004
10 9 8 7 6 5 4
Printed in the USA

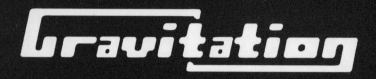

Volume 7

By
Maki Murakami

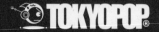

HAMBURG // LONDON // LOS ANGELES // TOKYO

CONTENTS

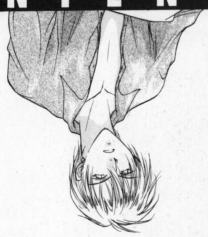

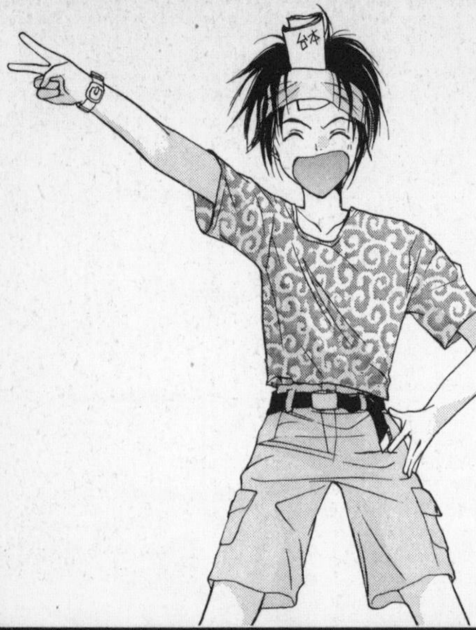
台本

GRAVITATION

THE MEMBERS OF THE GRAVITATION BAND

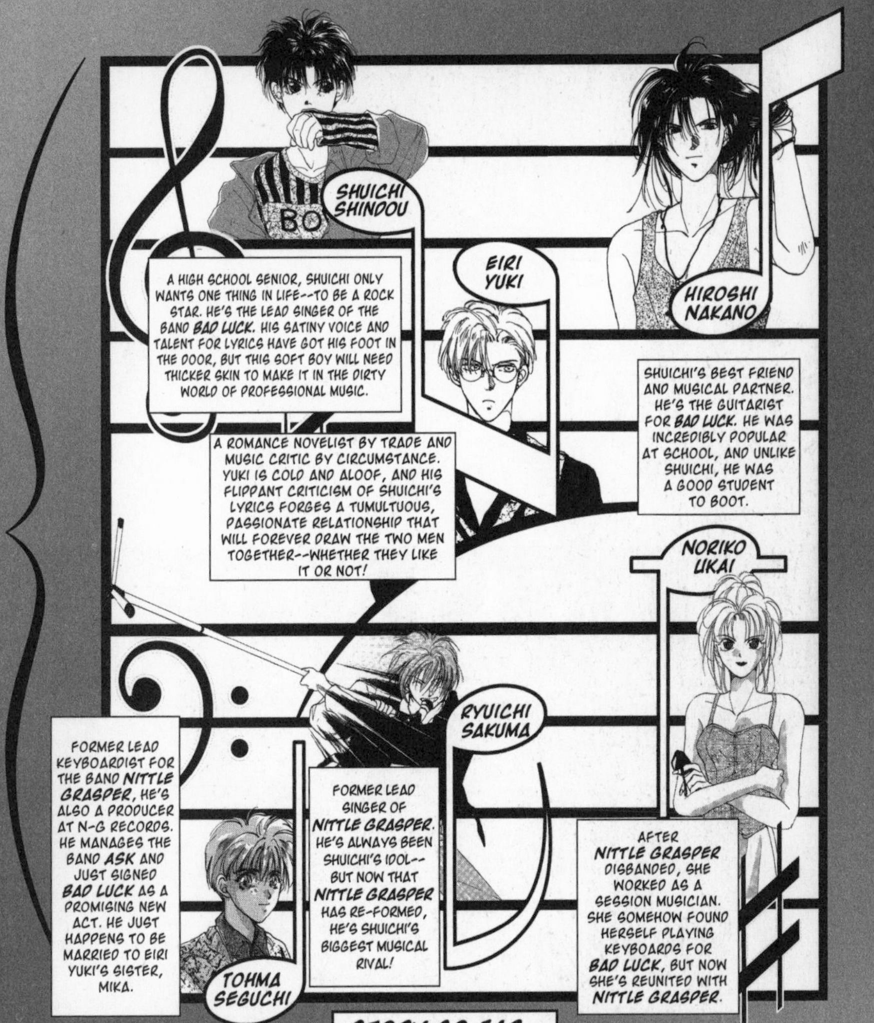

HIROSHI NAKANO
SHUICHI'S BEST FRIEND AND MUSICAL PARTNER. HE'S THE GUITARIST FOR BAD LUCK. HE WAS INCREDIBLY POPULAR AT SCHOOL, AND UNLIKE SHUICHI, HE WAS A GOOD STUDENT TO BOOT.
EIRI YUKI
A ROMANCE NOVELIST BY TRADE AND MUSIC CRITIC BY CIRCUMSTANCE. YUKI IS COLD AND ALOOF, AND HIS FLIPPANT CRITICISM OF SHUICHI'S LYRICS FORGES A TUMULTUOUS, PASSIONATE RELATIONSHIP THAT WILL FOREVER DRAW THE TWO MEN TOGETHER--WHETHER THEY LIKE IT OR NOT!
SHUICHI SHINDOU
A HIGH SCHOOL SENIOR, SHUICHI ONLY WANTS ONE THING IN LIFE--TO BE A ROCK STAR. HE'S THE LEAD SINGER OF THE BAND BAD LUCK. HIS SATINY VOICE AND TALENT FOR LYRICS HAVE GOT HIS FOOT IN THE DOOR, BUT THIS SOFT BOY WILL NEED THICKER SKIN TO MAKE IT IN THE DIRTY WORLD OF PROFESSIONAL MUSIC.
BO
NORIKO UKAI
AFTER NITTLE GRASPER DISBANDED, SHE WORKED AS A SESSION MUSICIAN. SHE SOMEHOW FOUND HERSELF PLAYING KEYBOARDS FOR BAD LUCK, BUT NOW SHE'S REUNITED WITH NITTLE GRASPER.
RYUICHI SAKUMA
FORMER LEAD SINGER OF NITTLE GRASPER. HE'S ALWAYS BEEN SHUICHI'S IDOL--BUT NOW THAT NITTLE GRASPER HAS RE-FORMED, HE'S SHUICHI'S BIGGEST MUSICAL RIVAL!
TOHMA SEGUCHI
FORMER LEAD KEYBOARDIST FOR THE BAND NITTLE GRASPER, HE'S ALSO A PRODUCER AT N-G RECORDS. HE MANAGES THE BAND ASK AND JUST SIGNED BAD LUCK AS A PROMISING NEW ACT. HE JUST HAPPENS TO BE MARRIED TO EIRI YUKI'S SISTER, MIKA.

STORY SO FAR...

SHUICHI SHINDOU IS DETERMINED TO BE A ROCK STAR...AND HE'S OFF TO A BLAZING START! HIS BAND, BAD LUCK, HAS JUST BEEN SIGNED TO THE N-G RECORD LABEL, AND THEIR FIRST SINGLE IS BURNING UP THE CHARTS! WITH THE ADDITION OF HIS NEW MANAGER--THE GUN-TOTING AMERICAN MANIAC NAMED "K"--SHUICHI IS POISED TO TAKE THE WORLD HOSTAGE! BUT THINGS ARE THROWN INTO DISACCORD WHEN THE LEGENDARY BAND NITTLE GRASPER ANNOUNCES THEY ARE REUNITING! NOW SHUICHI WILL HAVE TO GO HEAD-TO-HEAD WITH HIS IDOL, RYUICHI SAKUMA. ALL THE WHILE, SHUICHI IS DESPERATE TO KEEP HIS ROLLER-COASTER RELATIONSHIP WITH THE MYSTERIOUS WRITER EIRI YUKI AFLAME. BUT THEIR SECRET ROMANCE HAS HIT A FEW JARRING NOTES, PROVING THAT LOVE ISN'T ALWAYS HARMONIOUS. CONFRONTED BY A VORACIOUS PACK OF REPORTERS, YUKI SURPRISINGLY ADMITS TO A SHOCKED WORLD THAT HE AND SHUICHI ARE INDEED LOVERS! WILL THE ENSUING SCANDAL BE TOO HOT FOR EVERYONE TO HANDLE? CAN SHUICHI PREVENT HIS CAREER FROM SPIRALING INTO A BLACK HOLE? ARE SHUICHI AND YUKI DESTINED TO DRIFT APART, OR WILL THEY REMAIN INEXORABLY INTERTWINED, HELD TOGETHER BY A FORCE AS STRONG AS GRAVITY?

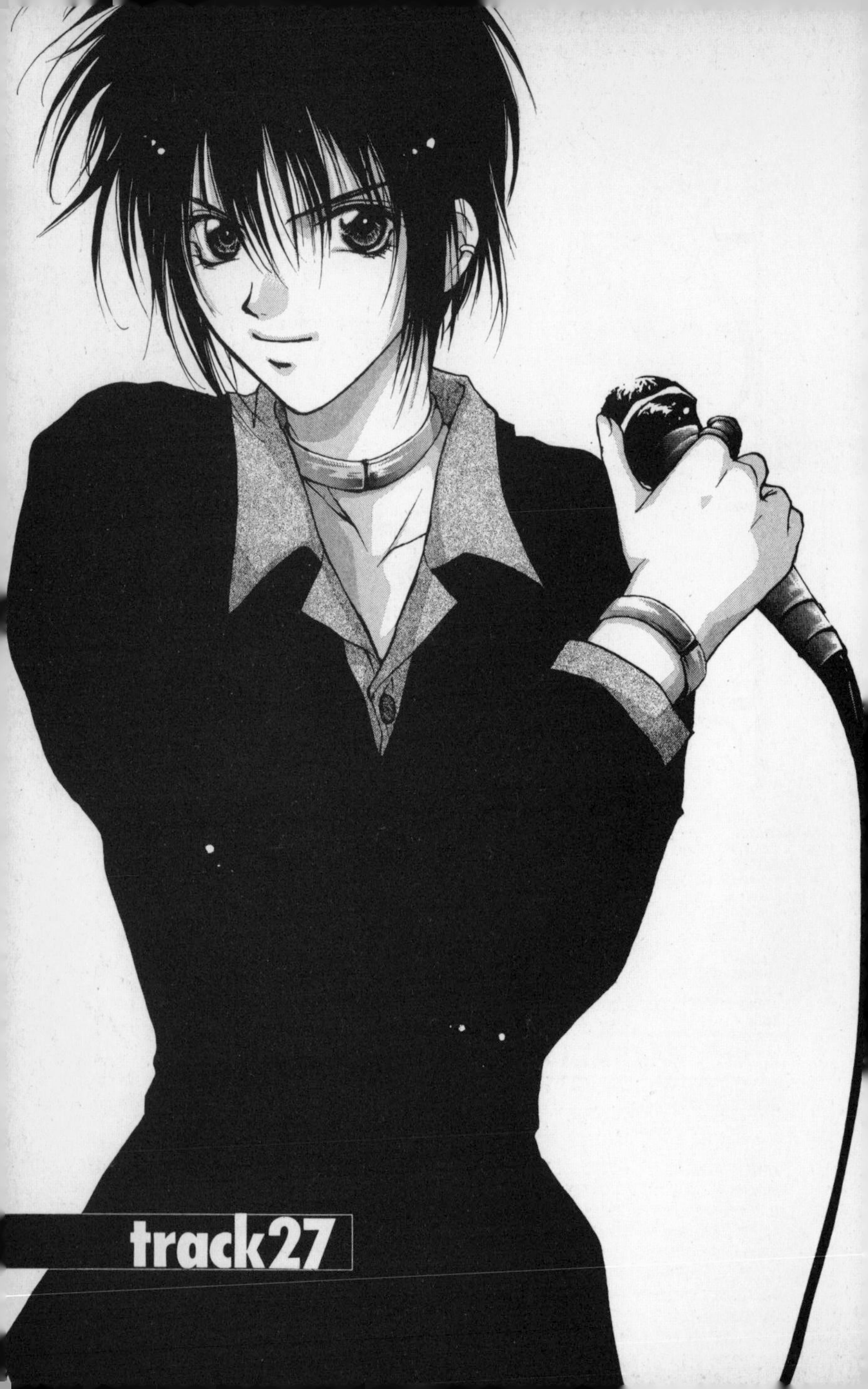
track27

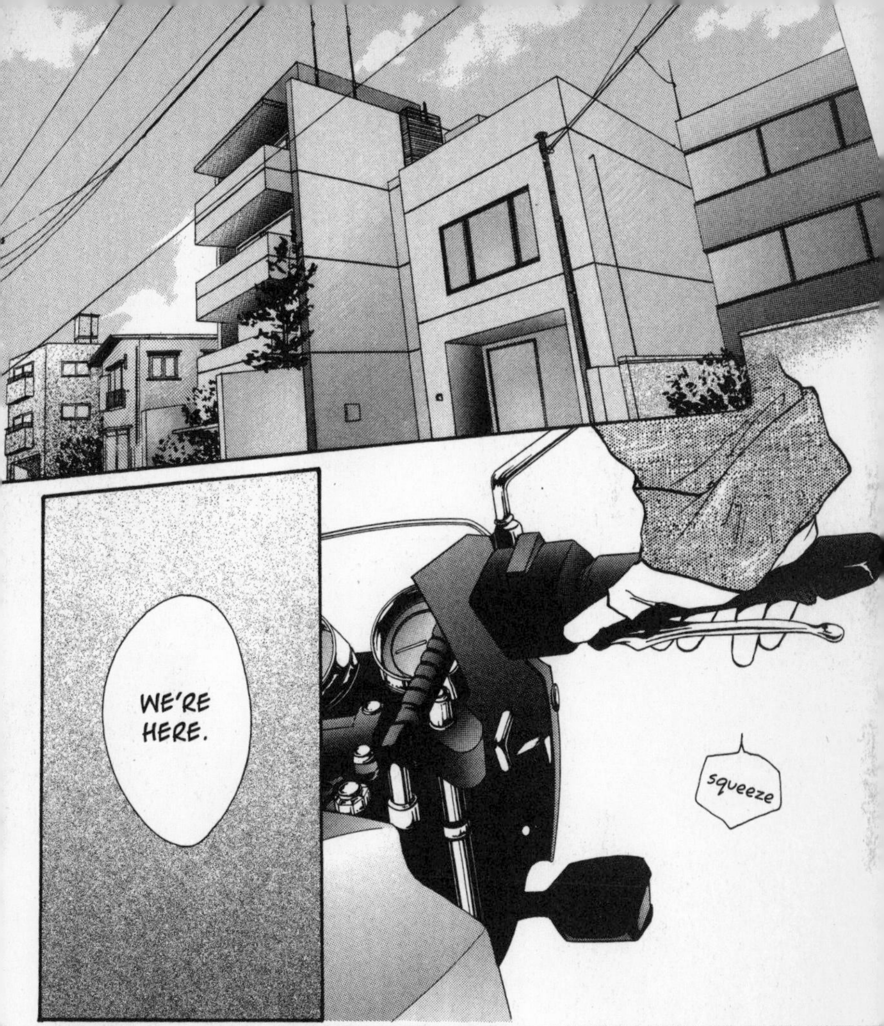
squeeze
WE'RE HERE.

ABOUT GRAVITATION TRACK 27

Let's see...what can I say about Track 27...? Oh, by the way, long time no see, everybody! Thanks for remaining loyal, my dear readers. Thanks to you, *Gravitation* has now reached Volume 7. As you well know, it's a strange manga, but I hope you continue reading it to the end. In this chapter, I've taken to drawing eyeballs in a rather peculiar way. Somehow, it doesn't match with my usual style. Since this new method takes a large amount of time anyway, after chapter 27, I've reverted to a more vague style of rendering eyes. I guess I don't have much perseverance. Speaking of not matching, I use a lot of tone and shading that doesn't seem to match, but I can't compromise on this point. If I don't use gray tones, it would get ugly. My assistants are cutting their lives short on the shading alone, but I intend to keep doing it. Keep up the good work, team!

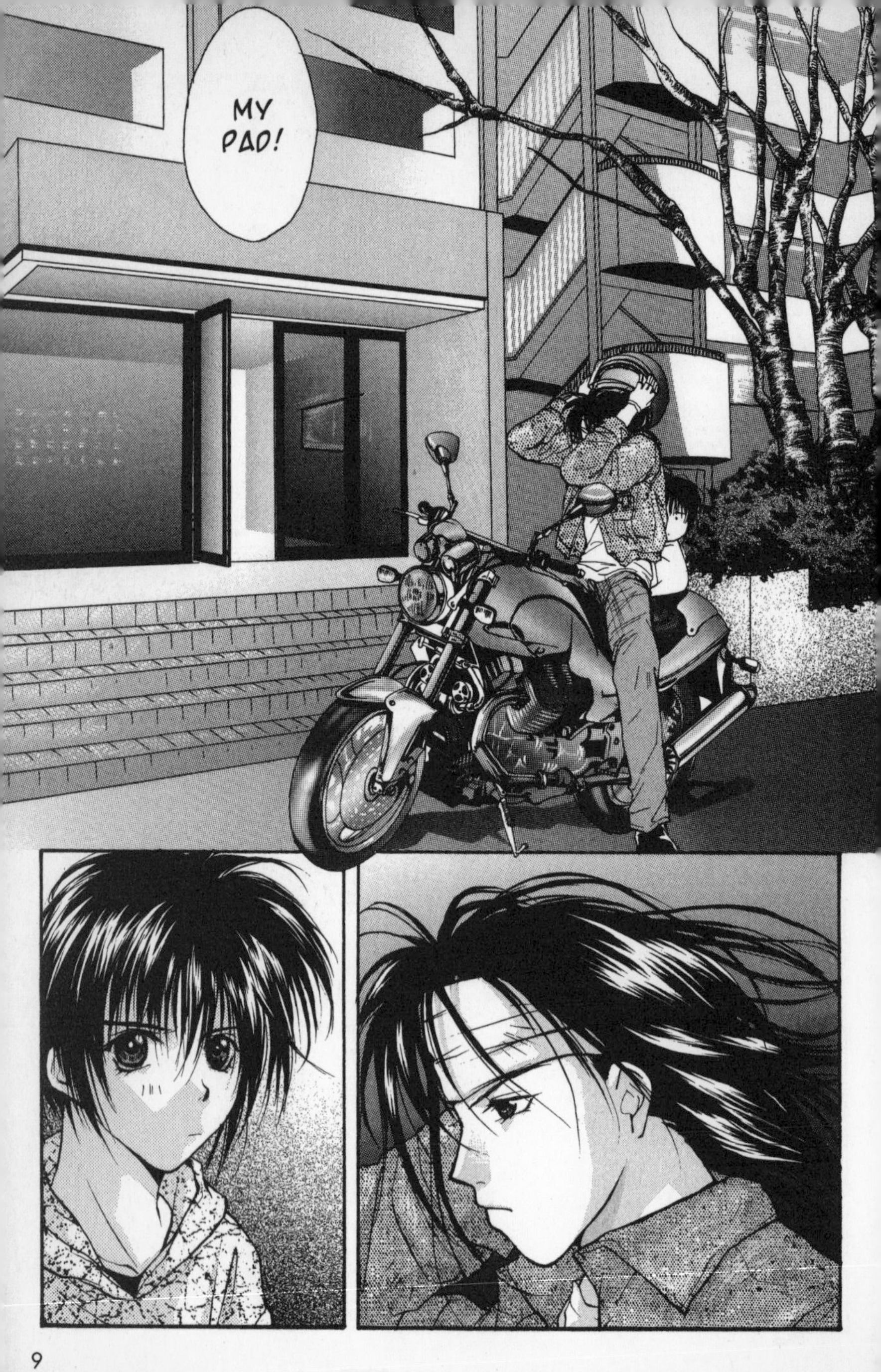
MY DAD!

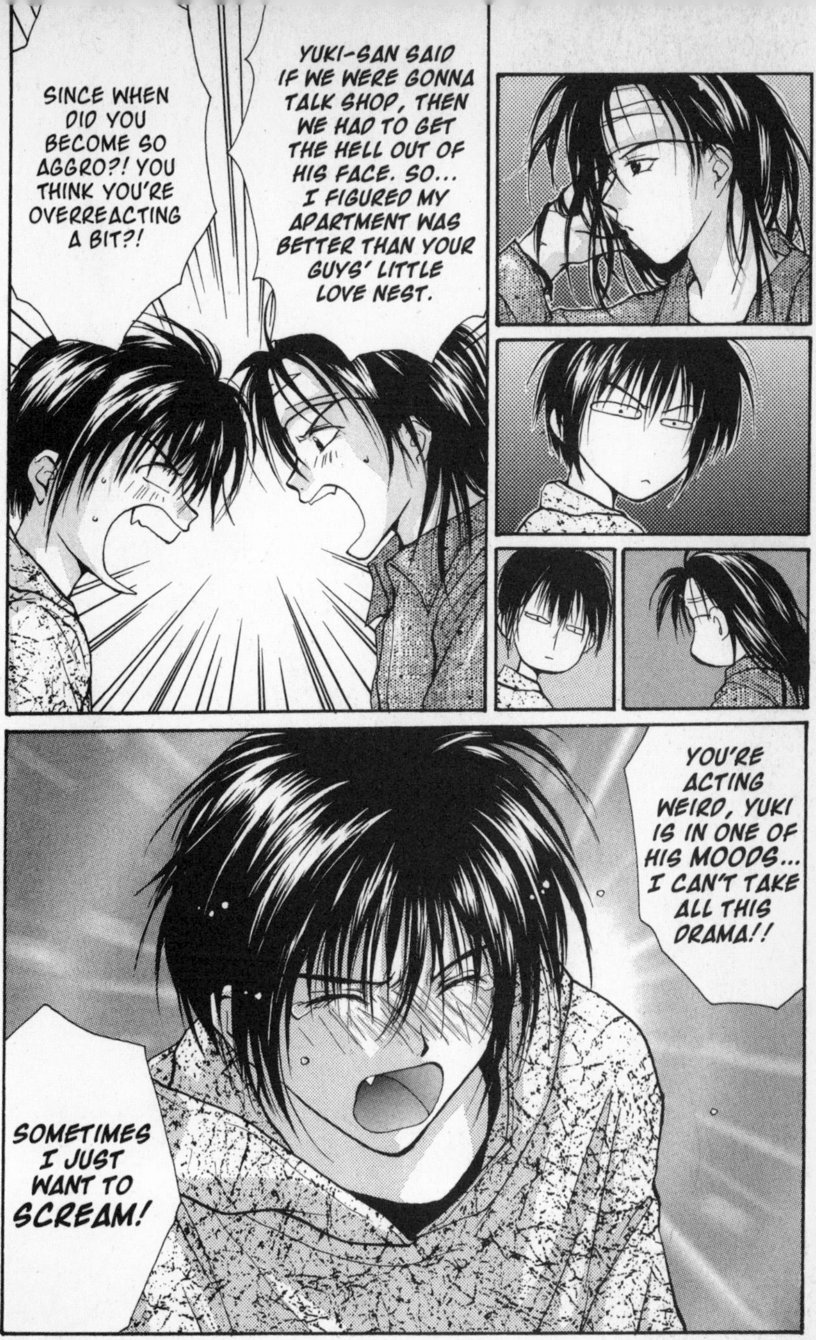
YUKI-SAN SAID IF WE WERE GONNA TALK SHOP, THEN WE HAD TO GET THE HELL OUT OF HIS FACE. SO... I FIGURED MY APARTMENT WAS BETTER THAN YOUR GUYS' LITTLE LOVE NEST.
SINCE WHEN DID YOU BECOME SO AGGRO?! YOU THINK YOU'RE OVERREACTING A BIT?!
YOU'RE ACTING WEIRD, YUKI IS IN ONE OF HIS MOODS... I CAN'T TAKE ALL THIS DRAMA!!
SOMETIMES I JUST WANT TO SCREAM!

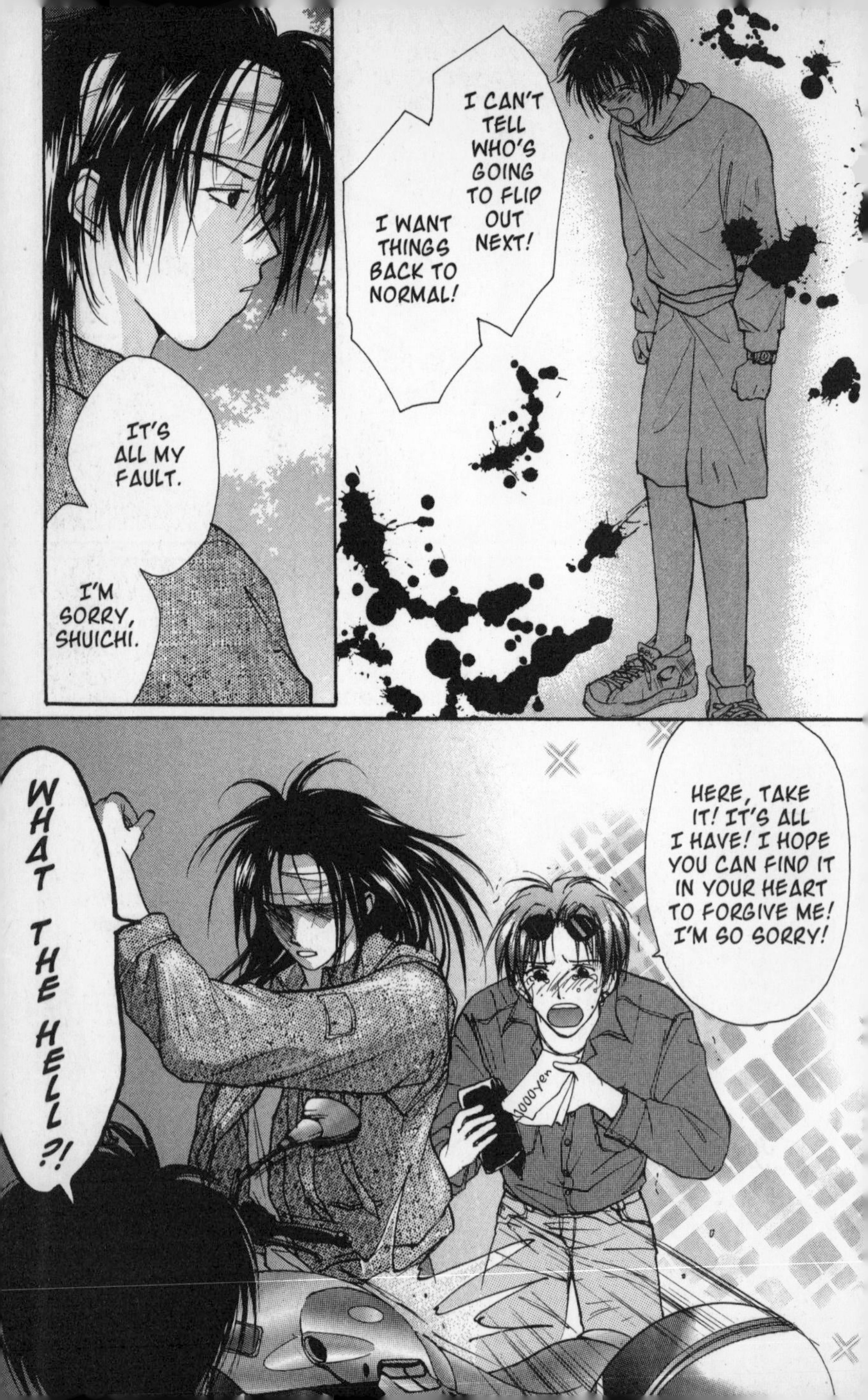
I CAN'T TELL WHO'S GOING TO FLIP OUT NEXT!
I WANT THINGS BACK TO NORMAL!
IT'S ALL MY FAULT.
I'M SORRY, SHUICHI.
HERE, TAKE IT! IT'S ALL I HAVE! I HOPE YOU CAN FIND IT IN YOUR HEART TO FORGIVE ME! I'M SO SORRY!
WHAT THE HELL?!

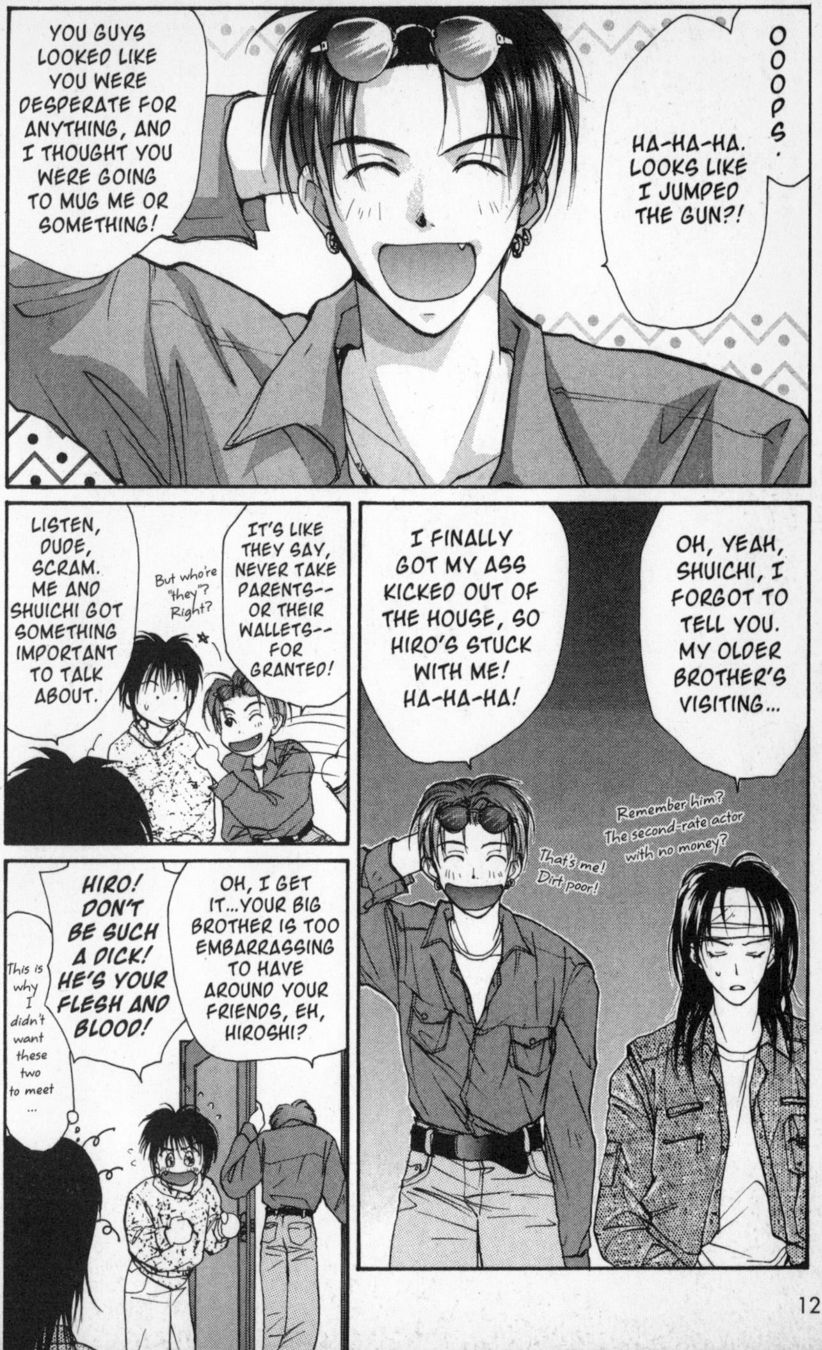
OOOPS.
HA-HA-HA. LOOKS LIKE I JUMPED THE GUN?!
YOU GUYS LOOKED LIKE YOU WERE DESPERATE FOR ANYTHING, AND I THOUGHT YOU WERE GOING TO MUG ME OR SOMETHING!
OH, YEAH, SHUICHI, I FORGOT TO TELL YOU. MY OLDER BROTHER'S VISITING...
I FINALLY GOT MY ASS KICKED OUT OF THE HOUSE, SO HIRO'S STUCK WITH ME! HA-HA-HA!
Remember him? The second-rate actor with no money?
That's me! Dirt poor!
IT'S LIKE THEY SAY, NEVER TAKE PARENTS--OR THEIR WALLETS--FOR GRANTED!
But who're "they"? Right?
LISTEN, DUDE, SCRAM. ME AND SHUICHI GOT SOMETHING IMPORTANT TO TALK ABOUT.
OH, I GET IT...YOUR BIG BROTHER IS TOO EMBARRASSING TO HAVE AROUND YOUR FRIENDS, EH, HIROSHI?
HIRO! DON'T BE SUCH A DICK! HE'S YOUR FLESH AND BLOOD!
This is why I didn't want these two to meet ...

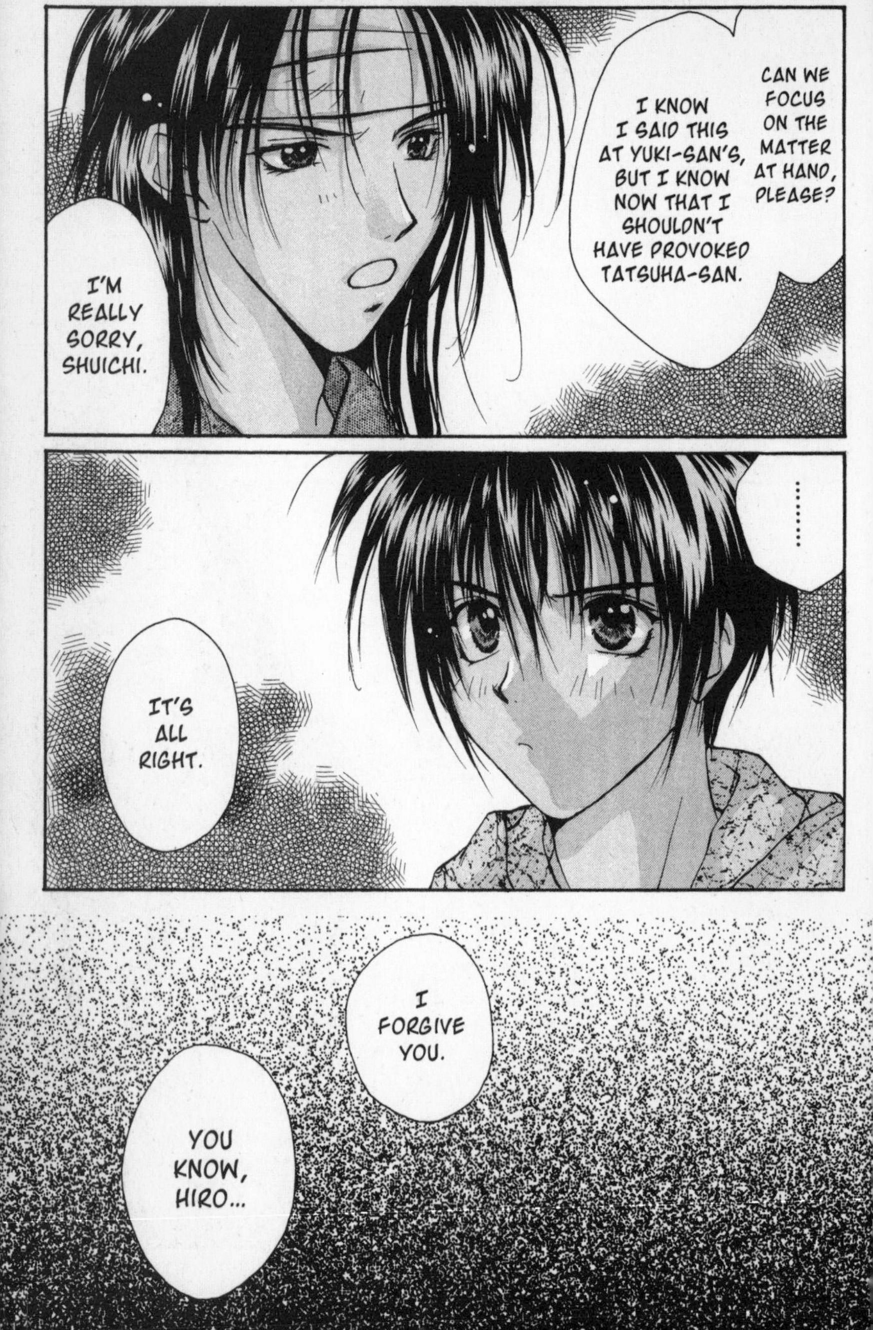
CAN WE FOCUS ON THE MATTER AT HAND, PLEASE?
I KNOW I SAID THIS AT YUKI-SAN'S, BUT I KNOW NOW THAT I SHOULDN'T HAVE PROVOKED TATSUHA-SAN.
I'M REALLY SORRY, SHUICHI.
....
IT'S ALL RIGHT.
I FORGIVE YOU.
YOU KNOW, HIRO...

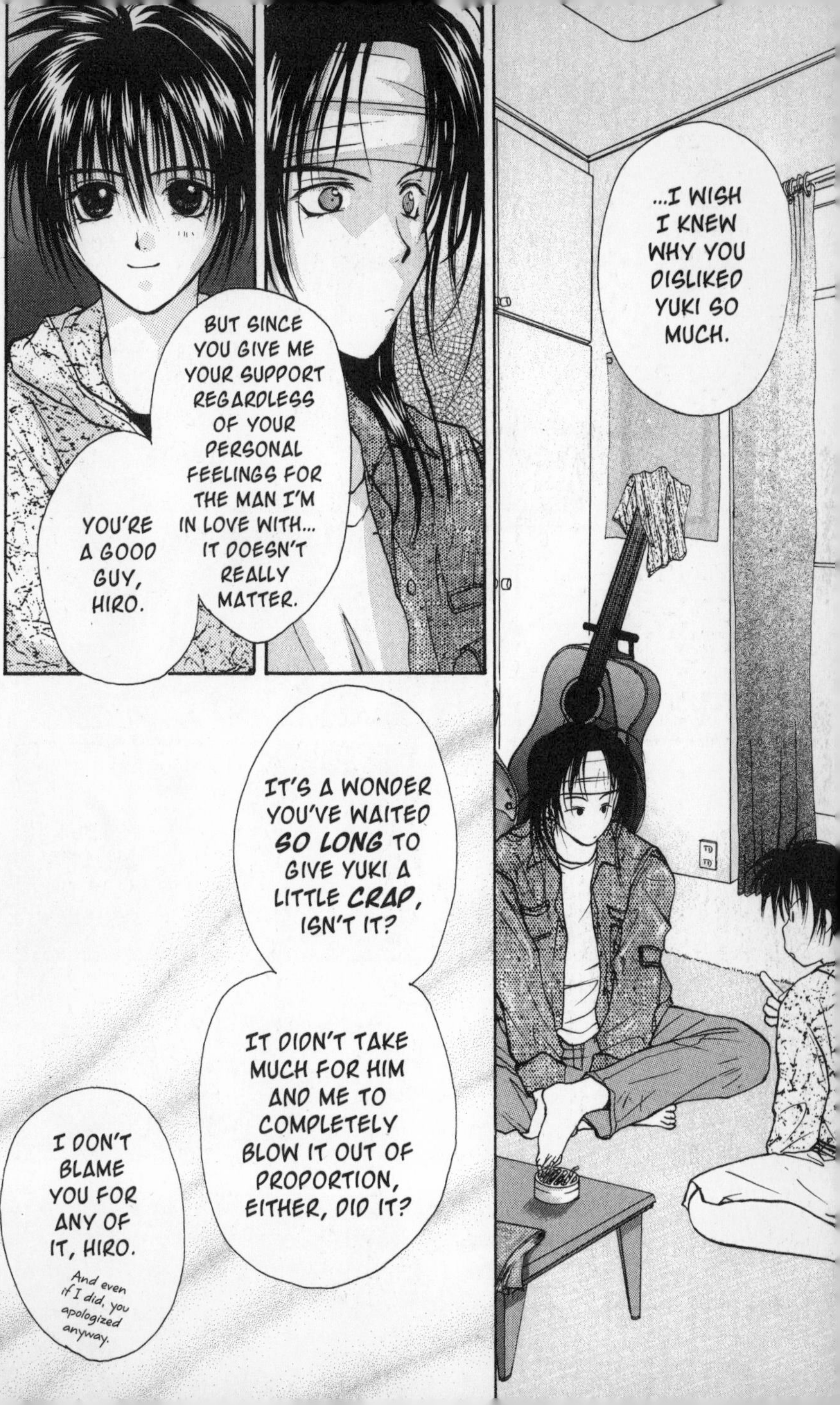
...I WISH I KNEW WHY YOU DISLIKED YUKI SO MUCH.
BUT SINCE YOU GIVE ME YOUR SUPPORT REGARDLESS OF YOUR PERSONAL FEELINGS FOR THE MAN I'M IN LOVE WITH... IT DOESN'T REALLY MATTER.
YOU'RE A GOOD GUY, HIRO.
IT'S A WONDER YOU'VE WAITED SO LONG TO GIVE YUKI A LITTLE CRAP, ISN'T IT?
IT DIDN'T TAKE MUCH FOR HIM AND ME TO COMPLETELY BLOW IT OUT OF PROPORTION, EITHER, DID IT?
I DON'T BLAME YOU FOR ANY OF IT, HIRO.
And even if I did, you apologized anyway.

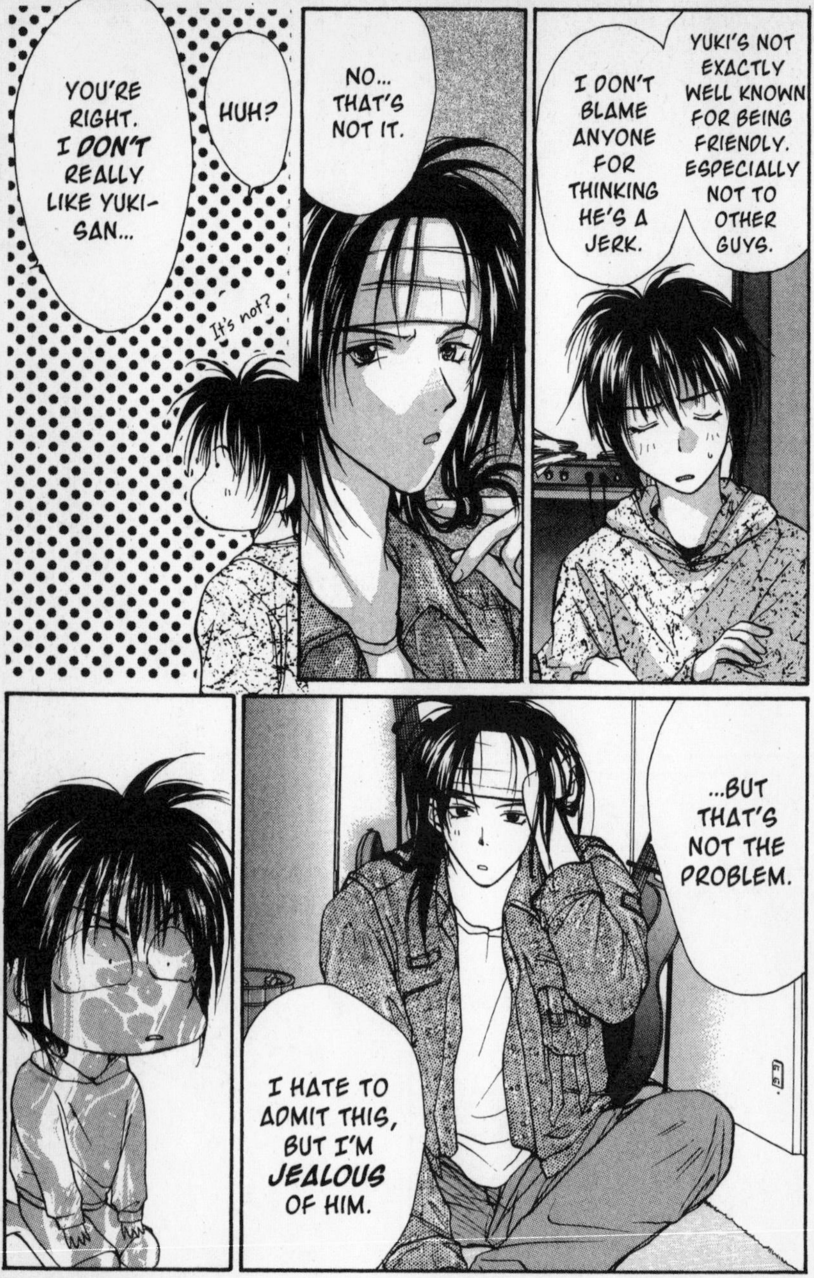
YUKI'S NOT EXACTLY WELL KNOWN FOR BEING FRIENDLY. ESPECIALLY NOT TO OTHER GUYS.
I DON'T BLAME ANYONE FOR THINKING HE'S A JERK.
NO... THAT'S NOT IT.
HUH?
It's not?
YOU'RE RIGHT. I DON'T REALLY LIKE YUKI-SAN...
...BUT THAT'S NOT THE PROBLEM.
I HATE TO ADMIT THIS, BUT I'M JEALOUS OF HIM.

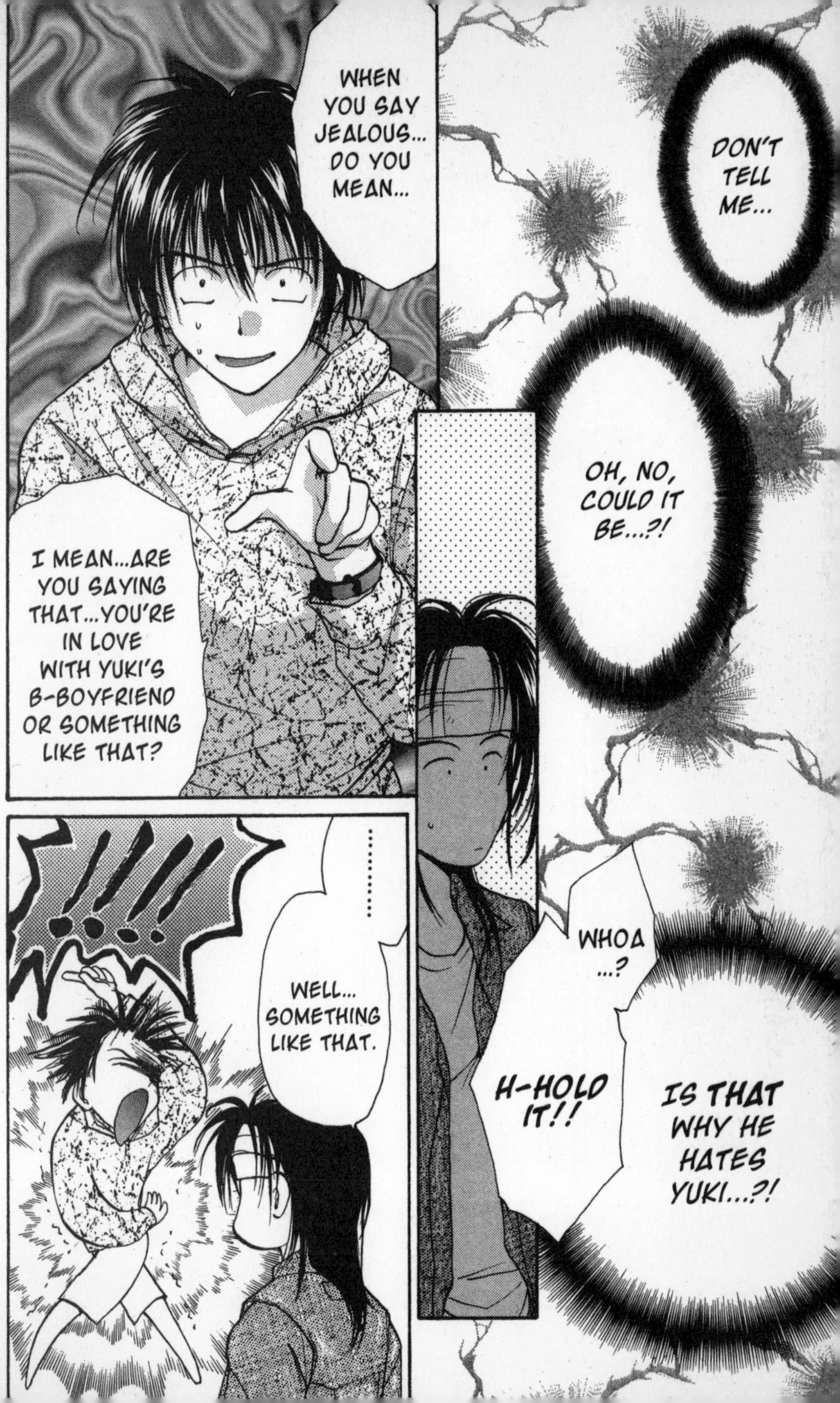
DON'T TELL ME...
OH, NO, COULD IT BE...?!
WHOA ...?
H-HOLD IT!!
IS THAT WHY HE HATES YUKI...?!
WHEN YOU SAY JEALOUS... DO YOU MEAN...
I MEAN...ARE YOU SAYING THAT...YOU'RE IN LOVE WITH YUKI'S B-BOYFRIEND OR SOMETHING LIKE THAT?
!!!
......
WELL... SOMETHING LIKE THAT.

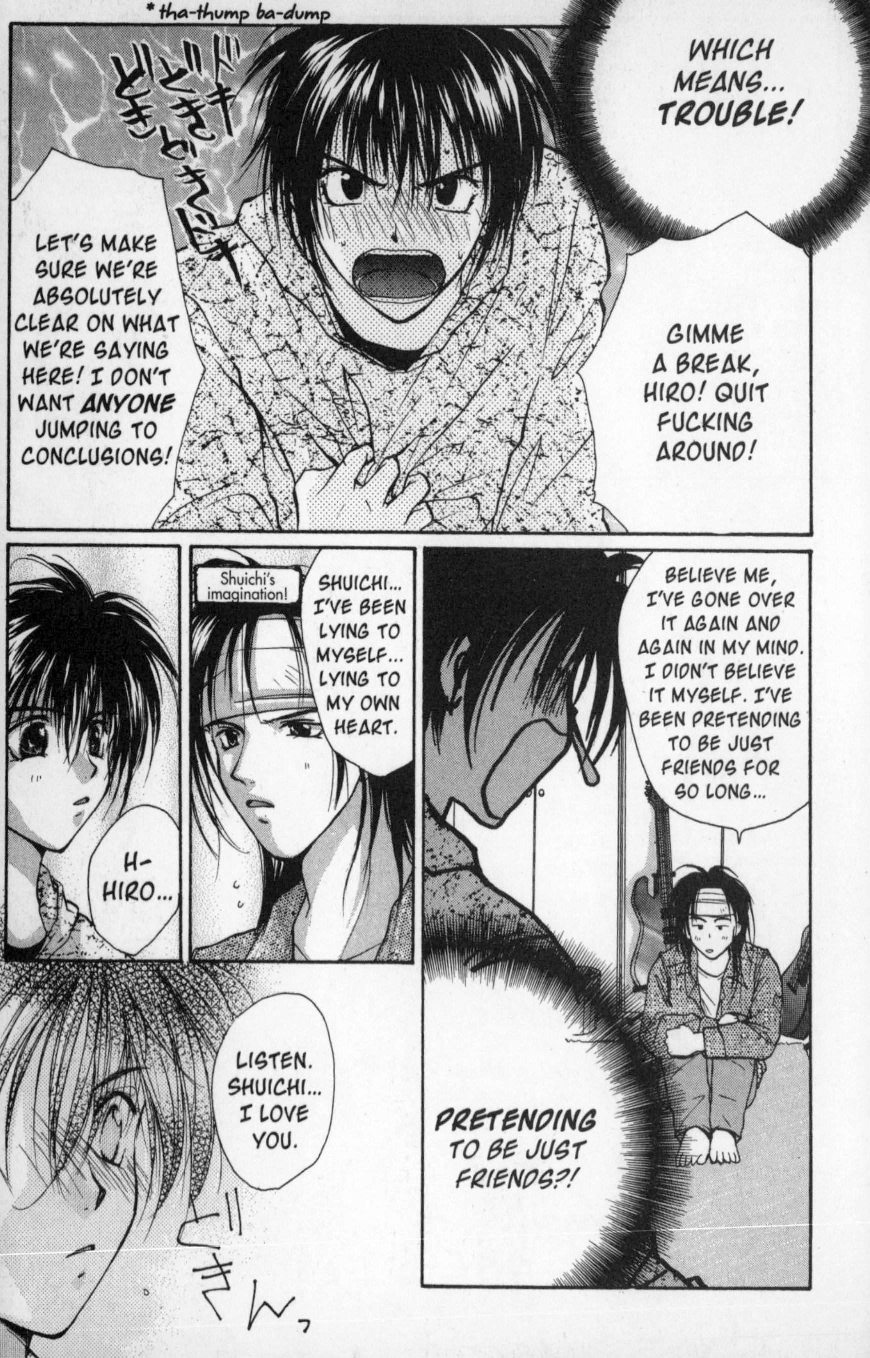
* tha-thump ba-dump
WHICH MEANS... TROUBLE!
ドキ どき どき どきドキ
GIMME A BREAK, HIRO! QUIT FUCKING AROUND!
LET'S MAKE SURE WE'RE ABSOLUTELY CLEAR ON WHAT WE'RE SAYING HERE! I DON'T WANT **ANYONE** JUMPING TO CONCLUSIONS!
BELIEVE ME, I'VE GONE OVER IT AGAIN AND AGAIN IN MY MIND. I DIDN'T BELIEVE IT MYSELF. I'VE BEEN PRETENDING TO BE JUST FRIENDS FOR SO LONG...
PRETENDING TO BE JUST FRIENDS?!
Shuichi's imagination!
SHUICHI... I'VE BEEN LYING TO MYSELF... LYING TO MY OWN HEART.
H-HIRO...
LISTEN. SHUICHI... I LOVE YOU.
どきん

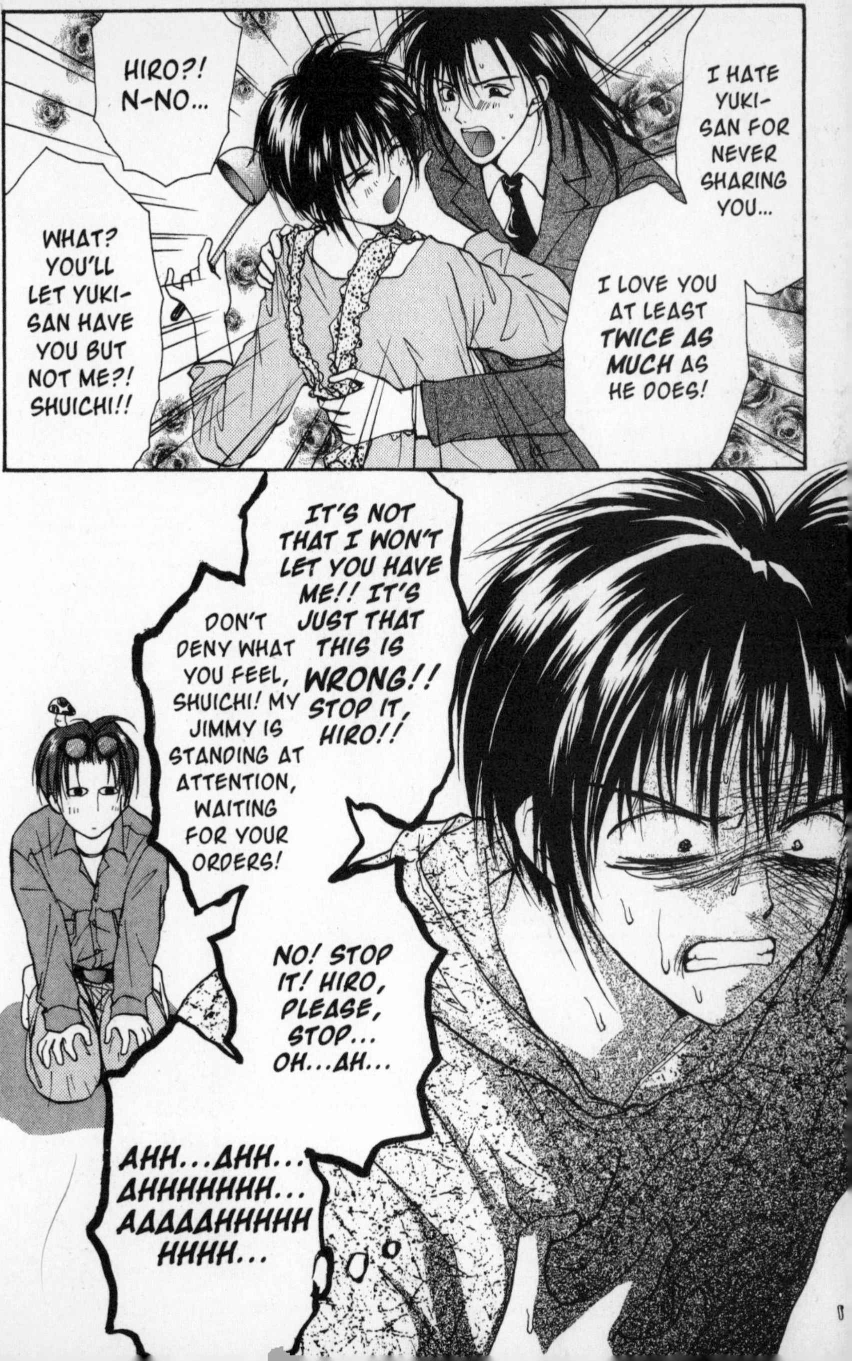
I HATE YUKI-SAN FOR NEVER SHARING YOU...
HIRO?! N-NO...
I LOVE YOU AT LEAST TWICE AS MUCH AS HE DOES!
WHAT? YOU'LL LET YUKI-SAN HAVE YOU BUT NOT ME?! SHUICHI!!
IT'S NOT THAT I WON'T LET YOU HAVE ME!! IT'S JUST THAT THIS IS WRONG!! STOP IT, HIRO!!
DON'T DENY WHAT YOU FEEL, SHUICHI! MY JIMMY IS STANDING AT ATTENTION, WAITING FOR YOUR ORDERS!
NO! STOP IT! HIRO, PLEASE, STOP... OH...AH...
AHH...AHH... AHHHHHHH... AAAAAHHHHH HHHH...

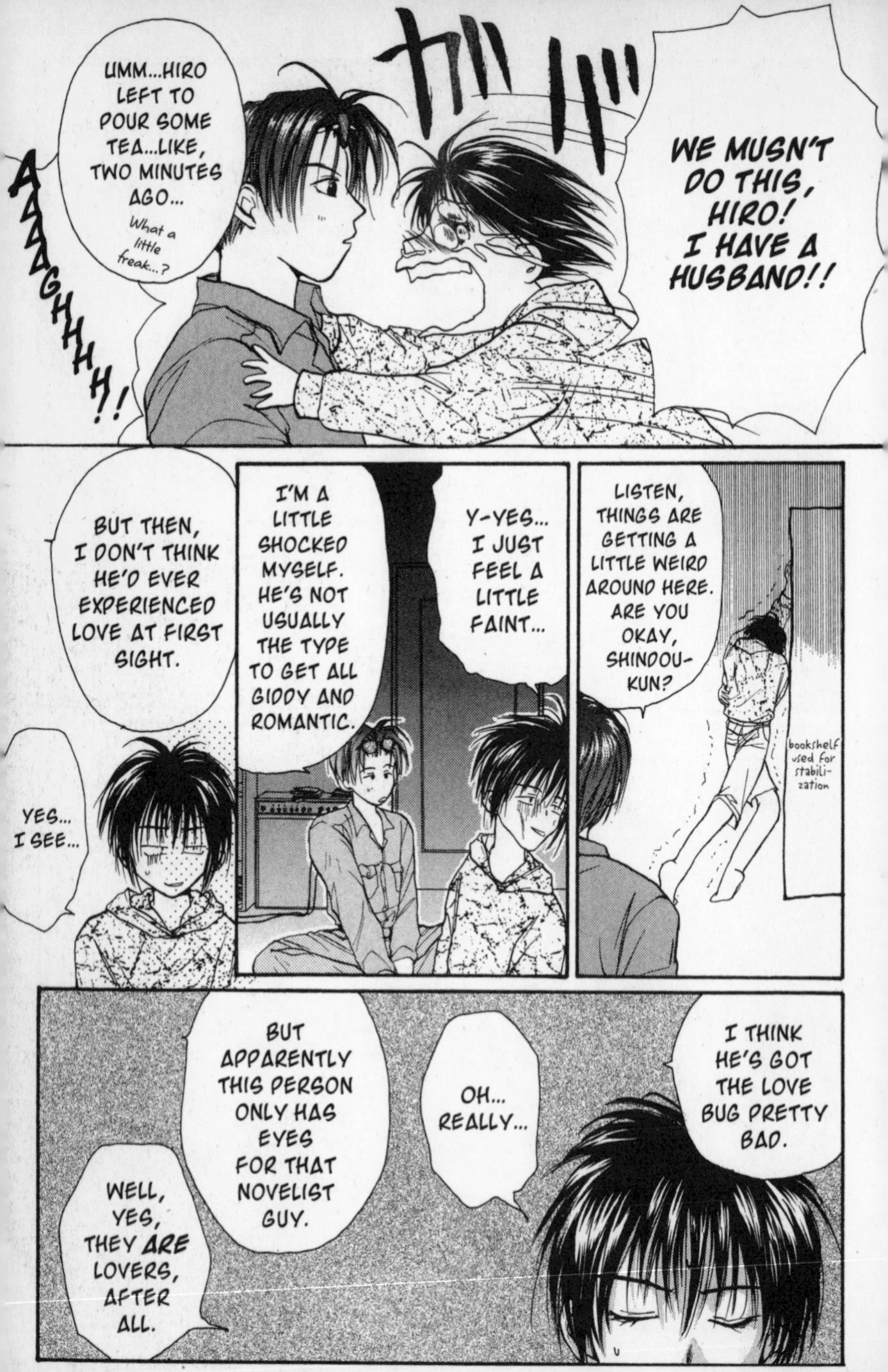
WE MUSN'T DO THIS, HIRO! I HAVE A HUSBAND!!
UMM...HIRO LEFT TO POUR SOME TEA...LIKE, TWO MINUTES AGO...
What a little freak...?
AAAAGHHHH?!
LISTEN, THINGS ARE GETTING A LITTLE WEIRD AROUND HERE. ARE YOU OKAY, SHINDOU-KUN?
bookshelf used for stabilization
Y-YES... I JUST FEEL A LITTLE FAINT...
I'M A LITTLE SHOCKED MYSELF. HE'S NOT USUALLY THE TYPE TO GET ALL GIDDY AND ROMANTIC.
BUT THEN, I DON'T THINK HE'D EVER EXPERIENCED LOVE AT FIRST SIGHT.
YES... I SEE...
I THINK HE'S GOT THE LOVE BUG PRETTY BAD.
OH... REALLY...
BUT APPARENTLY THIS PERSON ONLY HAS EYES FOR THAT NOVELIST GUY.
WELL, YES, THEY ARE LOVERS, AFTER ALL.

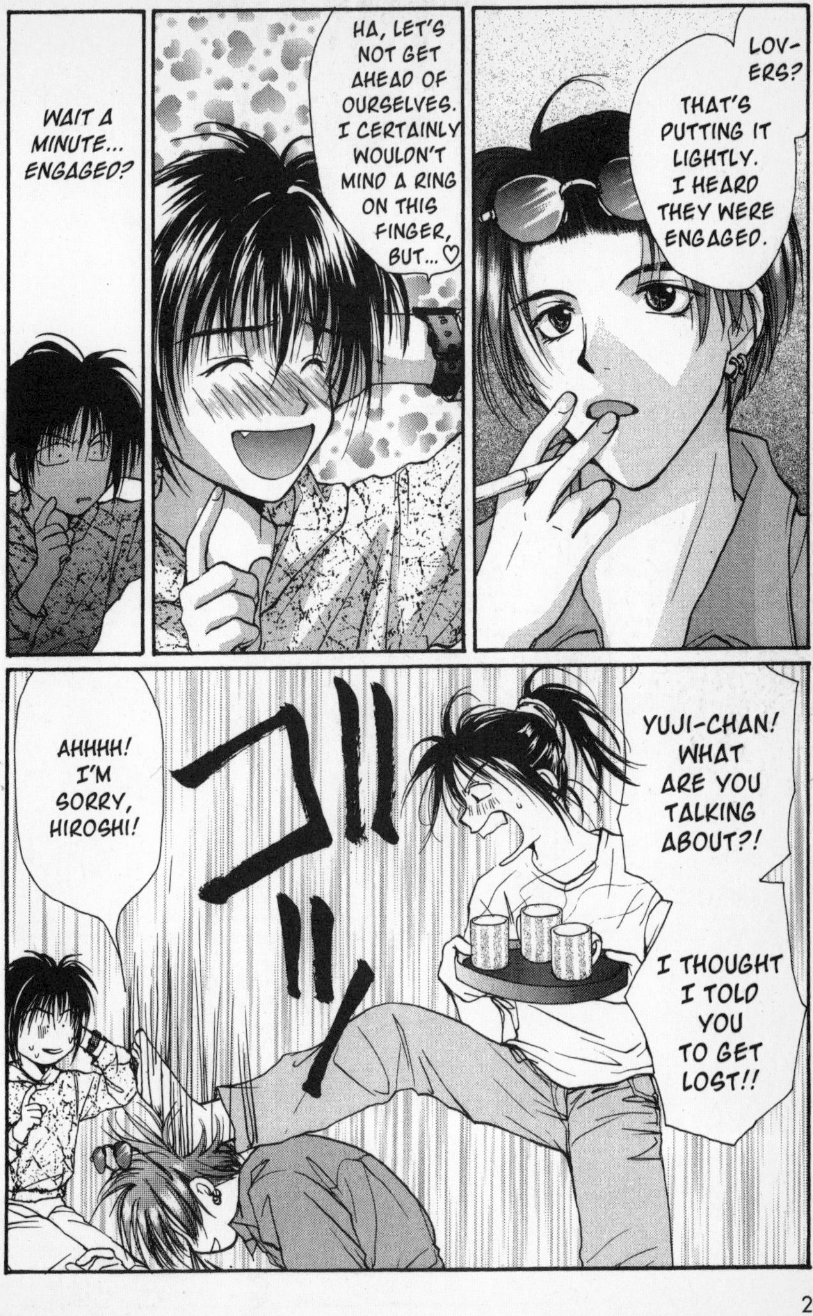
LOVERS?
THAT'S PUTTING IT LIGHTLY. I HEARD THEY WERE ENGAGED.
HA, LET'S NOT GET AHEAD OF OURSELVES. I CERTAINLY WOULDN'T MIND A RING ON THIS FINGER, BUT...♡
WAIT A MINUTE... ENGAGED?
YUJI-CHAN! WHAT ARE YOU TALKING ABOUT?!
I THOUGHT I TOLD YOU TO GET LOST!!
ゴッ
AHHHH! I'M SORRY, HIROSHI!

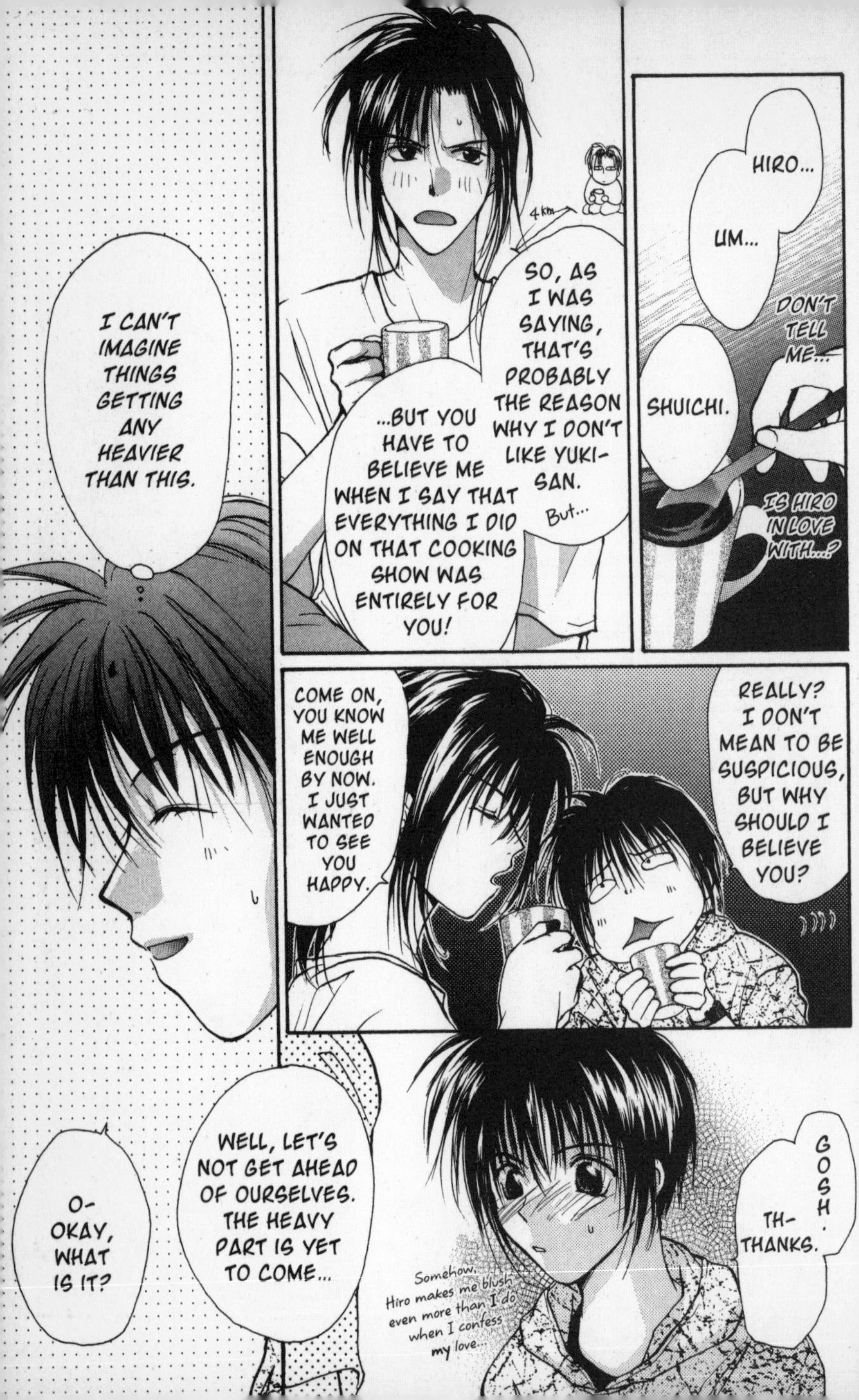
HIRO...
UM...
DON'T TELL ME...
SHUICHI.
IS HIRO IN LOVE WITH...?
4 km
SO, AS I WAS SAYING, THAT'S PROBABLY THE REASON WHY I DON'T LIKE YUKI-SAN.
But...
...BUT YOU HAVE TO BELIEVE ME WHEN I SAY THAT EVERYTHING I DID ON THAT COOKING SHOW WAS ENTIRELY FOR YOU!
REALLY? I DON'T MEAN TO BE SUSPICIOUS, BUT WHY SHOULD I BELIEVE YOU?
COME ON, YOU KNOW ME WELL ENOUGH BY NOW. I JUST WANTED TO SEE YOU HAPPY.
GOSH.
TH-THANKS.
Somehow, Hiro makes me blush even more than I do when I confess my love...
I CAN'T IMAGINE THINGS GETTING ANY HEAVIER THAN THIS.
WELL, LET'S NOT GET AHEAD OF OURSELVES. THE HEAVY PART IS YET TO COME...
O-OKAY, WHAT IS IT?

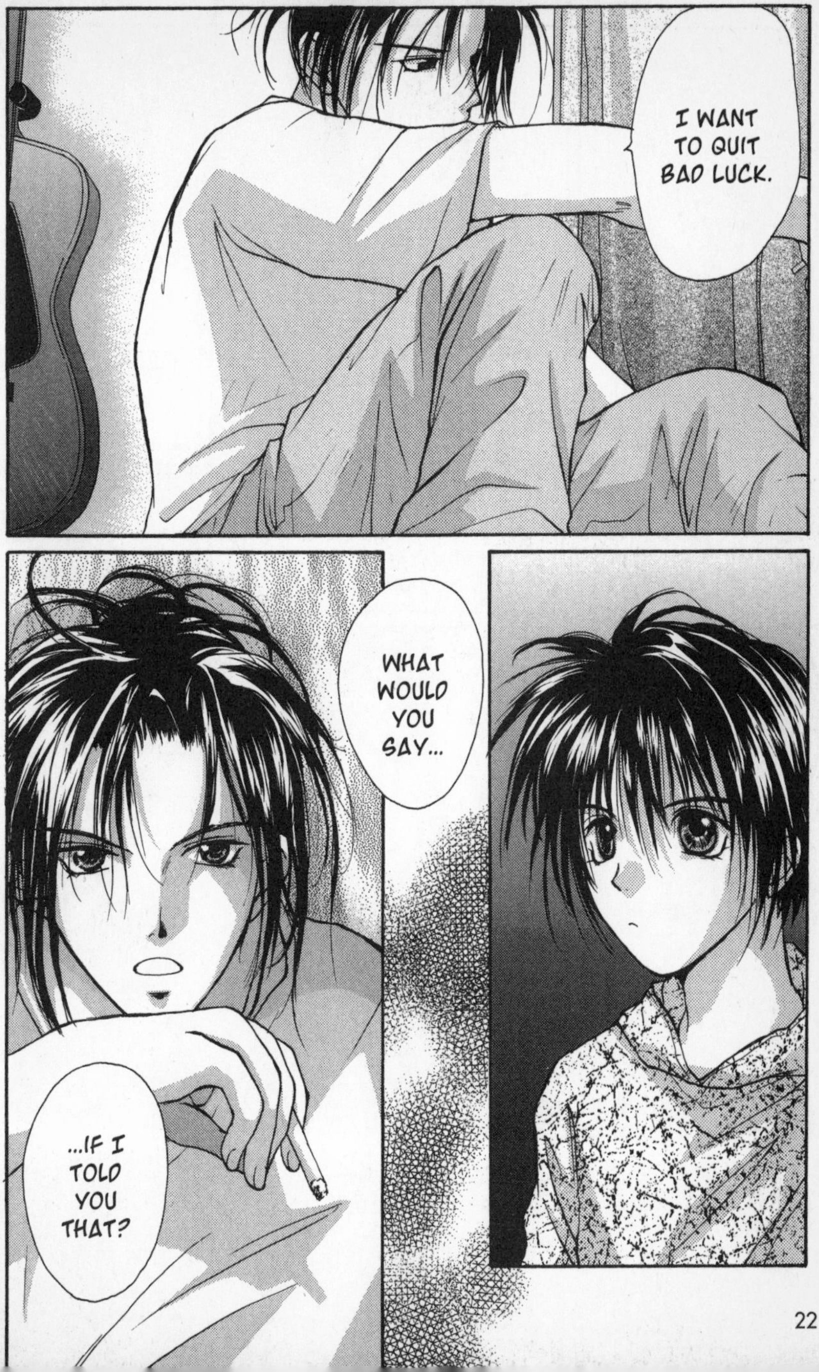
I WANT TO QUIT BAD LUCK.
WHAT WOULD YOU SAY...
...IF I TOLD YOU THAT?

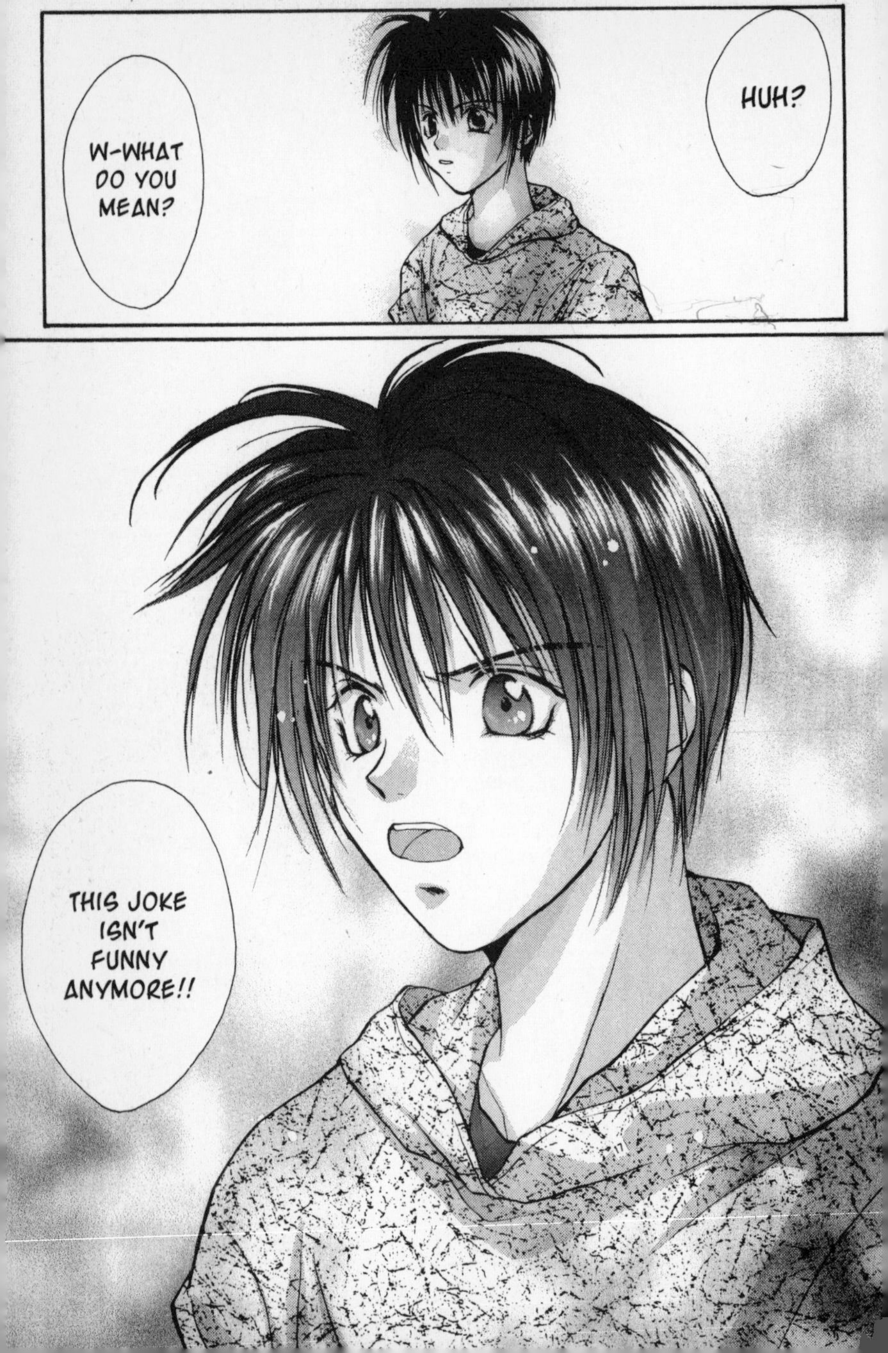
HUH?
W-WHAT DO YOU MEAN?
THIS JOKE ISN'T FUNNY ANYMORE!!

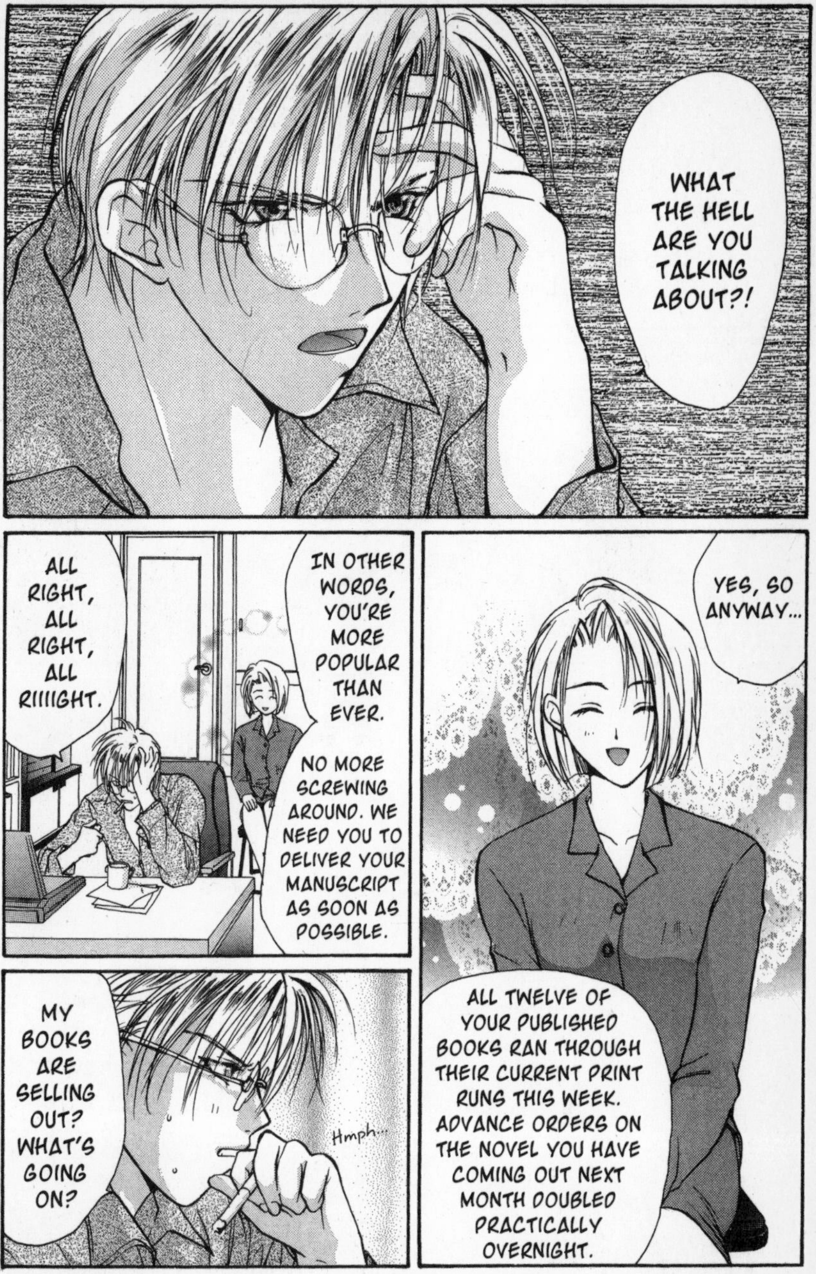
WHAT THE HELL ARE YOU TALKING ABOUT?!
YES, SO ANYWAY...
ALL TWELVE OF YOUR PUBLISHED BOOKS RAN THROUGH THEIR CURRENT PRINT RUNS THIS WEEK. ADVANCE ORDERS ON THE NOVEL YOU HAVE COMING OUT NEXT MONTH DOUBLED PRACTICALLY OVERNIGHT.
IN OTHER WORDS, YOU'RE MORE POPULAR THAN EVER.
NO MORE SCREWING AROUND. WE NEED YOU TO DELIVER YOUR MANUSCRIPT AS SOON AS POSSIBLE.
ALL RIGHT, ALL RIGHT, ALL RIIIIGHT.
Hmph...
MY BOOKS ARE SELLING OUT? WHAT'S GOING ON?

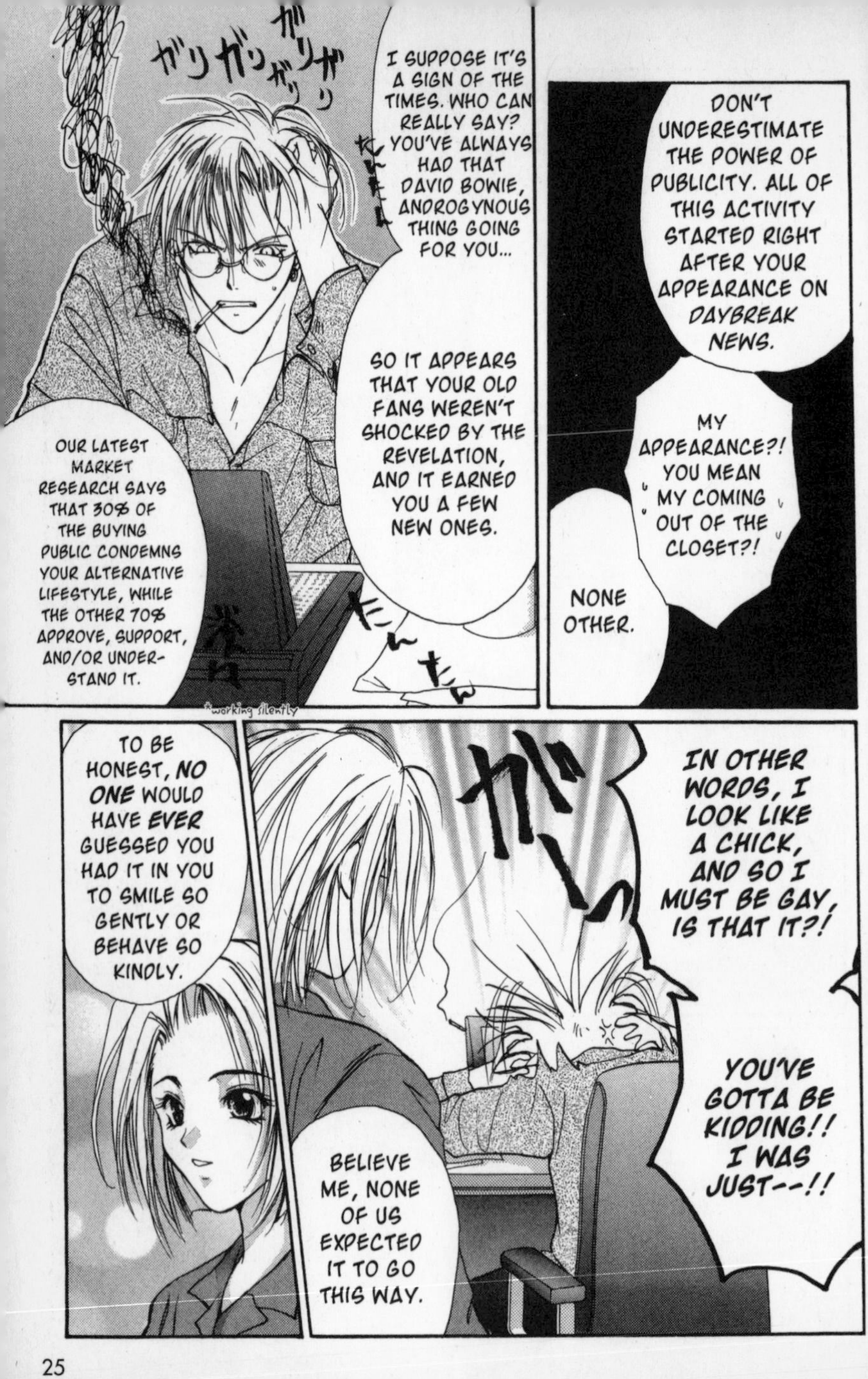
DON'T UNDERESTIMATE THE POWER OF PUBLICITY. ALL OF THIS ACTIVITY STARTED RIGHT AFTER YOUR APPEARANCE ON DAYBREAK NEWS.
MY APPEARANCE?! YOU MEAN MY COMING OUT OF THE CLOSET?!
NONE OTHER.
I SUPPOSE IT'S A SIGN OF THE TIMES. WHO CAN REALLY SAY? YOU'VE ALWAYS HAD THAT DAVID BOWIE, ANDROGYNOUS THING GOING FOR YOU...
SO IT APPEARS THAT YOUR OLD FANS WEREN'T SHOCKED BY THE REVELATION, AND IT EARNED YOU A FEW NEW ONES.
OUR LATEST MARKET RESEARCH SAYS THAT 30% OF THE BUYING PUBLIC CONDEMNS YOUR ALTERNATIVE LIFESTYLE, WHILE THE OTHER 70% APPROVE, SUPPORT, AND/OR UNDERSTAND IT.
*working silently
IN OTHER WORDS, I LOOK LIKE A CHICK, AND SO I MUST BE GAY, IS THAT IT?!
YOU'VE GOTTA BE KIDDING!! I WAS JUST--!!
BELIEVE ME, NONE OF US EXPECTED IT TO GO THIS WAY.
TO BE HONEST, NO ONE WOULD HAVE EVER GUESSED YOU HAD IT IN YOU TO SMILE SO GENTLY OR BEHAVE SO KINDLY.

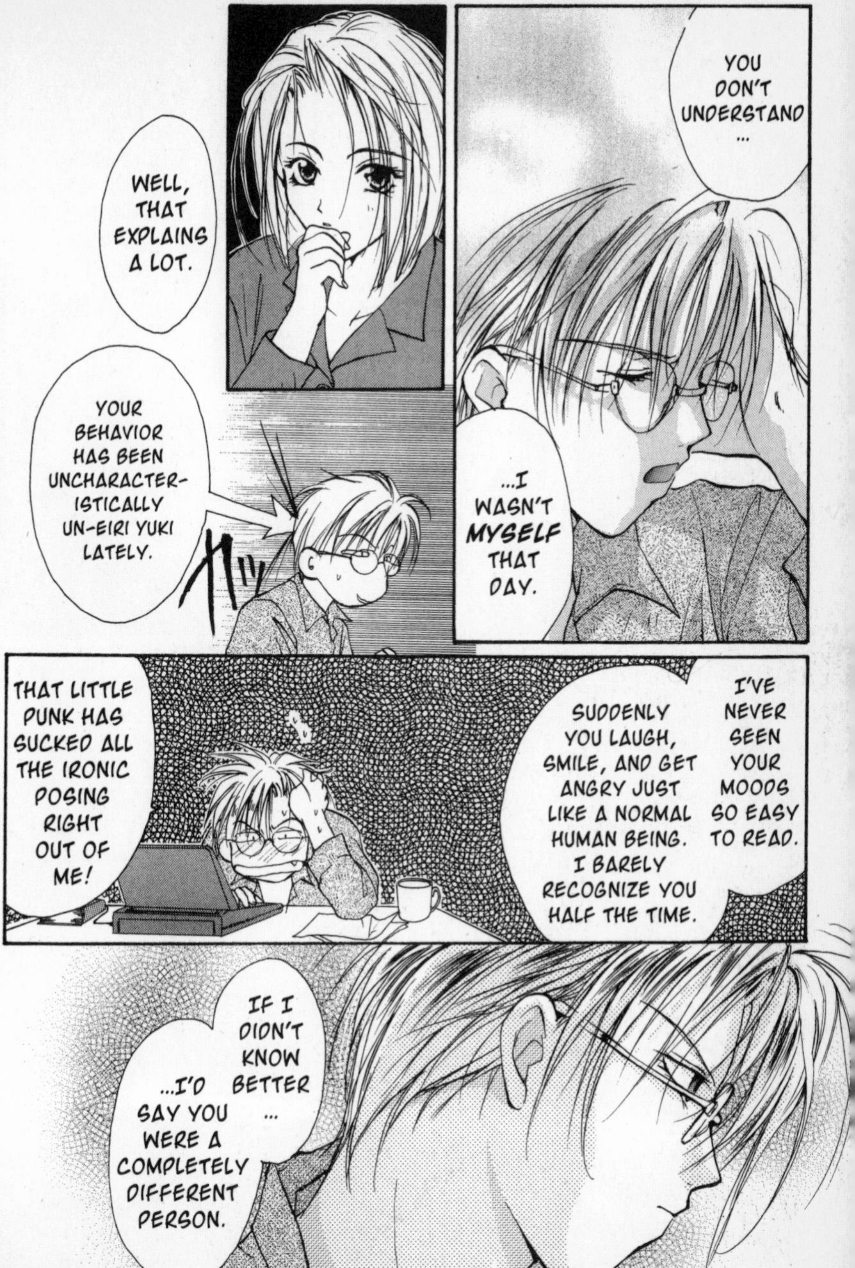
YOU DON'T UNDERSTAND...
...I WASN'T MYSELF THAT DAY.
WELL, THAT EXPLAINS A LOT.
YOUR BEHAVIOR HAS BEEN UNCHARACTER-ISTICALLY UN-EIRI YUKI LATELY.
I'VE NEVER SEEN YOUR MOODS SO EASY TO READ.
SUDDENLY YOU LAUGH, SMILE, AND GET ANGRY JUST LIKE A NORMAL HUMAN BEING. I BARELY RECOGNIZE YOU HALF THE TIME.
THAT LITTLE PUNK HAS SUCKED ALL THE IRONIC POSING RIGHT OUT OF ME!
IF I DIDN'T KNOW BETTER...
...I'D SAY YOU WERE A COMPLETELY DIFFERENT PERSON.

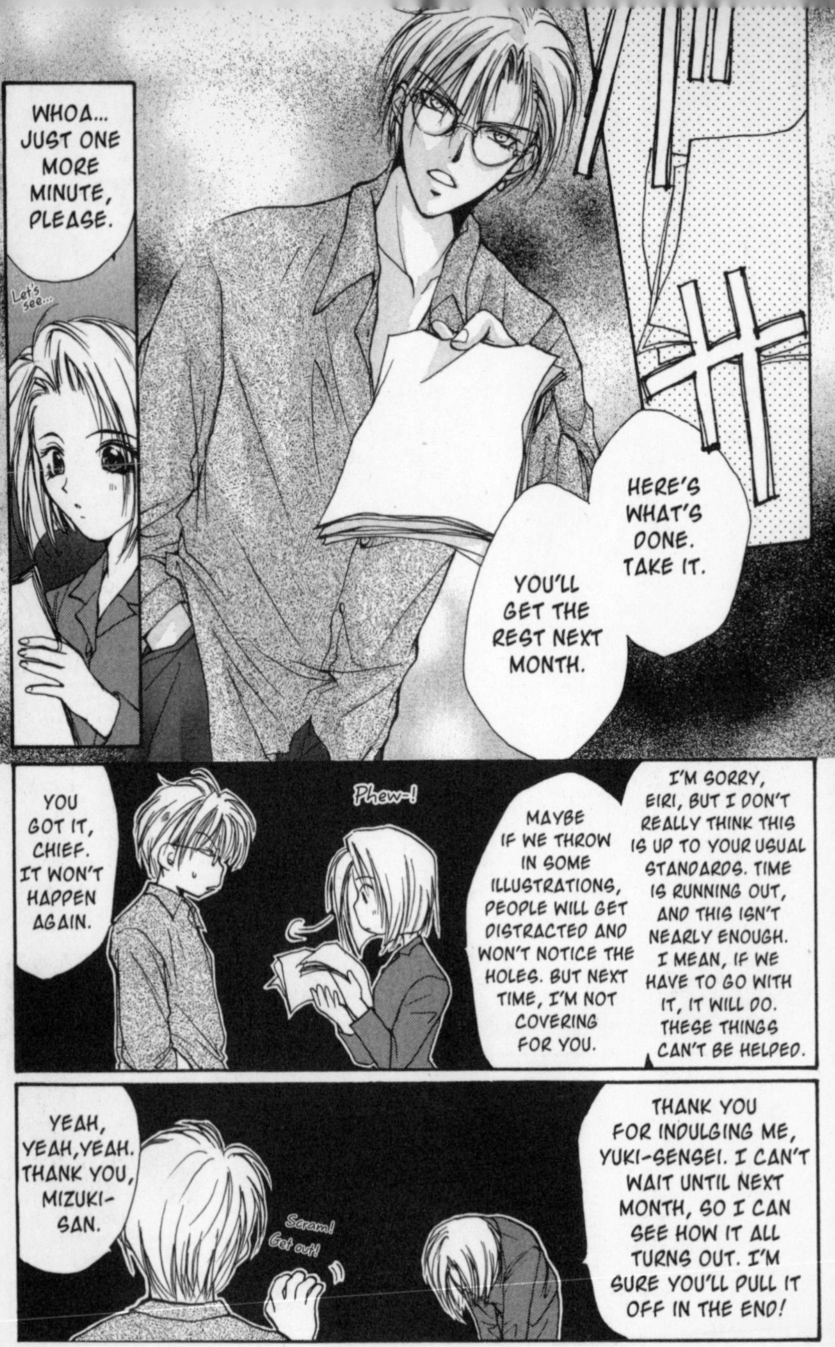
HERE'S WHAT'S DONE. TAKE IT.
YOU'LL GET THE REST NEXT MONTH.
WHOA... JUST ONE MORE MINUTE, PLEASE.
Let's see...
I'M SORRY, EIRI, BUT I DON'T REALLY THINK THIS IS UP TO YOUR USUAL STANDARDS. TIME IS RUNNING OUT, AND THIS ISN'T NEARLY ENOUGH. I MEAN, IF WE HAVE TO GO WITH IT, IT WILL DO. THESE THINGS CAN'T BE HELPED.
MAYBE IF WE THROW IN SOME ILLUSTRATIONS, PEOPLE WILL GET DISTRACTED AND WON'T NOTICE THE HOLES. BUT NEXT TIME, I'M NOT COVERING FOR YOU.
Phew-!
YOU GOT IT, CHIEF. IT WON'T HAPPEN AGAIN.
THANK YOU FOR INDULGING ME, YUKI-SENSEI. I CAN'T WAIT UNTIL NEXT MONTH, SO I CAN SEE HOW IT ALL TURNS OUT. I'M SURE YOU'LL PULL IT OFF IN THE END!
Scram! Get out!
YEAH, YEAH,YEAH. THANK YOU, MIZUKI-SAN.

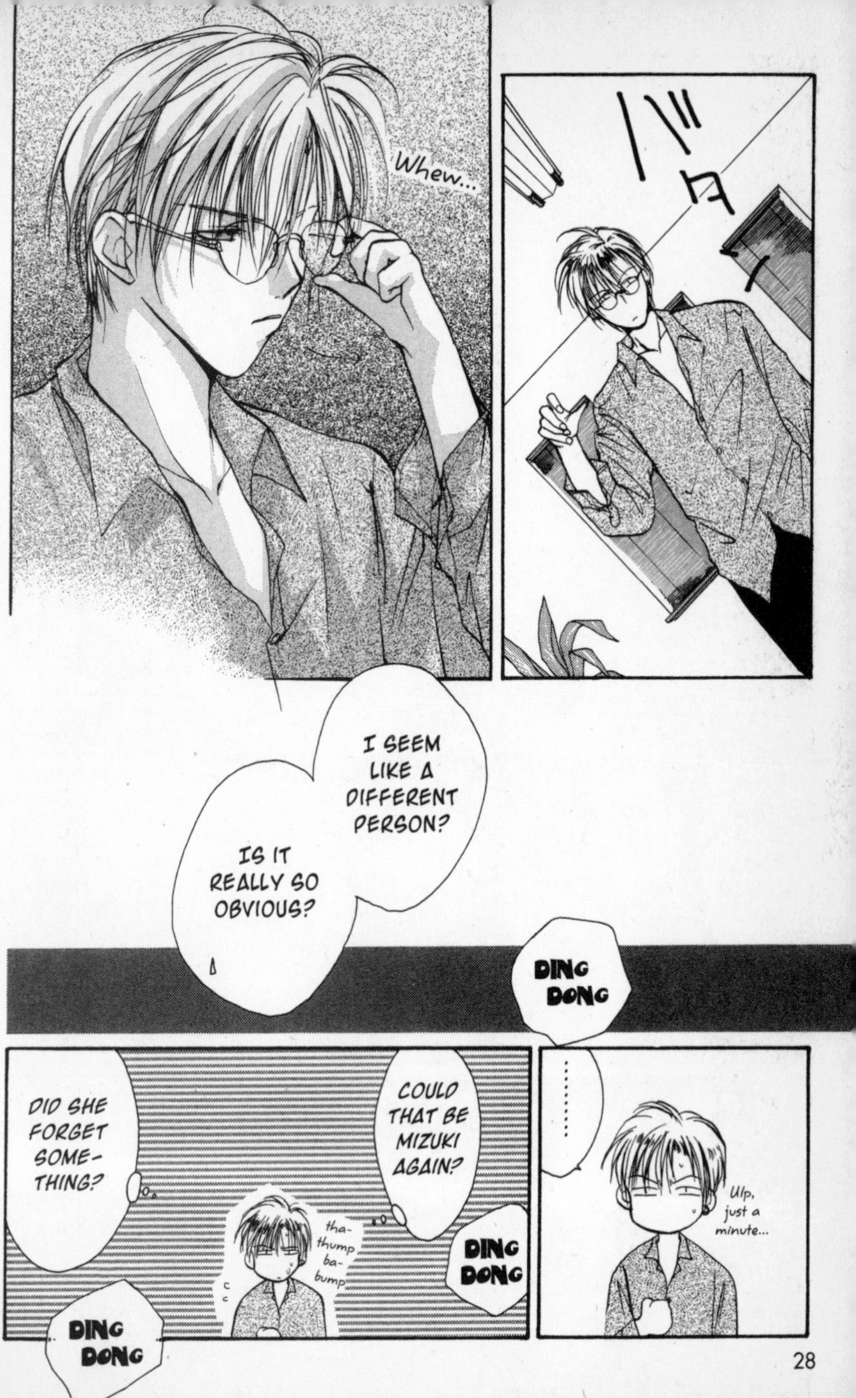
バタン
Whew...
I SEEM LIKE A DIFFERENT PERSON?
IS IT REALLY SO OBVIOUS?
DING DONG
......
Ulp, just a minute...
COULD THAT BE MIZUKI AGAIN?
DING DONG
DID SHE FORGET SOME-THING?
tha-thump ba-bump
DING DONG

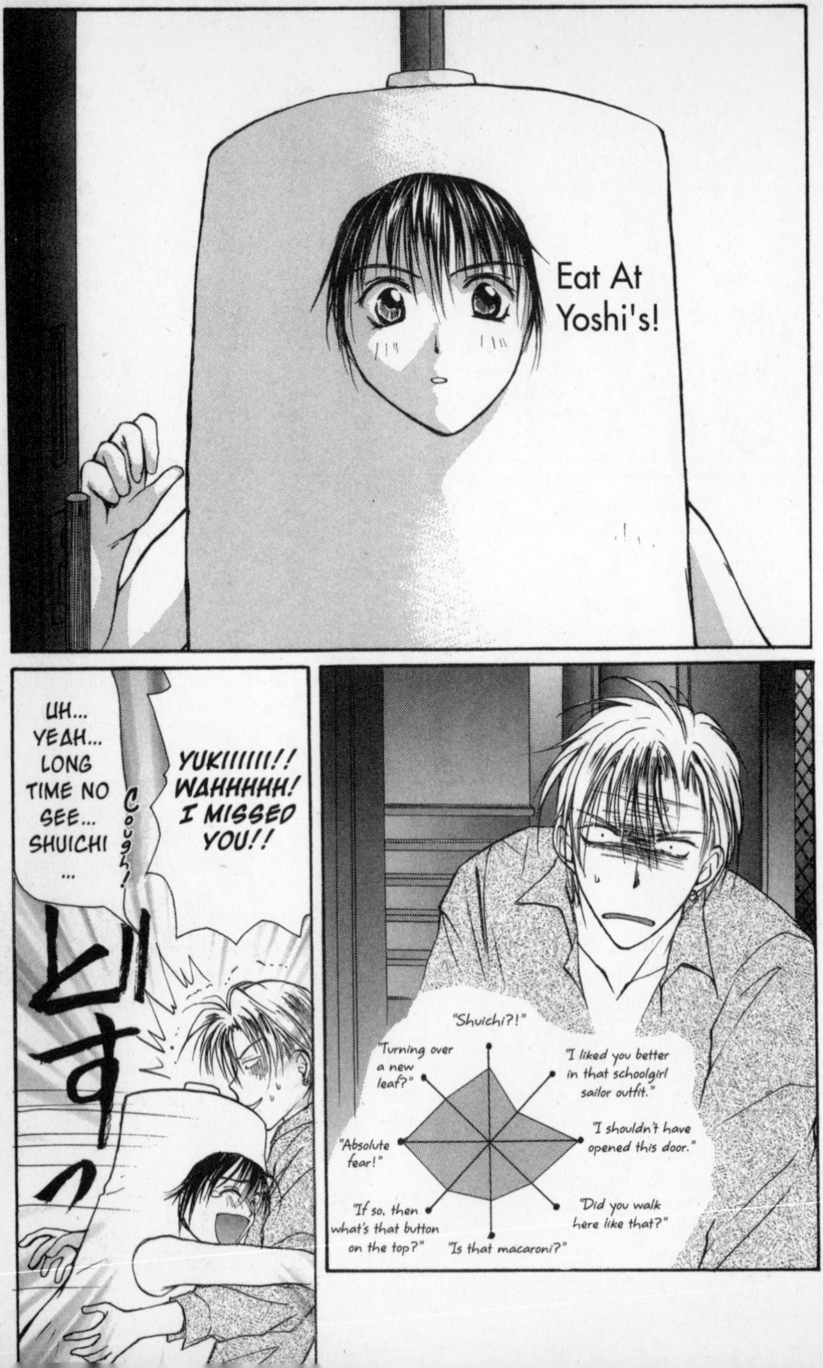
Eat At Yoshi's!
"Shuichi?!"
"I liked you better in that schoolgirl sailor outfit."
"I shouldn't have opened this door."
"Did you walk here like that?"
"Is that macaroni?"
"If so, then what's that button on the top?"
"Absolute fear!"
"Turning over a new leaf?"
YUKIIIIII!! WAHHHHH! I MISSED YOU!!
UH... YEAH... LONG TIME NO SEE... SHUICHI ...
Cough!
どすっ

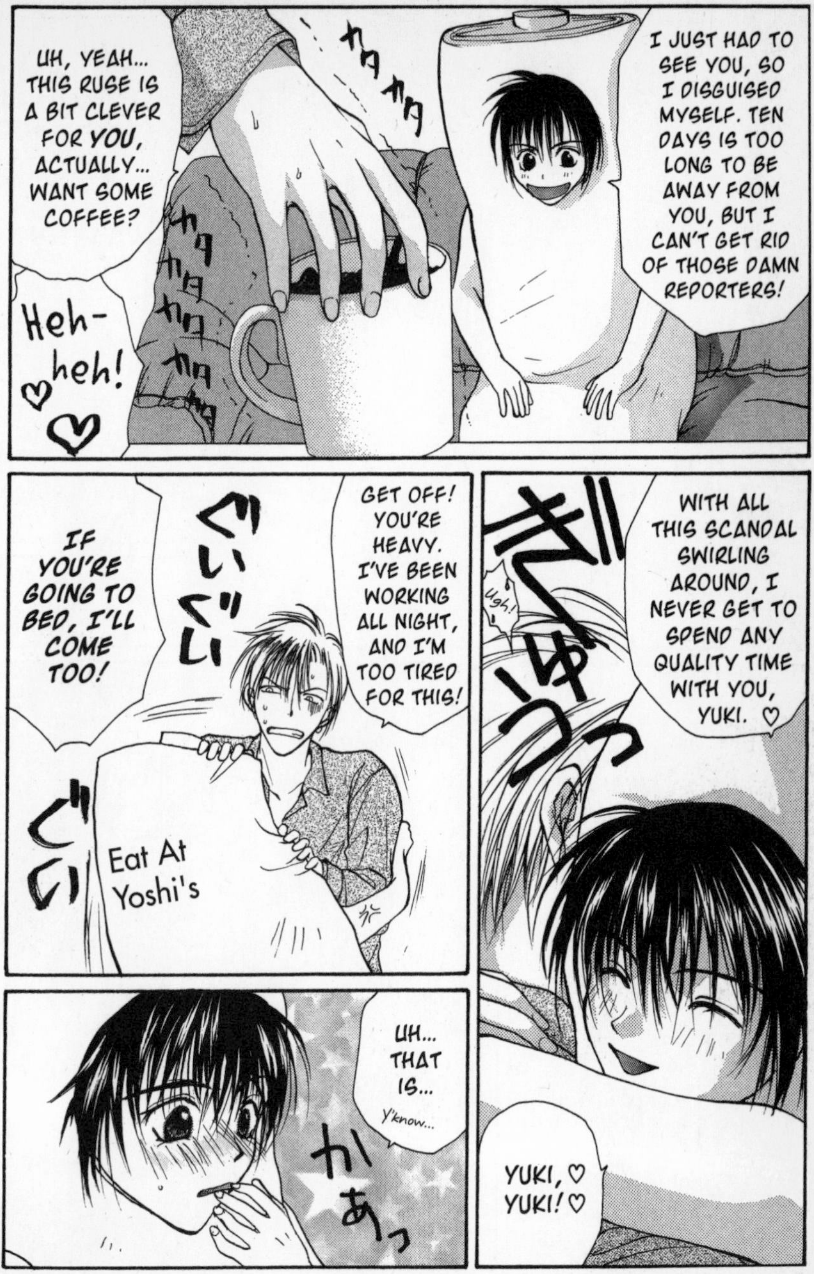
I JUST HAD TO SEE YOU, SO I DISGUISED MYSELF. TEN DAYS IS TOO LONG TO BE AWAY FROM YOU, BUT I CAN'T GET RID OF THOSE DAMN REPORTERS!
カタカタ
カタカタカタカタ
UH, YEAH... THIS RUSE IS A BIT CLEVER FOR YOU, ACTUALLY... WANT SOME COFFEE?
Heh-heh! ♡
WITH ALL THIS SCANDAL SWIRLING AROUND, I NEVER GET TO SPEND ANY QUALITY TIME WITH YOU, YUKI. ♡
Ugh!
ぎゅうっ
YUKI, ♡ YUKI! ♡
GET OFF! YOU'RE HEAVY. I'VE BEEN WORKING ALL NIGHT, AND I'M TOO TIRED FOR THIS!
ぐいぐい
IF YOU'RE GOING TO BED, I'LL COME TOO!
ぐい
Eat At Yoshi's
UH... THAT IS...
Y'know...
かあっ

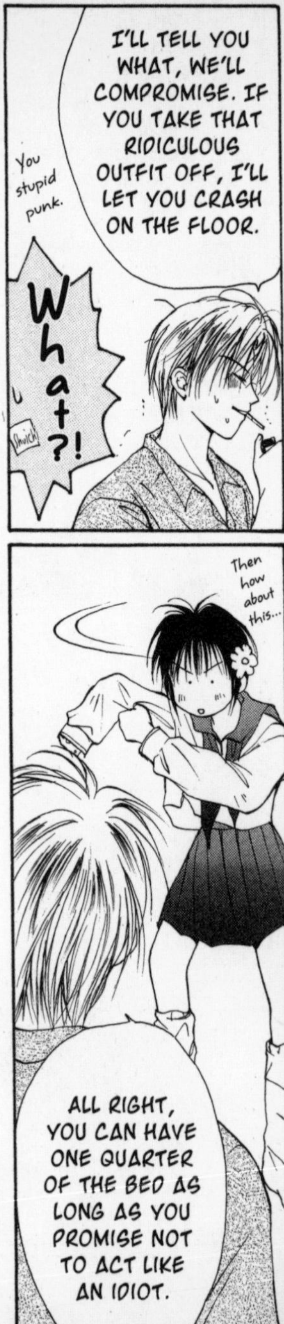
I'LL TELL YOU WHAT, WE'LL COMPROMISE. IF YOU TAKE THAT RIDICULOUS OUTFIT OFF, I'LL LET YOU CRASH ON THE FLOOR.
You stupid punk.
What?!
Shuichi
Then how about this...
ALL RIGHT, YOU CAN HAVE ONE QUARTER OF THE BED AS LONG AS YOU PROMISE NOT TO ACT LIKE AN IDIOT.
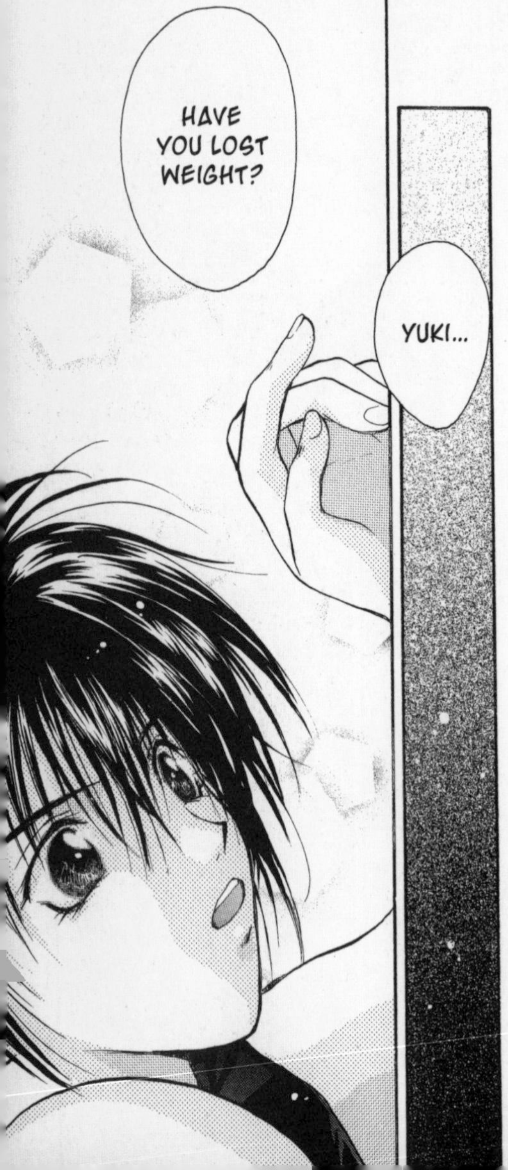
HAVE YOU LOST WEIGHT?
YUKI...

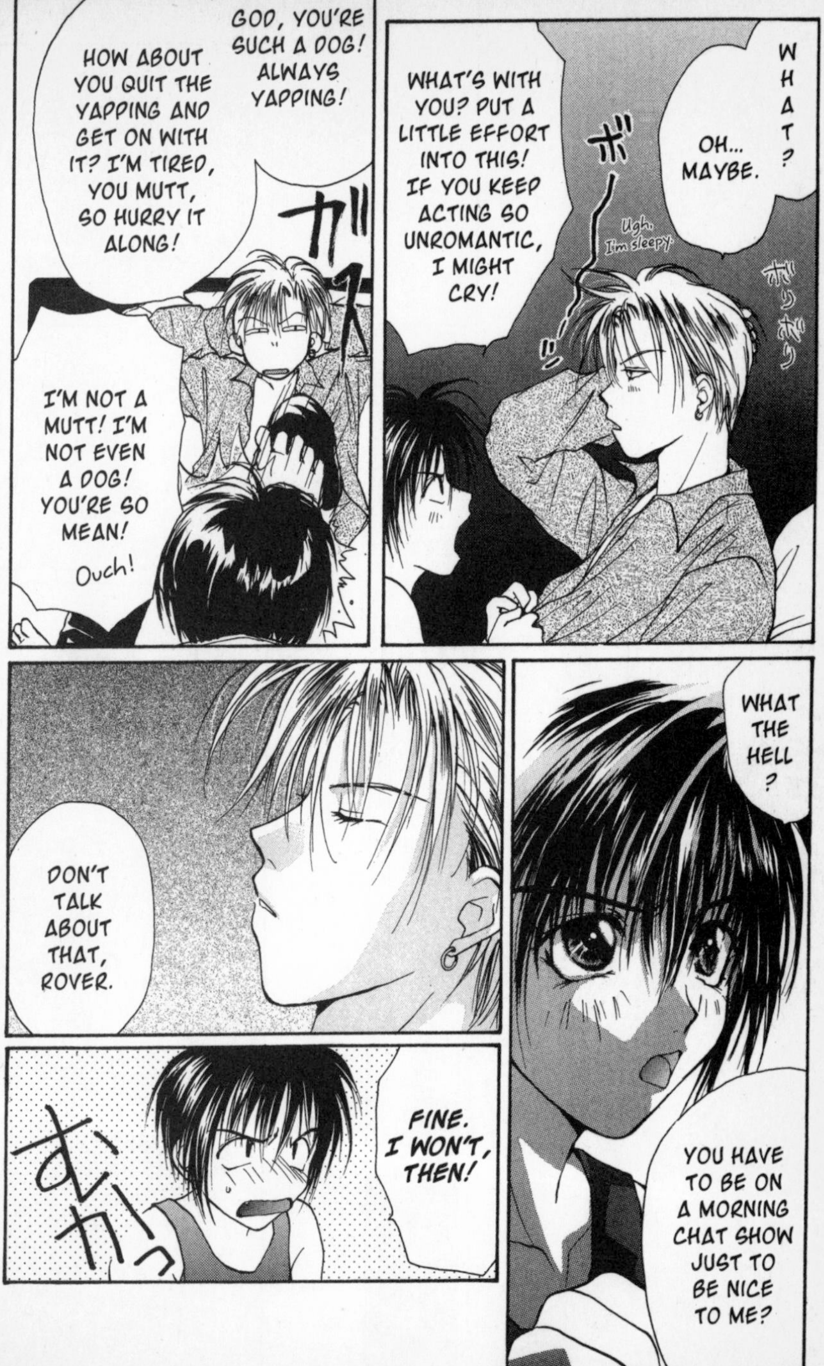
WHAT?
OH... MAYBE.
Ugh. I'm sleepy.
WHAT'S WITH YOU? PUT A LITTLE EFFORT INTO THIS! IF YOU KEEP ACTING SO UNROMANTIC, I MIGHT CRY!
GOD, YOU'RE SUCH A DOG! ALWAYS YAPPING!
HOW ABOUT YOU QUIT THE YAPPING AND GET ON WITH IT? I'M TIRED, YOU MUTT, SO HURRY IT ALONG!
I'M NOT A MUTT! I'M NOT EVEN A DOG! YOU'RE SO MEAN!
Ouch!
WHAT THE HELL?
YOU HAVE TO BE ON A MORNING CHAT SHOW JUST TO BE NICE TO ME?
DON'T TALK ABOUT THAT, ROVER.
FINE. I WON'T, THEN!

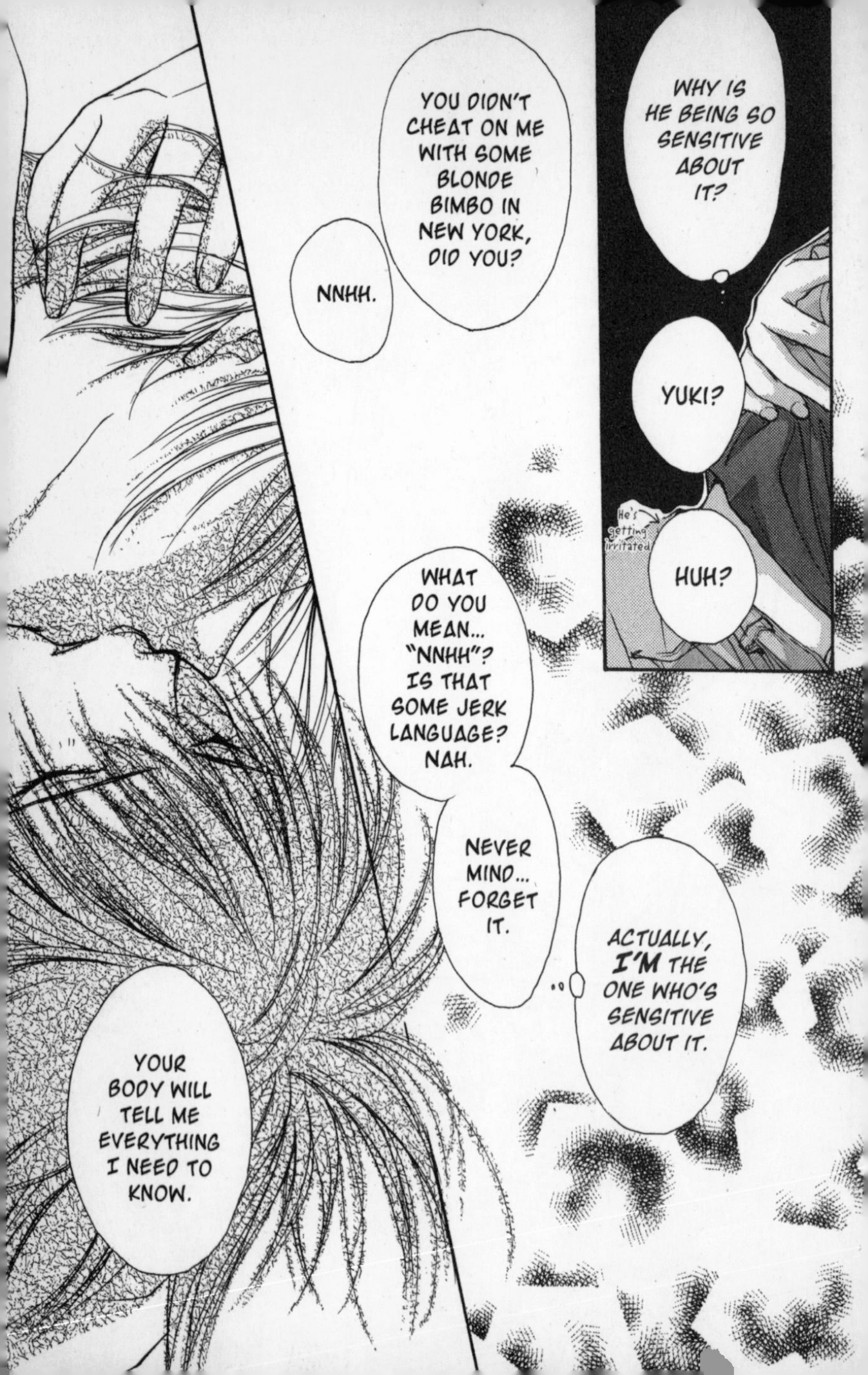
WHY IS HE BEING SO SENSITIVE ABOUT IT?
YUKI?
He's getting irritated
HUH?
YOU DIDN'T CHEAT ON ME WITH SOME BLONDE BIMBO IN NEW YORK, DID YOU?
NNHH.
WHAT DO YOU MEAN... "NNHH"? IS THAT SOME JERK LANGUAGE? NAH.
NEVER MIND... FORGET IT.
ACTUALLY, I'M THE ONE WHO'S SENSITIVE ABOUT IT.
YOUR BODY WILL TELL ME EVERYTHING I NEED TO KNOW.

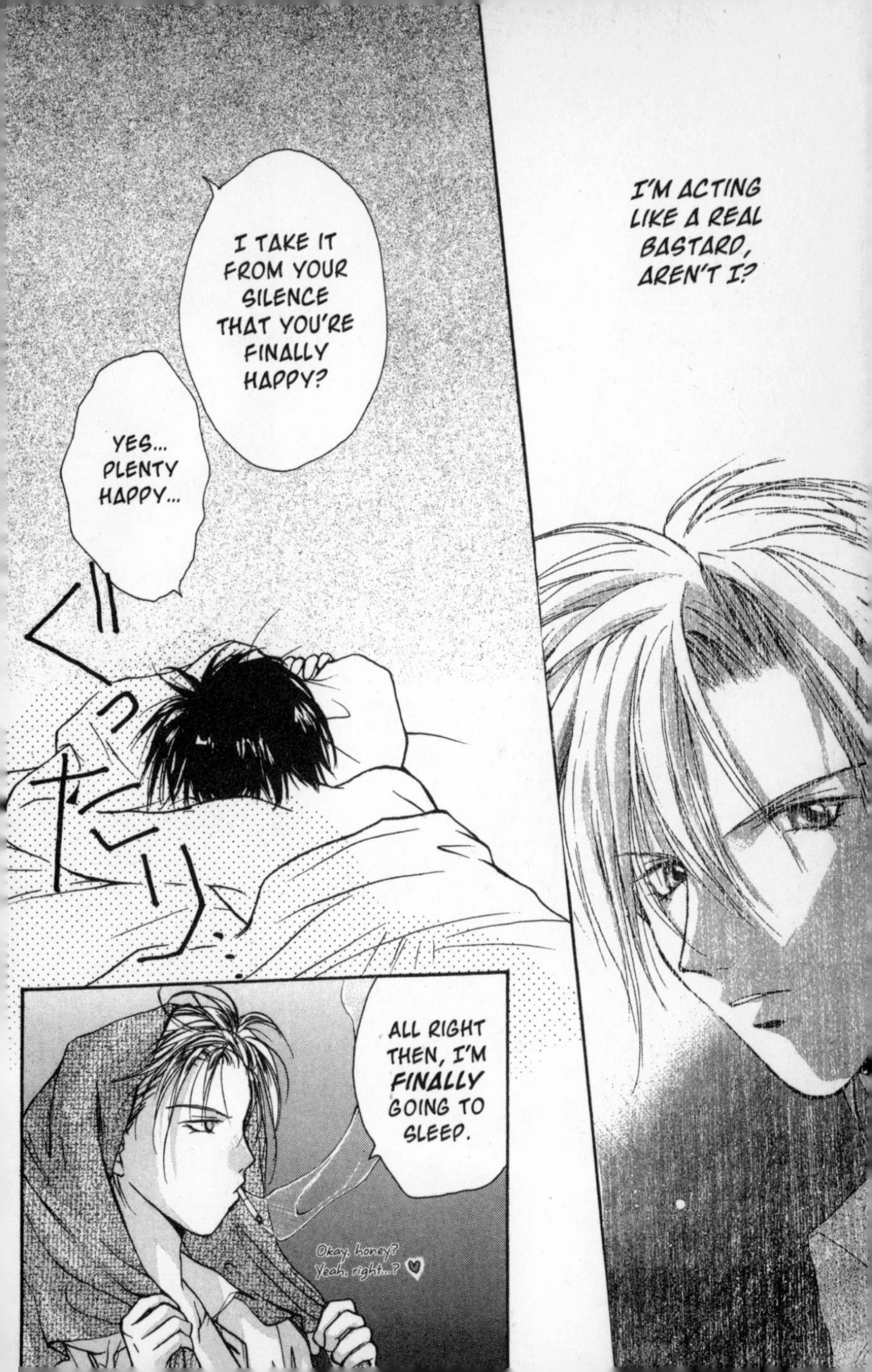
I'M ACTING LIKE A REAL BASTARD, AREN'T I?
I TAKE IT FROM YOUR SILENCE THAT YOU'RE FINALLY HAPPY?
YES... PLENTY HAPPY...
ALL RIGHT THEN, I'M FINALLY GOING TO SLEEP.
Okay, honey? Yeah, right...? ♥

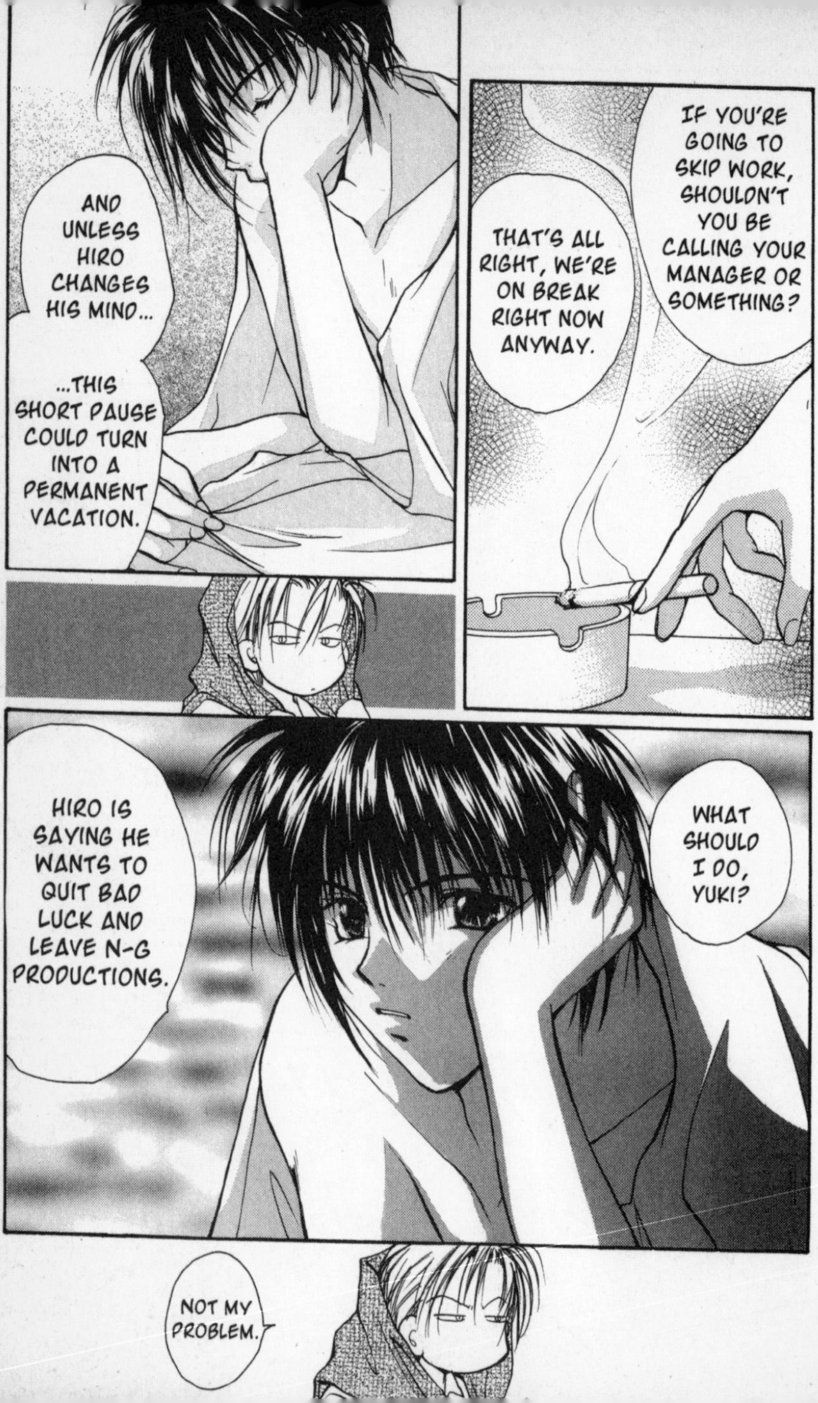
IF YOU'RE GOING TO SKIP WORK, SHOULDN'T YOU BE CALLING YOUR MANAGER OR SOMETHING?
THAT'S ALL RIGHT, WE'RE ON BREAK RIGHT NOW ANYWAY.
AND UNLESS HIRO CHANGES HIS MIND...
...THIS SHORT PAUSE COULD TURN INTO A PERMANENT VACATION.
WHAT SHOULD I DO, YUKI?
HIRO IS SAYING HE WANTS TO QUIT BAD LUCK AND LEAVE N-G PRODUCTIONS.
NOT MY PROBLEM.

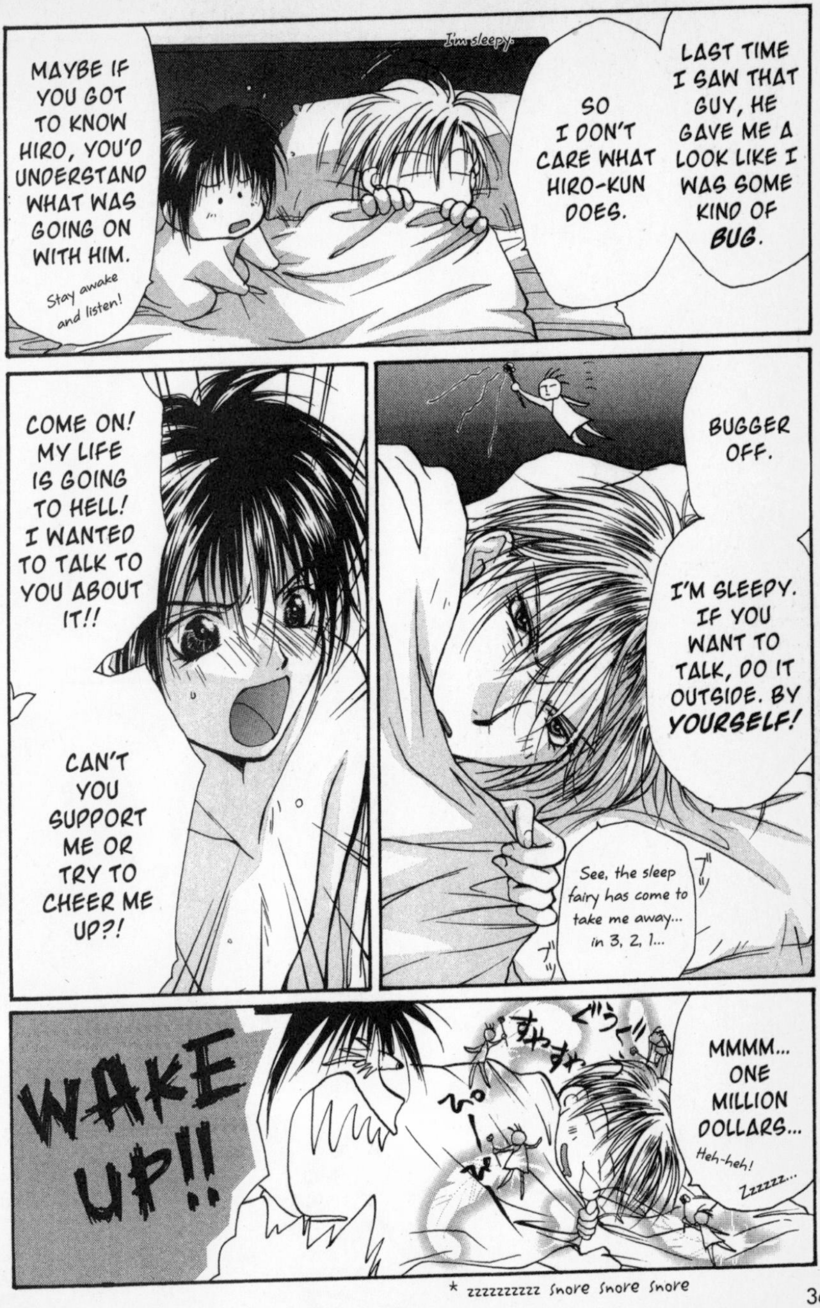
LAST TIME I SAW THAT GUY, HE GAVE ME A LOOK LIKE I WAS SOME KIND OF BUG.
I'm sleepy.
SO I DON'T CARE WHAT HIRO-KUN DOES.
MAYBE IF YOU GOT TO KNOW HIRO, YOU'D UNDERSTAND WHAT WAS GOING ON WITH HIM.
Stay awake and listen!
BUGGER OFF.
I'M SLEEPY. IF YOU WANT TO TALK, DO IT OUTSIDE. BY YOURSELF!
See, the sleep fairy has come to take me away... in 3, 2, 1...
COME ON! MY LIFE IS GOING TO HELL! I WANTED TO TALK TO YOU ABOUT IT!!
CAN'T YOU SUPPORT ME OR TRY TO CHEER ME UP?!
MMMM... ONE MILLION DOLLARS...
Heh-heh!
Zzzzzz...
ぐう～!!
すやすや
WAKE UP!!

* zzzzzzzzzz snore snore snore

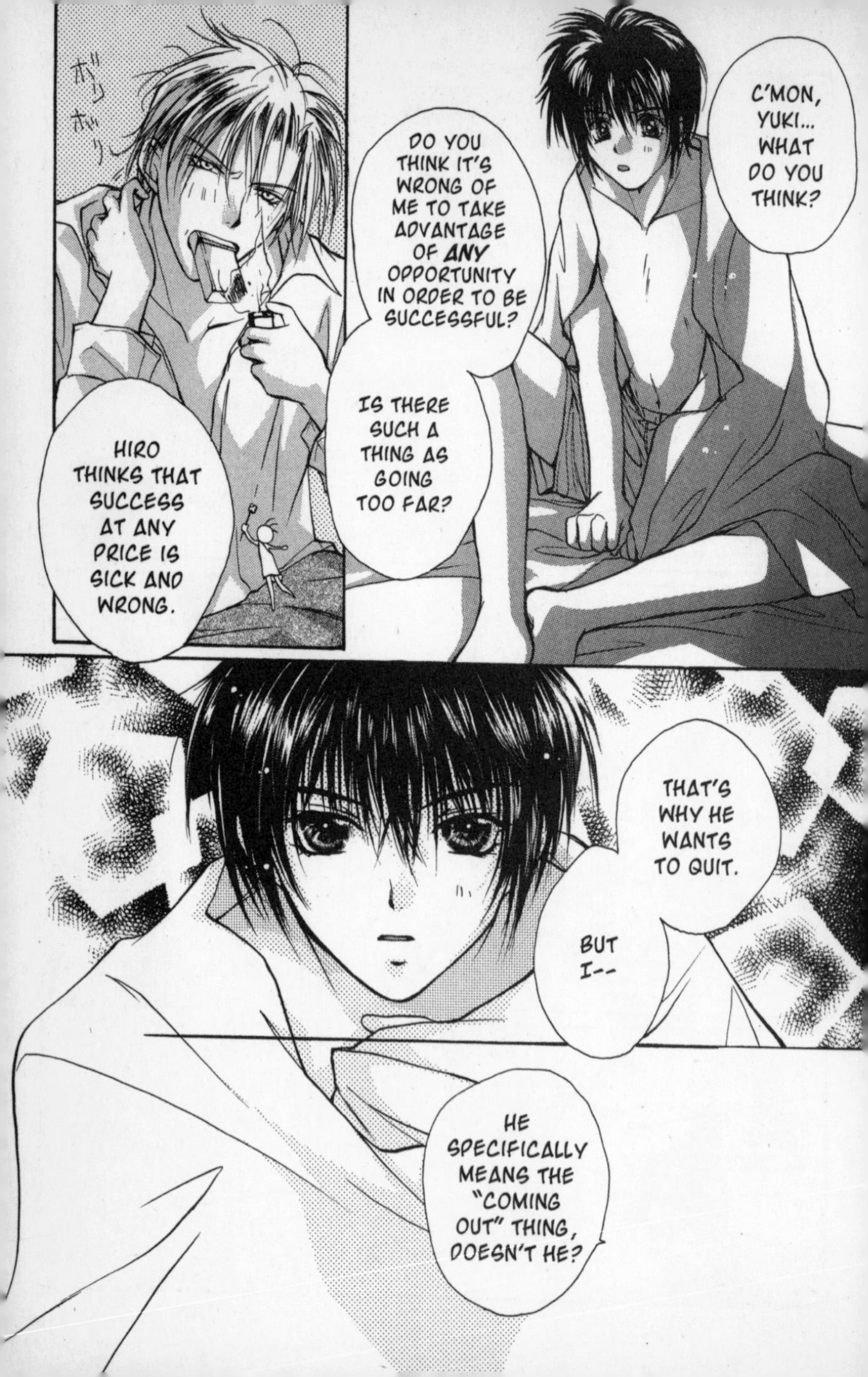
C'MON, YUKI... WHAT DO YOU THINK?
DO YOU THINK IT'S WRONG OF ME TO TAKE ADVANTAGE OF **ANY** OPPORTUNITY IN ORDER TO BE SUCCESSFUL?
IS THERE SUCH A THING AS GOING TOO FAR?
ボリボリ
HIRO THINKS THAT SUCCESS AT ANY PRICE IS SICK AND WRONG.
THAT'S WHY HE WANTS TO QUIT.
BUT I--
HE SPECIFICALLY MEANS THE "COMING OUT" THING, DOESN'T HE?

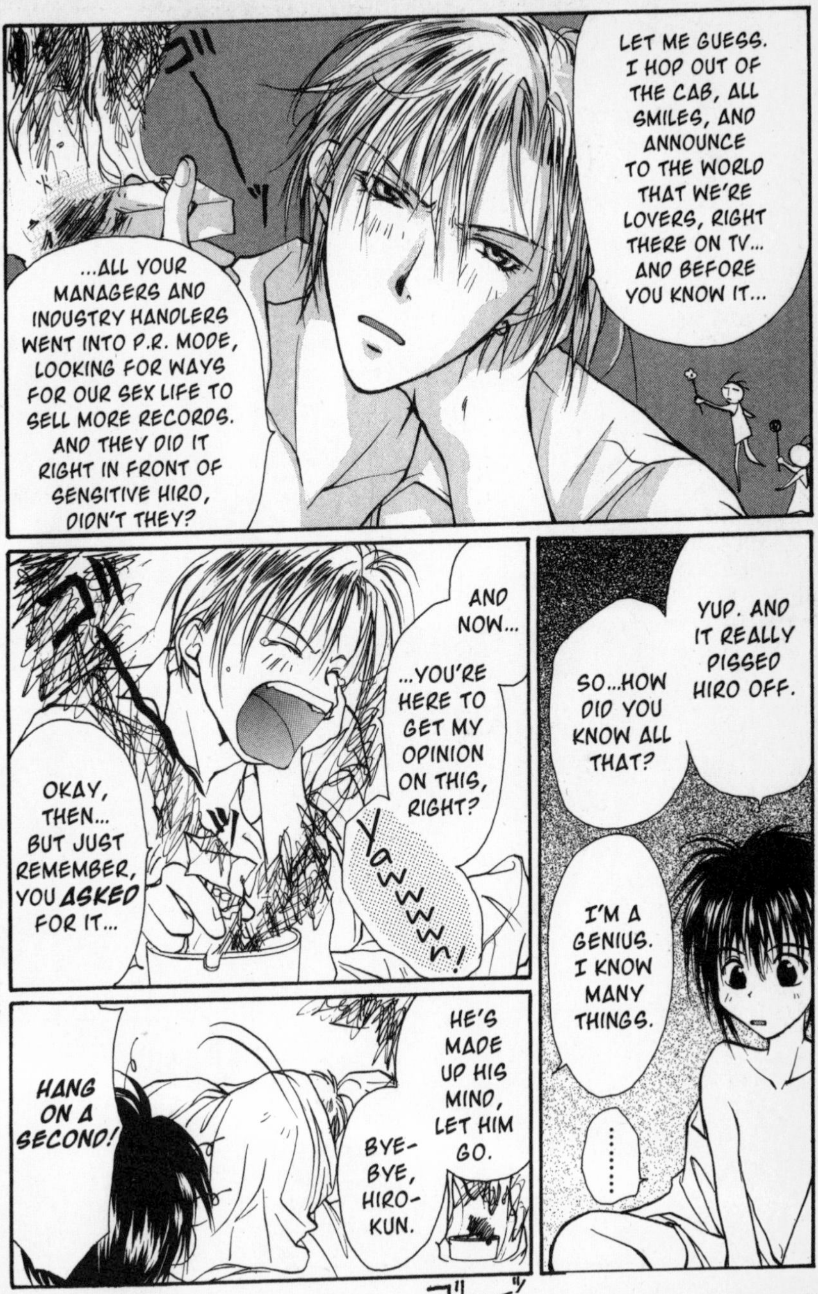
LET ME GUESS. I HOP OUT OF THE CAB, ALL SMILES, AND ANNOUNCE TO THE WORLD THAT WE'RE LOVERS, RIGHT THERE ON TV... AND BEFORE YOU KNOW IT...
...ALL YOUR MANAGERS AND INDUSTRY HANDLERS WENT INTO P.R. MODE, LOOKING FOR WAYS FOR OUR SEX LIFE TO SELL MORE RECORDS. AND THEY DID IT RIGHT IN FRONT OF SENSITIVE HIRO, DIDN'T THEY?
YUP. AND IT REALLY PISSED HIRO OFF.
SO...HOW DID YOU KNOW ALL THAT?
I'M A GENIUS. I KNOW MANY THINGS.
......
AND NOW...
...YOU'RE HERE TO GET MY OPINION ON THIS, RIGHT?
Yawwwwn!
OKAY, THEN... BUT JUST REMEMBER, YOU **ASKED** FOR IT...
HE'S MADE UP HIS MIND, LET HIM GO.
BYE-BYE, HIRO-KUN.
HANG ON A SECOND!

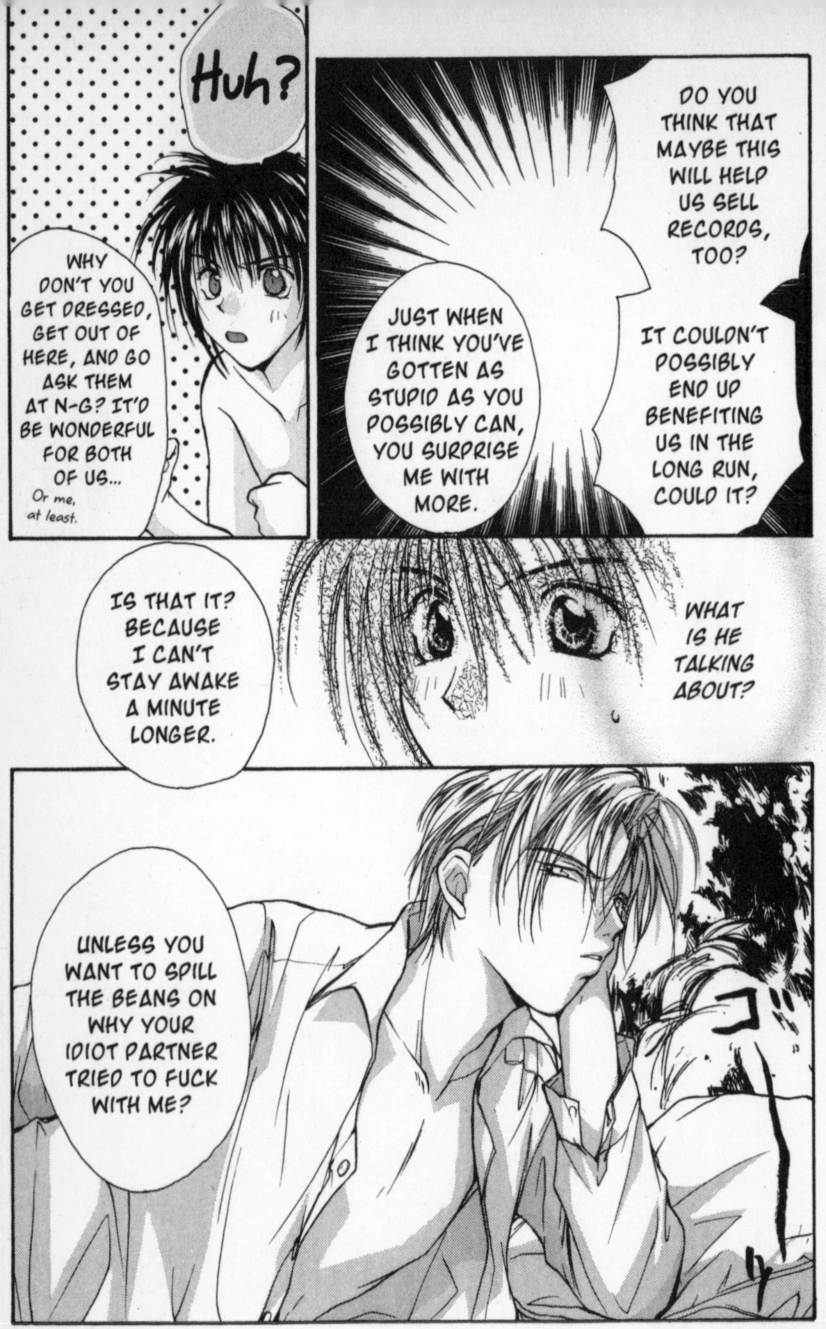
DO YOU THINK THAT MAYBE THIS WILL HELP US SELL RECORDS, TOO?
IT COULDN'T POSSIBLY END UP BENEFITING US IN THE LONG RUN, COULD IT?
JUST WHEN I THINK YOU'VE GOTTEN AS STUPID AS YOU POSSIBLY CAN, YOU SURPRISE ME WITH MORE.
Huh?
WHY DON'T YOU GET DRESSED, GET OUT OF HERE, AND GO ASK THEM AT N-G? IT'D BE WONDERFUL FOR BOTH OF US...
Or me, at least.
WHAT IS HE TALKING ABOUT?
IS THAT IT? BECAUSE I CAN'T STAY AWAKE A MINUTE LONGER.
UNLESS YOU WANT TO SPILL THE BEANS ON WHY YOUR IDIOT PARTNER TRIED TO FUCK WITH ME?

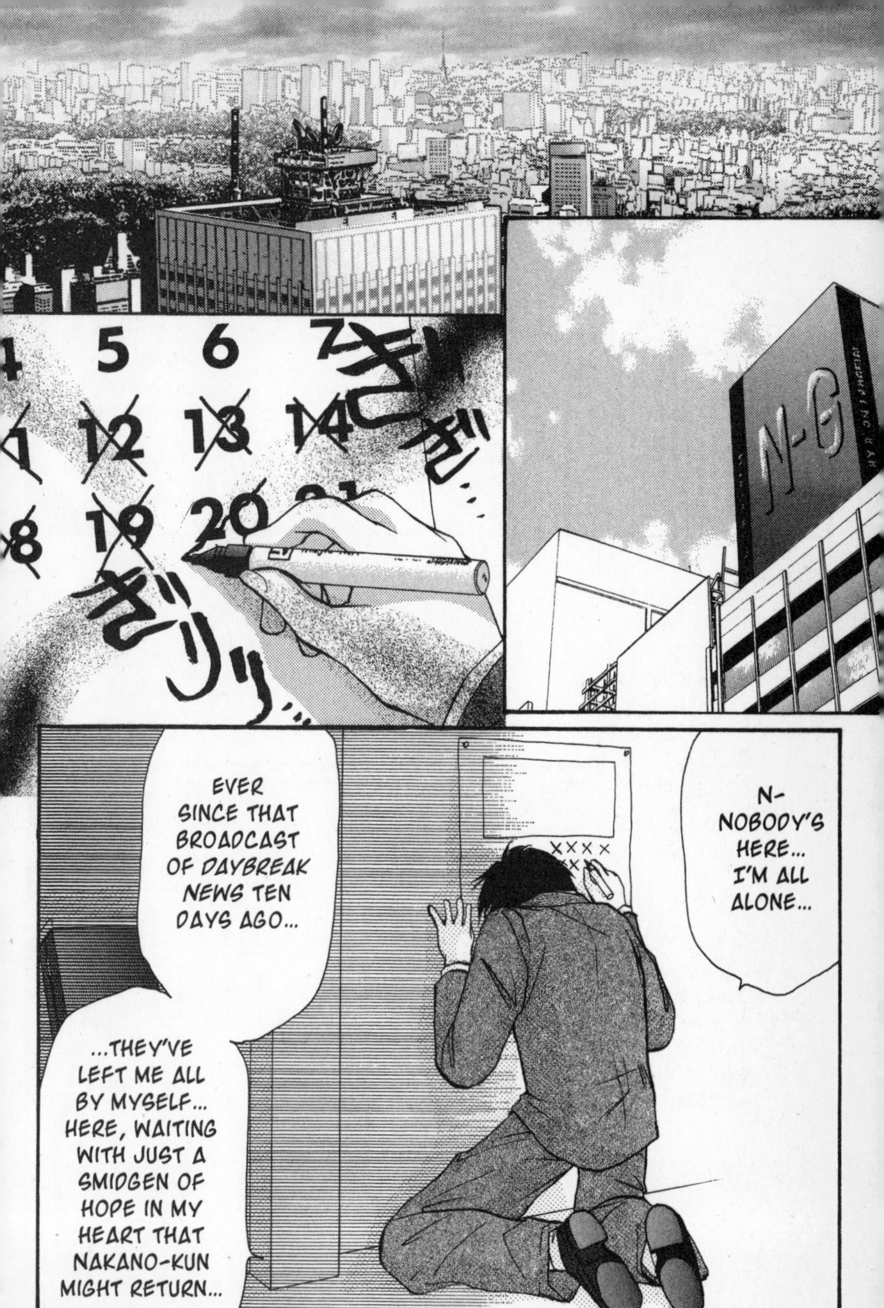
ぎりり…
N-NOBODY'S HERE... I'M ALL ALONE...
EVER SINCE THAT BROADCAST OF DAYBREAK NEWS TEN DAYS AGO...
...THEY'VE LEFT ME ALL BY MYSELF... HERE, WAITING WITH JUST A SMIDGEN OF HOPE IN MY HEART THAT NAKANO-KUN MIGHT RETURN...

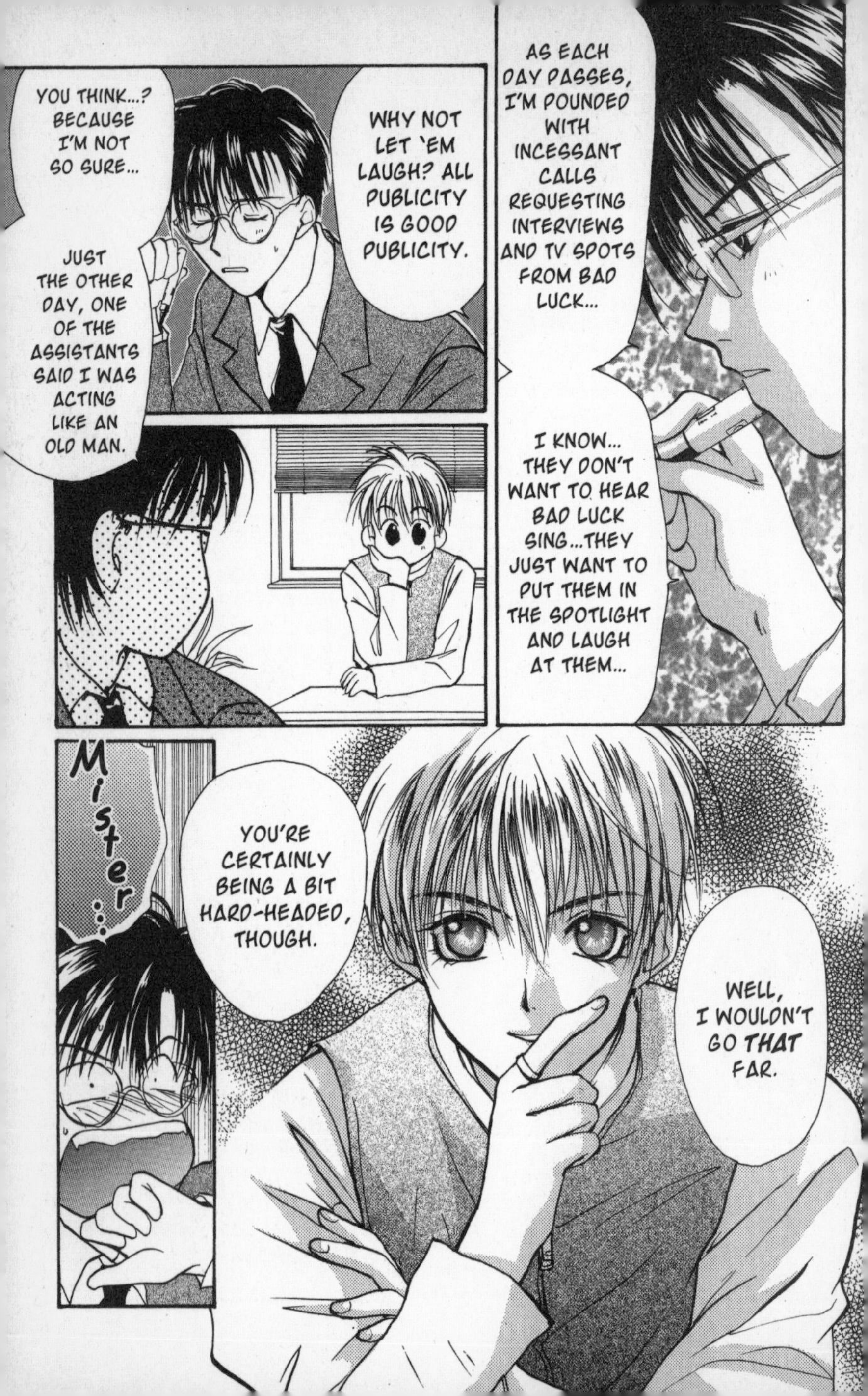
AS EACH DAY PASSES, I'M POUNDED WITH INCESSANT CALLS REQUESTING INTERVIEWS AND TV SPOTS FROM BAD LUCK...
I KNOW... THEY DON'T WANT TO HEAR BAD LUCK SING...THEY JUST WANT TO PUT THEM IN THE SPOTLIGHT AND LAUGH AT THEM...
WHY NOT LET 'EM LAUGH? ALL PUBLICITY IS GOOD PUBLICITY.
YOU THINK...? BECAUSE I'M NOT SO SURE...
JUST THE OTHER DAY, ONE OF THE ASSISTANTS SAID I WAS ACTING LIKE AN OLD MAN.
YOU'RE CERTAINLY BEING A BIT HARD-HEADED, THOUGH.
WELL, I WOULDN'T GO **THAT** FAR.
Mister...

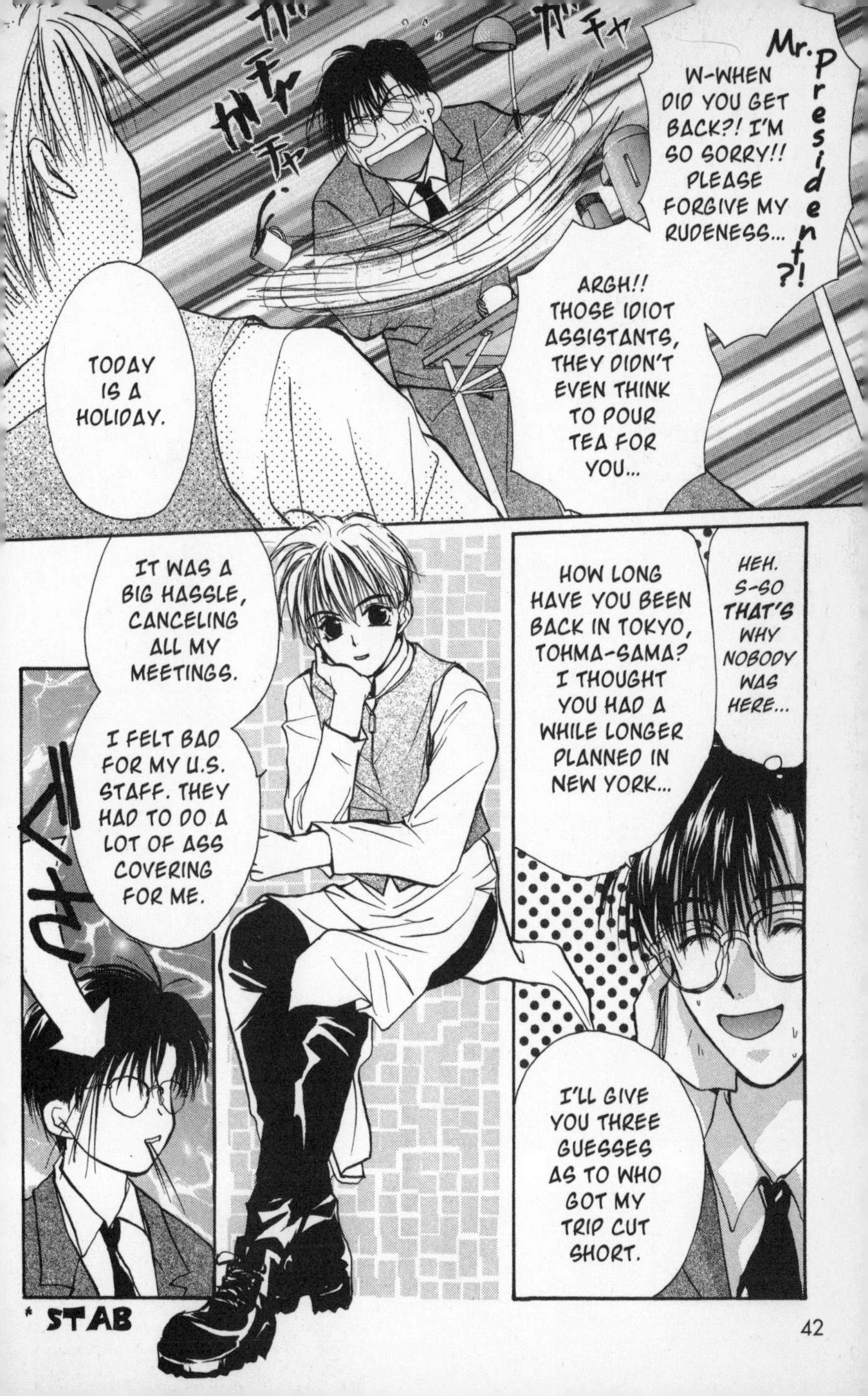

ガチャ
Mr. President?!
W-WHEN DID YOU GET BACK?! I'M SO SORRY!! PLEASE FORGIVE MY RUDENESS...
ARGH!! THOSE IDIOT ASSISTANTS, THEY DIDN'T EVEN THINK TO POUR TEA FOR YOU...
ガチャガチャ
TODAY IS A HOLIDAY.
HEH. S-SO THAT'S WHY NOBODY WAS HERE...
HOW LONG HAVE YOU BEEN BACK IN TOKYO, TOHMA-SAMA? I THOUGHT YOU HAD A WHILE LONGER PLANNED IN NEW YORK...
I'LL GIVE YOU THREE GUESSES AS TO WHO GOT MY TRIP CUT SHORT.
IT WAS A BIG HASSLE, CANCELING ALL MY MEETINGS.
I FELT BAD FOR MY U.S. STAFF. THEY HAD TO DO A LOT OF ASS COVERING FOR ME.
* STAB

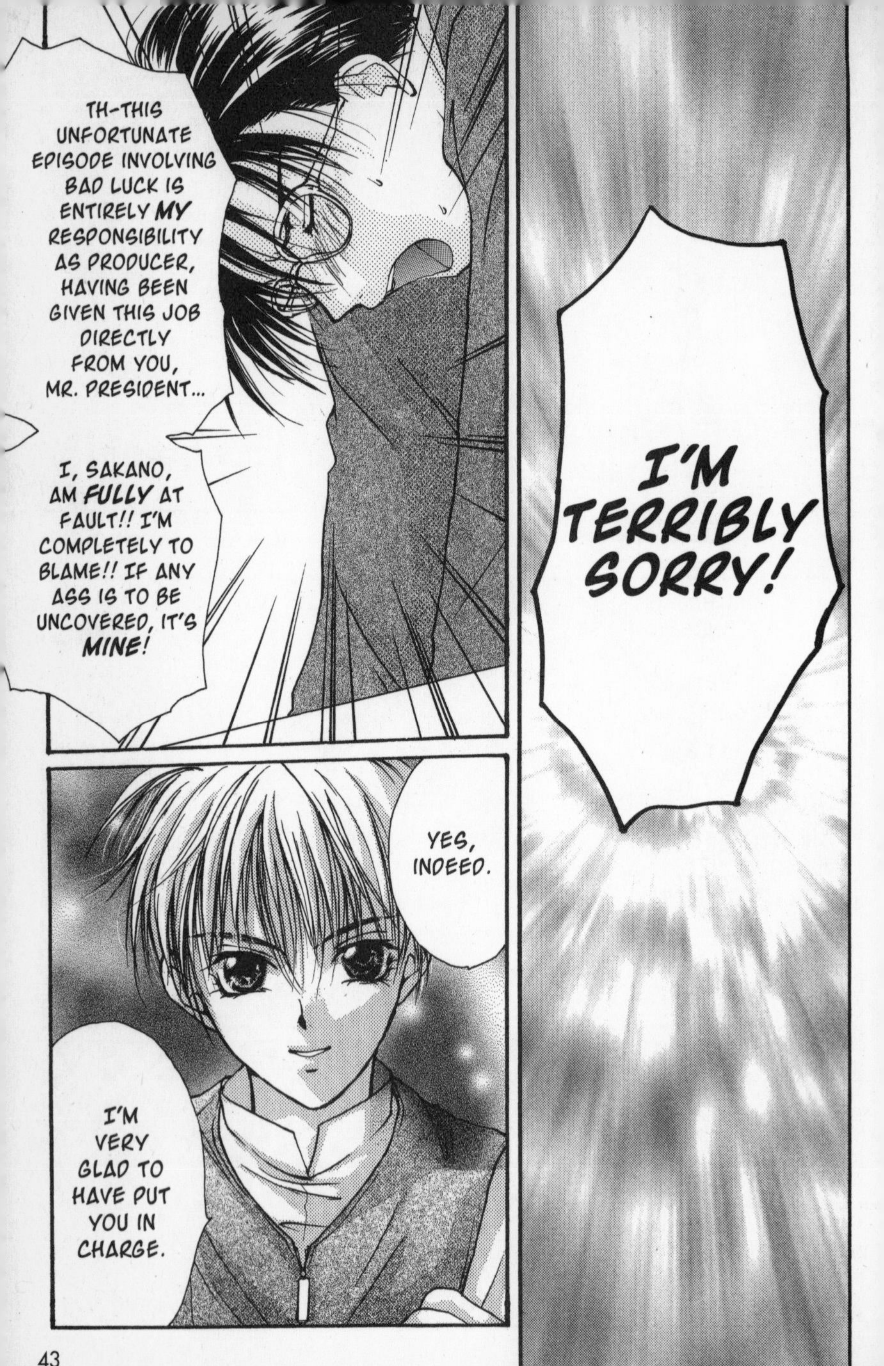
I'M TERRIBLY SORRY!
TH-THIS UNFORTUNATE EPISODE INVOLVING BAD LUCK IS ENTIRELY MY RESPONSIBILITY AS PRODUCER, HAVING BEEN GIVEN THIS JOB DIRECTLY FROM YOU, MR. PRESIDENT...
I, SAKANO, AM FULLY AT FAULT!! I'M COMPLETELY TO BLAME!! IF ANY ASS IS TO BE UNCOVERED, IT'S MINE!
YES, INDEED.
I'M VERY GLAD TO HAVE PUT YOU IN CHARGE.

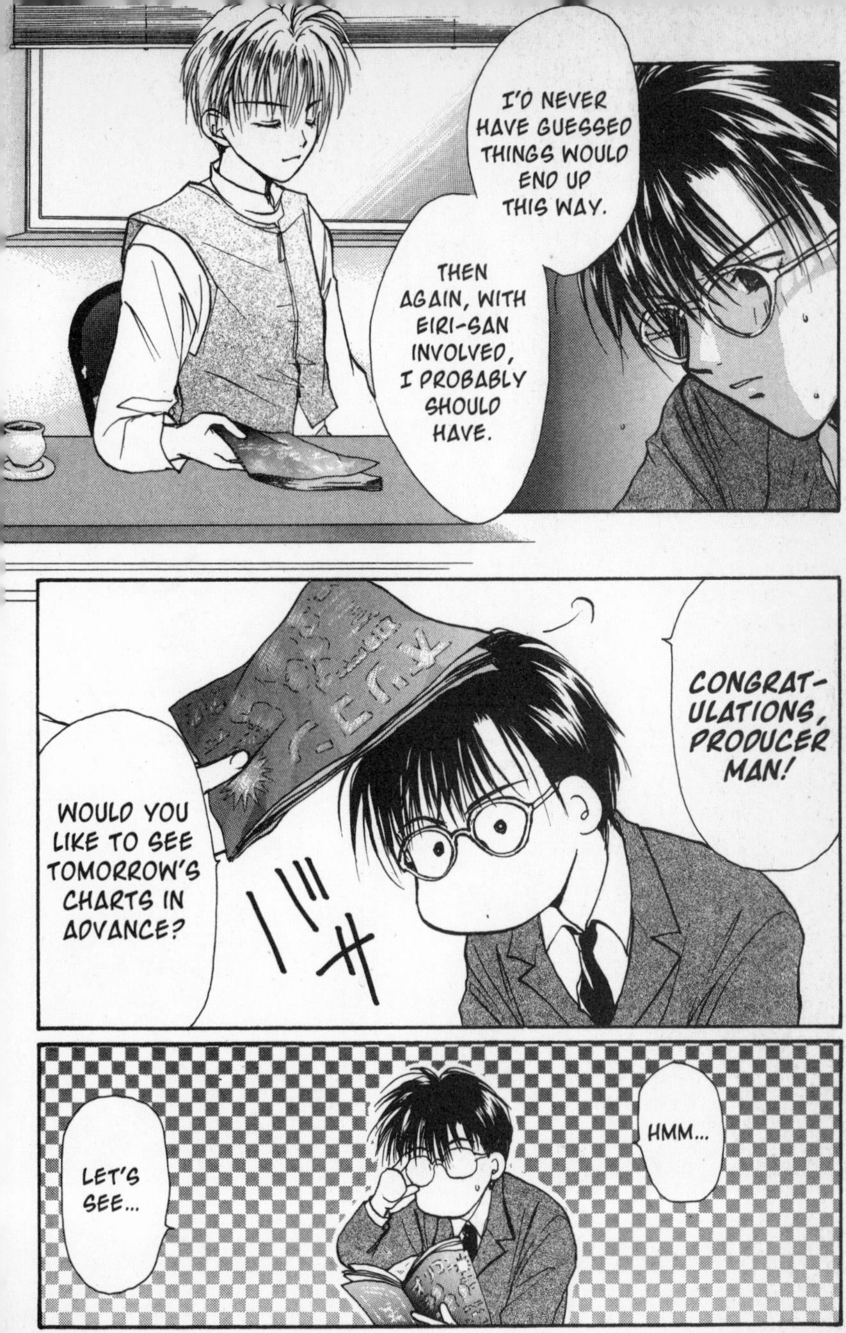
I'D NEVER HAVE GUESSED THINGS WOULD END UP THIS WAY.
THEN AGAIN, WITH EIRI-SAN INVOLVED, I PROBABLY SHOULD HAVE.
CONGRAT-ULATIONS, PRODUCER MAN!
WOULD YOU LIKE TO SEE TOMORROW'S CHARTS IN ADVANCE?
HMM...
LET'S SEE...

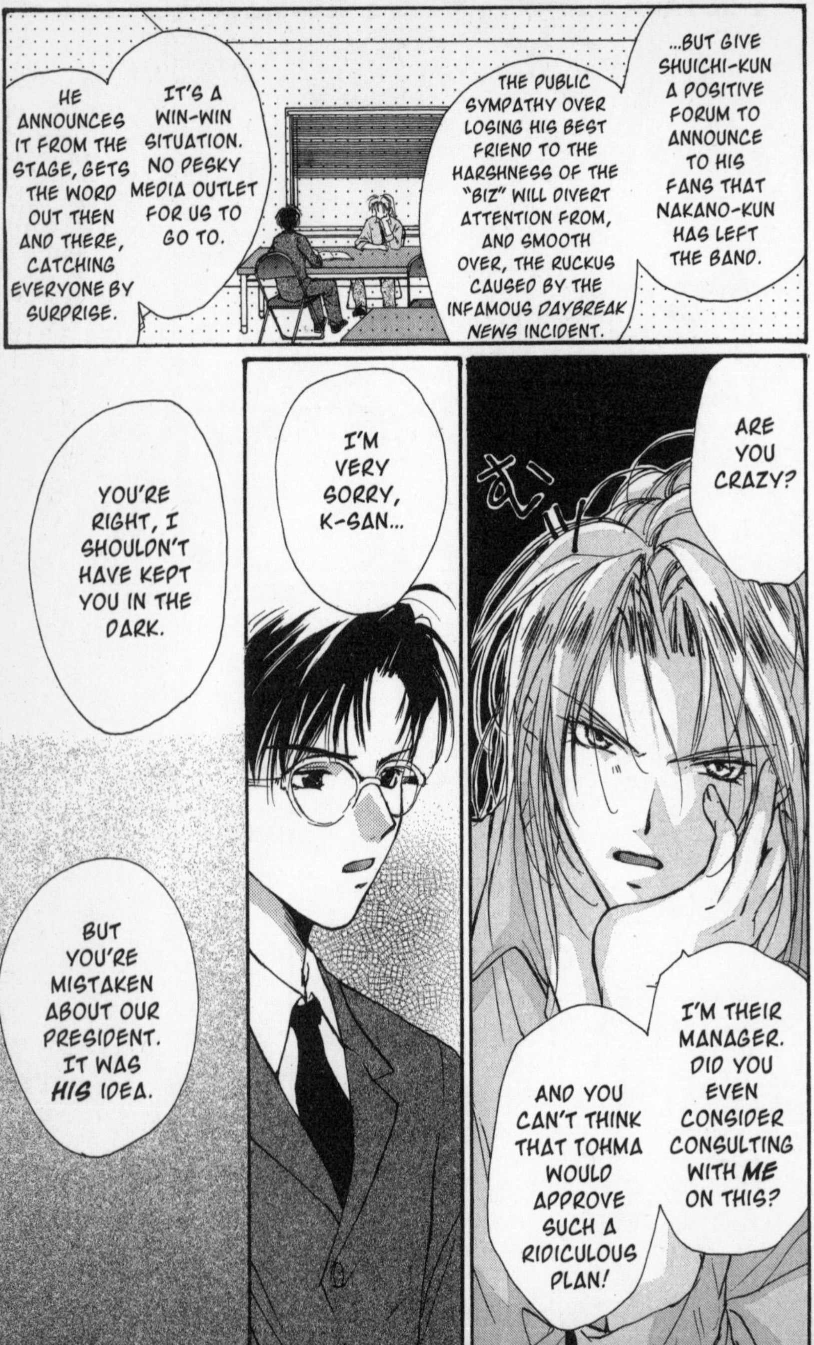
...BUT GIVE SHUICHI-KUN A POSITIVE FORUM TO ANNOUNCE TO HIS FANS THAT NAKANO-KUN HAS LEFT THE BAND.
THE PUBLIC SYMPATHY OVER LOSING HIS BEST FRIEND TO THE HARSHNESS OF THE "BIZ" WILL DIVERT ATTENTION FROM, AND SMOOTH OVER, THE RUCKUS CAUSED BY THE INFAMOUS *DAYBREAK NEWS* INCIDENT.
IT'S A WIN-WIN SITUATION. NO PESKY MEDIA OUTLET FOR US TO GO TO.
HE ANNOUNCES IT FROM THE STAGE, GETS THE WORD OUT THEN AND THERE, CATCHING EVERYONE BY SURPRISE.
ARE YOU CRAZY?
I'M THEIR MANAGER. DID YOU EVEN CONSIDER CONSULTING WITH *ME* ON THIS?
AND YOU CAN'T THINK THAT TOHMA WOULD APPROVE SUCH A RIDICULOUS PLAN!
I'M VERY SORRY, K-SAN...
YOU'RE RIGHT, I SHOULDN'T HAVE KEPT YOU IN THE DARK.
BUT YOU'RE MISTAKEN ABOUT OUR PRESIDENT. IT WAS ***HIS*** IDEA.

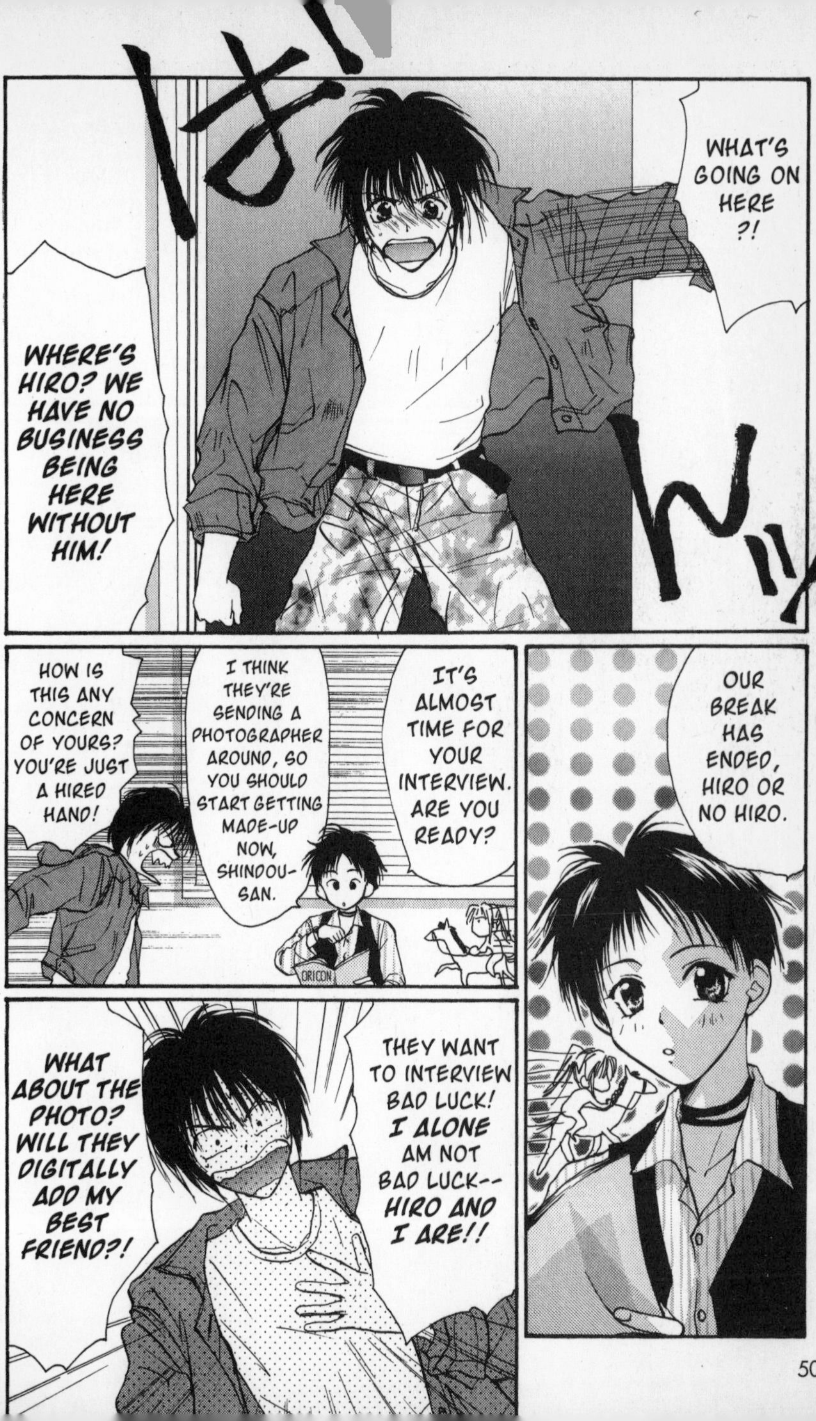
ば
WHAT'S GOING ON HERE ?!
WHERE'S HIRO? WE HAVE NO BUSINESS BEING HERE WITHOUT HIM!
んッ
OUR BREAK HAS ENDED, HIRO OR NO HIRO.
IT'S ALMOST TIME FOR YOUR INTERVIEW. ARE YOU READY?
I THINK THEY'RE SENDING A PHOTOGRAPHER AROUND, SO YOU SHOULD START GETTING MADE-UP NOW, SHINDOU-SAN.
HOW IS THIS ANY CONCERN OF YOURS? YOU'RE JUST A HIRED HAND!
ORICON
THEY WANT TO INTERVIEW BAD LUCK! I ALONE AM NOT BAD LUCK--HIRO AND I ARE!!
WHAT ABOUT THE PHOTO? WILL THEY DIGITALLY ADD MY BEST FRIEND?!

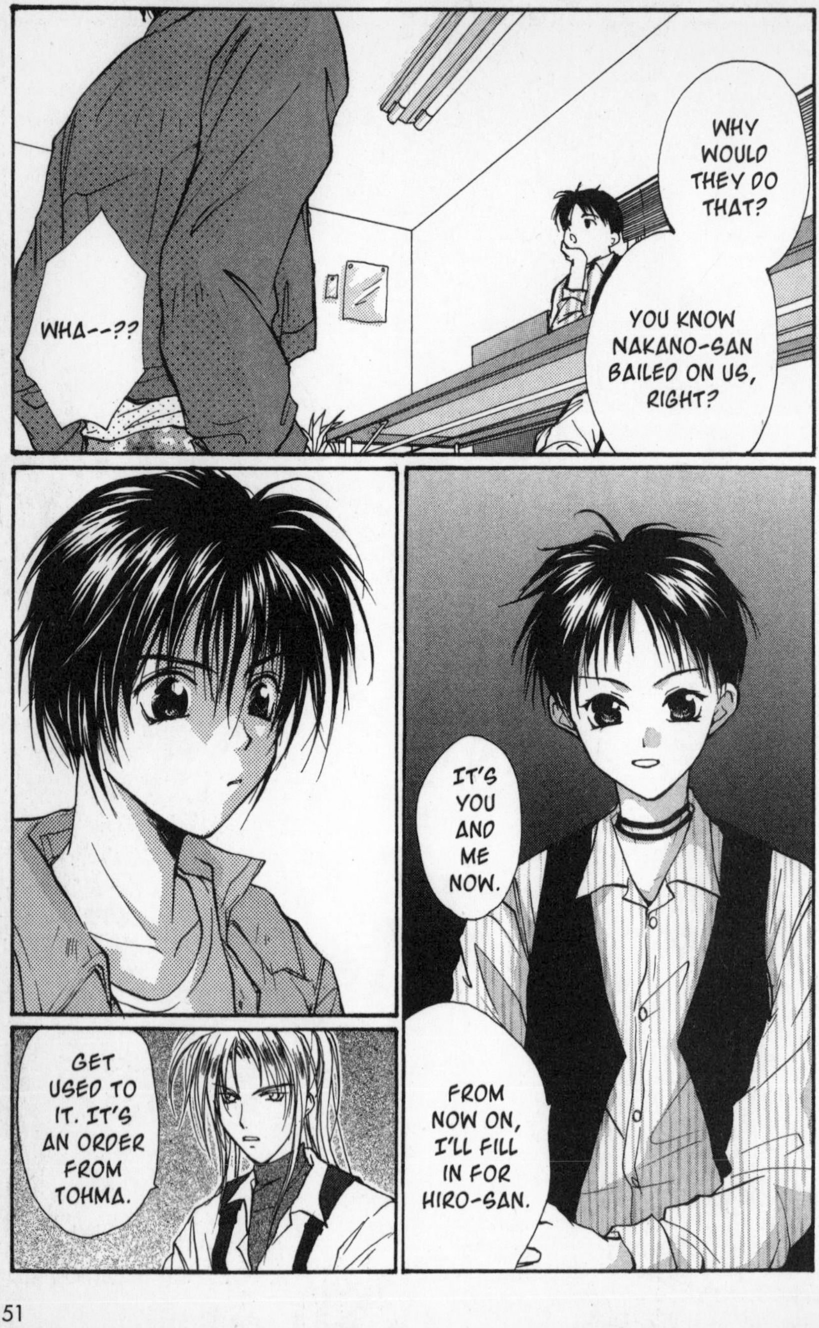
WHY WOULD THEY DO THAT?
YOU KNOW NAKANO-SAN BAILED ON US, RIGHT?
WHA--??
IT'S YOU AND ME NOW.
FROM NOW ON, I'LL FILL IN FOR HIRO-SAN.
GET USED TO IT. IT'S AN ORDER FROM TOHMA.

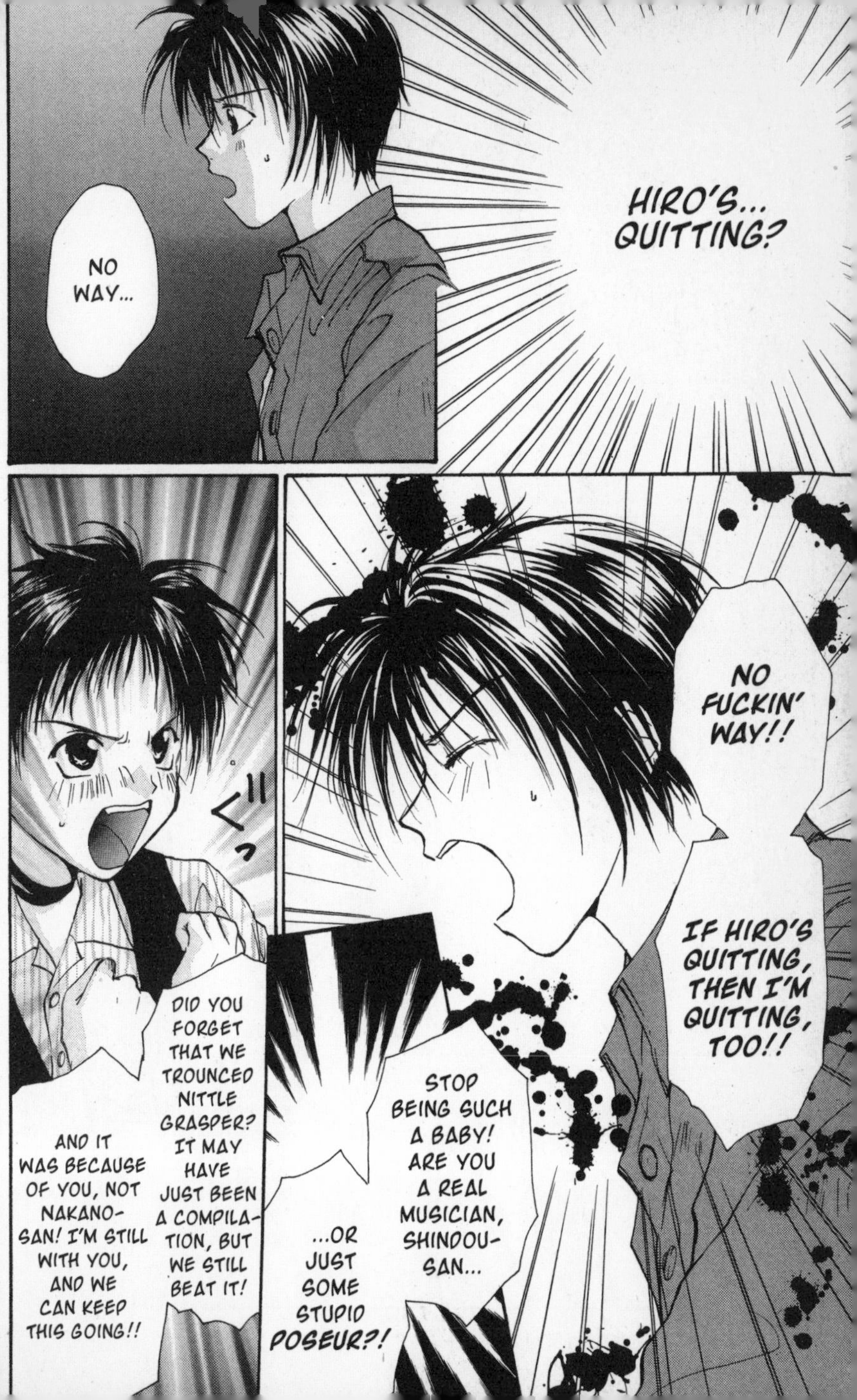
HIRO'S... QUITTING?
NO WAY...
NO FUCKIN' WAY!!
IF HIRO'S QUITTING, THEN I'M QUITTING, TOO!!
STOP BEING SUCH A BABY! ARE YOU A REAL MUSICIAN, SHINDOU-SAN...
...OR JUST SOME STUPID POSEUR?!
ぐっ
DID YOU FORGET THAT WE TROUNCED NITTLE GRASPER? IT MAY HAVE JUST BEEN A COMPILATION, BUT WE STILL BEAT IT!
AND IT WAS BECAUSE OF YOU, NOT NAKANO-SAN! I'M STILL WITH YOU, AND WE CAN KEEP THIS GOING!!

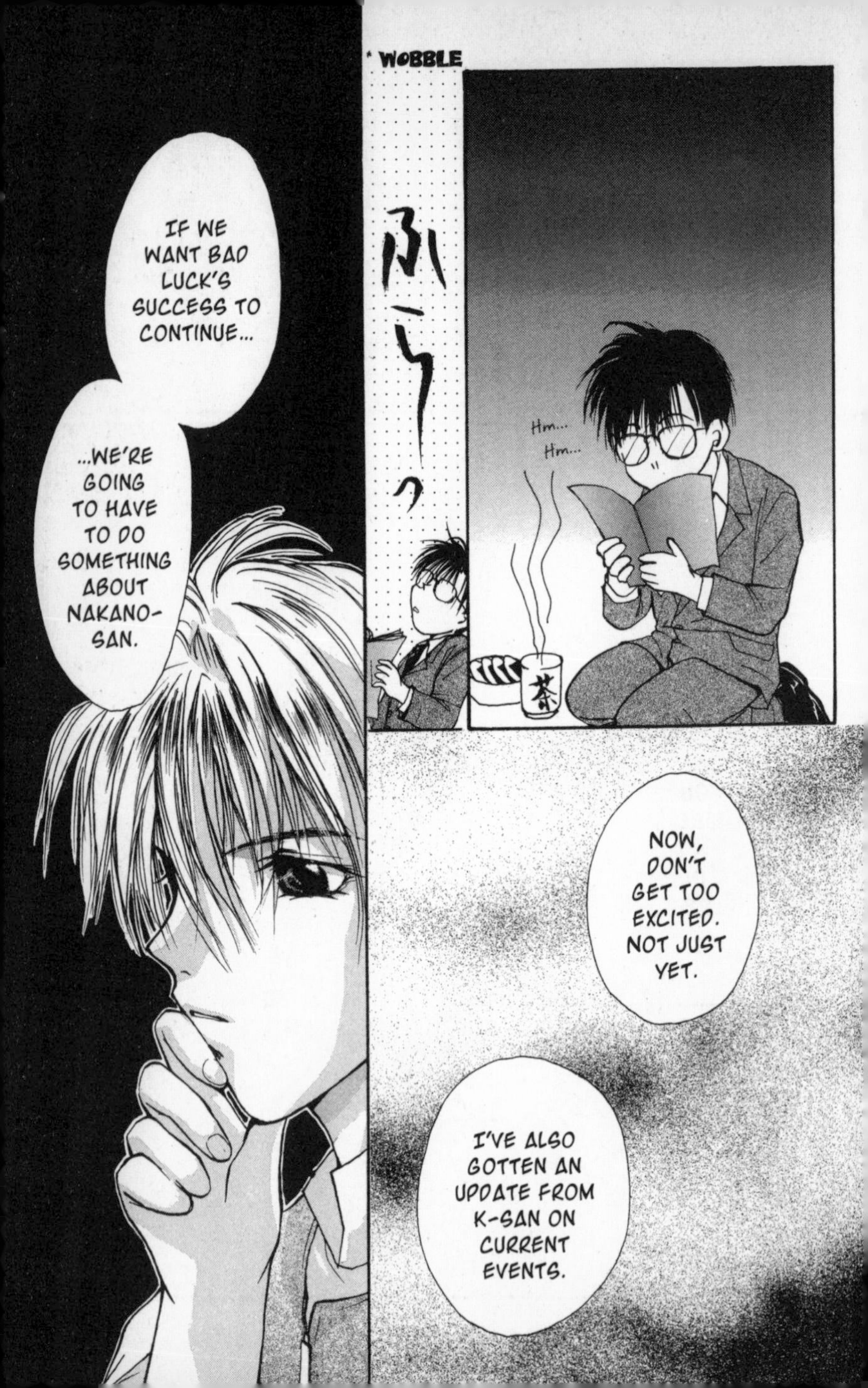
* WOBBLE
Hm... Hm...
NOW, DON'T GET TOO EXCITED. NOT JUST YET.
I'VE ALSO GOTTEN AN UPDATE FROM K-SAN ON CURRENT EVENTS.
IF WE WANT BAD LUCK'S SUCCESS TO CONTINUE...
...WE'RE GOING TO HAVE TO DO SOMETHING ABOUT NAKANO-SAN.

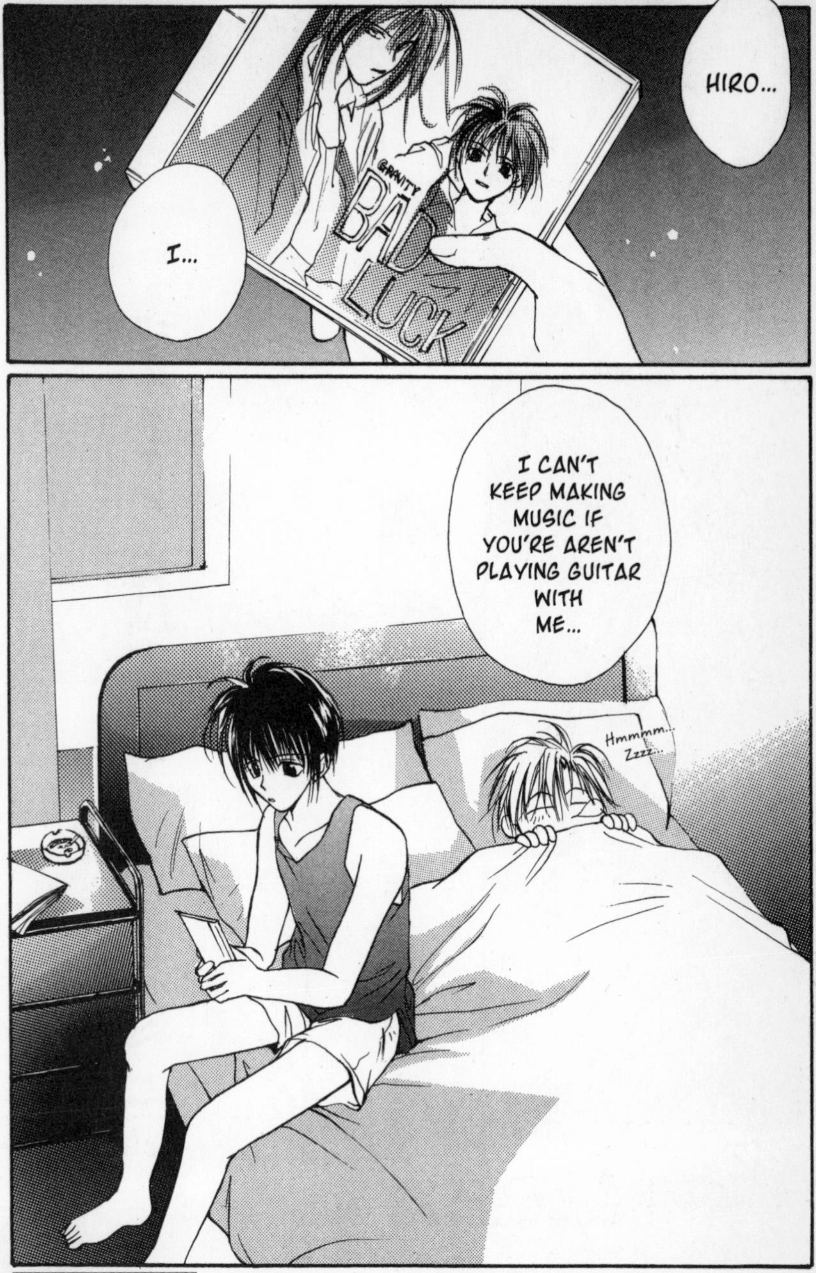
HIRO...
I...
GRAVITY
BAD LUCK
I CAN'T KEEP MAKING MUSIC IF YOU'RE AREN'T PLAYING GUITAR WITH ME...
Hmmmm... Zzzz...

track27 END

track28

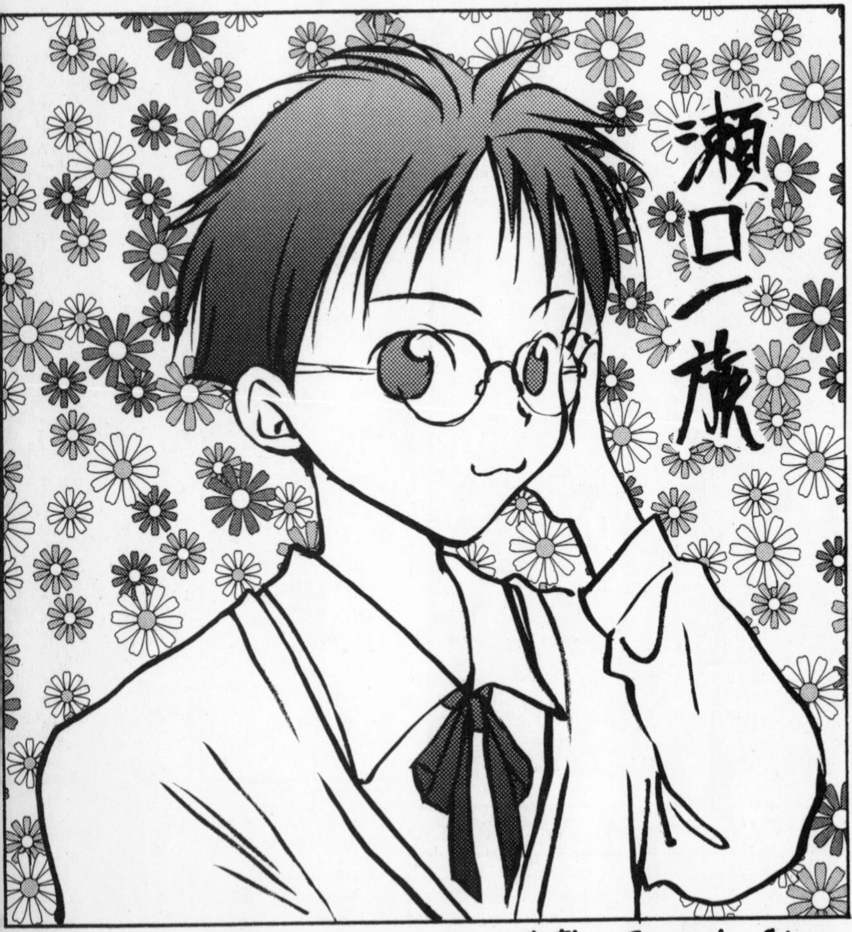
瀬口一族

* The Seguchi Clan

Gravitation

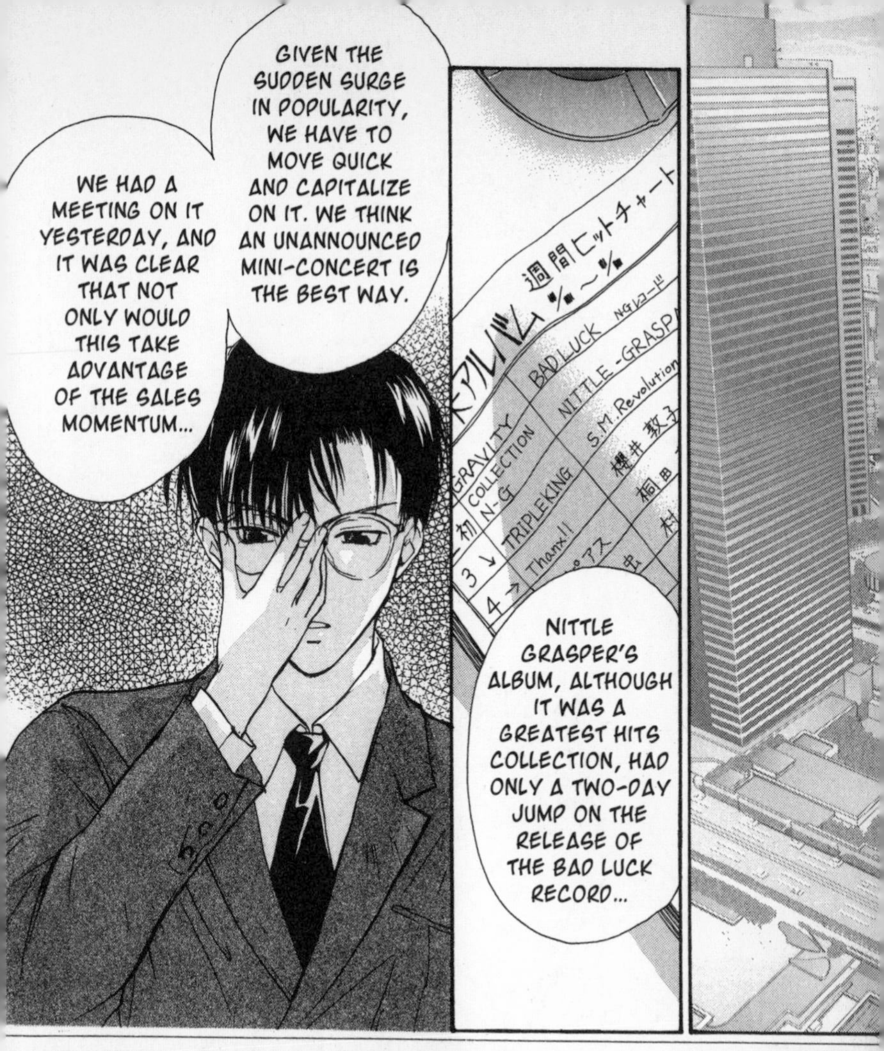
週間ヒットチャート
BAD LUCK
NGレコード
GRAVITY
COLLECTION
N-G
NITTLE-GRASP
TRIPLEKING
S.M.Revolution
Thanx!!
NITTLE GRASPER'S ALBUM, ALTHOUGH IT WAS A GREATEST HITS COLLECTION, HAD ONLY A TWO-DAY JUMP ON THE RELEASE OF THE BAD LUCK RECORD...
GIVEN THE SUDDEN SURGE IN POPULARITY, WE HAVE TO MOVE QUICK AND CAPITALIZE ON IT. WE THINK AN UNANNOUNCED MINI-CONCERT IS THE BEST WAY.
WE HAD A MEETING ON IT YESTERDAY, AND IT WAS CLEAR THAT NOT ONLY WOULD THIS TAKE ADVANTAGE OF THE SALES MOMENTUM...

ABOUT GRAVITATION TRACK 28

But actually it doesn't have much to do with this specific chapter.

About Sakano-san: He has quite a dedicated following. He's also a relatively masochistic fellow. I don't know if that's a good thing. I mean, he has a huge three-meter high poster of Seguchi Tohma in his living room, made from a photograph he secretly took himself. He folds his suits very neatly and puts them next to his pillow before going to bed. He sits in proper Japanese style at the end of each day and writes a letter chastising himself about the day's mistakes. I'll bet he'd go to sleep wearing his suit if he could, and he probably talks to his boss in his sleep..."Oh, yes, Mr. President!" I wouldn't even be surprised if he jams a pillow between his legs while having impure thoughts about Seguchi-san, and then commutes to N-G Productions on a bicycle (an old lady bike, not a cool one). I bet there's all sorts of dirty stuff like that lurking in his closet. So, anyway, I designate him "the character who matches with flowers the best." Mr. Super-White Sakano. And when am I ever going to give him a first name?

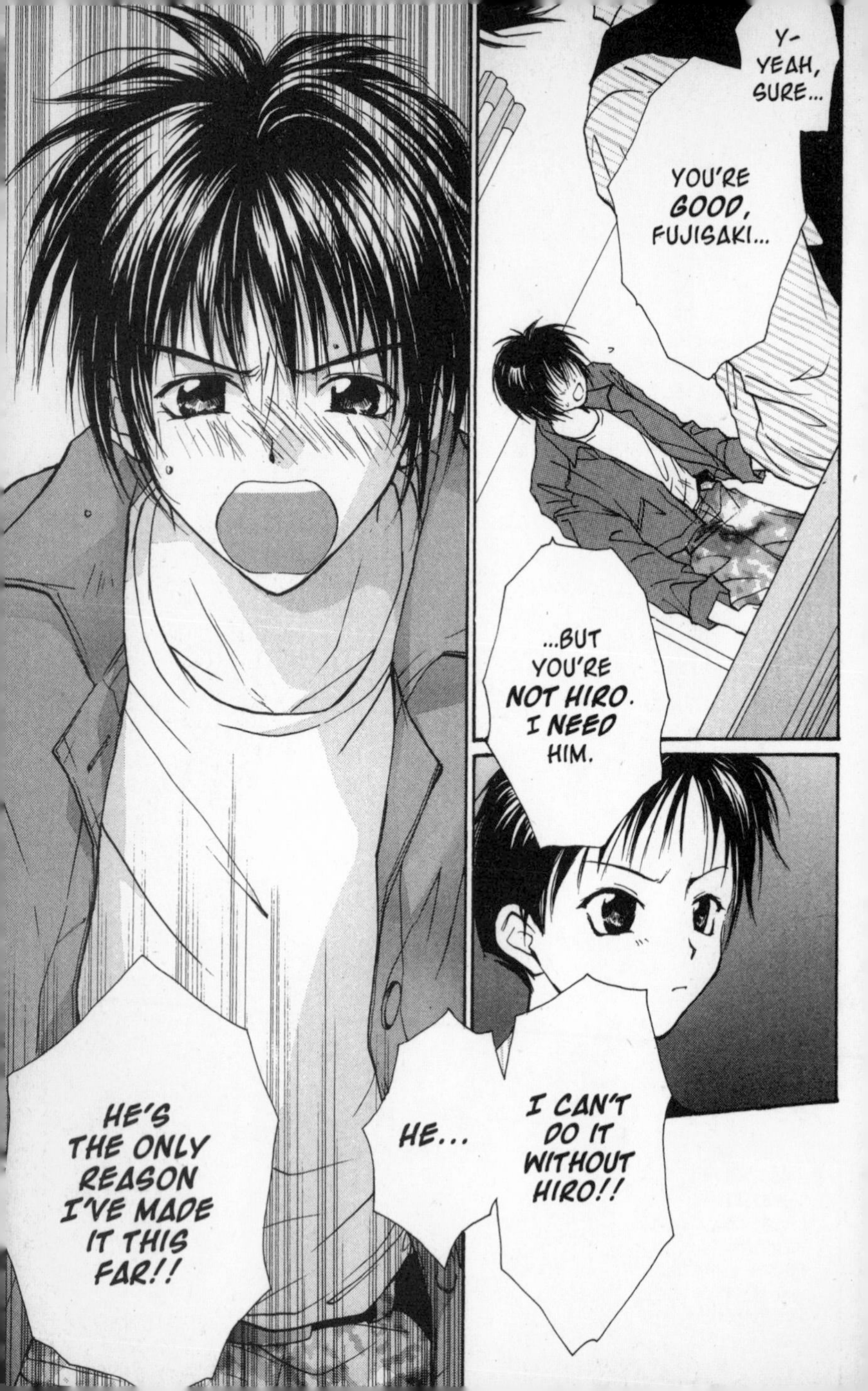
Y-YEAH, SURE...
YOU'RE GOOD, FUJISAKI...
...BUT YOU'RE NOT HIRO. I NEED HIM.
I CAN'T DO IT WITHOUT HIRO!!
HE...
HE'S THE ONLY REASON I'VE MADE IT THIS FAR!!

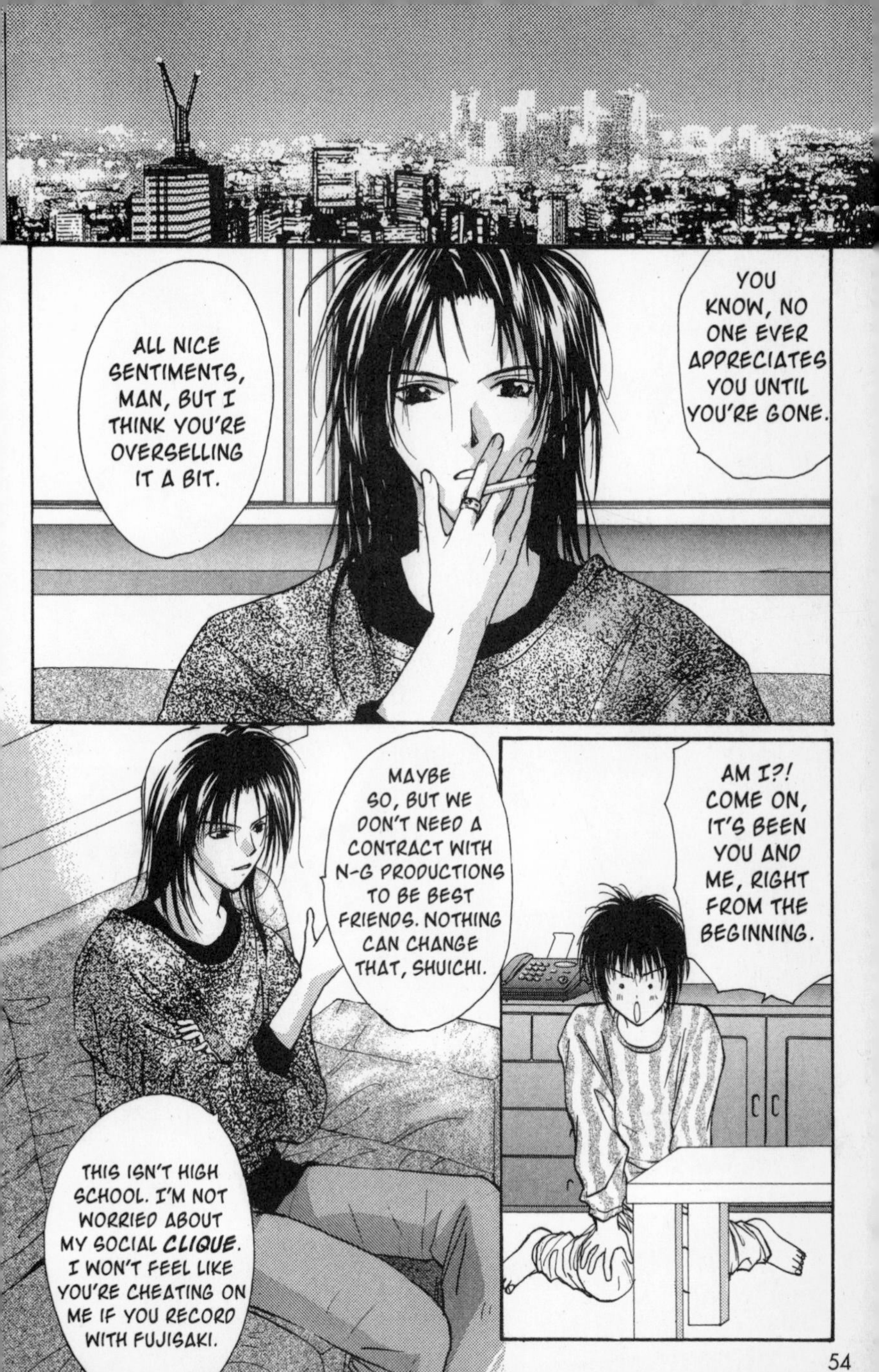

YOU KNOW, NO ONE EVER APPRECIATES YOU UNTIL YOU'RE GONE.
ALL NICE SENTIMENTS, MAN, BUT I THINK YOU'RE OVERSELLING IT A BIT.
AM I?! COME ON, IT'S BEEN YOU AND ME, RIGHT FROM THE BEGINNING.
MAYBE SO, BUT WE DON'T NEED A CONTRACT WITH N-G PRODUCTIONS TO BE BEST FRIENDS. NOTHING CAN CHANGE THAT, SHUICHI.
THIS ISN'T HIGH SCHOOL. I'M NOT WORRIED ABOUT MY SOCIAL *CLIQUE*. I WON'T FEEL LIKE YOU'RE CHEATING ON ME IF YOU RECORD WITH FUJISAKI.

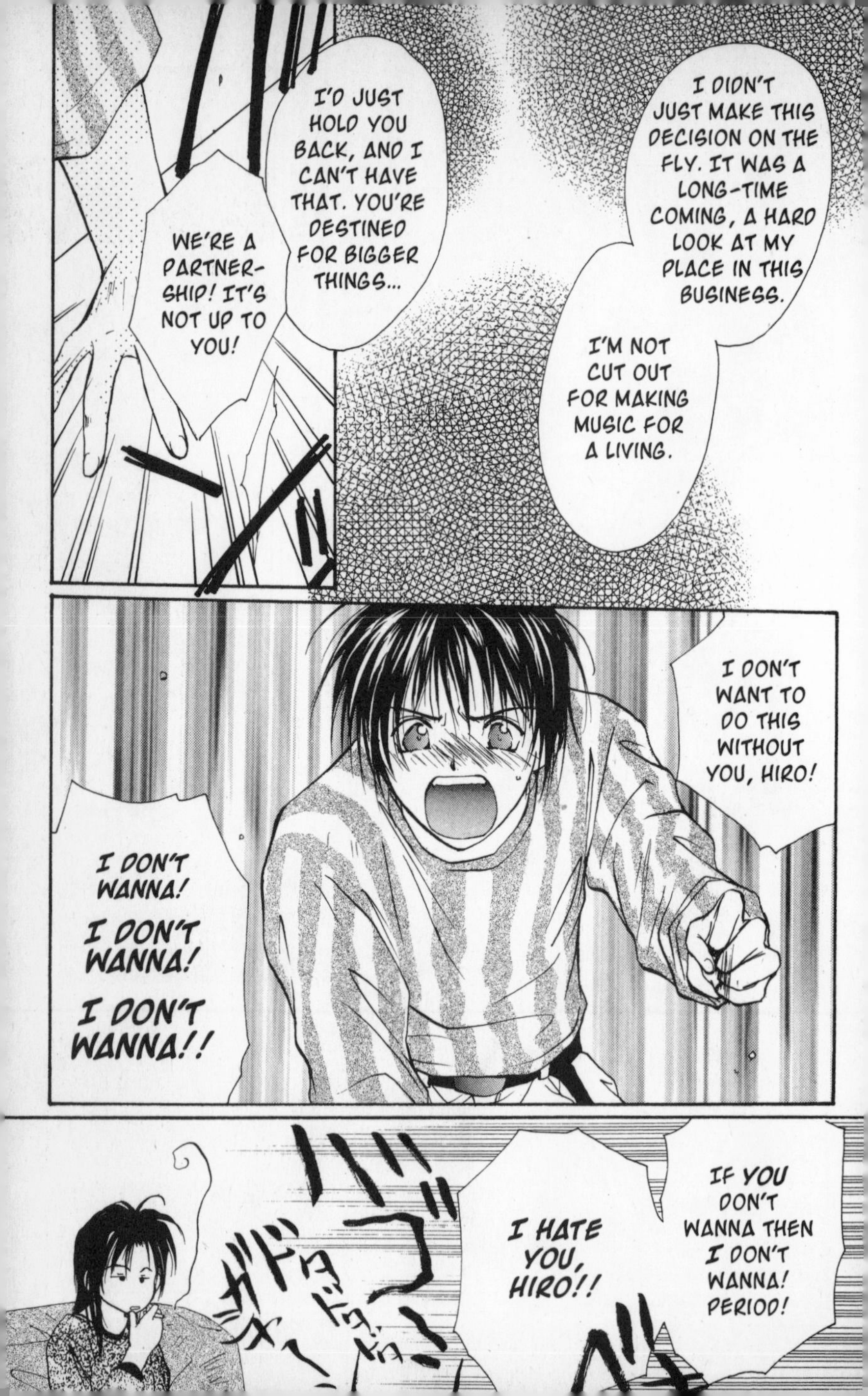
I DIDN'T JUST MAKE THIS DECISION ON THE FLY. IT WAS A LONG-TIME COMING, A HARD LOOK AT MY PLACE IN THIS BUSINESS.
I'M NOT CUT OUT FOR MAKING MUSIC FOR A LIVING.
I'D JUST HOLD YOU BACK, AND I CAN'T HAVE THAT. YOU'RE DESTINED FOR BIGGER THINGS...
WE'RE A PARTNER-SHIP! IT'S NOT UP TO YOU!
I DON'T WANT TO DO THIS WITHOUT YOU, HIRO!
I DON'T WANNA!
I DON'T WANNA!
I DON'T WANNA!!
IF YOU DON'T WANNA THEN I DON'T WANNA! PERIOD!
I HATE YOU, HIRO!!

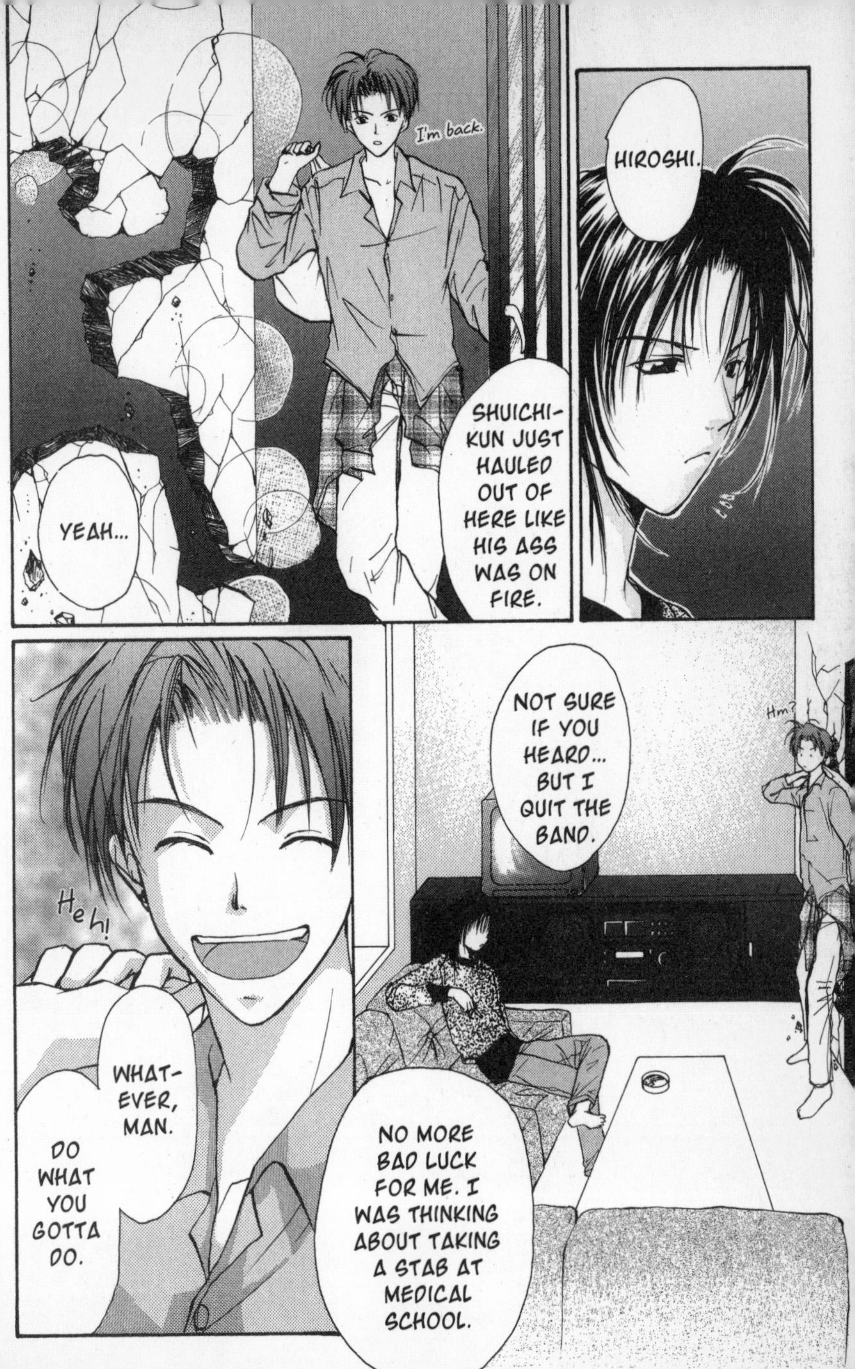
HIROSHI.
SHUICHI-KUN JUST HAULED OUT OF HERE LIKE HIS ASS WAS ON FIRE.
I'm back.
YEAH...
Hm?
NOT SURE IF YOU HEARD... BUT I QUIT THE BAND.
NO MORE BAD LUCK FOR ME. I WAS THINKING ABOUT TAKING A STAB AT MEDICAL SCHOOL.
Heh!
WHAT-EVER, MAN.
DO WHAT YOU GOTTA DO.

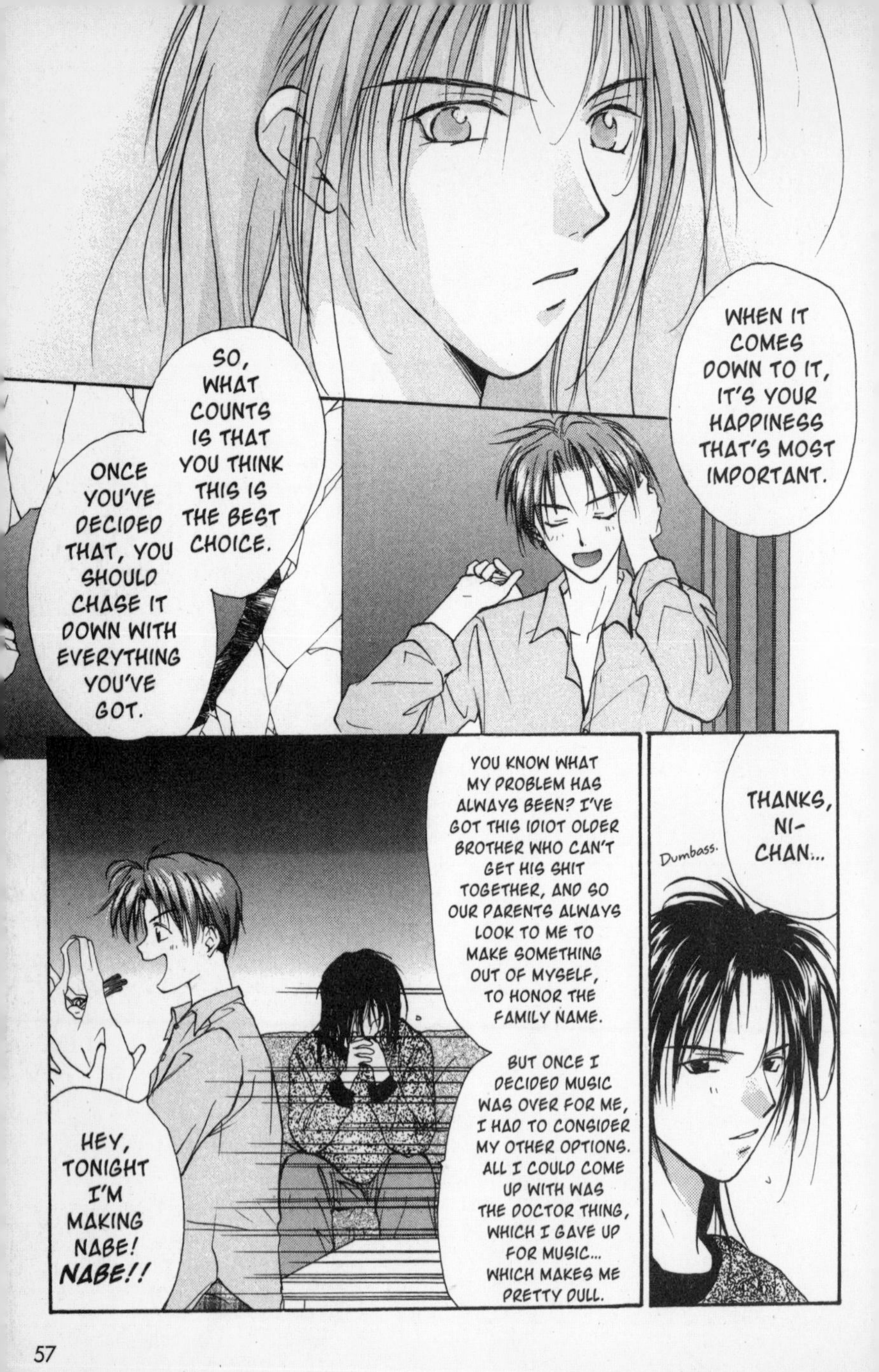
WHEN IT COMES DOWN TO IT, IT'S YOUR HAPPINESS THAT'S MOST IMPORTANT.
SO, WHAT COUNTS IS THAT YOU THINK THIS IS THE BEST CHOICE.
ONCE YOU'VE DECIDED THAT, YOU SHOULD CHASE IT DOWN WITH EVERYTHING YOU'VE GOT.
THANKS, NI-CHAN...
Dumbass.
YOU KNOW WHAT MY PROBLEM HAS ALWAYS BEEN? I'VE GOT THIS IDIOT OLDER BROTHER WHO CAN'T GET HIS SHIT TOGETHER, AND SO OUR PARENTS ALWAYS LOOK TO ME TO MAKE SOMETHING OUT OF MYSELF, TO HONOR THE FAMILY NAME.
BUT ONCE I DECIDED MUSIC WAS OVER FOR ME, I HAD TO CONSIDER MY OTHER OPTIONS. ALL I COULD COME UP WITH WAS THE DOCTOR THING, WHICH I GAVE UP FOR MUSIC... WHICH MAKES ME PRETTY DULL.
HEY, TONIGHT I'M MAKING NABE! NABE!!

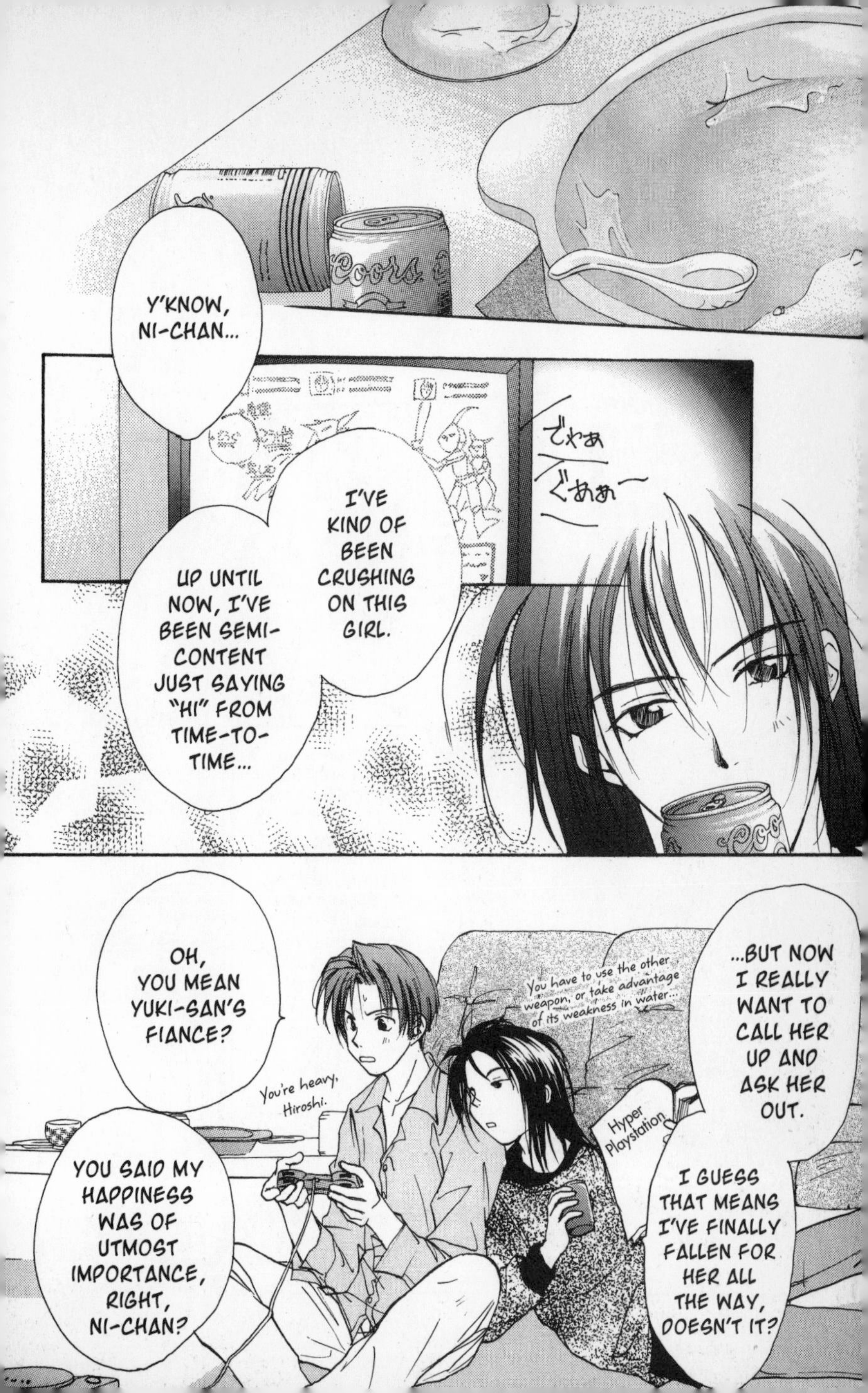
Y'KNOW, NI-CHAN...
でやあ
ぐあぁ~
I'VE KIND OF BEEN CRUSHING ON THIS GIRL.
UP UNTIL NOW, I'VE BEEN SEMI-CONTENT JUST SAYING "HI" FROM TIME-TO-TIME...
...BUT NOW I REALLY WANT TO CALL HER UP AND ASK HER OUT.
I GUESS THAT MEANS I'VE FINALLY FALLEN FOR HER ALL THE WAY, DOESN'T IT?
You have to use the other weapon, or take advantage of its weakness in water...
Hyper Playstation
OH, YOU MEAN YUKI-SAN'S FIANCE?
You're heavy, Hiroshi.
YOU SAID MY HAPPINESS WAS OF UTMOST IMPORTANCE, RIGHT, NI-CHAN?

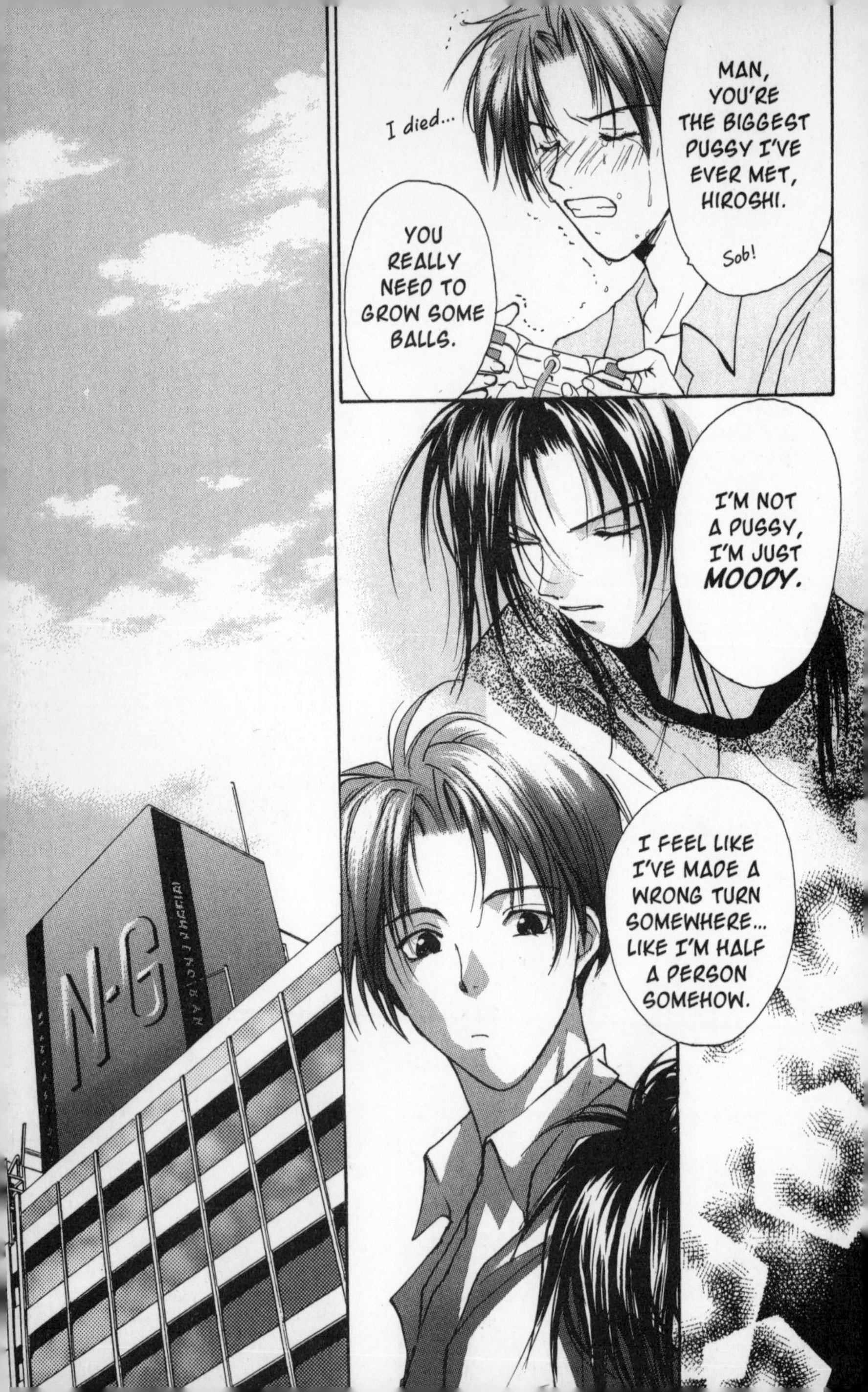
MAN, YOU'RE THE BIGGEST PUSSY I'VE EVER MET, HIROSHI.
Sob!
I died...
YOU REALLY NEED TO GROW SOME BALLS.
I'M NOT A PUSSY, I'M JUST MOODY.
I FEEL LIKE I'VE MADE A WRONG TURN SOMEWHERE... LIKE I'M HALF A PERSON SOMEHOW.
N-G

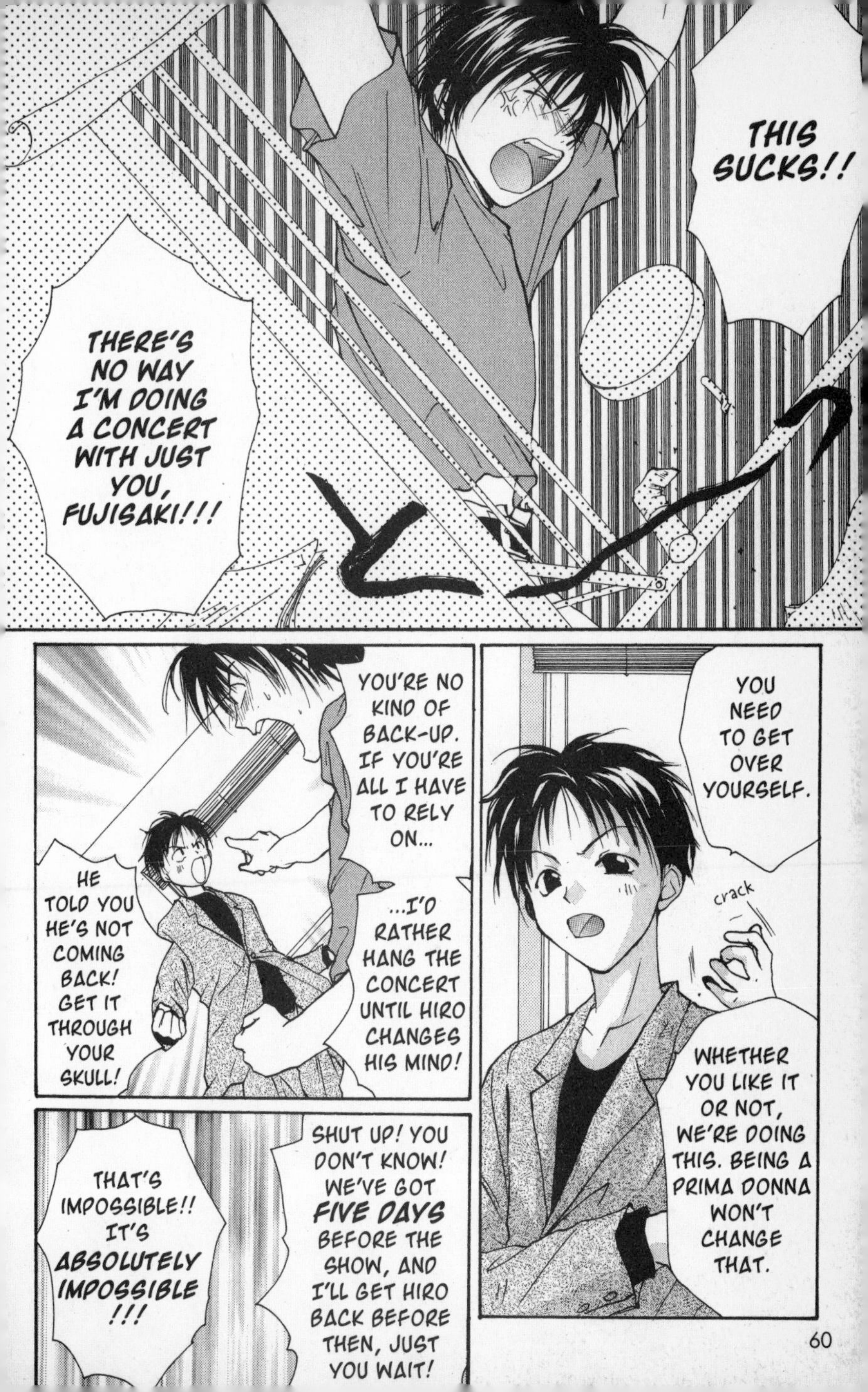
THIS SUCKS!!
THERE'S NO WAY I'M DOING A CONCERT WITH JUST YOU, FUJISAKI!!!
YOU NEED TO GET OVER YOURSELF.
crack
WHETHER YOU LIKE IT OR NOT, WE'RE DOING THIS. BEING A PRIMA DONNA WON'T CHANGE THAT.
YOU'RE NO KIND OF BACK-UP. IF YOU'RE ALL I HAVE TO RELY ON...
...I'D RATHER HANG THE CONCERT UNTIL HIRO CHANGES HIS MIND!
HE TOLD YOU HE'S NOT COMING BACK! GET IT THROUGH YOUR SKULL!
SHUT UP! YOU DON'T KNOW! WE'VE GOT FIVE DAYS BEFORE THE SHOW, AND I'LL GET HIRO BACK BEFORE THEN, JUST YOU WAIT!
THAT'S IMPOSSIBLE!! IT'S ABSOLUTELY IMPOSSIBLE!!!

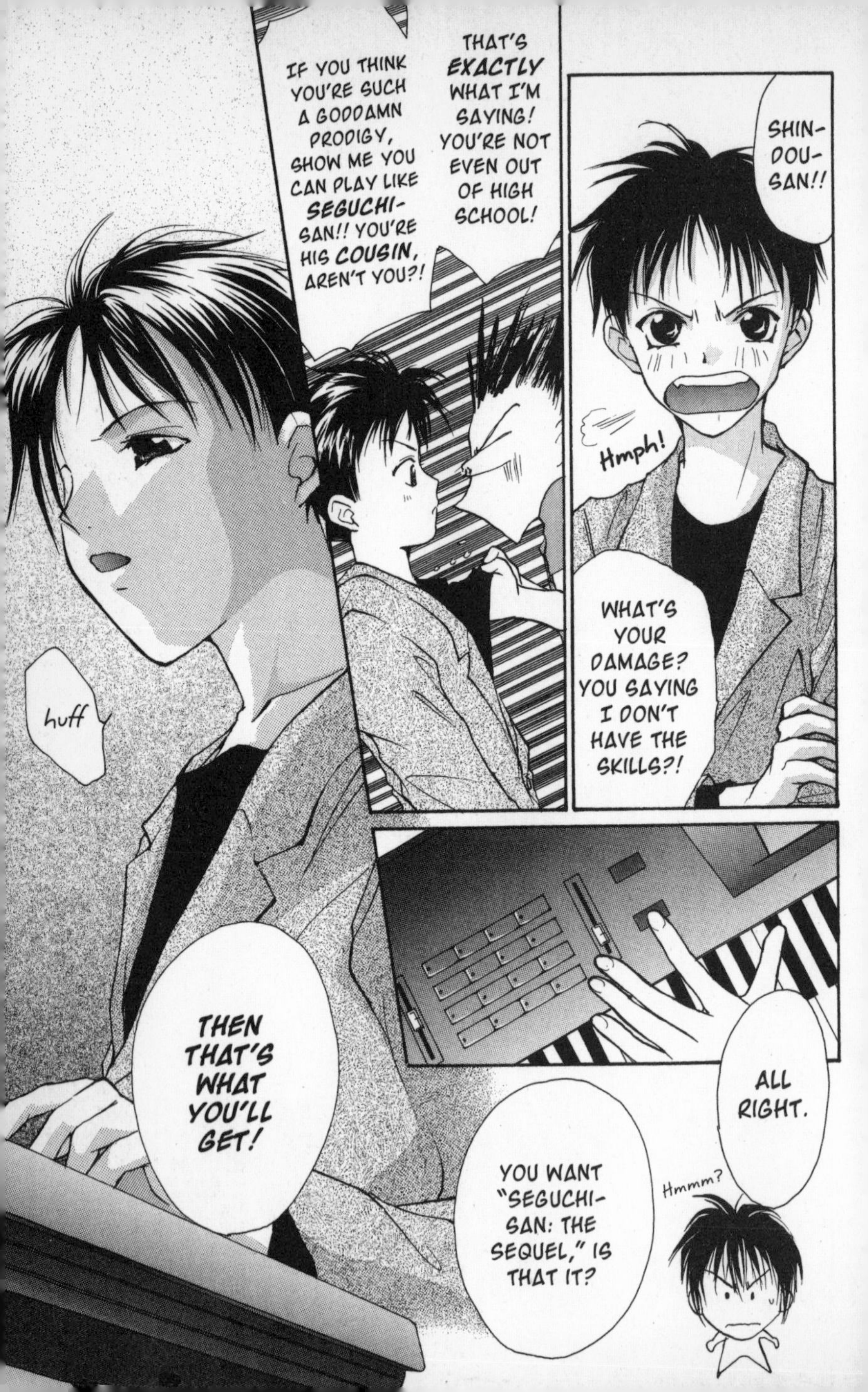
SHIN-DOU-SAN!!
Hmph!
WHAT'S YOUR DAMAGE? YOU SAYING I DON'T HAVE THE SKILLS?!
THAT'S EXACTLY WHAT I'M SAYING! YOU'RE NOT EVEN OUT OF HIGH SCHOOL!
IF YOU THINK YOU'RE SUCH A GODDAMN PRODIGY, SHOW ME YOU CAN PLAY LIKE SEGUCHI-SAN!! YOU'RE HIS COUSIN, AREN'T YOU?!
huff
ALL RIGHT.
YOU WANT "SEGUCHI-SAN: THE SEQUEL," IS THAT IT?
Hmmm?
THEN THAT'S WHAT YOU'LL GET!

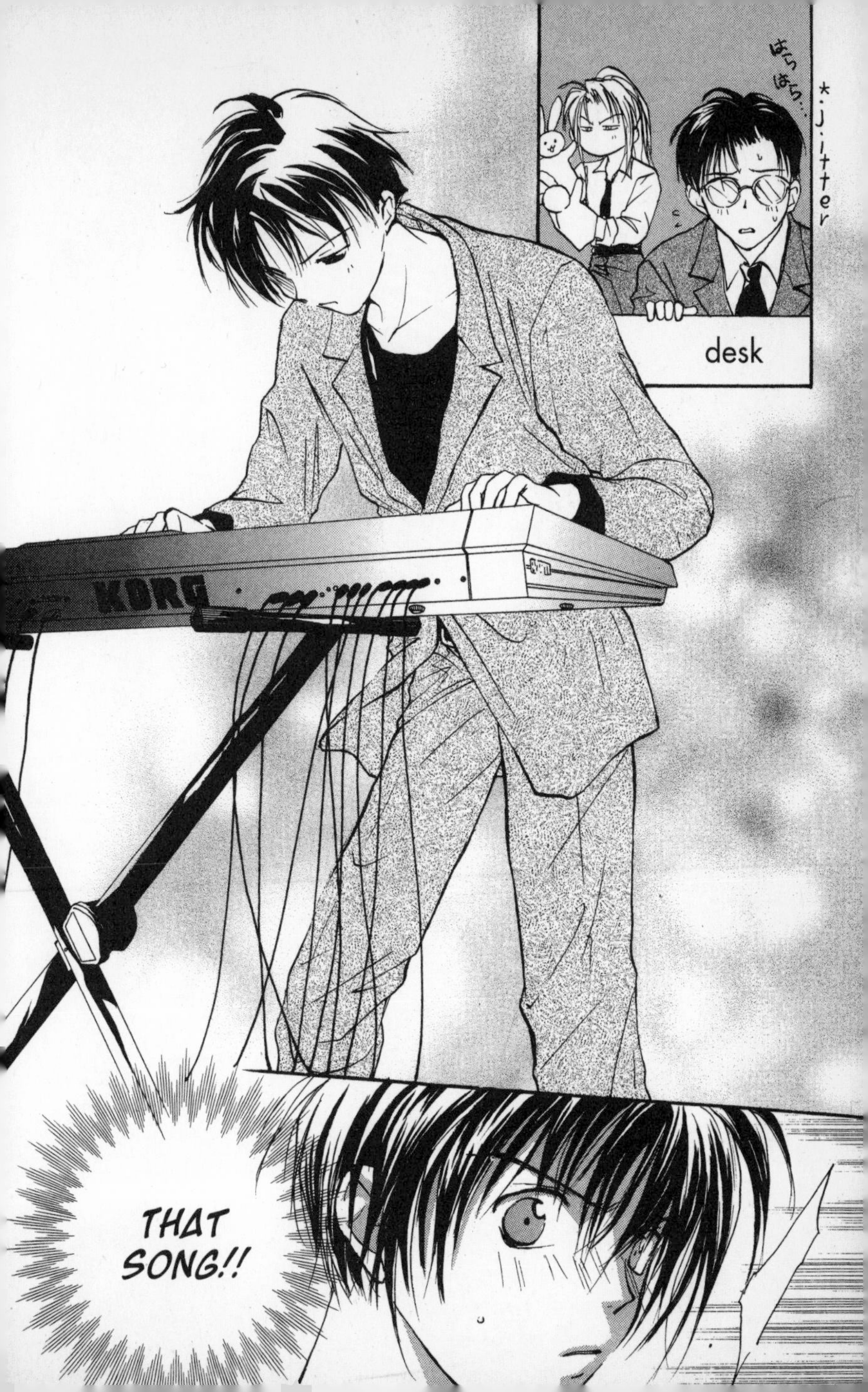
はらはら…
*jitter
desk
KORG
THAT SONG!!

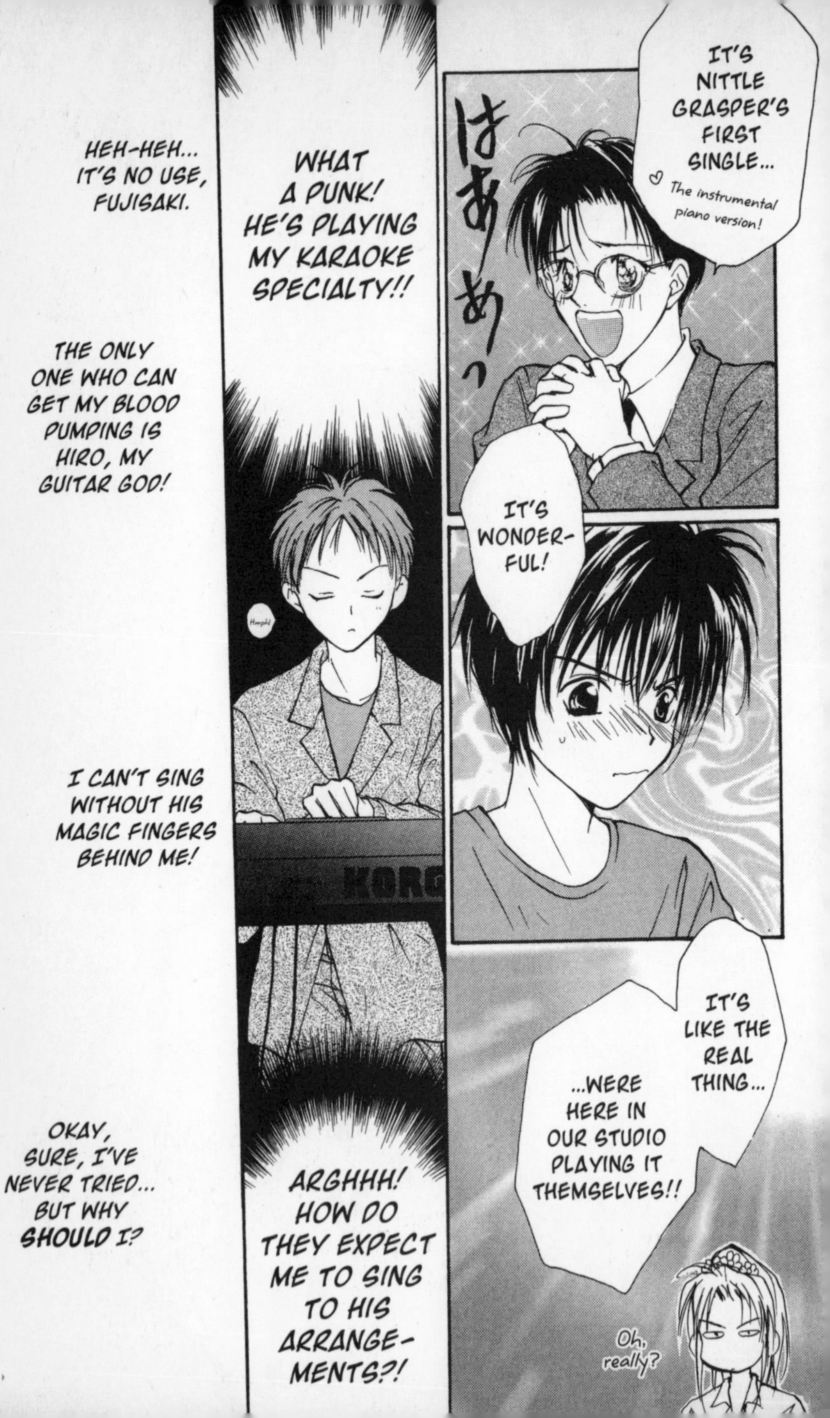
IT'S NITTLE GRASPER'S FIRST SINGLE...
♡ The instrumental piano version!
はあっ
IT'S WONDERFUL!
IT'S LIKE THE REAL THING...
...WERE HERE IN OUR STUDIO PLAYING IT THEMSELVES!!
Oh, really?
WHAT A PUNK! HE'S PLAYING MY KARAOKE SPECIALTY!!
Hmph!
ARGHHH! HOW DO THEY EXPECT ME TO SING TO HIS ARRANGE-MENTS?!
HEH-HEH... IT'S NO USE, FUJISAKI.
THE ONLY ONE WHO CAN GET MY BLOOD PUMPING IS HIRO, MY GUITAR GOD!
I CAN'T SING WITHOUT HIS MAGIC FINGERS BEHIND ME!
OKAY, SURE, I'VE NEVER TRIED... BUT WHY SHOULD I?

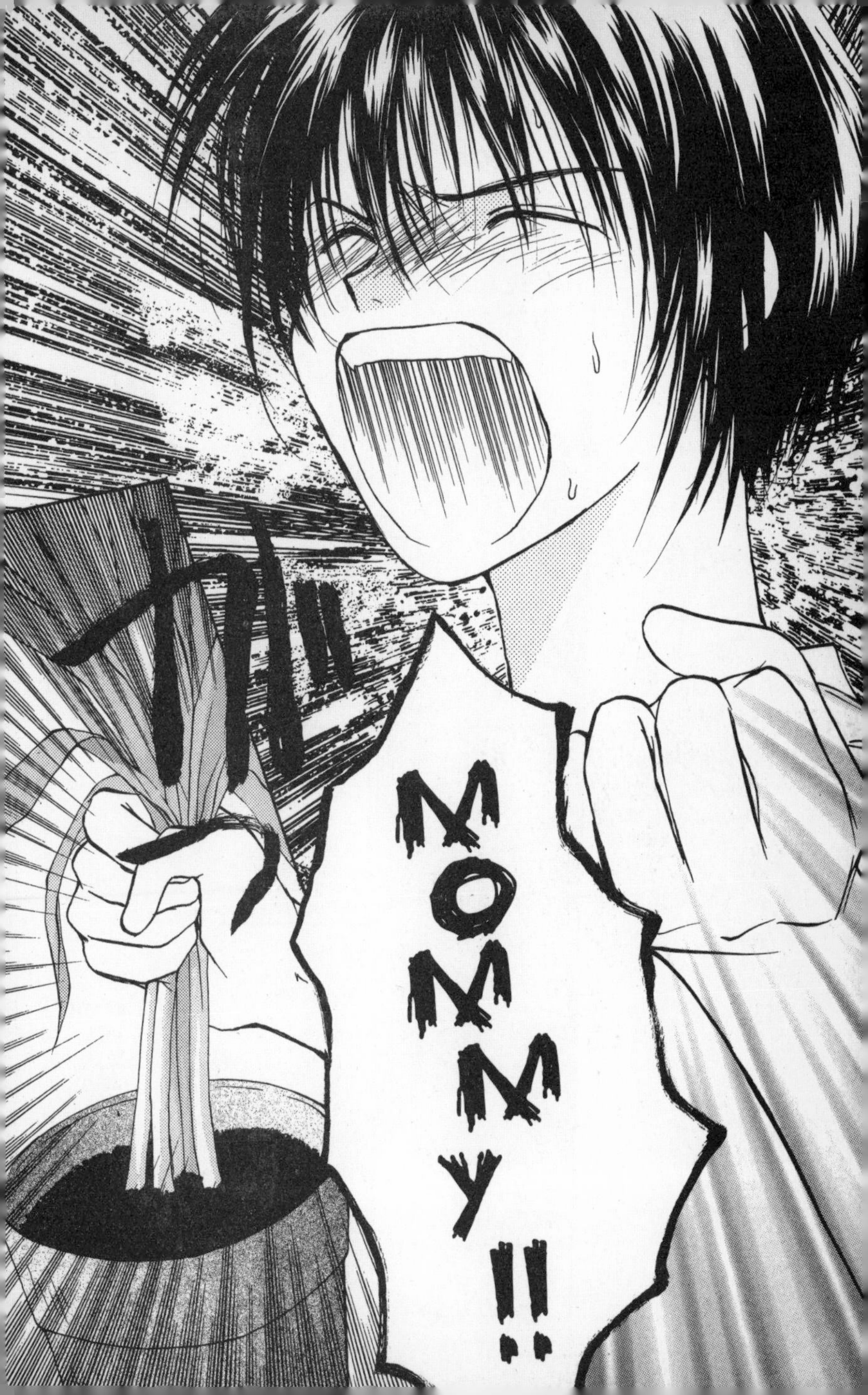
MOMMY!!

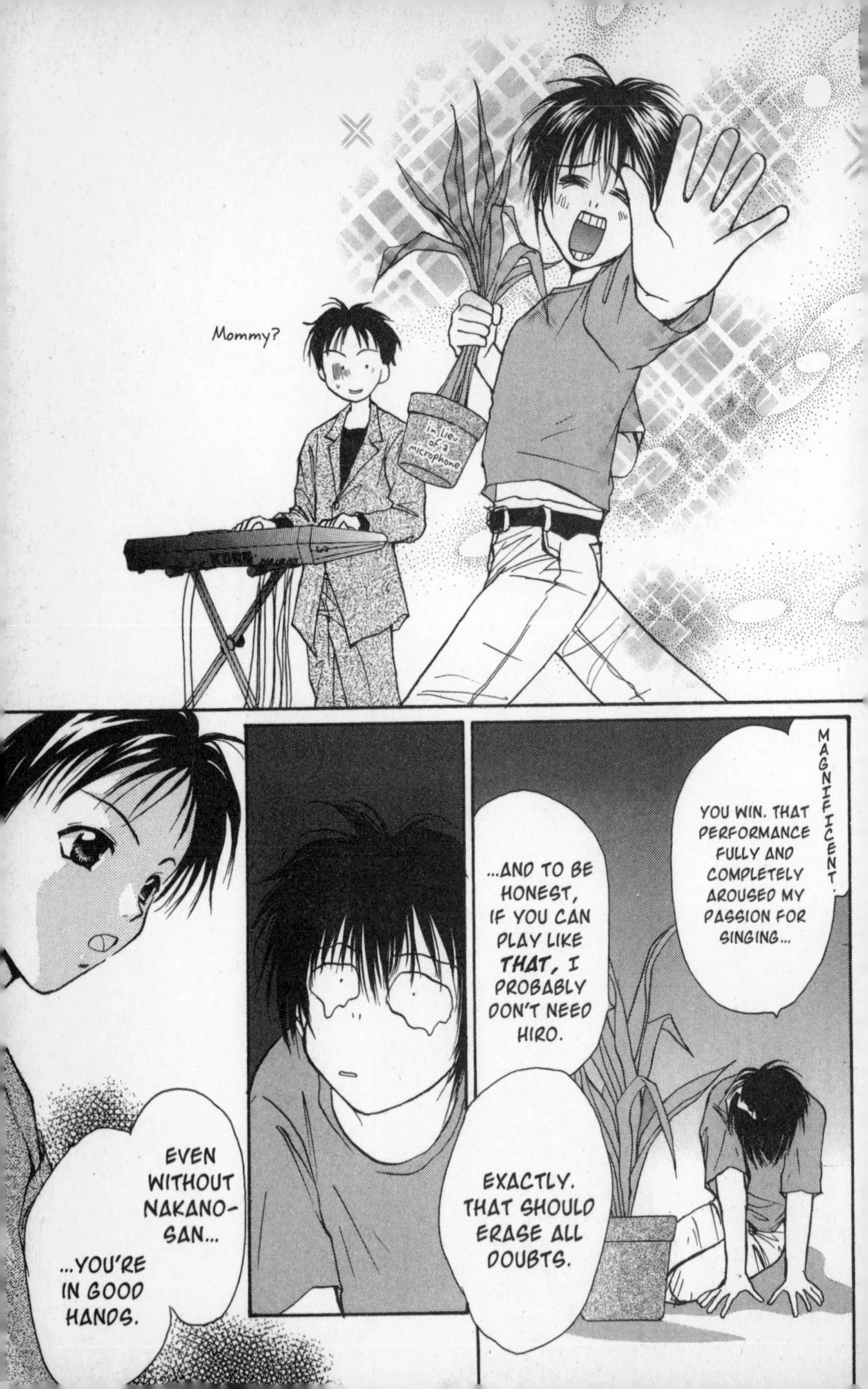
Mommy?
In lieu of a microphone
MAGNIFICENT.
YOU WIN. THAT PERFORMANCE FULLY AND COMPLETELY AROUSED MY PASSION FOR SINGING...
...AND TO BE HONEST, IF YOU CAN PLAY LIKE **THAT**, I PROBABLY DON'T NEED HIRO.
EXACTLY. THAT SHOULD ERASE ALL DOUBTS.
EVEN WITHOUT NAKANO-SAN...
...YOU'RE IN GOOD HANDS.

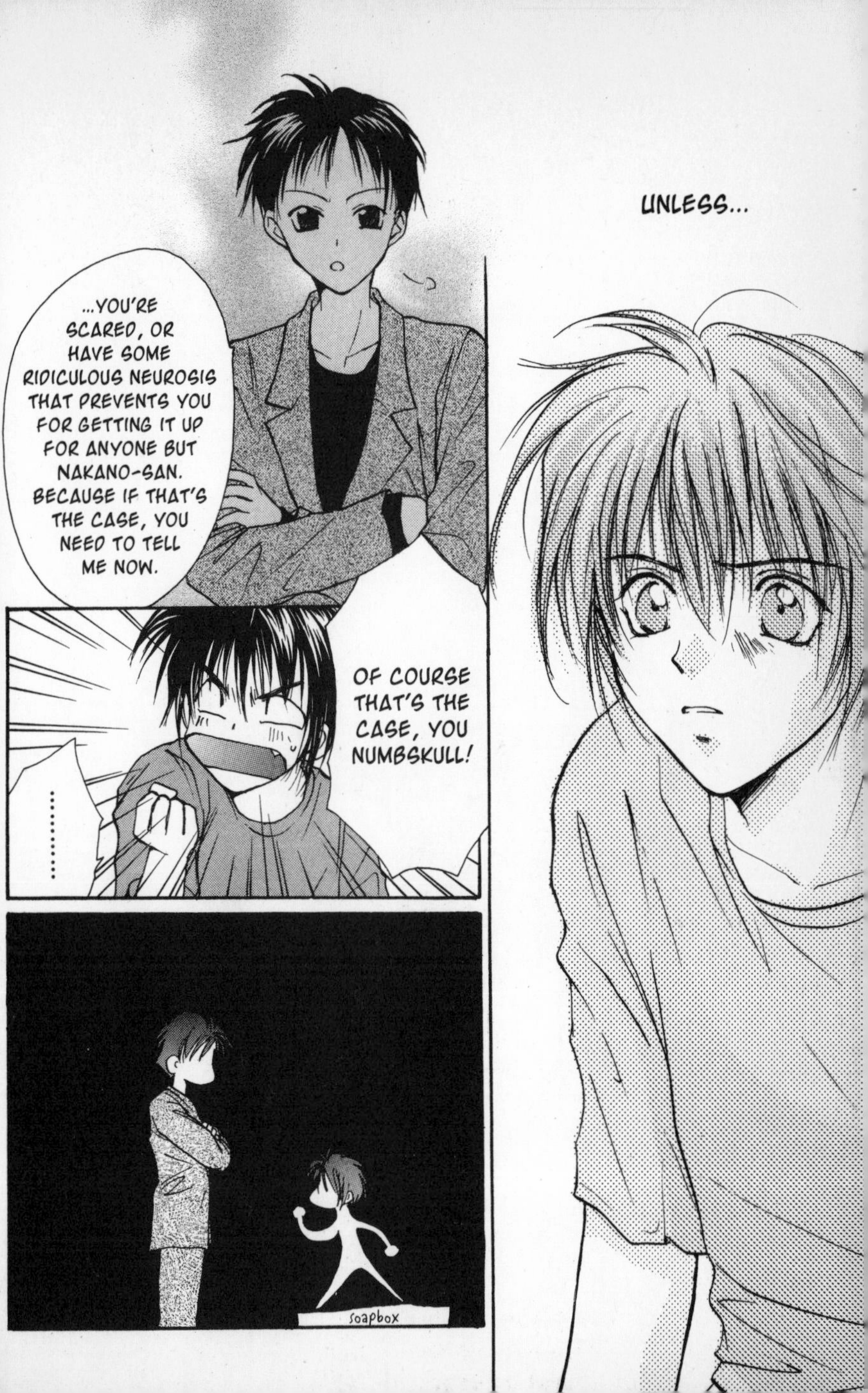
UNLESS...
...YOU'RE SCARED, OR HAVE SOME RIDICULOUS NEUROSIS THAT PREVENTS YOU FOR GETTING IT UP FOR ANYONE BUT NAKANO-SAN. BECAUSE IF THAT'S THE CASE, YOU NEED TO TELL ME NOW.
OF COURSE THAT'S THE CASE, YOU NUMBSKULL!
......
soapbox

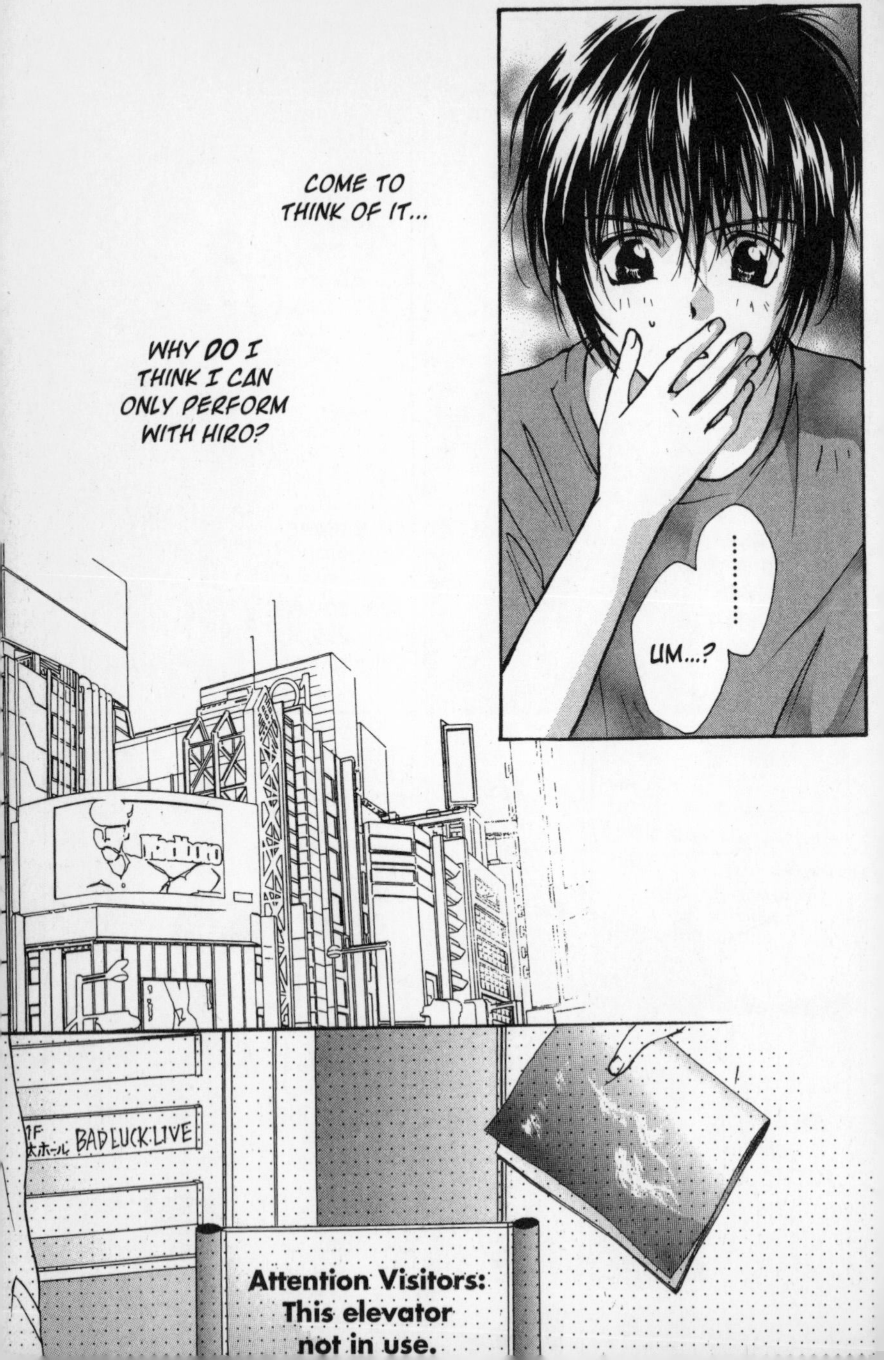
......
UM...?
COME TO THINK OF IT...
WHY DO I THINK I CAN ONLY PERFORM WITH HIRO?
Marlboro
1F 大ホール BAD LUCK LIVE
Attention Visitors: This elevator not in use.

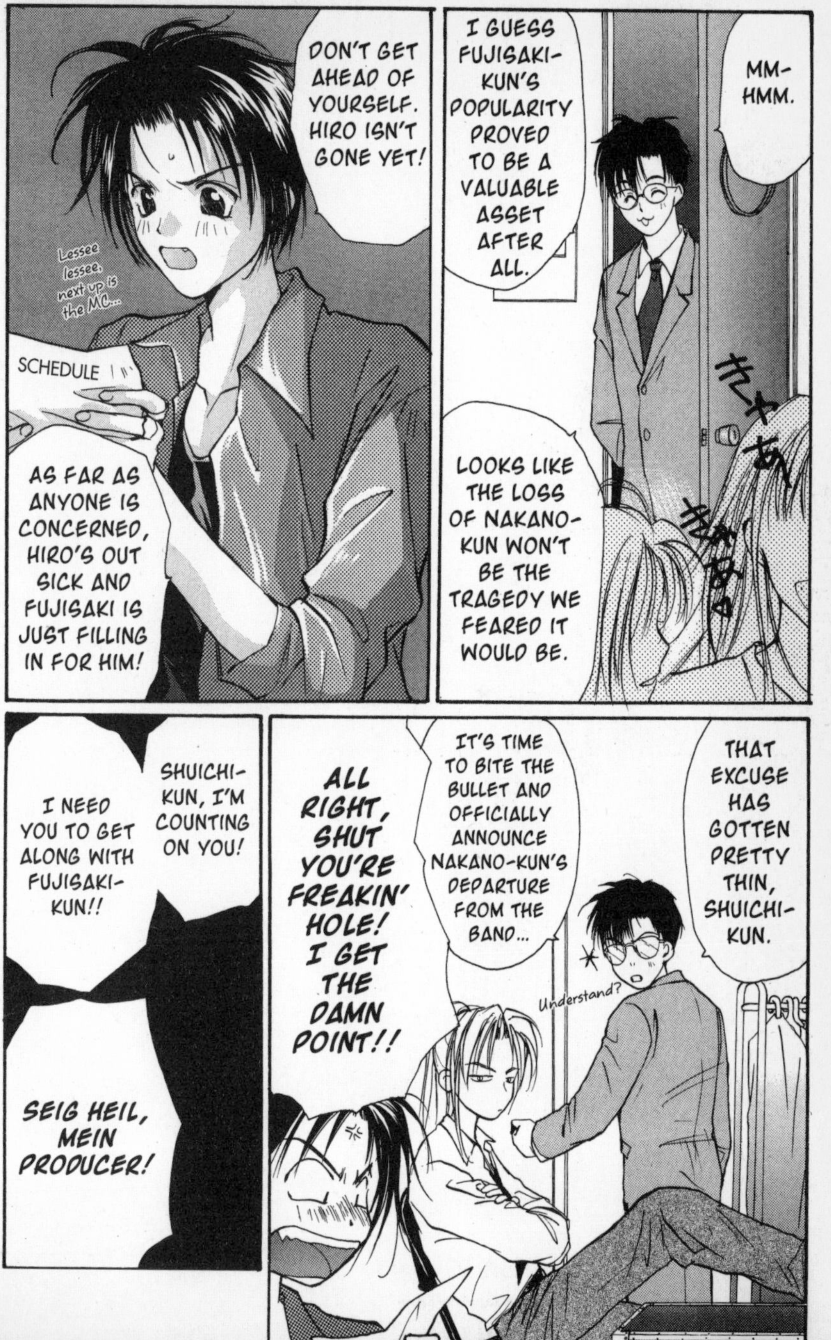
MM-HMM.
I GUESS FUJISAKI-KUN'S POPULARITY PROVED TO BE A VALUABLE ASSET AFTER ALL.
きゃあ
LOOKS LIKE THE LOSS OF NAKANO-KUN WON'T BE THE TRAGEDY WE FEARED IT WOULD BE.
DON'T GET AHEAD OF YOURSELF. HIRO ISN'T GONE YET!
Lessee lessee, next up is the MC...
SCHEDULE
AS FAR AS ANYONE IS CONCERNED, HIRO'S OUT SICK AND FUJISAKI IS JUST FILLING IN FOR HIM!
THAT EXCUSE HAS GOTTEN PRETTY THIN, SHUICHI-KUN.
IT'S TIME TO BITE THE BULLET AND OFFICIALLY ANNOUNCE NAKANO-KUN'S DEPARTURE FROM THE BAND...
Understand?
ALL RIGHT, SHUT YOU'RE FREAKIN' HOLE! I GET THE DAMN POINT!!
SHUICHI-KUN, I'M COUNTING ON YOU!
I NEED YOU TO GET ALONG WITH FUJISAKI-KUN!!
SEIG HEIL, MEIN PRODUCER!

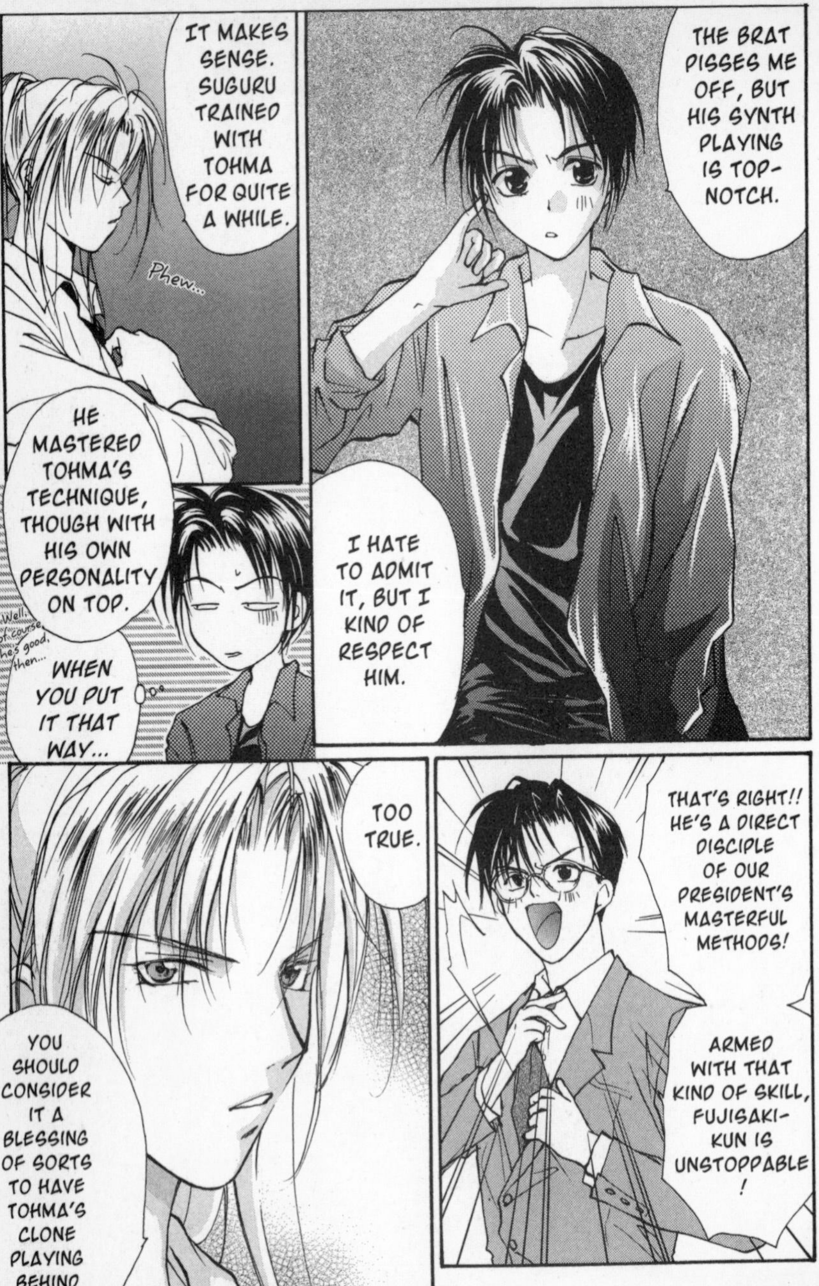
THE BRAT PISSES ME OFF, BUT HIS SYNTH PLAYING IS TOP-NOTCH.
I HATE TO ADMIT IT, BUT I KIND OF RESPECT HIM.
IT MAKES SENSE. SUGURU TRAINED WITH TOHMA FOR QUITE A WHILE.
Phew...
HE MASTERED TOHMA'S TECHNIQUE, THOUGH WITH HIS OWN PERSONALITY ON TOP.
Well, of course he's good, then...
WHEN YOU PUT IT THAT WAY...
THAT'S RIGHT!! HE'S A DIRECT DISCIPLE OF OUR PRESIDENT'S MASTERFUL METHODS!
ARMED WITH THAT KIND OF SKILL, FUJISAKI-KUN IS UNSTOPPABLE!
TOO TRUE.
YOU SHOULD CONSIDER IT A BLESSING OF SORTS TO HAVE TOHMA'S CLONE PLAYING BEHIND YOU.

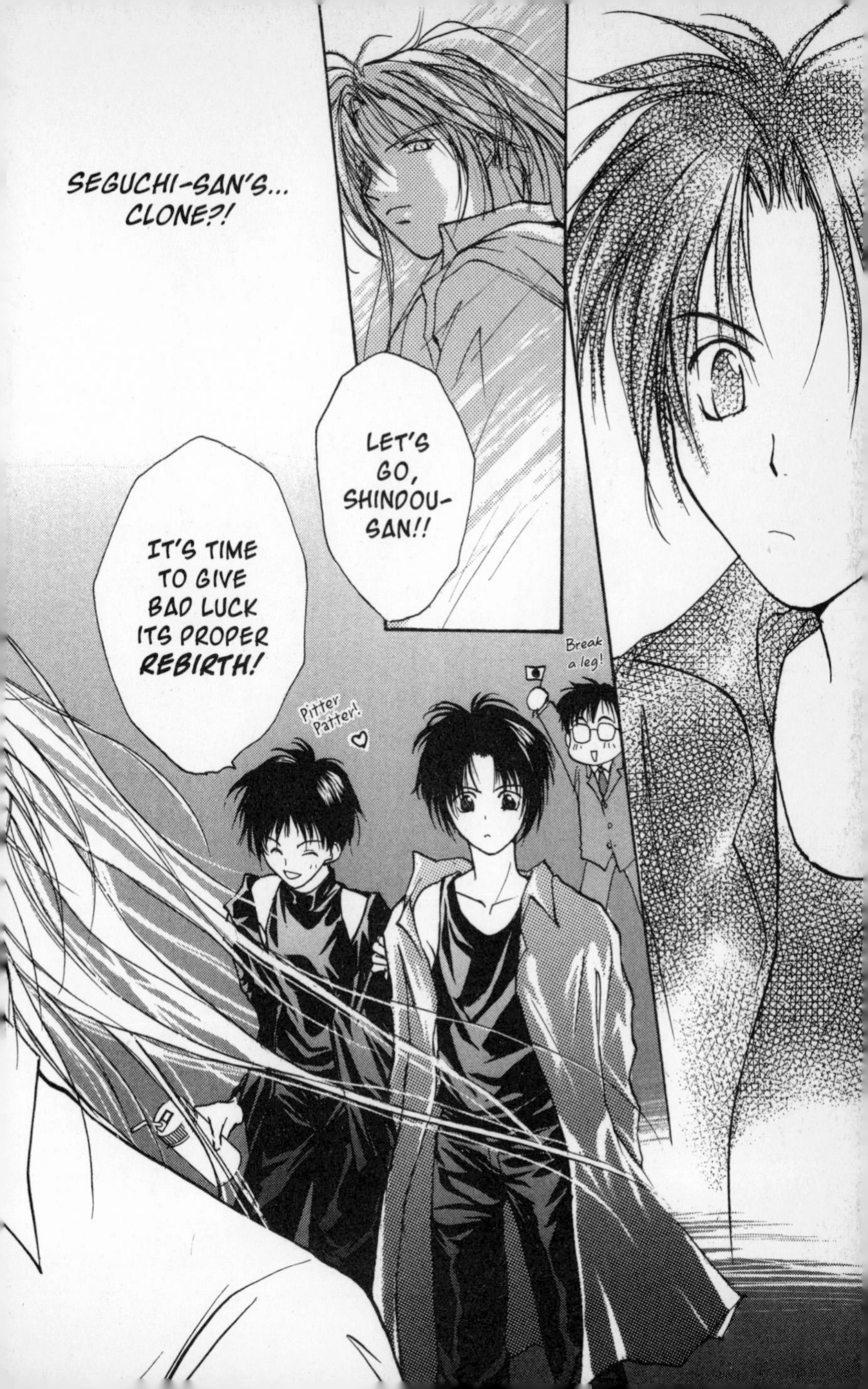
SEGUCHI-SAN'S... CLONE?!
LET'S GO, SHINDOU-SAN!!
IT'S TIME TO GIVE BAD LUCK ITS PROPER REBIRTH!
Break a leg!
Pitter Patter!

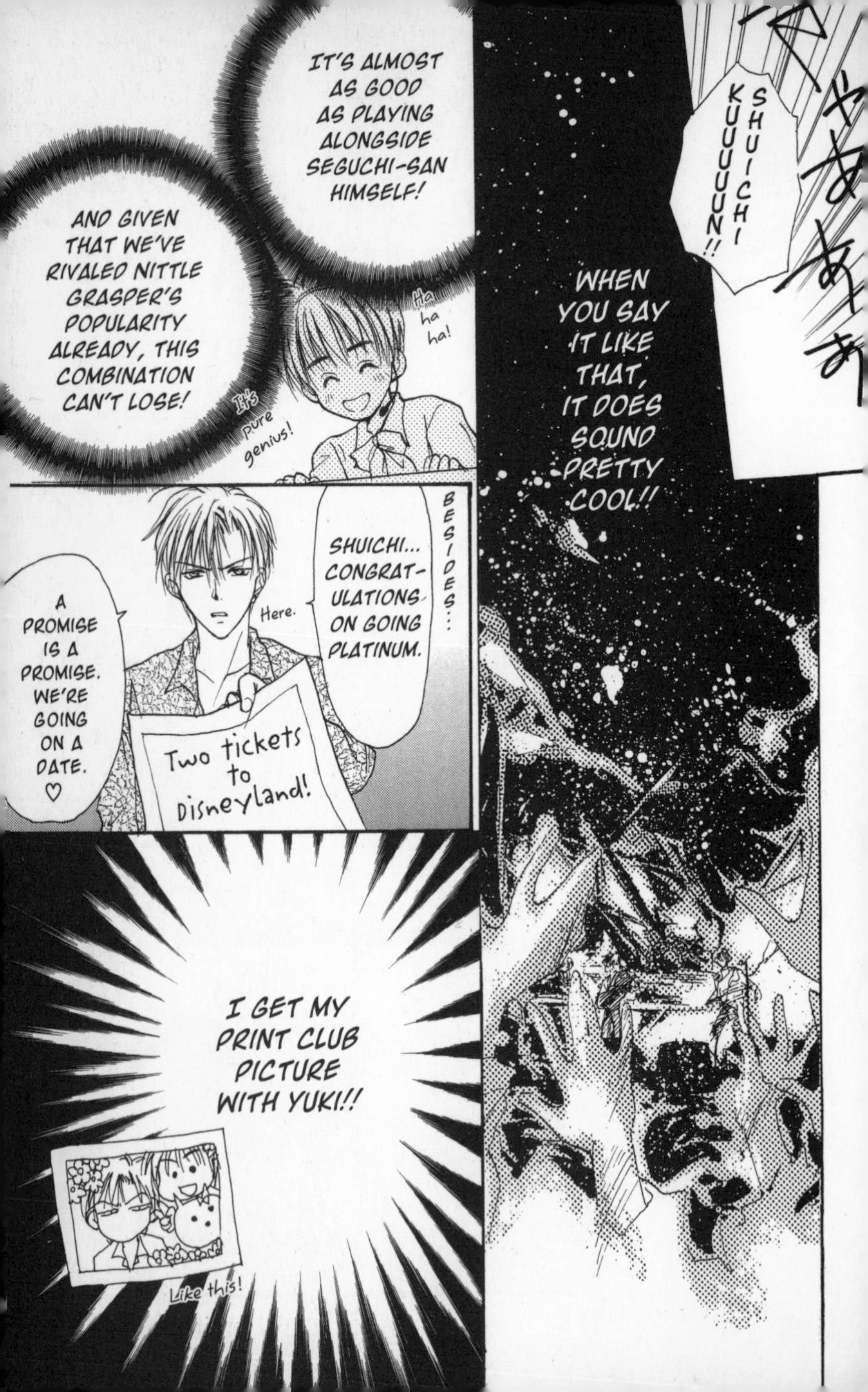

やあああ
SHUICHI KUUUUUUN!!
WHEN YOU SAY IT LIKE THAT, IT DOES SOUND PRETTY COOL!!
IT'S ALMOST AS GOOD AS PLAYING ALONGSIDE SEGUCHI-SAN HIMSELF!
Ha ha ha!
AND GIVEN THAT WE'VE RIVALED NITTLE GRASPER'S POPULARITY ALREADY, THIS COMBINATION CAN'T LOSE!
It's pure genius!
BESIDES...
SHUICHI... CONGRATULATIONS ON GOING PLATINUM.
Here.
A PROMISE IS A PROMISE. WE'RE GOING ON A DATE. ♡
Two tickets to Disneyland!
I GET MY PRINT CLUB PICTURE WITH YUKI!!
Like this!

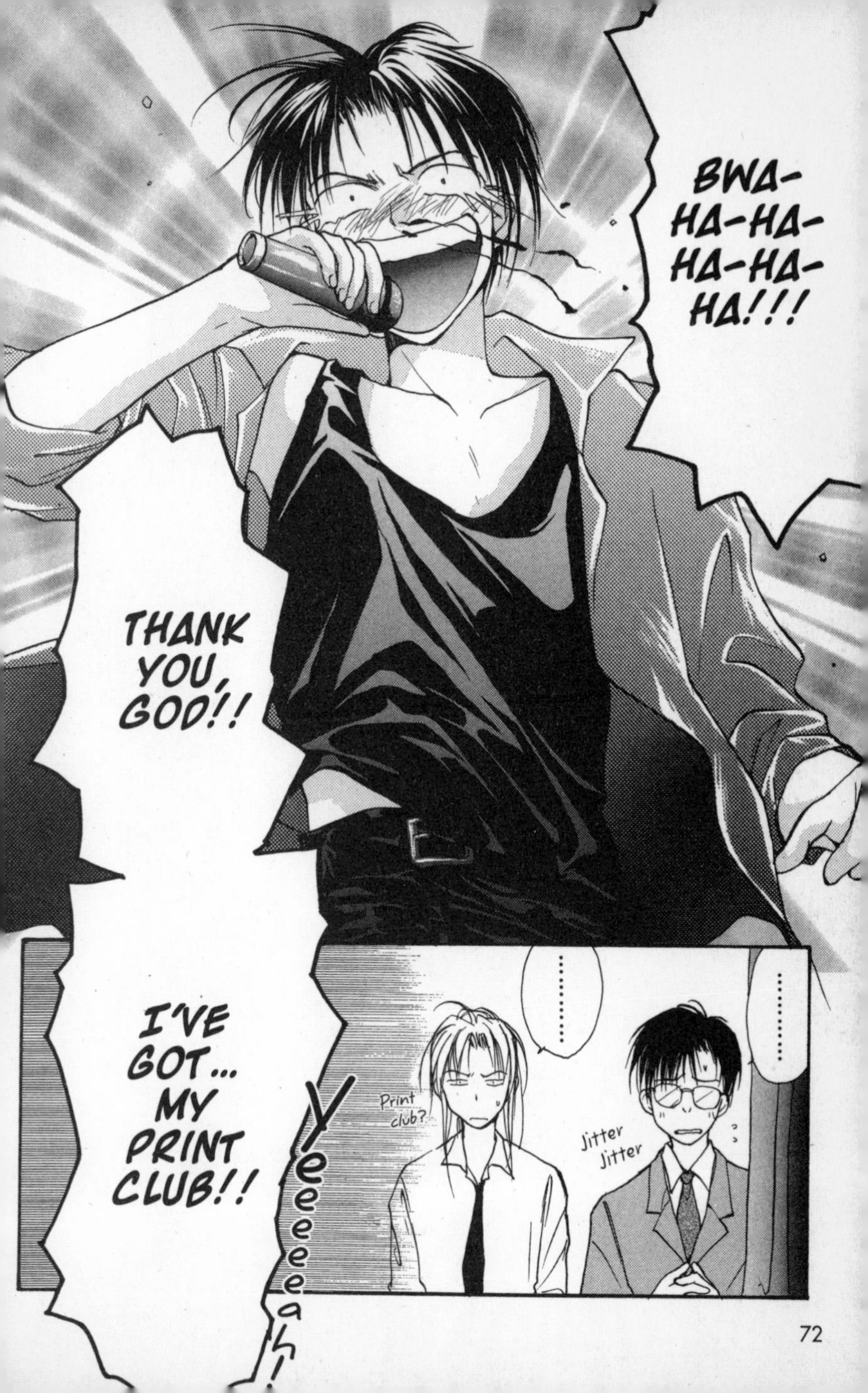
BWA-HA-HA-HA-HA-HA!!!
THANK YOU, GOD!!
I'VE GOT... MY PRINT CLUB!!
Yeeeeeeah!
......
......
Print club?
Jitter Jitter

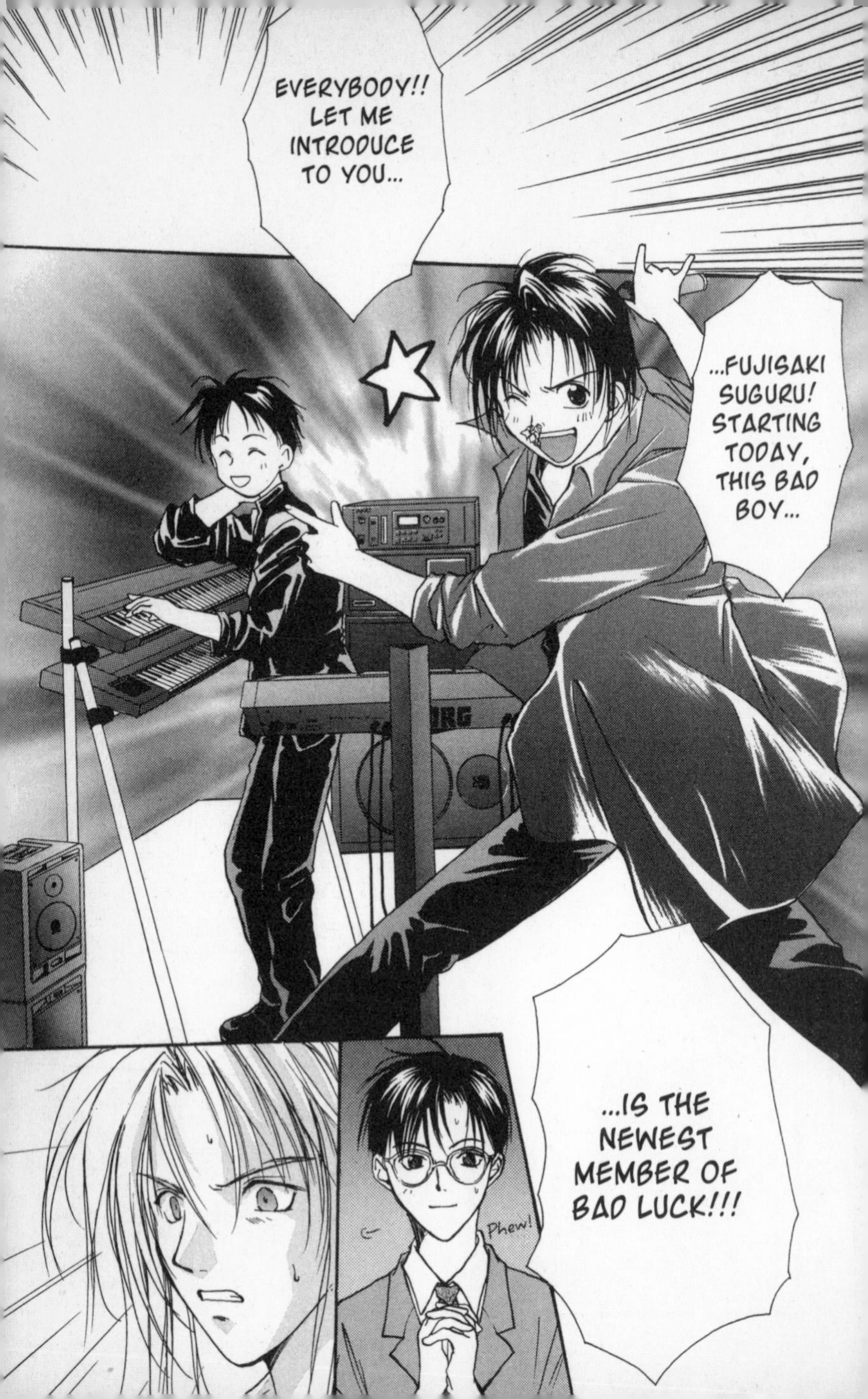
EVERYBODY!! LET ME INTRODUCE TO YOU...
...FUJISAKI SUGURU! STARTING TODAY, THIS BAD BOY...
...IS THE NEWEST MEMBER OF BAD LUCK!!!
Phew!

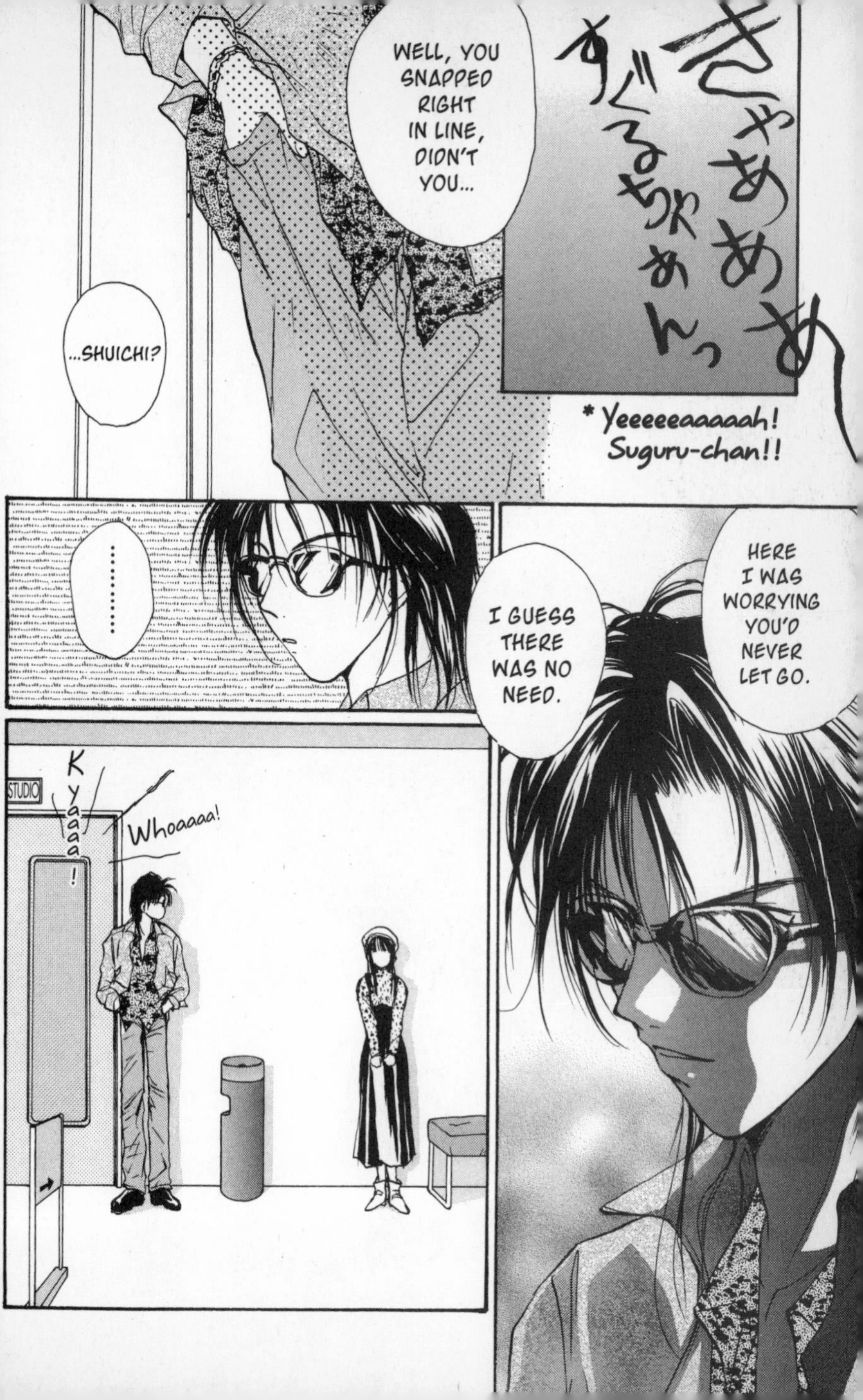
きゃあああ
すぐるちゃあんっ
* Yeeeeeaaaaaah! Suguru-chan!!
WELL, YOU SNAPPED RIGHT IN LINE, DIDN'T YOU...
...SHUICHI?
HERE I WAS WORRYING YOU'D NEVER LET GO.
I GUESS THERE WAS NO NEED.
....
STUDIO
Kyaaaa!
Whoaaaa!

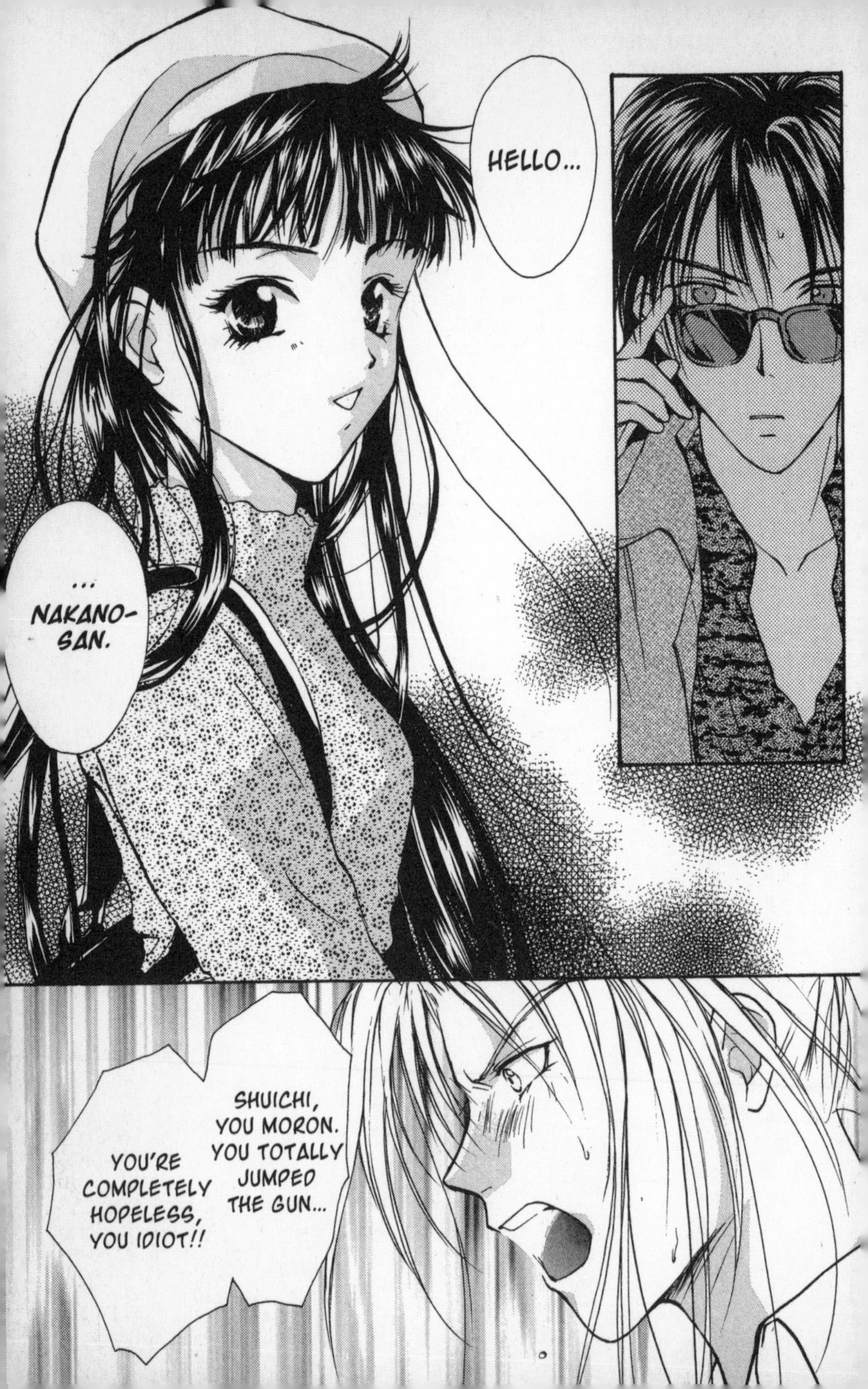
HELLO...
... NAKANO-SAN.
SHUICHI, YOU MORON. YOU TOTALLY JUMPED THE GUN...
YOU'RE COMPLETELY HOPELESS, YOU IDIOT!!

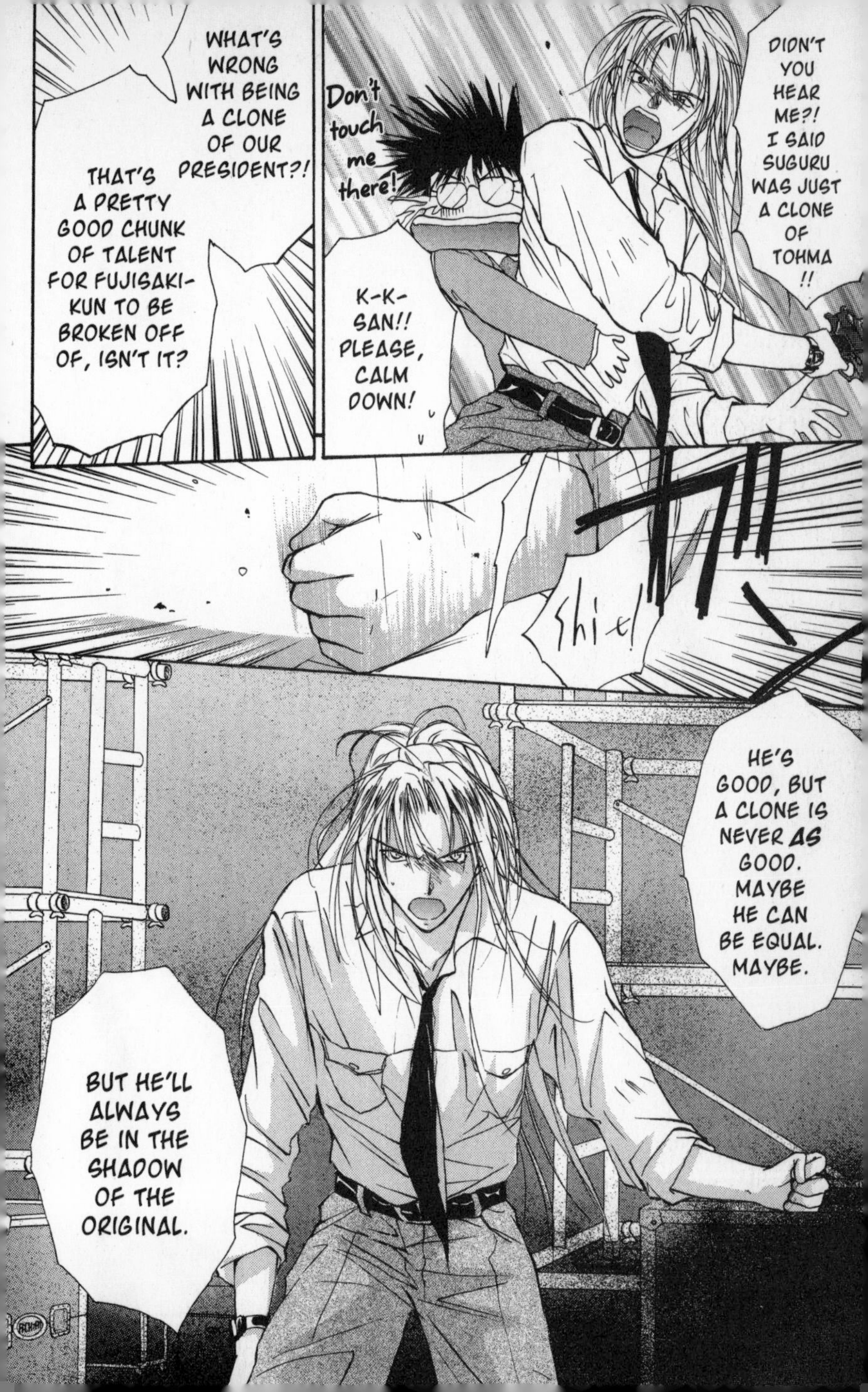
DIDN'T YOU HEAR ME?! I SAID SUGURU WAS JUST A CLONE OF TOHMA !!
Don't touch me there!
K-K-SAN!! PLEASE, CALM DOWN!
WHAT'S WRONG WITH BEING A CLONE OF OUR PRESIDENT?!
THAT'S A PRETTY GOOD CHUNK OF TALENT FOR FUJISAKI-KUN TO BE BROKEN OFF OF, ISN'T IT?
Shi-t!
HE'S GOOD, BUT A CLONE IS NEVER AS GOOD. MAYBE HE CAN BE EQUAL. MAYBE.
BUT HE'LL ALWAYS BE IN THE SHADOW OF THE ORIGINAL.

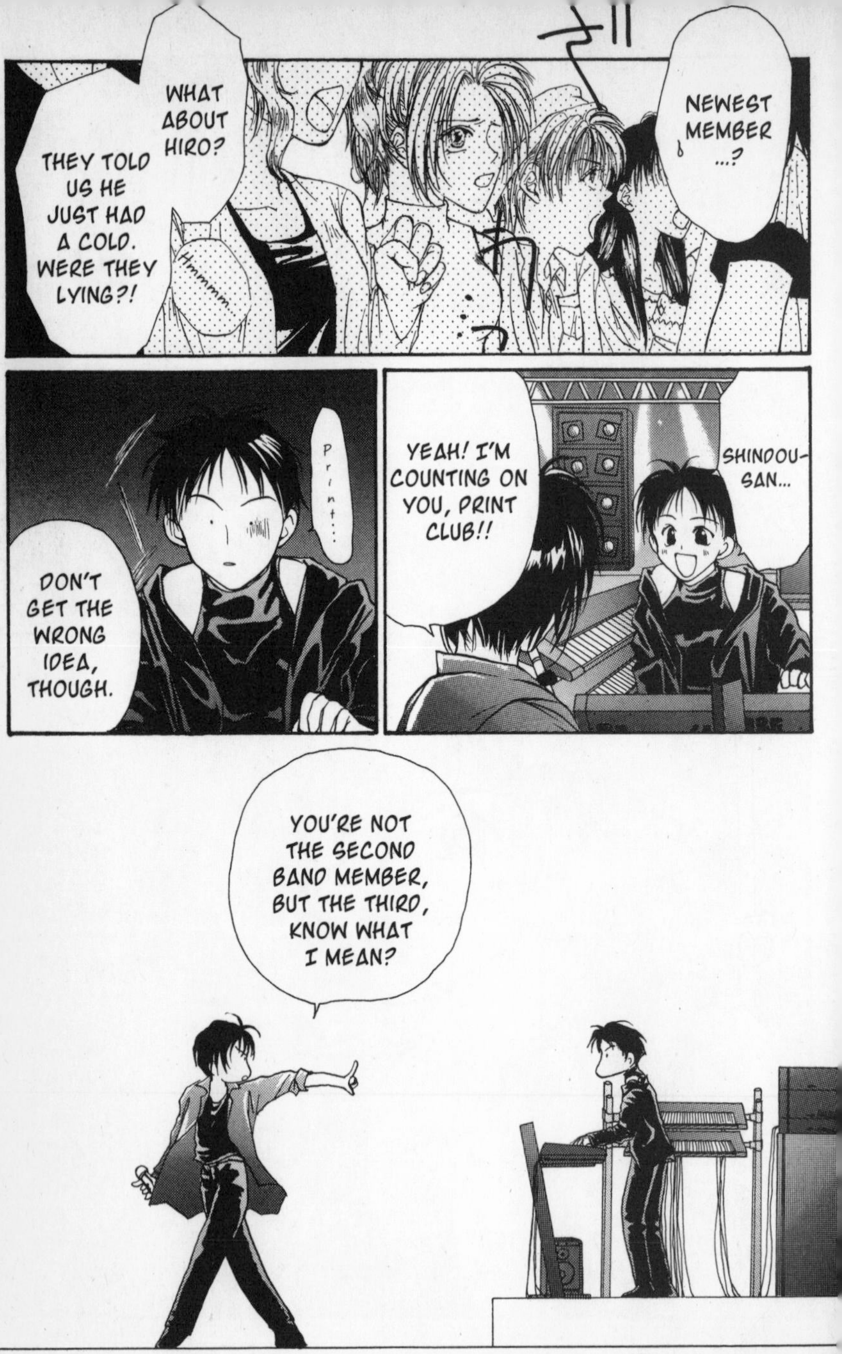
NEWEST MEMBER ...?
WHAT ABOUT HIRO?
THEY TOLD US HE JUST HAD A COLD. WERE THEY LYING?!
Hmmmm.
SHINDOU-SAN...
YEAH! I'M COUNTING ON YOU, PRINT CLUB!!
Print...
DON'T GET THE WRONG IDEA, THOUGH.
YOU'RE NOT THE SECOND BAND MEMBER, BUT THE THIRD, KNOW WHAT I MEAN?

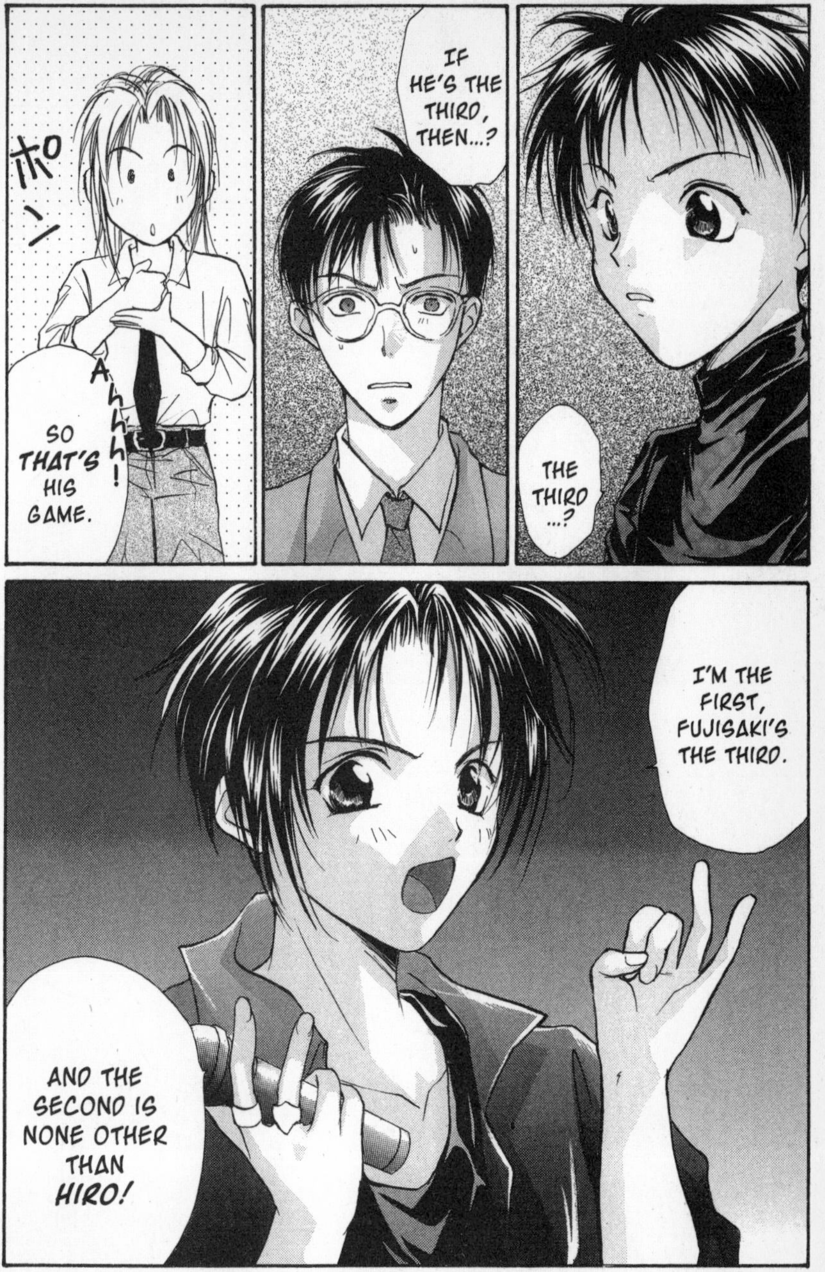
THE THIRD ...?
IF HE'S THE THIRD, THEN...?
ポン
Ahhh!
SO **THAT'S** HIS GAME.
I'M THE FIRST, FUJISAKI'S THE THIRD.
AND THE SECOND IS NONE OTHER THAN **HIRO!**

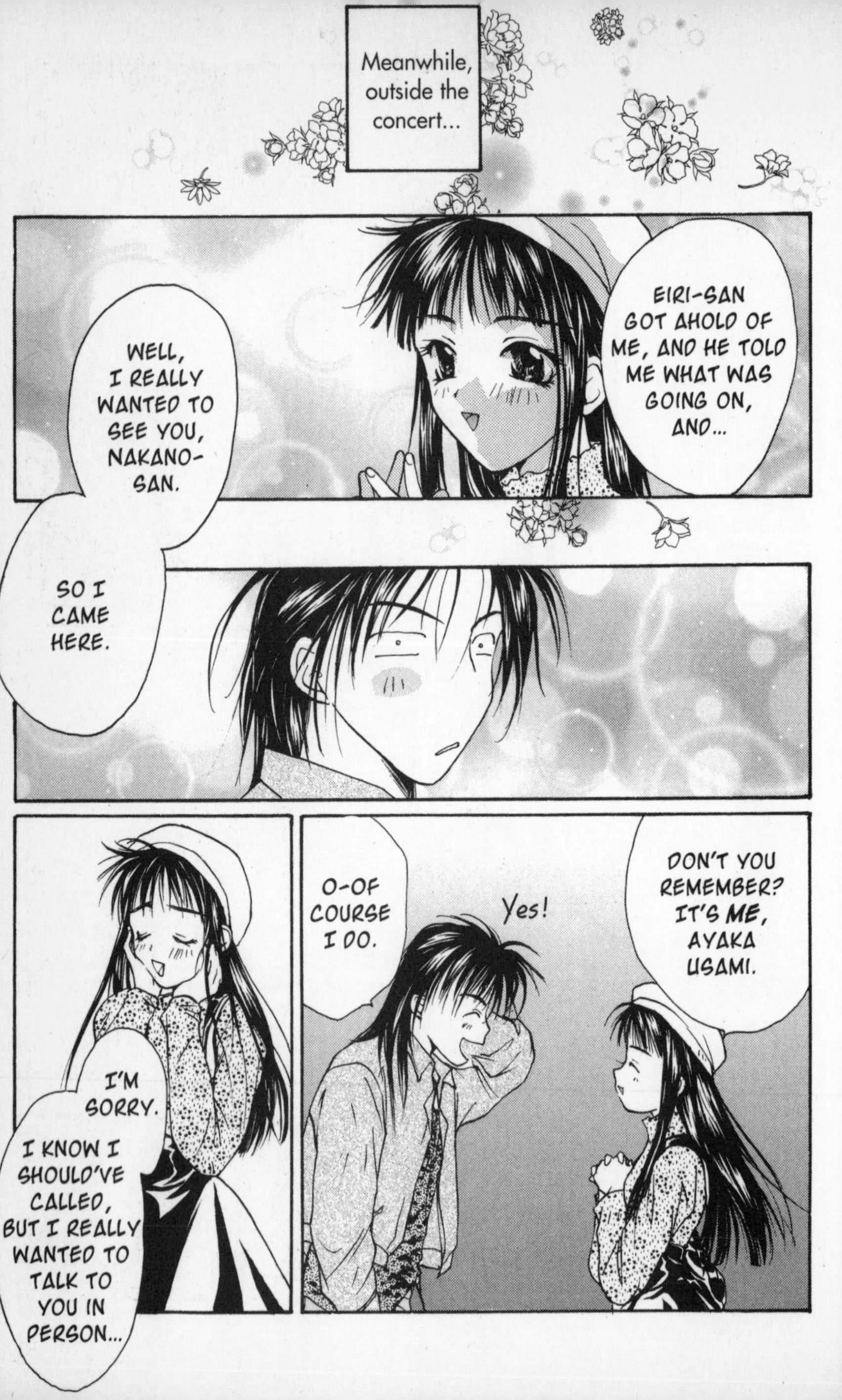
Meanwhile, outside the concert...
EIRI-SAN GOT AHOLD OF ME, AND HE TOLD ME WHAT WAS GOING ON, AND...
WELL, I REALLY WANTED TO SEE YOU, NAKANO-SAN.
SO I CAME HERE.
DON'T YOU REMEMBER? IT'S *ME*, AYAKA USAMI.
Yes!
O-OF COURSE I DO.
I'M SORRY.
I KNOW I SHOULD'VE CALLED, BUT I REALLY WANTED TO TALK TO YOU IN PERSON...

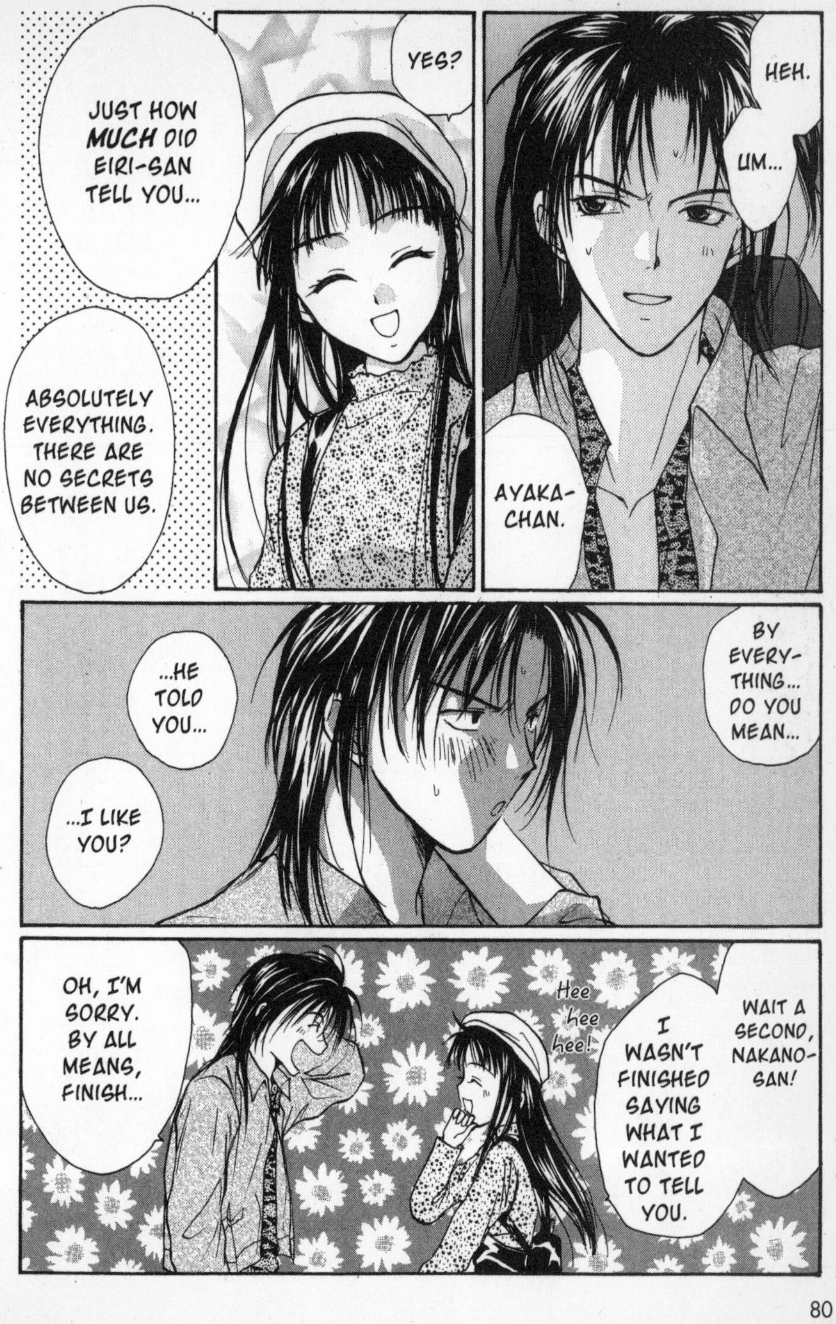
HEH.
UM...
AYAKA-CHAN.
YES?
JUST HOW MUCH DID EIRI-SAN TELL YOU...
ABSOLUTELY EVERYTHING. THERE ARE NO SECRETS BETWEEN US.
BY EVERY-THING... DO YOU MEAN...
...HE TOLD YOU...
...I LIKE YOU?
WAIT A SECOND, NAKANO-SAN!
I WASN'T FINISHED SAYING WHAT I WANTED TO TELL YOU.
Hee hee hee!
OH, I'M SORRY. BY ALL MEANS, FINISH...

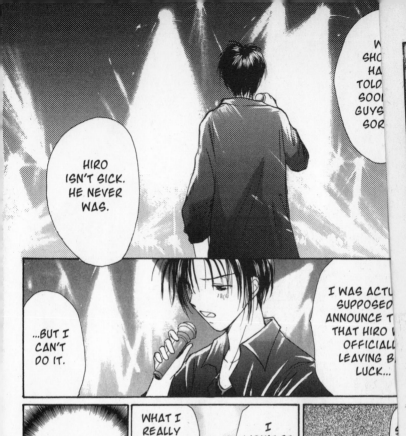

HIRO ISN'T SICK. HE NEVER WAS.

W SHO HA TOLD SOO GUYS SOR

I WAS ACTU SUPPOSED ANNOUNCE T THAT HIRO OFFICIALL LEAVING B LUCK...

...BUT I CAN'T DO IT.

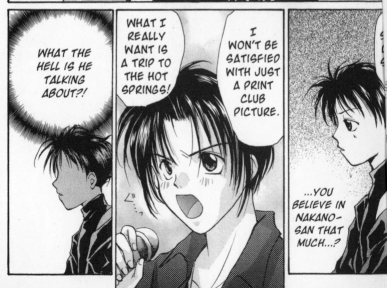

WHAT THE HELL IS HE TALKING ABOUT?!

WHAT I REALLY WANT IS A TRIP TO THE HOT SPRINGS!

I WON'T BE SATISFIED WITH JUST A PRINT CLUB PICTURE.

...YOU BELIEVE IN NAKANO-SAN THAT MUCH...?

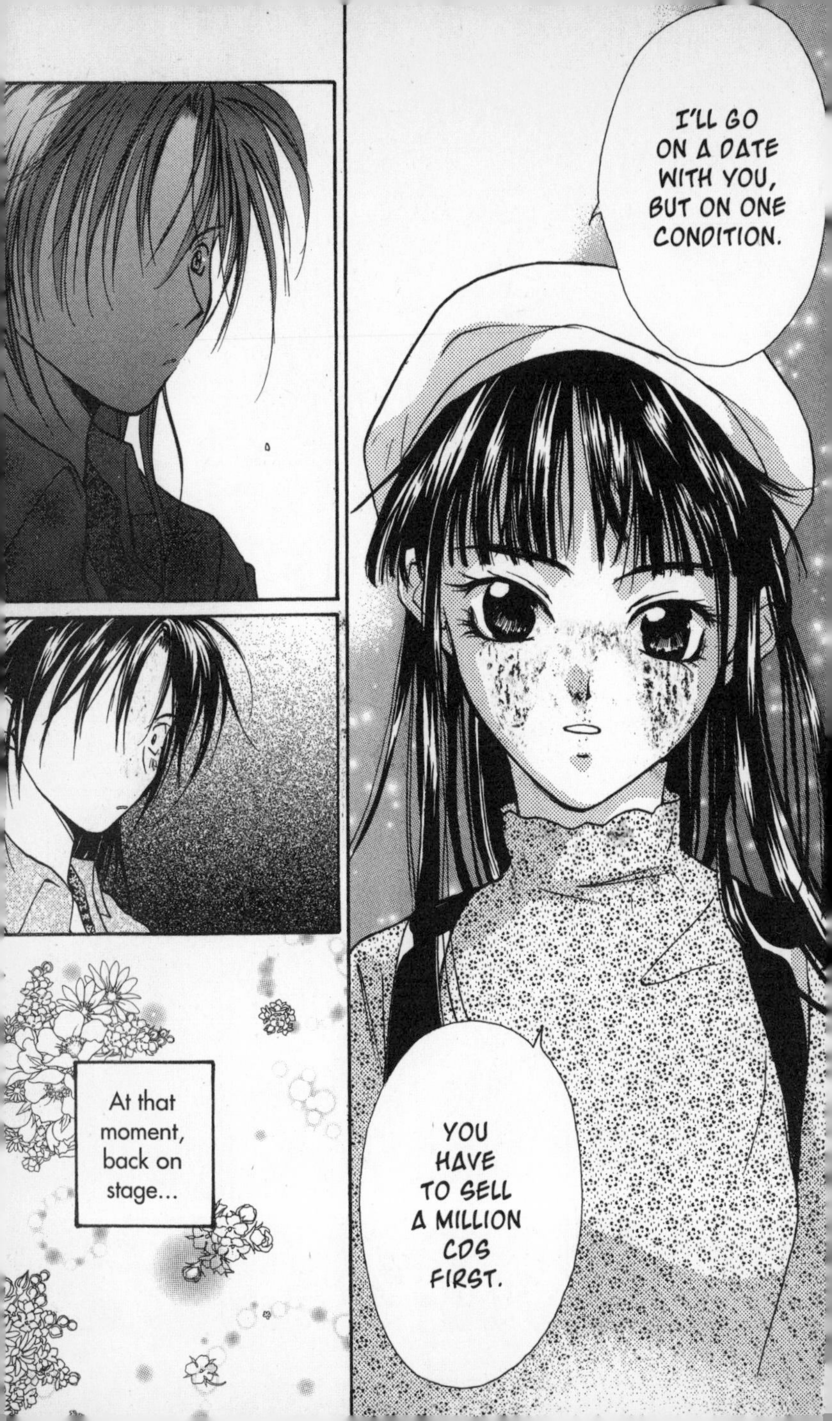
I'LL GO ON A DATE WITH YOU, BUT ON ONE CONDITION.
YOU HAVE TO SELL A MILLION CDS FIRST.
At that moment, back on stage...

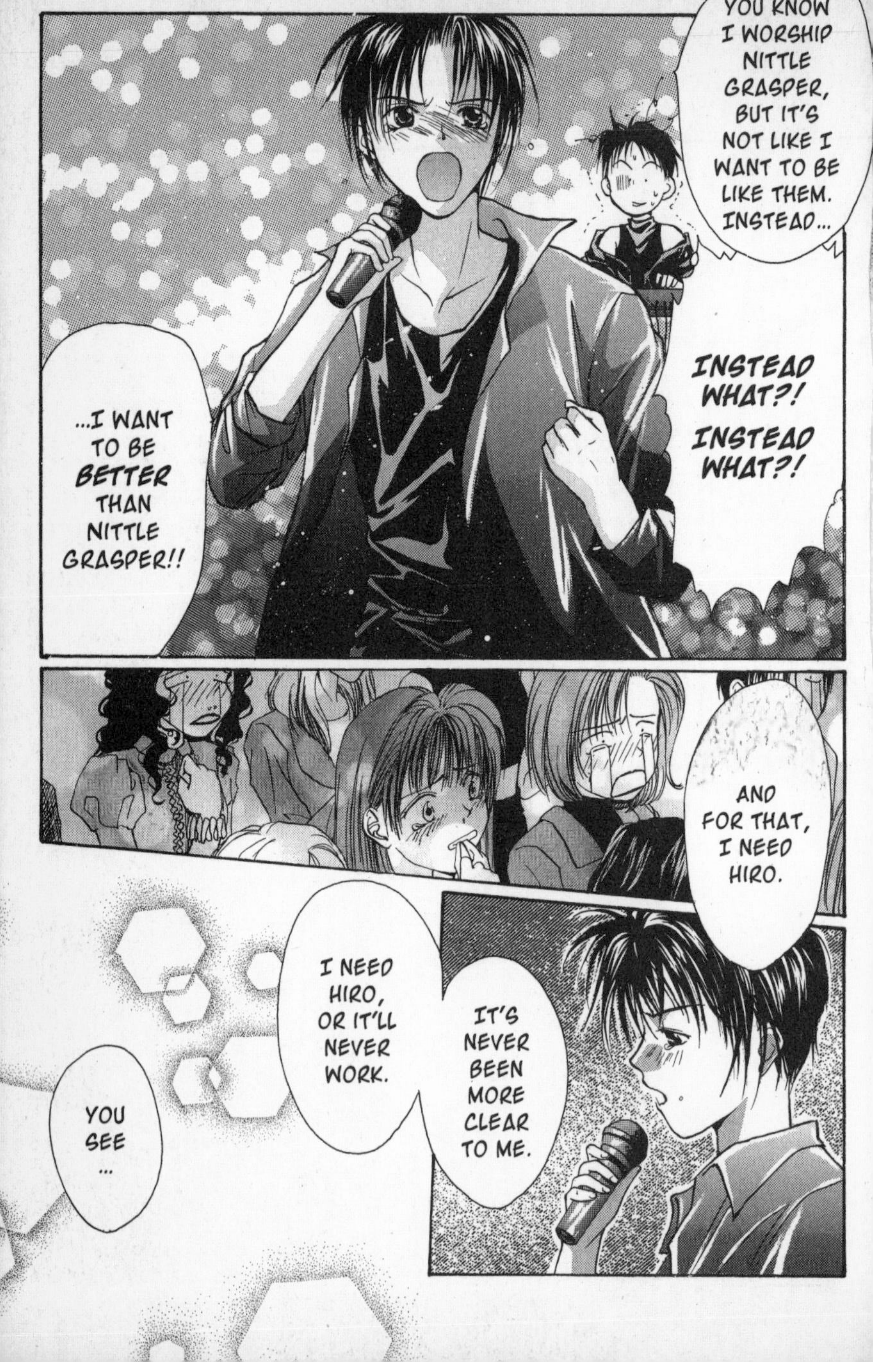
YOU KNOW I WORSHIP NITTLE GRASPER, BUT IT'S NOT LIKE I WANT TO BE LIKE THEM. INSTEAD...
INSTEAD WHAT?! INSTEAD WHAT?!
...I WANT TO BE BETTER THAN NITTLE GRASPER!!
AND FOR THAT, I NEED HIRO.
IT'S NEVER BEEN MORE CLEAR TO ME.
I NEED HIRO, OR IT'LL NEVER WORK.
YOU SEE ...

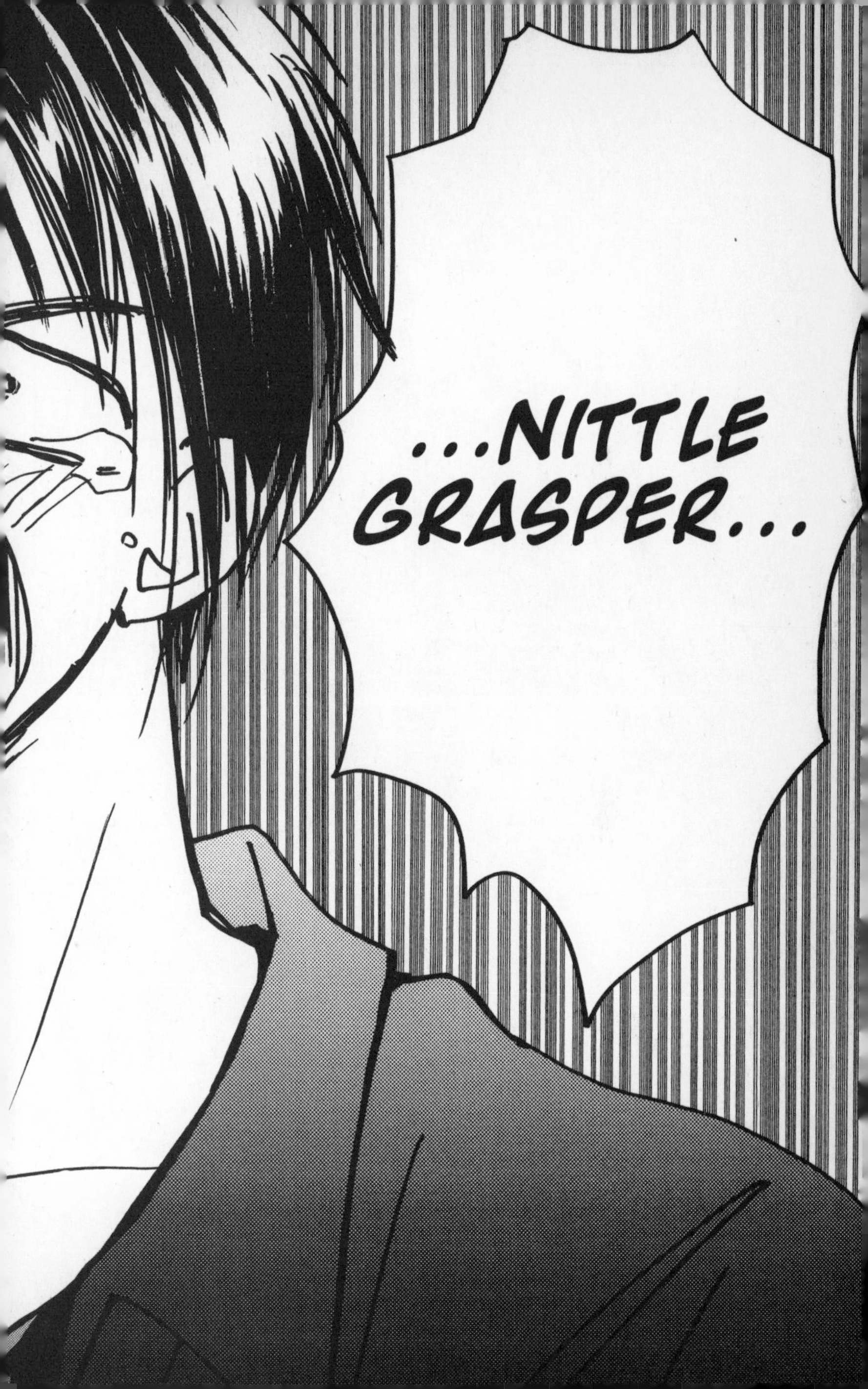
...NITTLE GRASPER...

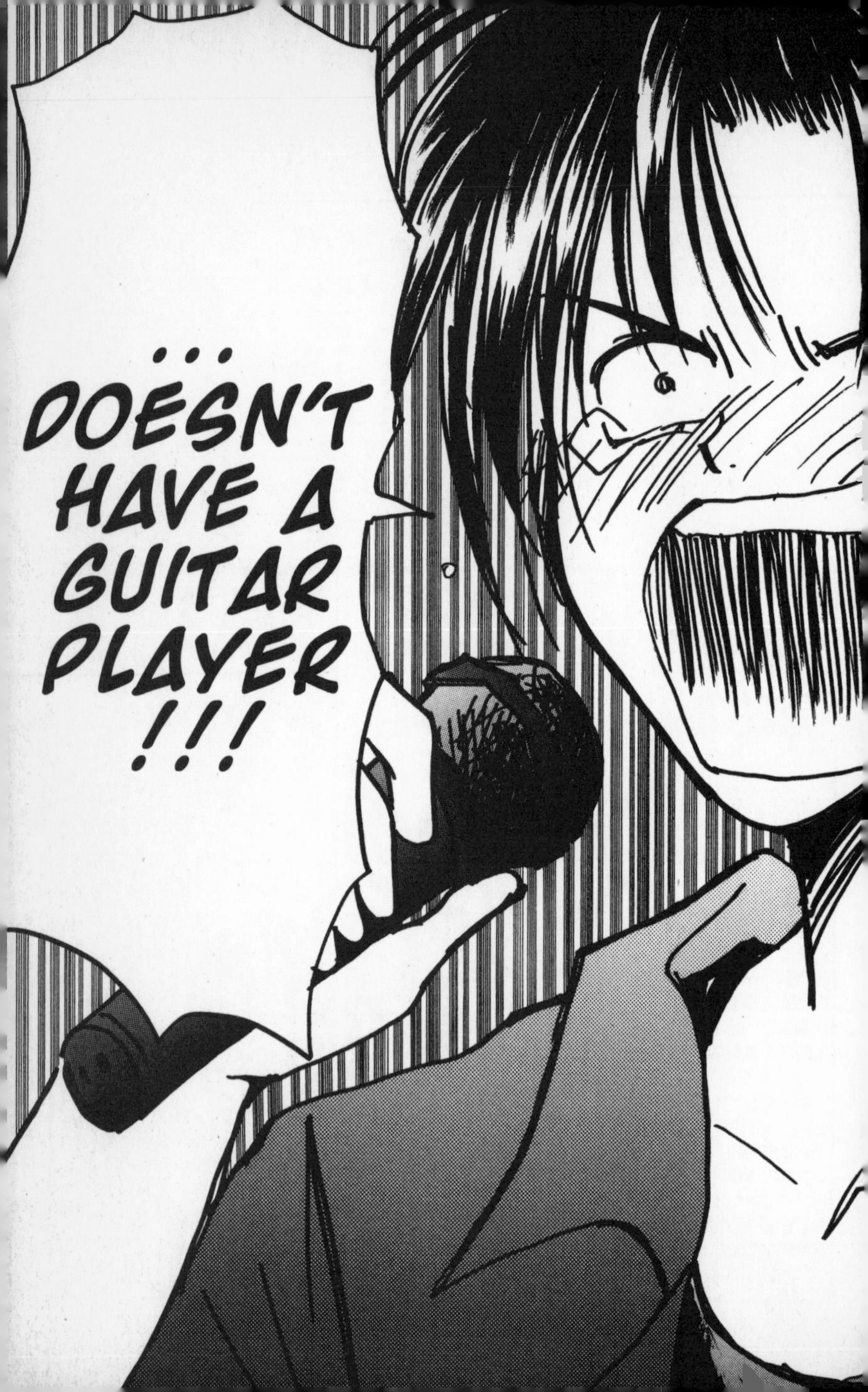
...DOESN'T HAVE A GUITAR PLAYER!!!

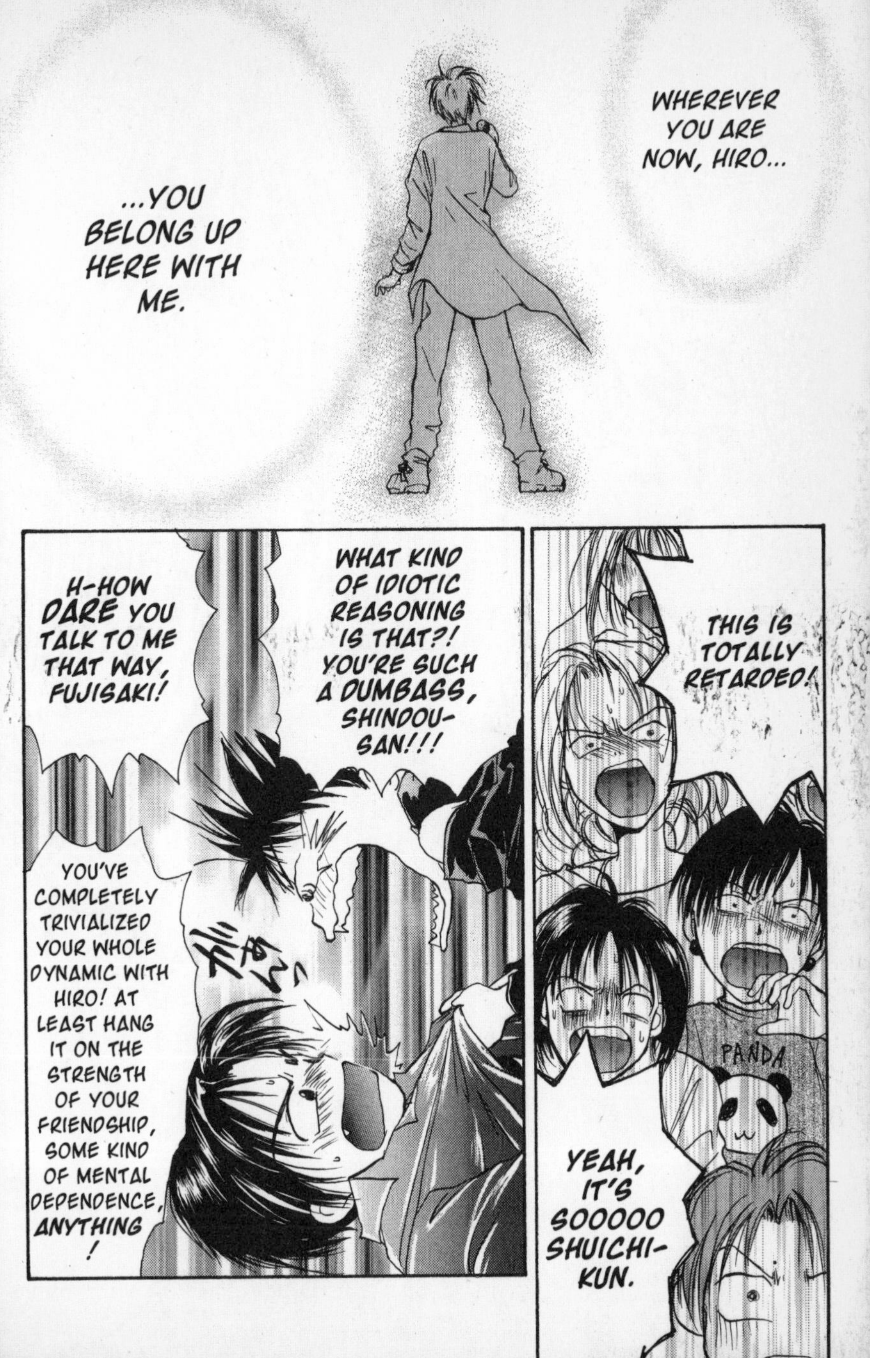
WHEREVER YOU ARE NOW, HIRO...
...YOU BELONG UP HERE WITH ME.
THIS IS TOTALLY RETARDED!
PANDA
YEAH, IT'S SOOOOO SHUICHI-KUN.
WHAT KIND OF IDIOTIC REASONING IS THAT?! YOU'RE SUCH A DUMBASS, SHINDOU-SAN!!!
H-HOW DARE YOU TALK TO ME THAT WAY, FUJISAKI!
YOU'VE COMPLETELY TRIVIALIZED YOUR WHOLE DYNAMIC WITH HIRO! AT LEAST HANG IT ON THE STRENGTH OF YOUR FRIENDSHIP, SOME KIND OF MENTAL DEPENDENCE, ANYTHING!

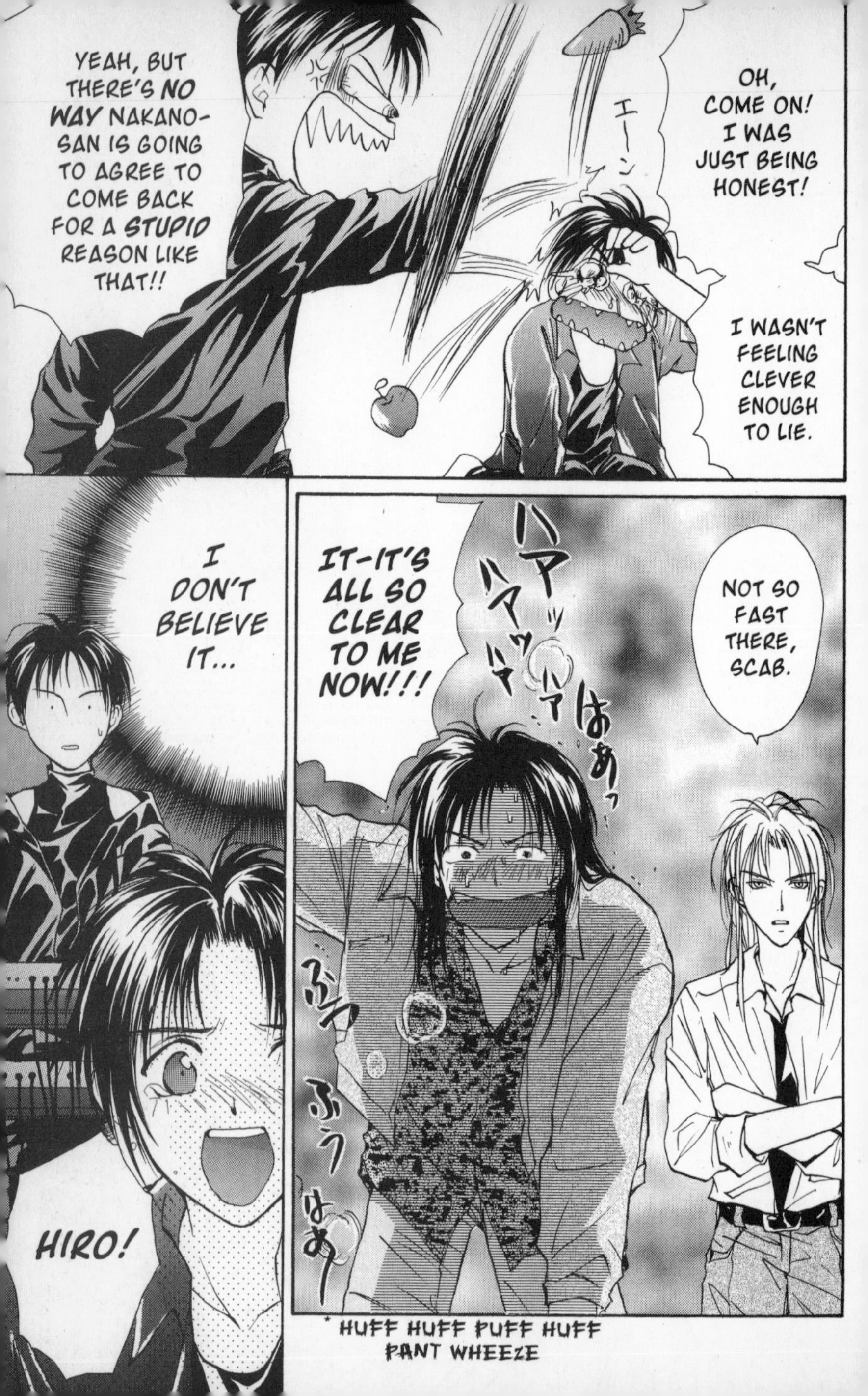
OH, COME ON! I WAS JUST BEING HONEST!
エーン
I WASN'T FEELING CLEVER ENOUGH TO LIE.
YEAH, BUT THERE'S NO WAY NAKANO-SAN IS GOING TO AGREE TO COME BACK FOR A STUPID REASON LIKE THAT!!
NOT SO FAST THERE, SCAB.
ハアッ ハアッ ハア
はあっ
IT-IT'S ALL SO CLEAR TO ME NOW!!!
ふぅ ふう はあっ
I DON'T BELIEVE IT...
HIRO!
* HUFF HUFF PUFF HUFF PANT WHEEZE

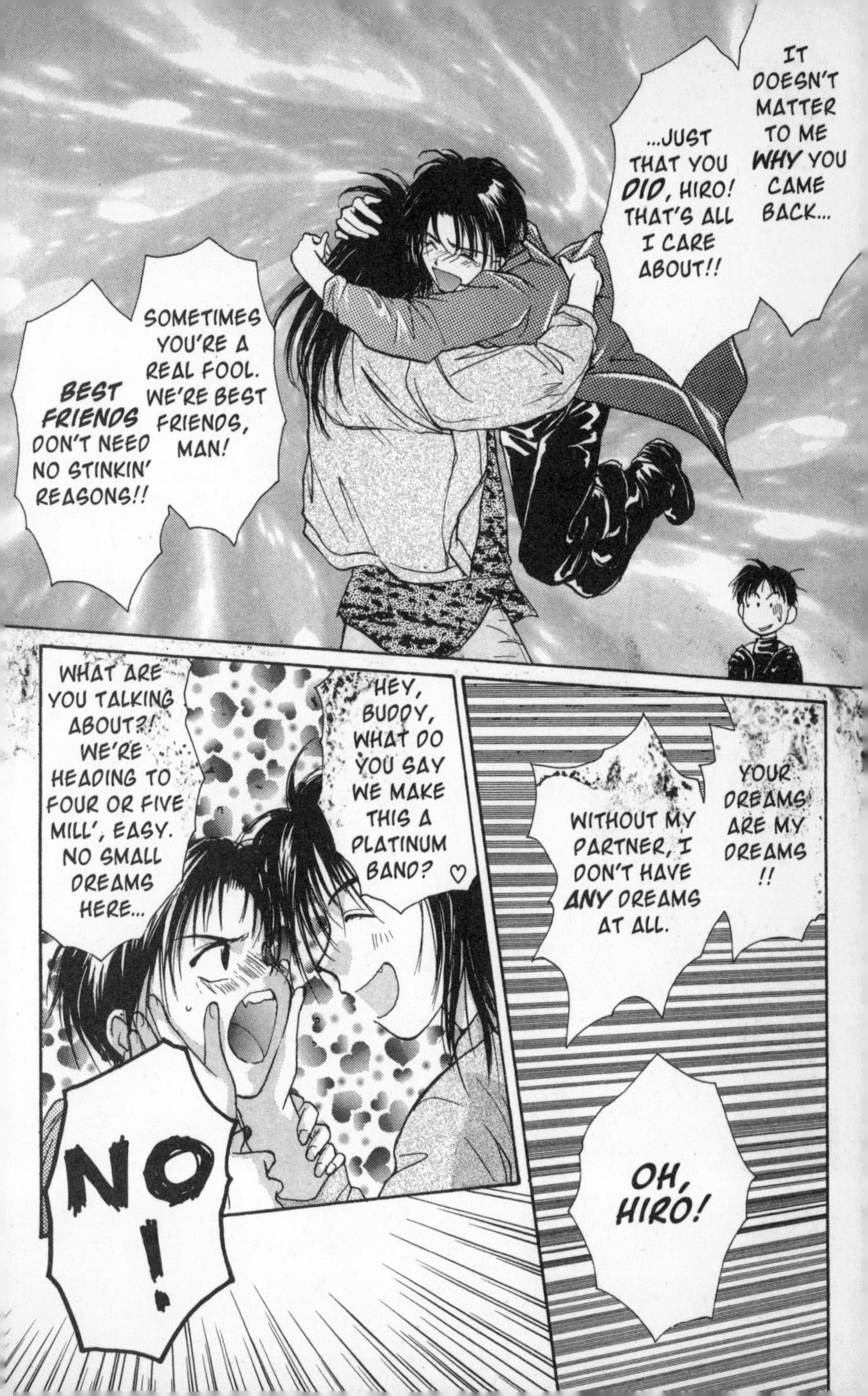
IT DOESN'T MATTER TO ME WHY YOU CAME BACK...
...JUST THAT YOU DID, HIRO! THAT'S ALL I CARE ABOUT!!
SOMETIMES YOU'RE A REAL FOOL. WE'RE BEST FRIENDS, MAN!
BEST FRIENDS DON'T NEED NO STINKIN' REASONS!!
YOUR DREAMS ARE MY DREAMS!!
WITHOUT MY PARTNER, I DON'T HAVE ANY DREAMS AT ALL.
OH, HIRO!
HEY, BUDDY, WHAT DO YOU SAY WE MAKE THIS A PLATINUM BAND? ♡
WHAT ARE YOU TALKING ABOUT?! WE'RE HEADING TO FOUR OR FIVE MILL', EASY. NO SMALL DREAMS HERE...
NO!

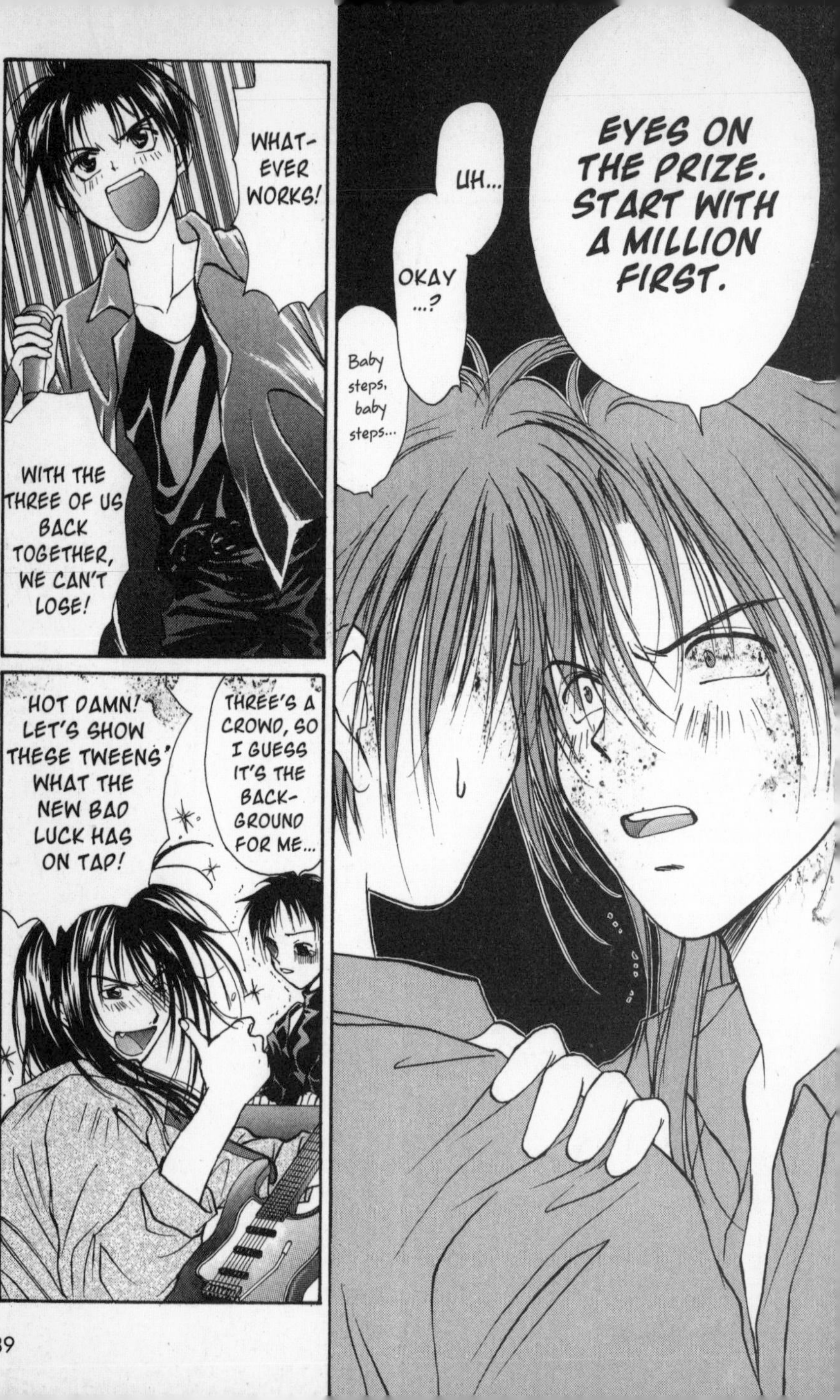
EYES ON THE PRIZE. START WITH A MILLION FIRST.
UH...
OKAY ...?
Baby steps, baby steps...
WHAT-EVER WORKS!
WITH THE THREE OF US BACK TOGETHER, WE CAN'T LOSE!
THREE'S A CROWD, SO I GUESS IT'S THE BACK-GROUND FOR ME...
"HOT DAMN! LET'S SHOW THESE TWEENS" WHAT THE NEW BAD LUCK HAS ON TAP!

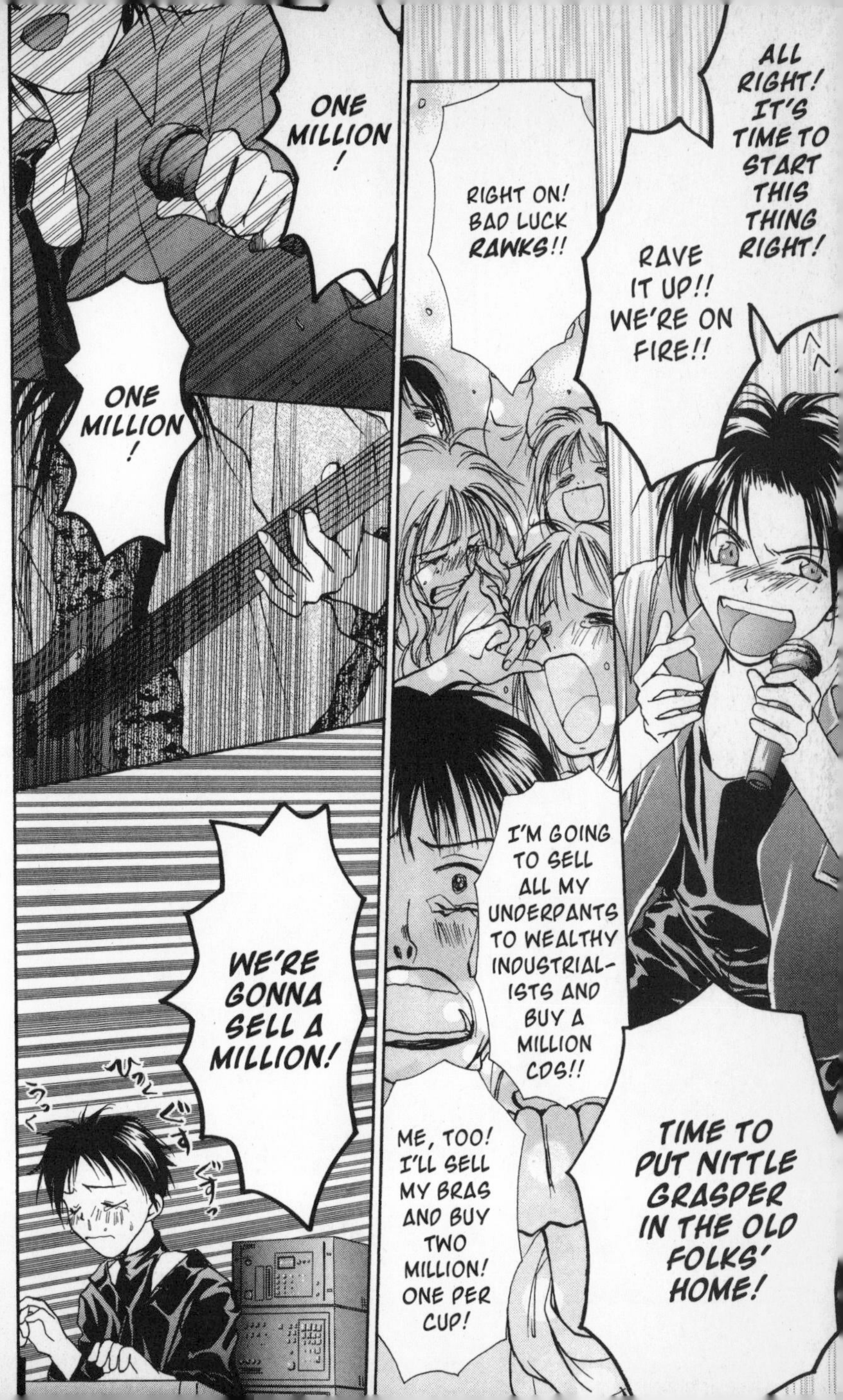
ALL RIGHT! IT'S TIME TO START THIS THING RIGHT!
RAVE IT UP!! WE'RE ON FIRE!!
RIGHT ON! BAD LUCK RAWKS!!
I'M GOING TO SELL ALL MY UNDERPANTS TO WEALTHY INDUSTRIAL-ISTS AND BUY A MILLION CDS!!
TIME TO PUT NITTLE GRASPER IN THE OLD FOLKS' HOME!
ME, TOO! I'LL SELL MY BRAS AND BUY TWO MILLION! ONE PER CUP!
ONE MILLION!
ONE MILLION!
WE'RE GONNA SELL A MILLION!

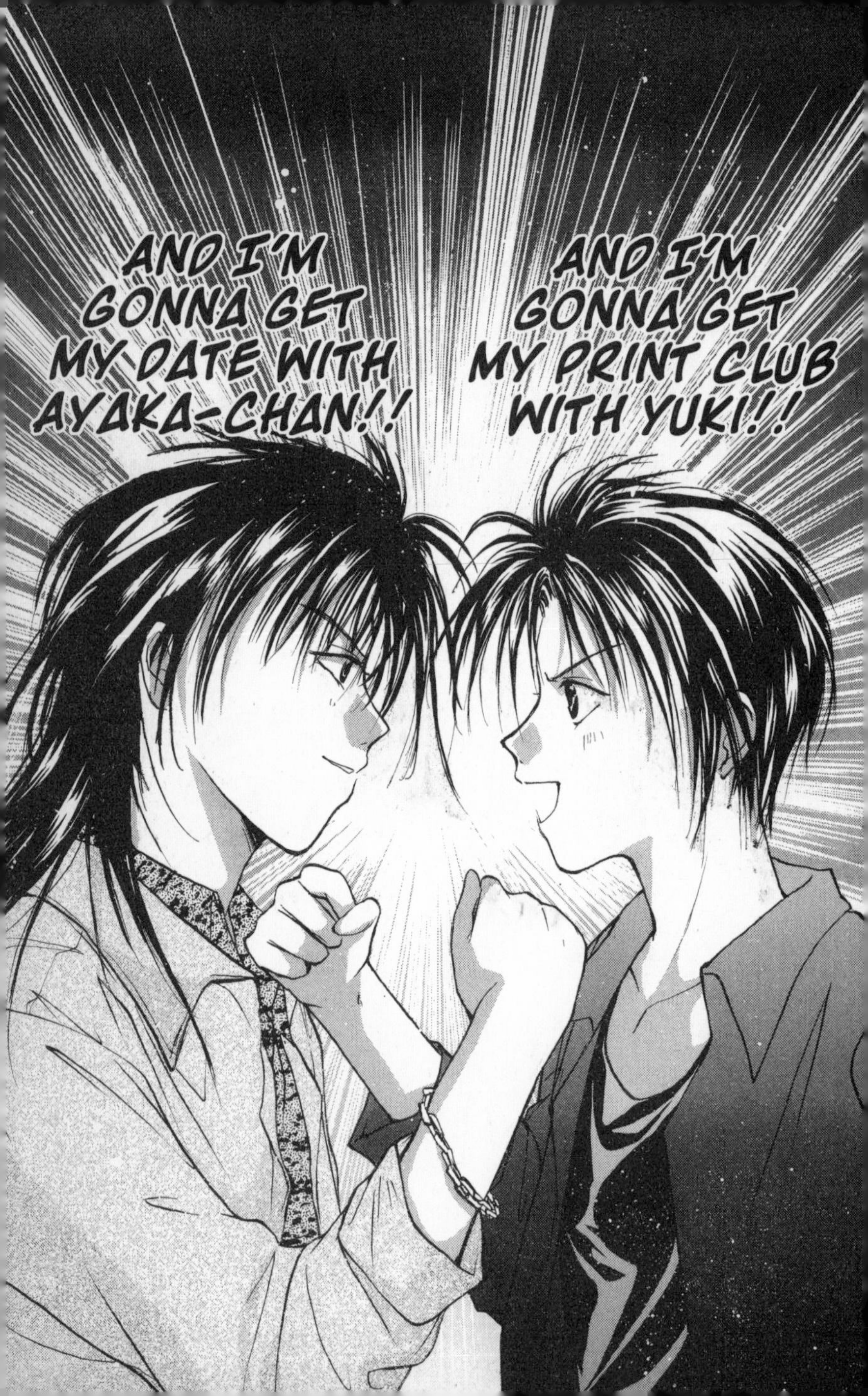
AND I'M GONNA GET MY PRINT CLUB WITH YUKI!!
AND I'M GONNA GET MY DATE WITH AYAKA-CHAN!!

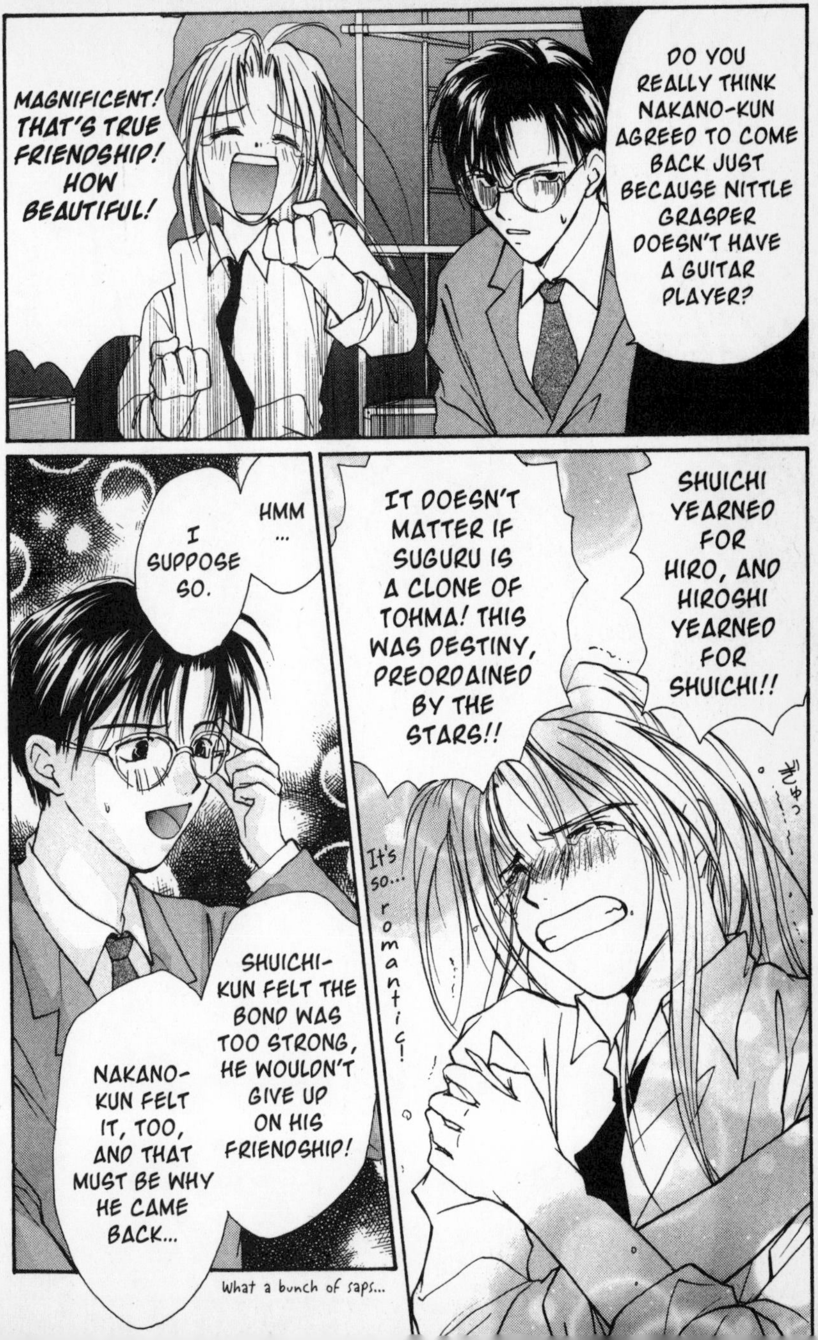
DO YOU REALLY THINK NAKANO-KUN AGREED TO COME BACK JUST BECAUSE NITTLE GRASPER DOESN'T HAVE A GUITAR PLAYER?
MAGNIFICENT! THAT'S TRUE FRIENDSHIP! HOW BEAUTIFUL!
SHUICHI YEARNED FOR HIRO, AND HIROSHI YEARNED FOR SHUICHI!!
IT DOESN'T MATTER IF SUGURU IS A CLONE OF TOHMA! THIS WAS DESTINY, PREORDAINED BY THE STARS!!
It's so... romantic!
HMM...
I SUPPOSE SO.
SHUICHI-KUN FELT THE BOND WAS TOO STRONG, HE WOULDN'T GIVE UP ON HIS FRIENDSHIP!
NAKANO-KUN FELT IT, TOO, AND THAT MUST BE WHY HE CAME BACK...
What a bunch of saps...

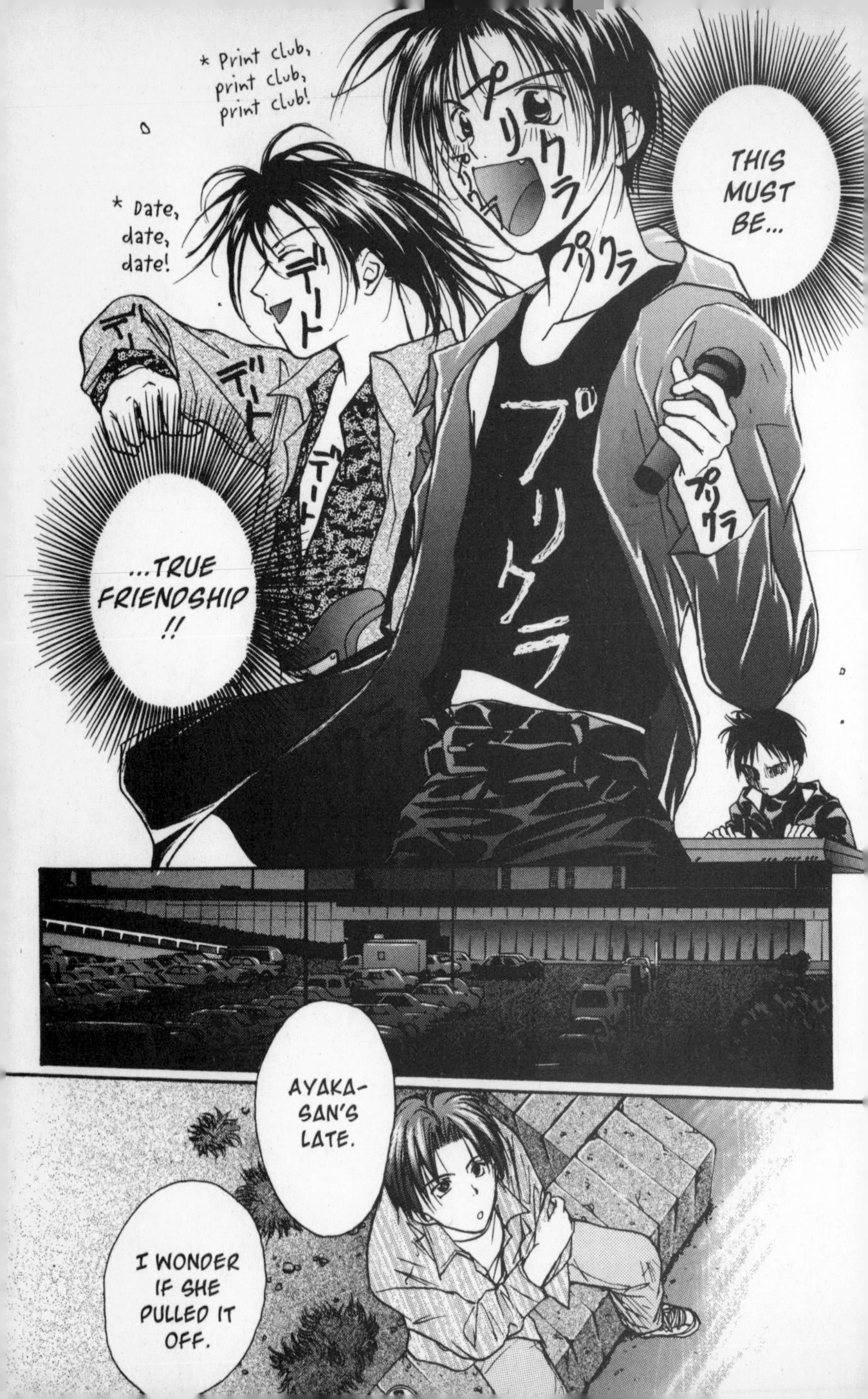

THIS MUST BE...
プリクラ
* Print club, print club, print club!
...TRUE FRIENDSHIP !!
デート
* Date, date, date!
AYAKA-SAN'S LATE.
I WONDER IF SHE PULLED IT OFF.

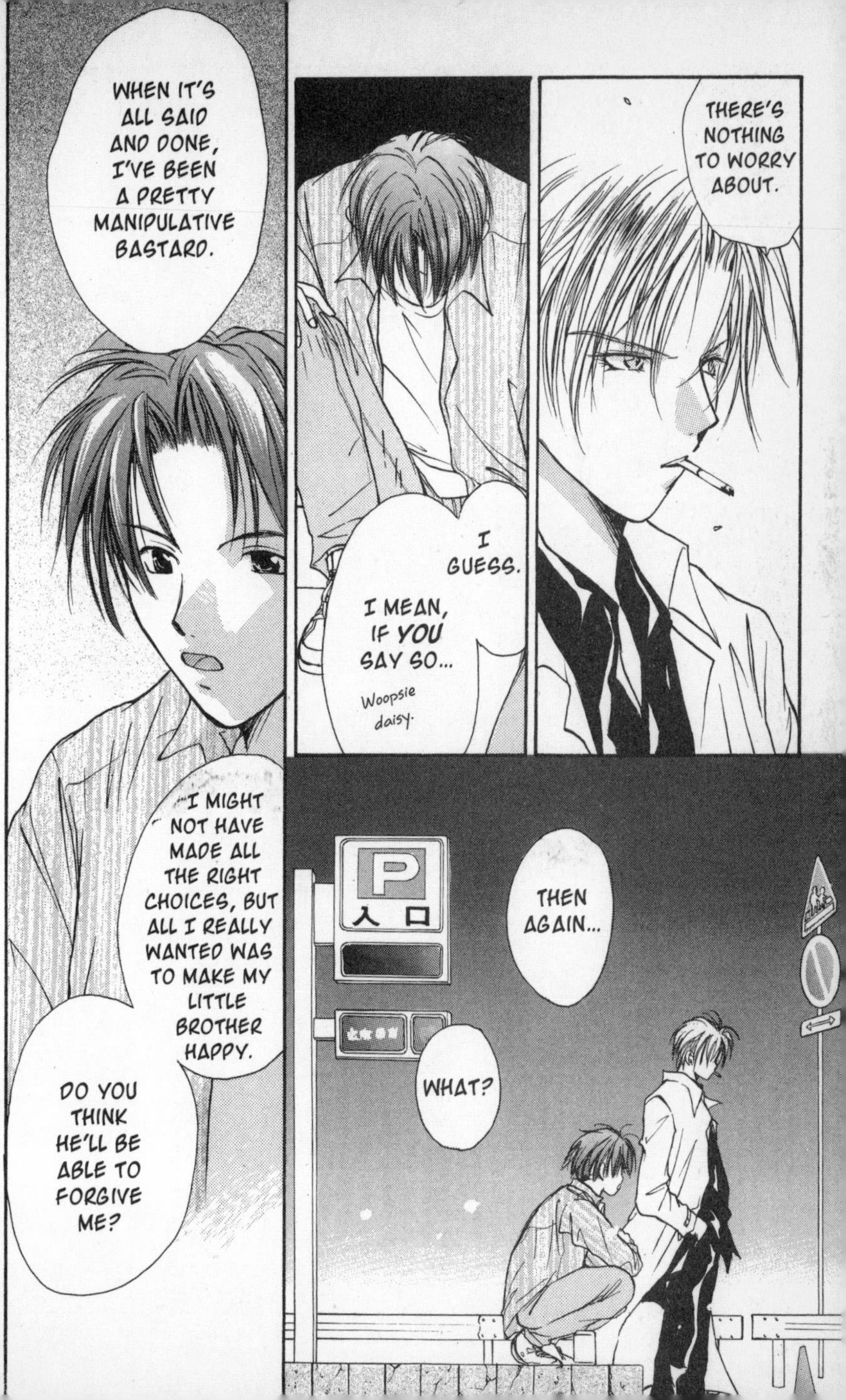
THERE'S NOTHING TO WORRY ABOUT.
I GUESS.
I MEAN, IF *YOU* SAY SO...
Woopsie daisy.
THEN AGAIN...
入口
WHAT?
WHEN IT'S ALL SAID AND DONE, I'VE BEEN A PRETTY MANIPULATIVE BASTARD.
I MIGHT NOT HAVE MADE ALL THE RIGHT CHOICES, BUT ALL I REALLY WANTED WAS TO MAKE MY LITTLE BROTHER HAPPY.
DO YOU THINK HE'LL BE ABLE TO FORGIVE ME?

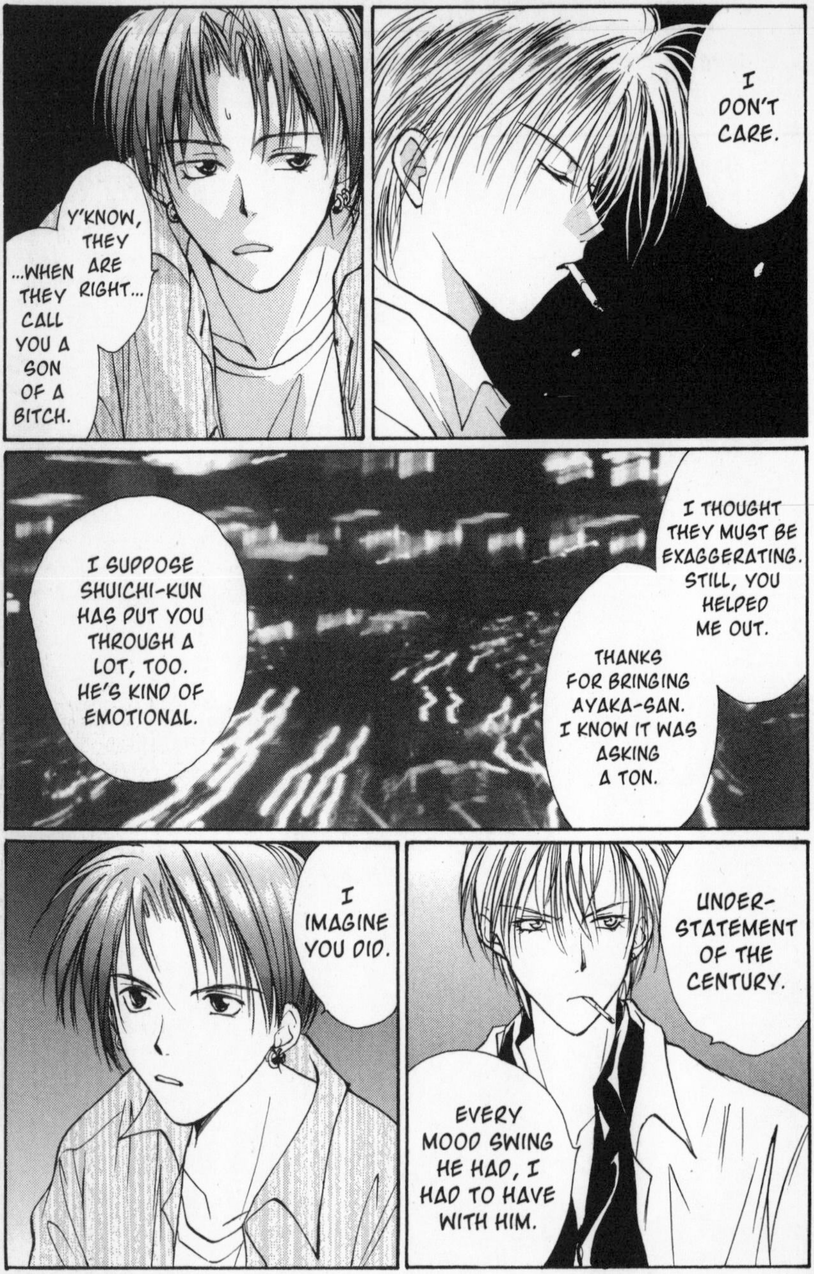
I DON'T CARE.
Y'KNOW, THEY ARE RIGHT...
...WHEN THEY CALL YOU A SON OF A BITCH.
I THOUGHT THEY MUST BE EXAGGERATING. STILL, YOU HELPED ME OUT.
THANKS FOR BRINGING AYAKA-SAN. I KNOW IT WAS ASKING A TON.
I SUPPOSE SHUICHI-KUN HAS PUT YOU THROUGH A LOT, TOO. HE'S KIND OF EMOTIONAL.
UNDER-STATEMENT OF THE CENTURY.
EVERY MOOD SWING HE HAD, I HAD TO HAVE WITH HIM.
I IMAGINE YOU DID.

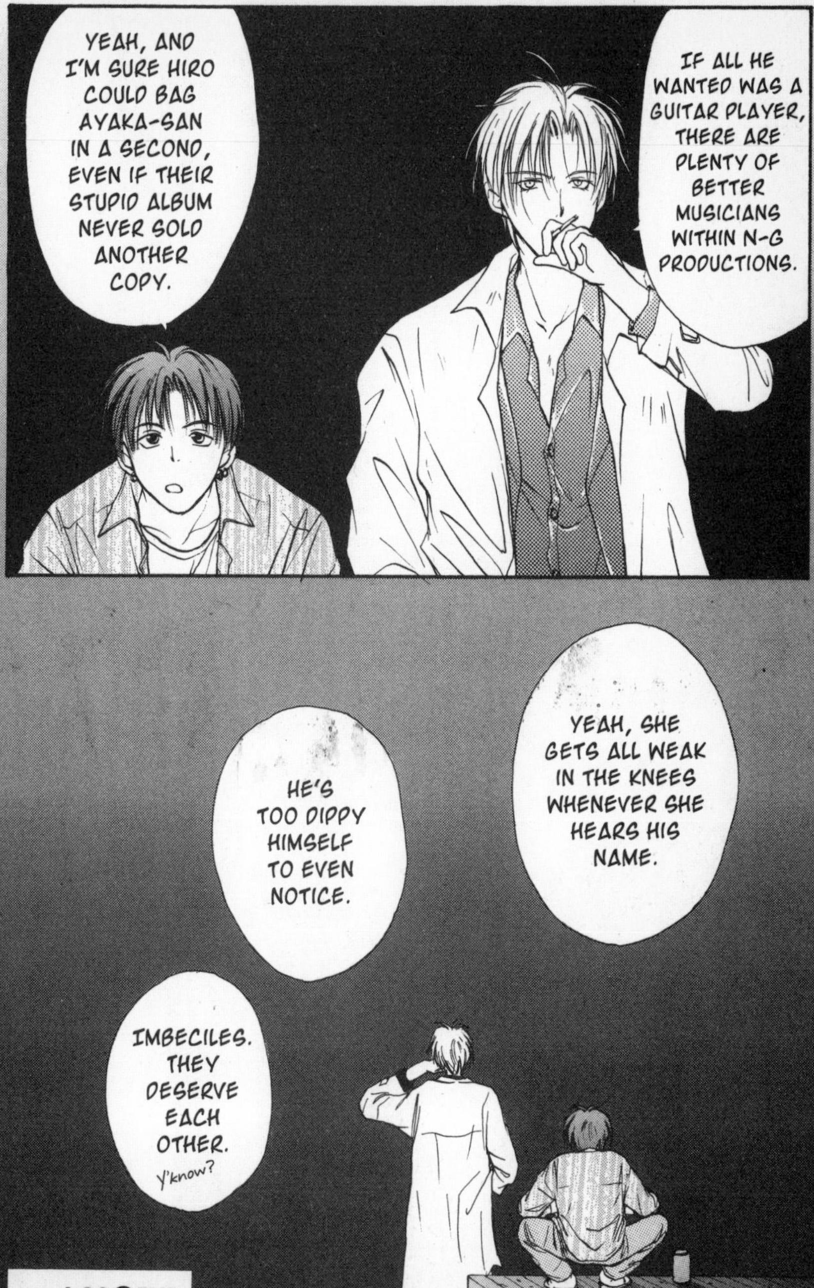
IF ALL HE WANTED WAS A GUITAR PLAYER, THERE ARE PLENTY OF BETTER MUSICIANS WITHIN N-G PRODUCTIONS.
YEAH, AND I'M SURE HIRO COULD BAG AYAKA-SAN IN A SECOND, EVEN IF THEIR STUDIO ALBUM NEVER SOLD ANOTHER COPY.
YEAH, SHE GETS ALL WEAK IN THE KNEES WHENEVER SHE HEARS HIS NAME.
HE'S TOO DIPPY HIMSELF TO EVEN NOTICE.
IMBECILES. THEY DESERVE EACH OTHER.
Y'know?
track28▶END

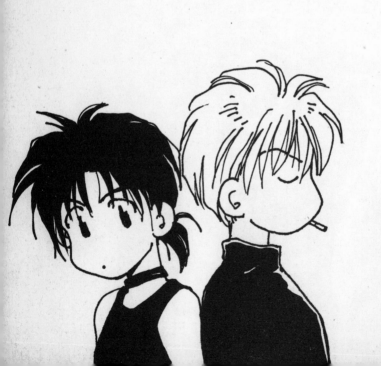

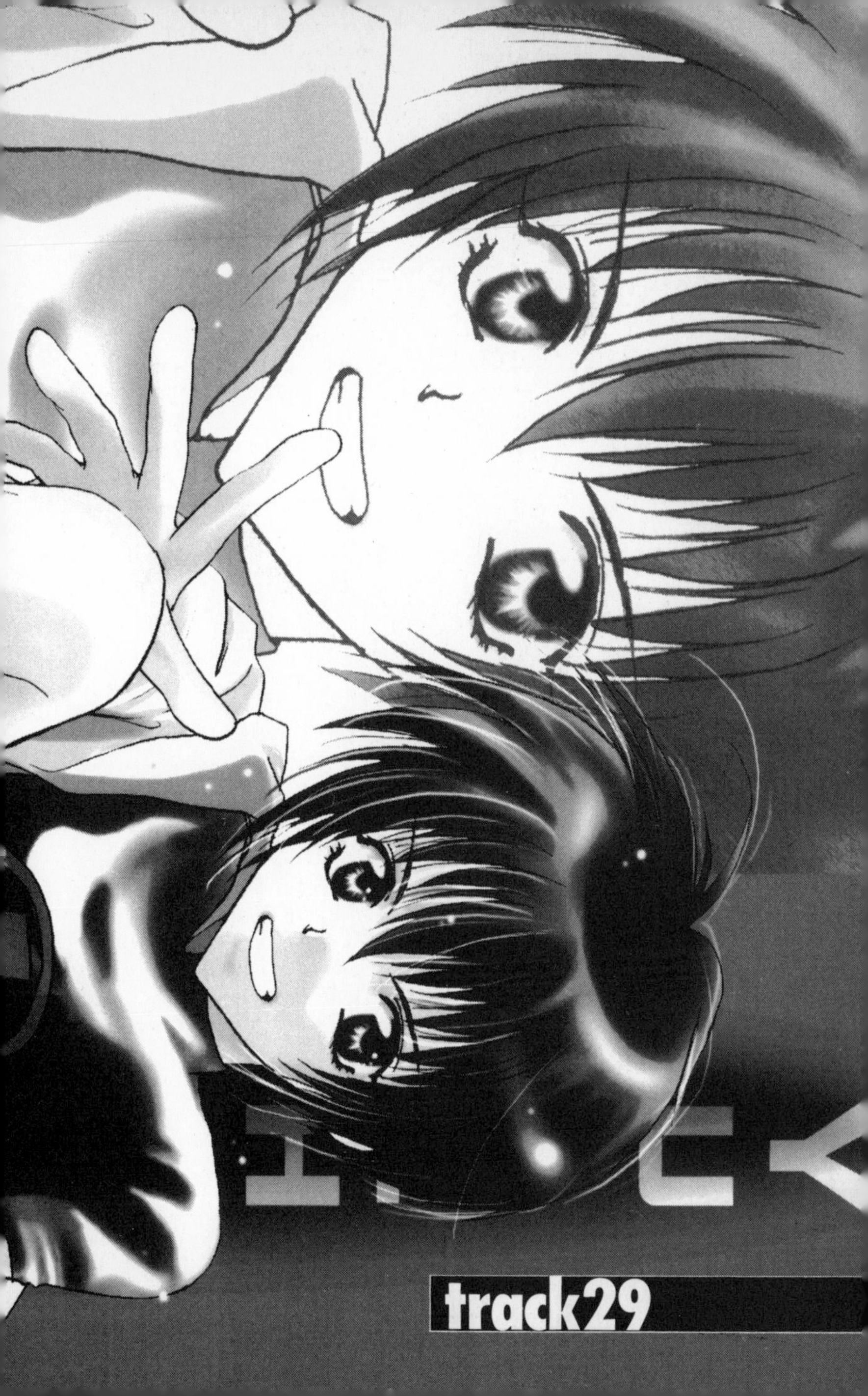
track29

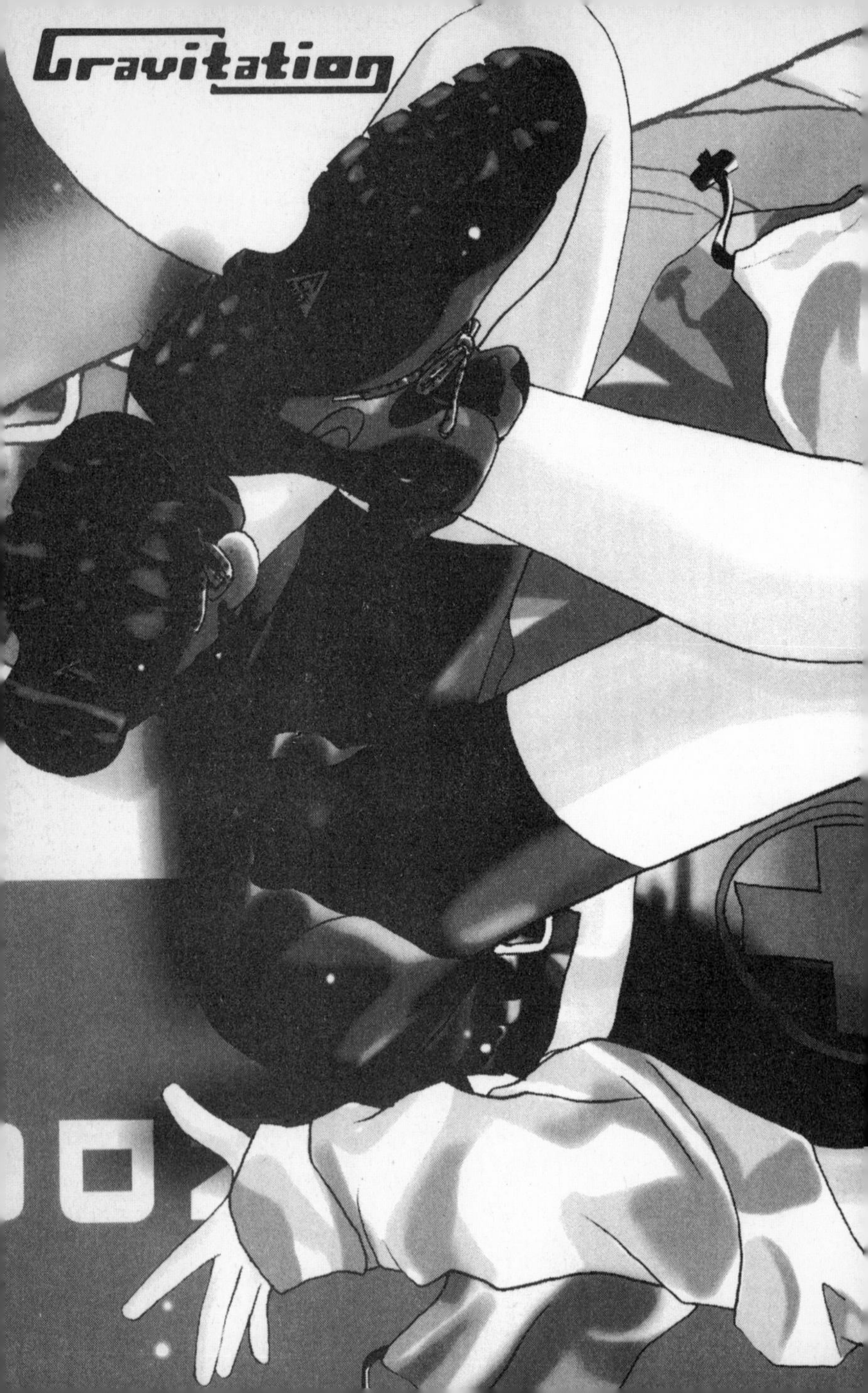
Gravitation

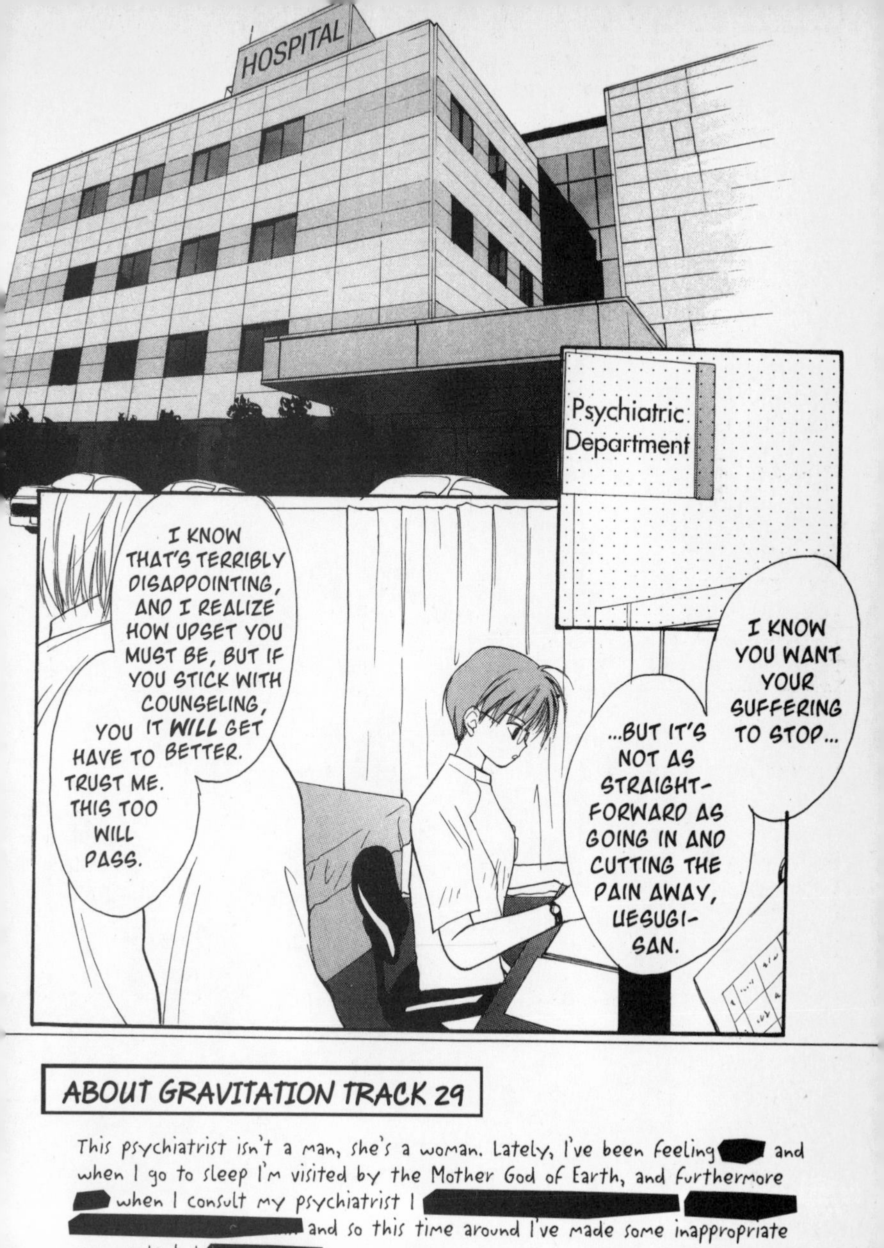
HOSPITAL
Psychiatric Department
I KNOW YOU WANT YOUR SUFFERING TO STOP...
...BUT IT'S NOT AS STRAIGHT-FORWARD AS GOING IN AND CUTTING THE PAIN AWAY, UESUGI-SAN.
I KNOW THAT'S TERRIBLY DISAPPOINTING, AND I REALIZE HOW UPSET YOU MUST BE, BUT IF YOU STICK WITH COUNSELING, IT WILL GET BETTER.
YOU HAVE TO TRUST ME. THIS TOO WILL PASS.

ABOUT GRAVITATION TRACK 29

This psychiatrist isn't a man, she's a woman. Lately, I've been feeling [redacted] and when I go to sleep I'm visited by the Mother God of Earth, and furthermore [redacted] when I consult my psychiatrist I [redacted] and so this time around I've made some inappropriate comments, but [redacted]

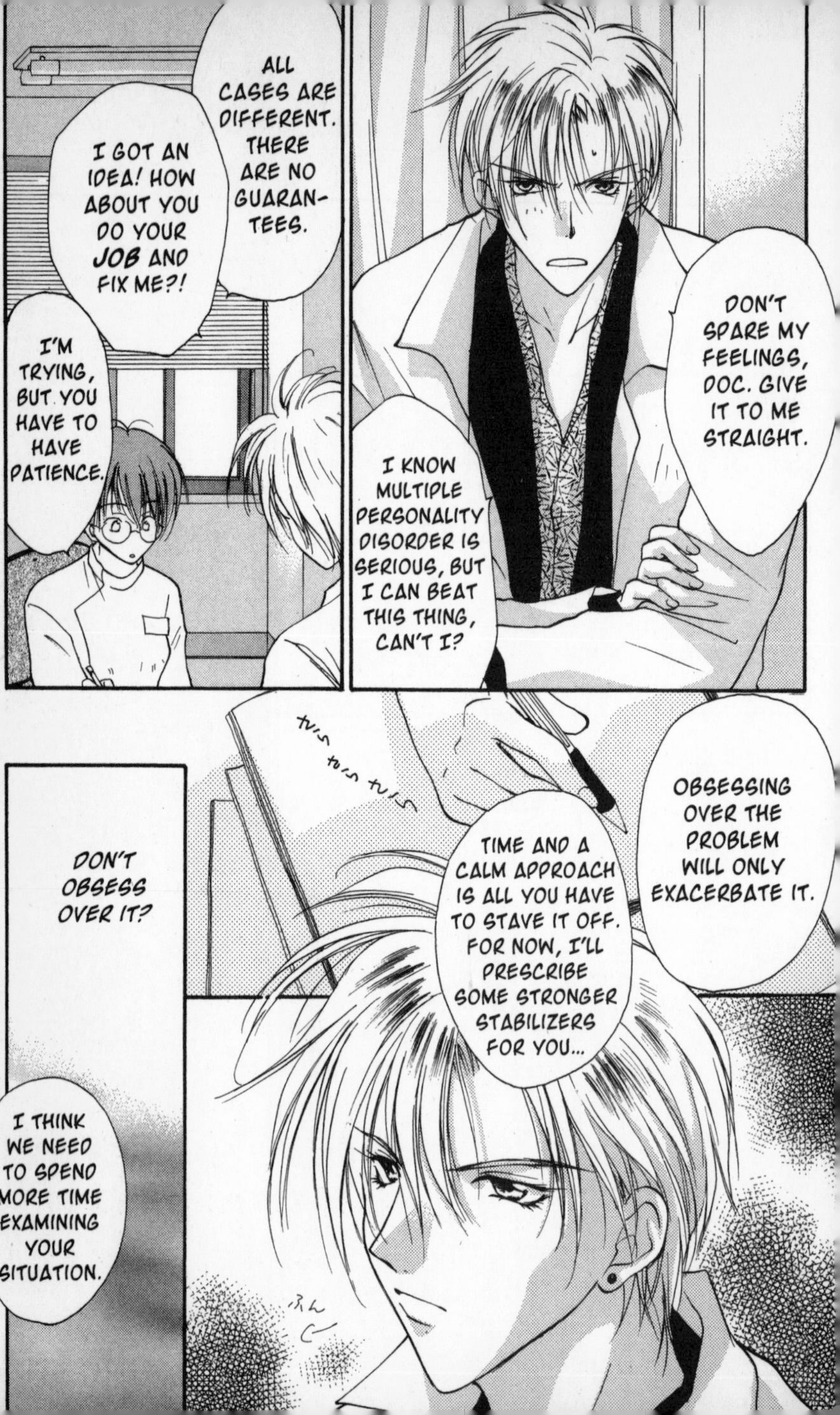
DON'T SPARE MY FEELINGS, DOC. GIVE IT TO ME STRAIGHT.
I KNOW MULTIPLE PERSONALITY DISORDER IS SERIOUS, BUT I CAN BEAT THIS THING, CAN'T I?
ALL CASES ARE DIFFERENT. THERE ARE NO GUARAN-TEES.
I GOT AN IDEA! HOW ABOUT YOU DO YOUR *JOB* AND FIX ME?!
I'M TRYING, BUT YOU HAVE TO HAVE PATIENCE.
OBSESSING OVER THE PROBLEM WILL ONLY EXACERBATE IT.
TIME AND A CALM APPROACH IS ALL YOU HAVE TO STAVE IT OFF. FOR NOW, I'LL PRESCRIBE SOME STRONGER STABILIZERS FOR YOU...
DON'T OBSESS OVER IT?
I THINK WE NEED TO SPEND MORE TIME EXAMINING YOUR SITUATION.
ふん

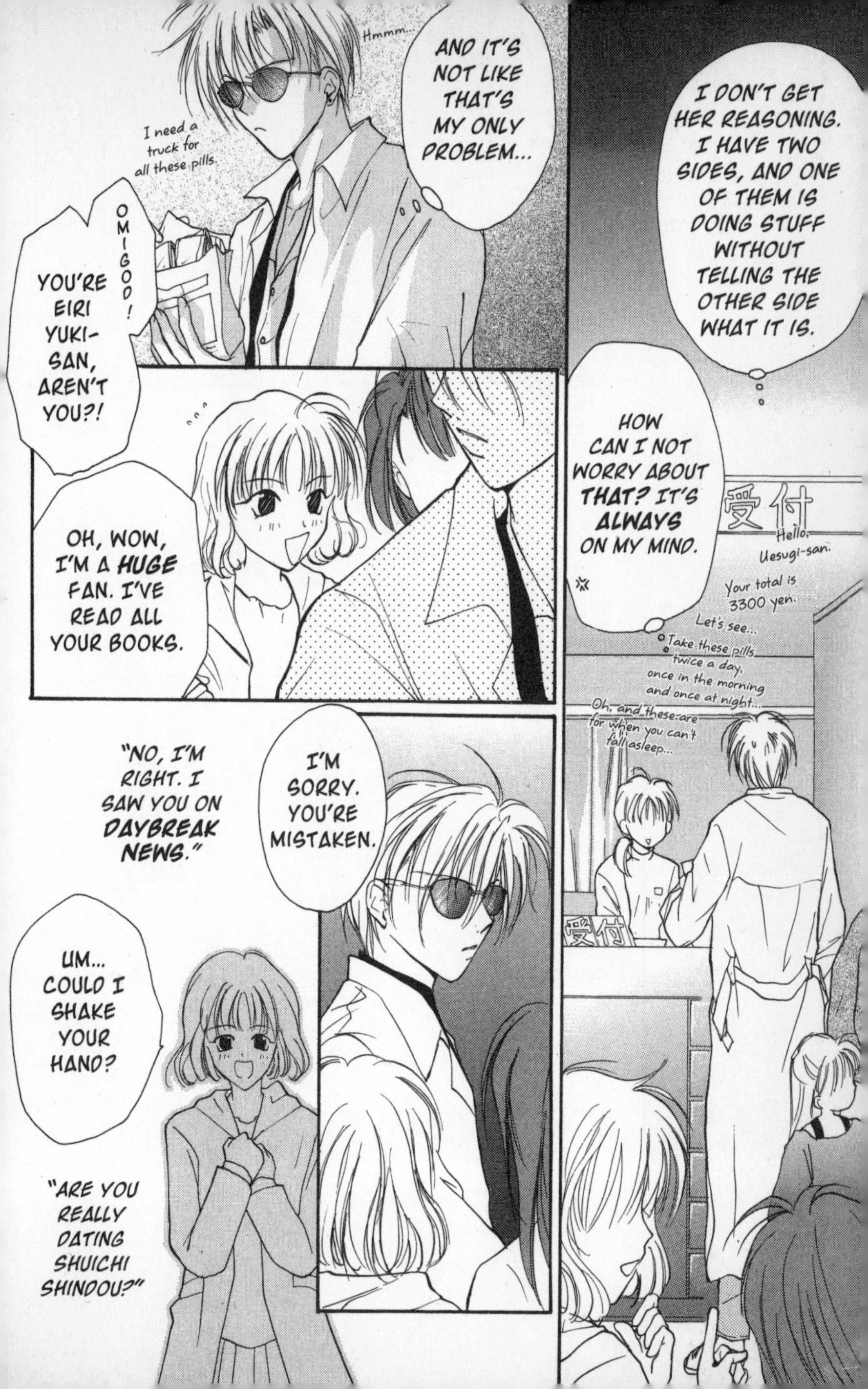
I DON'T GET HER REASONING. I HAVE TWO SIDES, AND ONE OF THEM IS DOING STUFF WITHOUT TELLING THE OTHER SIDE WHAT IT IS.
HOW CAN I NOT WORRY ABOUT THAT? IT'S ALWAYS ON MY MIND.
受付
Hello, Uesugi-san.
Your total is 3300 yen.
Let's see...
Take these pills twice a day, once in the morning and once at night...
Oh, and these are for when you can't fall asleep...
受付
Hmmm...
AND IT'S NOT LIKE THAT'S MY ONLY PROBLEM...
I need a truck for all these pills.
OMIGOD!
YOU'RE EIRI YUKI-SAN, AREN'T YOU?!
OH, WOW, I'M A HUGE FAN. I'VE READ ALL YOUR BOOKS.
I'M SORRY. YOU'RE MISTAKEN.
"NO, I'M RIGHT. I SAW YOU ON DAYBREAK NEWS."
UM... COULD I SHAKE YOUR HAND?
"ARE YOU REALLY DATING SHUICHI SHINDOU?"

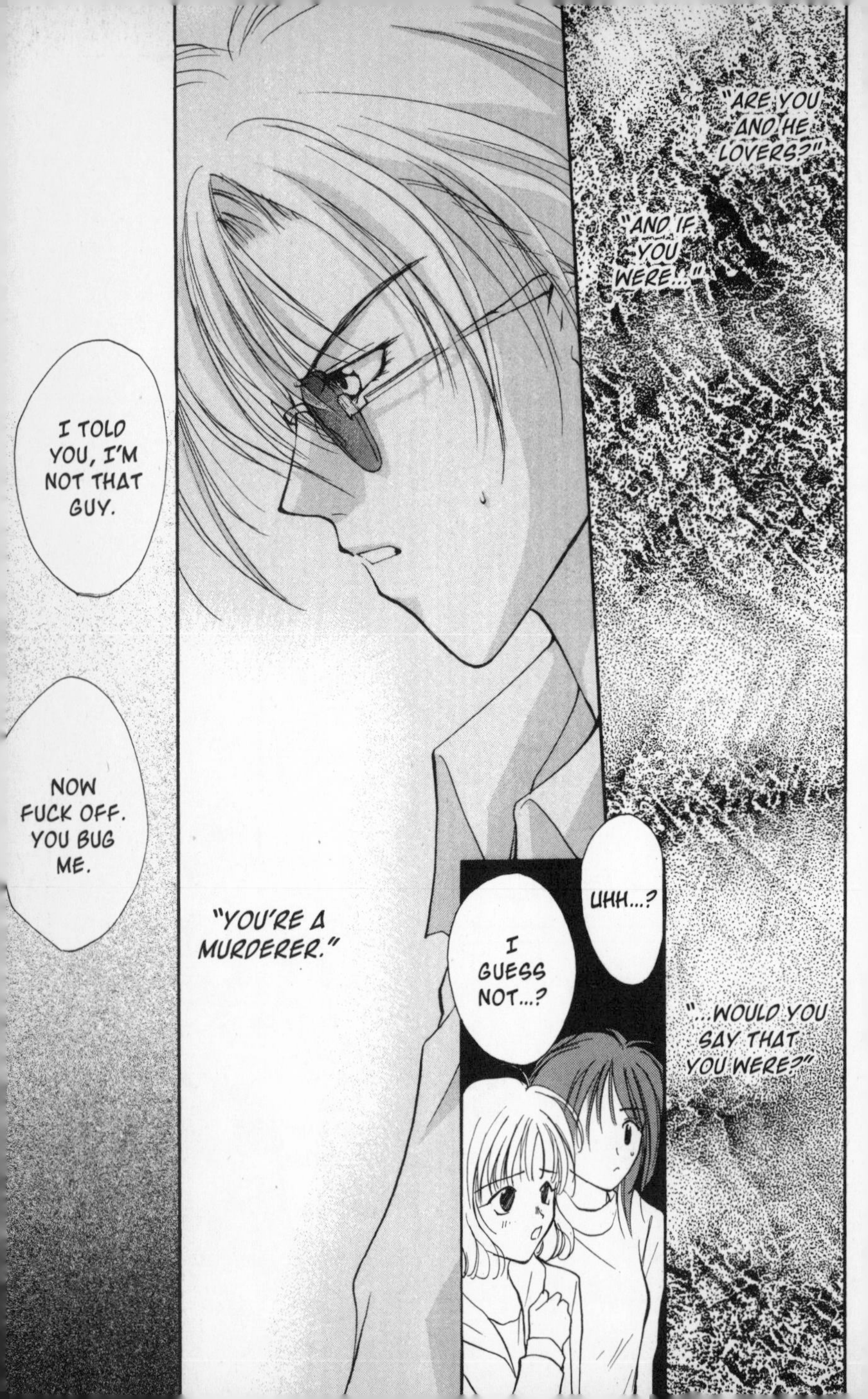
"ARE YOU AND HE LOVERS?"
"AND IF YOU WERE..."
"...WOULD YOU SAY THAT YOU WERE?"
UHH...?
I GUESS NOT...?
"YOU'RE A MURDERER."
I TOLD YOU, I'M NOT THAT GUY.
NOW FUCK OFF. YOU BUG ME.

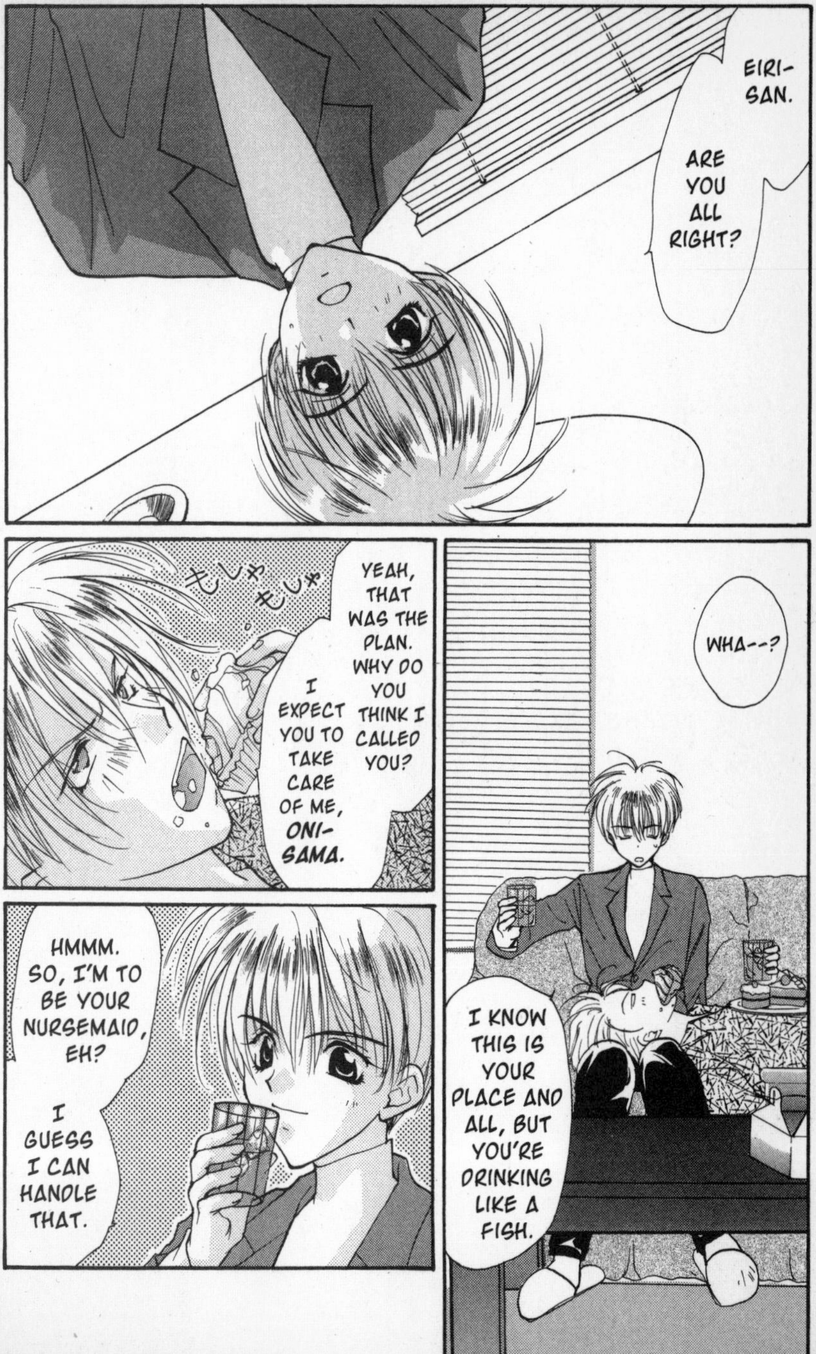
EIRI-SAN.
ARE YOU ALL RIGHT?
WHA--?
I KNOW THIS IS YOUR PLACE AND ALL, BUT YOU'RE DRINKING LIKE A FISH.
もしゃ もしゃ
YEAH, THAT WAS THE PLAN. WHY DO YOU THINK I CALLED YOU?
I EXPECT YOU TO TAKE CARE OF ME, ONI-SAMA.
HMMM. SO, I'M TO BE YOUR NURSEMAID, EH?
I GUESS I CAN HANDLE THAT.

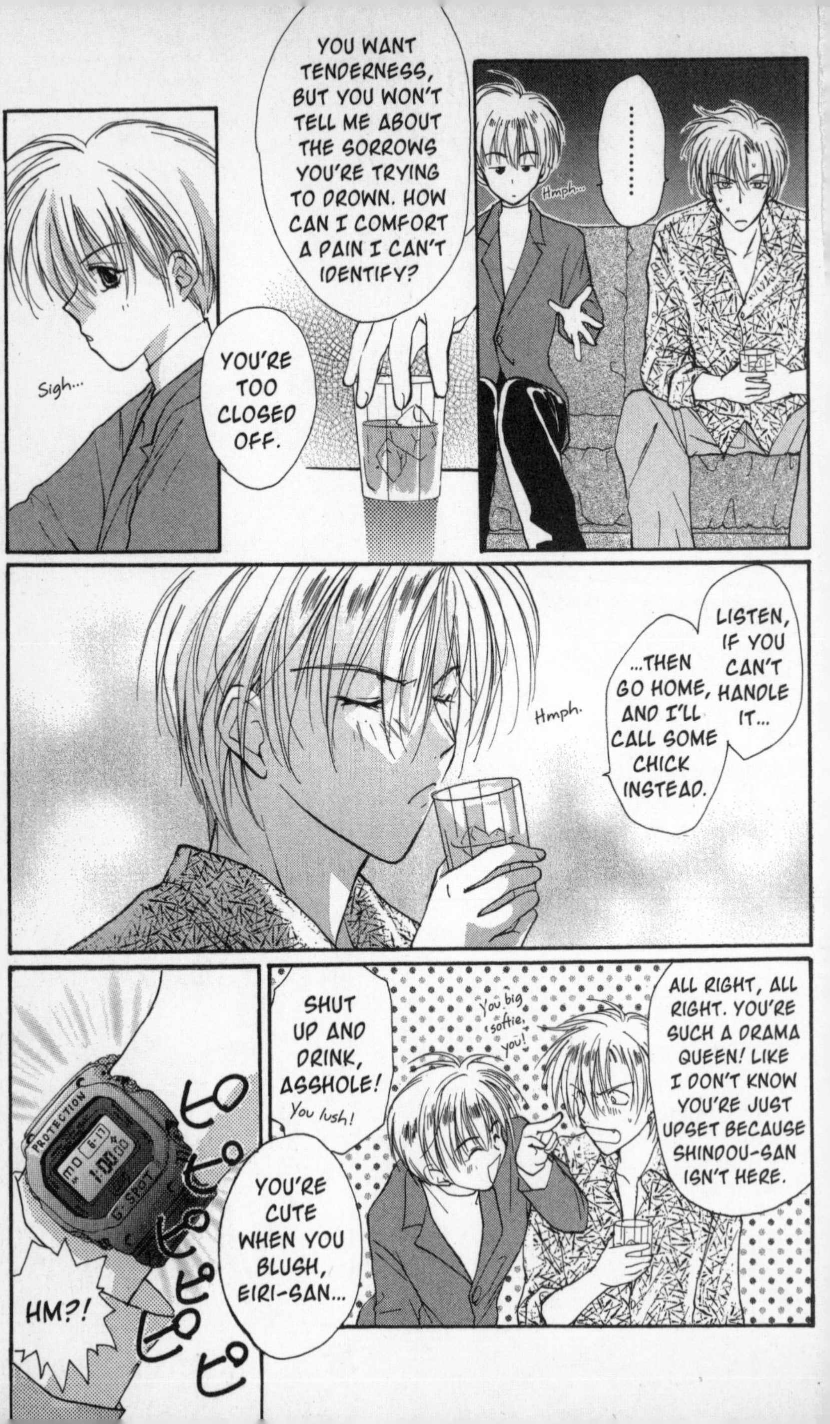
......
Hmph...
YOU WANT TENDERNESS, BUT YOU WON'T TELL ME ABOUT THE SORROWS YOU'RE TRYING TO DROWN. HOW CAN I COMFORT A PAIN I CAN'T IDENTIFY?
YOU'RE TOO CLOSED OFF.
Sigh...
LISTEN, IF YOU CAN'T HANDLE IT...
...THEN GO HOME, AND I'LL CALL SOME CHICK INSTEAD.
Hmph.
ALL RIGHT, ALL RIGHT. YOU'RE SUCH A DRAMA QUEEN! LIKE I DON'T KNOW YOU'RE JUST UPSET BECAUSE SHINDOU-SAN ISN'T HERE.
You big softie, you!
SHUT UP AND DRINK, ASSHOLE!
You lush!
YOU'RE CUTE WHEN YOU BLUSH, EIRI-SAN...
PROTECTION
ピピピピピピピ
HM?!

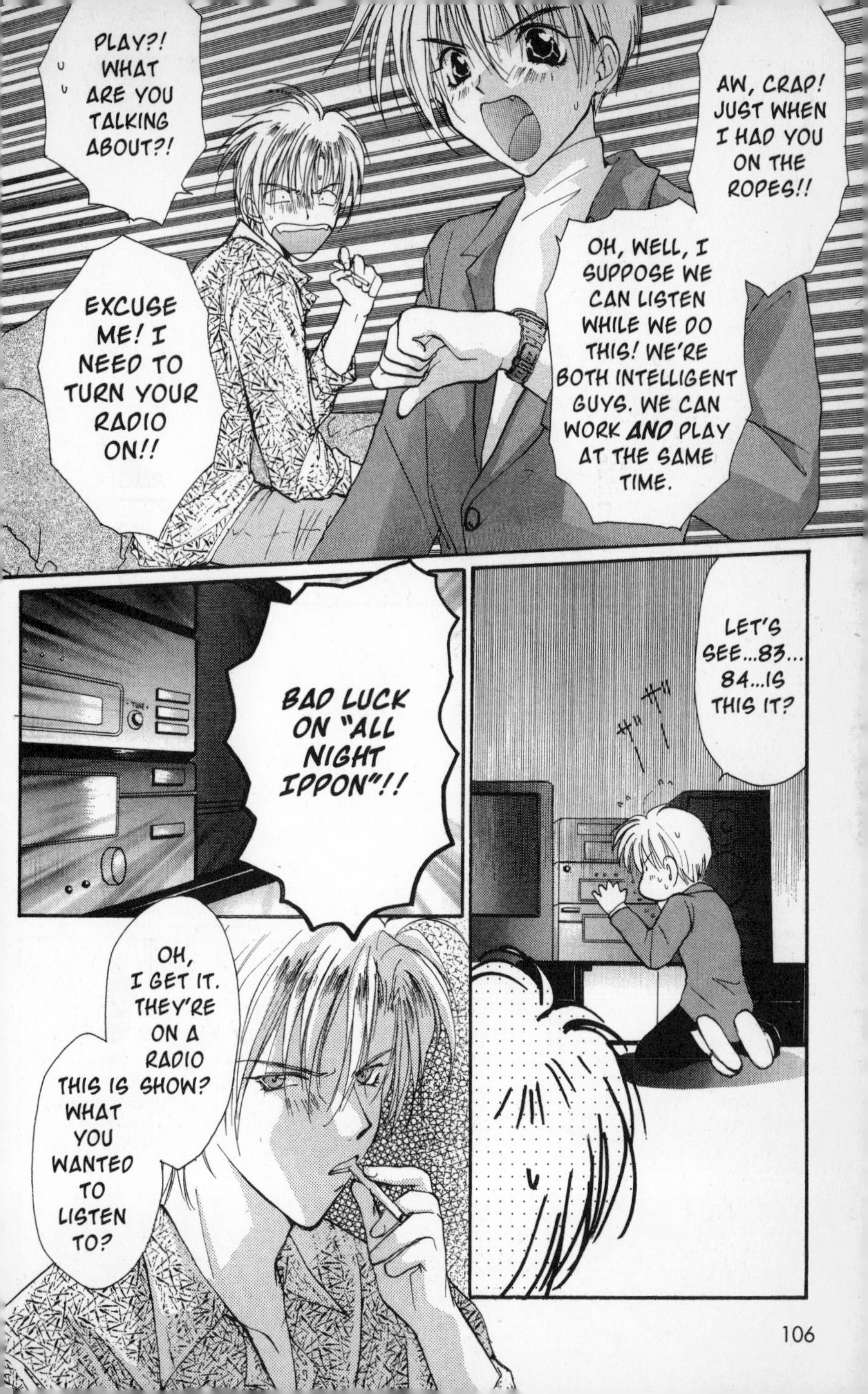
AW, CRAP! JUST WHEN I HAD YOU ON THE ROPES!!
OH, WELL, I SUPPOSE WE CAN LISTEN WHILE WE DO THIS! WE'RE BOTH INTELLIGENT GUYS. WE CAN WORK **AND** PLAY AT THE SAME TIME.
PLAY?! WHAT ARE YOU TALKING ABOUT?!
EXCUSE ME! I NEED TO TURN YOUR RADIO ON!!
LET'S SEE...83...84...IS THIS IT?
BAD LUCK ON "ALL NIGHT IPPON"!!
OH, I GET IT. THEY'RE ON A RADIO SHOW? THIS IS WHAT YOU WANTED TO LISTEN TO?

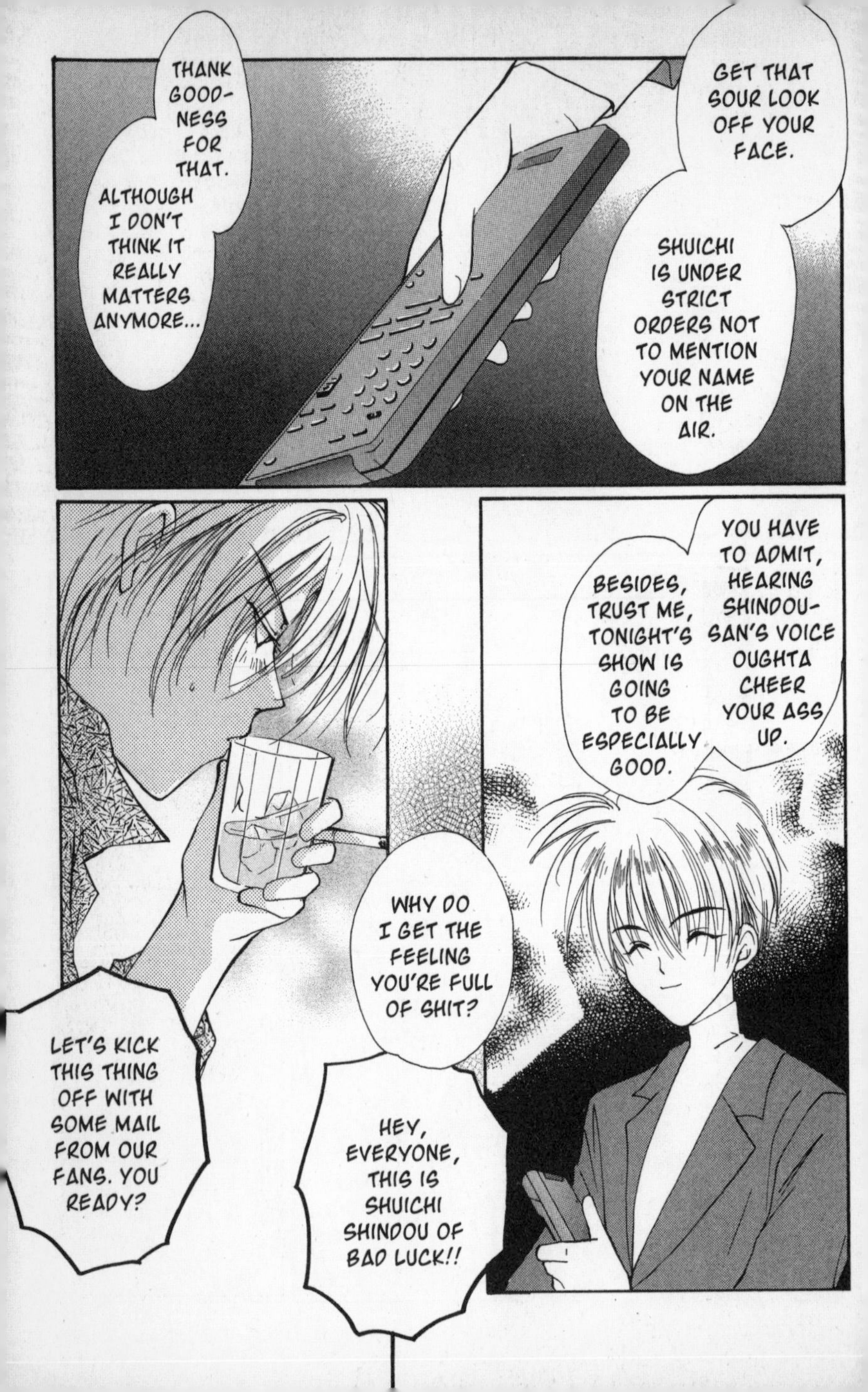
GET THAT SOUR LOOK OFF YOUR FACE.
SHUICHI IS UNDER STRICT ORDERS NOT TO MENTION YOUR NAME ON THE AIR.
THANK GOOD-NESS FOR THAT.
ALTHOUGH I DON'T THINK IT REALLY MATTERS ANYMORE...
YOU HAVE TO ADMIT, HEARING SHINDOU-SAN'S VOICE OUGHTA CHEER YOUR ASS UP.
BESIDES, TRUST ME, TONIGHT'S SHOW IS GOING TO BE ESPECIALLY GOOD.
WHY DO I GET THE FEELING YOU'RE FULL OF SHIT?
HEY, EVERYONE, THIS IS SHUICHI SHINDOU OF BAD LUCK!!
LET'S KICK THIS THING OFF WITH SOME MAIL FROM OUR FANS. YOU READY?

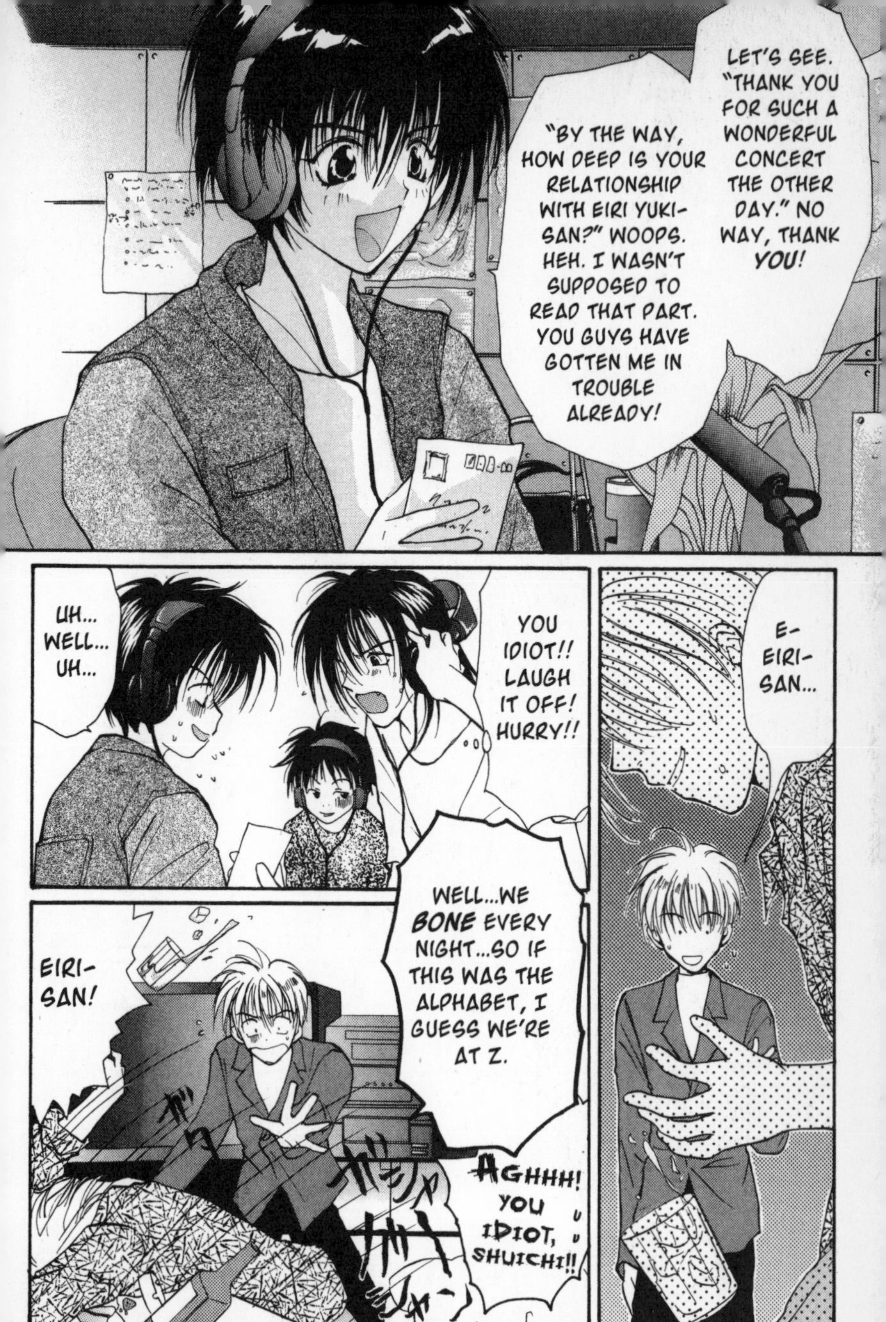
LET'S SEE. "THANK YOU FOR SUCH A WONDERFUL CONCERT THE OTHER DAY." NO WAY, THANK *YOU*!
"BY THE WAY, HOW DEEP IS YOUR RELATIONSHIP WITH EIRI YUKI-SAN?" WOOPS. HEH. I WASN'T SUPPOSED TO READ THAT PART. YOU GUYS HAVE GOTTEN ME IN TROUBLE ALREADY!
E-EIRI-SAN...
YOU IDIOT!! LAUGH IT OFF! HURRY!!
UH... WELL... UH...
WELL...WE **BONE** EVERY NIGHT...SO IF THIS WAS THE ALPHABET, I GUESS WE'RE AT Z.
EIRI-SAN!
AGHHH! YOU IDIOT, SHUICHI!!

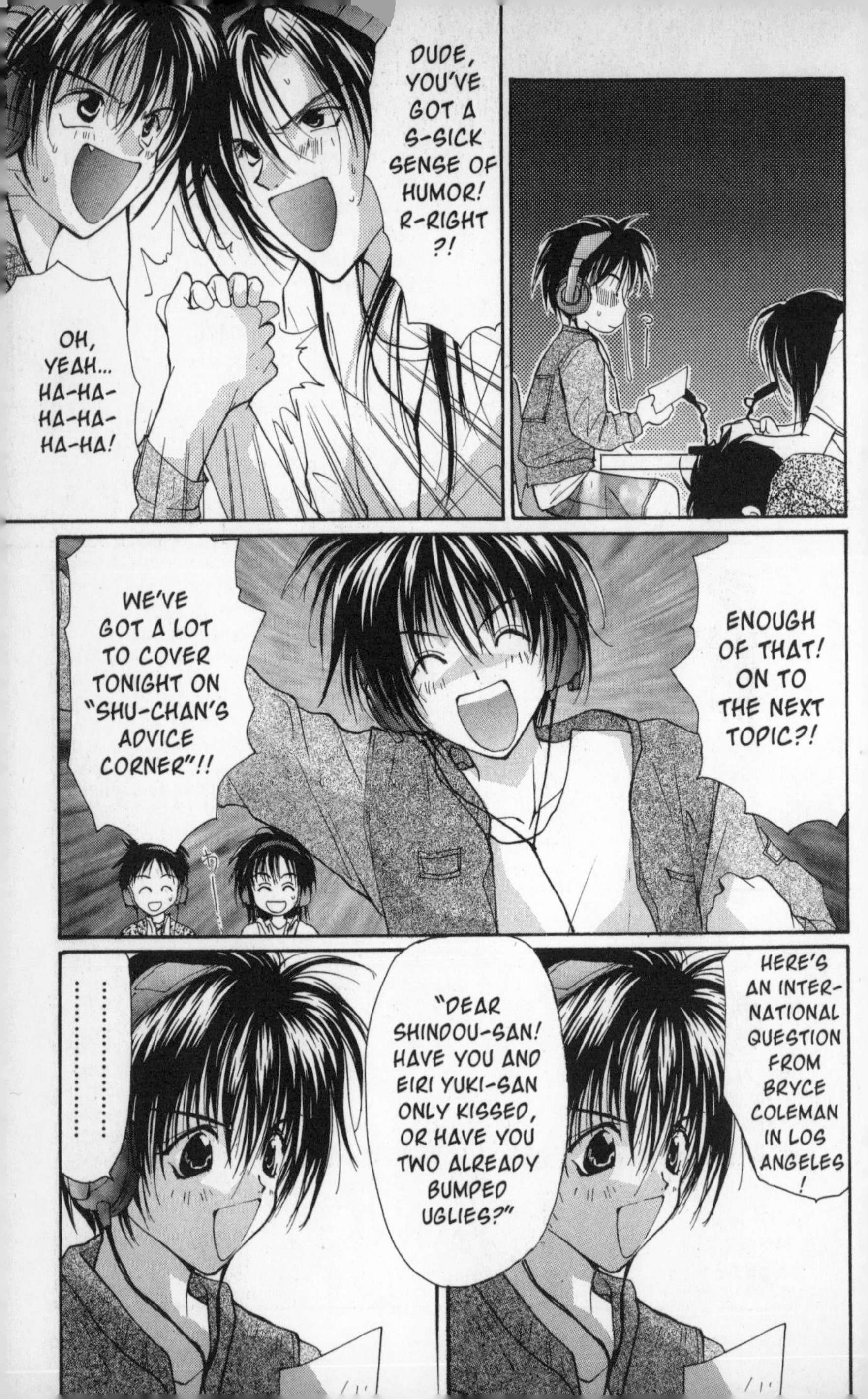
DUDE, YOU'VE GOT A S-SICK SENSE OF HUMOR! R-RIGHT?!
OH, YEAH... HA-HA-HA-HA-HA-HA!
ENOUGH OF THAT! ON TO THE NEXT TOPIC?!
WE'VE GOT A LOT TO COVER TONIGHT ON "SHU-CHAN'S ADVICE CORNER"!!
HERE'S AN INTER-NATIONAL QUESTION FROM BRYCE COLEMAN IN LOS ANGELES!
"DEAR SHINDOU-SAN! HAVE YOU AND EIRI YUKI-SAN ONLY KISSED, OR HAVE YOU TWO ALREADY BUMPED UGLIES?"
......

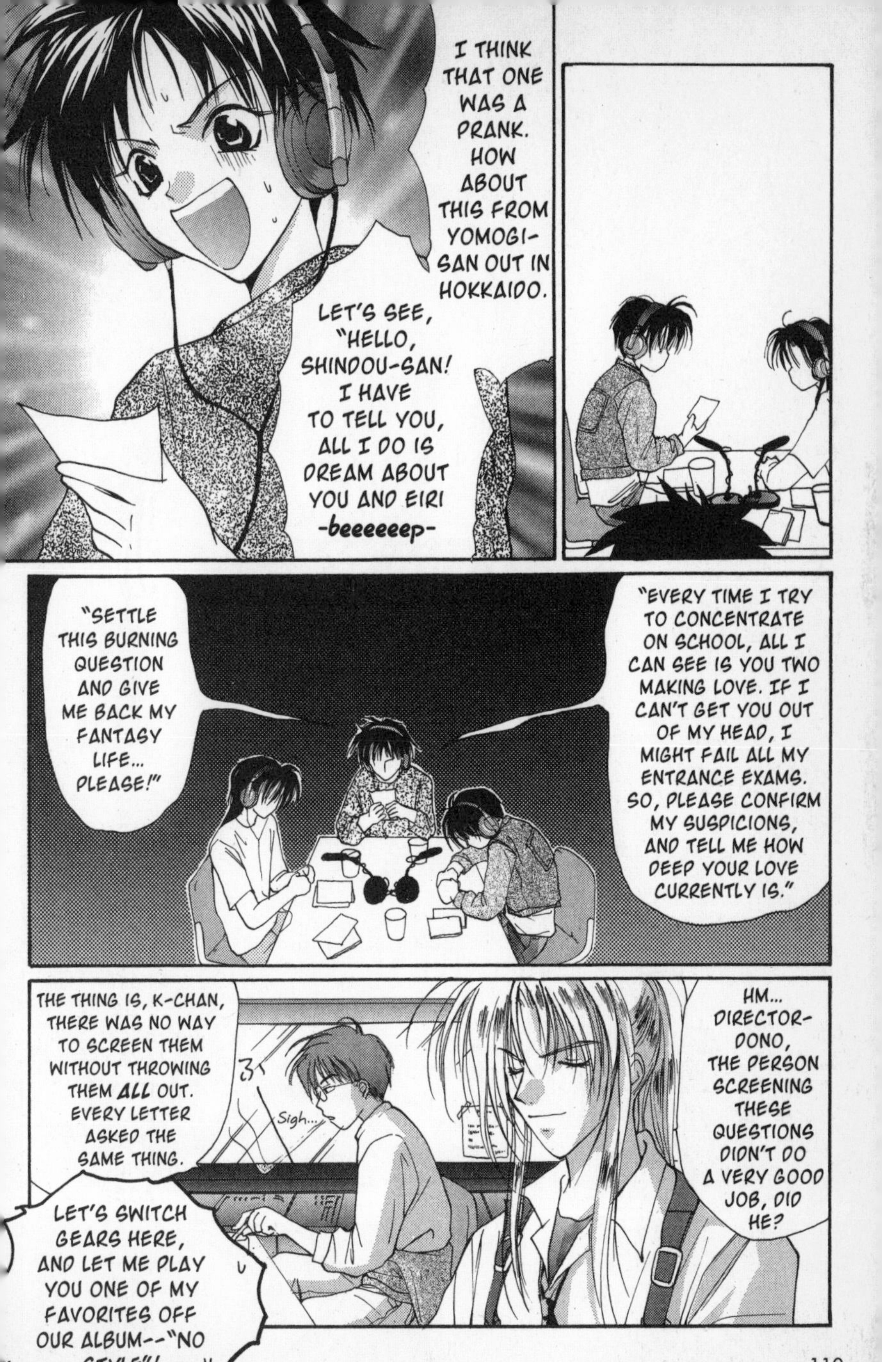
I THINK THAT ONE WAS A PRANK. HOW ABOUT THIS FROM YOMOGI-SAN OUT IN HOKKAIDO.
LET'S SEE, "HELLO, SHINDOU-SAN! I HAVE TO TELL YOU, ALL I DO IS DREAM ABOUT YOU AND EIRI -beeeeeep-
"EVERY TIME I TRY TO CONCENTRATE ON SCHOOL, ALL I CAN SEE IS YOU TWO MAKING LOVE. IF I CAN'T GET YOU OUT OF MY HEAD, I MIGHT FAIL ALL MY ENTRANCE EXAMS. SO, PLEASE CONFIRM MY SUSPICIONS, AND TELL ME HOW DEEP YOUR LOVE CURRENTLY IS."
"SETTLE THIS BURNING QUESTION AND GIVE ME BACK MY FANTASY LIFE... PLEASE!"
HM... DIRECTOR-DONO, THE PERSON SCREENING THESE QUESTIONS DIDN'T DO A VERY GOOD JOB, DID HE?
THE THING IS, K-CHAN, THERE WAS NO WAY TO SCREEN THEM WITHOUT THROWING THEM ALL OUT. EVERY LETTER ASKED THE SAME THING.
Sigh...
LET'S SWITCH GEARS HERE, AND LET ME PLAY YOU ONE OF MY FAVORITES OFF OUR ALBUM--"NO STYLE"!

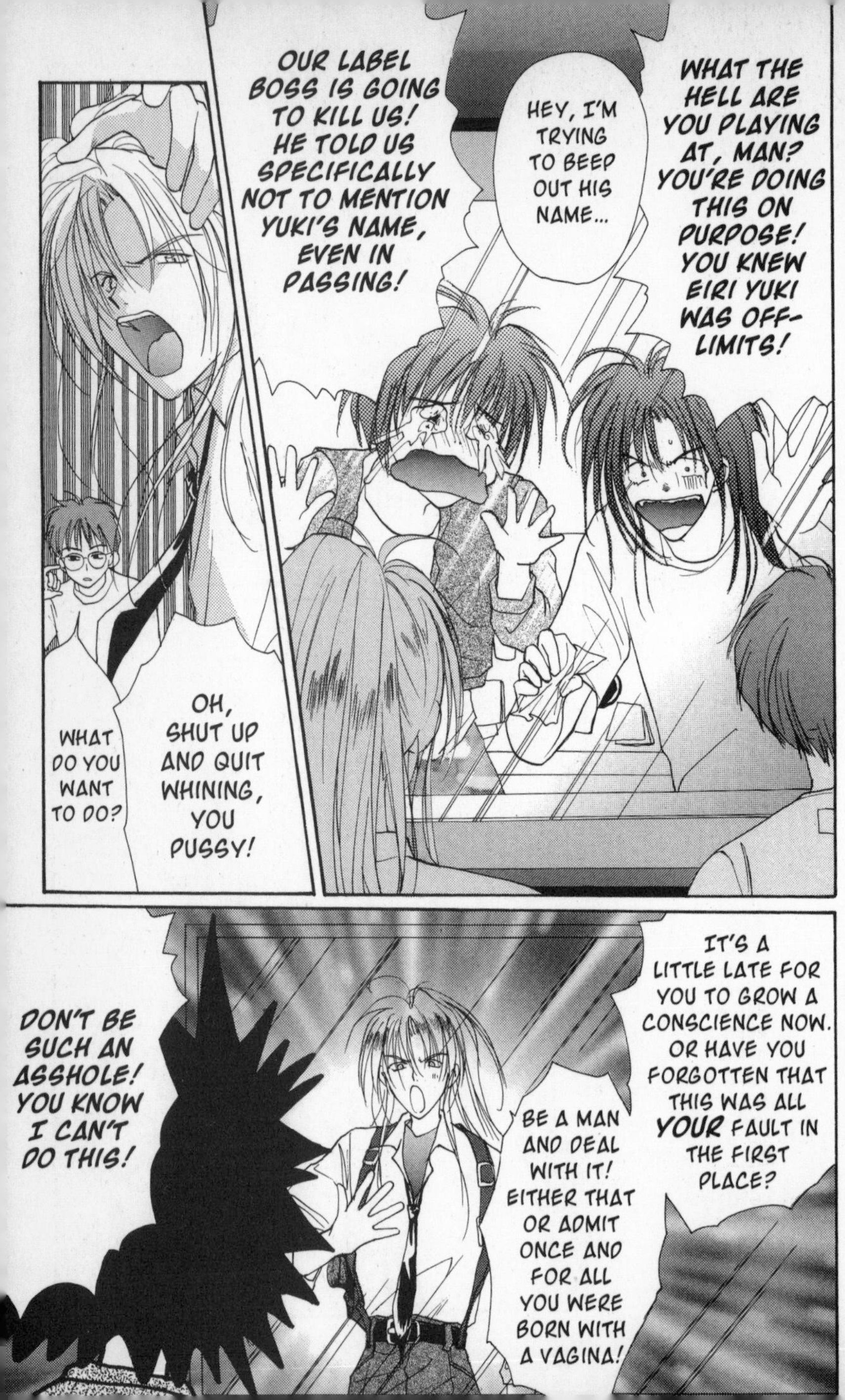
WHAT THE HELL ARE YOU PLAYING AT, MAN? YOU'RE DOING THIS ON PURPOSE! YOU KNEW EIRI YUKI WAS OFF-LIMITS!
HEY, I'M TRYING TO BEEP OUT HIS NAME...
OUR LABEL BOSS IS GOING TO KILL US! HE TOLD US SPECIFICALLY NOT TO MENTION YUKI'S NAME, EVEN IN PASSING!
OH, SHUT UP AND QUIT WHINING, YOU PUSSY!
WHAT DO YOU WANT TO DO?
IT'S A LITTLE LATE FOR YOU TO GROW A CONSCIENCE NOW. OR HAVE YOU FORGOTTEN THAT THIS WAS ALL YOUR FAULT IN THE FIRST PLACE?
BE A MAN AND DEAL WITH IT! EITHER THAT OR ADMIT ONCE AND FOR ALL YOU WERE BORN WITH A VAGINA!
DON'T BE SUCH AN ASSHOLE! YOU KNOW I CAN'T DO THIS!

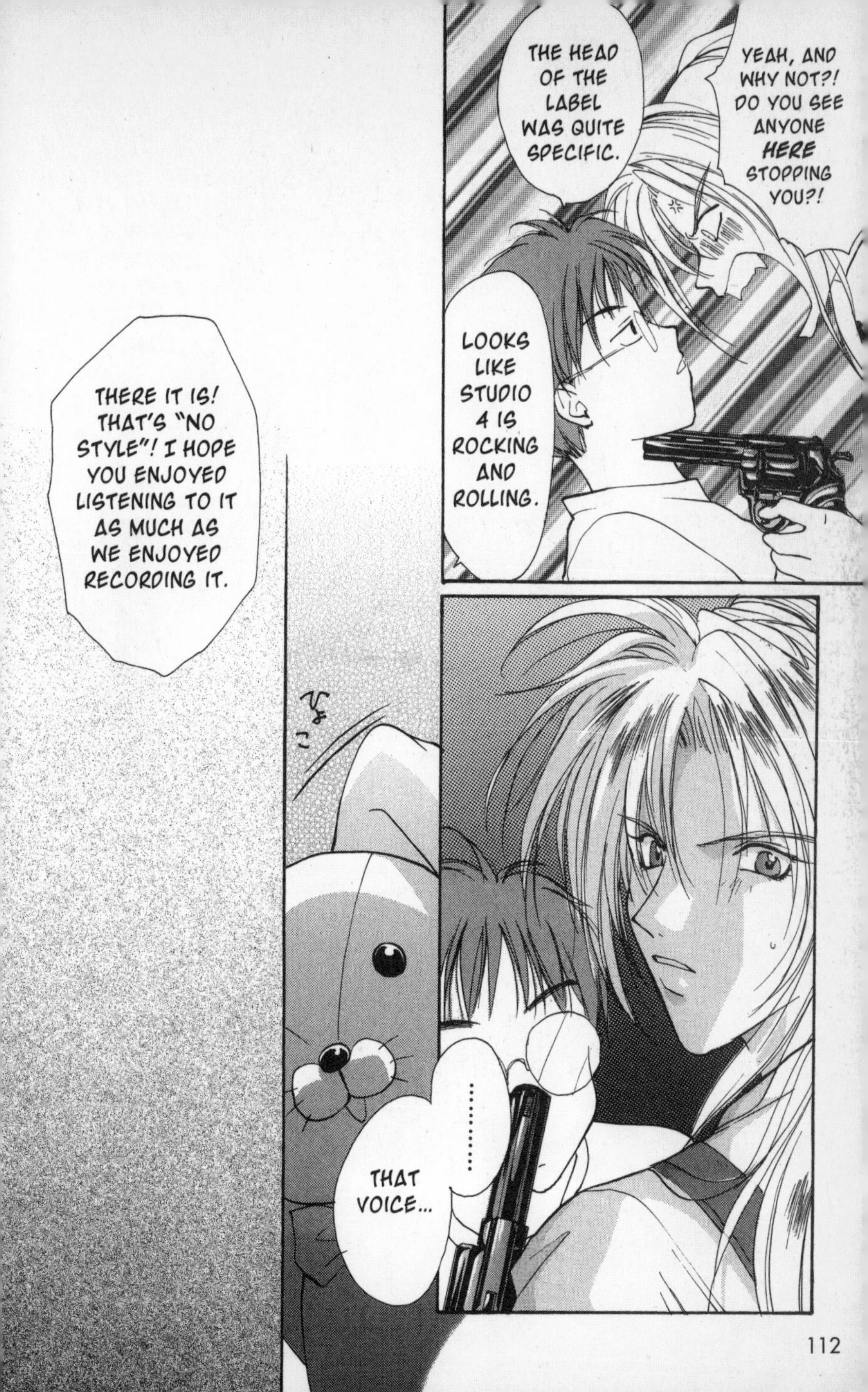
YEAH, AND WHY NOT?! DO YOU SEE ANYONE **HERE** STOPPING YOU?!
THE HEAD OF THE LABEL WAS QUITE SPECIFIC.
LOOKS LIKE STUDIO 4 IS ROCKING AND ROLLING.
ひょこ
......
THAT VOICE...
THERE IT IS! THAT'S "NO STYLE"! I HOPE YOU ENJOYED LISTENING TO IT AS MUCH AS WE ENJOYED RECORDING IT.

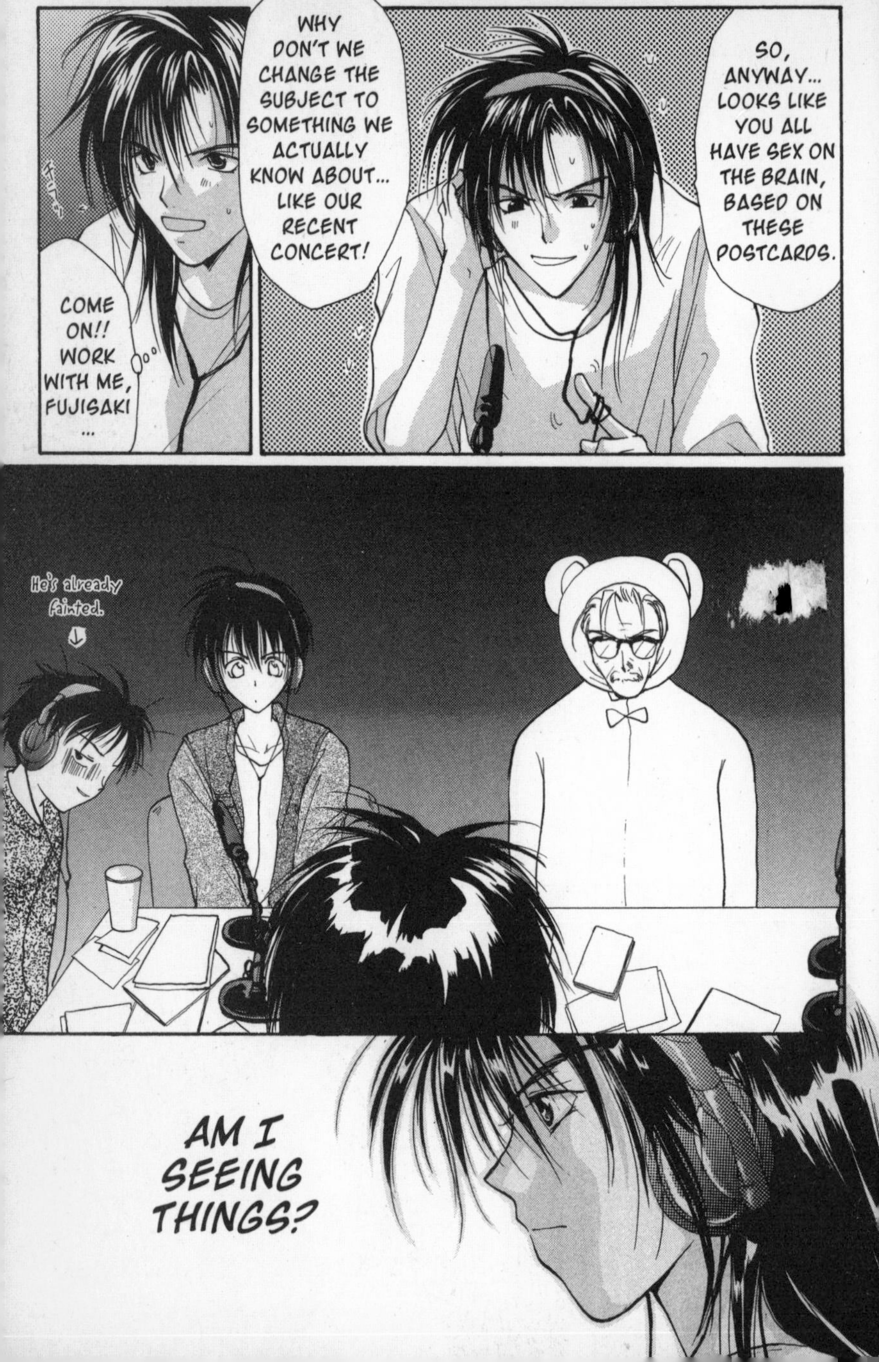
SO, ANYWAY... LOOKS LIKE YOU ALL HAVE SEX ON THE BRAIN, BASED ON THESE POSTCARDS.
WHY DON'T WE CHANGE THE SUBJECT TO SOMETHING WE ACTUALLY KNOW ABOUT... LIKE OUR RECENT CONCERT!
COME ON!! WORK WITH ME, FUJISAKI...
He's already fainted.
AM I SEEING THINGS?

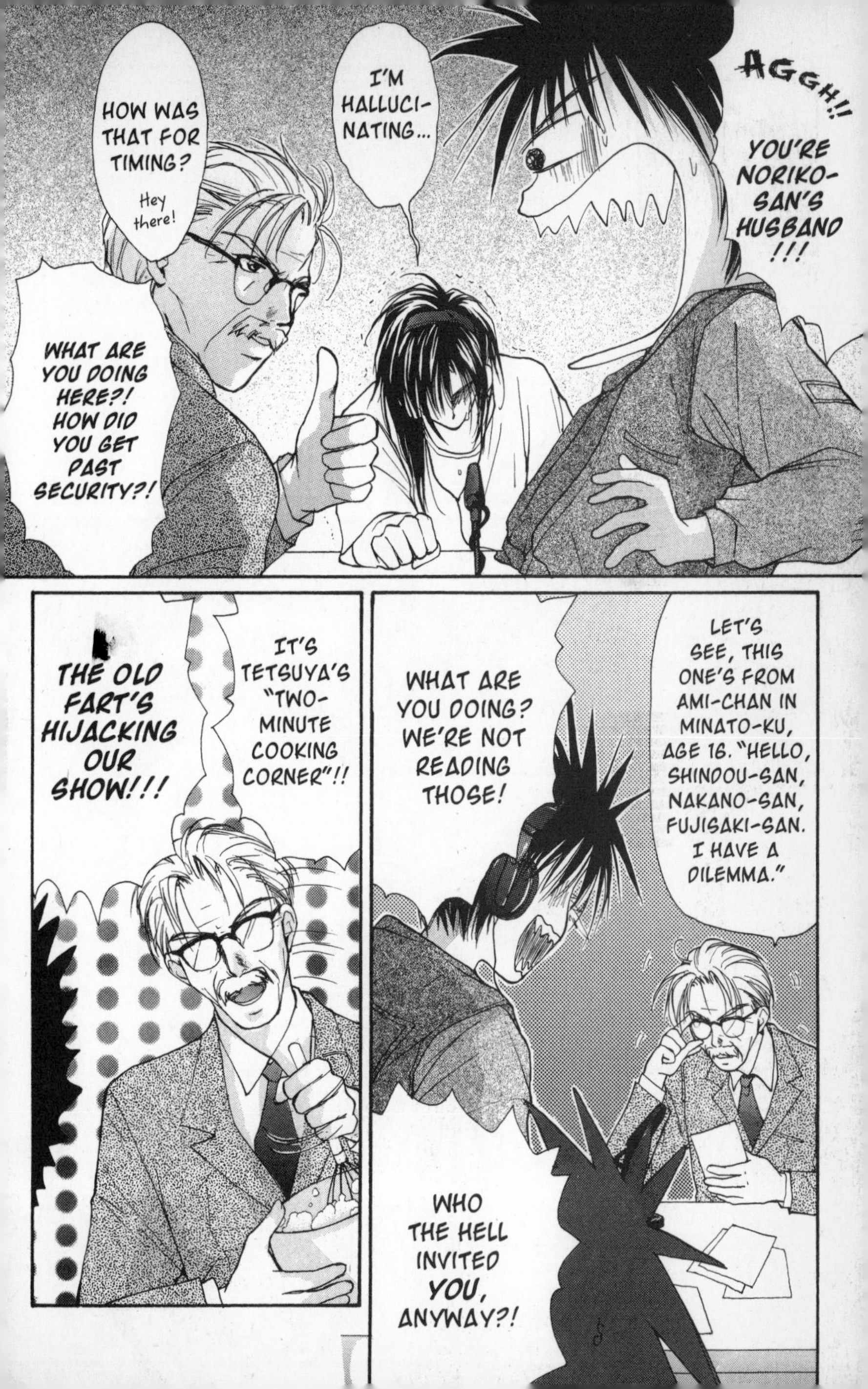
AGGH!!
YOU'RE NORIKO-SAN'S HUSBAND!!!
I'M HALLUCI-NATING...
HOW WAS THAT FOR TIMING?
Hey there!
WHAT ARE YOU DOING HERE?! HOW DID YOU GET PAST SECURITY?!
LET'S SEE, THIS ONE'S FROM AMI-CHAN IN MINATO-KU, AGE 16. "HELLO, SHINDOU-SAN, NAKANO-SAN, FUJISAKI-SAN. I HAVE A DILEMMA."
WHAT ARE YOU DOING? WE'RE NOT READING THOSE!
WHO THE HELL INVITED YOU, ANYWAY?!
IT'S TETSUYA'S "TWO-MINUTE COOKING CORNER"!!
THE OLD FART'S HIJACKING OUR SHOW!!!

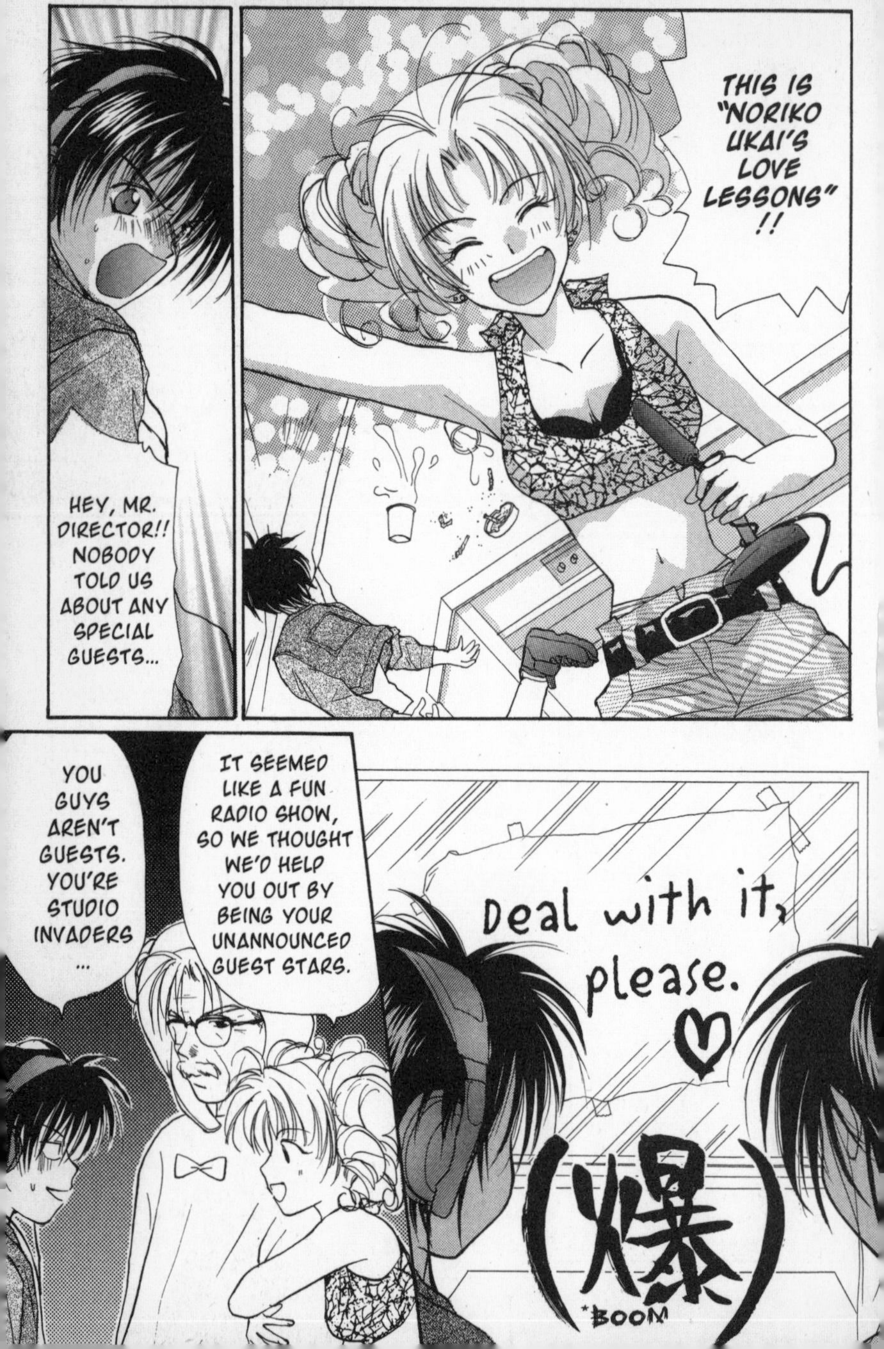
THIS IS "NORIKO UKAI'S LOVE LESSONS" !!
HEY, MR. DIRECTOR!! NOBODY TOLD US ABOUT ANY SPECIAL GUESTS...
Deal with it, please. ♥
(爆)
*BOOM
IT SEEMED LIKE A FUN RADIO SHOW, SO WE THOUGHT WE'D HELP YOU OUT BY BEING YOUR UNANNOUNCED GUEST STARS.
YOU GUYS AREN'T GUESTS. YOU'RE STUDIO INVADERS ...

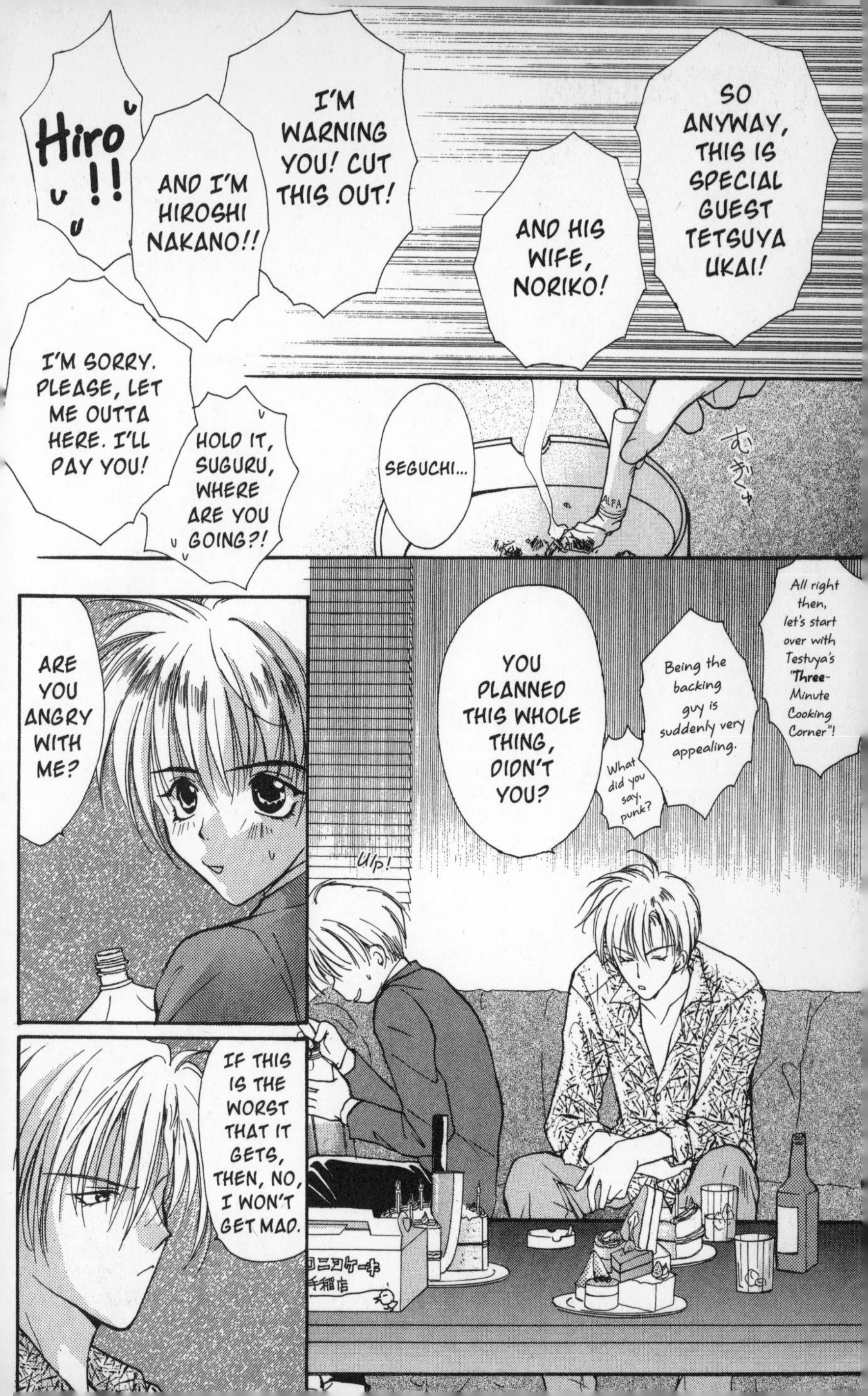
SO ANYWAY, THIS IS SPECIAL GUEST TETSUYA UKAI!
AND HIS WIFE, NORIKO!
I'M WARNING YOU! CUT THIS OUT!
AND I'M HIROSHI NAKANO!!
Hiro!!
I'M SORRY. PLEASE, LET ME OUTTA HERE. I'LL PAY YOU!
HOLD IT, SUGURU, WHERE ARE YOU GOING?!
むぎゅ
SEGUCHI...
All right then, let's start over with Testuya's "Three-Minute Cooking Corner"!
Being the backing guy is suddenly very appealing.
What did you say, punk?
YOU PLANNED THIS WHOLE THING, DIDN'T YOU?
Ulp!
ARE YOU ANGRY WITH ME?
IF THIS IS THE WORST THAT IT GETS, THEN, NO, I WON'T GET MAD.

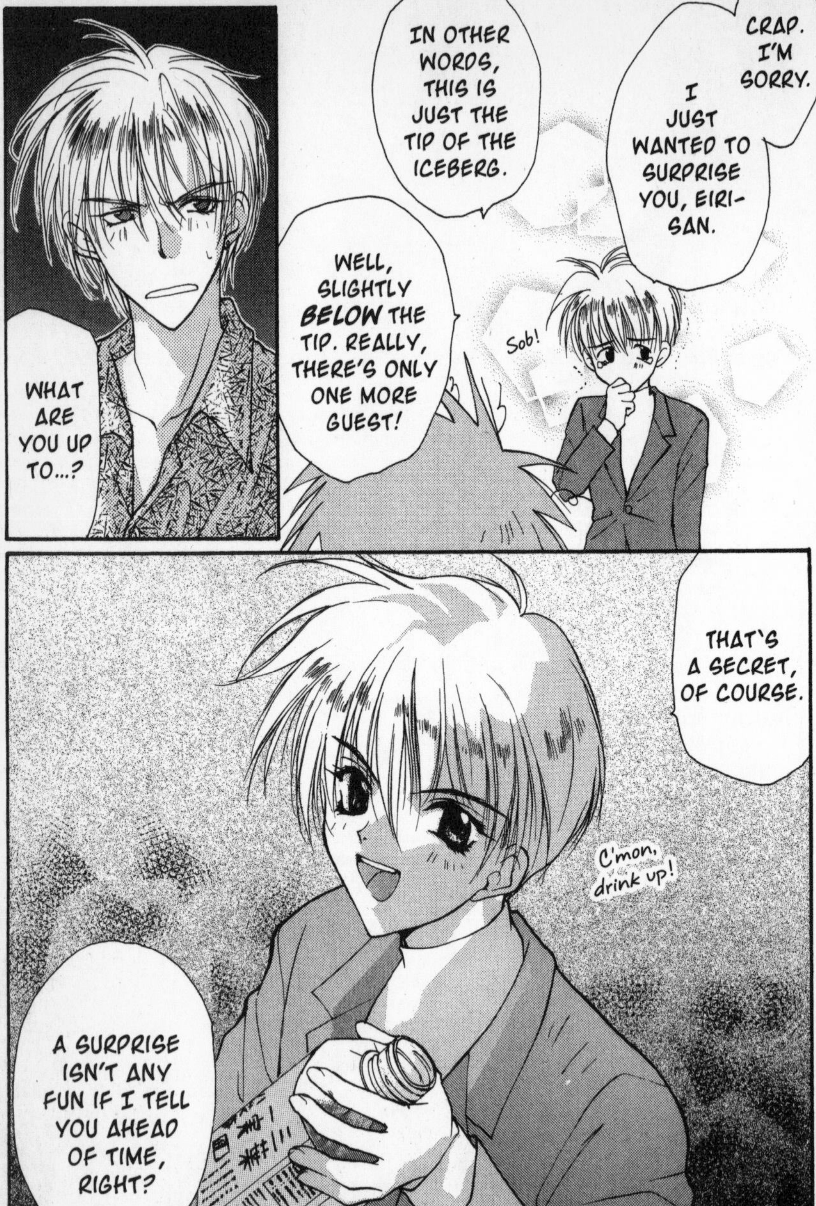
CRAP. I'M SORRY.
I JUST WANTED TO SURPRISE YOU, EIRI-SAN.
IN OTHER WORDS, THIS IS JUST THE TIP OF THE ICEBERG.
Sob!
WELL, SLIGHTLY **BELOW** THE TIP. REALLY, THERE'S ONLY ONE MORE GUEST!
WHAT ARE YOU UP TO...?
THAT'S A SECRET, OF COURSE.
C'mon, drink up!
A SURPRISE ISN'T ANY FUN IF I TELL YOU AHEAD OF TIME, RIGHT?

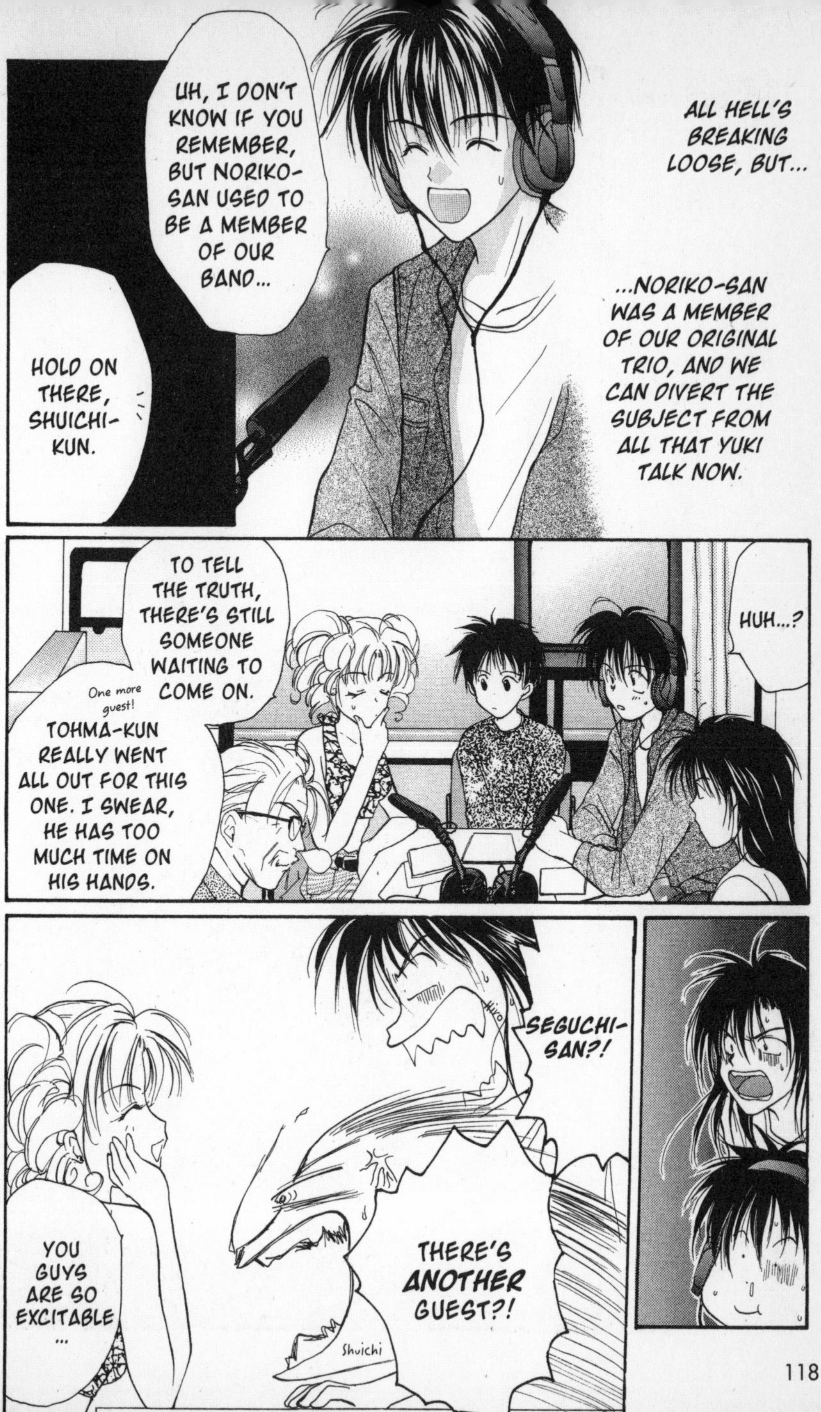
ALL HELL'S BREAKING LOOSE, BUT...
UH, I DON'T KNOW IF YOU REMEMBER, BUT NORIKO-SAN USED TO BE A MEMBER OF OUR BAND...
...NORIKO-SAN WAS A MEMBER OF OUR ORIGINAL TRIO, AND WE CAN DIVERT THE SUBJECT FROM ALL THAT YUKI TALK NOW.
HOLD ON THERE, SHUICHI-KUN.
HUH...?
TO TELL THE TRUTH, THERE'S STILL SOMEONE WAITING TO COME ON.
One more guest!
TOHMA-KUN REALLY WENT ALL OUT FOR THIS ONE. I SWEAR, HE HAS TOO MUCH TIME ON HIS HANDS.
Hiro
SEGUCHI-SAN?!
THERE'S ANOTHER GUEST?!
Shuichi
YOU GUYS ARE SO EXCITABLE ...

SIDEBAR

Eiri-san's Big Sister

In other words, I'm talking about Mika-san. Because I've drawn her face completely different than the last time, I figured I'd better point it out. I mean, she's pretty much a completely different person now, and I've received a truckload of complaints from readers.

To be honest, I've changed Shuichi's face to impossible proportions, too, but well, in Mika-san's case, I go back to a theory that she is Eiri with a wig and make-up. Which, to be honest, makes it kind of tough. Oh, well, it's just a fantasy anyway.

Then again, I think I might revert her back to her original face in her next appearance... What do you think? Is that okay? I can't draw the way I used to anymore!! Well, of course not. We're all just human beings! Kyaaa! I'll try harder!!

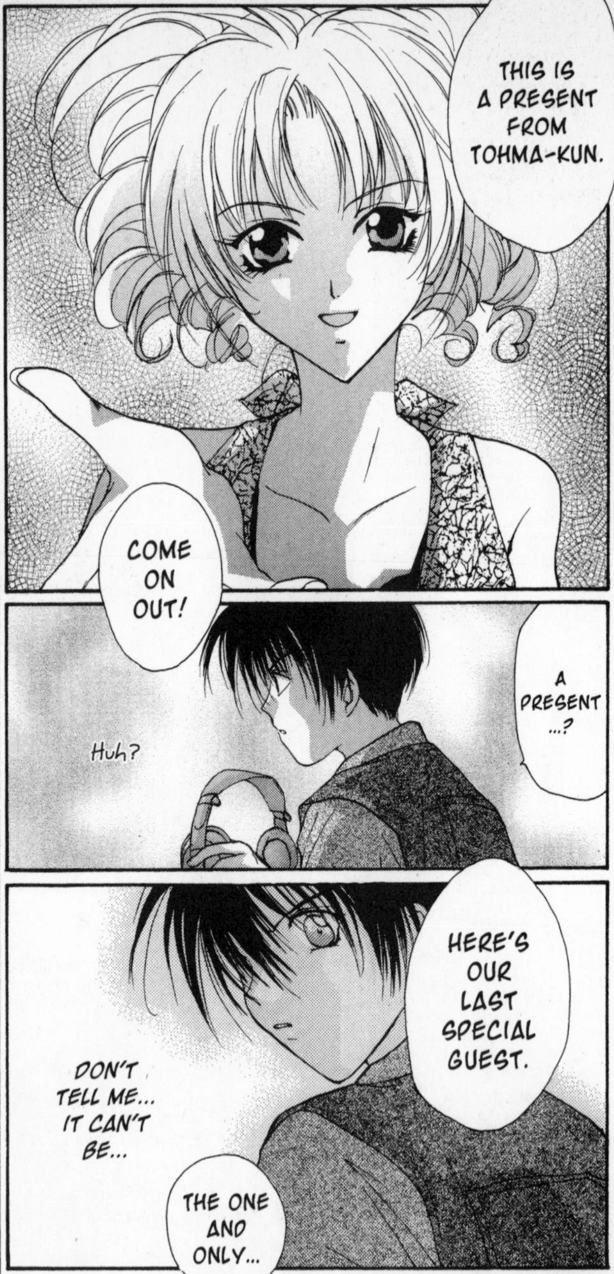
THIS IS A PRESENT FROM TOHMA-KUN.
COME ON OUT!
A PRESENT ...?
Huh?
HERE'S OUR LAST SPECIAL GUEST.
THE ONE AND ONLY...
DON'T TELL ME... IT CAN'T BE...

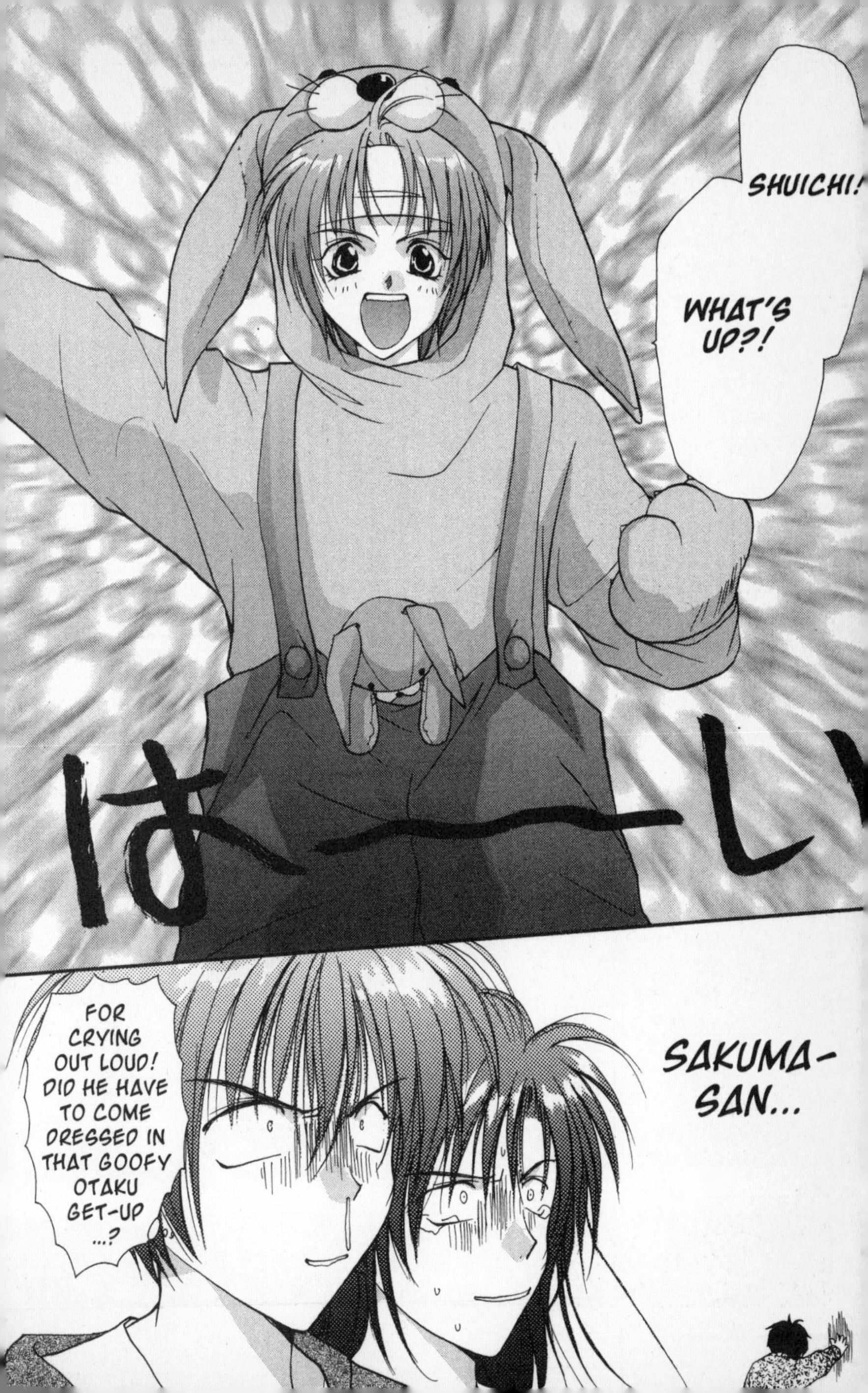

SHUICHI!
WHAT'S UP?!
はーーい
SAKUMA-SAN...
FOR CRYING OUT LOUD! DID HE HAVE TO COME DRESSED IN THAT GOOFY OTAKU GET-UP ...?

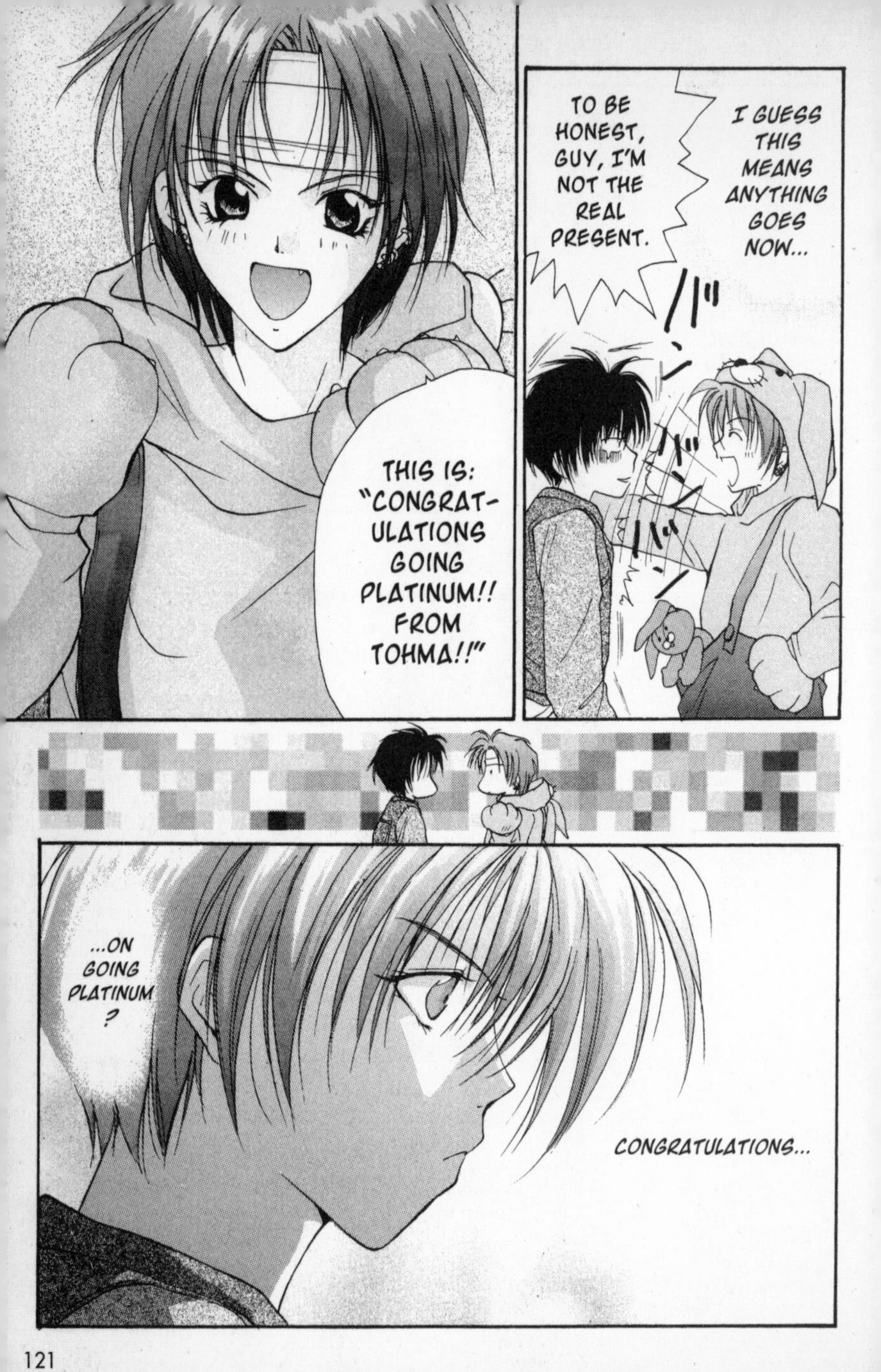
I GUESS THIS MEANS ANYTHING GOES NOW...
TO BE HONEST, GUY, I'M NOT THE REAL PRESENT.
THIS IS: "CONGRAT-ULATIONS GOING PLATINUM!! FROM TOHMA!!"
CONGRATULATIONS...
...ON GOING PLATINUM?

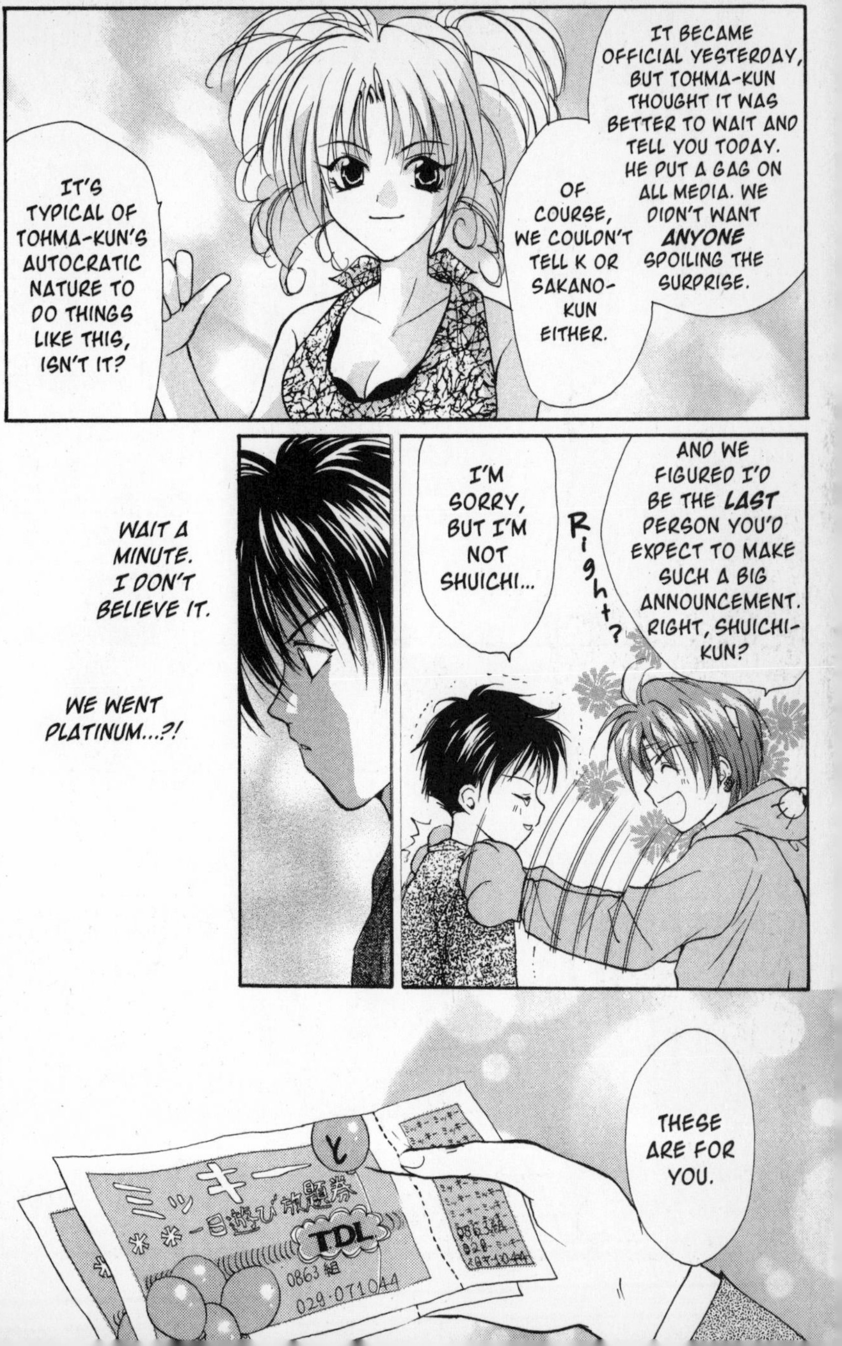
IT BECAME OFFICIAL YESTERDAY, BUT TOHMA-KUN THOUGHT IT WAS BETTER TO WAIT AND TELL YOU TODAY. HE PUT A GAG ON ALL MEDIA. WE DIDN'T WANT ***ANYONE*** SPOILING THE SURPRISE.
OF COURSE, WE COULDN'T TELL K OR SAKANO-KUN EITHER.
IT'S TYPICAL OF TOHMA-KUN'S AUTOCRATIC NATURE TO DO THINGS LIKE THIS, ISN'T IT?
AND WE FIGURED I'D BE THE ***LAST*** PERSON YOU'D EXPECT TO MAKE SUCH A BIG ANNOUNCEMENT. RIGHT, SHUICHI-KUN?
Right?
I'M SORRY, BUT I'M NOT SHUICHI...
WAIT A MINUTE. I DON'T BELIEVE IT.
WE WENT PLATINUM...?!
THESE ARE FOR YOU.
ミッキー
一日遊び放題券
TDL
0863組
029-071044

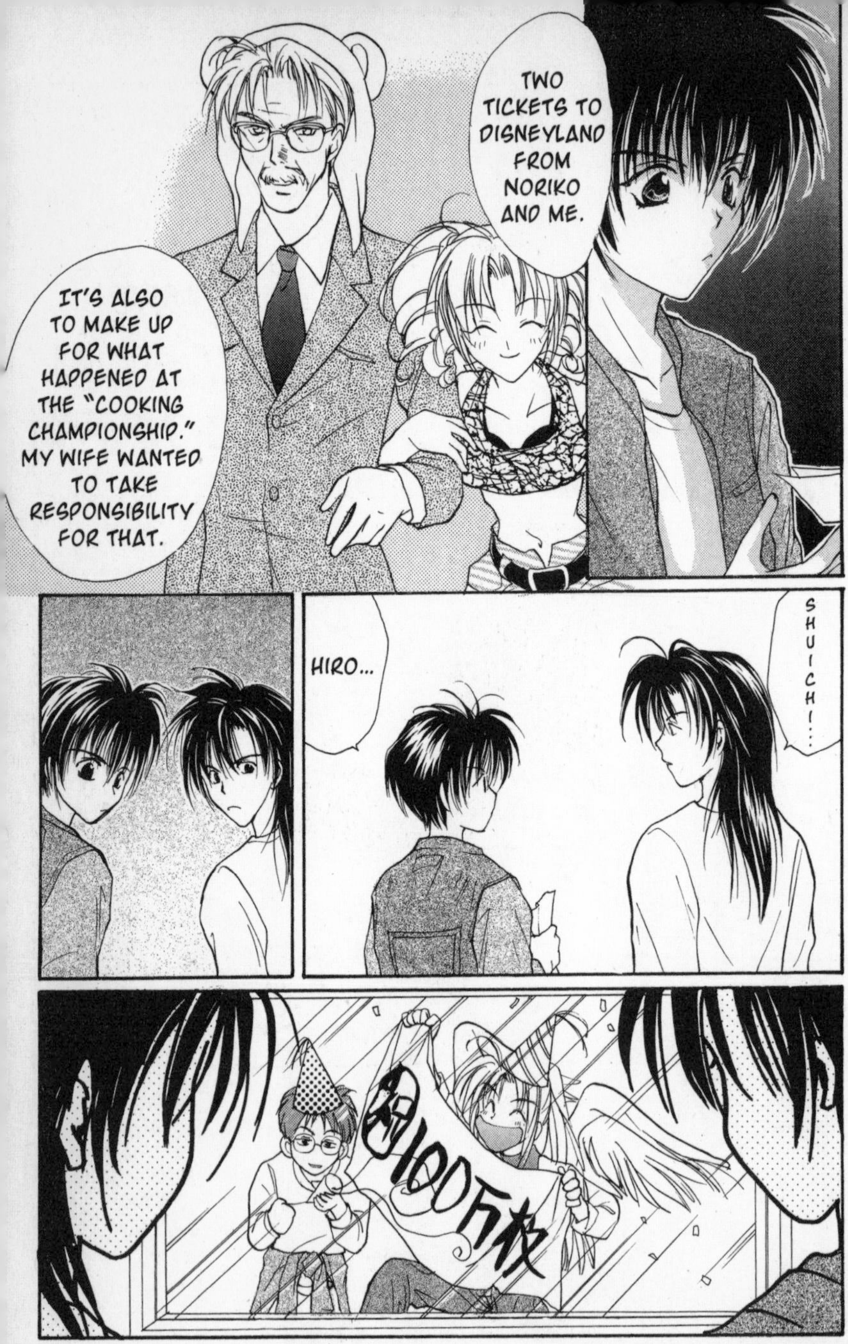
TWO TICKETS TO DISNEYLAND FROM NORIKO AND ME.
IT'S ALSO TO MAKE UP FOR WHAT HAPPENED AT THE "COOKING CHAMPIONSHIP." MY WIFE WANTED TO TAKE RESPONSIBILITY FOR THAT.
SHUICHI...
HIRO...
100万枚

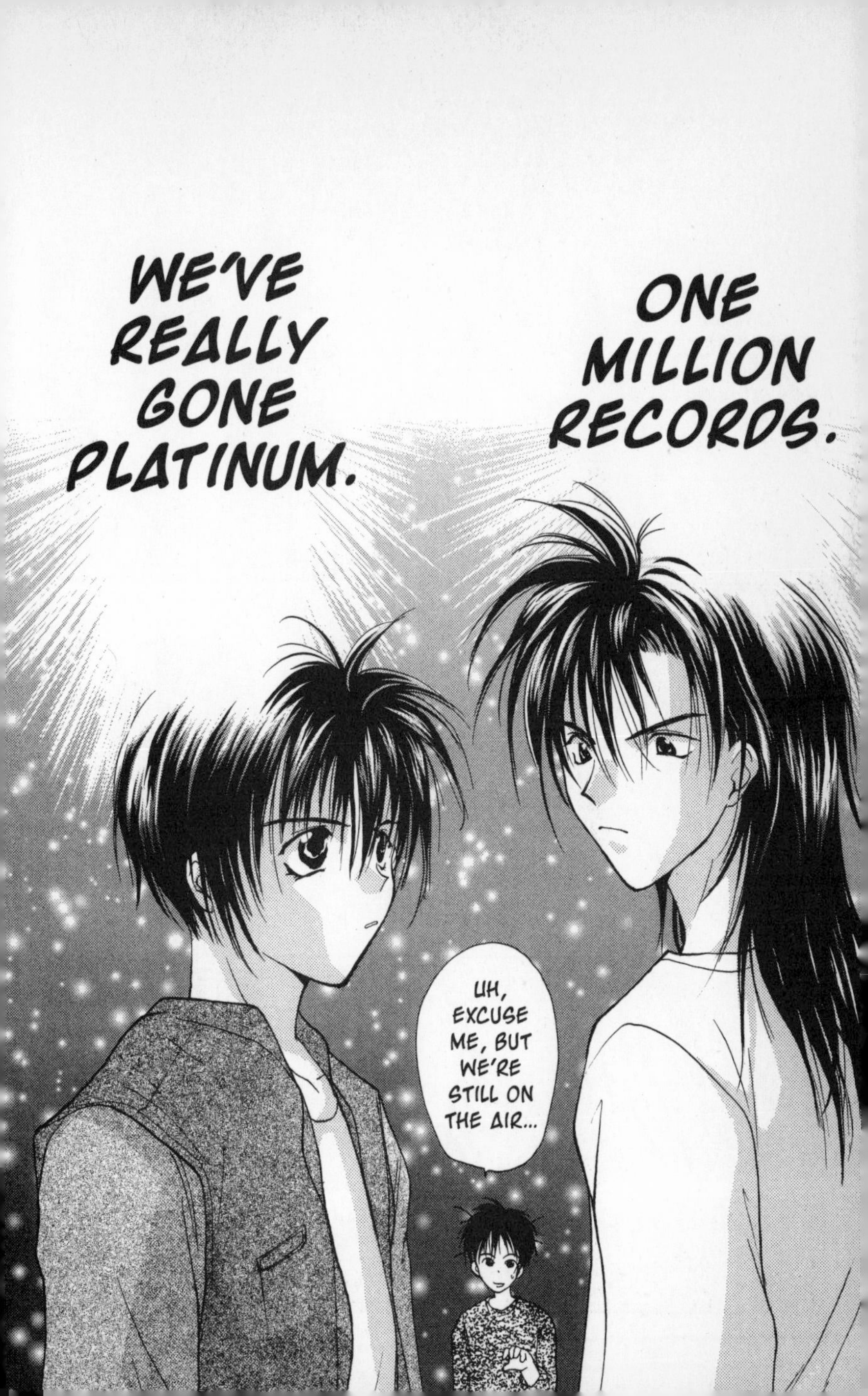
ONE MILLION RECORDS.
WE'VE REALLY GONE PLATINUM.
UH, EXCUSE ME, BUT WE'RE STILL ON THE AIR...

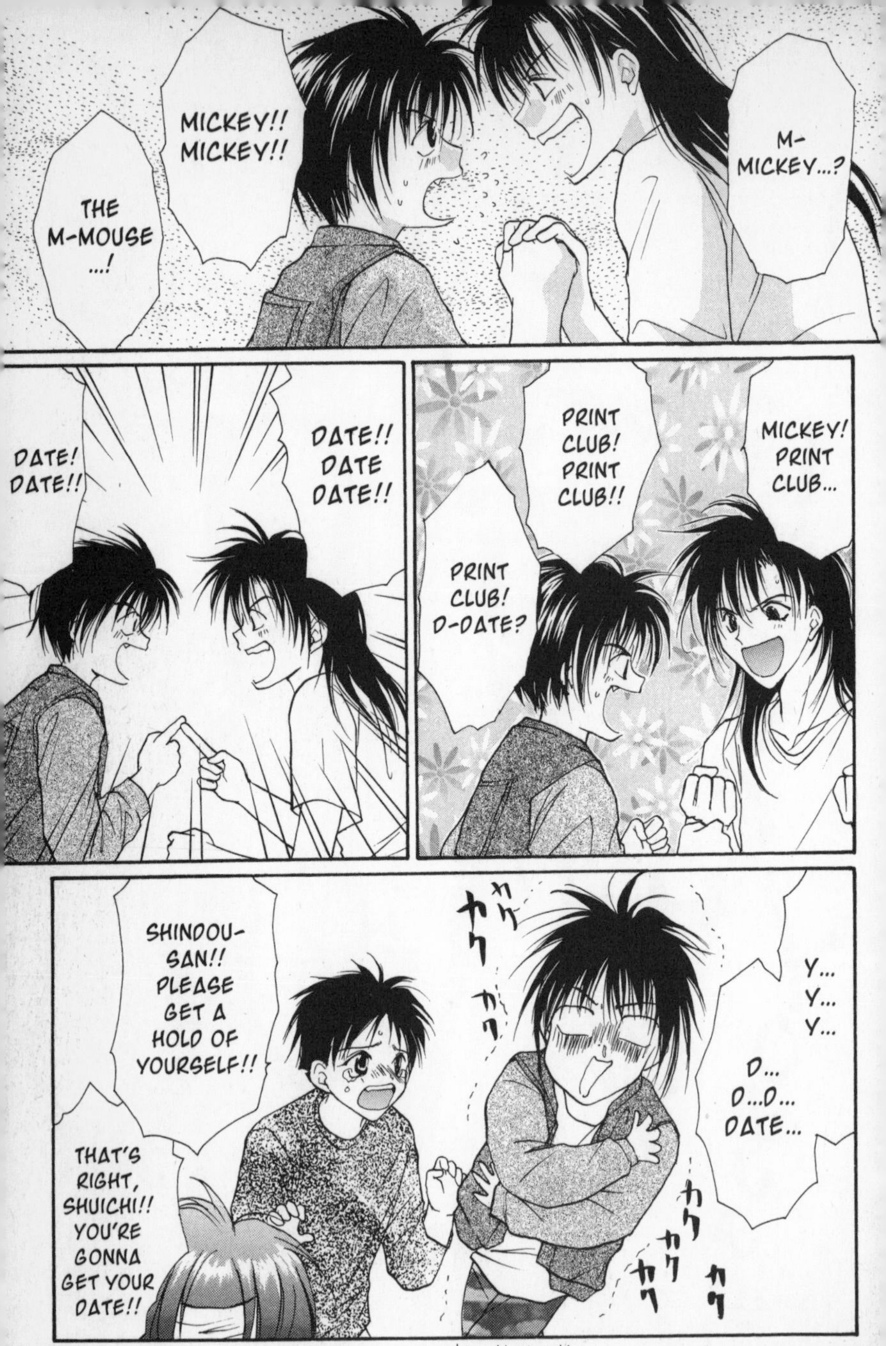
M- MICKEY...?
MICKEY!! MICKEY!!
THE M-MOUSE ...!
MICKEY! PRINT CLUB...
PRINT CLUB! PRINT CLUB!!
PRINT CLUB! D-DATE?
DATE!! DATE DATE!!
DATE! DATE!!
Y... Y... Y...
D... D...D... DATE...
カク カク
カク カク カク カク
SHINDOU-SAN!! PLEASE GET A HOLD OF YOURSELF!!
THAT'S RIGHT, SHUICHI!! YOU'RE GONNA GET YOUR DATE!!

*tremble tremble

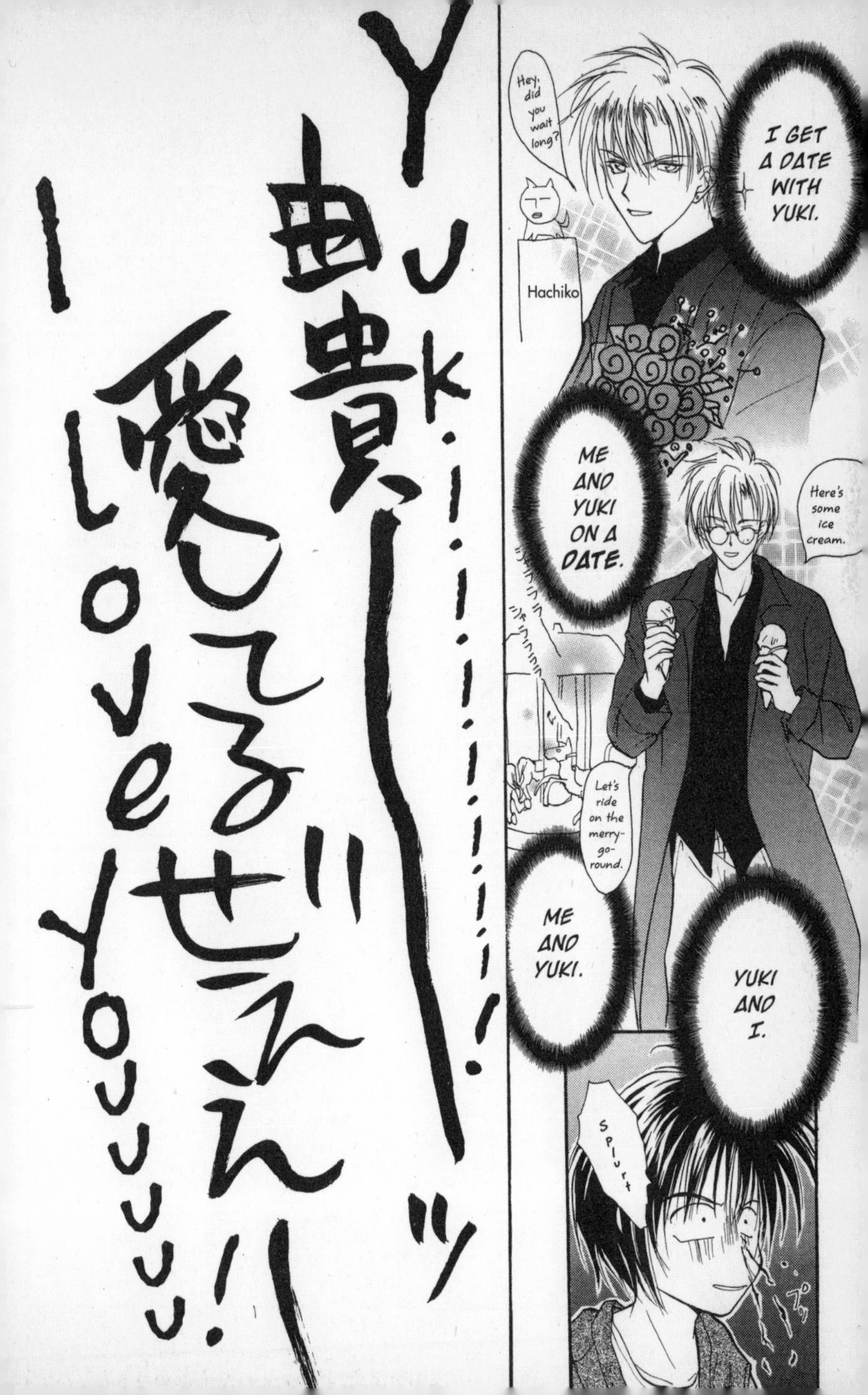
I GET A DATE WITH YUKI.
Hey, did you wait long?
Hachiko
Here's some ice cream.
ME AND YUKI ON A DATE.
Let's ride on the merry-go-round.
YUKI AND I.
ME AND YUKI.
Splurt
YUKI!!!!!!!!!
I LOVE YOUUUUU!

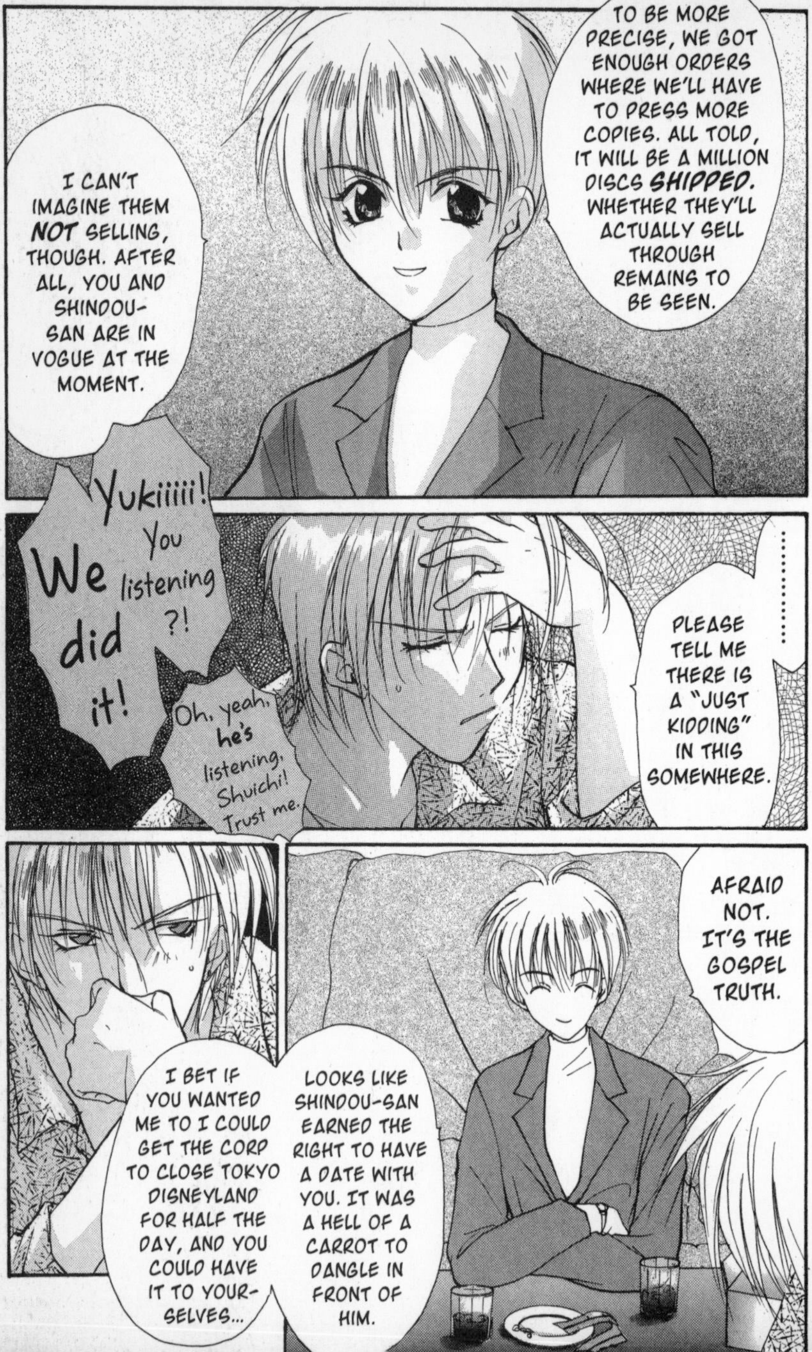
TO BE MORE PRECISE, WE GOT ENOUGH ORDERS WHERE WE'LL HAVE TO PRESS MORE COPIES. ALL TOLD, IT WILL BE A MILLION DISCS SHIPPED. WHETHER THEY'LL ACTUALLY SELL THROUGH REMAINS TO BE SEEN.
I CAN'T IMAGINE THEM NOT SELLING, THOUGH. AFTER ALL, YOU AND SHINDOU-SAN ARE IN VOGUE AT THE MOMENT.
......
PLEASE TELL ME THERE IS A "JUST KIDDING" IN THIS SOMEWHERE.
Yukiiiii! We did it! You listening?!
Oh, yeah, he's listening, Shuichi! Trust me.
AFRAID NOT. IT'S THE GOSPEL TRUTH.
LOOKS LIKE SHINDOU-SAN EARNED THE RIGHT TO HAVE A DATE WITH YOU. IT WAS A HELL OF A CARROT TO DANGLE IN FRONT OF HIM.
I BET IF YOU WANTED ME TO I COULD GET THE CORP TO CLOSE TOKYO DISNEYLAND FOR HALF THE DAY, AND YOU COULD HAVE IT TO YOURSELVES...

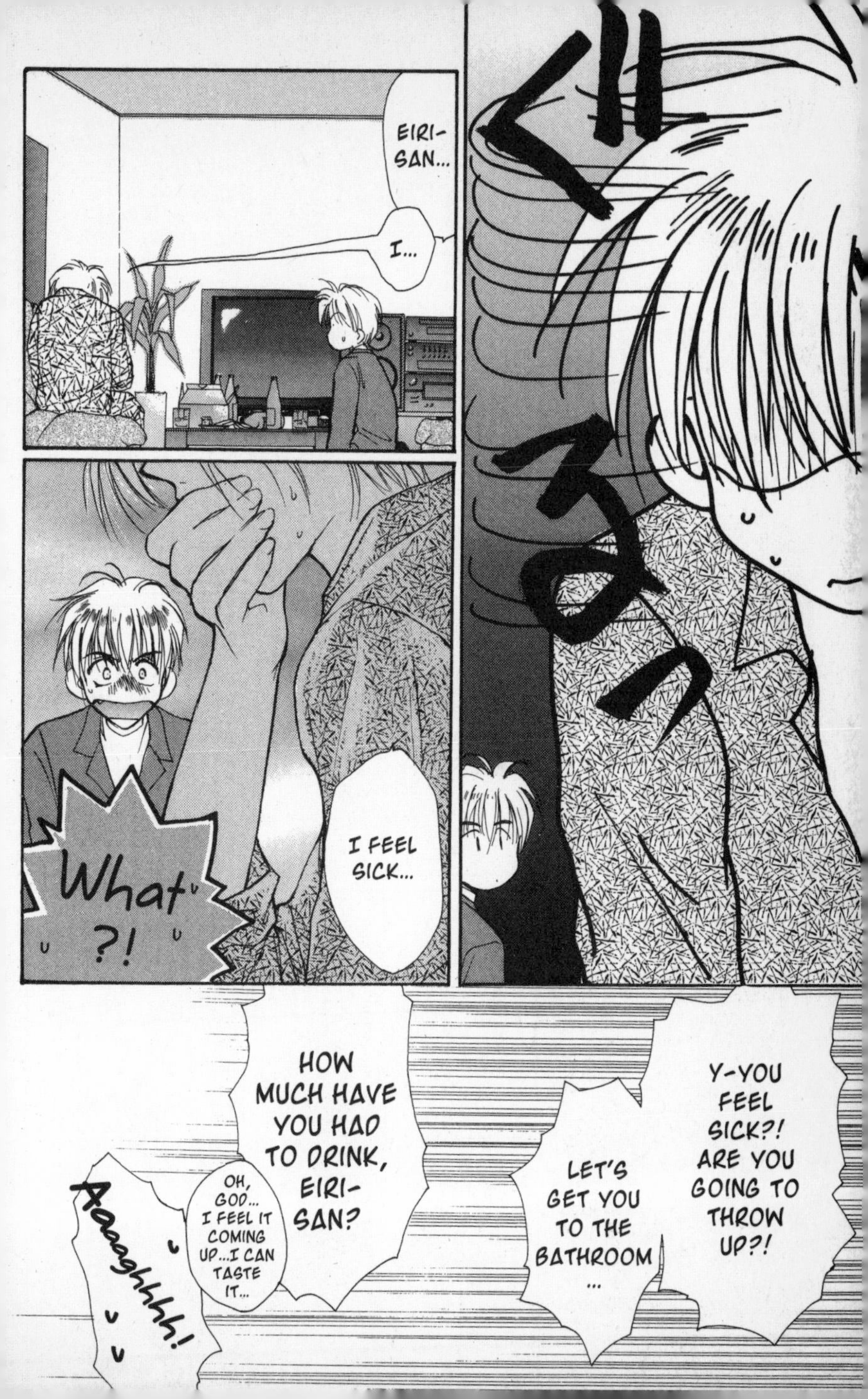
EIRI-SAN...
I...
I FEEL SICK...
What?!
Y-YOU FEEL SICK?! ARE YOU GOING TO THROW UP?!
LET'S GET YOU TO THE BATHROOM...
HOW MUCH HAVE YOU HAD TO DRINK, EIRI-SAN?
OH, GOD... I FEEL IT COMING UP...I CAN TASTE IT...
Aaaaghhhh!

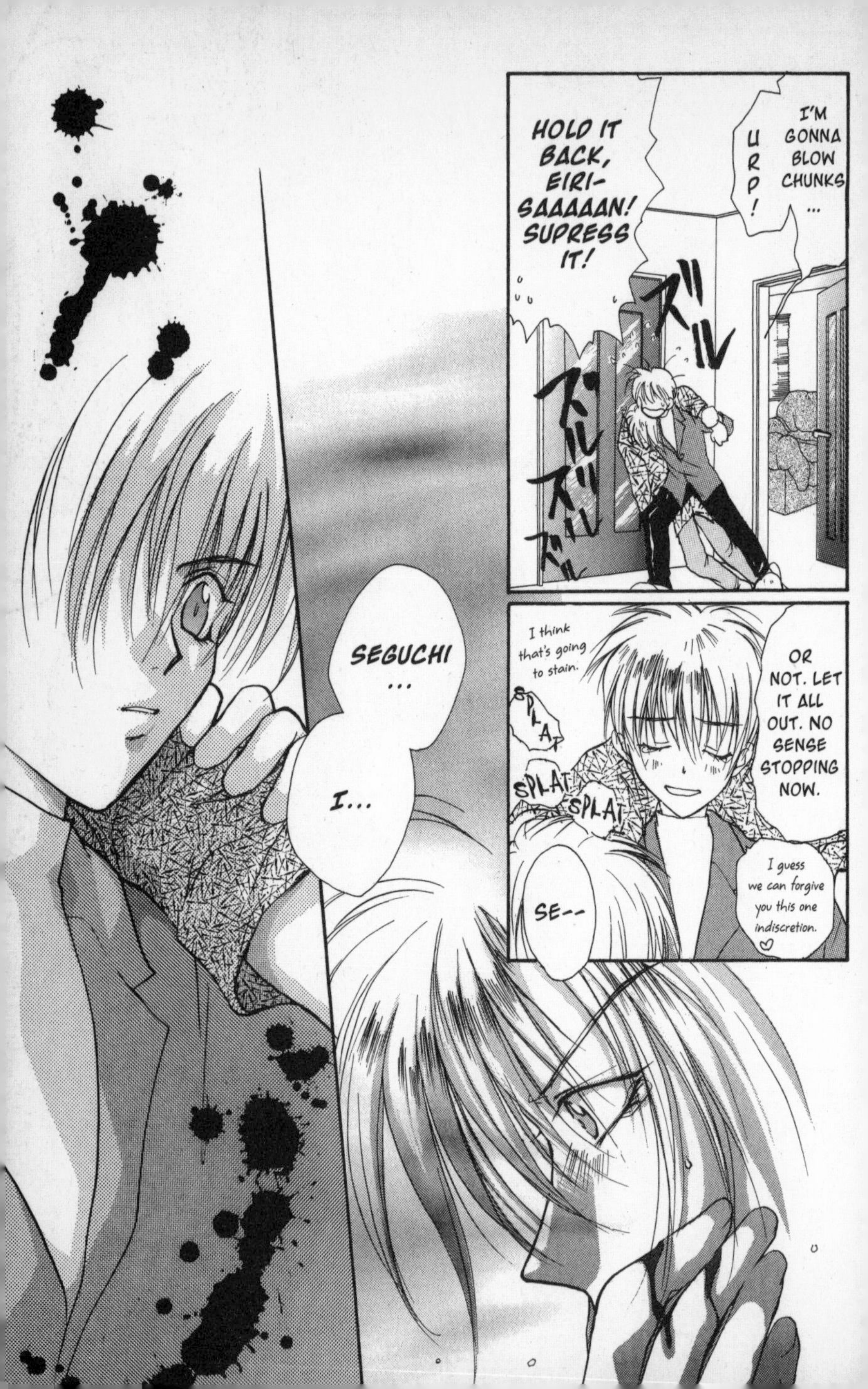

I'M GONNA BLOW CHUNKS...
URP!
HOLD IT BACK, EIRI-SAAAAAN! SUPRESS IT!
ズル
OR NOT. LET IT ALL OUT. NO SENSE STOPPING NOW.
I think that's going to stain.
SPLAT
SPLAT
SPLAT
I guess we can forgive you this one indiscretion.
SE--
SEGUCHI ...
I...

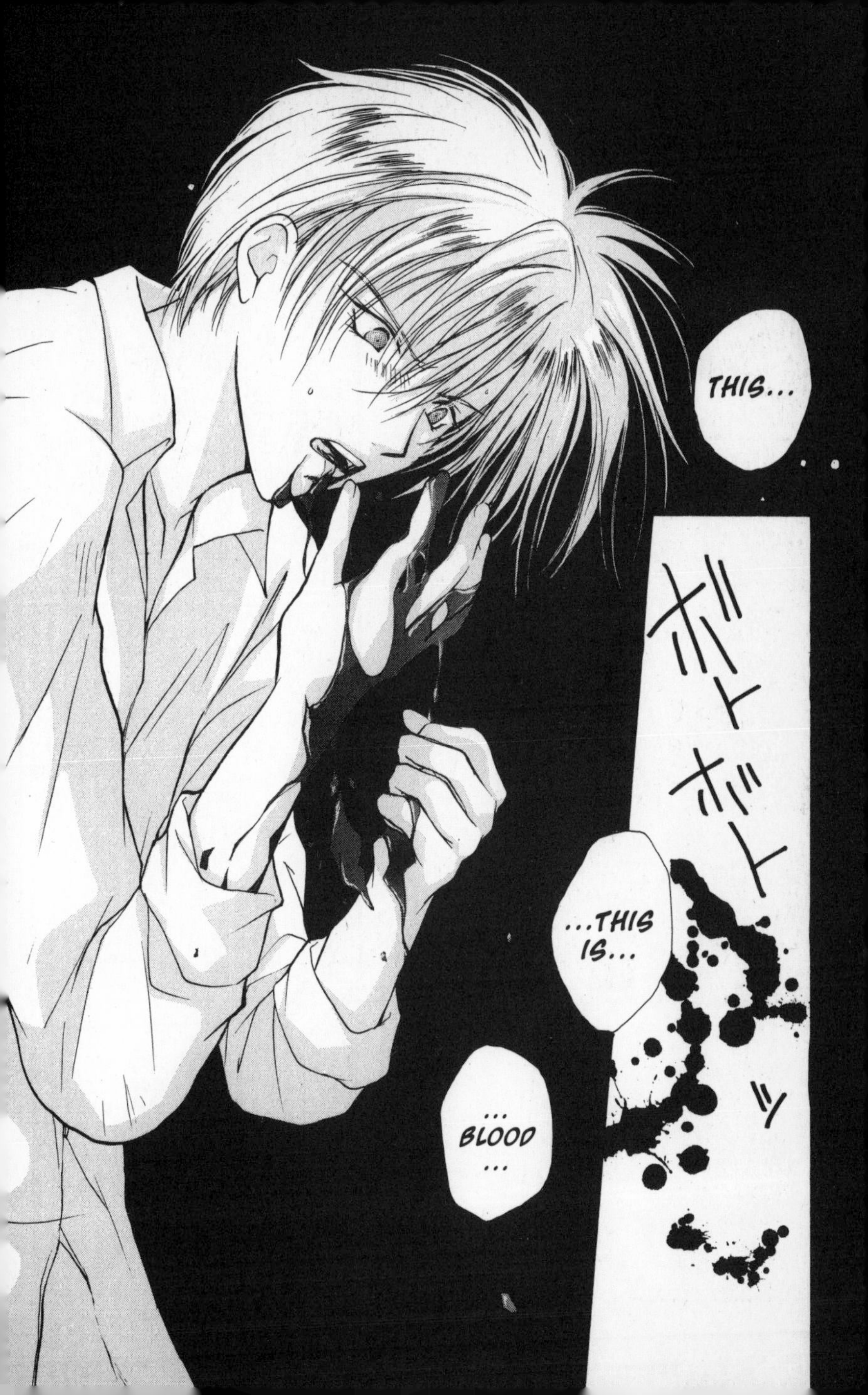
THIS...
ボトボトッ
...THIS IS...
... BLOOD ...

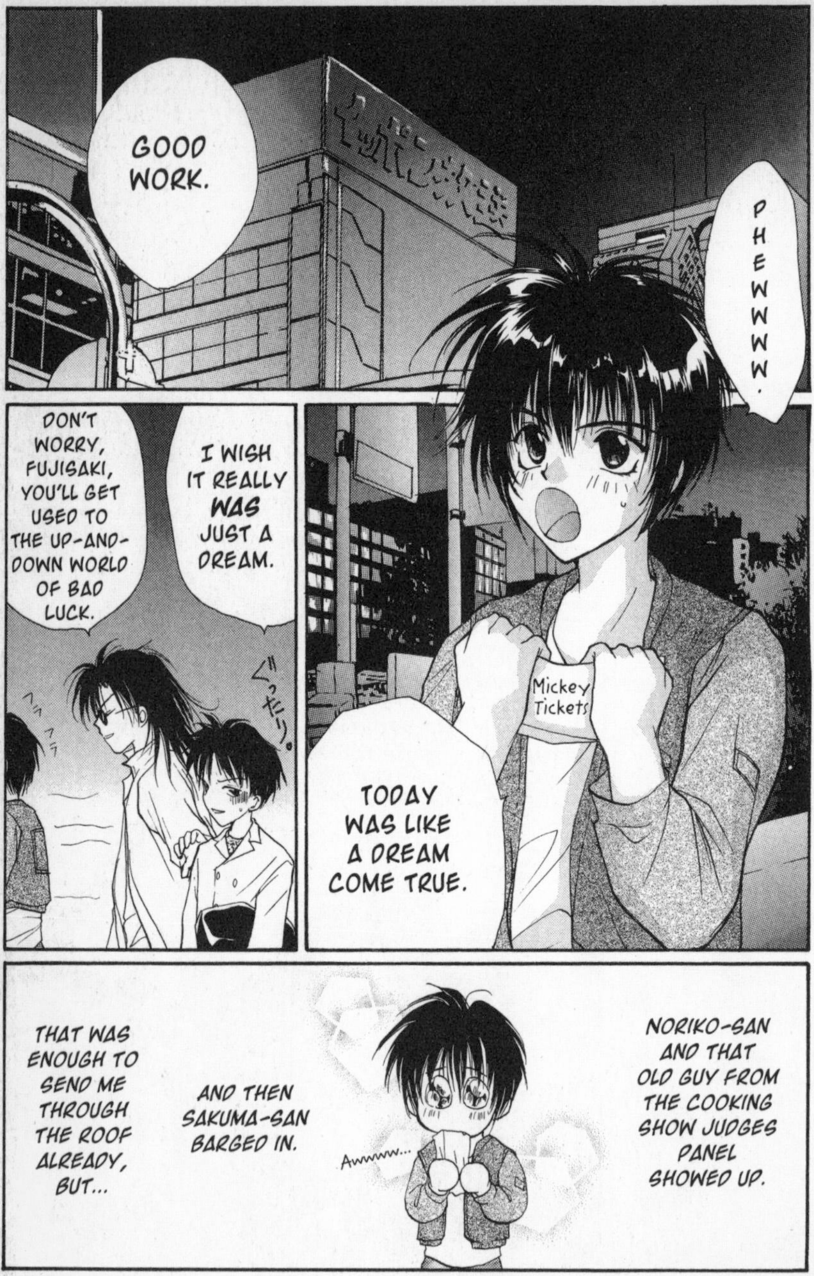
PHEWWWW.
GOOD WORK.
Mickey Tickets
TODAY WAS LIKE A DREAM COME TRUE.
I WISH IT REALLY **WAS** JUST A DREAM.
DON'T WORRY, FUJISAKI, YOU'LL GET USED TO THE UP-AND-DOWN WORLD OF BAD LUCK.
ぐったり。
NORIKO-SAN AND THAT OLD GUY FROM THE COOKING SHOW JUDGES PANEL SHOWED UP.
AND THEN SAKUMA-SAN BARGED IN.
Awwww...
THAT WAS ENOUGH TO SEND ME THROUGH THE ROOF ALREADY, BUT...

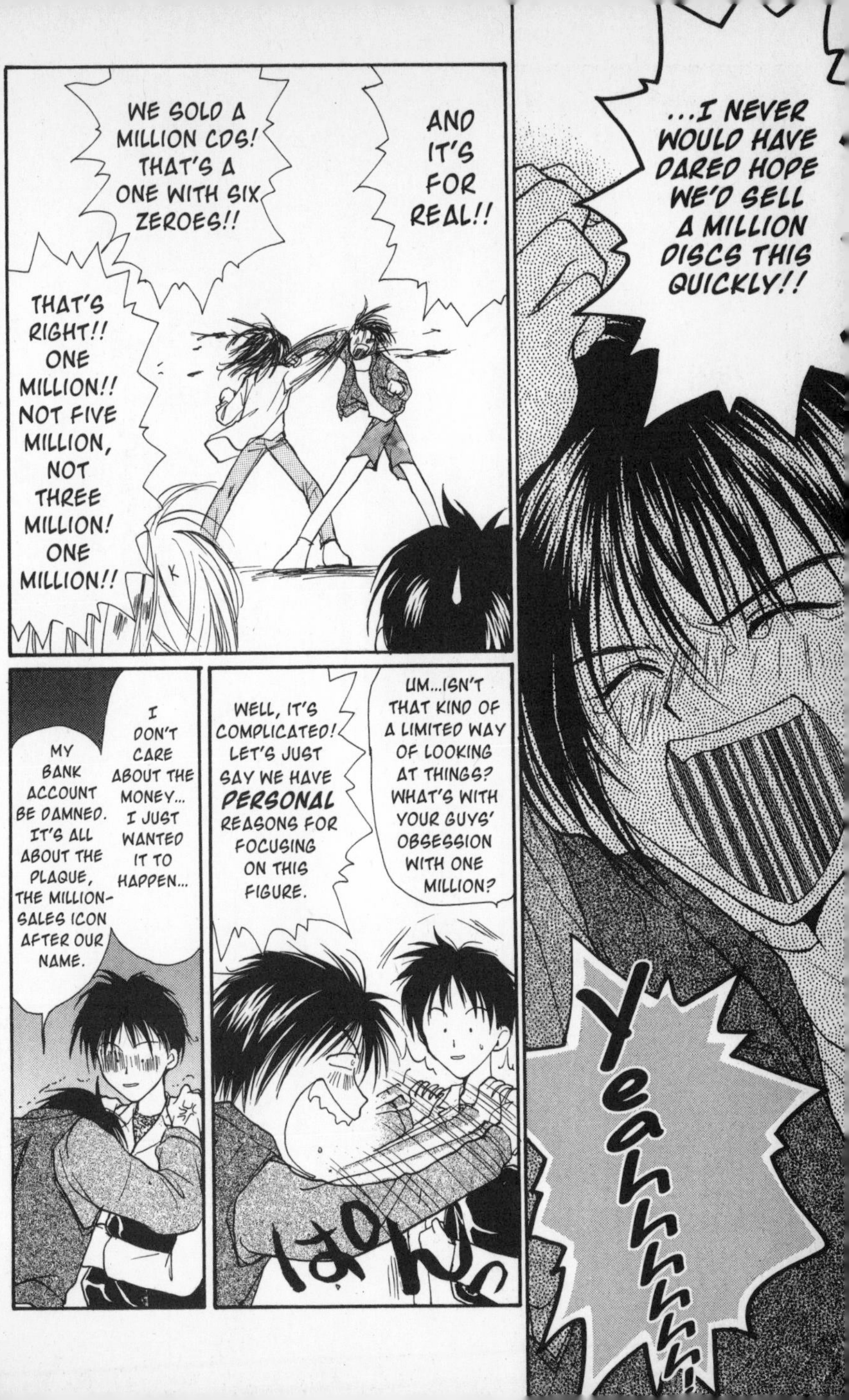
...I NEVER WOULD HAVE DARED HOPE WE'D SELL A MILLION DISCS THIS QUICKLY!!
Yeahhhhhhh!
AND IT'S FOR REAL!!
WE SOLD A MILLION CDS! THAT'S A ONE WITH SIX ZEROES!!
THAT'S RIGHT!! ONE MILLION!! NOT FIVE MILLION, NOT THREE MILLION! ONE MILLION!!
UM...ISN'T THAT KIND OF A LIMITED WAY OF LOOKING AT THINGS? WHAT'S WITH YOUR GUYS' OBSESSION WITH ONE MILLION?
WELL, IT'S COMPLICATED! LET'S JUST SAY WE HAVE PERSONAL REASONS FOR FOCUSING ON THIS FIGURE.
I DON'T CARE ABOUT THE MONEY... I JUST WANTED IT TO HAPPEN...
MY BANK ACCOUNT BE DAMNED. IT'S ALL ABOUT THE PLAQUE, THE MILLION-SALES ICON AFTER OUR NAME.

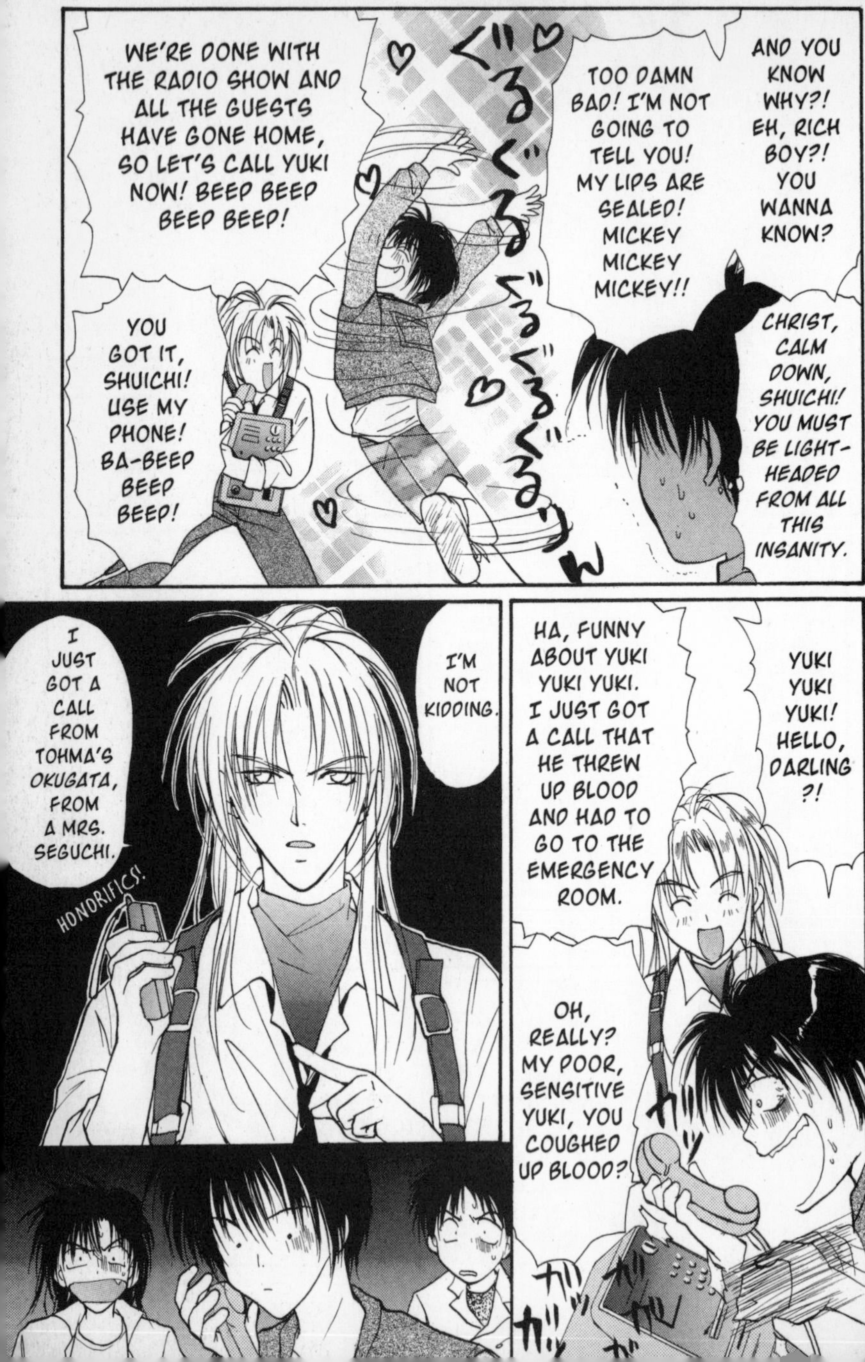
AND YOU KNOW WHY?! EH, RICH BOY?! YOU WANNA KNOW?
TOO DAMN BAD! I'M NOT GOING TO TELL YOU! MY LIPS ARE SEALED! MICKEY MICKEY MICKEY!!
WE'RE DONE WITH THE RADIO SHOW AND ALL THE GUESTS HAVE GONE HOME, SO LET'S CALL YUKI NOW! BEEP BEEP BEEP BEEP!
CHRIST, CALM DOWN, SHUICHI! YOU MUST BE LIGHT-HEADED FROM ALL THIS INSANITY.
YOU GOT IT, SHUICHI! USE MY PHONE! BA-BEEP BEEP BEEP!
YUKI YUKI YUKI! HELLO, DARLING?!
HA, FUNNY ABOUT YUKI YUKI YUKI. I JUST GOT A CALL THAT HE THREW UP BLOOD AND HAD TO GO TO THE EMERGENCY ROOM.
OH, REALLY? MY POOR, SENSITIVE YUKI, YOU COUGHED UP BLOOD?
I'M NOT KIDDING.
I JUST GOT A CALL FROM TOHMA'S OKUGATA, FROM A MRS. SEGUCHI.
HONORIFICS!

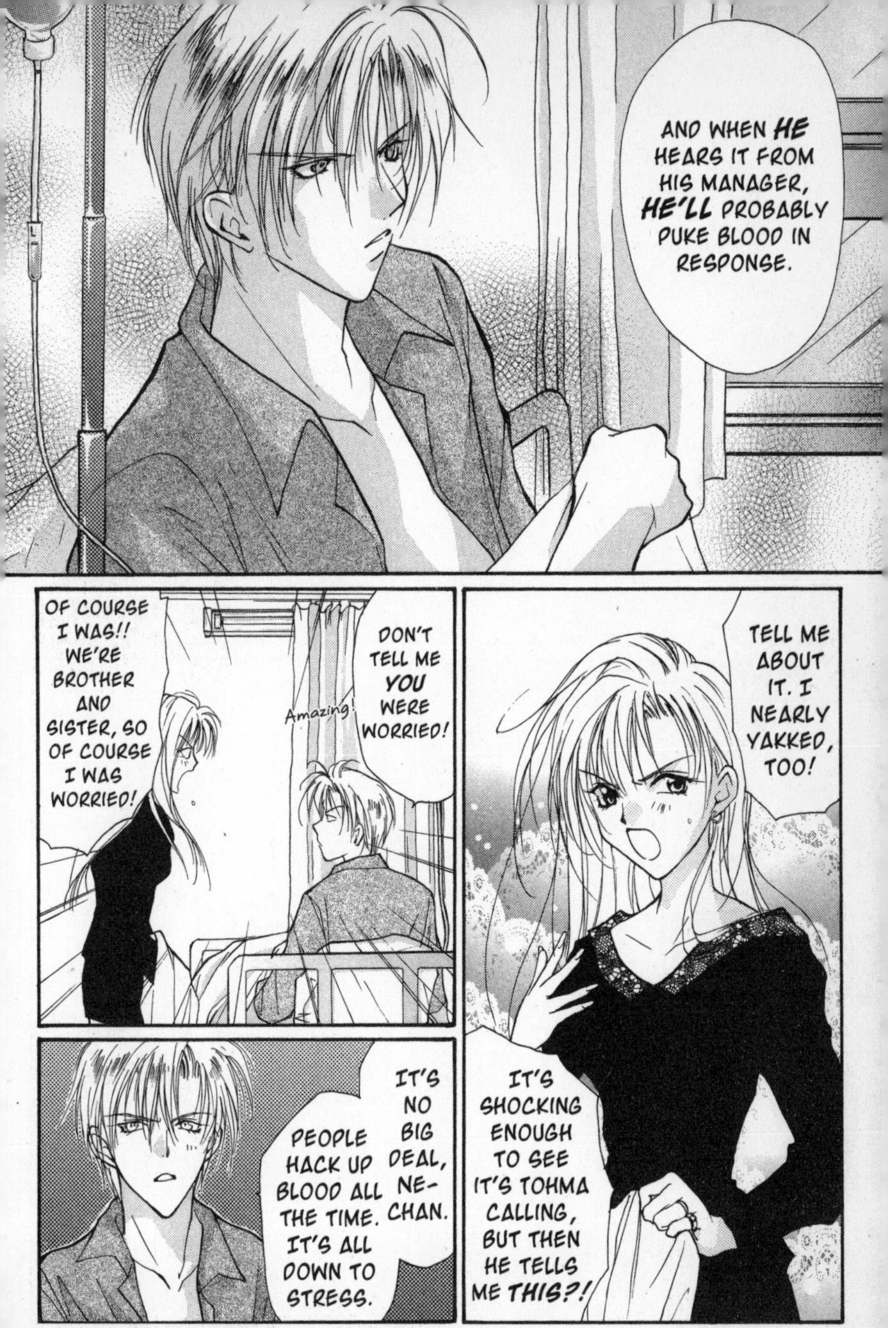
AND WHEN **HE** HEARS IT FROM HIS MANAGER, **HE'LL** PROBABLY PUKE BLOOD IN RESPONSE.
TELL ME ABOUT IT. I NEARLY YAKKED, TOO!
IT'S SHOCKING ENOUGH TO SEE IT'S TOHMA CALLING, BUT THEN HE TELLS ME ***THIS?!***
DON'T TELL ME ***YOU*** WERE WORRIED!
Amazing!
OF COURSE I WAS!! WE'RE BROTHER AND SISTER, SO OF COURSE I WAS WORRIED!
IT'S NO BIG DEAL, NE-CHAN.
PEOPLE HACK UP BLOOD ALL THE TIME. IT'S ALL DOWN TO STRESS.

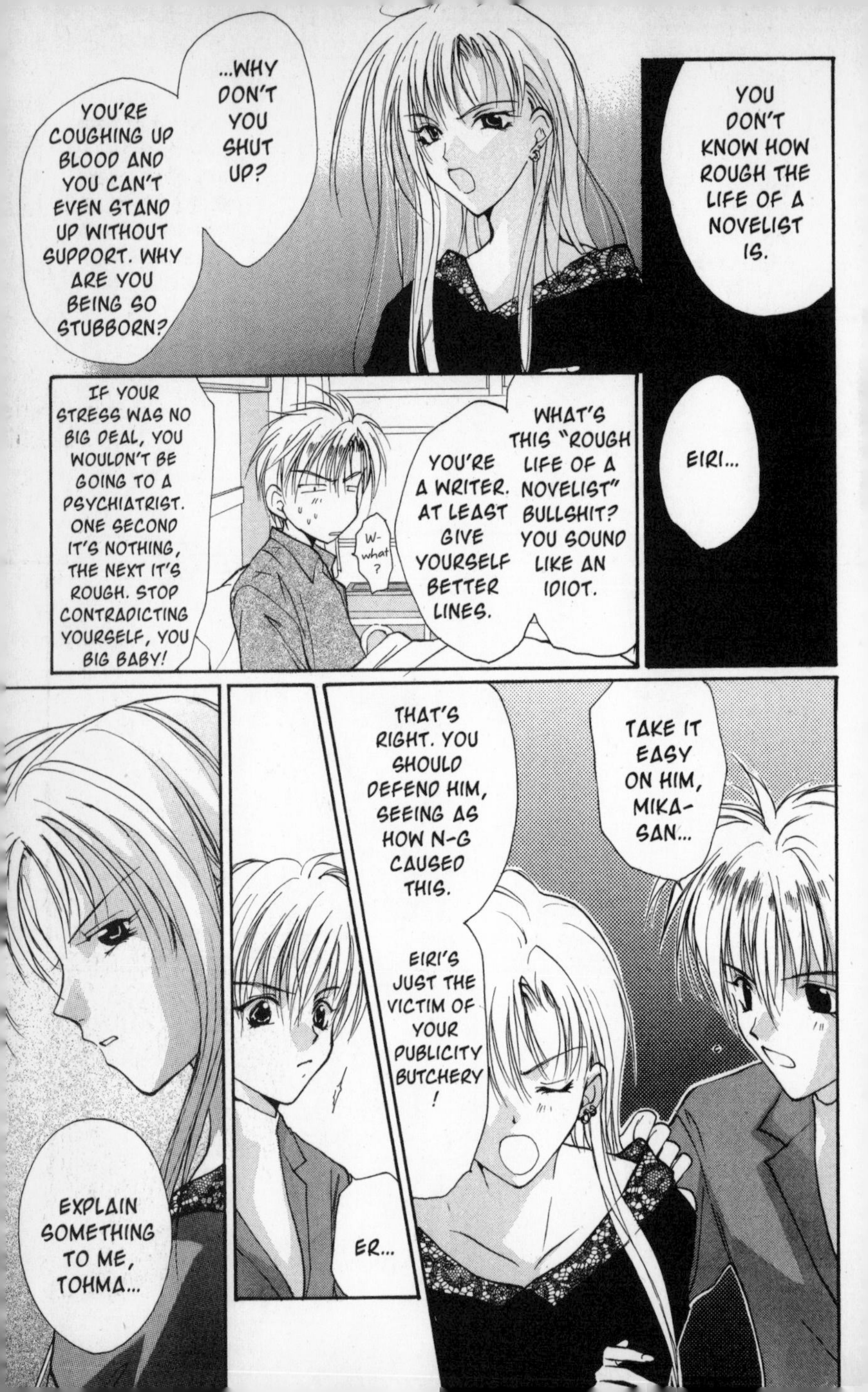
YOU DON'T KNOW HOW ROUGH THE LIFE OF A NOVELIST IS.
EIRI...
...WHY DON'T YOU SHUT UP?
YOU'RE COUGHING UP BLOOD AND YOU CAN'T EVEN STAND UP WITHOUT SUPPORT. WHY ARE YOU BEING SO STUBBORN?
WHAT'S THIS "ROUGH LIFE OF A NOVELIST" BULLSHIT? YOU SOUND LIKE AN IDIOT.
YOU'RE A WRITER. AT LEAST GIVE YOURSELF BETTER LINES.
W-what?
IF YOUR STRESS WAS NO BIG DEAL, YOU WOULDN'T BE GOING TO A PSYCHIATRIST. ONE SECOND IT'S NOTHING, THE NEXT IT'S ROUGH. STOP CONTRADICTING YOURSELF, YOU BIG BABY!
TAKE IT EASY ON HIM, MIKA-SAN...
THAT'S RIGHT. YOU SHOULD DEFEND HIM, SEEING AS HOW N-G CAUSED THIS.
EIRI'S JUST THE VICTIM OF YOUR PUBLICITY BUTCHERY!
ER...
EXPLAIN SOMETHING TO ME, TOHMA...

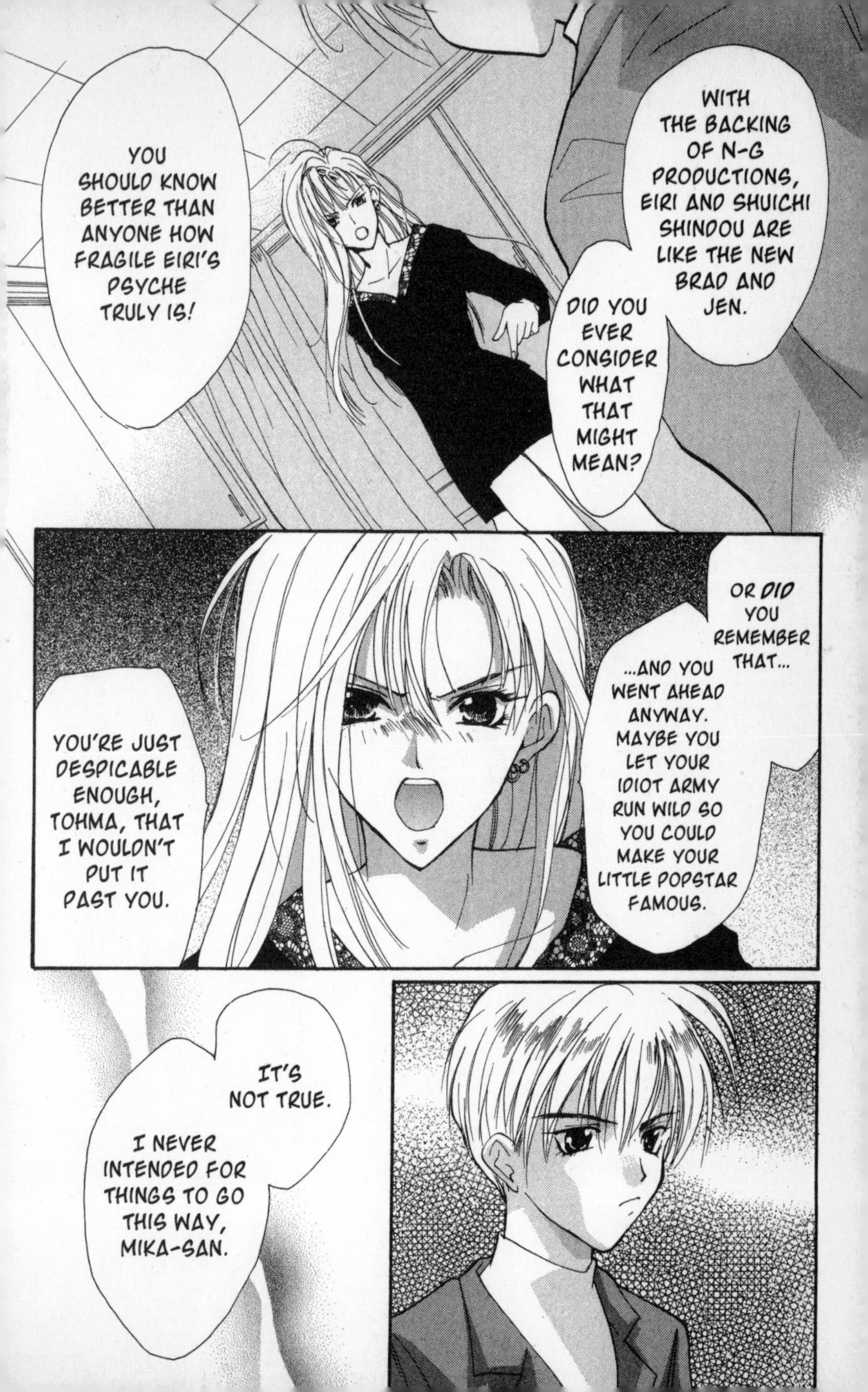
WITH THE BACKING OF N-G PRODUCTIONS, EIRI AND SHUICHI SHINDOU ARE LIKE THE NEW BRAD AND JEN.
DID YOU EVER CONSIDER WHAT THAT MIGHT MEAN?
YOU SHOULD KNOW BETTER THAN ANYONE HOW FRAGILE EIRI'S PSYCHE TRULY IS!
OR *DID* YOU REMEMBER THAT...
...AND YOU WENT AHEAD ANYWAY. MAYBE YOU LET YOUR IDIOT ARMY RUN WILD SO YOU COULD MAKE YOUR LITTLE POPSTAR FAMOUS.
YOU'RE JUST DESPICABLE ENOUGH, TOHMA, THAT I WOULDN'T PUT IT PAST YOU.
IT'S NOT TRUE.
I NEVER INTENDED FOR THINGS TO GO THIS WAY, MIKA-SAN.

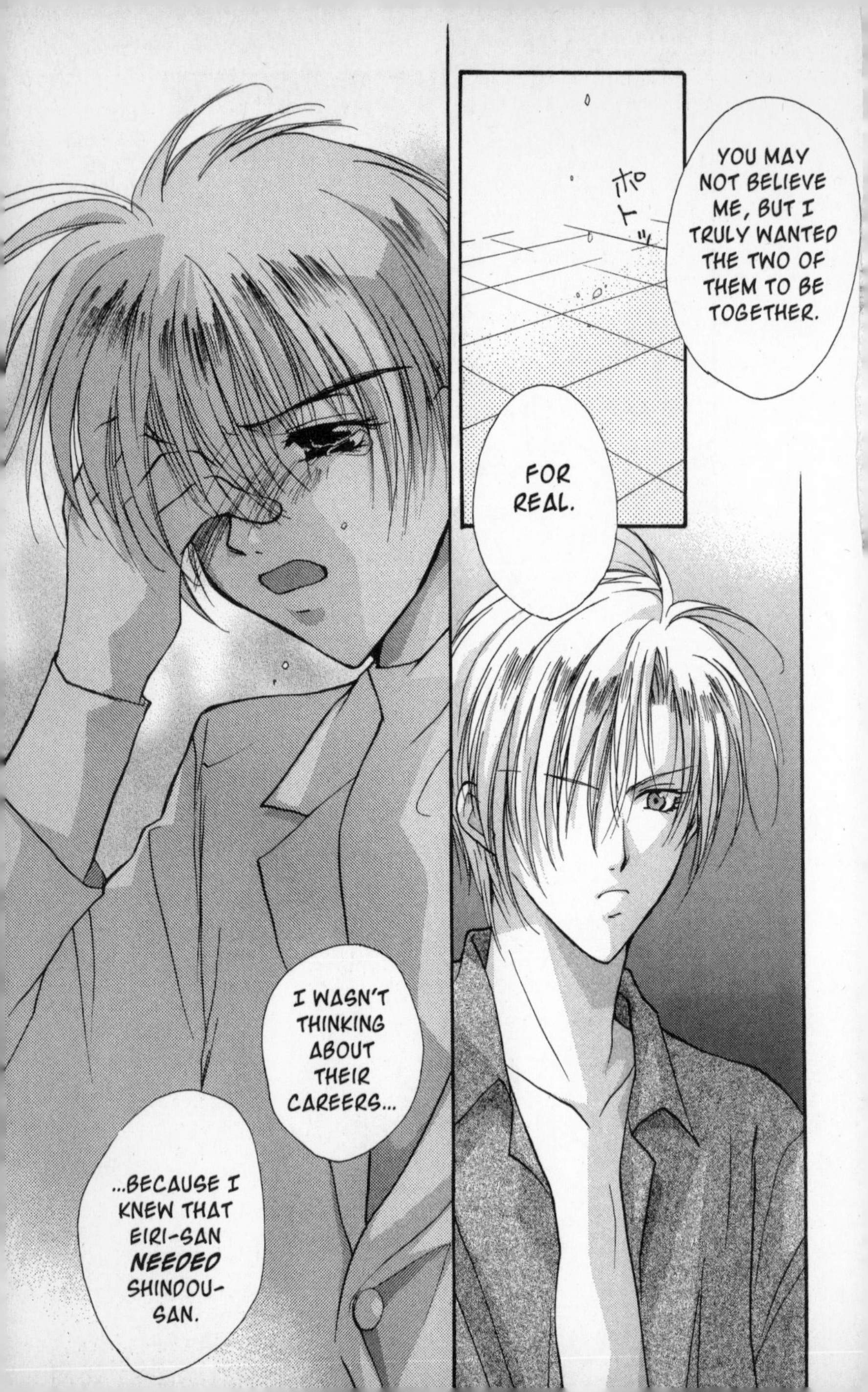
ポトッ
YOU MAY NOT BELIEVE ME, BUT I TRULY WANTED THE TWO OF THEM TO BE TOGETHER.
FOR REAL.
I WASN'T THINKING ABOUT THEIR CAREERS...
...BECAUSE I KNEW THAT EIRI-SAN *NEEDED* SHINDOU-SAN.

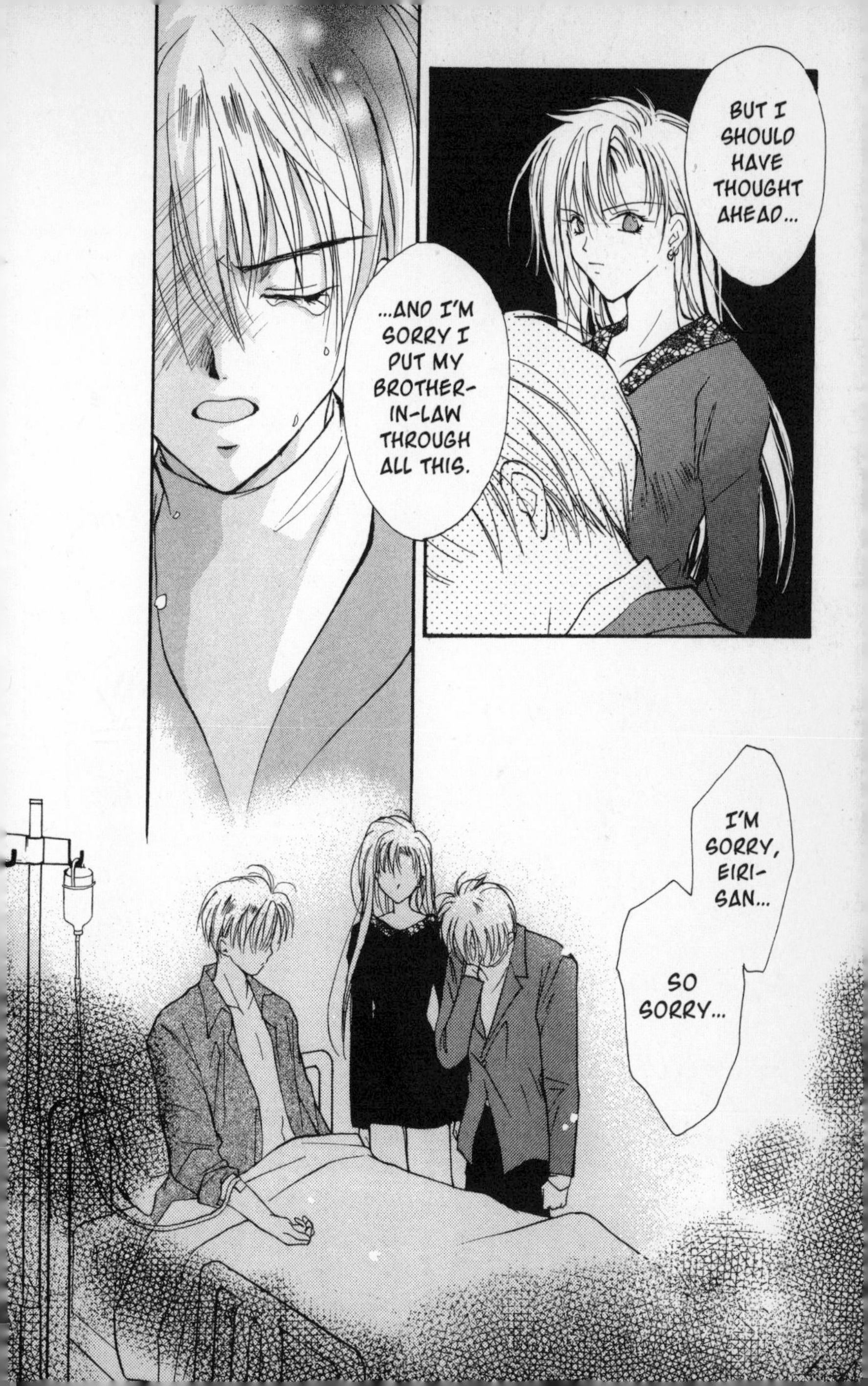
BUT I SHOULD HAVE THOUGHT AHEAD...
...AND I'M SORRY I PUT MY BROTHER-IN-LAW THROUGH ALL THIS.
I'M SORRY, EIRI-SAN...
SO SORRY...

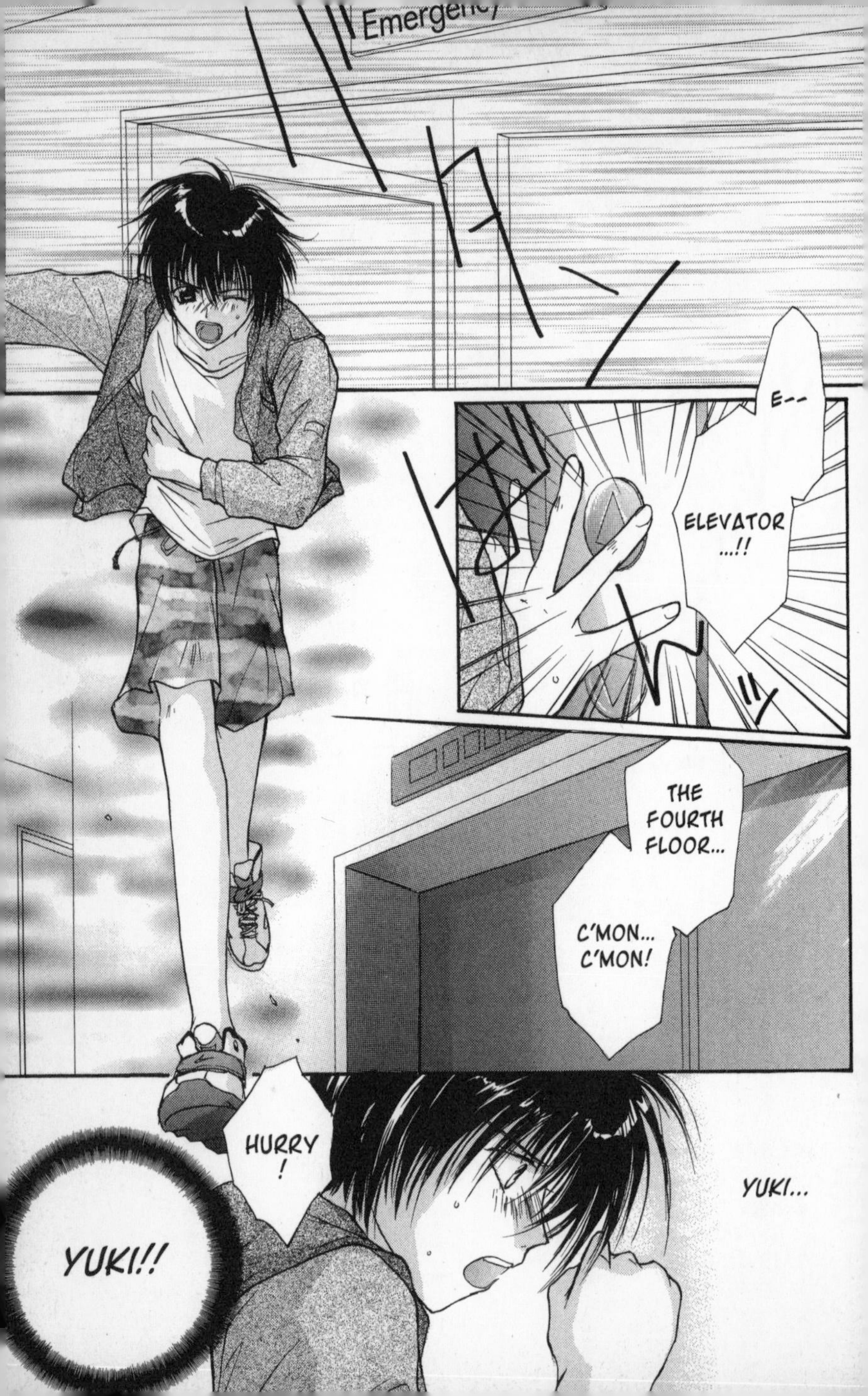
Emergency
E-- ELEVATOR ...!!
THE FOURTH FLOOR...
C'MON... C'MON!
YUKI...
HURRY!
YUKI!!

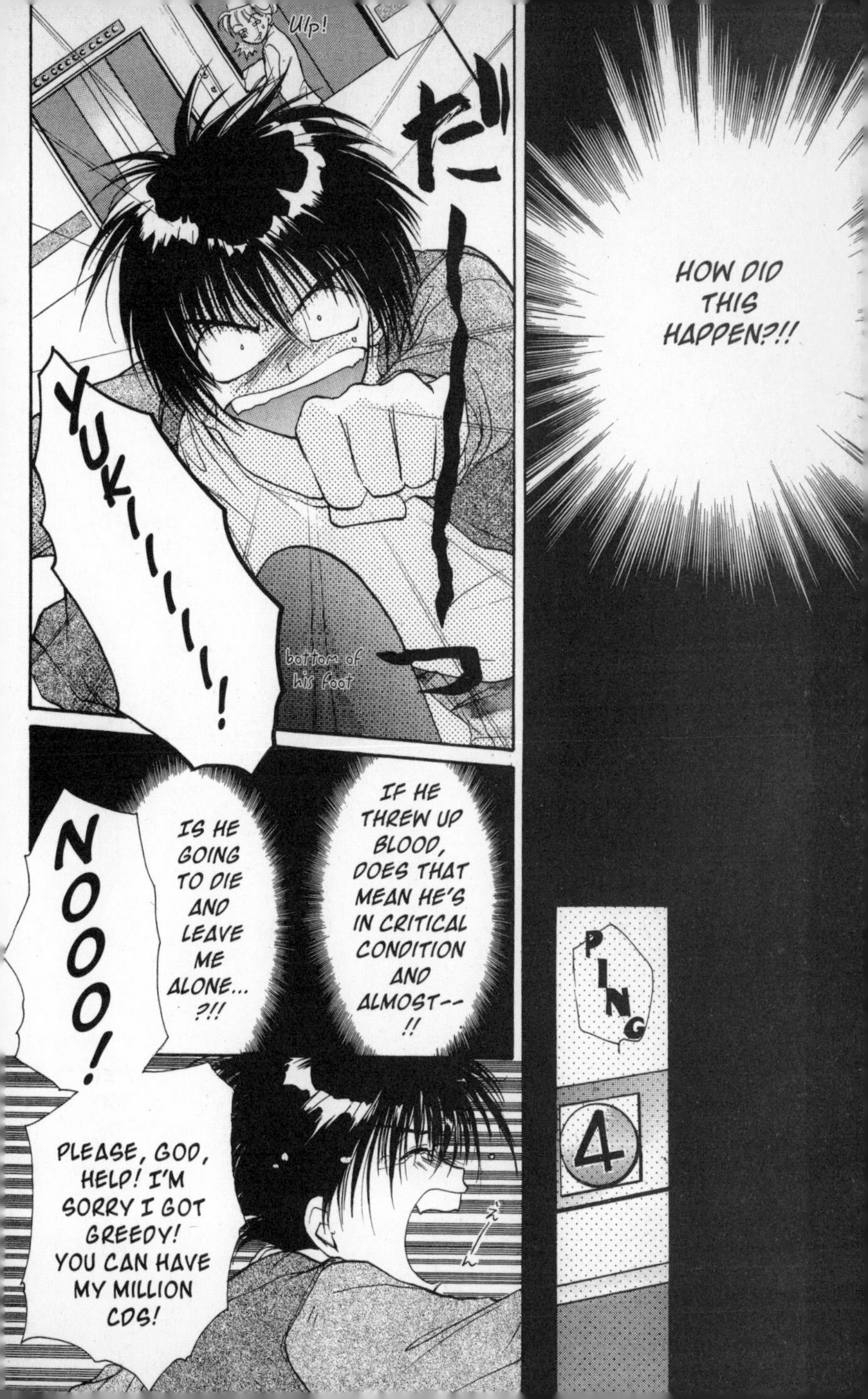
HOW DID THIS HAPPEN?!!
PING
4
Ulp!
YUKI-I-I-I-I-I!
bottom of his foot
IF HE THREW UP BLOOD, DOES THAT MEAN HE'S IN CRITICAL CONDITION AND ALMOST-- !!
IS HE GOING TO DIE AND LEAVE ME ALONE... ?!!
NOOOO!
PLEASE, GOD, HELP! I'M SORRY I GOT GREEDY! YOU CAN HAVE MY MILLION CDS!

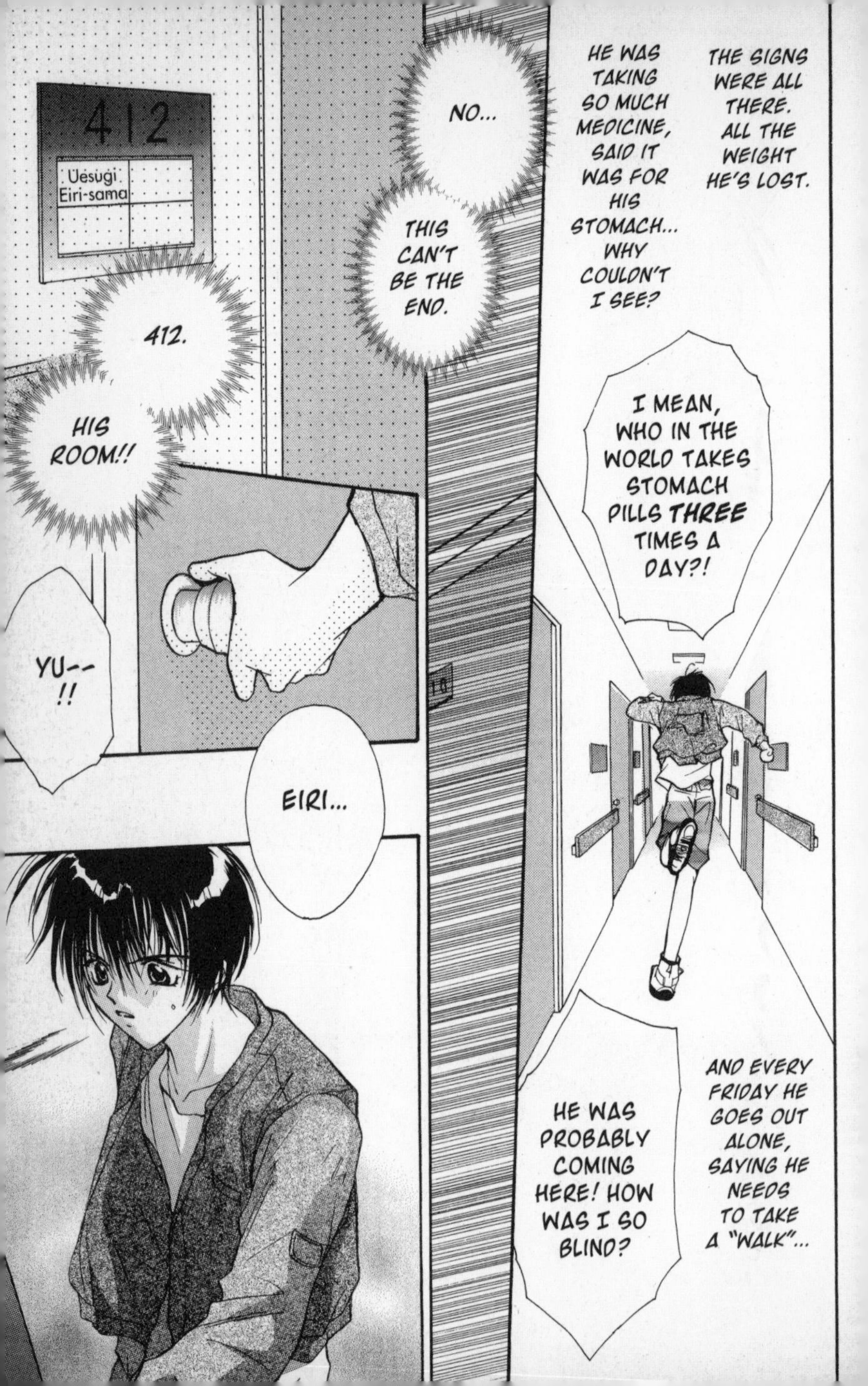
THE SIGNS WERE ALL THERE. ALL THE WEIGHT HE'S LOST.
HE WAS TAKING SO MUCH MEDICINE, SAID IT WAS FOR HIS STOMACH... WHY COULDN'T I SEE?
I MEAN, WHO IN THE WORLD TAKES STOMACH PILLS THREE TIMES A DAY?!
AND EVERY FRIDAY HE GOES OUT ALONE, SAYING HE NEEDS TO TAKE A "WALK"...
HE WAS PROBABLY COMING HERE! HOW WAS I SO BLIND?
NO...
THIS CAN'T BE THE END.
412
Uesugi Eiri-sama
412.
HIS ROOM!!
YU--!!
EIRI...

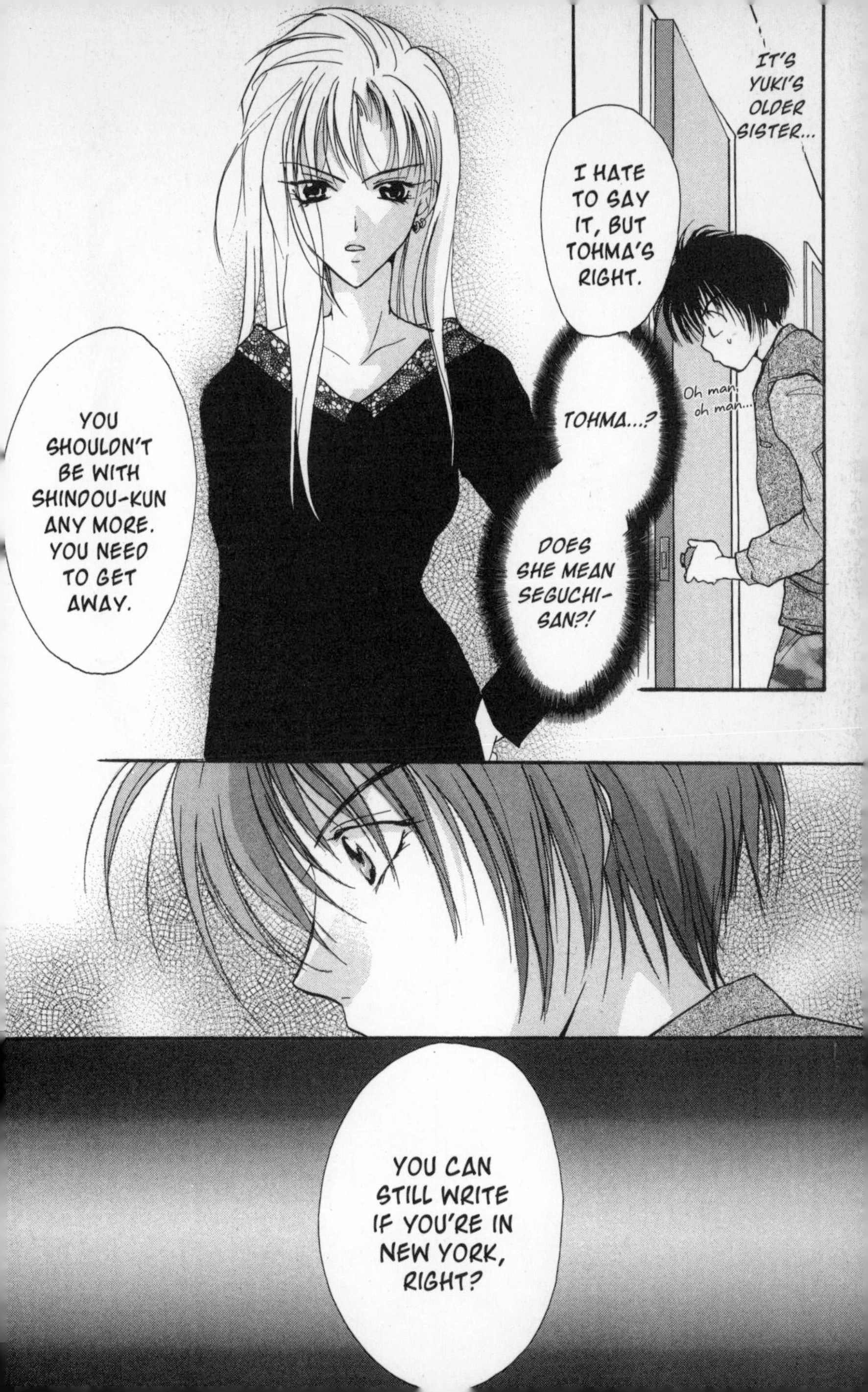
IT'S YUKI'S OLDER SISTER...
I HATE TO SAY IT, BUT TOHMA'S RIGHT.
Oh man, oh man...
TOHMA...?
DOES SHE MEAN SEGUCHI-SAN?!
YOU SHOULDN'T BE WITH SHINDOU-KUN ANY MORE. YOU NEED TO GET AWAY.
YOU CAN STILL WRITE IF YOU'RE IN NEW YORK, RIGHT?

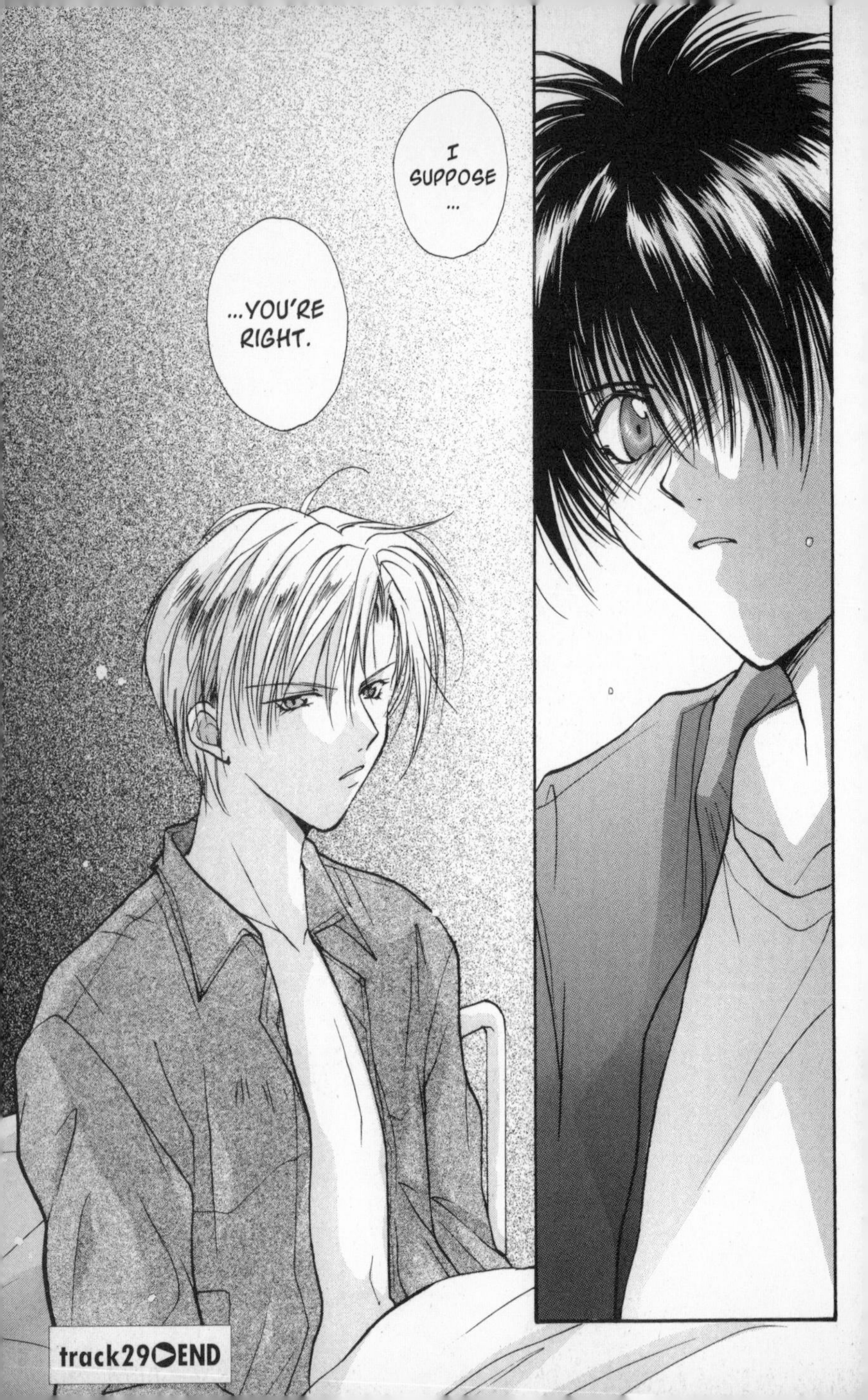
I SUPPOSE ...
...YOU'RE RIGHT.
track29▶END

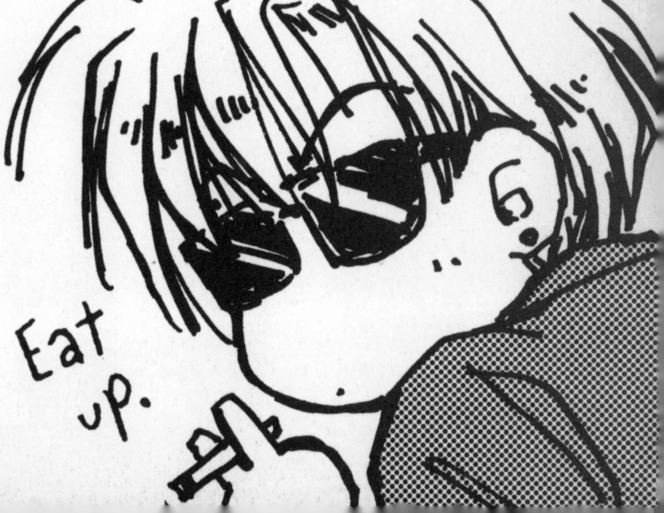
Eat up.

Gravitation

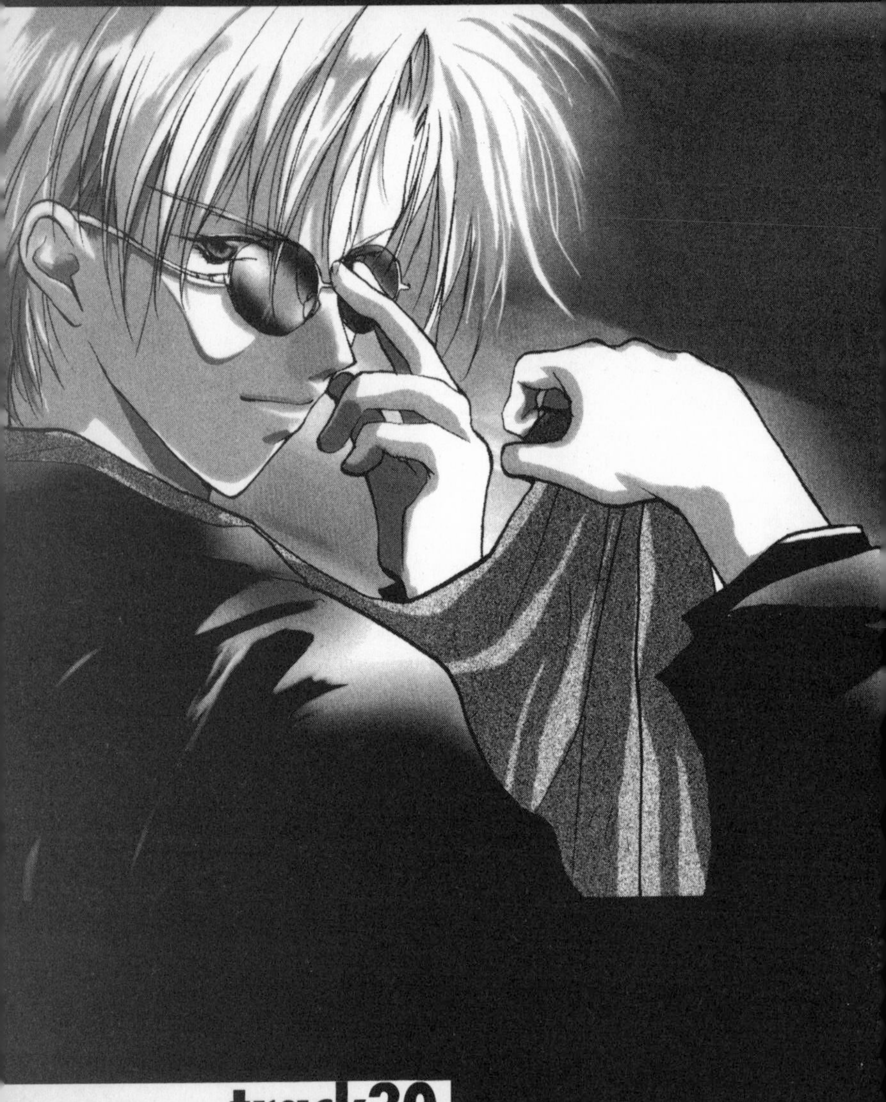

track30

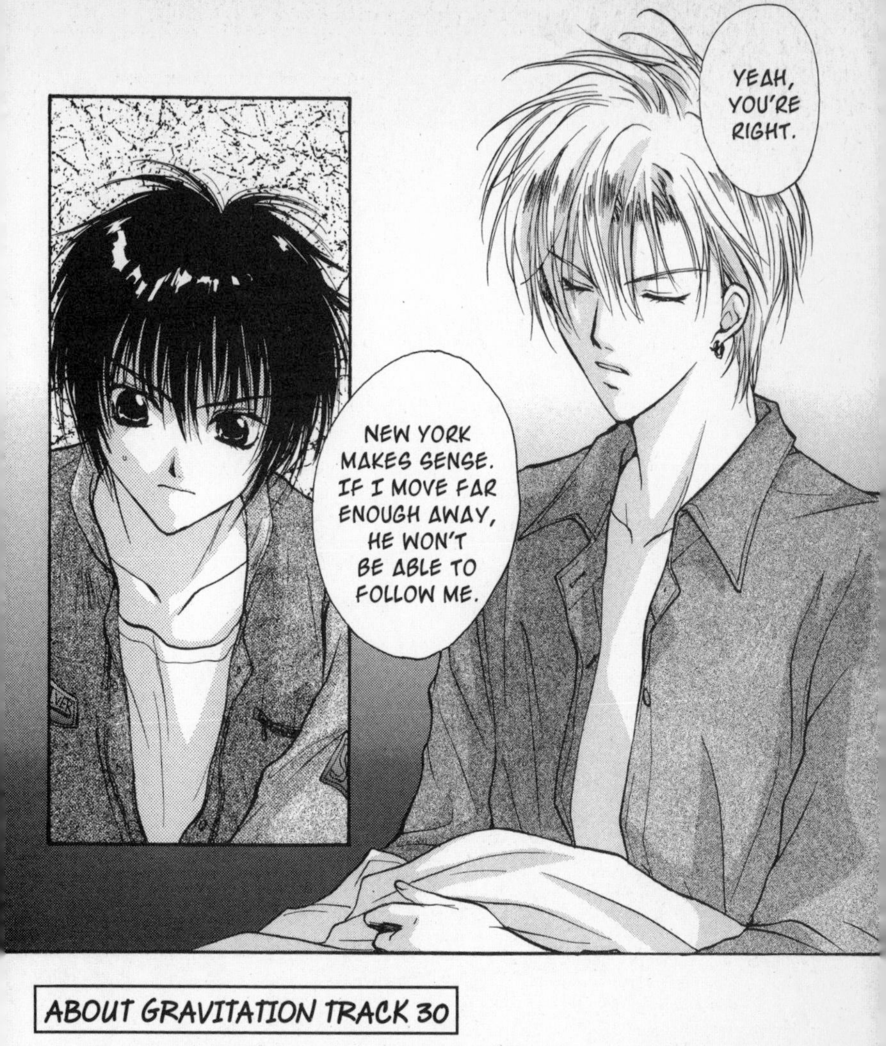
YEAH, YOU'RE RIGHT.
NEW YORK MAKES SENSE. IF I MOVE FAR ENOUGH AWAY, HE WON'T BE ABLE TO FOLLOW ME.

ABOUT GRAVITATION TRACK 30

30!! Track 30?! Wow!! Amazing! We've made it to number 30!! When I started *Gravitation*, it never occurred to me that I'd get this far! I thought the story would probably get cancelled after 5 episodes, or maybe 10. But thanks to you, my loyal readers, we've made it to number 30!!

Which means that I've written 30 of these episode commentaries already...

So, anyway, in this episode, there are several things to watch for, including Shuichi desperately stuffing himself into a bag. Eiri's strange behavior is also something you don't want to miss. And then there's the impossible evolution in Mika's character. A person stuffing himself into a bag isn't something you get to see every day, is it? Anyhow, see you next chapter!

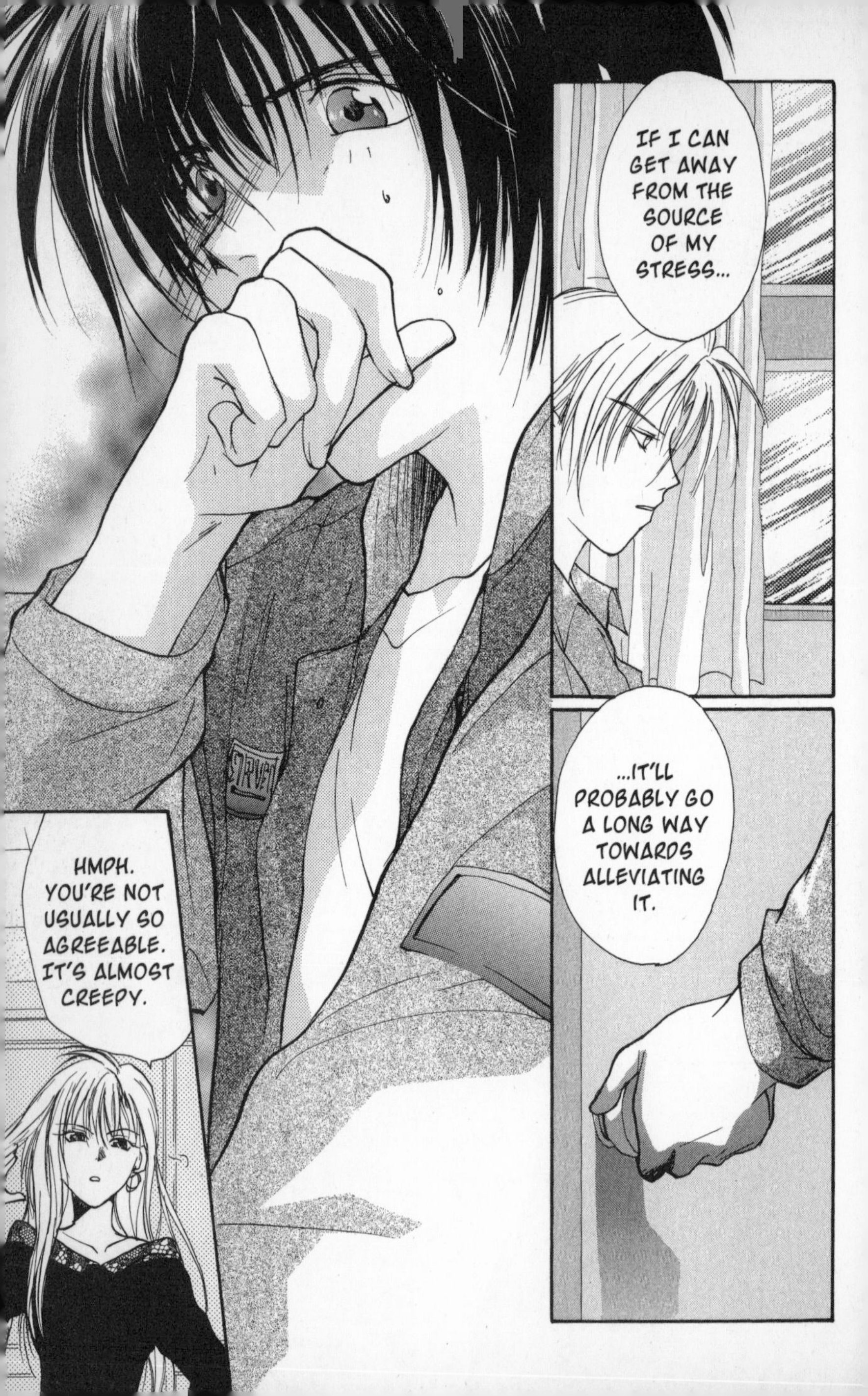
IF I CAN GET AWAY FROM THE SOURCE OF MY STRESS...
...IT'LL PROBABLY GO A LONG WAY TOWARDS ALLEVIATING IT.
HMPH. YOU'RE NOT USUALLY SO AGREEABLE. IT'S ALMOST CREEPY.

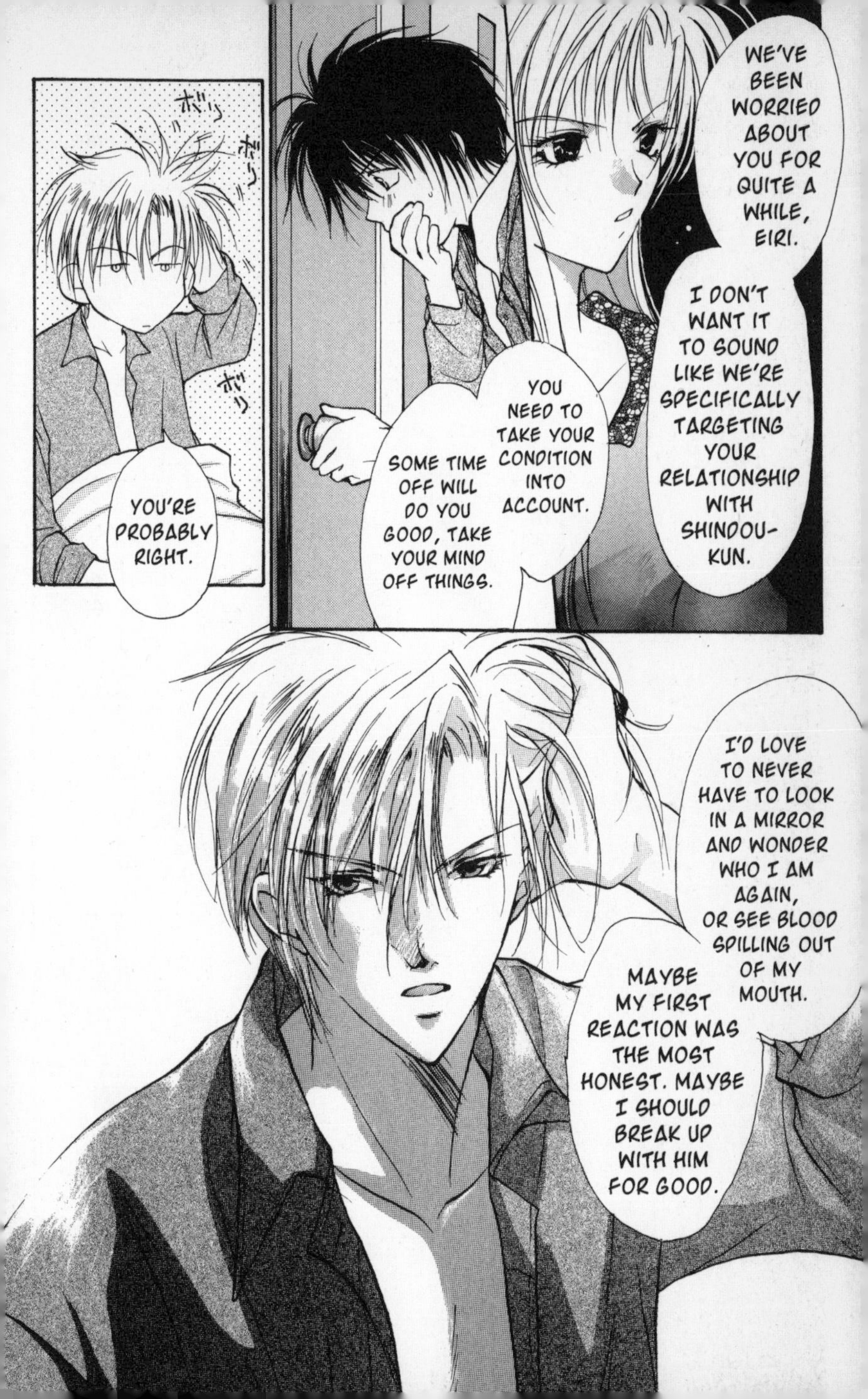
WE'VE BEEN WORRIED ABOUT YOU FOR QUITE A WHILE, EIRI.
I DON'T WANT IT TO SOUND LIKE WE'RE SPECIFICALLY TARGETING YOUR RELATIONSHIP WITH SHINDOU-KUN.
YOU NEED TO TAKE YOUR CONDITION INTO ACCOUNT.
SOME TIME OFF WILL DO YOU GOOD, TAKE YOUR MIND OFF THINGS.
ボリ
ボリ
ボリ
YOU'RE PROBABLY RIGHT.
I'D LOVE TO NEVER HAVE TO LOOK IN A MIRROR AND WONDER WHO I AM AGAIN, OR SEE BLOOD SPILLING OUT OF MY MOUTH.
MAYBE MY FIRST REACTION WAS THE MOST HONEST. MAYBE I SHOULD BREAK UP WITH HIM FOR GOOD.

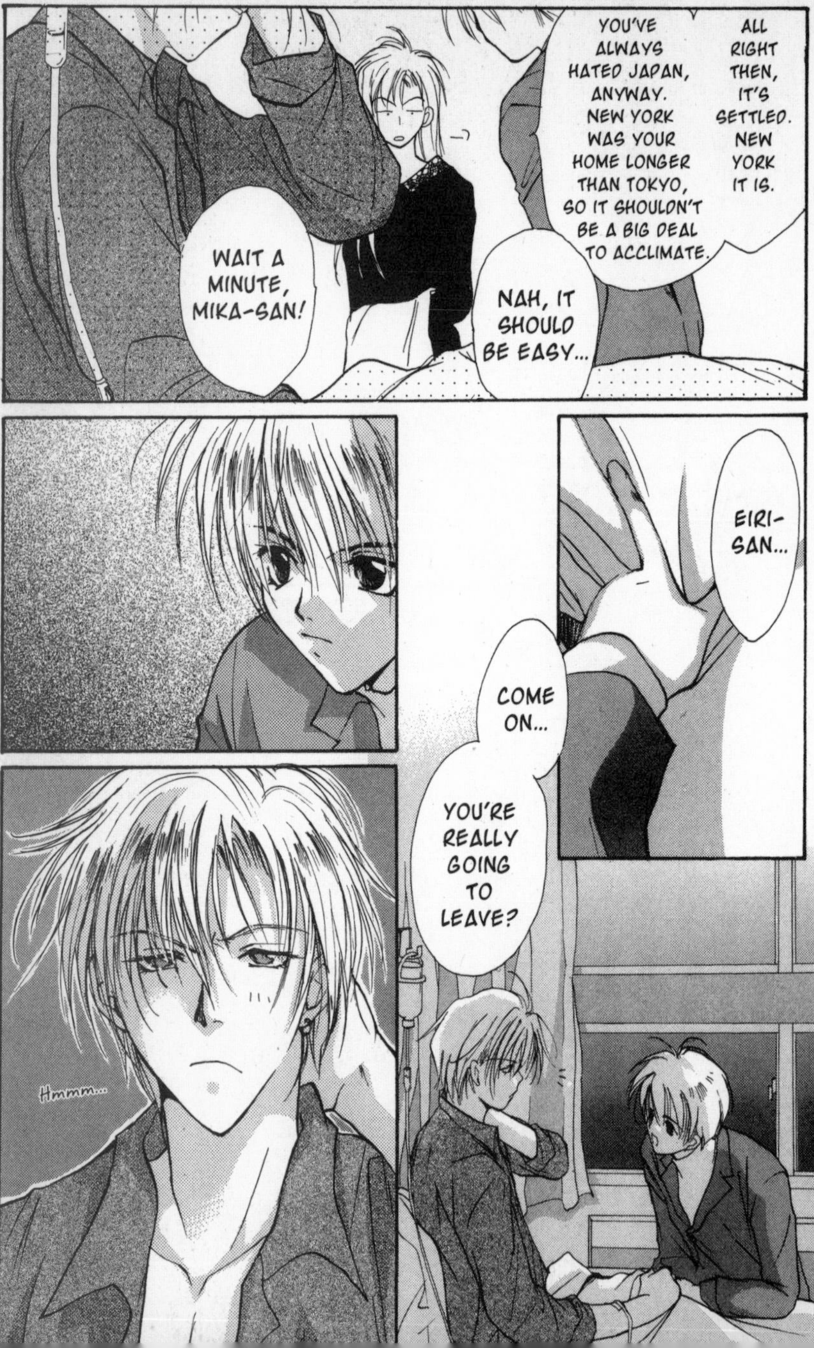
ALL RIGHT THEN, IT'S SETTLED. NEW YORK IT IS.
YOU'VE ALWAYS HATED JAPAN, ANYWAY. NEW YORK WAS YOUR HOME LONGER THAN TOKYO, SO IT SHOULDN'T BE A BIG DEAL TO ACCLIMATE.
NAH, IT SHOULD BE EASY...
WAIT A MINUTE, MIKA-SAN!
EIRI-SAN...
COME ON...
YOU'RE REALLY GOING TO LEAVE?
Hmmm...

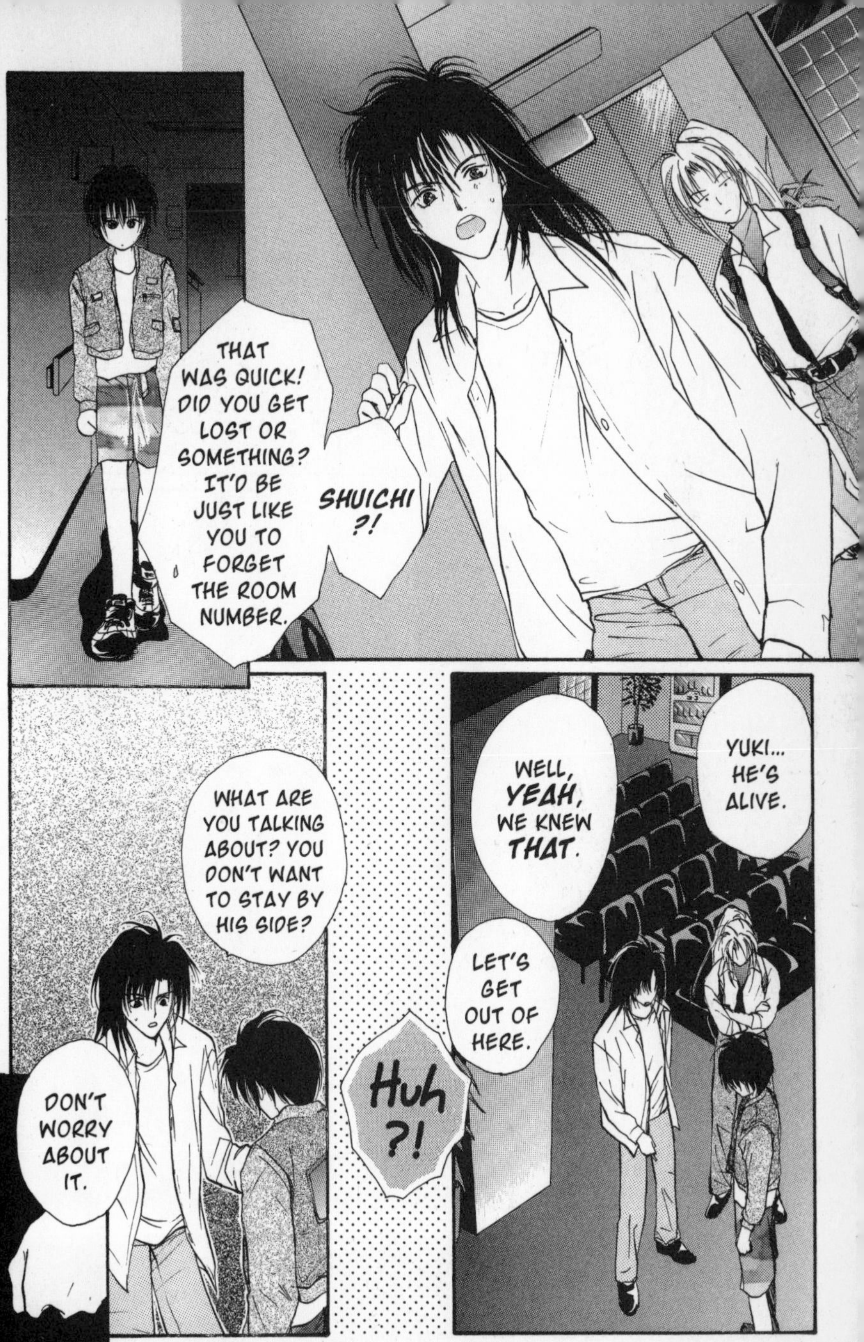

THAT WAS QUICK! DID YOU GET LOST OR SOMETHING? IT'D BE JUST LIKE YOU TO FORGET THE ROOM NUMBER.
SHUICHI ?!
YUKI... HE'S ALIVE.
WELL, YEAH, WE KNEW THAT.
LET'S GET OUT OF HERE.
Huh ?!
WHAT ARE YOU TALKING ABOUT? YOU DON'T WANT TO STAY BY HIS SIDE?
DON'T WORRY ABOUT IT.

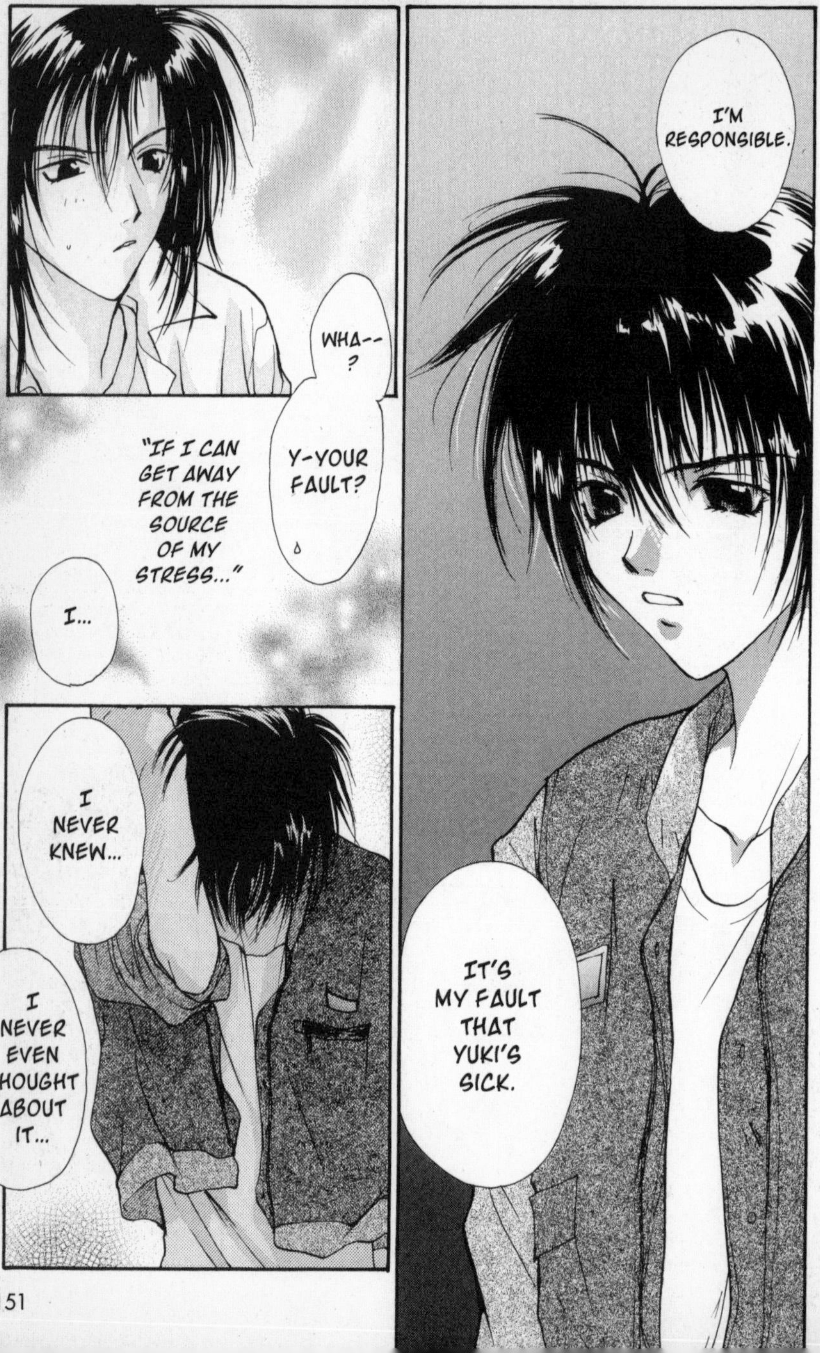
I'M RESPONSIBLE.
IT'S MY FAULT THAT YUKI'S SICK.
WHA--?
Y-YOUR FAULT?
"IF I CAN GET AWAY FROM THE SOURCE OF MY STRESS..."
I...
I NEVER KNEW...
I NEVER EVEN THOUGHT ABOUT IT...

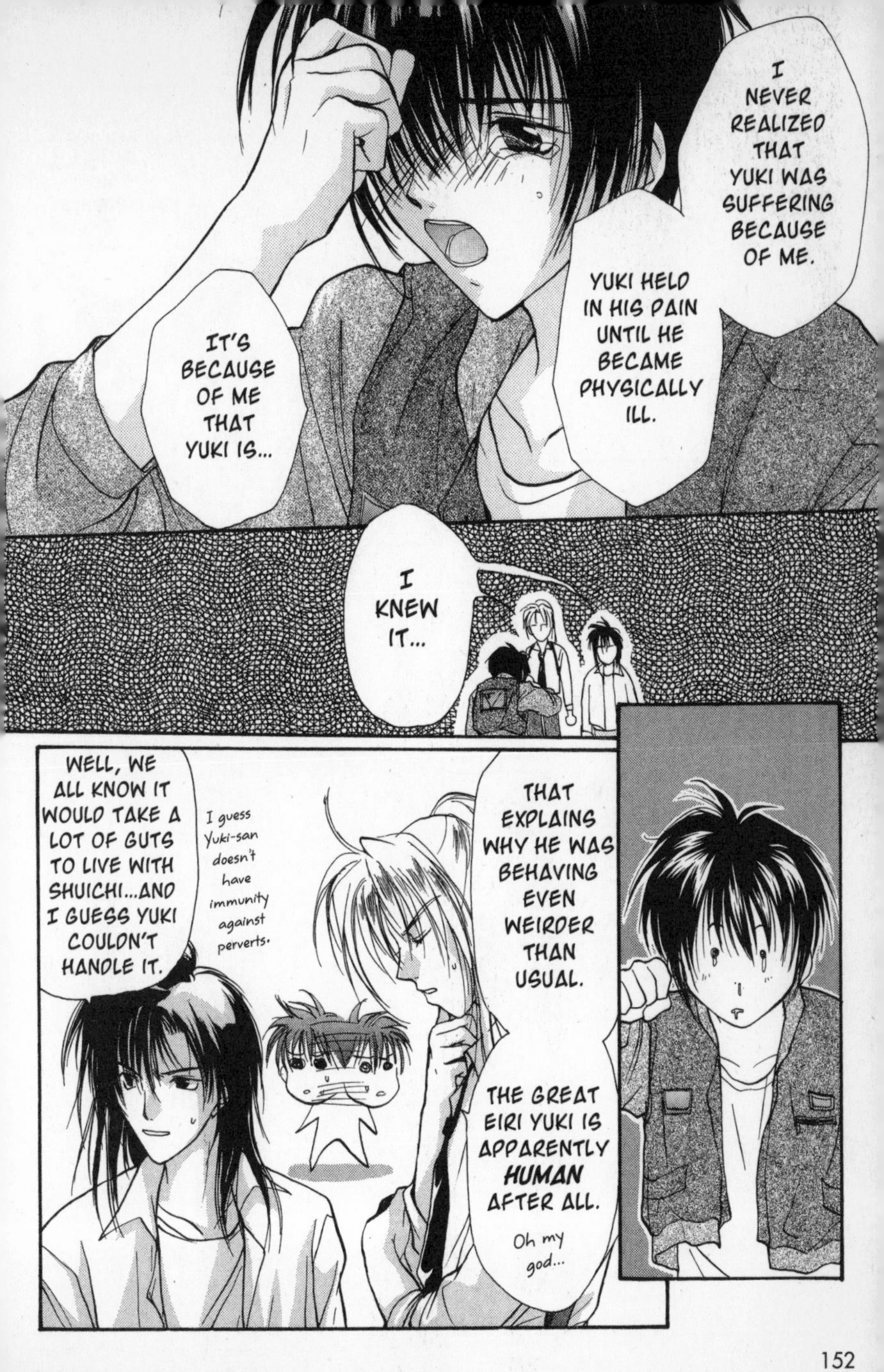
I NEVER REALIZED THAT YUKI WAS SUFFERING BECAUSE OF ME.
YUKI HELD IN HIS PAIN UNTIL HE BECAME PHYSICALLY ILL.
IT'S BECAUSE OF ME THAT YUKI IS...
I KNEW IT...
THAT EXPLAINS WHY HE WAS BEHAVING EVEN WEIRDER THAN USUAL.
THE GREAT EIRI YUKI IS APPARENTLY ***HUMAN*** AFTER ALL.
Oh my god...
WELL, WE ALL KNOW IT WOULD TAKE A LOT OF GUTS TO LIVE WITH SHUICHI...AND I GUESS YUKI COULDN'T HANDLE IT.
I guess Yuki-san doesn't have immunity against perverts.

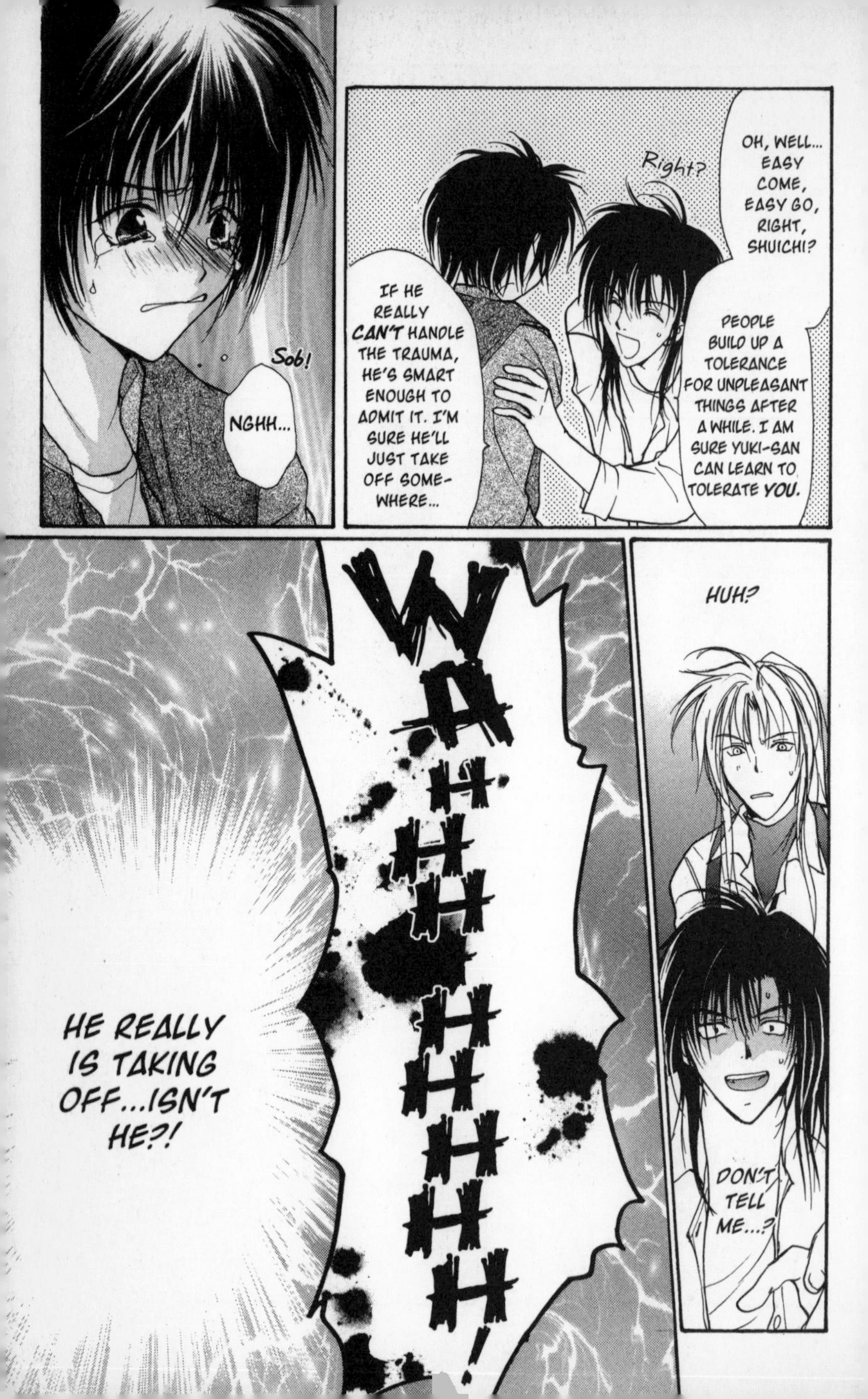
OH, WELL... EASY COME, EASY GO, RIGHT, SHUICHI?
Right?
PEOPLE BUILD UP A TOLERANCE FOR UNPLEASANT THINGS AFTER A WHILE. I AM SURE YUKI-SAN CAN LEARN TO TOLERATE YOU.
IF HE REALLY CAN'T HANDLE THE TRAUMA, HE'S SMART ENOUGH TO ADMIT IT. I'M SURE HE'LL JUST TAKE OFF SOME-WHERE...
Sob!
NGHH...
HUH?
DON'T TELL ME...?
WAHHHHHHHHHH!
HE REALLY IS TAKING OFF...ISN'T HE?!

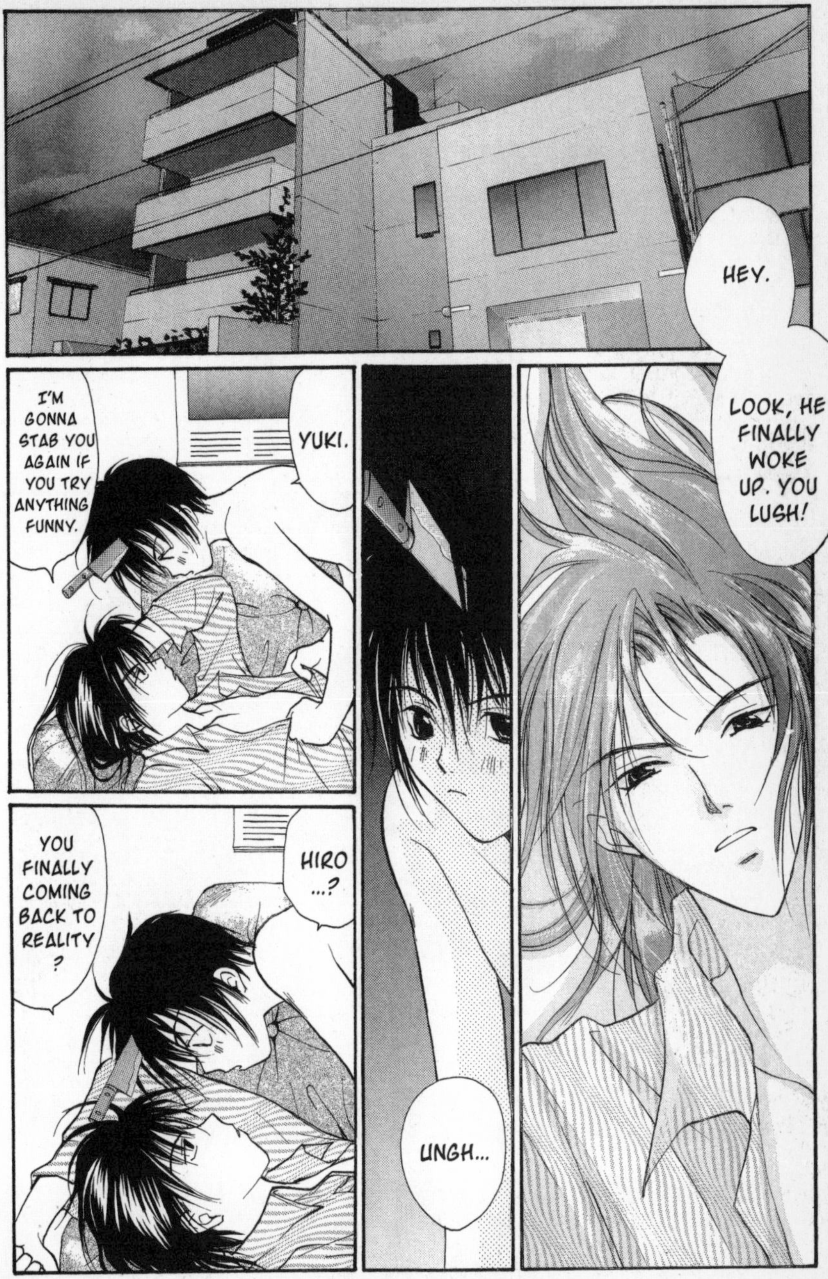
HEY.
LOOK, HE FINALLY WOKE UP. YOU LUSH!
UNGH...
YUKI.
I'M GONNA STAB YOU AGAIN IF YOU TRY ANYTHING FUNNY.
HIRO ...?
YOU FINALLY COMING BACK TO REALITY?

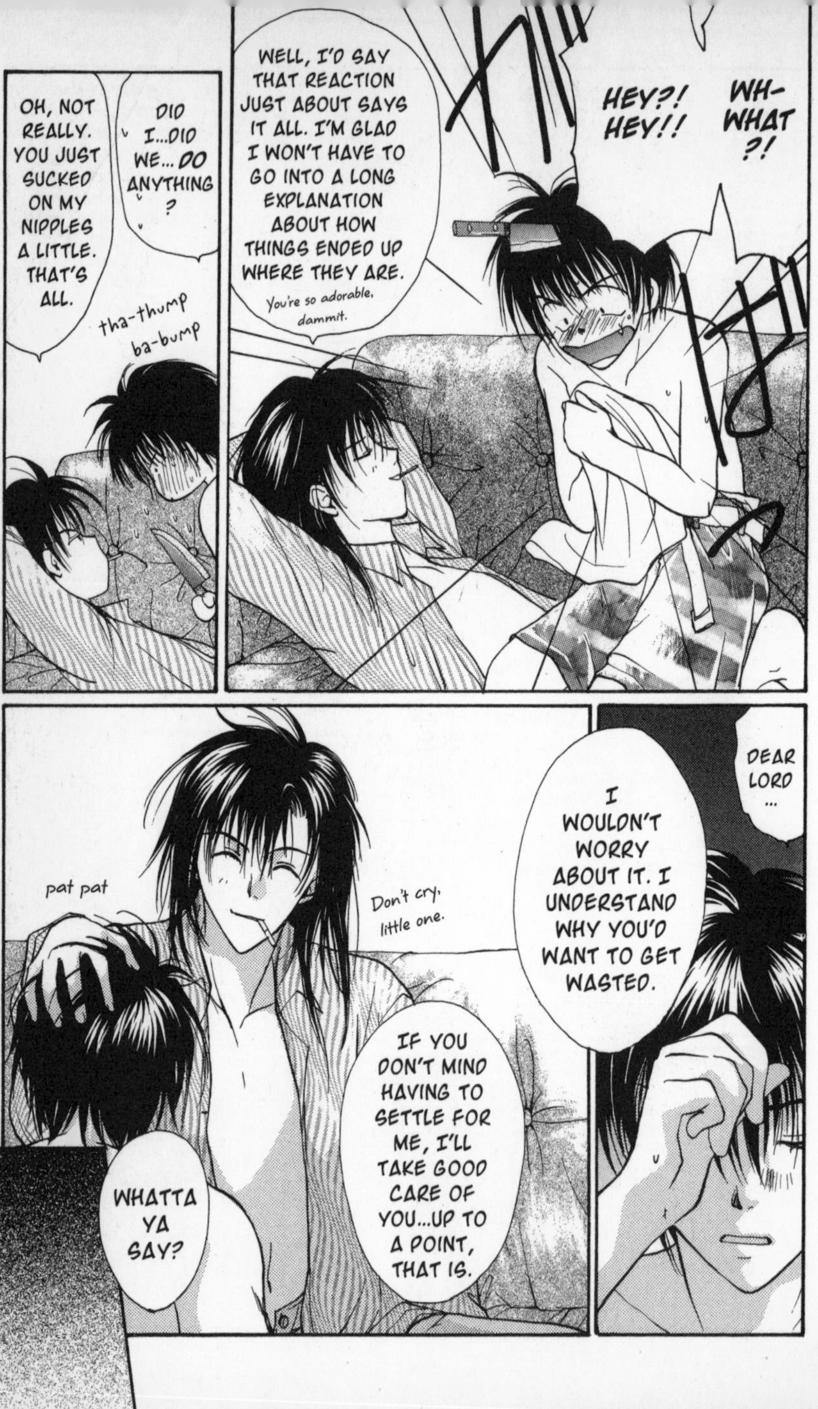
WH- WHAT ?!
HEY?! HEY!!
WELL, I'D SAY THAT REACTION JUST ABOUT SAYS IT ALL. I'M GLAD I WON'T HAVE TO GO INTO A LONG EXPLANATION ABOUT HOW THINGS ENDED UP WHERE THEY ARE.
You're so adorable, dammit.
DID I...DID WE...DO ANYTHING ?
OH, NOT REALLY. YOU JUST SUCKED ON MY NIPPLES A LITTLE. THAT'S ALL.
tha-thump
ba-bump
DEAR LORD ...
I WOULDN'T WORRY ABOUT IT. I UNDERSTAND WHY YOU'D WANT TO GET WASTED.
Don't cry, little one.
pat pat
IF YOU DON'T MIND HAVING TO SETTLE FOR ME, I'LL TAKE GOOD CARE OF YOU...UP TO A POINT, THAT IS.
WHATTA YA SAY?

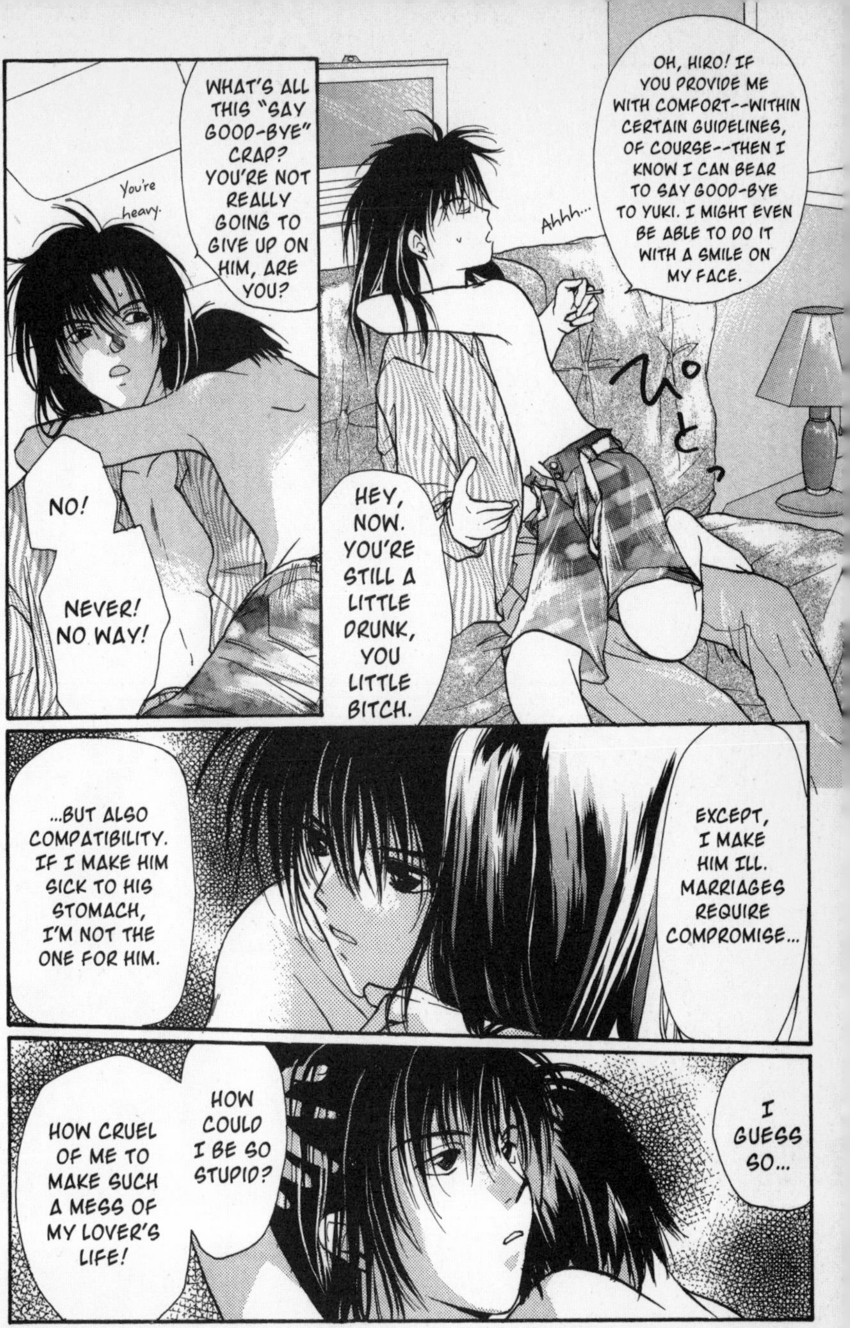
OH, HIRO! IF YOU PROVIDE ME WITH COMFORT--WITHIN CERTAIN GUIDELINES, OF COURSE--THEN I KNOW I CAN BEAR TO SAY GOOD-BYE TO YUKI. I MIGHT EVEN BE ABLE TO DO IT WITH A SMILE ON MY FACE.
Ahhh...
ぴとっ
HEY, NOW. YOU'RE STILL A LITTLE DRUNK, YOU LITTLE BITCH.
WHAT'S ALL THIS "SAY GOOD-BYE" CRAP? YOU'RE NOT REALLY GOING TO GIVE UP ON HIM, ARE YOU?
You're heavy.
NO!
NEVER! NO WAY!
EXCEPT, I MAKE HIM ILL. MARRIAGES REQUIRE COMPROMISE...
...BUT ALSO COMPATIBILITY. IF I MAKE HIM SICK TO HIS STOMACH, I'M NOT THE ONE FOR HIM.
I GUESS SO...
HOW COULD I BE SO STUPID?
HOW CRUEL OF ME TO MAKE SUCH A MESS OF MY LOVER'S LIFE!

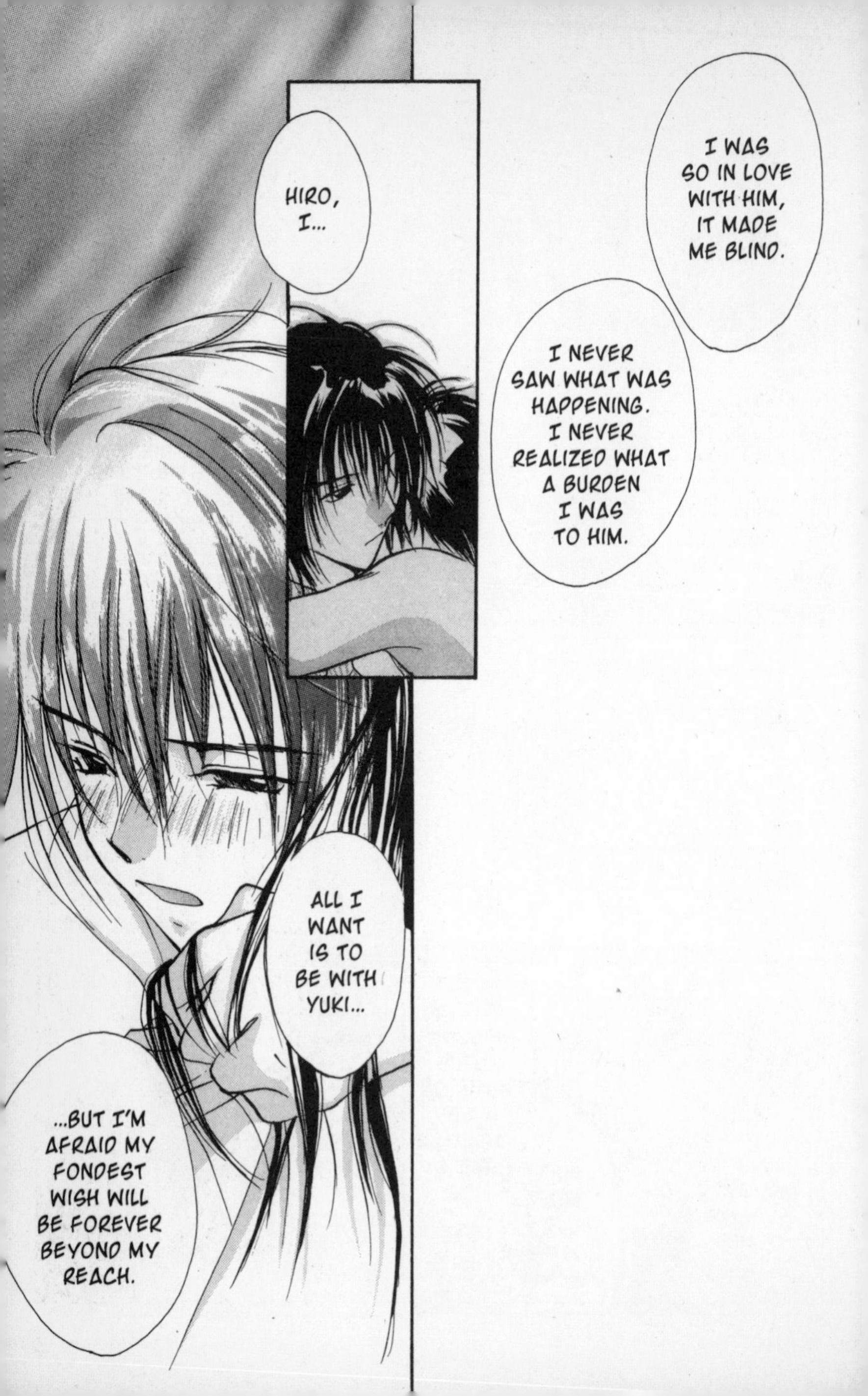
I WAS SO IN LOVE WITH HIM, IT MADE ME BLIND.
I NEVER SAW WHAT WAS HAPPENING. I NEVER REALIZED WHAT A BURDEN I WAS TO HIM.
HIRO, I...
ALL I WANT IS TO BE WITH YUKI...
...BUT I'M AFRAID MY FONDEST WISH WILL BE FOREVER BEYOND MY REACH.

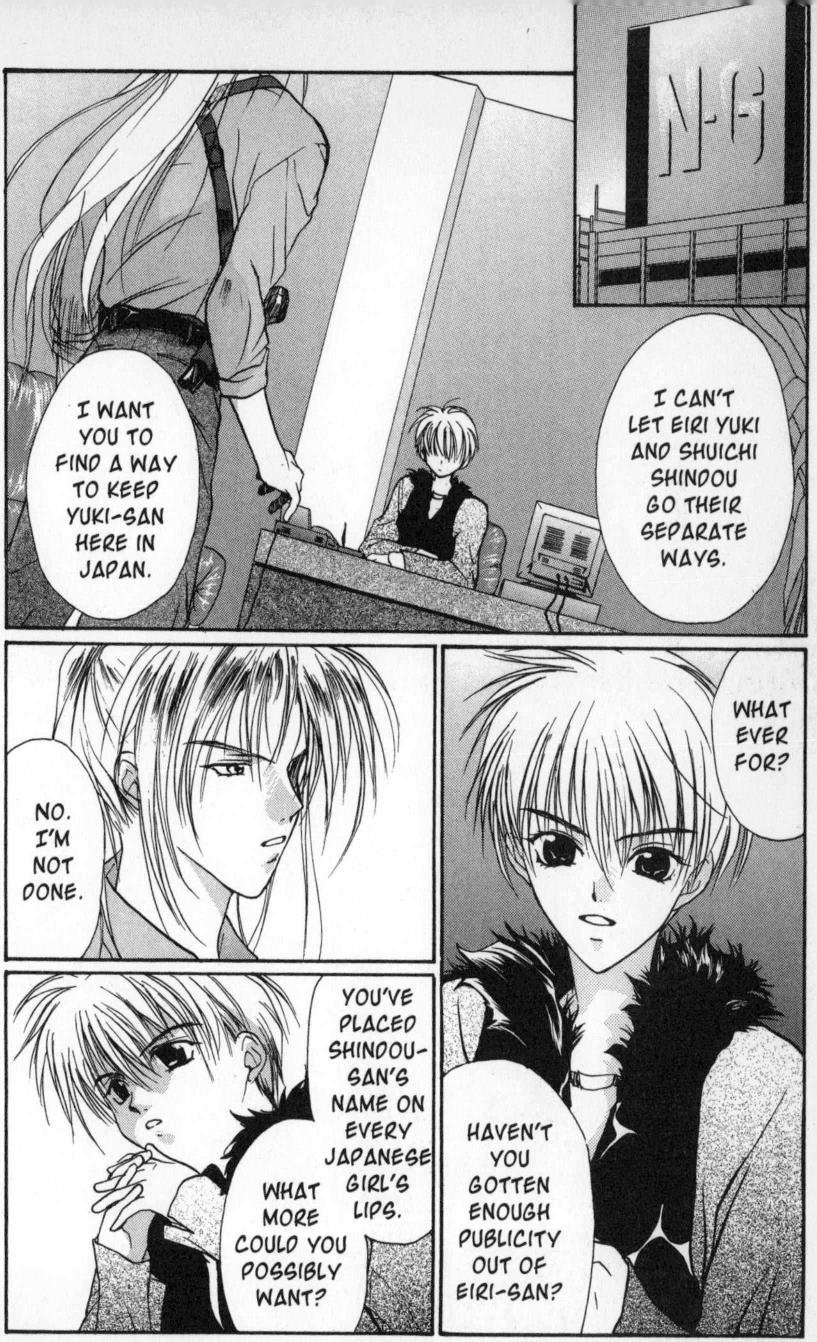
N-G
I CAN'T LET EIRI YUKI AND SHUICHI SHINDOU GO THEIR SEPARATE WAYS.
I WANT YOU TO FIND A WAY TO KEEP YUKI-SAN HERE IN JAPAN.
WHAT EVER FOR?
HAVEN'T YOU GOTTEN ENOUGH PUBLICITY OUT OF EIRI-SAN?
NO. I'M NOT DONE.
YOU'VE PLACED SHINDOU-SAN'S NAME ON EVERY JAPANESE GIRL'S LIPS.
WHAT MORE COULD YOU POSSIBLY WANT?

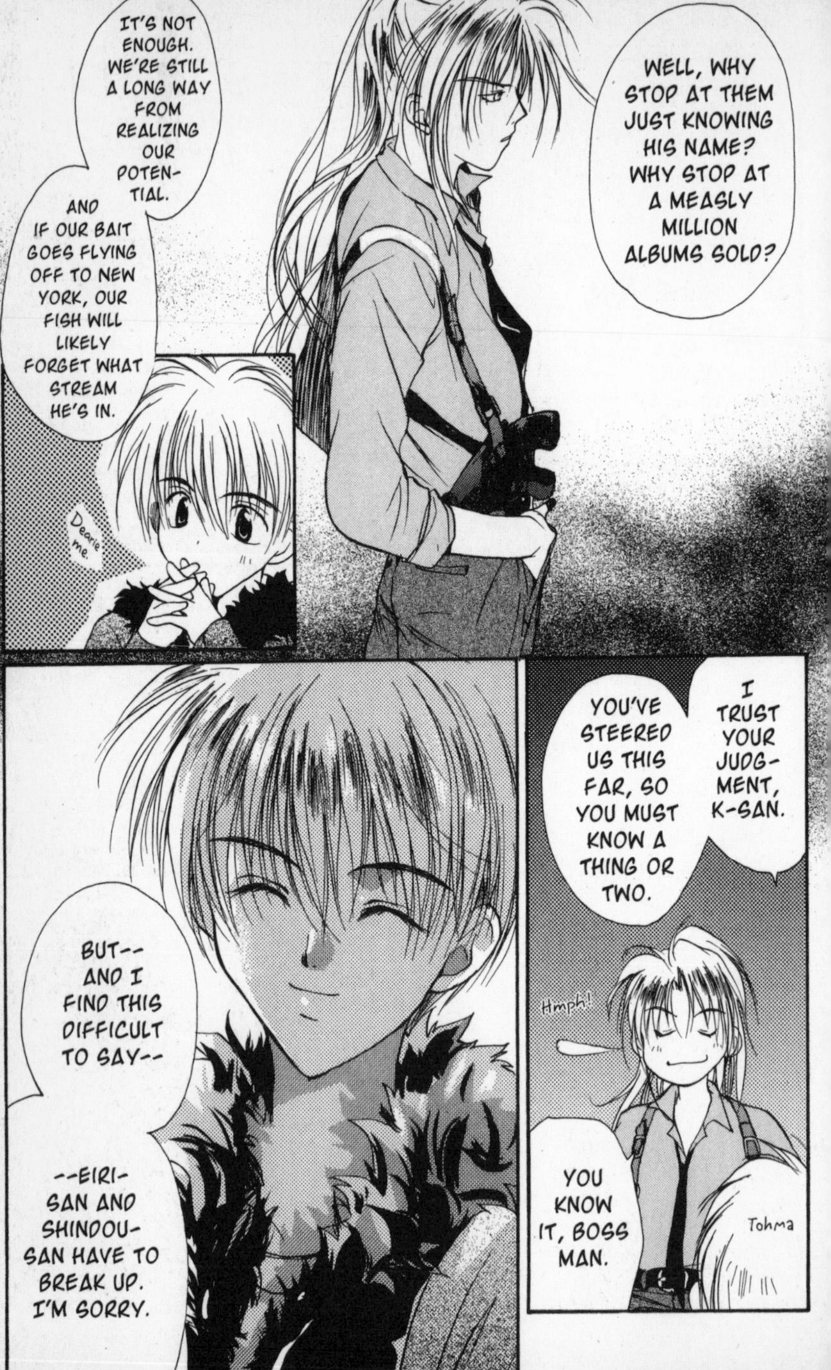
WELL, WHY STOP AT THEM JUST KNOWING HIS NAME? WHY STOP AT A MEASLY MILLION ALBUMS SOLO?
IT'S NOT ENOUGH. WE'RE STILL A LONG WAY FROM REALIZING OUR POTEN-TIAL.
AND IF OUR BAIT GOES FLYING OFF TO NEW YORK, OUR FISH WILL LIKELY FORGET WHAT STREAM HE'S IN.
Dearie me.
I TRUST YOUR JUDG-MENT, K-SAN.
YOU'VE STEERED US THIS FAR, SO YOU MUST KNOW A THING OR TWO.
Hmph!
YOU KNOW IT, BOSS MAN.
Tohma
BUT-- AND I FIND THIS DIFFICULT TO SAY--
--EIRI-SAN AND SHINDOU-SAN HAVE TO BREAK UP. I'M SORRY.

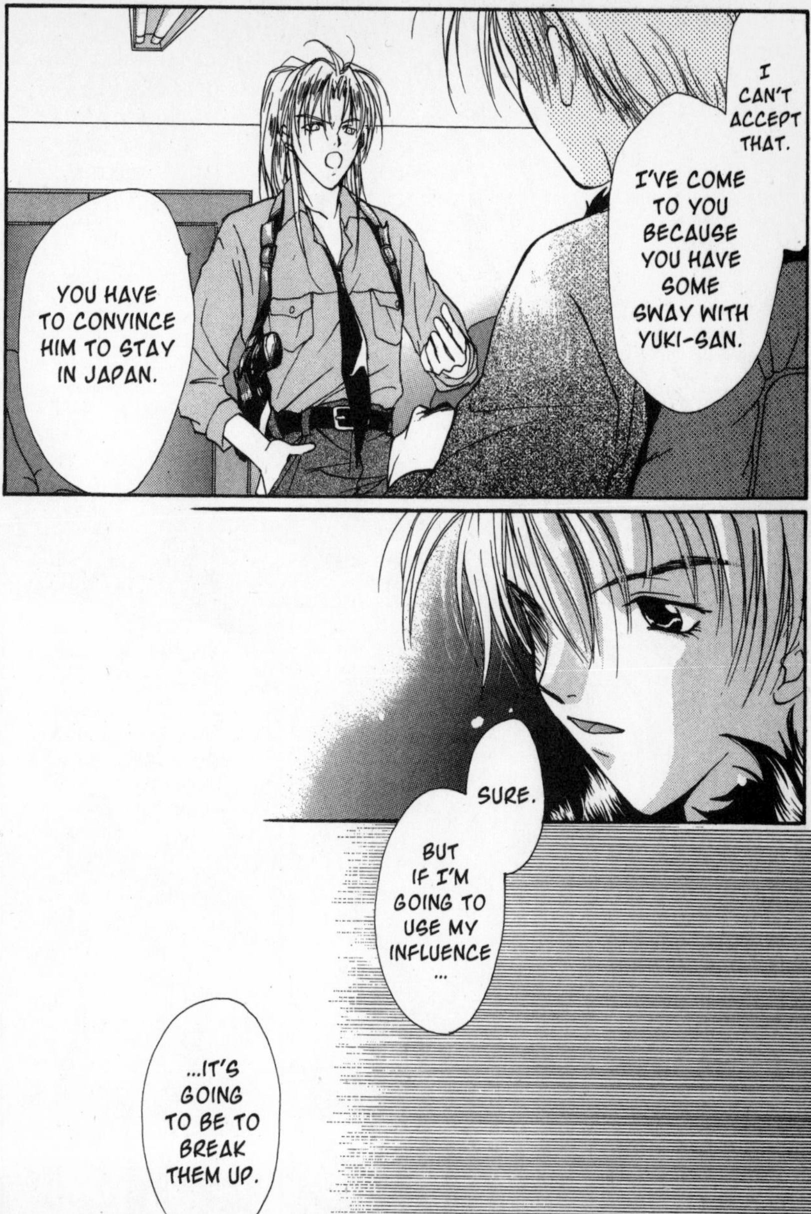
I CAN'T ACCEPT THAT.
I'VE COME TO YOU BECAUSE YOU HAVE SOME SWAY WITH YUKI-SAN.
YOU HAVE TO CONVINCE HIM TO STAY IN JAPAN.
SURE.
BUT IF I'M GOING TO USE MY INFLUENCE ...
...IT'S GOING TO BE TO BREAK THEM UP.

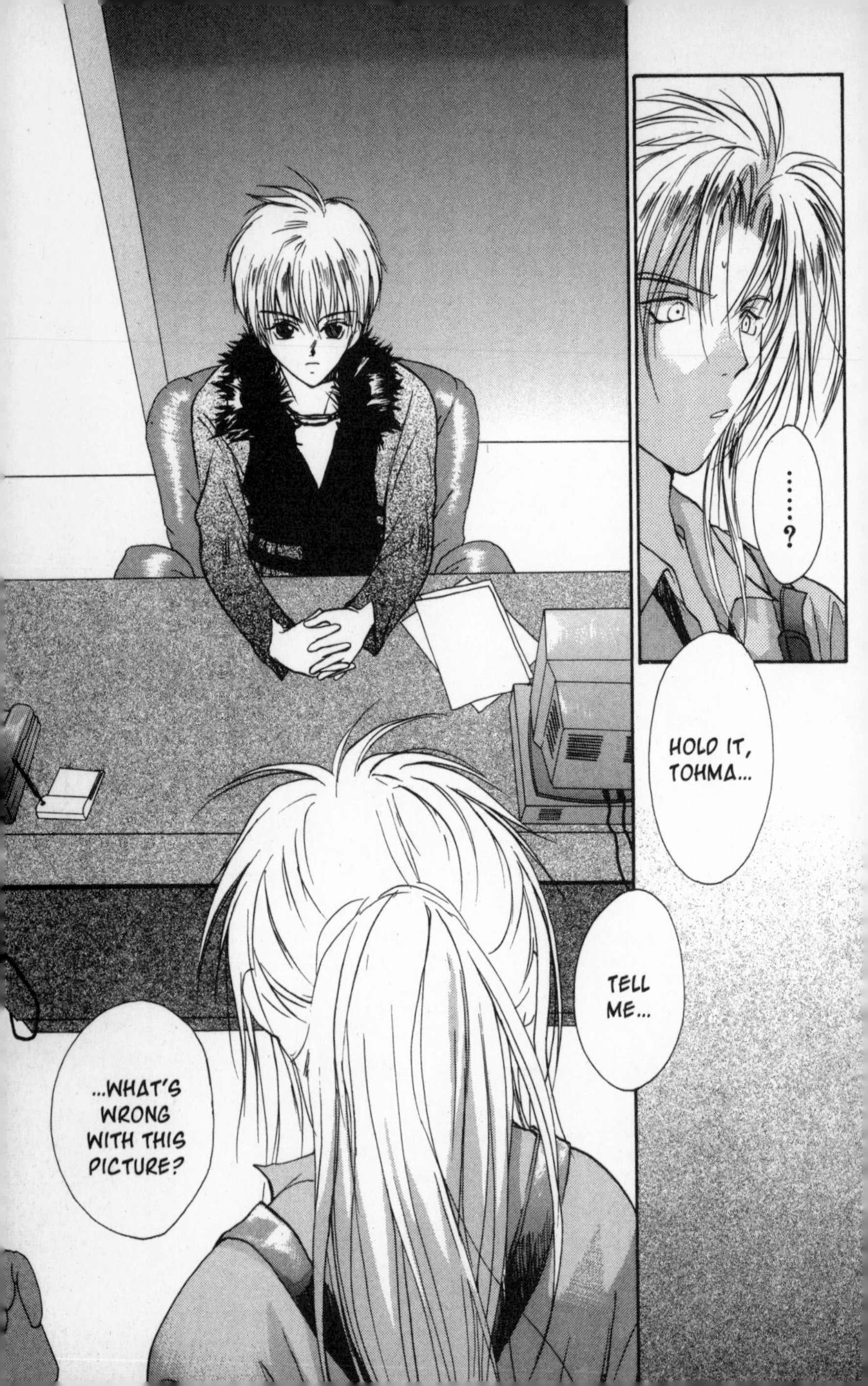
......?
HOLD IT, TOHMA...
TELL ME...
...WHAT'S WRONG WITH THIS PICTURE?

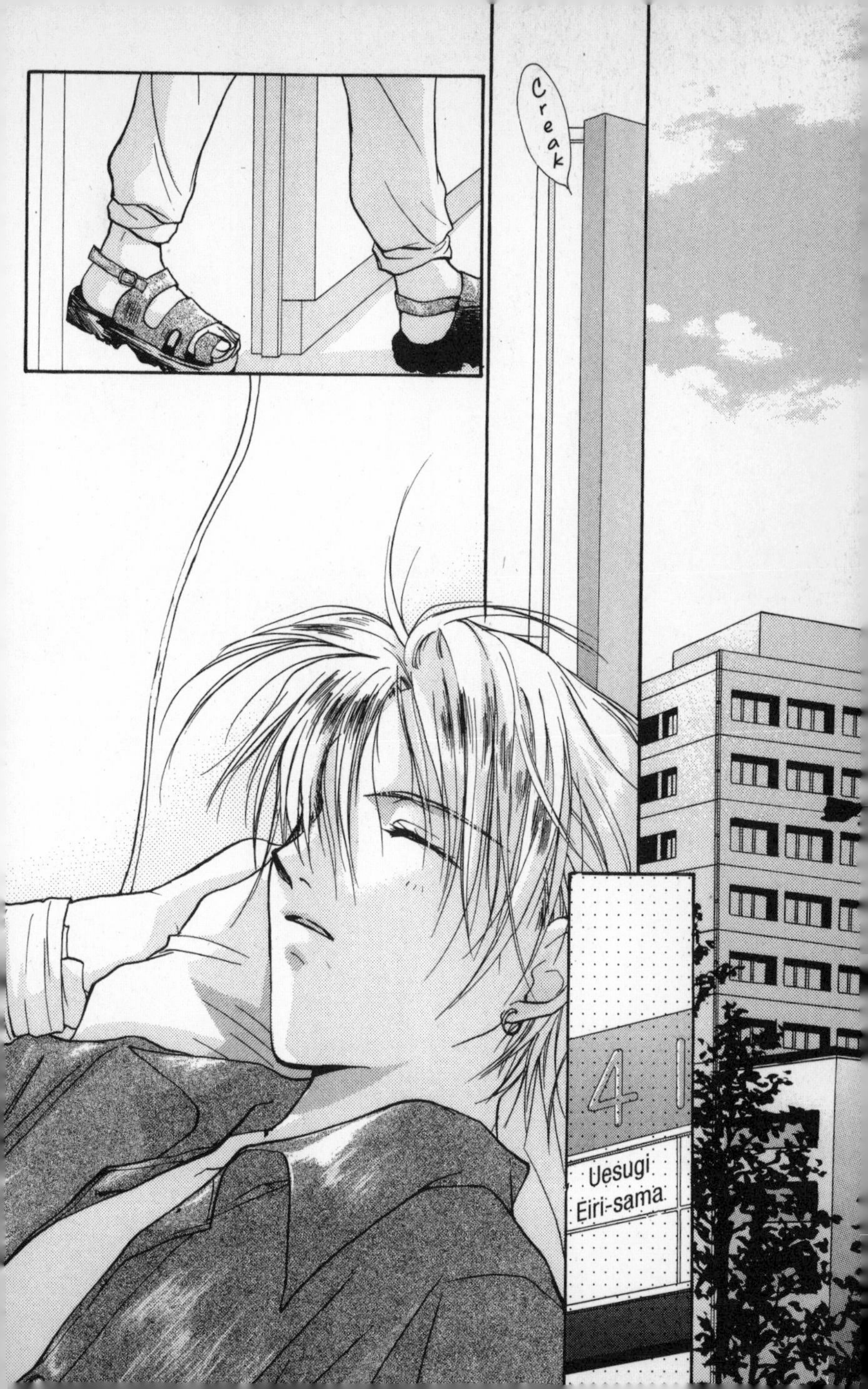
Creak
4
Uesugi
Eiri-sama

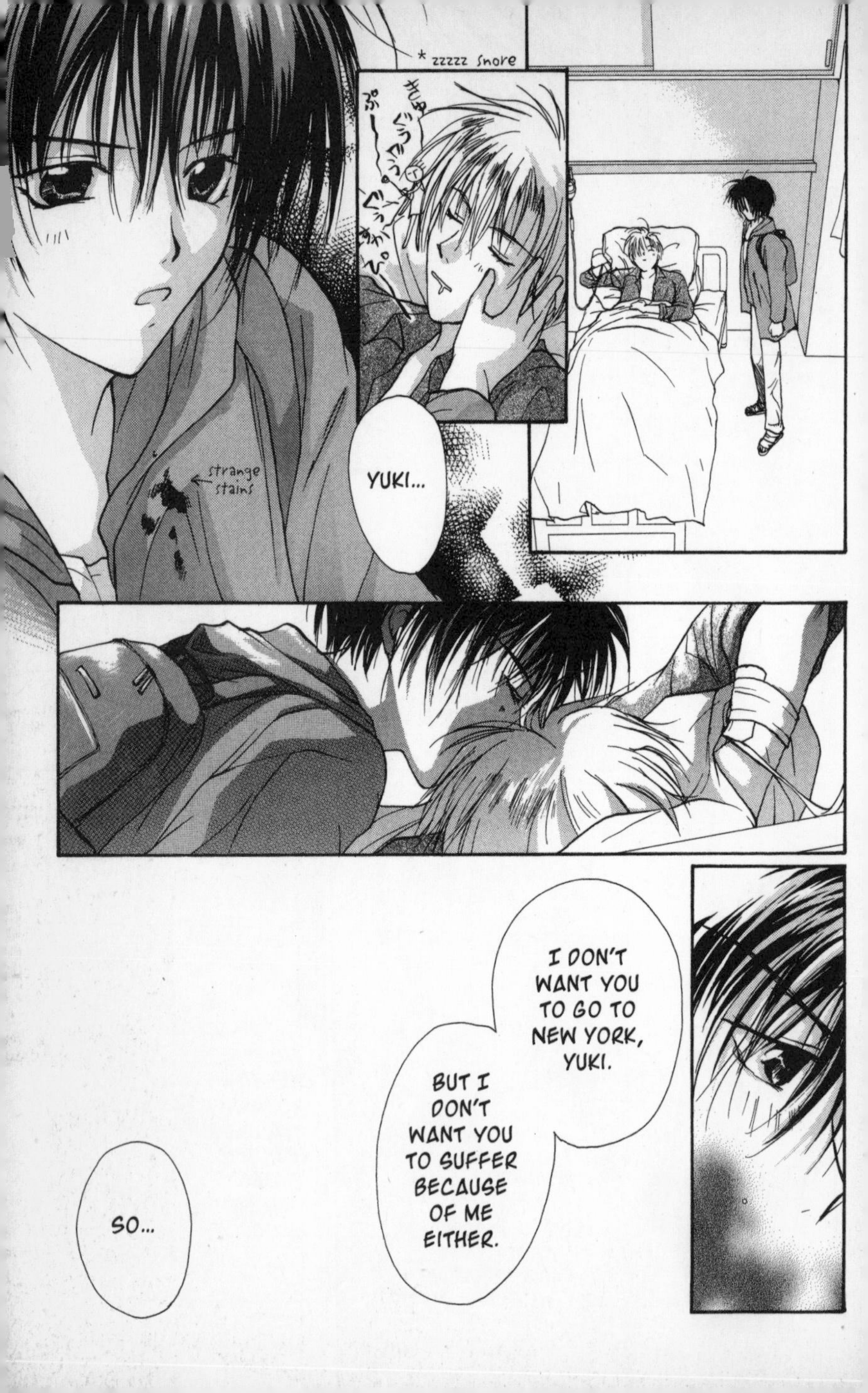
* zzzzz snore
strange stains
YUKI...
I DON'T WANT YOU TO GO TO NEW YORK, YUKI.
BUT I DON'T WANT YOU TO SUFFER BECAUSE OF ME EITHER.
SO...

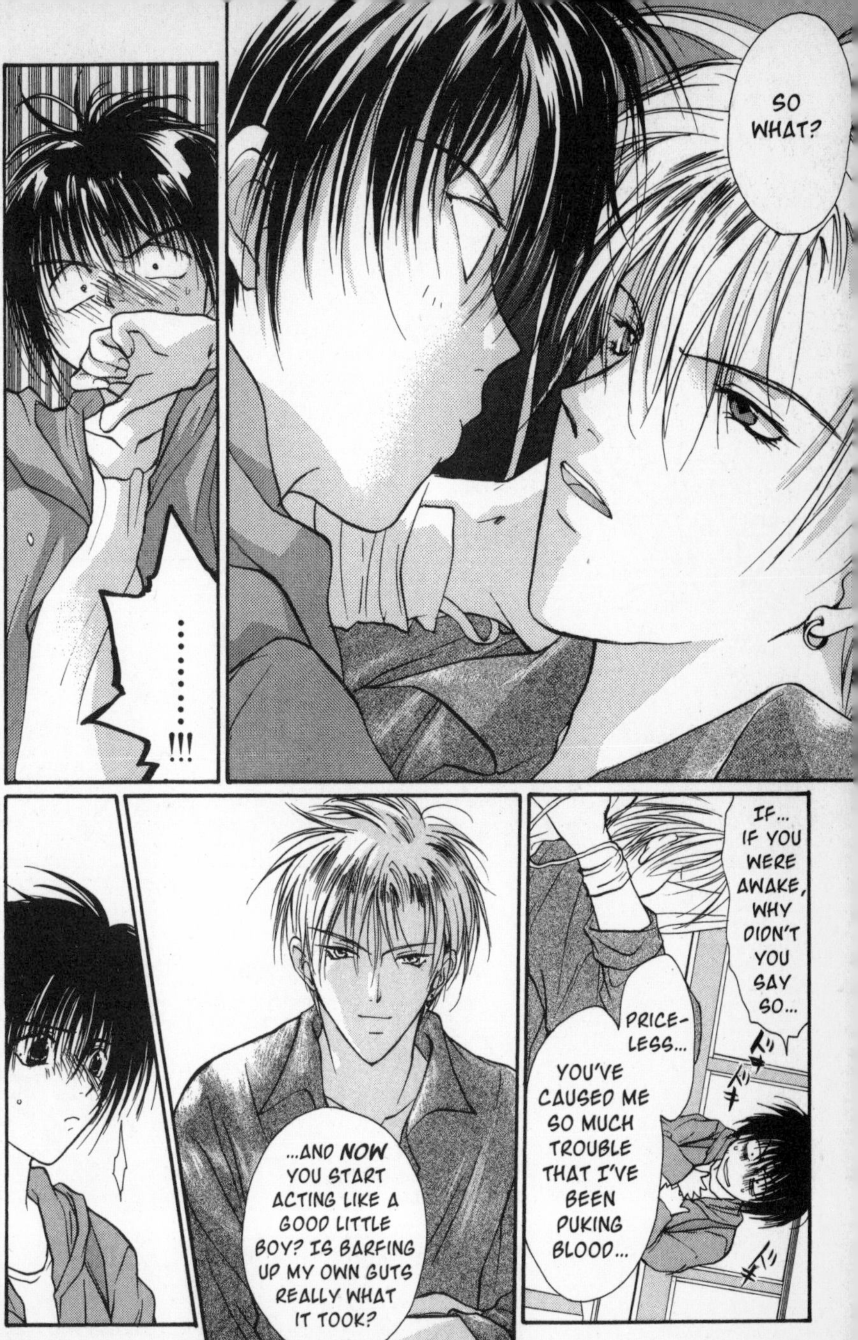
SO WHAT?
......!!!
IF... IF YOU WERE AWAKE, WHY DIDN'T YOU SAY SO...
PRICE-LESS... YOU'VE CAUSED ME SO MUCH TROUBLE THAT I'VE BEEN PUKING BLOOD...
...AND **NOW** YOU START ACTING LIKE A GOOD LITTLE BOY? IS BARFING UP MY OWN GUTS REALLY WHAT IT TOOK?

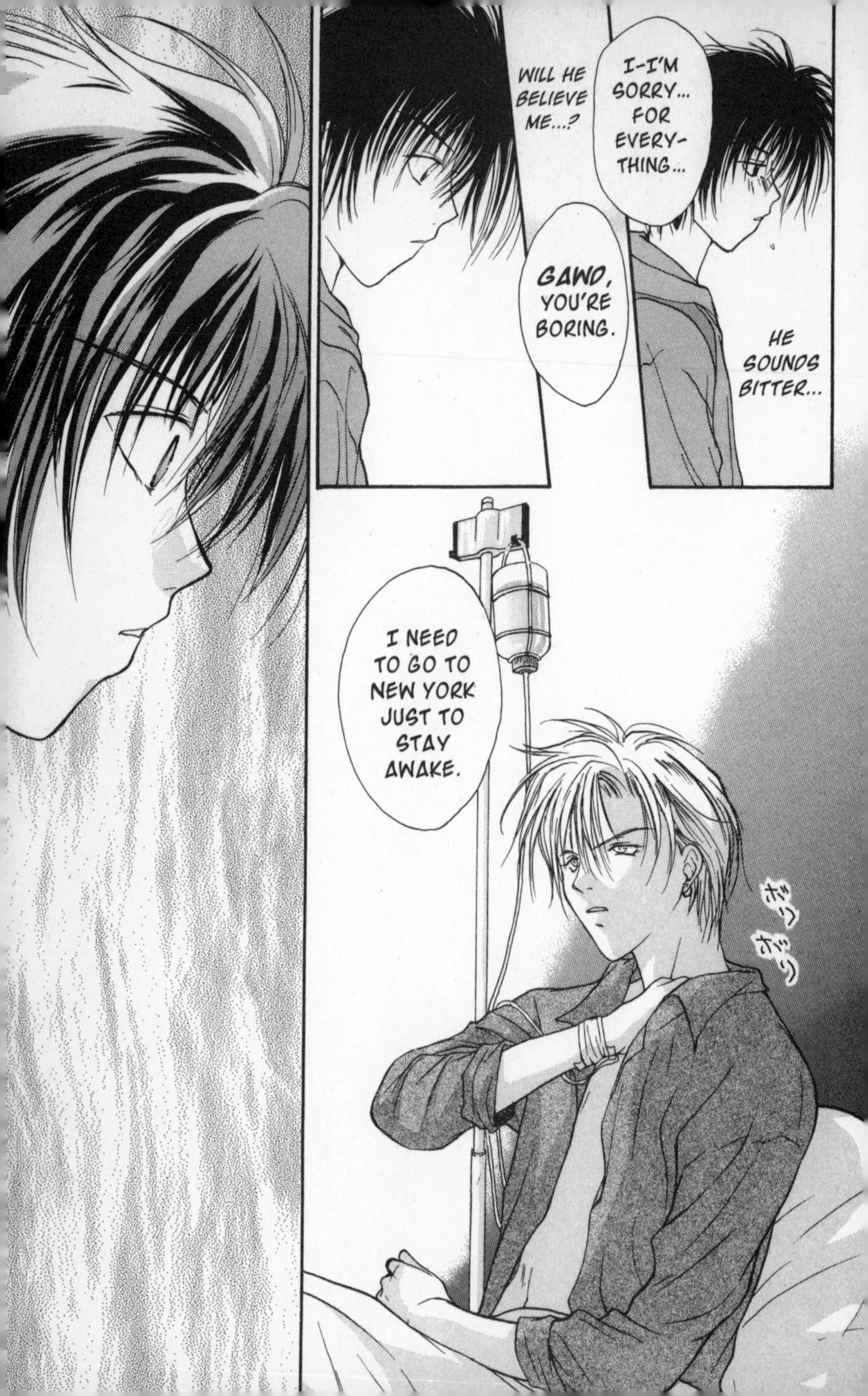
I-I'M SORRY... FOR EVERYTHING...
WILL HE BELIEVE ME...?
GAWD, YOU'RE BORING.
HE SOUNDS BITTER...
I NEED TO GO TO NEW YORK JUST TO STAY AWAKE.
ボリ ボリ

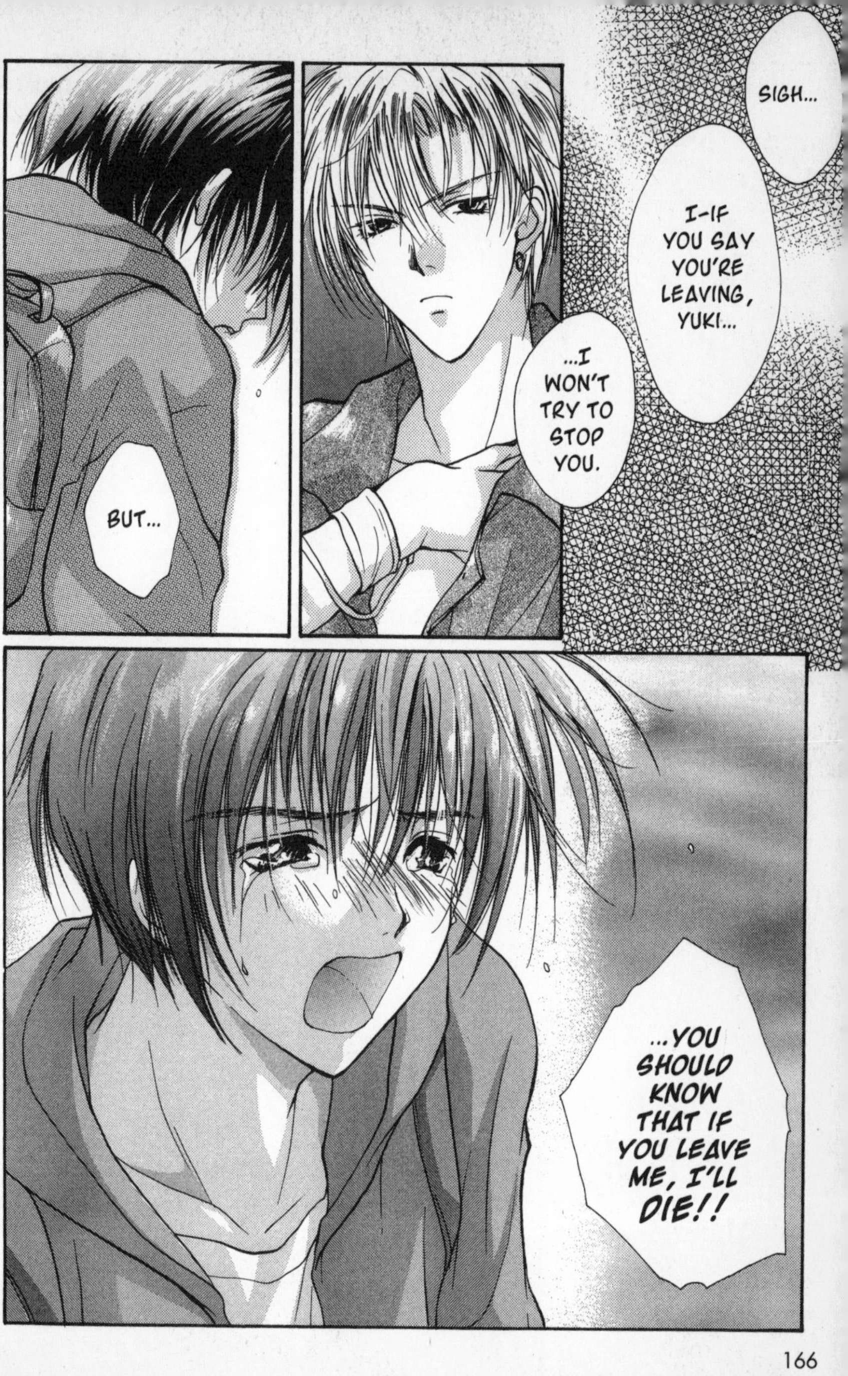
SIGH...
I-IF YOU SAY YOU'RE LEAVING, YUKI...
...I WON'T TRY TO STOP YOU.
BUT...
...YOU SHOULD KNOW THAT IF YOU LEAVE ME, I'LL DIE!!

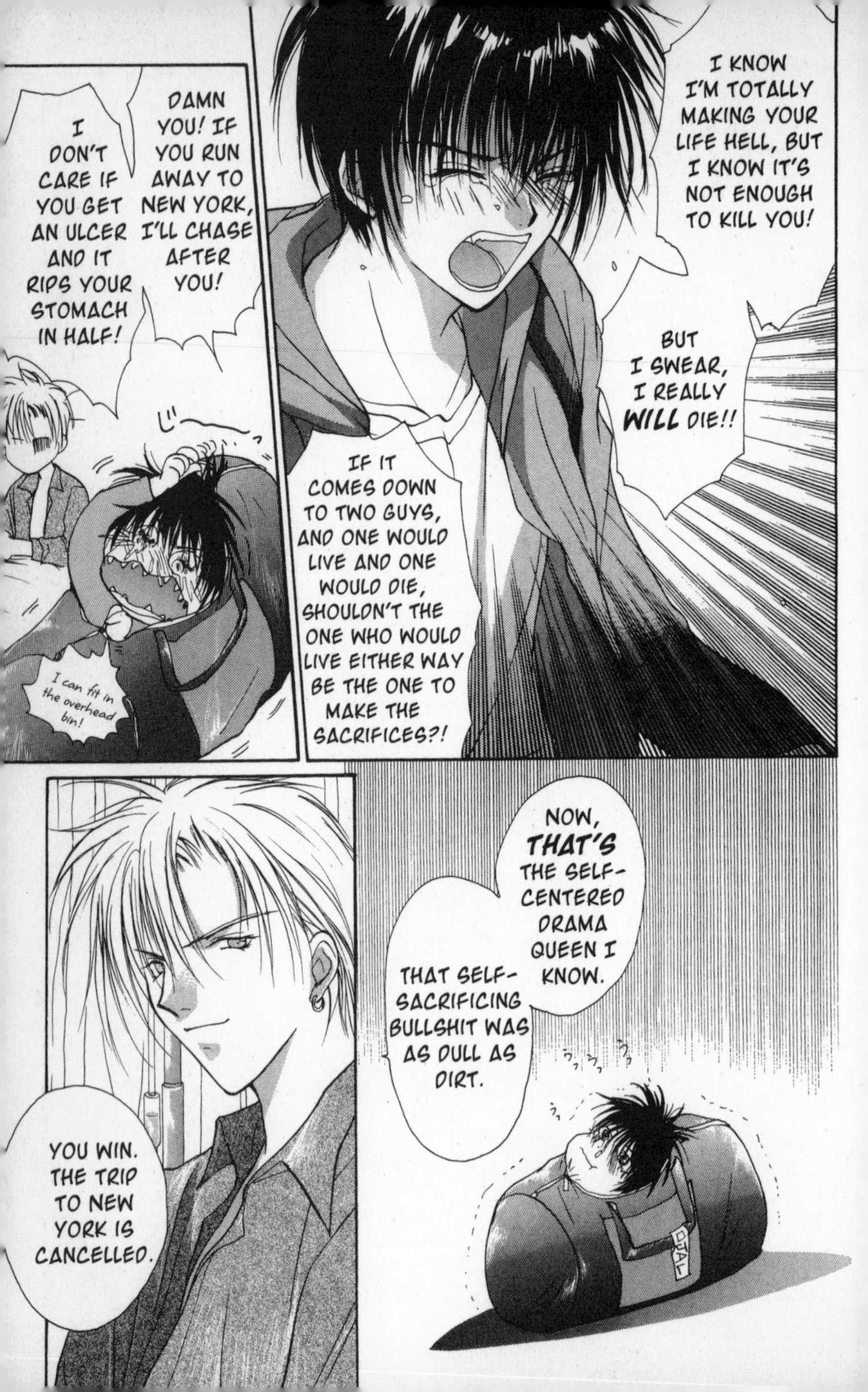
I KNOW I'M TOTALLY MAKING YOUR LIFE HELL, BUT I KNOW IT'S NOT ENOUGH TO KILL YOU!
BUT I SWEAR, I REALLY **WILL** DIE!!
IF IT COMES DOWN TO TWO GUYS, AND ONE WOULD LIVE AND ONE WOULD DIE, SHOULDN'T THE ONE WHO WOULD LIVE EITHER WAY BE THE ONE TO MAKE THE SACRIFICES?!
DAMN YOU! IF YOU RUN AWAY TO NEW YORK, I'LL CHASE AFTER YOU!
I DON'T CARE IF YOU GET AN ULCER AND IT RIPS YOUR STOMACH IN HALF!
I can fit in the overhead bin!
NOW, **THAT'S** THE SELF-CENTERED DRAMA QUEEN I KNOW.
THAT SELF-SACRIFICING BULLSHIT WAS AS DULL AS DIRT.
YOU WIN. THE TRIP TO NEW YORK IS CANCELLED.

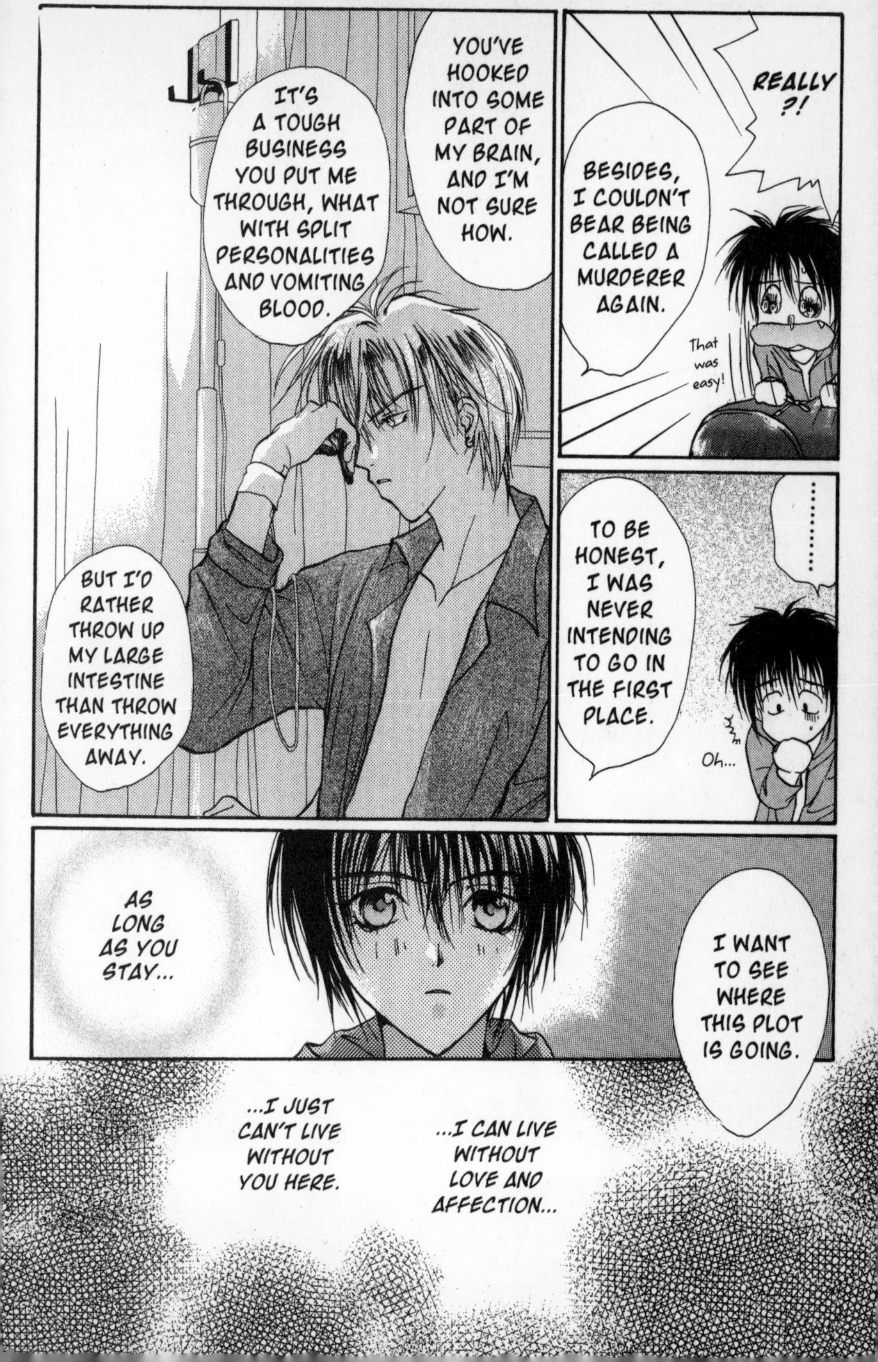
REALLY ?!
BESIDES, I COULDN'T BEAR BEING CALLED A MURDERER AGAIN.
That was easy!
......
TO BE HONEST, I WAS NEVER INTENDING TO GO IN THE FIRST PLACE.
Oh...
YOU'VE HOOKED INTO SOME PART OF MY BRAIN, AND I'M NOT SURE HOW.
IT'S A TOUGH BUSINESS YOU PUT ME THROUGH, WHAT WITH SPLIT PERSONALITIES AND VOMITING BLOOD.
BUT I'D RATHER THROW UP MY LARGE INTESTINE THAN THROW EVERYTHING AWAY.
I WANT TO SEE WHERE THIS PLOT IS GOING.
AS LONG AS YOU STAY...
...I CAN LIVE WITHOUT LOVE AND AFFECTION...
...I JUST CAN'T LIVE WITHOUT YOU HERE.

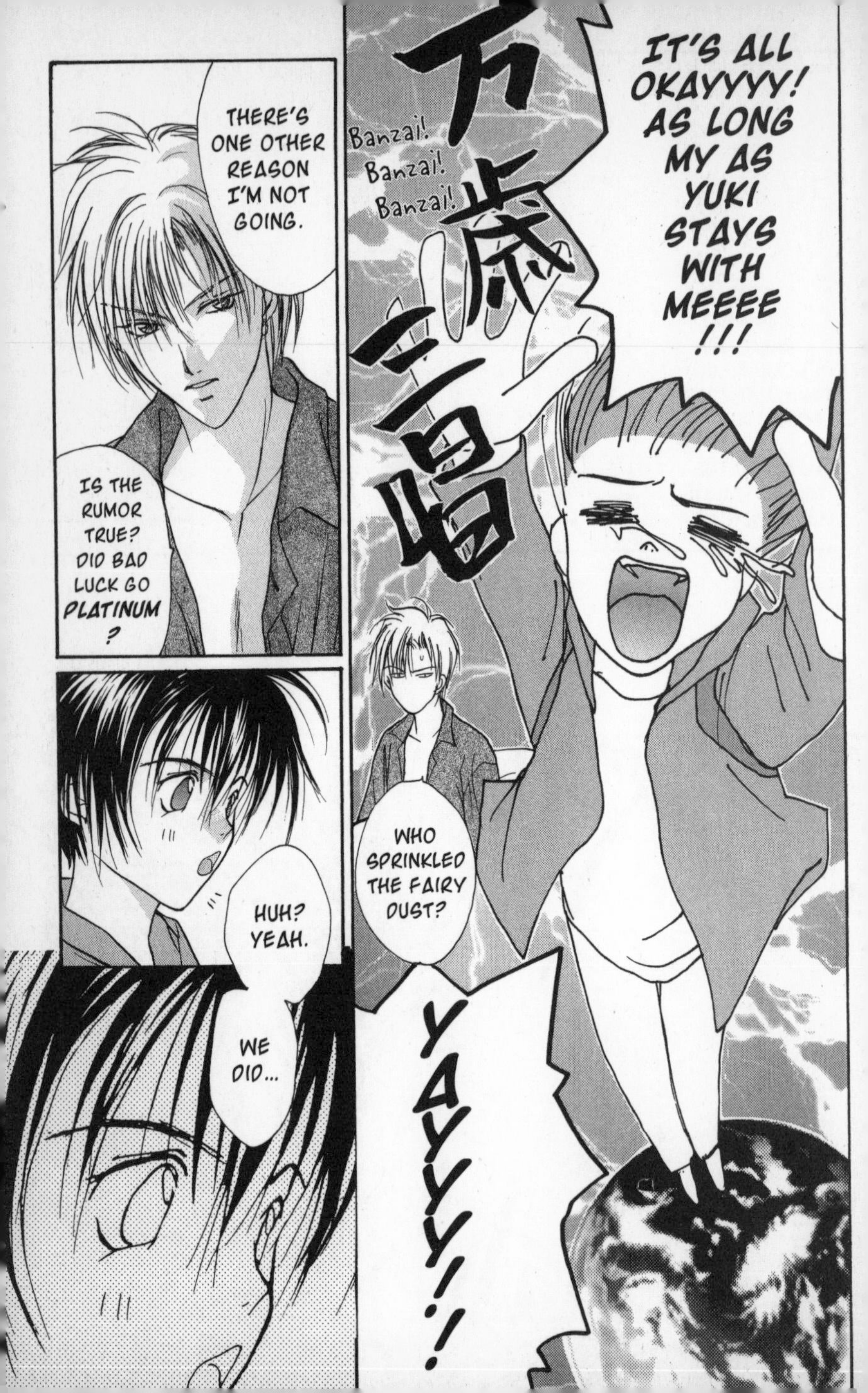
IT'S ALL OKAYYYY! AS LONG MY AS YUKI STAYS WITH MEEEE!!!
万歳三唱
Banzai! Banzai! Banzai!
YAYYYY!!!
WHO SPRINKLED THE FAIRY DUST?
THERE'S ONE OTHER REASON I'M NOT GOING.
IS THE RUMOR TRUE? DID BAD LUCK GO PLATINUM?
HUH? YEAH.
WE DID...

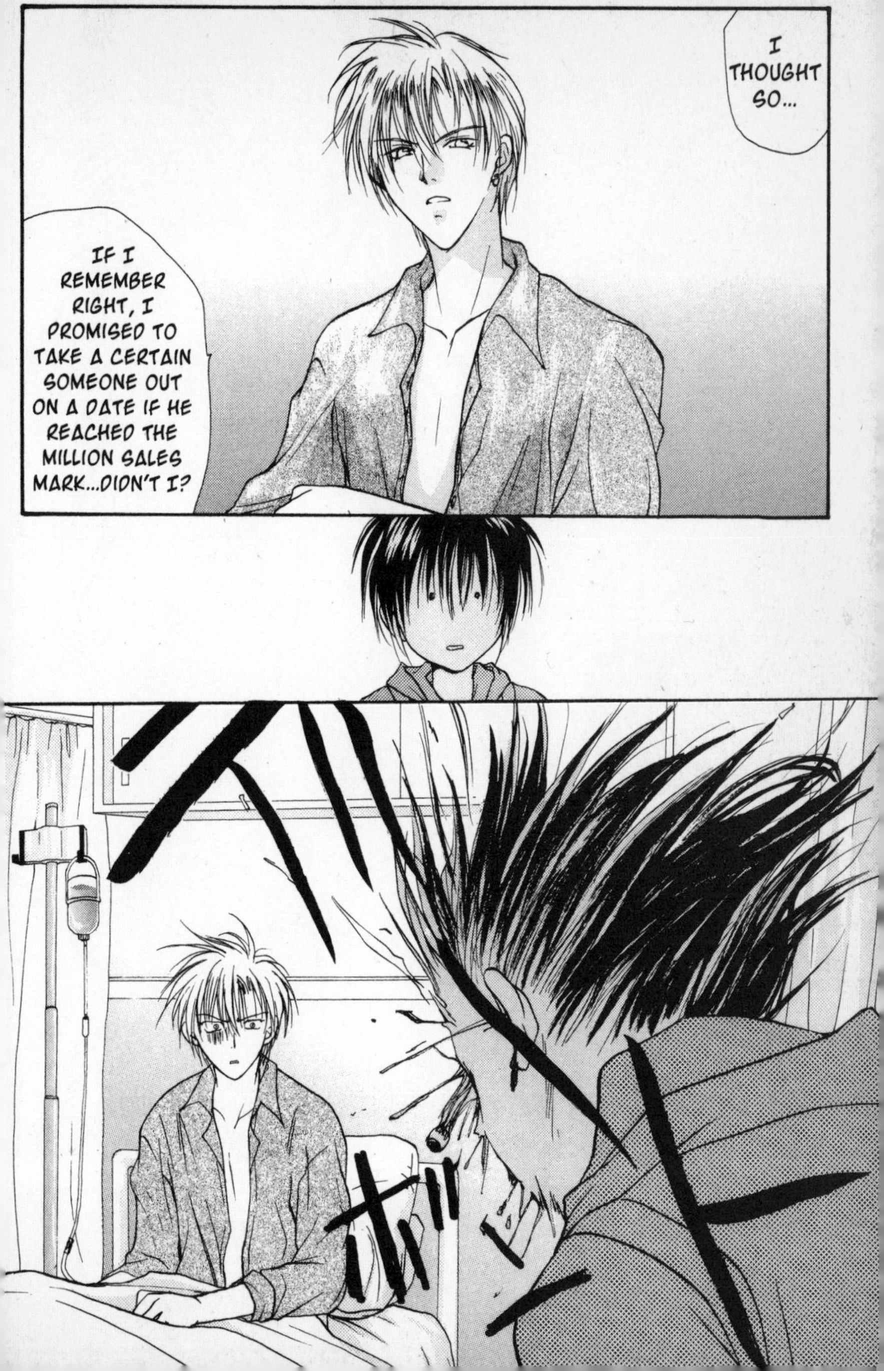
I THOUGHT SO...
IF I REMEMBER RIGHT, I PROMISED TO TAKE A CERTAIN SOMEONE OUT ON A DATE IF HE REACHED THE MILLION SALES MARK...DIDN'T I?

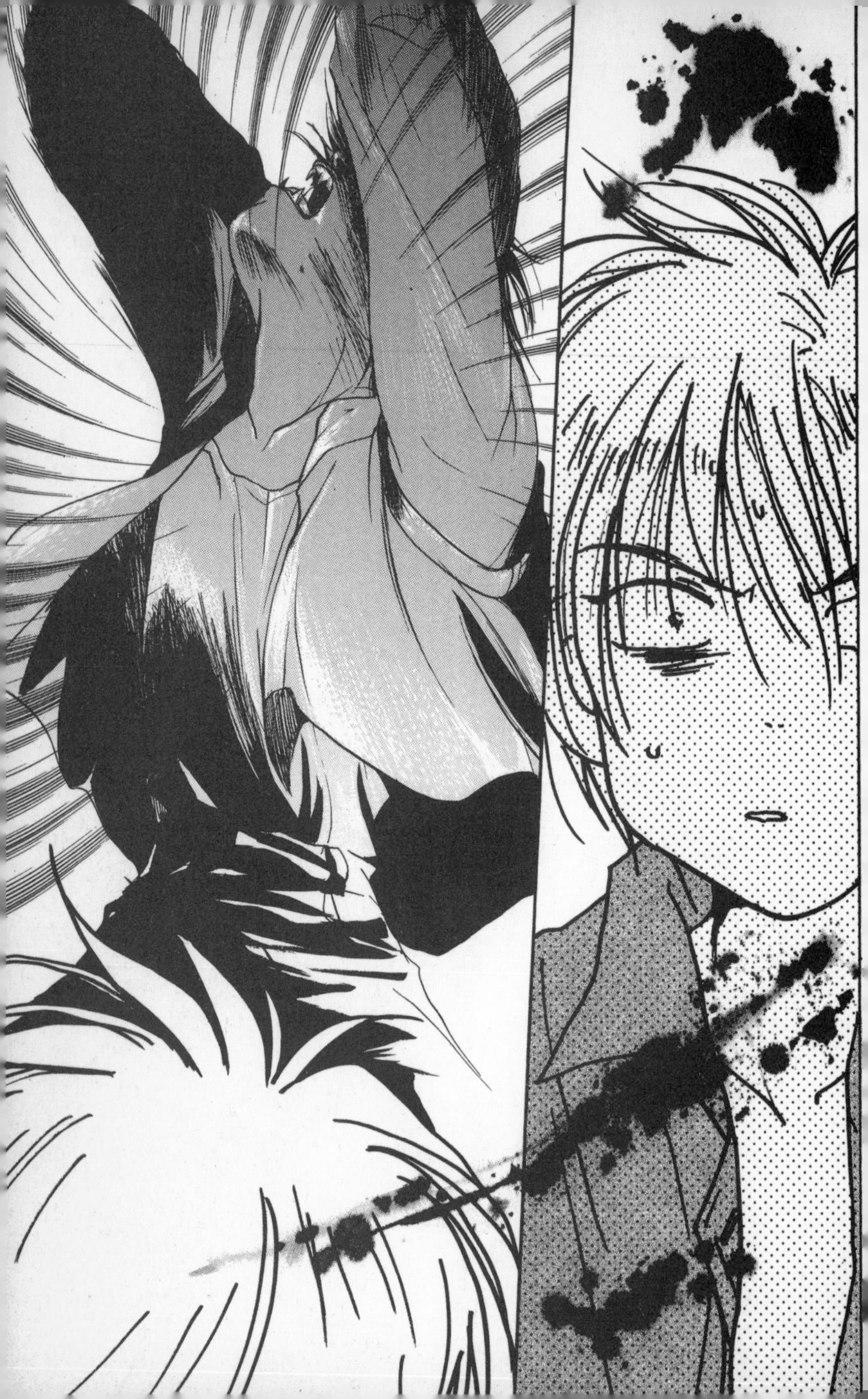

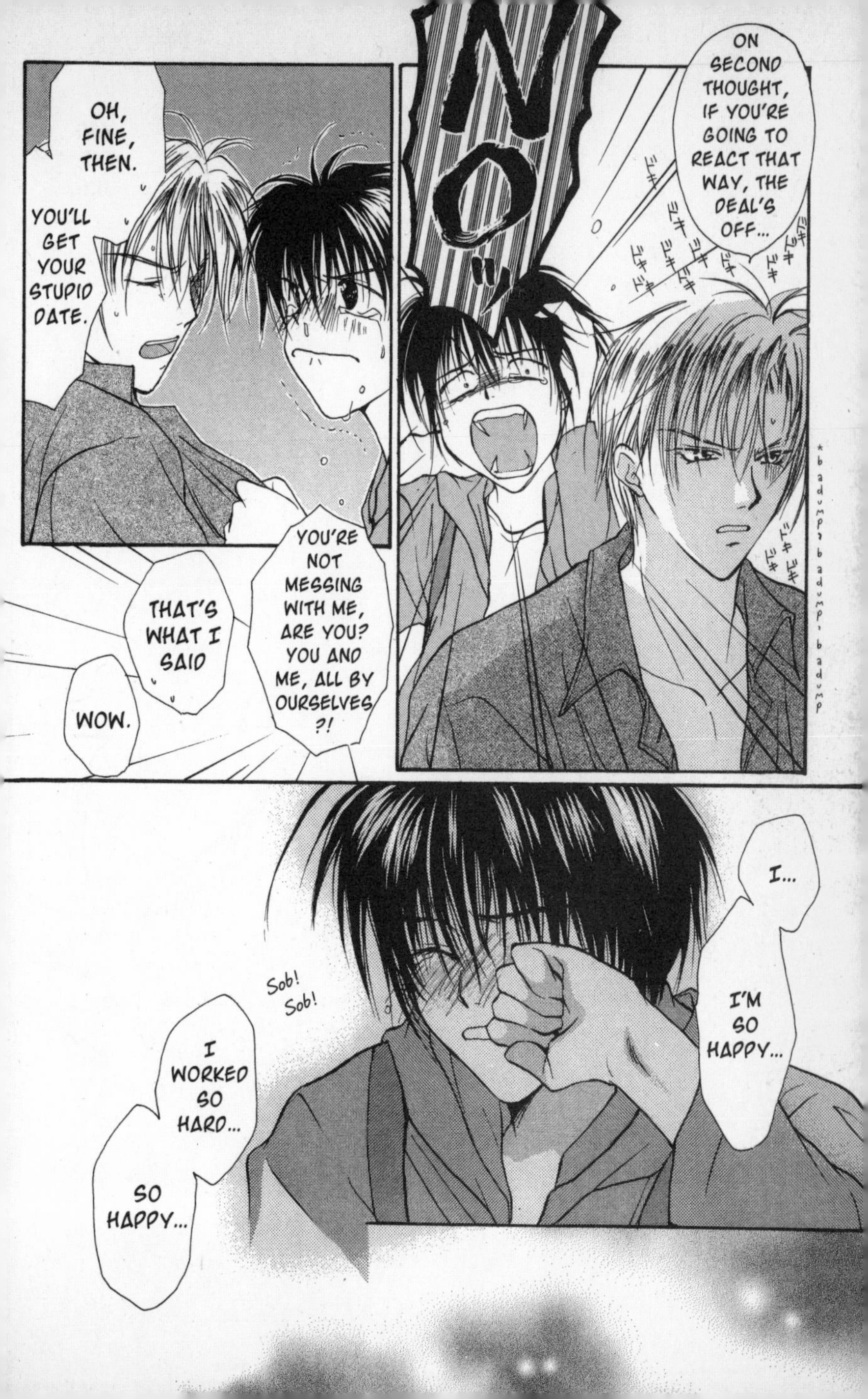
NO
ON SECOND THOUGHT, IF YOU'RE GOING TO REACT THAT WAY, THE DEAL'S OFF...
ドキ ドキ ドキ ドキ ドキ ドキ ドキ ドキ
ドキ ドキ ドキ ドキ
*badump badump badump
OH, FINE, THEN.
YOU'LL GET YOUR STUPID DATE.
YOU'RE NOT MESSING WITH ME, ARE YOU? YOU AND ME, ALL BY OURSELVES?!
THAT'S WHAT I SAID
WOW.
I...
I'M SO HAPPY...
Sob! Sob!
I WORKED SO HARD...
SO HAPPY...

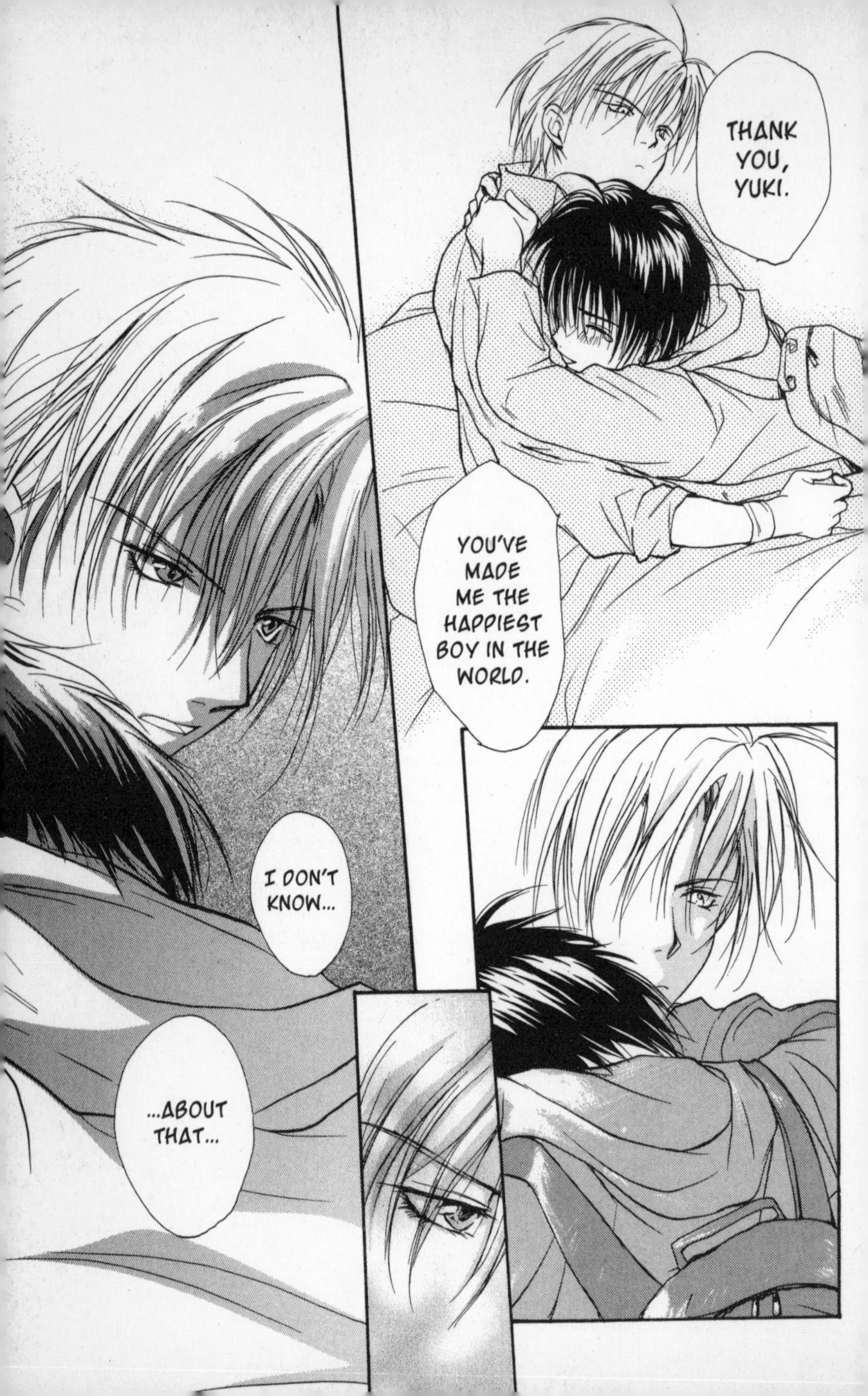
THANK YOU, YUKI.
YOU'VE MADE ME THE HAPPIEST BOY IN THE WORLD.
I DON'T KNOW...
...ABOUT THAT...

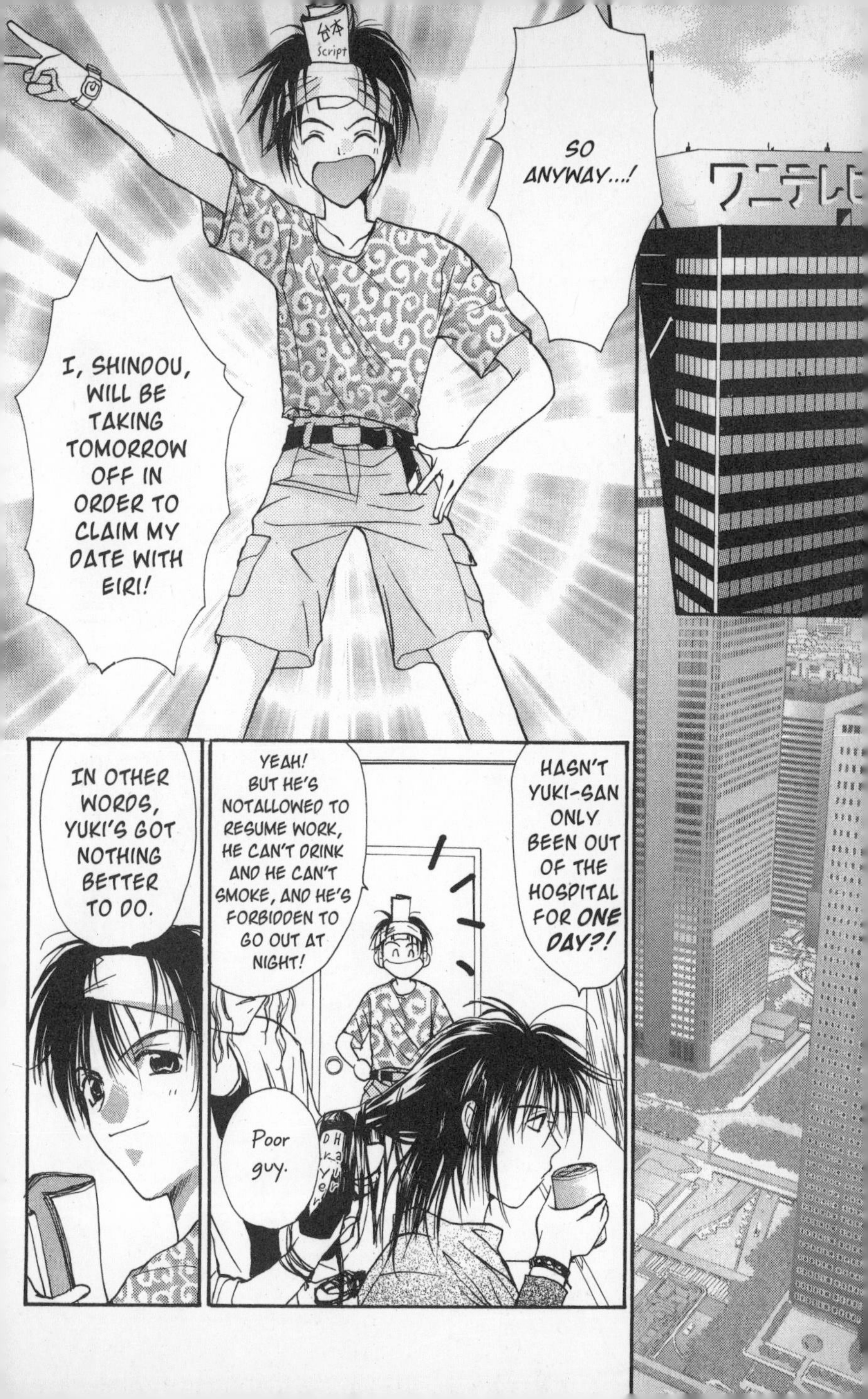
台本
Script
SO ANYWAY...!
I, SHINDOU, WILL BE TAKING TOMORROW OFF IN ORDER TO CLAIM MY DATE WITH EIRI!
HASN'T YUKI-SAN ONLY BEEN OUT OF THE HOSPITAL FOR ***ONE DAY?!***
YEAH! BUT HE'S NOTALLOWED TO RESUME WORK, HE CAN'T DRINK AND HE CAN'T SMOKE, AND HE'S FORBIDDEN TO GO OUT AT NIGHT!
Poor guy.
IN OTHER WORDS, YUKI'S GOT NOTHING BETTER TO DO.

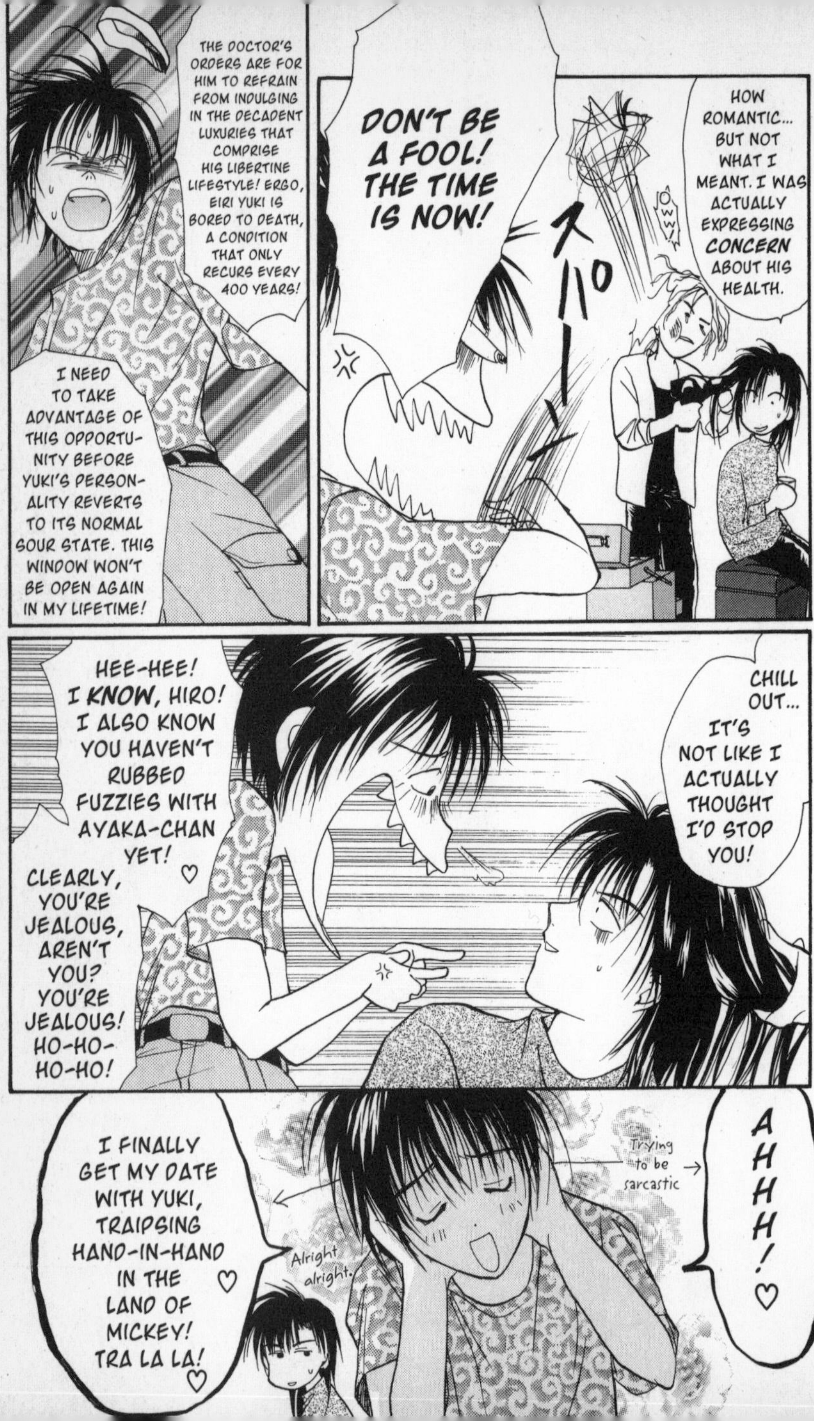
HOW ROMANTIC... BUT NOT WHAT I MEANT. I WAS ACTUALLY EXPRESSING CONCERN ABOUT HIS HEALTH.
OWW!
DON'T BE A FOOL! THE TIME IS NOW!
スパーン
THE DOCTOR'S ORDERS ARE FOR HIM TO REFRAIN FROM INDULGING IN THE DECADENT LUXURIES THAT COMPRISE HIS LIBERTINE LIFESTYLE! ERGO, EIRI YUKI IS BORED TO DEATH, A CONDITION THAT ONLY RECURS EVERY 400 YEARS!
I NEED TO TAKE ADVANTAGE OF THIS OPPORTUNITY BEFORE YUKI'S PERSONALITY REVERTS TO ITS NORMAL SOUR STATE. THIS WINDOW WON'T BE OPEN AGAIN IN MY LIFETIME!
CHILL OUT... IT'S NOT LIKE I ACTUALLY THOUGHT I'D STOP YOU!
HEE-HEE! I KNOW, HIRO! I ALSO KNOW YOU HAVEN'T RUBBED FUZZIES WITH AYAKA-CHAN YET! ♡
CLEARLY, YOU'RE JEALOUS, AREN'T YOU? YOU'RE JEALOUS! HO-HO-HO-HO!
AHHHH! ♡
Trying to be sarcastic
I FINALLY GET MY DATE WITH YUKI, TRAIPSING HAND-IN-HAND IN THE LAND OF MICKEY! TRA LA LA! ♡ ♡
Alright alright.

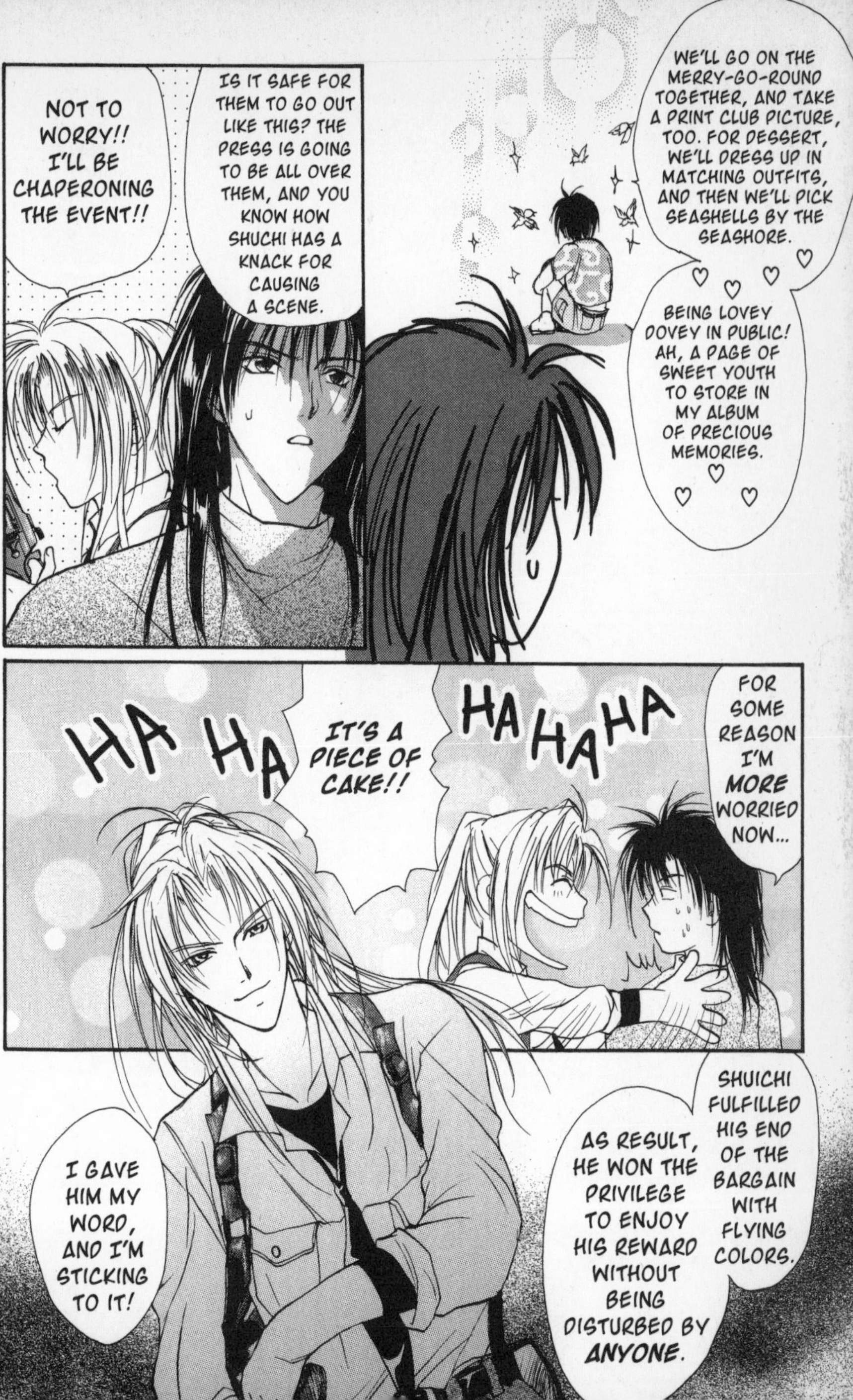
WE'LL GO ON THE MERRY-GO-ROUND TOGETHER, AND TAKE A PRINT CLUB PICTURE, TOO. FOR DESSERT, WE'LL DRESS UP IN MATCHING OUTFITS, AND THEN WE'LL PICK SEASHELLS BY THE SEASHORE. ♡ ♡ ♡ ♡
BEING LOVEY DOVEY IN PUBLIC! AH, A PAGE OF SWEET YOUTH TO STORE IN MY ALBUM OF PRECIOUS MEMORIES. ♡ ♡ ♡
IS IT SAFE FOR THEM TO GO OUT LIKE THIS? THE PRESS IS GOING TO BE ALL OVER THEM, AND YOU KNOW HOW SHUCHI HAS A KNACK FOR CAUSING A SCENE.
NOT TO WORRY!! I'LL BE CHAPERONING THE EVENT!!
FOR SOME REASON I'M ***MORE*** WORRIED NOW...
HA HA HA HA
IT'S A PIECE OF CAKE!!
HA HA HA
SHUICHI FULFILLED HIS END OF THE BARGAIN WITH FLYING COLORS.
AS RESULT, HE WON THE PRIVILEGE TO ENJOY HIS REWARD WITHOUT BEING DISTURBED BY ***ANYONE***.
I GAVE HIM MY WORD, AND I'M STICKING TO IT!

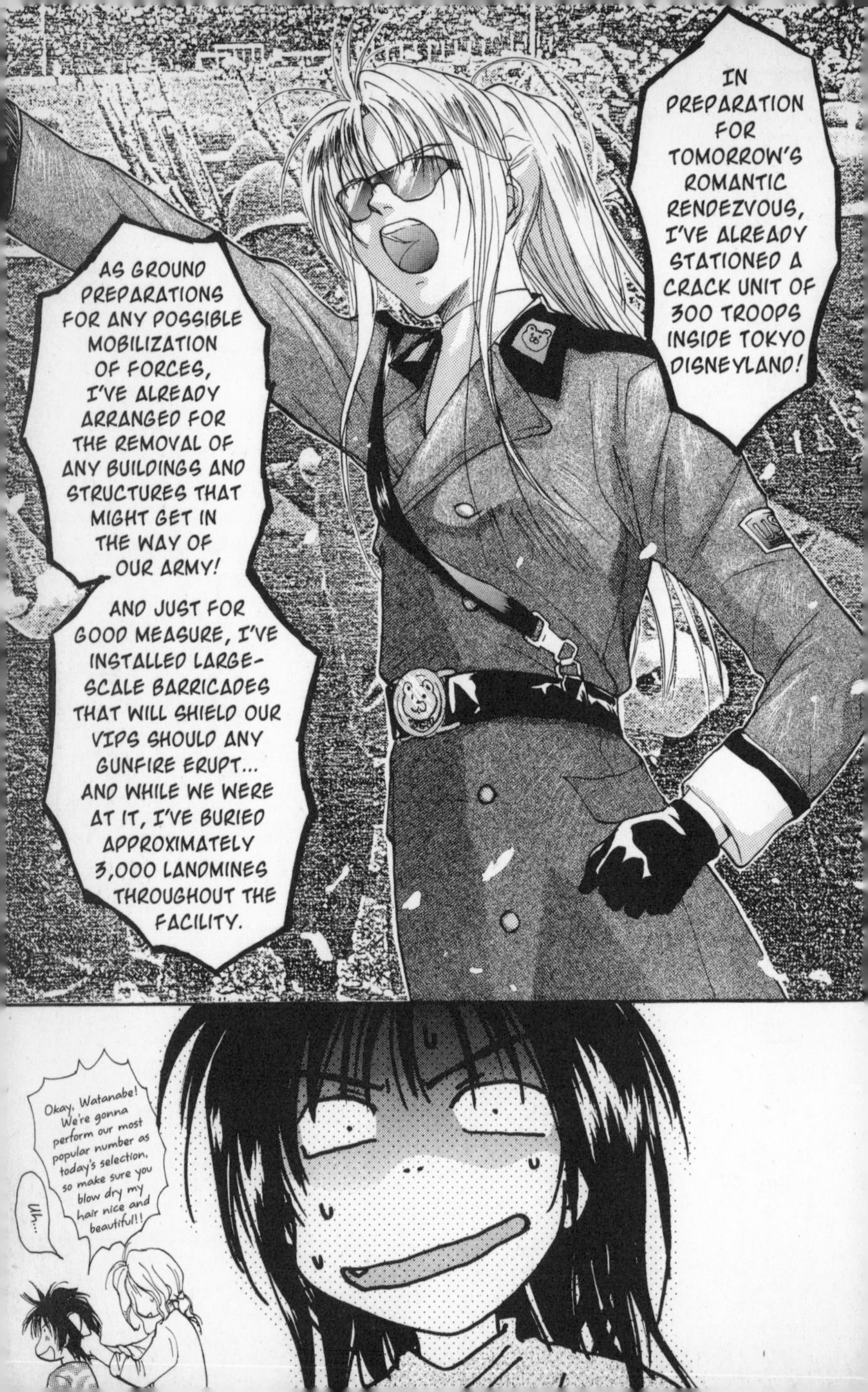
IN PREPARATION FOR TOMORROW'S ROMANTIC RENDEZVOUS, I'VE ALREADY STATIONED A CRACK UNIT OF 300 TROOPS INSIDE TOKYO DISNEYLAND!
AS GROUND PREPARATIONS FOR ANY POSSIBLE MOBILIZATION OF FORCES, I'VE ALREADY ARRANGED FOR THE REMOVAL OF ANY BUILDINGS AND STRUCTURES THAT MIGHT GET IN THE WAY OF OUR ARMY!
AND JUST FOR GOOD MEASURE, I'VE INSTALLED LARGE-SCALE BARRICADES THAT WILL SHIELD OUR VIPS SHOULD ANY GUNFIRE ERUPT... AND WHILE WE WERE AT IT, I'VE BURIED APPROXIMATELY 3,000 LANDMINES THROUGHOUT THE FACILITY.
Okay, Watanabe! We're gonna perform our most popular number as today's selection, so make sure you blow dry my hair nice and beautiful!!
Uh...

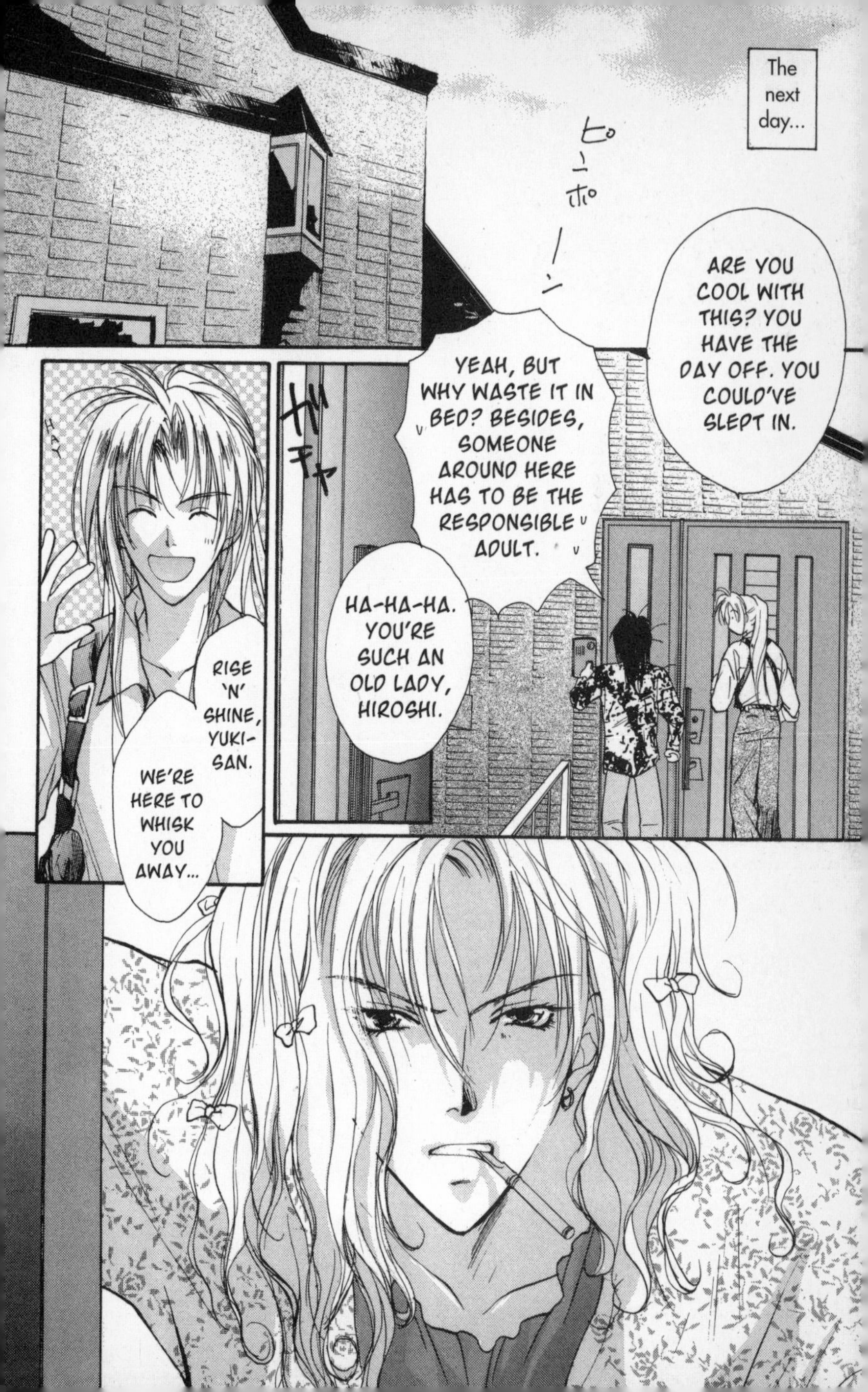
The next day...
ARE YOU COOL WITH THIS? YOU HAVE THE DAY OFF. YOU COULD'VE SLEPT IN.
YEAH, BUT WHY WASTE IT IN BED? BESIDES, SOMEONE AROUND HERE HAS TO BE THE RESPONSIBLE ADULT.
ガチャ
HA-HA-HA. YOU'RE SUCH AN OLD LADY, HIROSHI.
RISE 'N' SHINE, YUKI-SAN.
WE'RE HERE TO WHISK YOU AWAY...

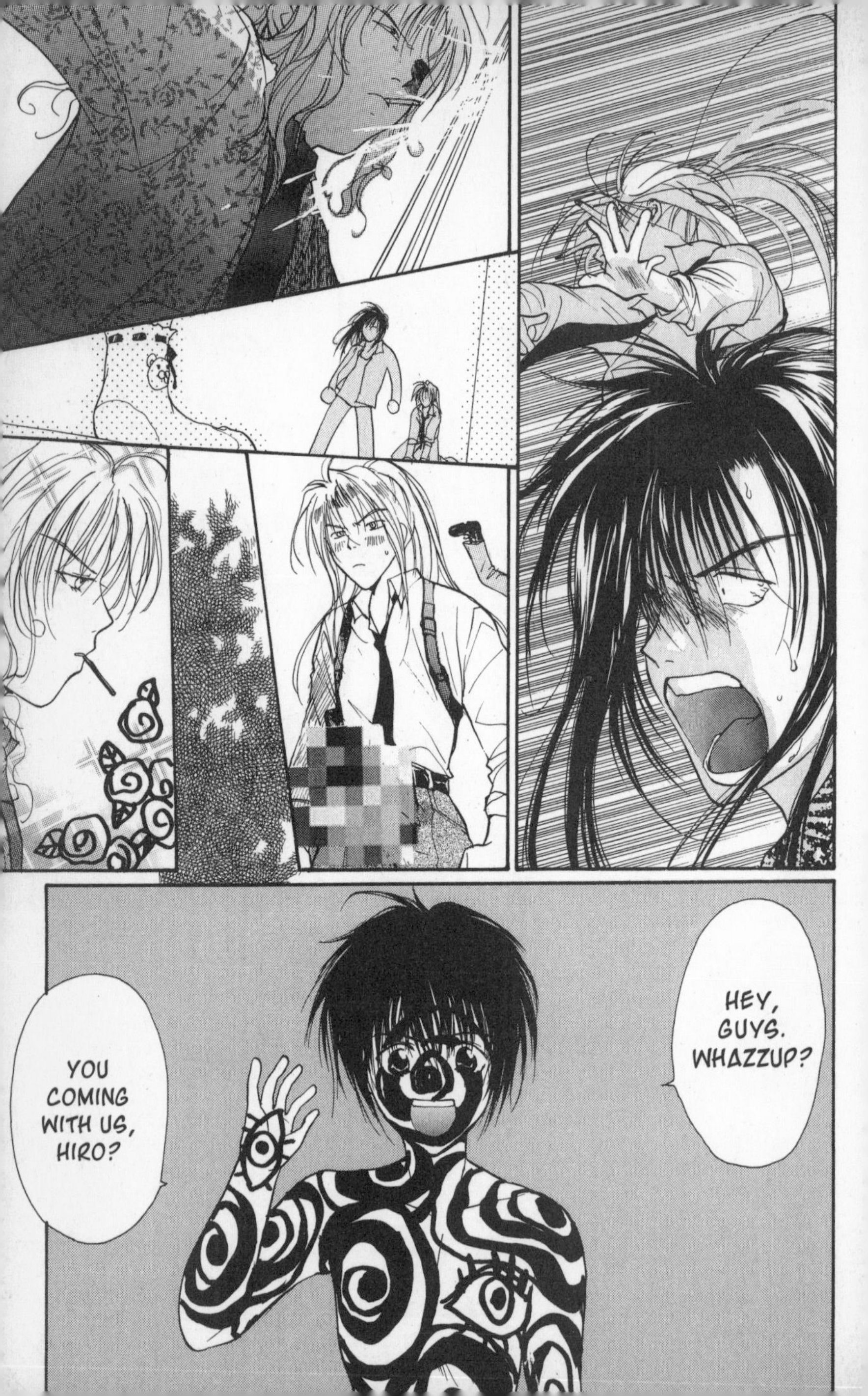
HEY, GUYS. WHAZZUP?
YOU COMING WITH US, HIRO?

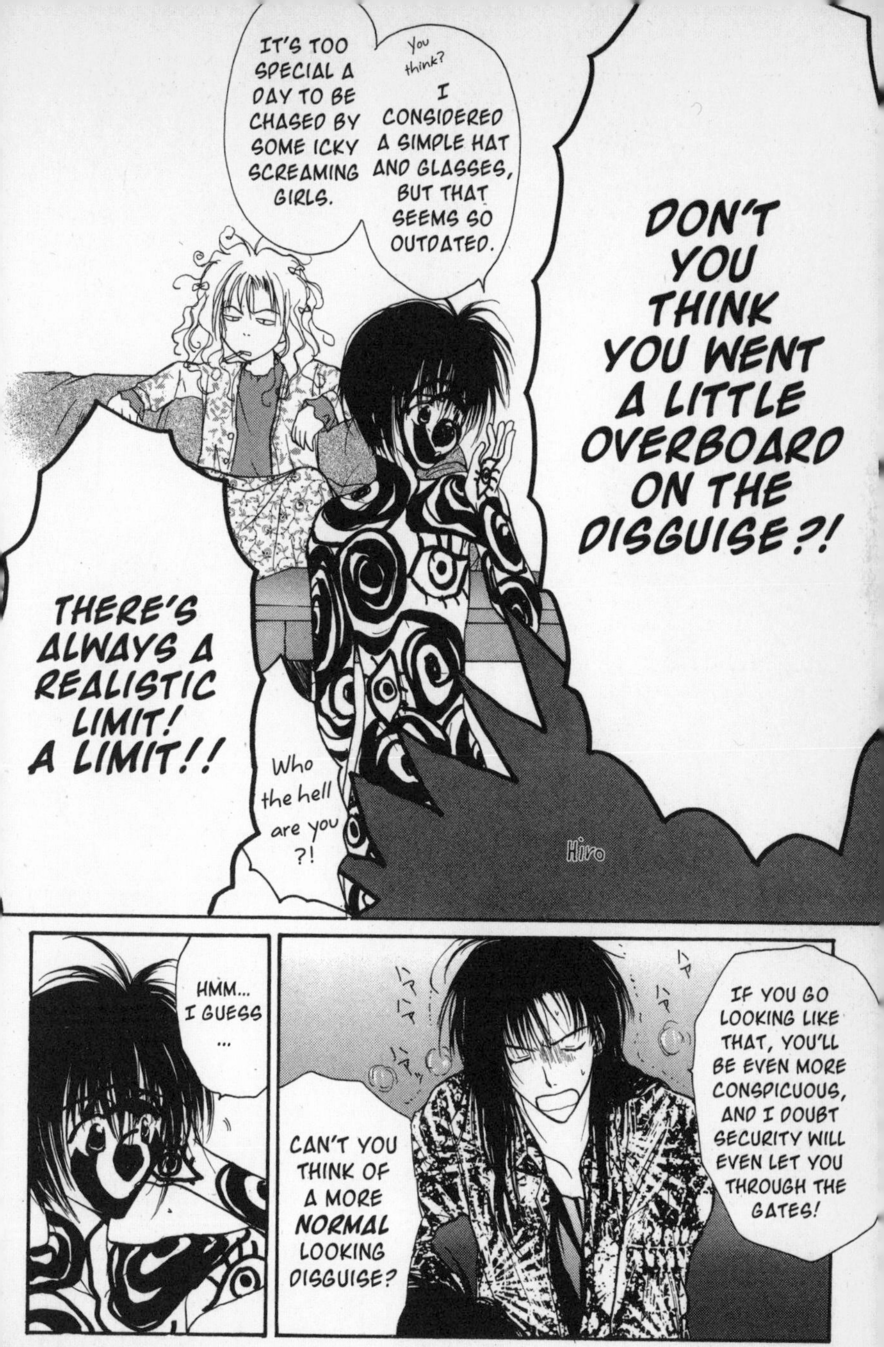

You think? I CONSIDERED A SIMPLE HAT AND GLASSES, BUT THAT SEEMS SO OUTDATED.
IT'S TOO SPECIAL A DAY TO BE CHASED BY SOME ICKY SCREAMING GIRLS.
DON'T YOU THINK YOU WENT A LITTLE OVERBOARD ON THE DISGUISE?!
Who the hell are you ?!
THERE'S ALWAYS A REALISTIC LIMIT! A LIMIT!!
Hiro
IF YOU GO LOOKING LIKE THAT, YOU'LL BE EVEN MORE CONSPICUOUS, AND I DOUBT SECURITY WILL EVEN LET YOU THROUGH THE GATES!
CAN'T YOU THINK OF A MORE NORMAL LOOKING DISGUISE?
HMM... I GUESS ...

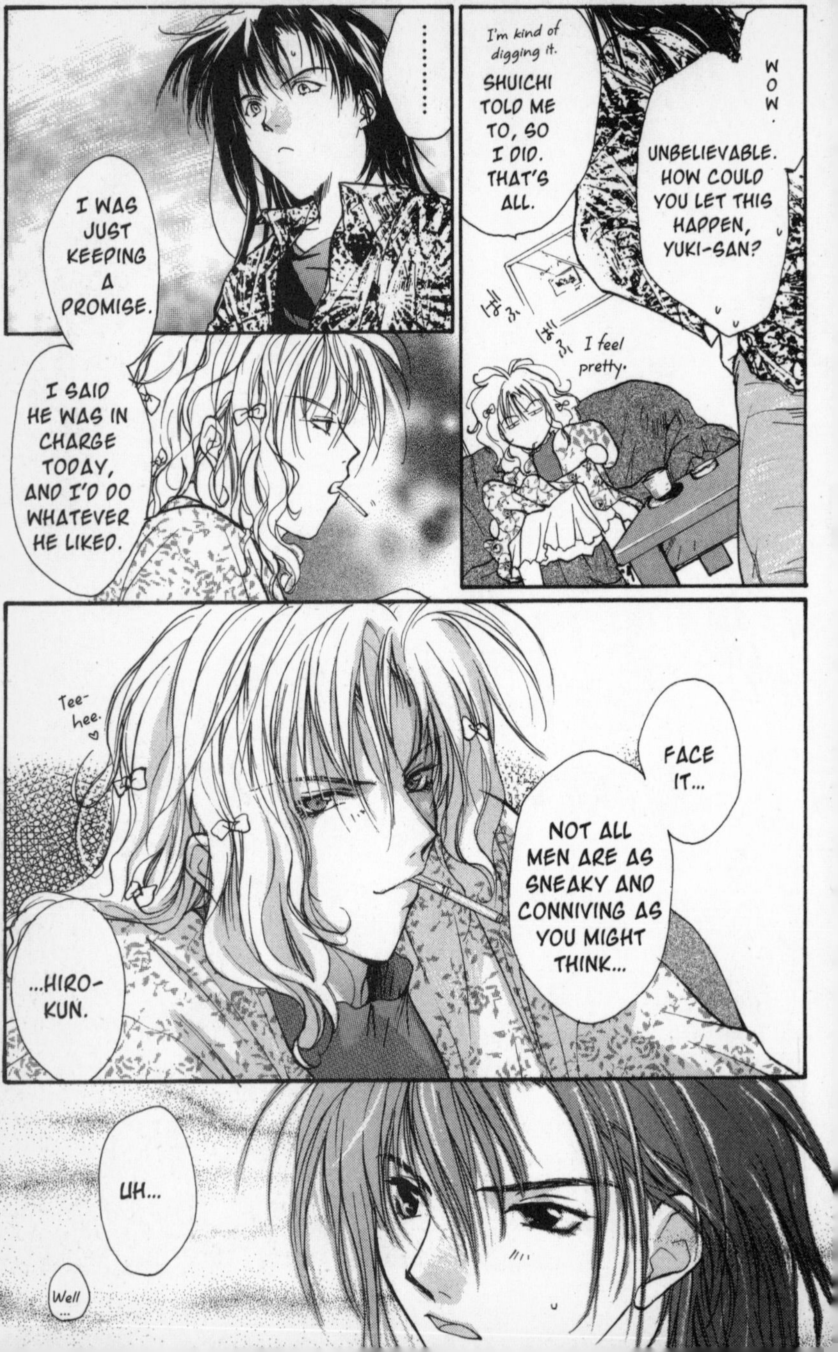
WOW.
UNBELIEVABLE. HOW COULD YOU LET THIS HAPPEN, YUKI-SAN?
ぱふ
ぱふ
I feel pretty.
SHUICHI TOLD ME TO, SO I DID. THAT'S ALL.
I'm kind of digging it.
......
I WAS JUST KEEPING A PROMISE.
I SAID HE WAS IN CHARGE TODAY, AND I'D DO WHATEVER HE LIKED.
FACE IT...
NOT ALL MEN ARE AS SNEAKY AND CONNIVING AS YOU MIGHT THINK...
...HIRO-KUN.
Tee-hee.
UH...
Well...

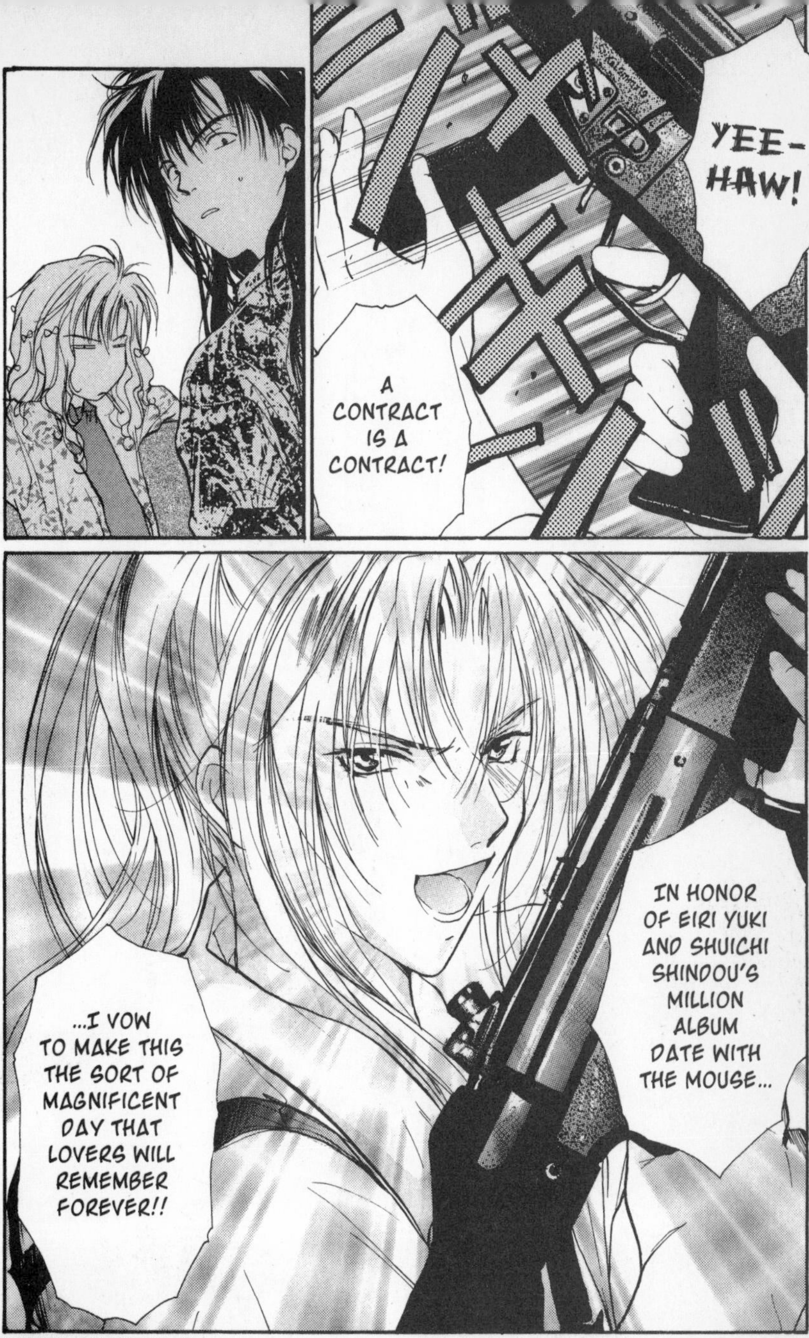
YEE-HAW!
A CONTRACT IS A CONTRACT!
IN HONOR OF EIRI YUKI AND SHUICHI SHINDOU'S MILLION ALBUM DATE WITH THE MOUSE...
...I VOW TO MAKE THIS THE SORT OF MAGNIFICENT DAY THAT LOVERS WILL REMEMBER FOREVER!!

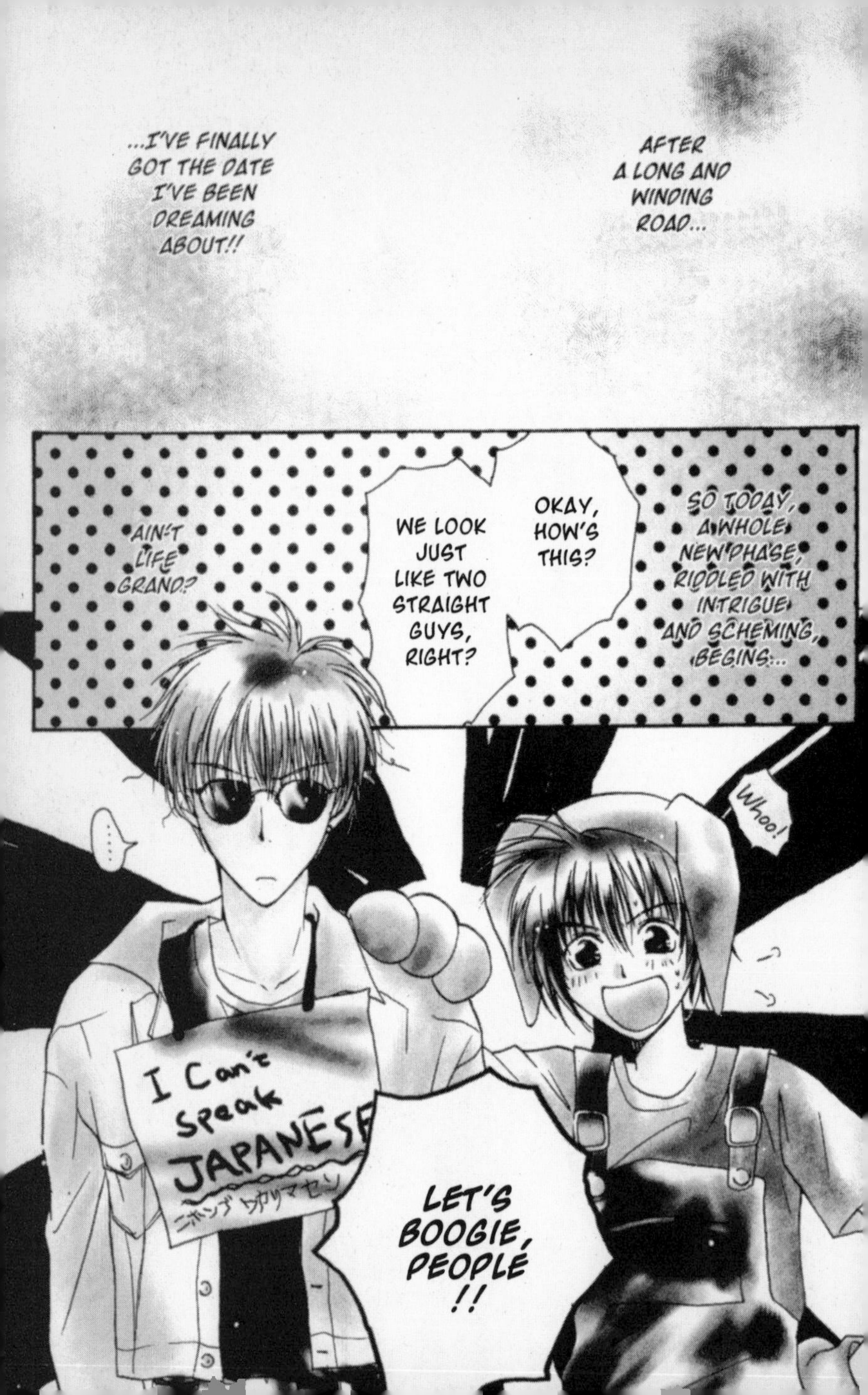
AFTER A LONG AND WINDING ROAD...
...I'VE FINALLY GOT THE DATE I'VE BEEN DREAMING ABOUT!!
SO TODAY, A WHOLE NEW PHASE, RIDDLED WITH INTRIGUE AND SCHEMING, BEGINS...
OKAY, HOW'S THIS?
WE LOOK JUST LIKE TWO STRAIGHT GUYS, RIGHT?
AIN'T LIFE GRAND?
Whoo!
...
I Can't Speak JAPANESE
ニホンゴ ワカリマセン
LET'S BOOGIE, PEOPLE!!

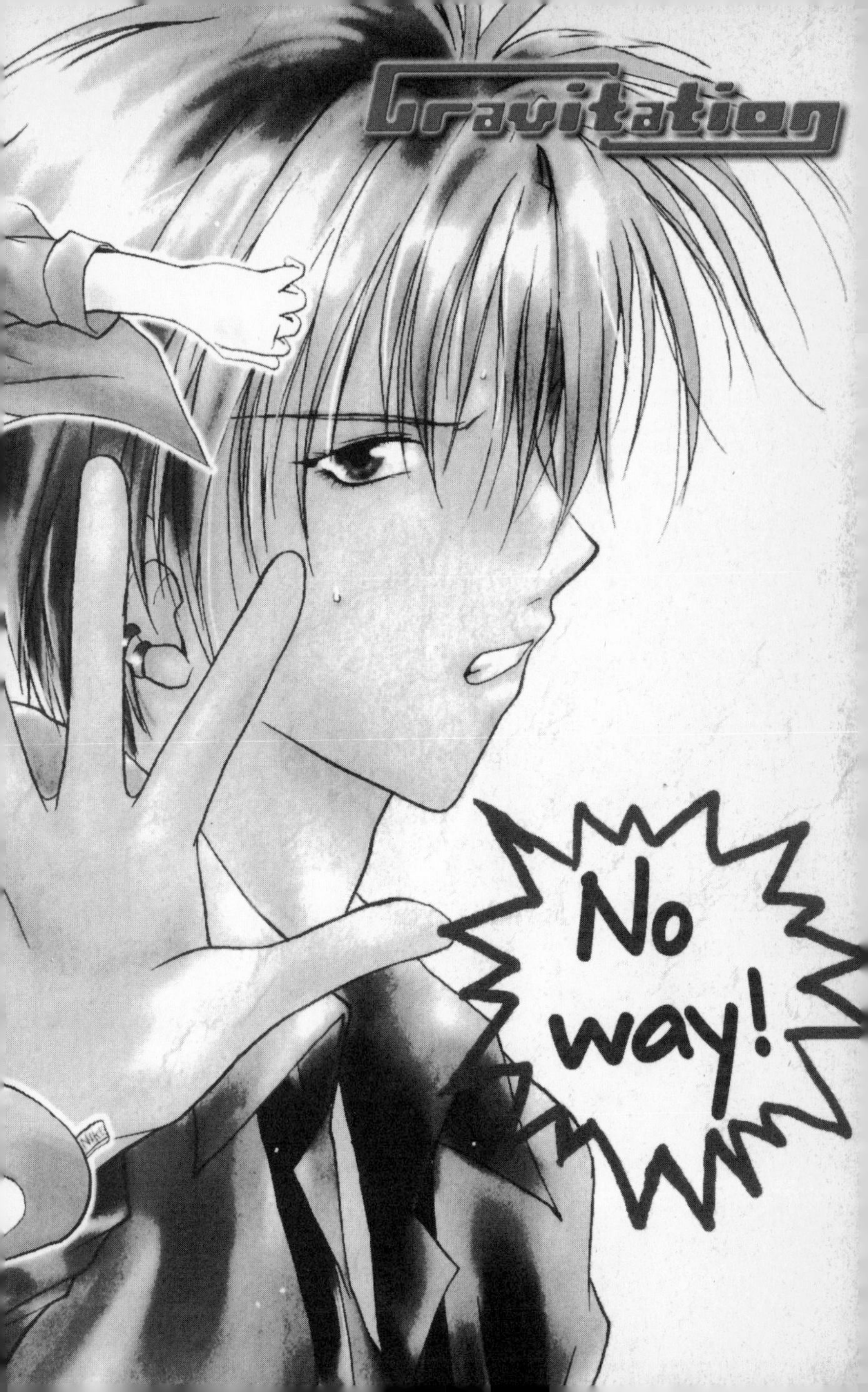
Gravitation
No way!

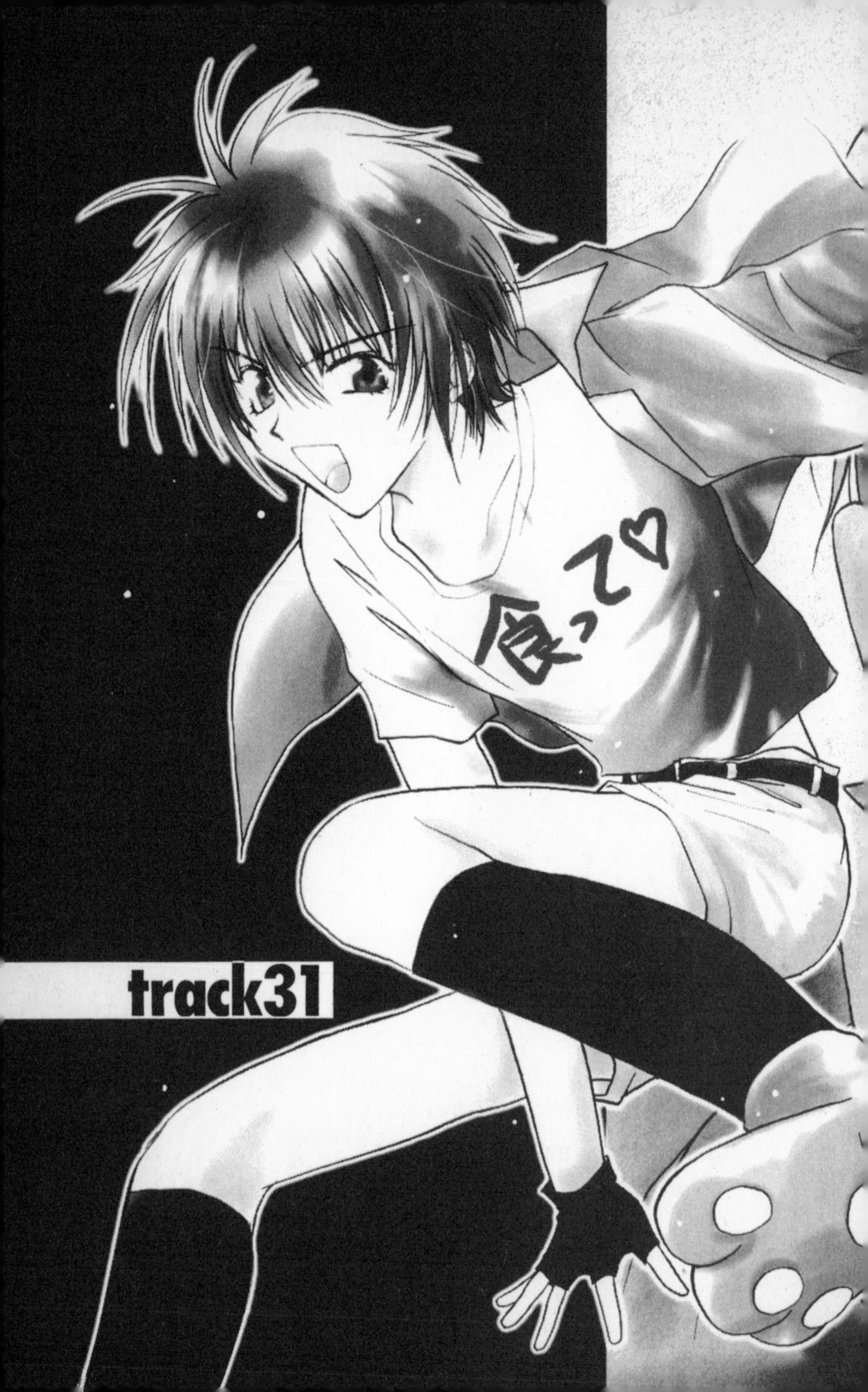
食って♡
track31

RELEASED TO THE PUBLIC FOR THE FIRST TIME! MURAKAMI MAKI'S ROAD TO AGONY: A SELF-PORTRAIT.

I file these ideas away, because they were just too original for my regular readership to handle.

① Why a dog...?

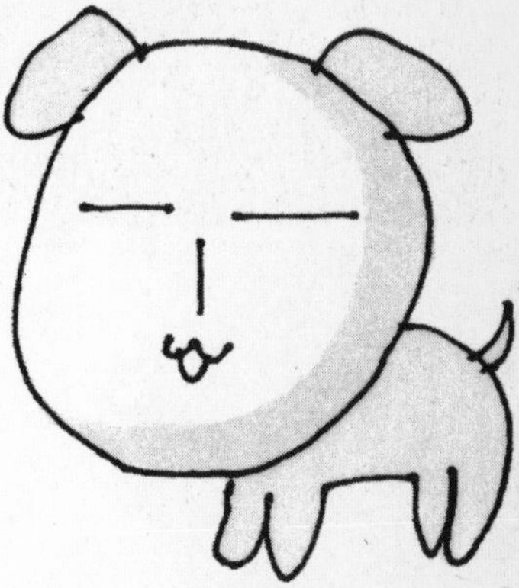

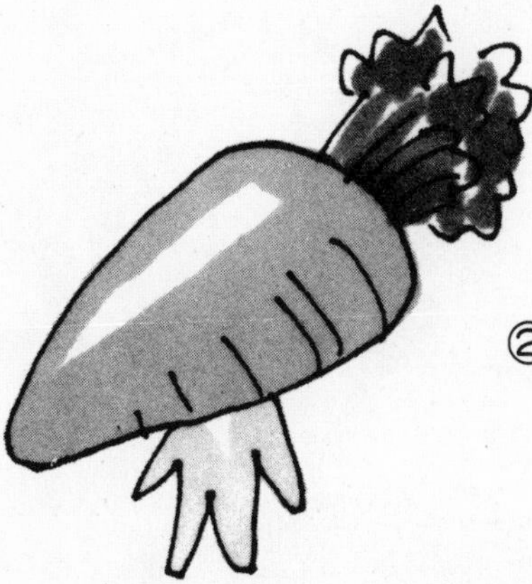

② Why a carrot...?

③ For some reason, I decided on this!! (see pg. 207 for the full explanation)

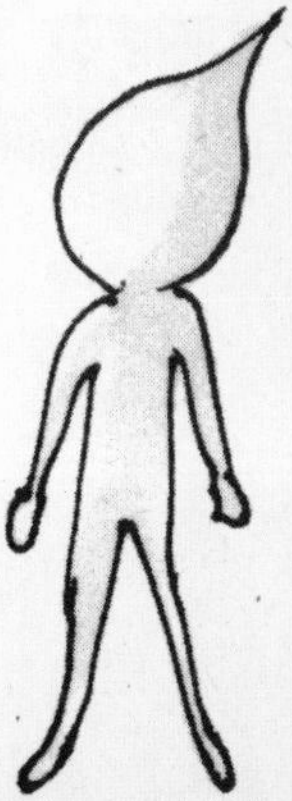

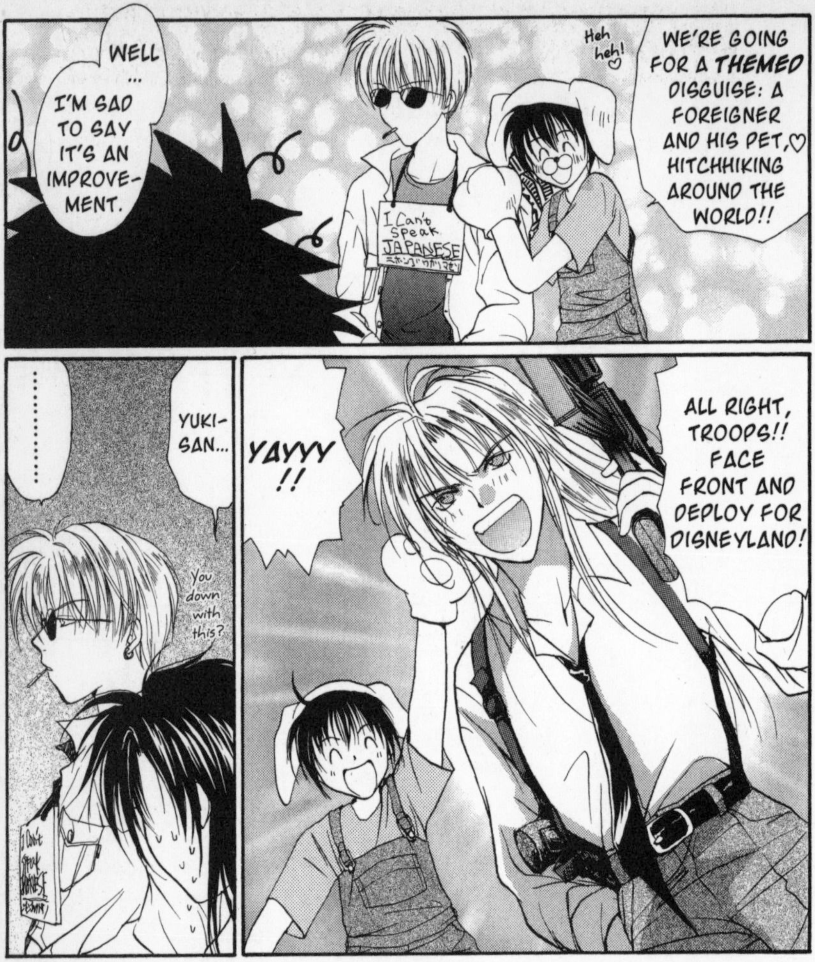
WE'RE GOING FOR A ***THEMED*** DISGUISE: A FOREIGNER AND HIS PET,♡ HITCHHIKING AROUND THE WORLD!!
Heh heh!♡
I Can't Speak JAPANESE
WELL ... I'M SAD TO SAY IT'S AN IMPROVEMENT.
ALL RIGHT, TROOPS!! FACE FRONT AND DEPLOY FOR DISNEYLAND!
YAYYY !!
YUKI-SAN...
....
You down with this?

ABOUT GRAVITATION TRACK 31

Well...somehow Volume 7 never really found its structure...it's all over the place. And this is how it ends up. It almost doesn't even feel like a young girls' manga anymore.

Originally this comic was intended to have more of a dark story. I wonder how things turned out the way that they have. K was supposed to be only a minor character, but look how important a role he plays now!! But I wonder about his capabilities as a manager for Bad Luck...

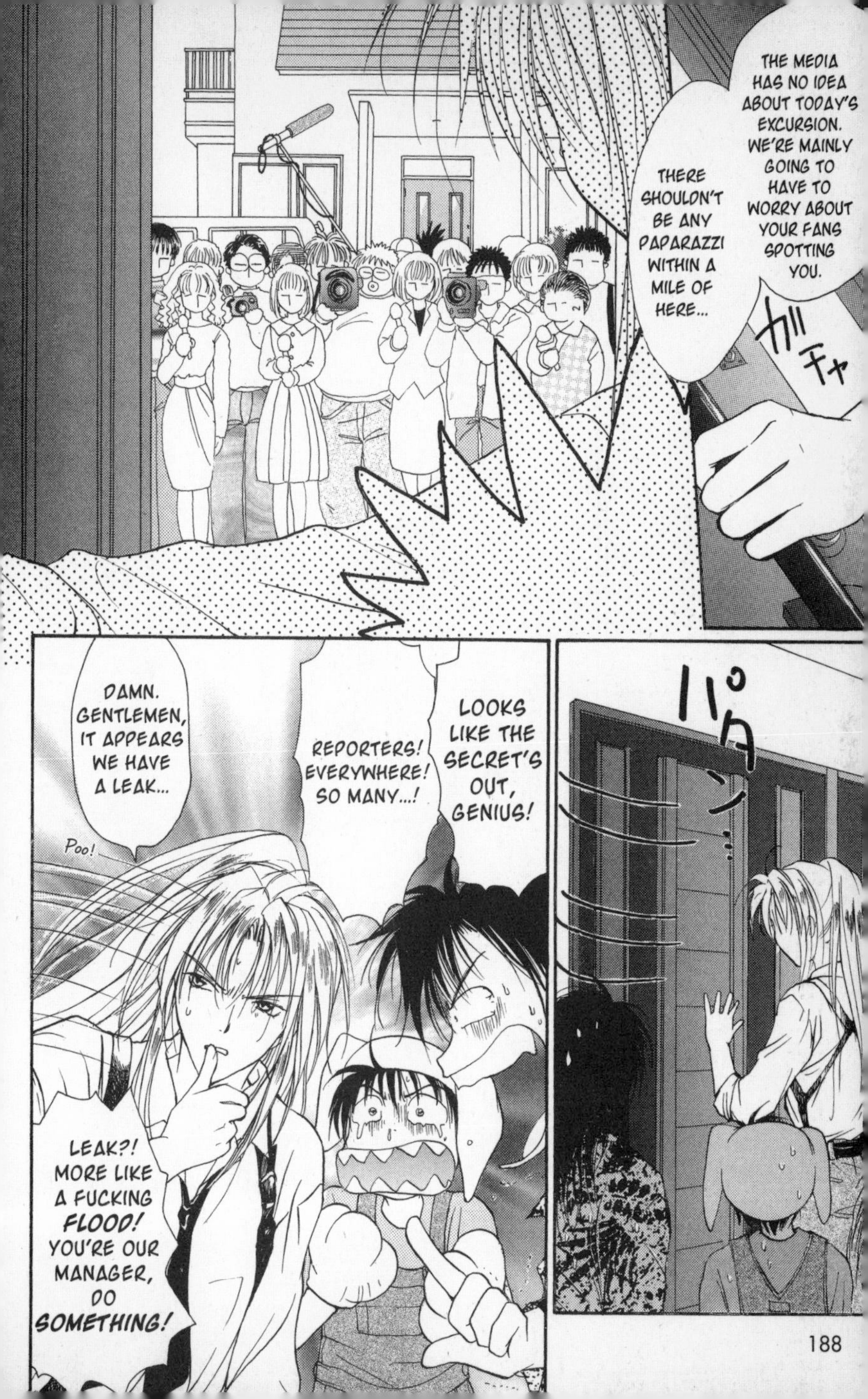
THE MEDIA HAS NO IDEA ABOUT TODAY'S EXCURSION. WE'RE MAINLY GOING TO HAVE TO WORRY ABOUT YOUR FANS SPOTTING YOU.
THERE SHOULDN'T BE ANY PAPARAZZI WITHIN A MILE OF HERE...
ガチャ
パタン…
LOOKS LIKE THE SECRET'S OUT, GENIUS!
REPORTERS! EVERYWHERE! SO MANY...!
DAMN. GENTLEMEN, IT APPEARS WE HAVE A LEAK...
Poo!
LEAK?! MORE LIKE A FUCKING **FLOOD!** YOU'RE OUR MANAGER, DO **SOMETHING!**

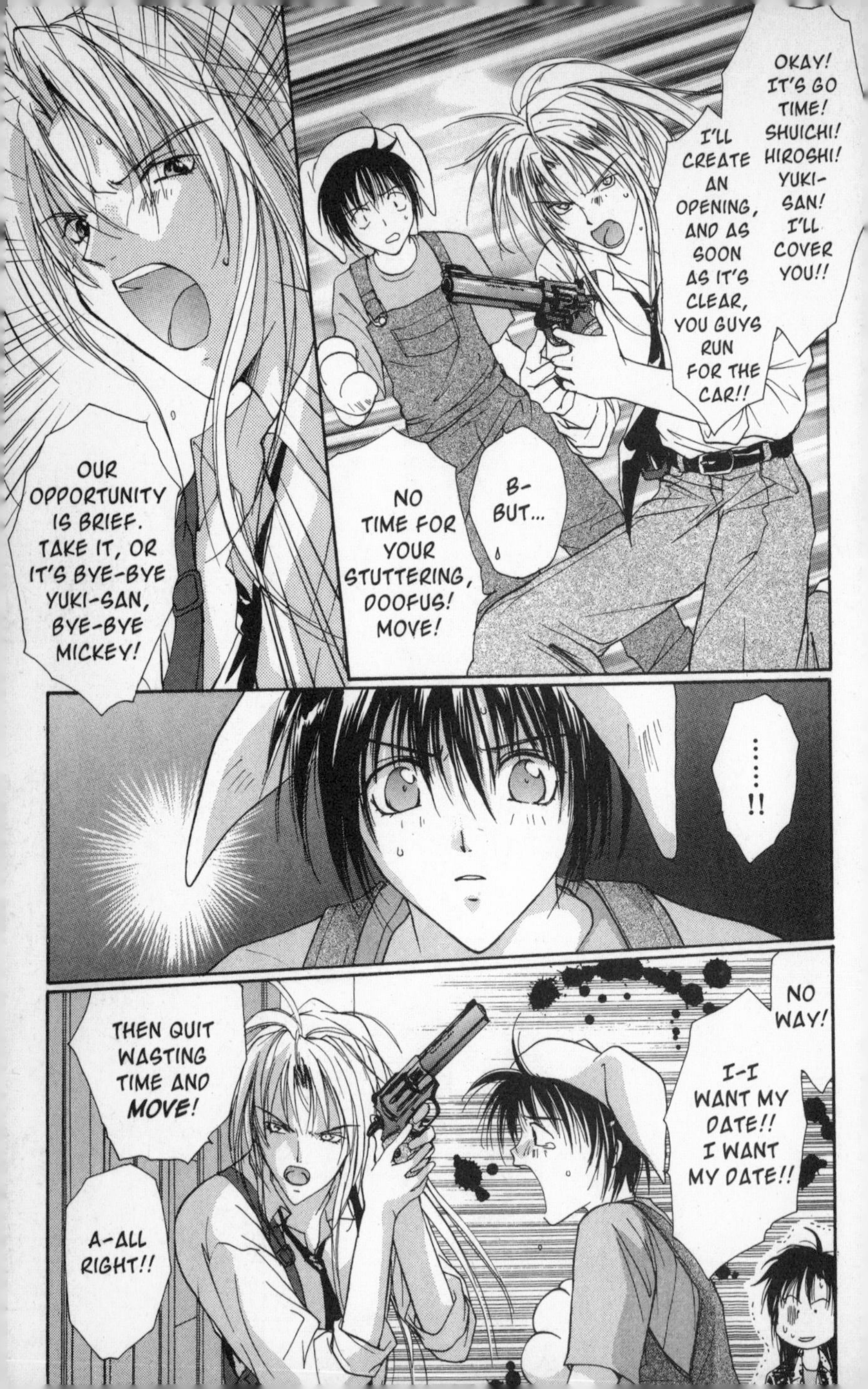
OKAY! IT'S GO TIME! SHUICHI! HIROSHI! YUKI-SAN! I'LL COVER YOU!!
I'LL CREATE AN OPENING, AND AS SOON AS IT'S CLEAR, YOU GUYS RUN FOR THE CAR!!
B-BUT...
NO TIME FOR YOUR STUTTERING, DOOFUS! MOVE!
OUR OPPORTUNITY IS BRIEF. TAKE IT, OR IT'S BYE-BYE YUKI-SAN, BYE-BYE MICKEY!
......!!
NO WAY!
I-I WANT MY DATE!! I WANT MY DATE!!
THEN QUIT WASTING TIME AND MOVE!
A-ALL RIGHT!!

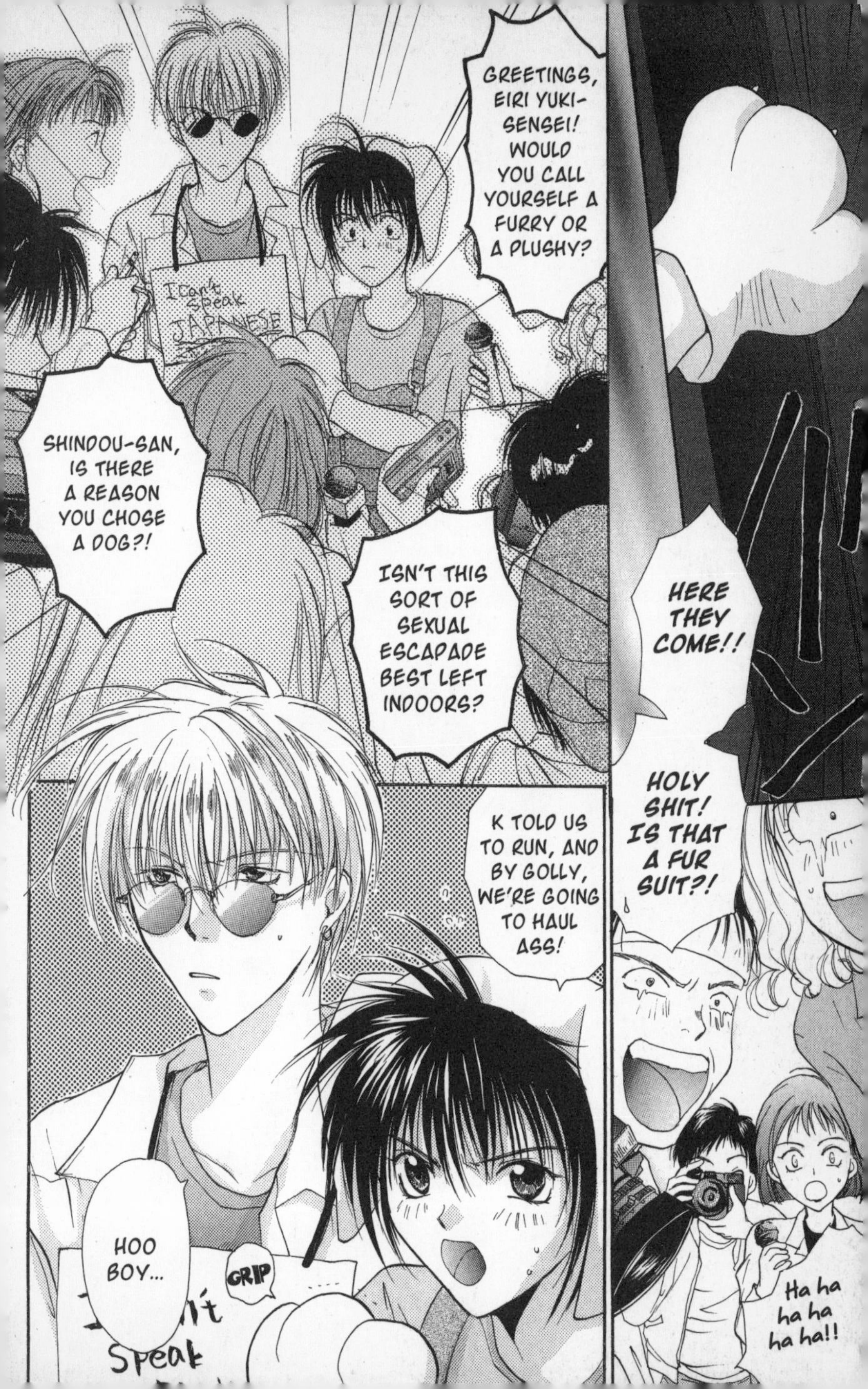
HERE THEY COME!!
GREETINGS, EIRI YUKI-SENSEI! WOULD YOU CALL YOURSELF A FURRY OR A PLUSHY?
I Can't Speak JAPANESE
SHINDOU-SAN, IS THERE A REASON YOU CHOSE A DOG?!
ISN'T THIS SORT OF SEXUAL ESCAPADE BEST LEFT INDOORS?
HOLY SHIT! IS THAT A FUR SUIT?!
Ha ha ha ha ha ha!!
K TOLD US TO RUN, AND BY GOLLY, WE'RE GOING TO HAUL ASS!
HOO BOY...
GRIP

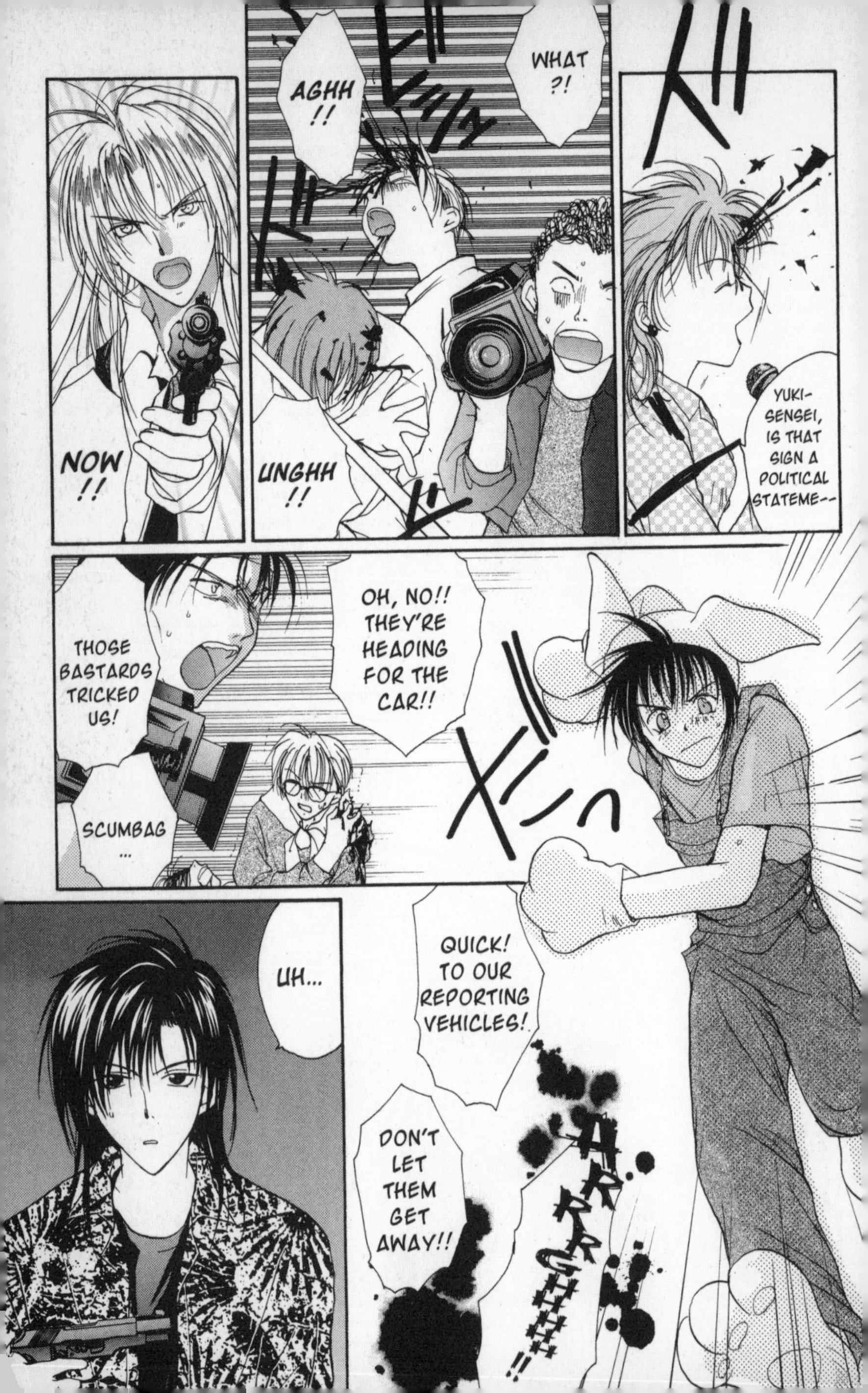
YUKI-SENSEI, IS THAT SIGN A POLITICAL STATEME--
WHAT ?!
AGHH !!
UNGHH !!
NOW !!
OH, NO!! THEY'RE HEADING FOR THE CAR!!
THOSE BASTARDS TRICKED US!
SCUMBAG ...
QUICK! TO OUR REPORTING VEHICLES!
DON'T LET THEM GET AWAY!!
ARRRGHHH!!
UH...

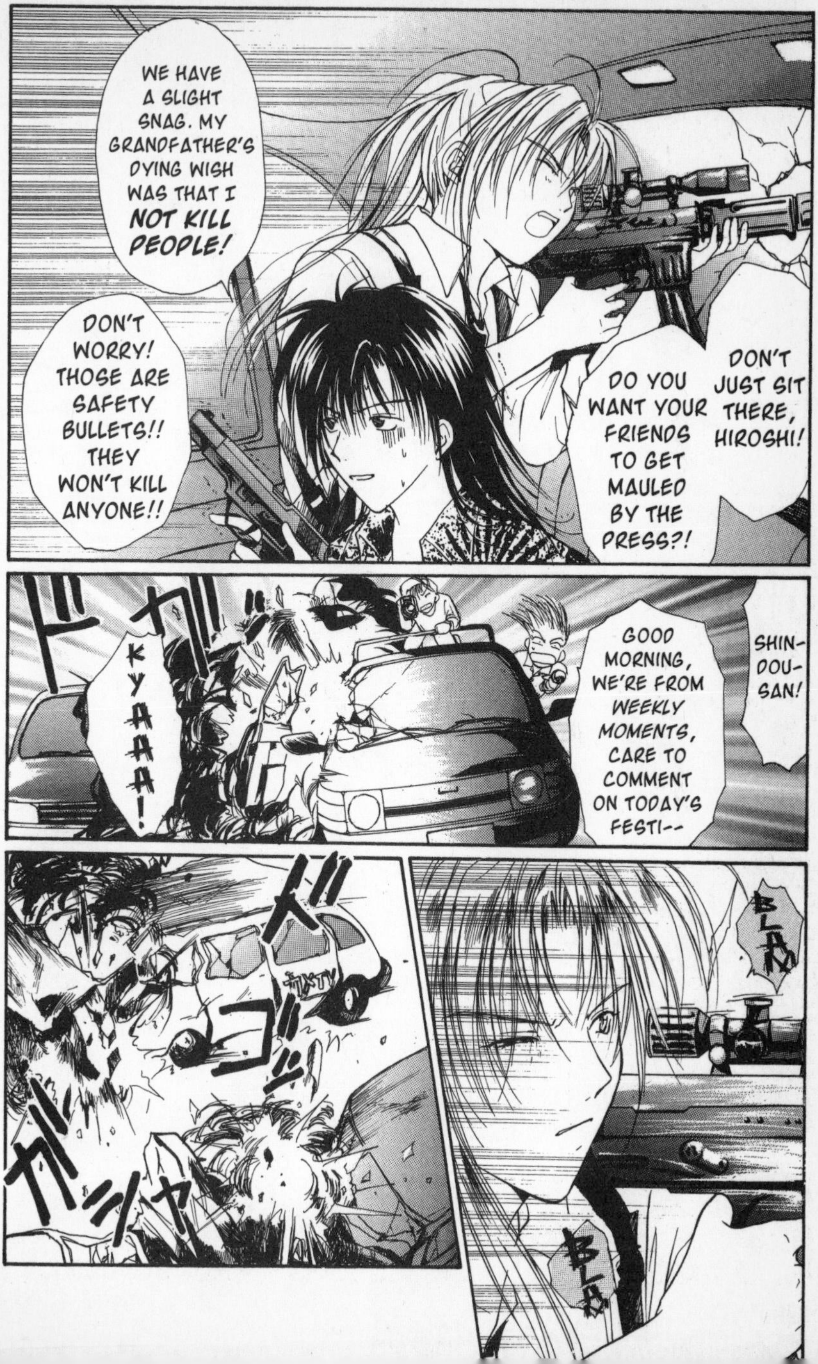
DON'T JUST SIT THERE, HIROSHI!
DO YOU WANT YOUR FRIENDS TO GET MAULED BY THE PRESS?!
WE HAVE A SLIGHT SNAG. MY GRANDFATHER'S DYING WISH WAS THAT I *NOT KILL PEOPLE!*
DON'T WORRY! THOSE ARE SAFETY BULLETS!! THEY WON'T KILL ANYONE!!
SHIN-DOU-SAN!
GOOD MORNING, WE'RE FROM WEEKLY MOMENTS, CARE TO COMMENT ON TODAY'S FESTI--
KYAAAAA!
BLAM
BLA

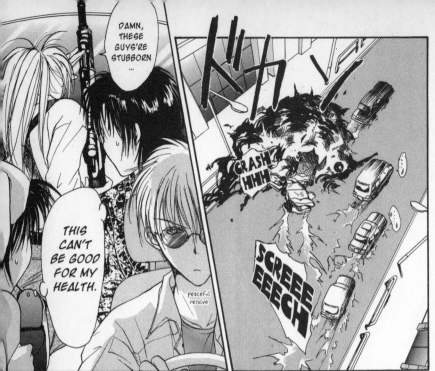

DAMN, THESE GUYS'RE STUBBORN...

THIS CAN'T BE GOOD FOR MY HEALTH.

peaceful resolve

ドカッ

CRASHHHH

SCREEE EEECH

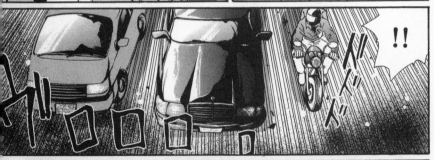

!!

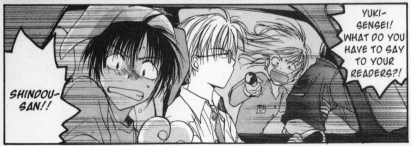

YUKI-SENSEI!! WHAT DO YOU HAVE TO SAY TO YOUR READERS?!

SHINDOU-SAN!!

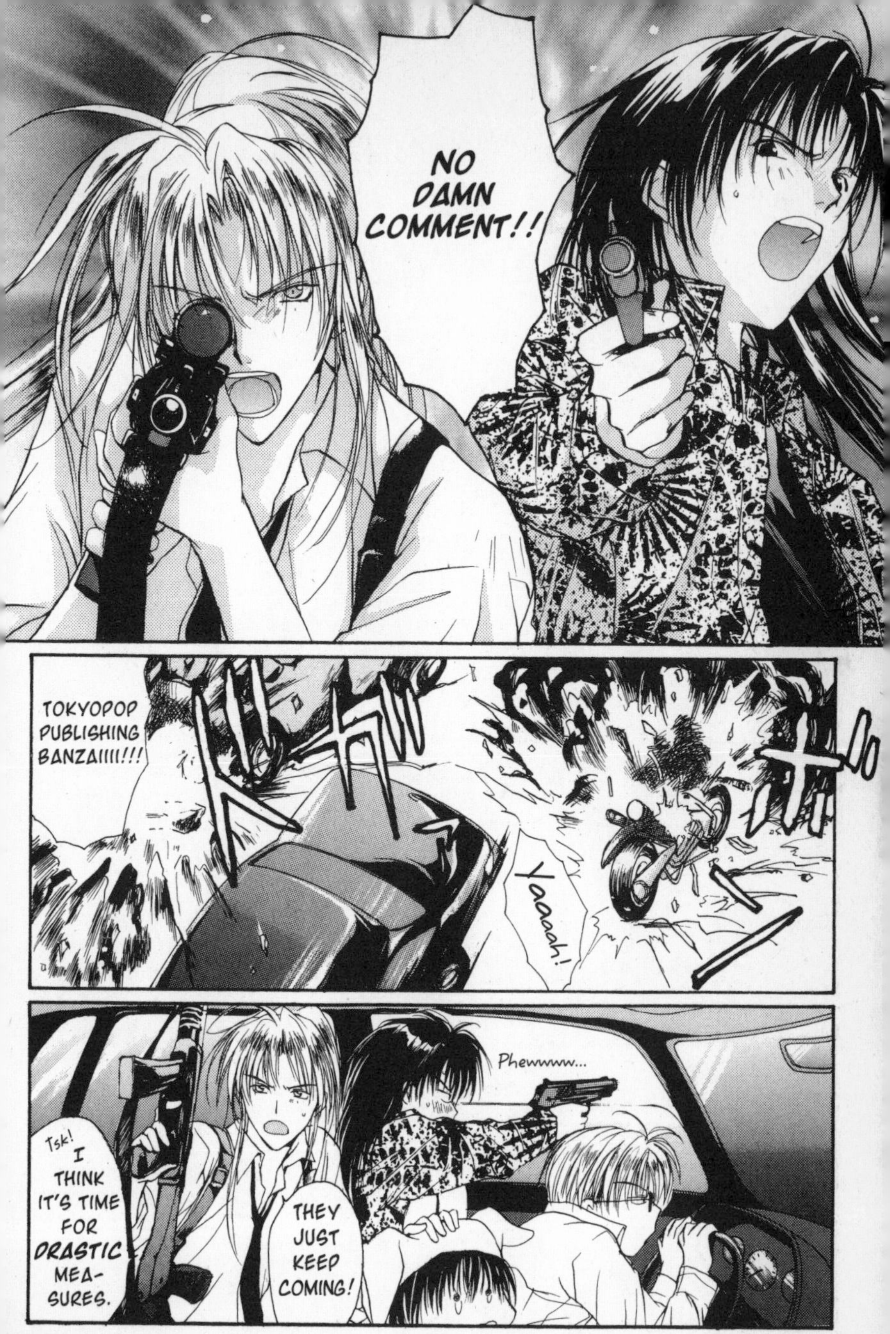
NO DAMN COMMENT!!
TOKYOPOP PUBLISHING BANZAIIII!!!
Yaaaah!
Phewwww...
THEY JUST KEEP COMING!
Tsk! I THINK IT'S TIME FOR DRASTIC MEA-SURES.

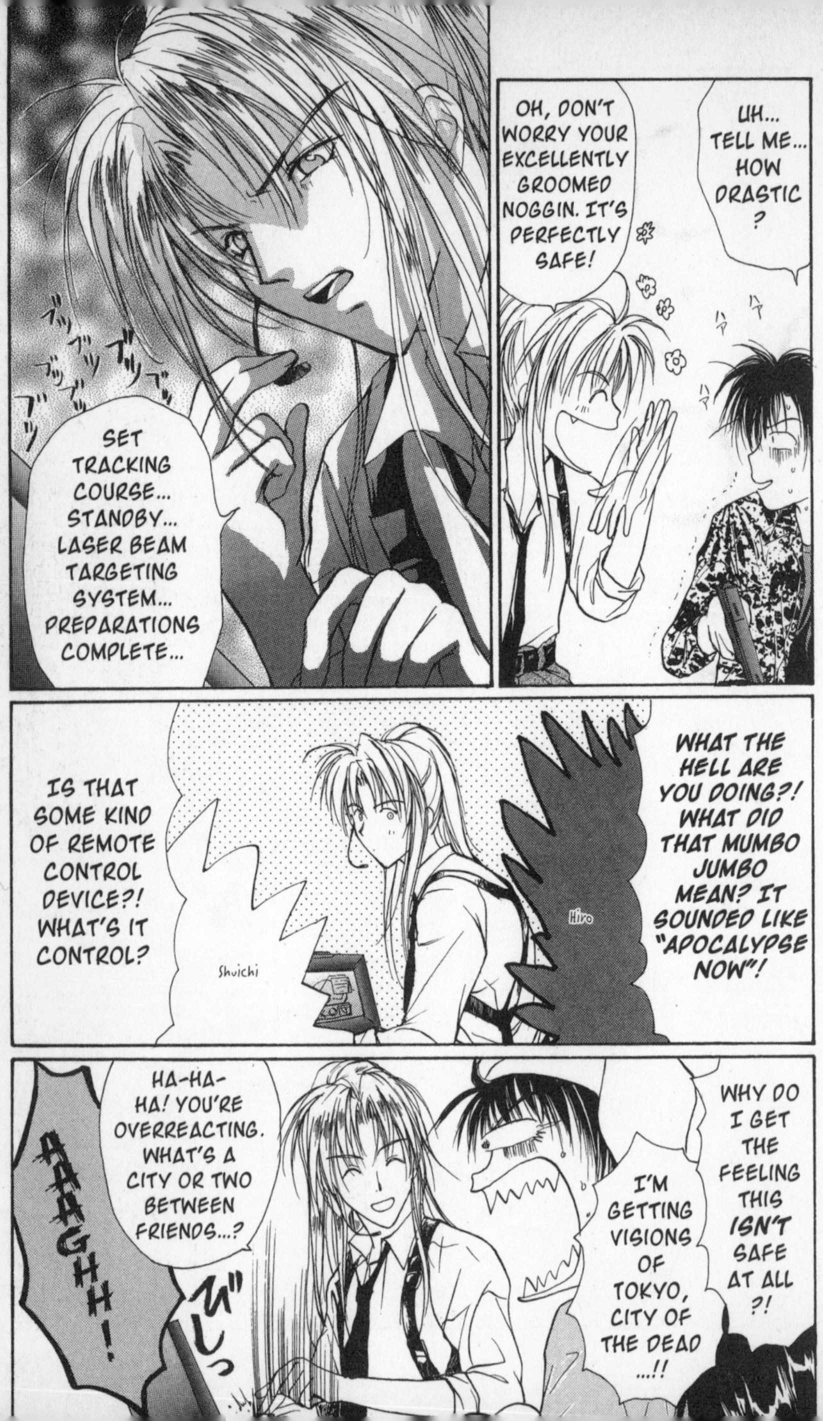
UH... TELL ME... HOW DRASTIC ?
OH, DON'T WORRY YOUR EXCELLENTLY GROOMED NOGGIN. IT'S PERFECTLY SAFE!
SET TRACKING COURSE... STANDBY... LASER BEAM TARGETING SYSTEM... PREPARATIONS COMPLETE...
WHAT THE HELL ARE YOU DOING?! WHAT DID THAT MUMBO JUMBO MEAN? IT SOUNDED LIKE "APOCALYPSE NOW"!
Hiro
IS THAT SOME KIND OF REMOTE CONTROL DEVICE?! WHAT'S IT CONTROL?
Shuichi
WHY DO I GET THE FEELING THIS ISN'T SAFE AT ALL ?!
I'M GETTING VISIONS OF TOKYO, CITY OF THE DEAD ...!!
HA-HA-HA! YOU'RE OVERREACTING. WHAT'S A CITY OR TWO BETWEEN FRIENDS...?
AAAGHH!
びしっ

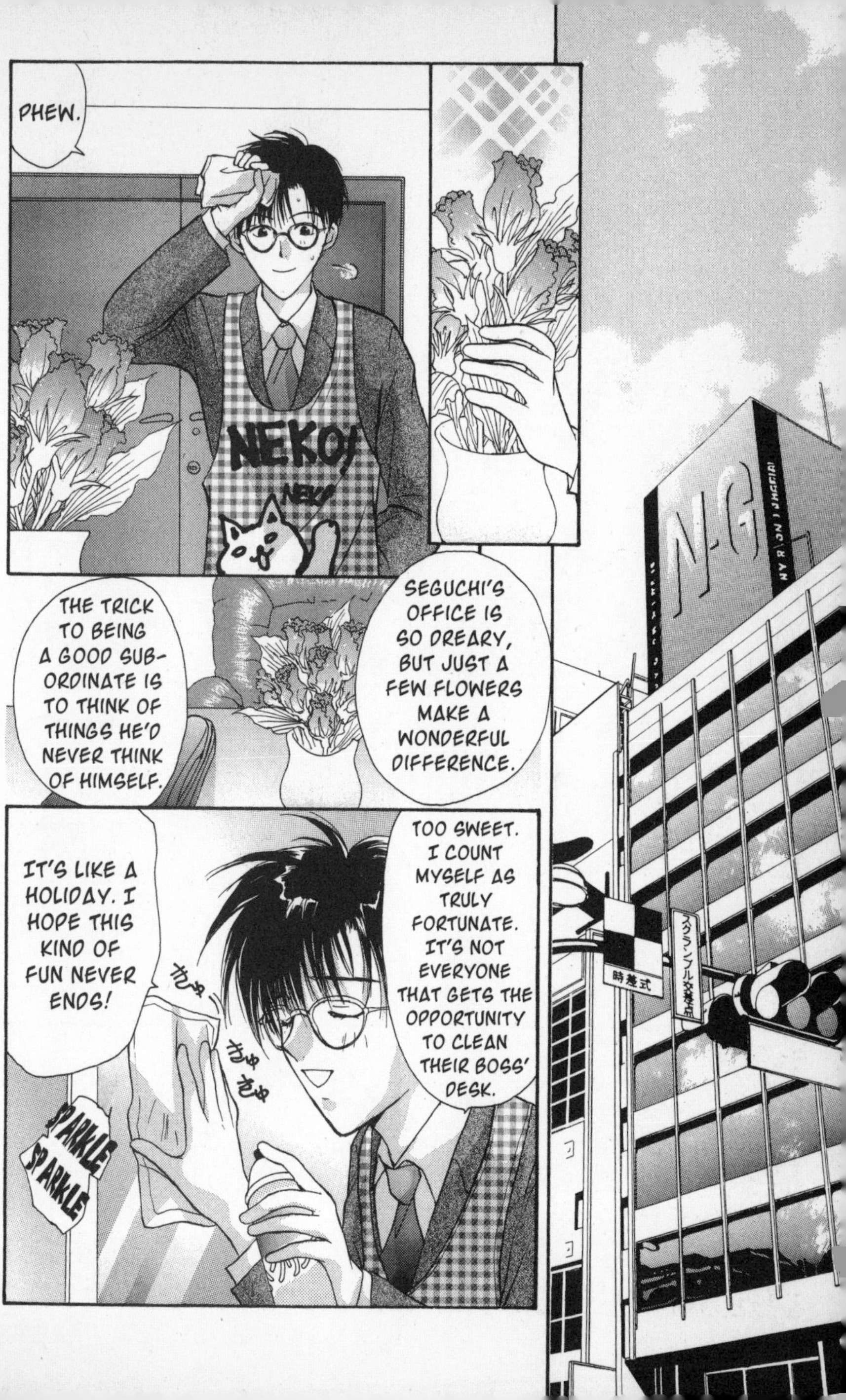
N-G
スクランブル交差点
時差式
PHEW.
SEGUCHI'S OFFICE IS SO DREARY, BUT JUST A FEW FLOWERS MAKE A WONDERFUL DIFFERENCE.
THE TRICK TO BEING A GOOD SUB-ORDINATE IS TO THINK OF THINGS HE'D NEVER THINK OF HIMSELF.
TOO SWEET. I COUNT MYSELF AS TRULY FORTUNATE. IT'S NOT EVERYONE THAT GETS THE OPPORTUNITY TO CLEAN THEIR BOSS' DESK.
IT'S LIKE A HOLIDAY. I HOPE THIS KIND OF FUN NEVER ENDS!
きゅ
きゅ
きゅ
SPARKLE
SPARKLE

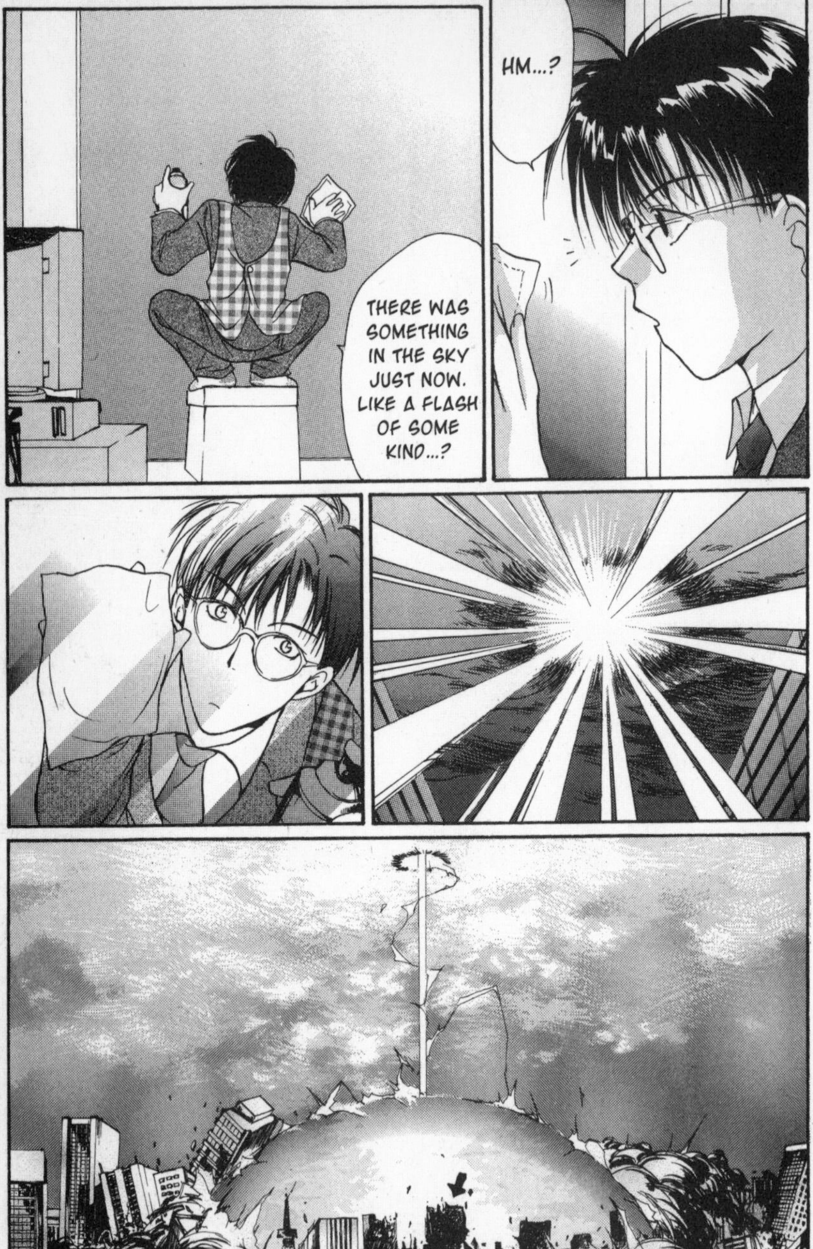
HM...?
THERE WAS SOMETHING IN THE SKY JUST NOW. LIKE A FLASH OF SOME KIND...?

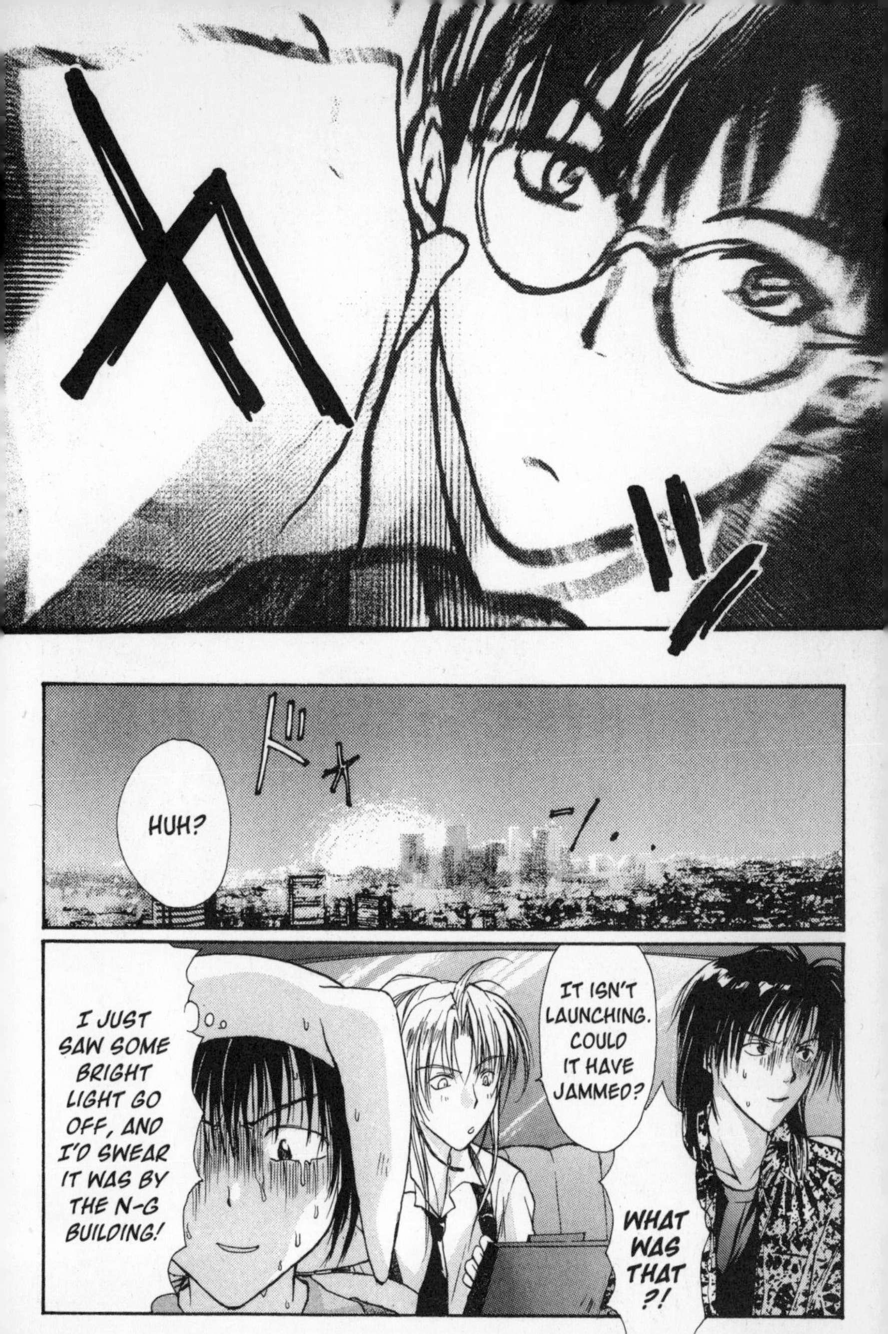
HUH?
WHAT WAS THAT?!
IT ISN'T LAUNCHING. COULD IT HAVE JAMMED?
I JUST SAW SOME BRIGHT LIGHT GO OFF, AND I'D SWEAR IT WAS BY THE N-G BUILDING!

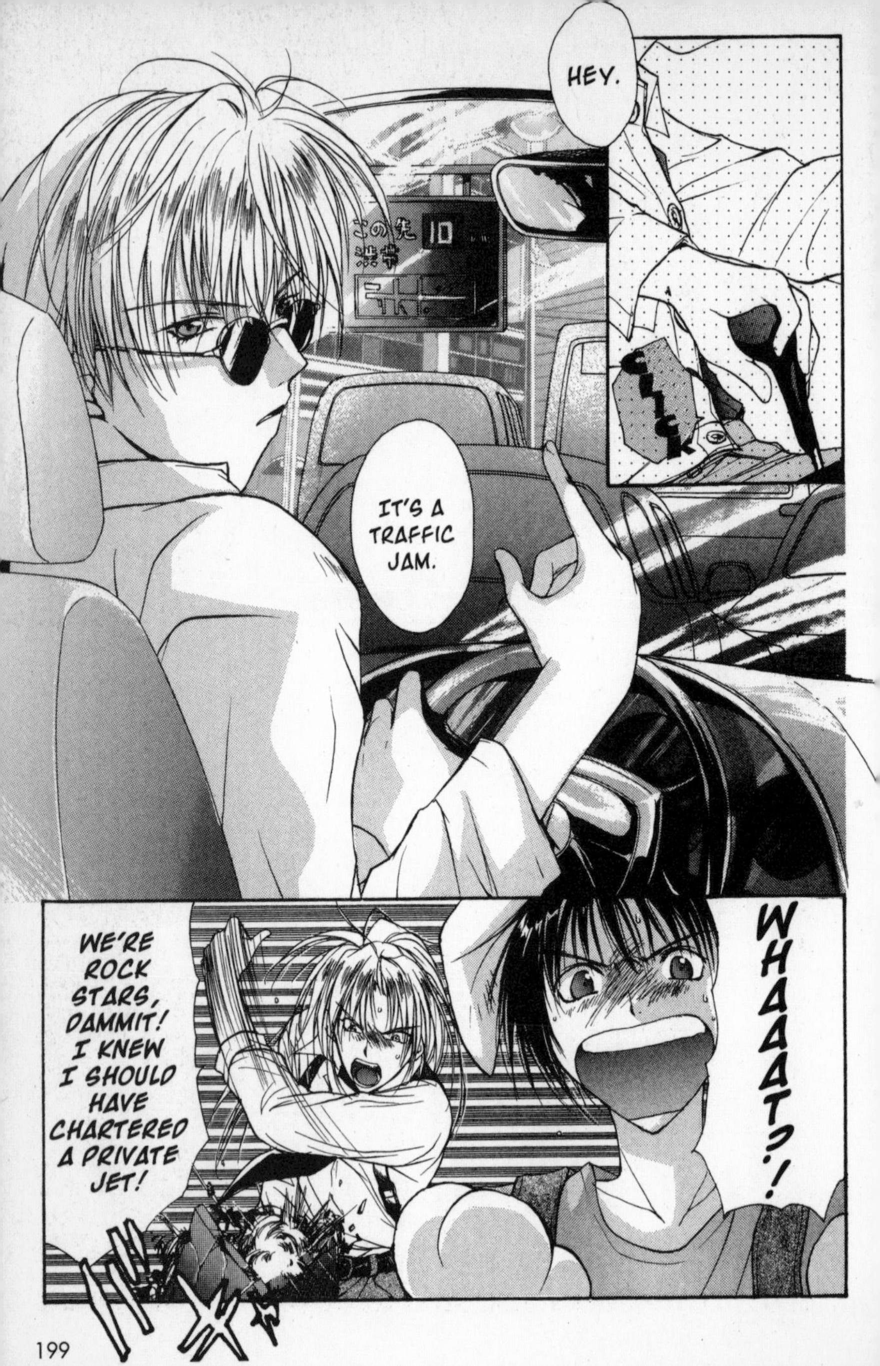
HEY.
CLICK
この先 10
渋滞
IT'S A TRAFFIC JAM.
WHAAAAT?!
WE'RE ROCK STARS, DAMMIT! I KNEW I SHOULD HAVE CHARTERED A PRIVATE JET!

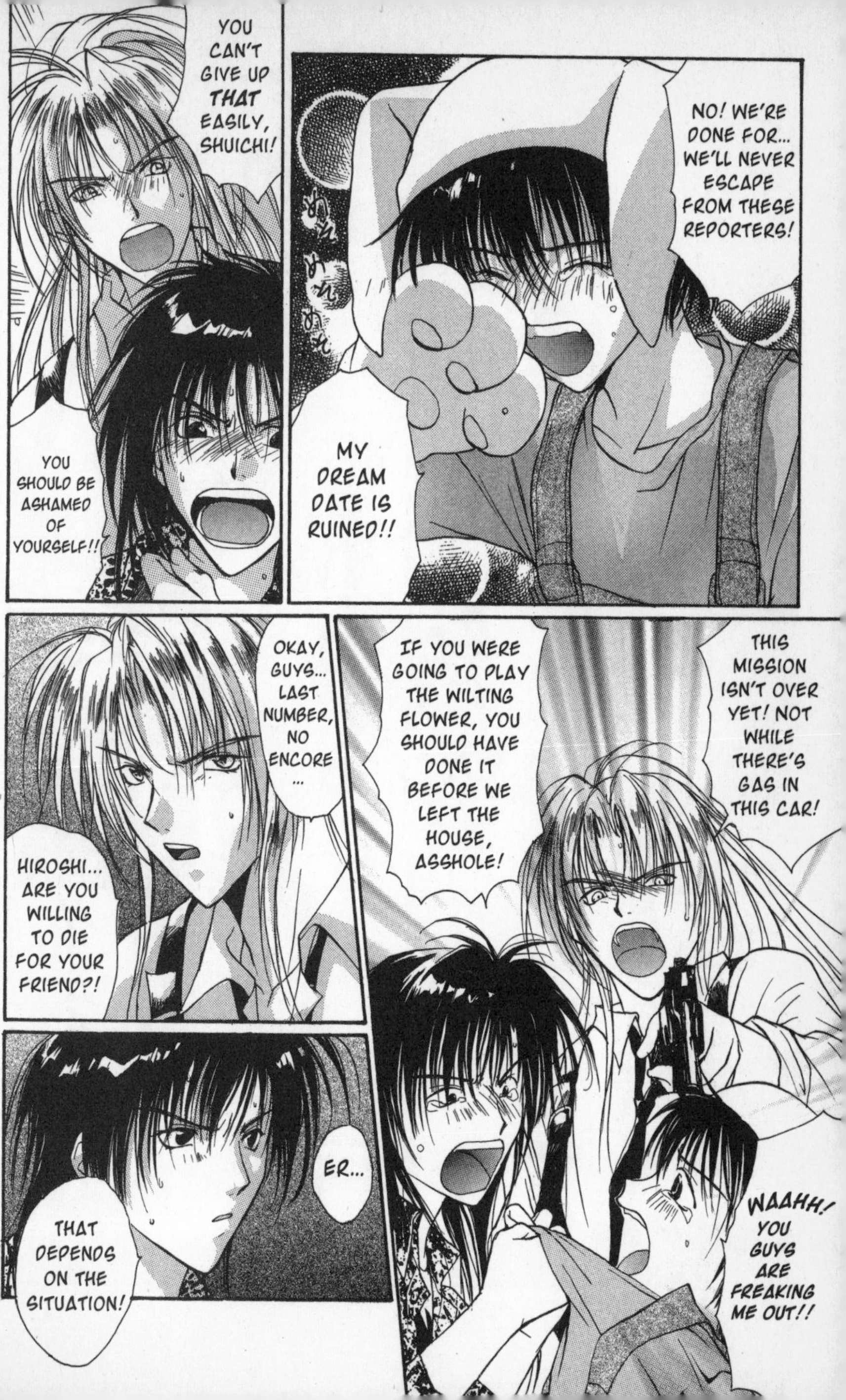
NO! WE'RE DONE FOR... WE'LL NEVER ESCAPE FROM THESE REPORTERS!
MY DREAM DATE IS RUINED!!
YOU CAN'T GIVE UP **THAT** EASILY, SHUICHI!
YOU SHOULD BE ASHAMED OF YOURSELF!!
THIS MISSION ISN'T OVER YET! NOT WHILE THERE'S GAS IN THIS CAR!
IF YOU WERE GOING TO PLAY THE WILTING FLOWER, YOU SHOULD HAVE DONE IT BEFORE WE LEFT THE HOUSE, ASSHOLE!
WAAHH! YOU GUYS ARE FREAKING ME OUT!!
OKAY, GUYS... LAST NUMBER, NO ENCORE ...
HIROSHI... ARE YOU WILLING TO DIE FOR YOUR FRIEND?!
ER...
THAT DEPENDS ON THE SITUATION!

*They're still inside the car.

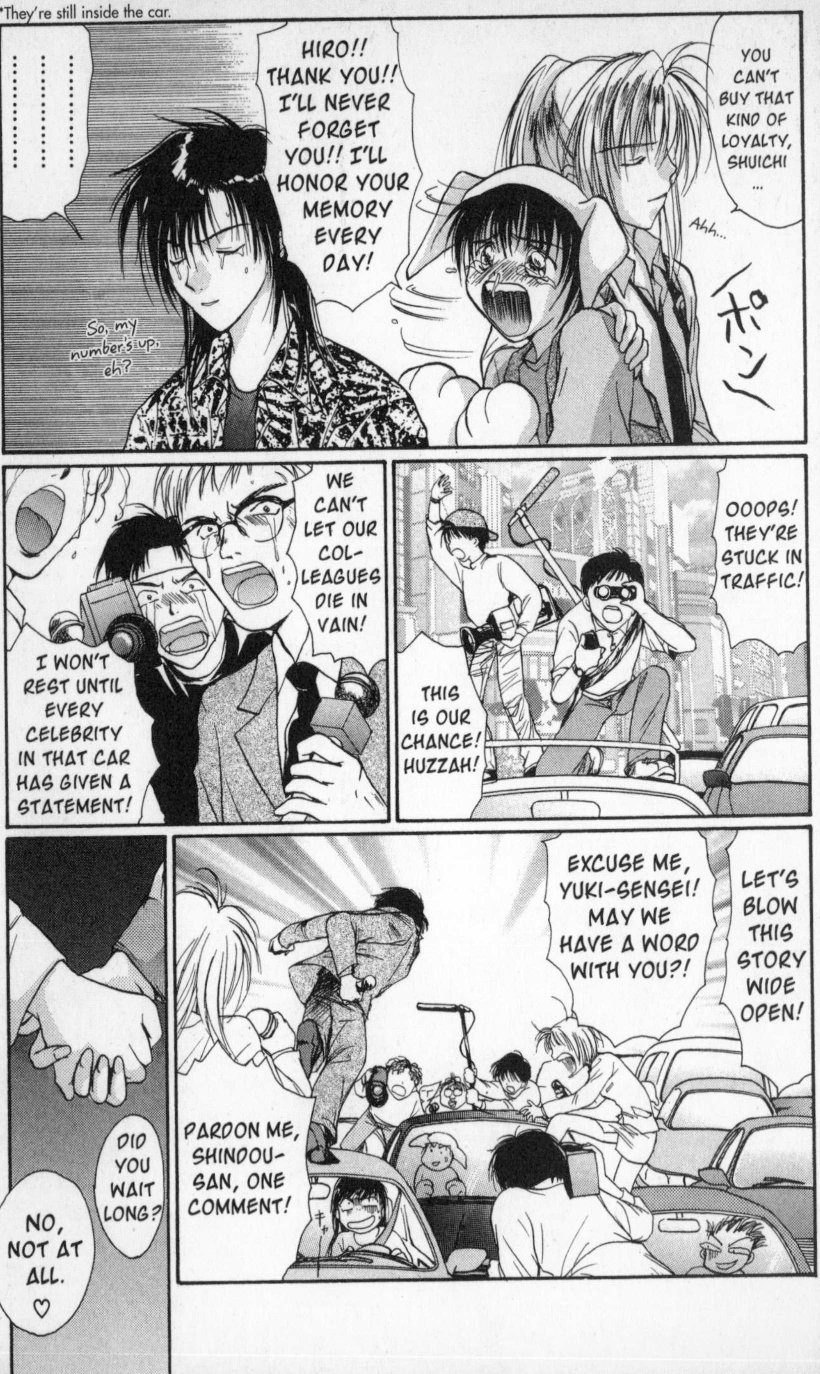
YOU CAN'T BUY THAT KIND OF LOYALTY, SHUICHI ...
Ahh...
ポン
HIRO!! THANK YOU!! I'LL NEVER FORGET YOU!! I'LL HONOR YOUR MEMORY EVERY DAY!
So, my number's up, eh?
......
OOOPS! THEY'RE STUCK IN TRAFFIC!
THIS IS OUR CHANCE! HUZZAH!
WE CAN'T LET OUR COL-LEAGUES DIE IN VAIN!
I WON'T REST UNTIL EVERY CELEBRITY IN THAT CAR HAS GIVEN A STATEMENT!
LET'S BLOW THIS STORY WIDE OPEN!
EXCUSE ME, YUKI-SENSEI! MAY WE HAVE A WORD WITH YOU?!
PARDON ME, SHINDOU-SAN, ONE COMMENT!
キャ
DID YOU WAIT LONG?
NO, NOT AT ALL. ♡

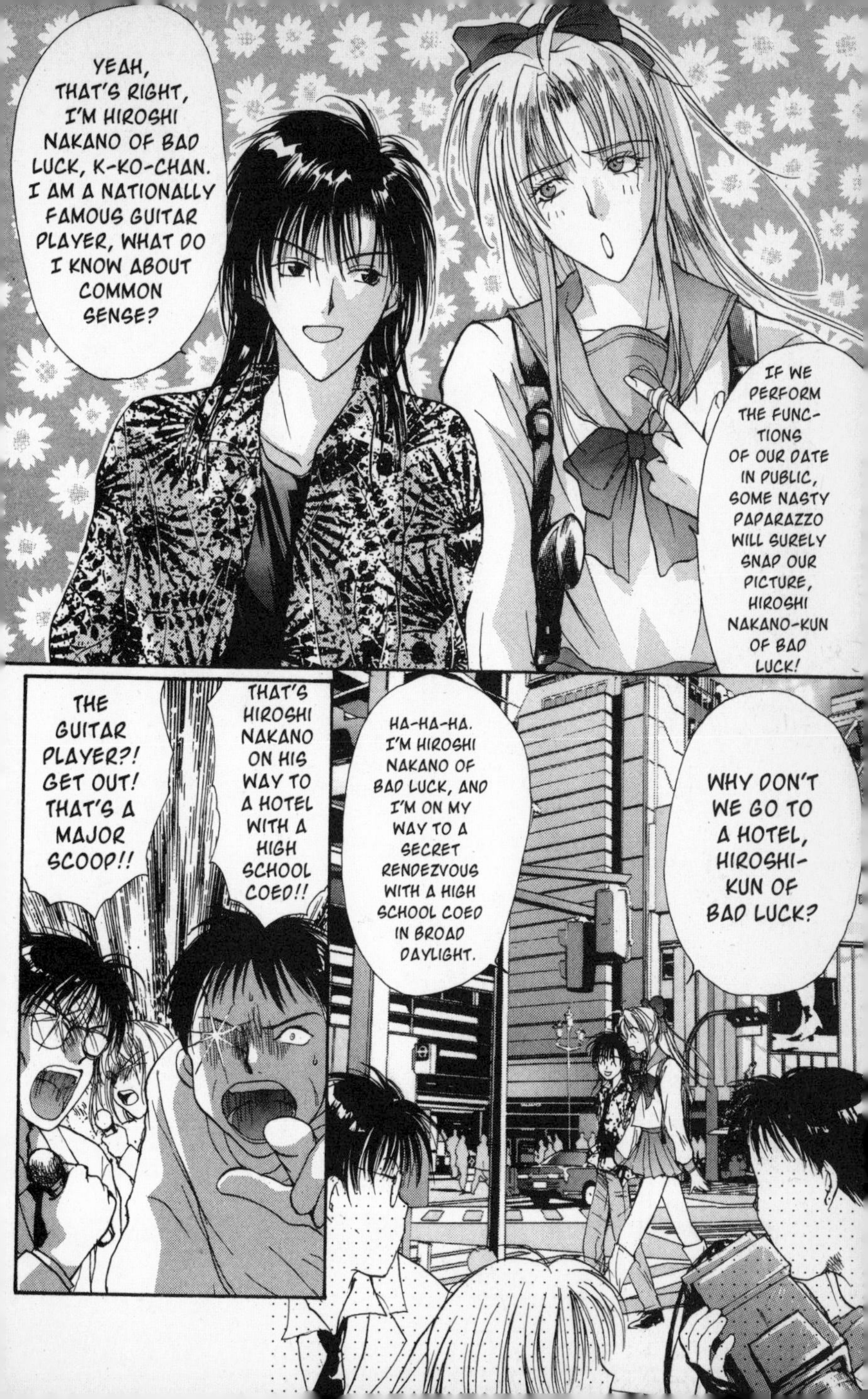
IF WE PERFORM THE FUNCTIONS OF OUR DATE IN PUBLIC, SOME NASTY PAPARAZZO WILL SURELY SNAP OUR PICTURE, HIROSHI NAKANO-KUN OF BAD LUCK!
YEAH, THAT'S RIGHT, I'M HIROSHI NAKANO OF BAD LUCK, K-KO-CHAN. I AM A NATIONALLY FAMOUS GUITAR PLAYER, WHAT DO I KNOW ABOUT COMMON SENSE?
WHY DON'T WE GO TO A HOTEL, HIROSHI-KUN OF BAD LUCK?
HA-HA-HA. I'M HIROSHI NAKANO OF BAD LUCK, AND I'M ON MY WAY TO A SECRET RENDEZVOUS WITH A HIGH SCHOOL COED IN BROAD DAYLIGHT.
THAT'S HIROSHI NAKANO ON HIS WAY TO A HOTEL WITH A HIGH SCHOOL COED!!
THE GUITAR PLAYER?! GET OUT! THAT'S A MAJOR SCOOP!!

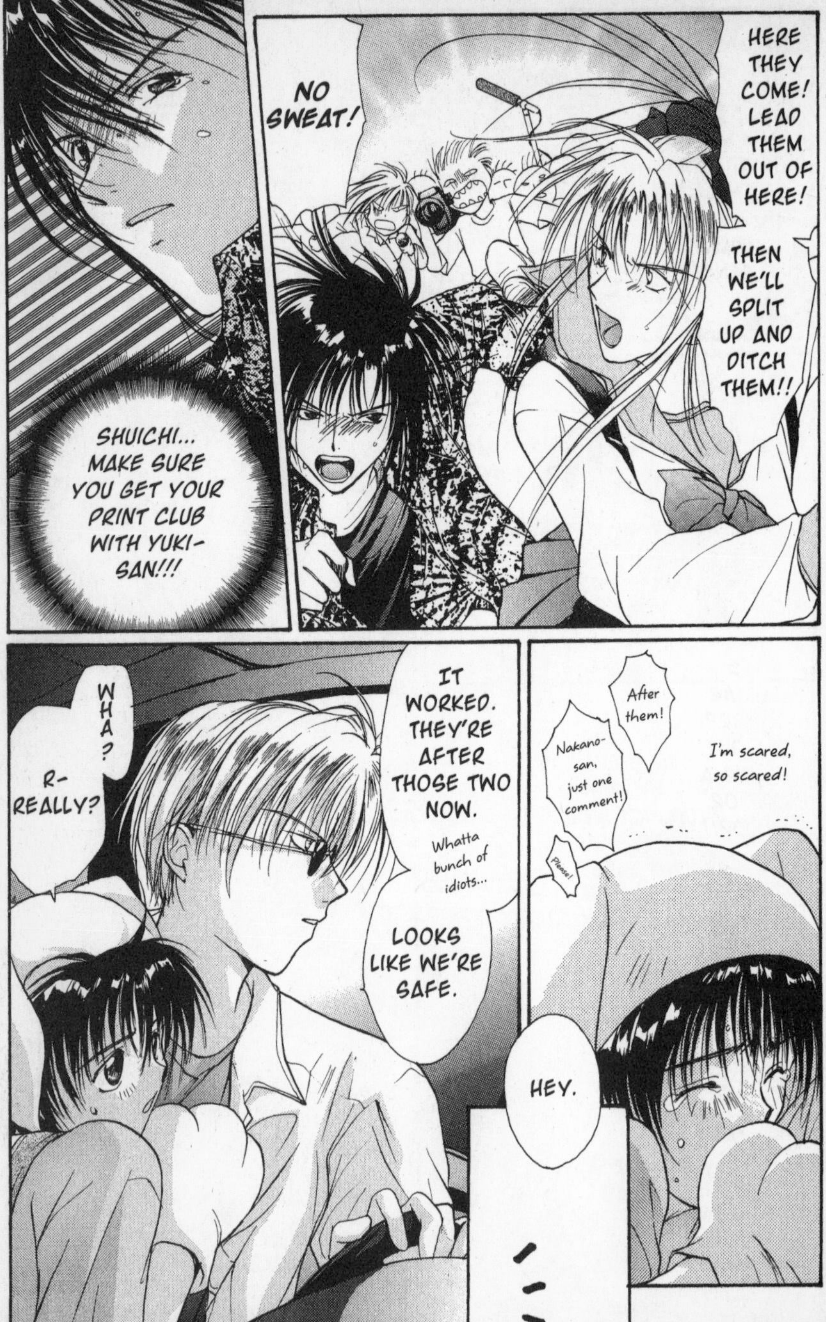
HERE THEY COME! LEAD THEM OUT OF HERE!
THEN WE'LL SPLIT UP AND DITCH THEM!!
NO SWEAT!
SHUICHI... MAKE SURE YOU GET YOUR PRINT CLUB WITH YUKI-SAN!!!
After them!
Nakano-san, just one comment!
Please!
I'm scared, so scared!
HEY.
IT WORKED. THEY'RE AFTER THOSE TWO NOW.
Whatta bunch of idiots...
LOOKS LIKE WE'RE SAFE.
WHA? R-REALLY?

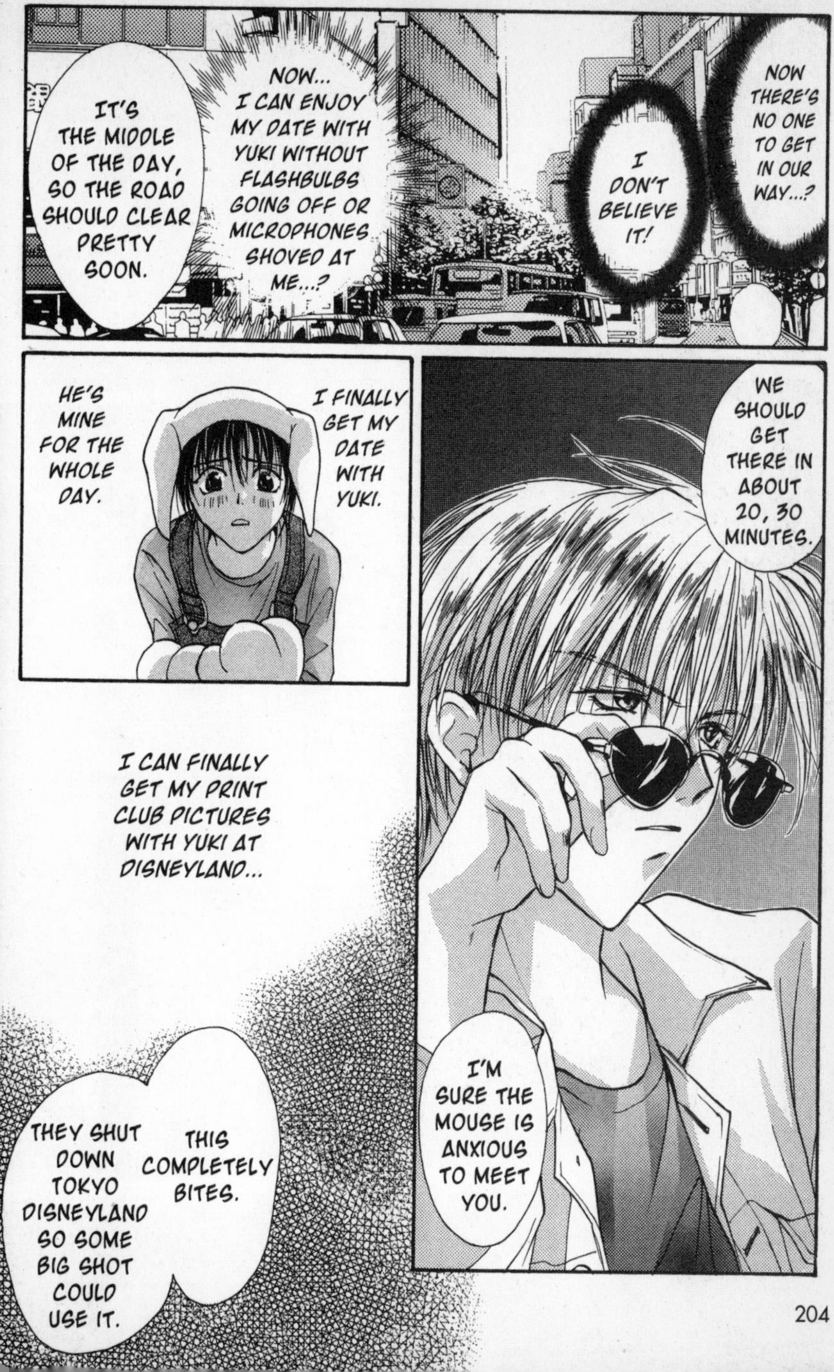
NOW THERE'S NO ONE TO GET IN OUR WAY...?
I DON'T BELIEVE IT!
NOW... I CAN ENJOY MY DATE WITH YUKI WITHOUT FLASHBULBS GOING OFF OR MICROPHONES SHOVED AT ME...?
IT'S THE MIDDLE OF THE DAY, SO THE ROAD SHOULD CLEAR PRETTY SOON.
WE SHOULD GET THERE IN ABOUT 20, 30 MINUTES.
I'M SURE THE MOUSE IS ANXIOUS TO MEET YOU.
I FINALLY GET MY DATE WITH YUKI.
HE'S MINE FOR THE WHOLE DAY.
I CAN FINALLY GET MY PRINT CLUB PICTURES WITH YUKI AT DISNEYLAND...
THIS COMPLETELY BITES.
THEY SHUT DOWN TOKYO DISNEYLAND SO SOME BIG SHOT COULD USE IT.

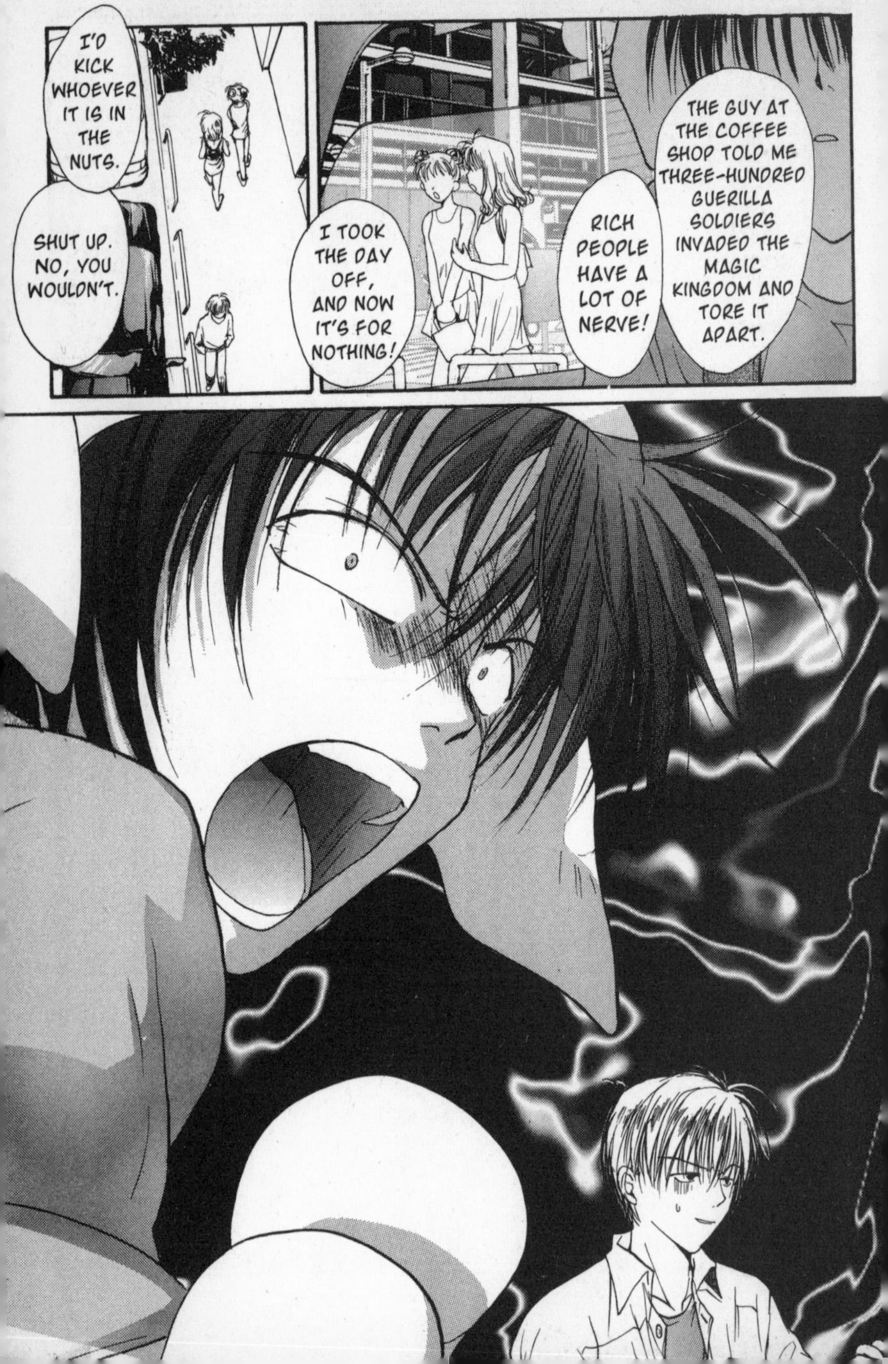
THE GUY AT THE COFFEE SHOP TOLD ME THREE-HUNDRED GUERILLA SOLDIERS INVADED THE MAGIC KINGDOM AND TORE IT APART.
RICH PEOPLE HAVE A LOT OF NERVE!
I TOOK THE DAY OFF, AND NOW IT'S FOR NOTHING!
I'D KICK WHOEVER IT IS IN THE NUTS.
SHUT UP. NO, YOU WOULDN'T.

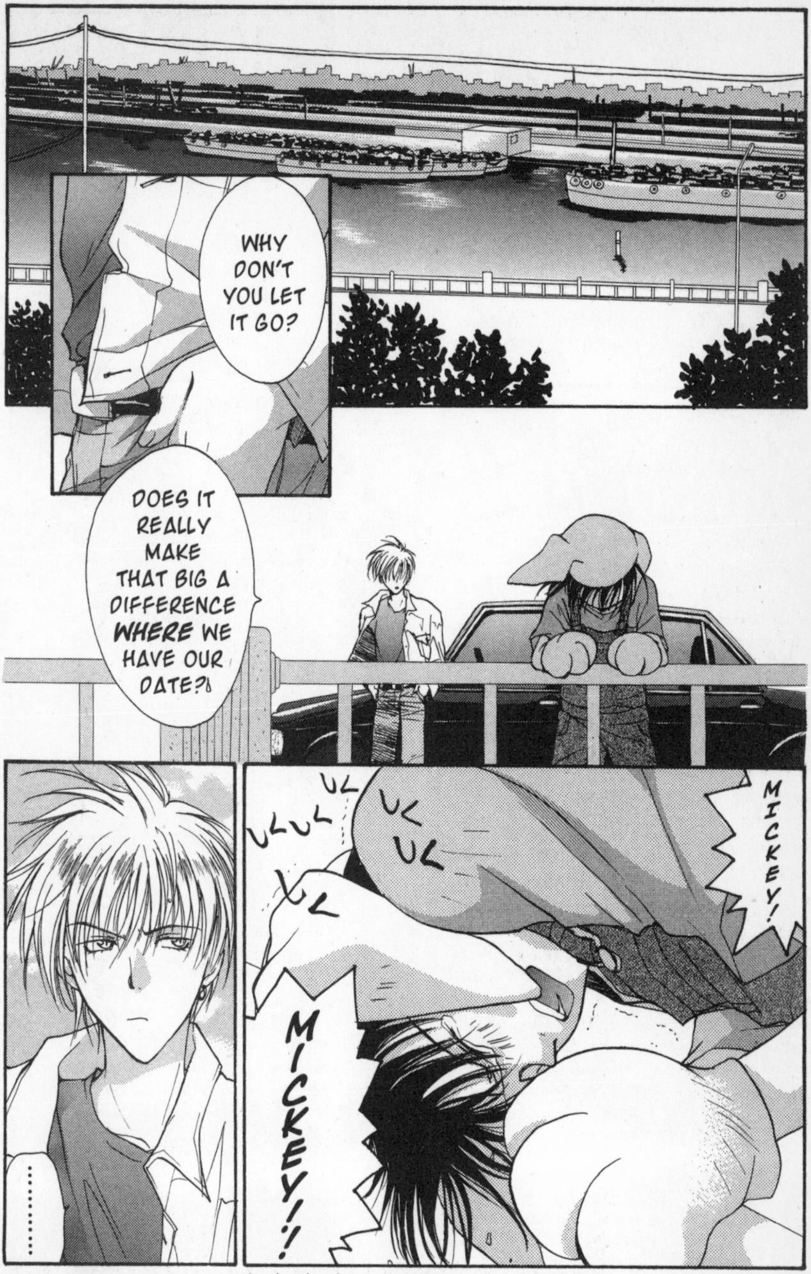
WHY DON'T YOU LET IT GO?
DOES IT REALLY MAKE THAT BIG A DIFFERENCE WHERE WE HAVE OUR DATE?!
MICKEY!
UL UL
ULULUL
UL
UL
MICKEY!!
......

* sob sob sob

About my self-portraits.

I actually like my self-portraits. Someone who is good at judging a person's character would interpret them as someone who envisions herself as something other than human, because she can't come up with the right words to describe herself as she really is. Then again, why should I? I'm a manga artist, after all, so why should I try to express myself though writing? I draw pictures for a living, and I can't fill this space with a lot of useless text. It's too hard, and, to be honest, a total pain in the ass. So, I use it to draw some pictures. But nooooo, that's not good enough either. Oh, heaven forbid. I can't do this. "Men In Black." "Love and Peace." If I were a space alien I could just hook on to some wavelength and it would do all the work for me. Wouldn't that be so easy? I guess I'm just going through some random thoughts here. But it's better than getting stuck with a blank page. Looking good! Approval ratings are up! So, as a result, it's good to have space aliens! I want to be a space alien! Yayyyy! So, anyway, this is how I drew myself in the end.

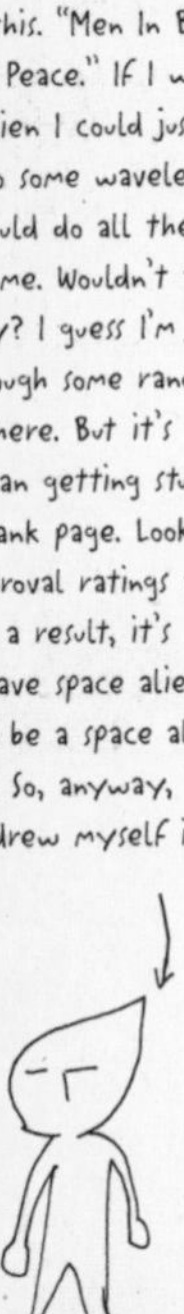

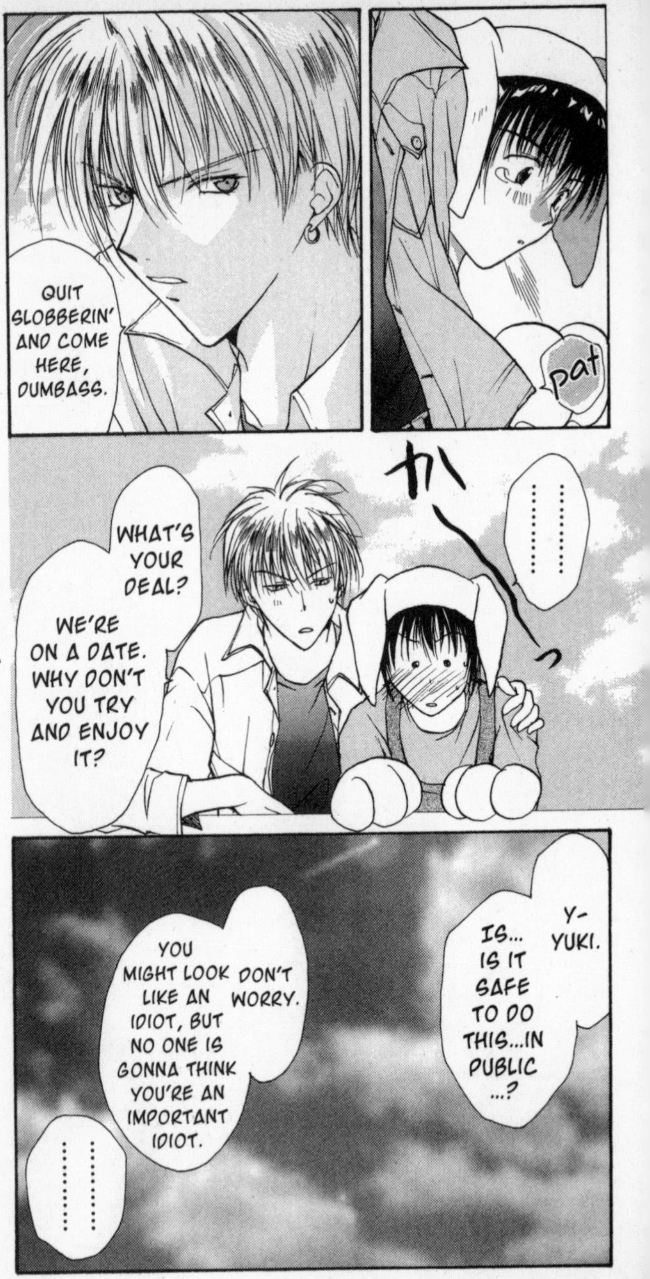
pat
QUIT SLOBBERIN' AND COME HERE, DUMBASS.
......
か〜
WHAT'S YOUR DEAL?
WE'RE ON A DATE. WHY DON'T YOU TRY AND ENJOY IT?
Y-YUKI.
IS... IS IT SAFE TO DO THIS...IN PUBLIC ...?
DON'T WORRY.
YOU MIGHT LOOK LIKE AN IDIOT, BUT NO ONE IS GONNA THINK YOU'RE AN IMPORTANT IDIOT.
......

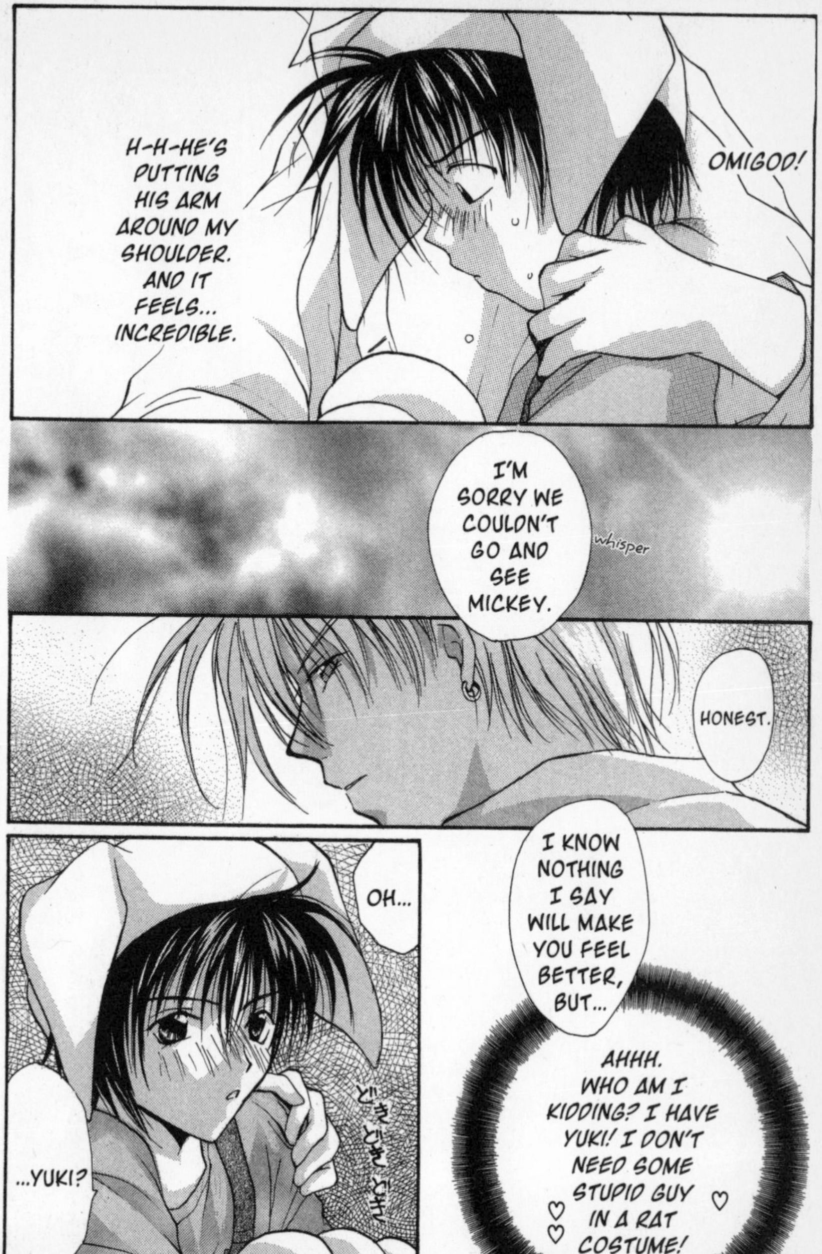
OMIGOD!
H-H-HE'S PUTTING HIS ARM AROUND MY SHOULDER. AND IT FEELS... INCREDIBLE.
I'M SORRY WE COULDN'T GO AND SEE MICKEY.
whisper
HONEST.
I KNOW NOTHING I SAY WILL MAKE YOU FEEL BETTER, BUT...
AHHH. WHO AM I KIDDING? I HAVE YUKI! I DON'T NEED SOME STUPID GUY IN A RAT COSTUME!
OH...
どき どき どき
...YUKI?

* Ba-dump Tha-thump

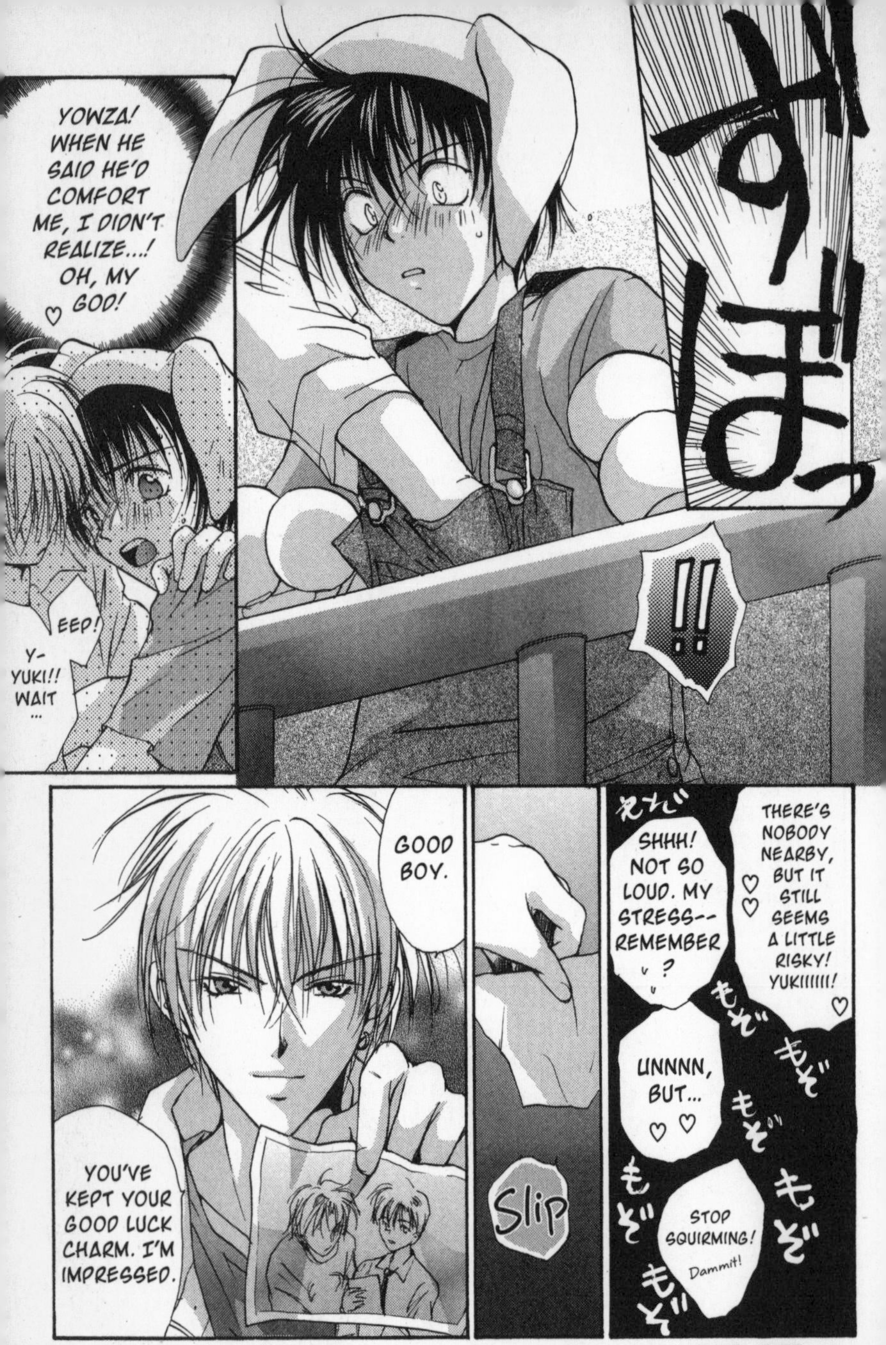
ずぼっ
!!
YOWZA! WHEN HE SAID HE'D COMFORT ME, I DIDN'T REALIZE...! OH, MY GOD! ♡
EEP!
Y-YUKI!! WAIT ...
THERE'S NOBODY NEARBY, BUT IT STILL SEEMS A LITTLE RISKY! YUKIIIIII! ♡ ♡ ♡
SHHH! NOT SO LOUD. MY STRESS--REMEMBER ?
もぞもぞ もぞもぞ もぞもぞ もぞもぞ
UNNNN, BUT... ♡ ♡
STOP SQUIRMING!
Dammit!
Slip
GOOD BOY.
YOU'VE KEPT YOUR GOOD LUCK CHARM. I'M IMPRESSED.

* GROPE GROPE GROPE GROPE

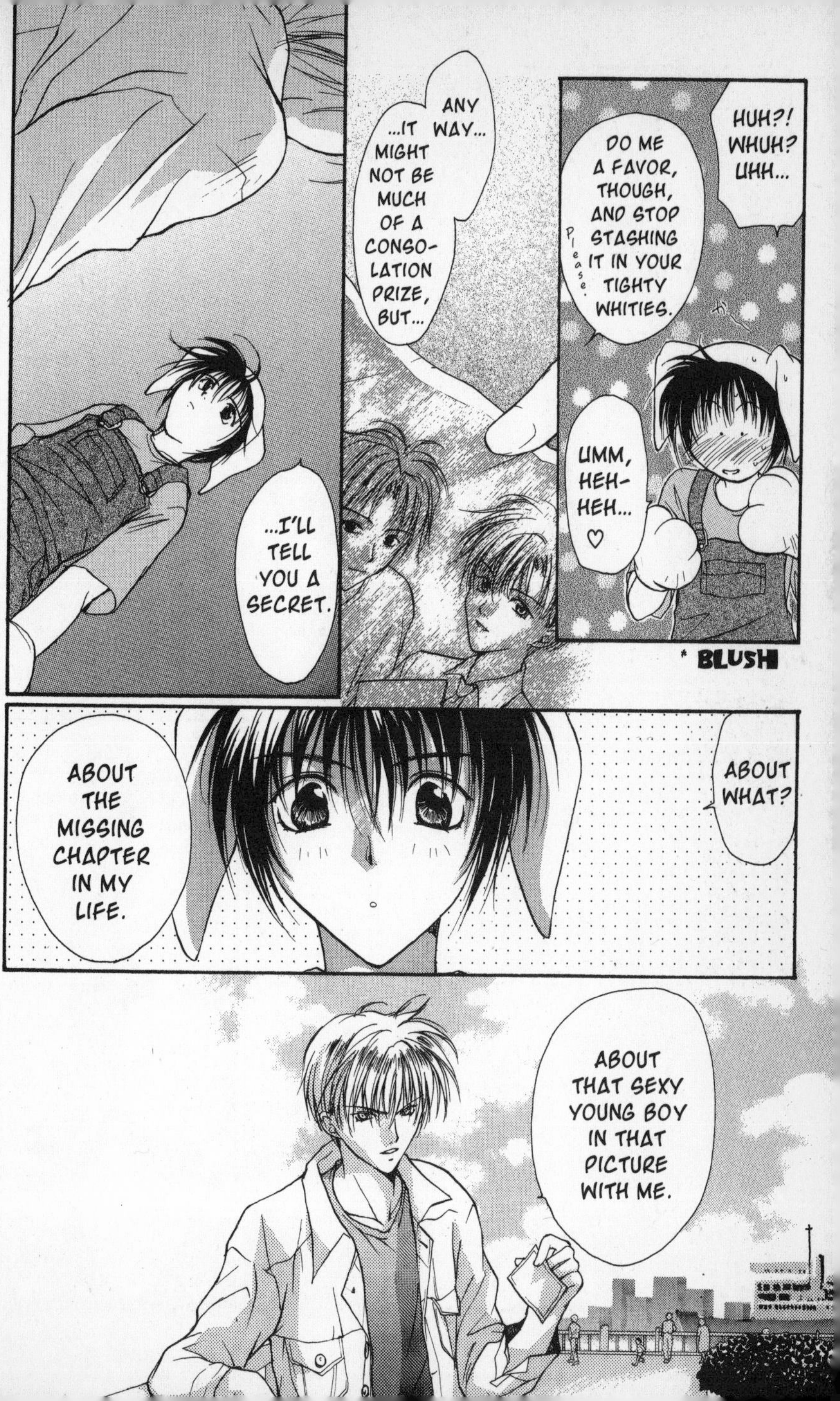
HUH?! WHUH? UHH...
DO ME A FAVOR, THOUGH, AND STOP STASHING IT IN YOUR TIGHTY WHITIES.
Please.
UMM, HEH-HEH... ♡
* BLUSH
ANYWAY... ...IT MIGHT NOT BE MUCH OF A CONSOLATION PRIZE, BUT...
...I'LL TELL YOU A SECRET.
ABOUT WHAT?
ABOUT THE MISSING CHAPTER IN MY LIFE.
ABOUT THAT SEXY YOUNG BOY IN THAT PICTURE WITH ME.

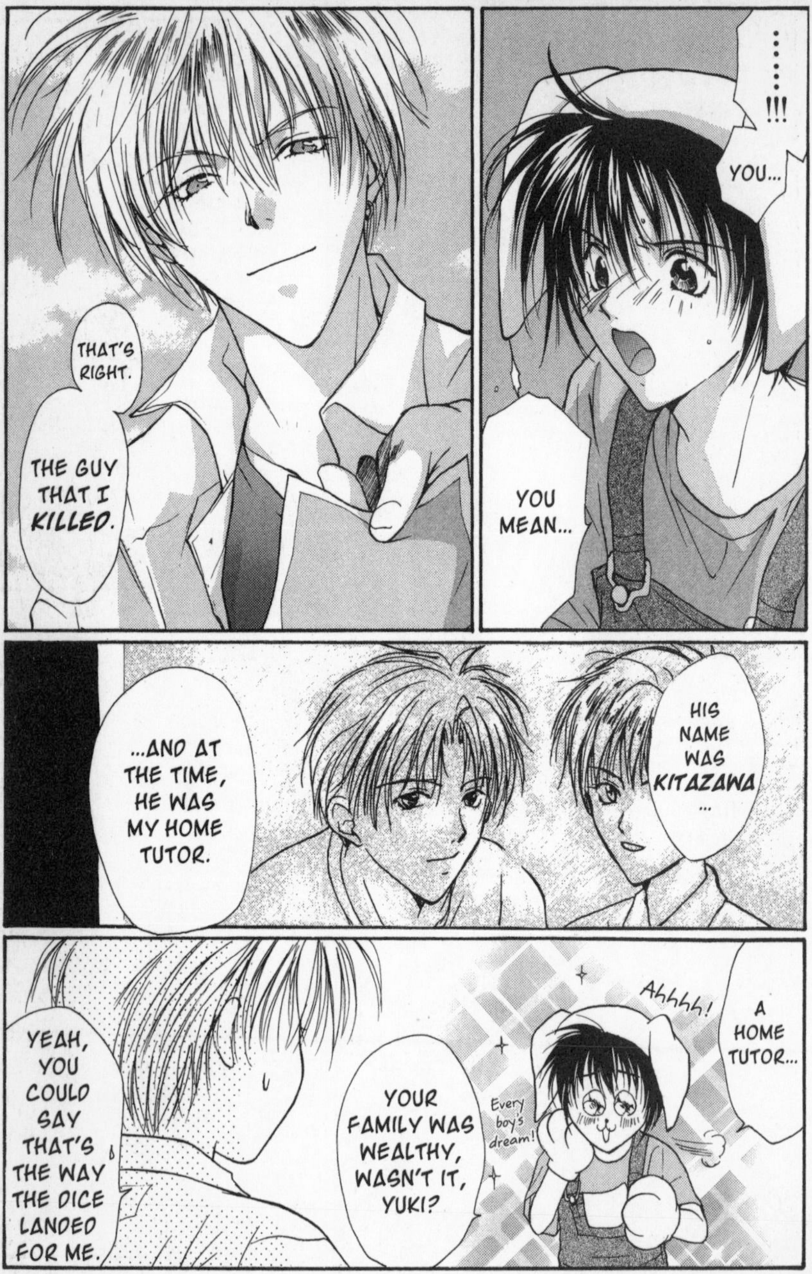
......!!!
YOU...
YOU MEAN...
THAT'S RIGHT.
THE GUY THAT I **KILLED**.
HIS NAME WAS **KITAZAWA** ...
...AND AT THE TIME, HE WAS MY HOME TUTOR.
A HOME TUTOR...
Ahhhh!
Every boy's dream!
YOUR FAMILY WAS WEALTHY, WASN'T IT, YUKI?
YEAH, YOU COULD SAY THAT'S THE WAY THE DICE LANDED FOR ME.

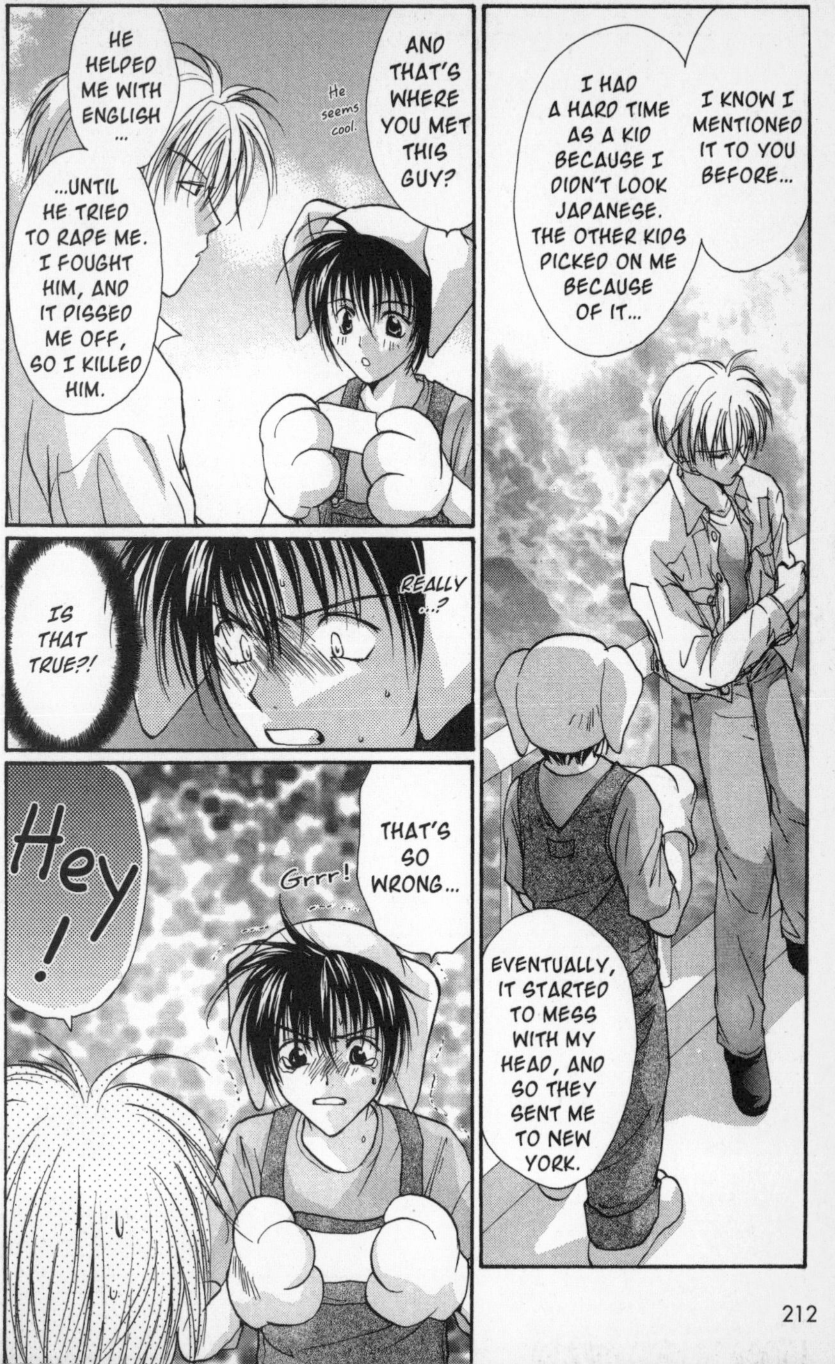

I KNOW I MENTIONED IT TO YOU BEFORE...
I HAD A HARD TIME AS A KID BECAUSE I DIDN'T LOOK JAPANESE. THE OTHER KIDS PICKED ON ME BECAUSE OF IT...
EVENTUALLY, IT STARTED TO MESS WITH MY HEAD, AND SO THEY SENT ME TO NEW YORK.
AND THAT'S WHERE YOU MET THIS GUY?
He seems cool.
HE HELPED ME WITH ENGLISH ...
...UNTIL HE TRIED TO RAPE ME. I FOUGHT HIM, AND IT PISSED ME OFF, SO I KILLED HIM.
REALLY ...?
IS THAT TRUE?!
THAT'S SO WRONG...
Grrr!
Hey!

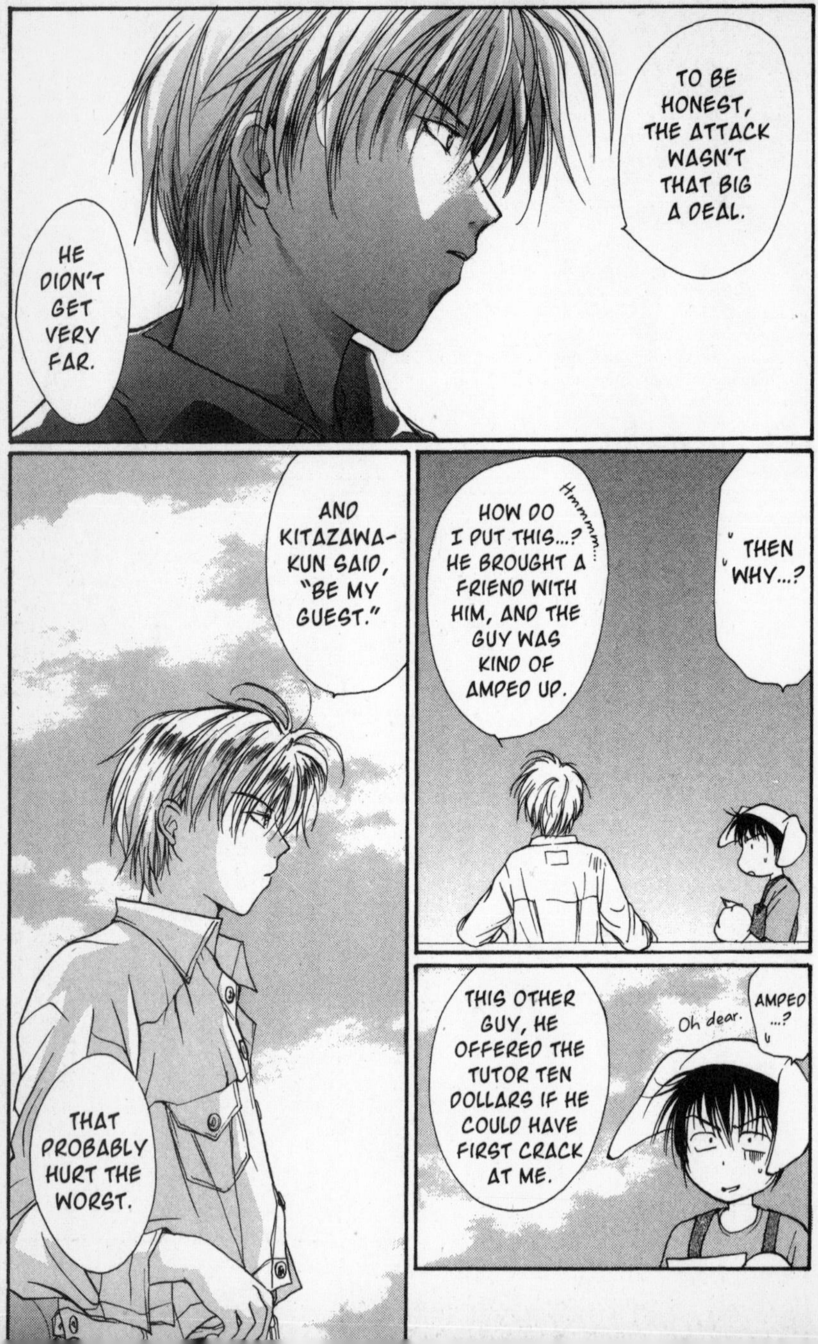
TO BE HONEST, THE ATTACK WASN'T THAT BIG A DEAL.
HE DIDN'T GET VERY FAR.
THEN WHY...?
Hmmmmm...
HOW DO I PUT THIS...? HE BROUGHT A FRIEND WITH HIM, AND THE GUY WAS KIND OF AMPED UP.
AMPED ...?
Oh dear.
THIS OTHER GUY, HE OFFERED THE TUTOR TEN DOLLARS IF HE COULD HAVE FIRST CRACK AT ME.
AND KITAZAWA-KUN SAID, "BE MY GUEST."
THAT PROBABLY HURT THE WORST.

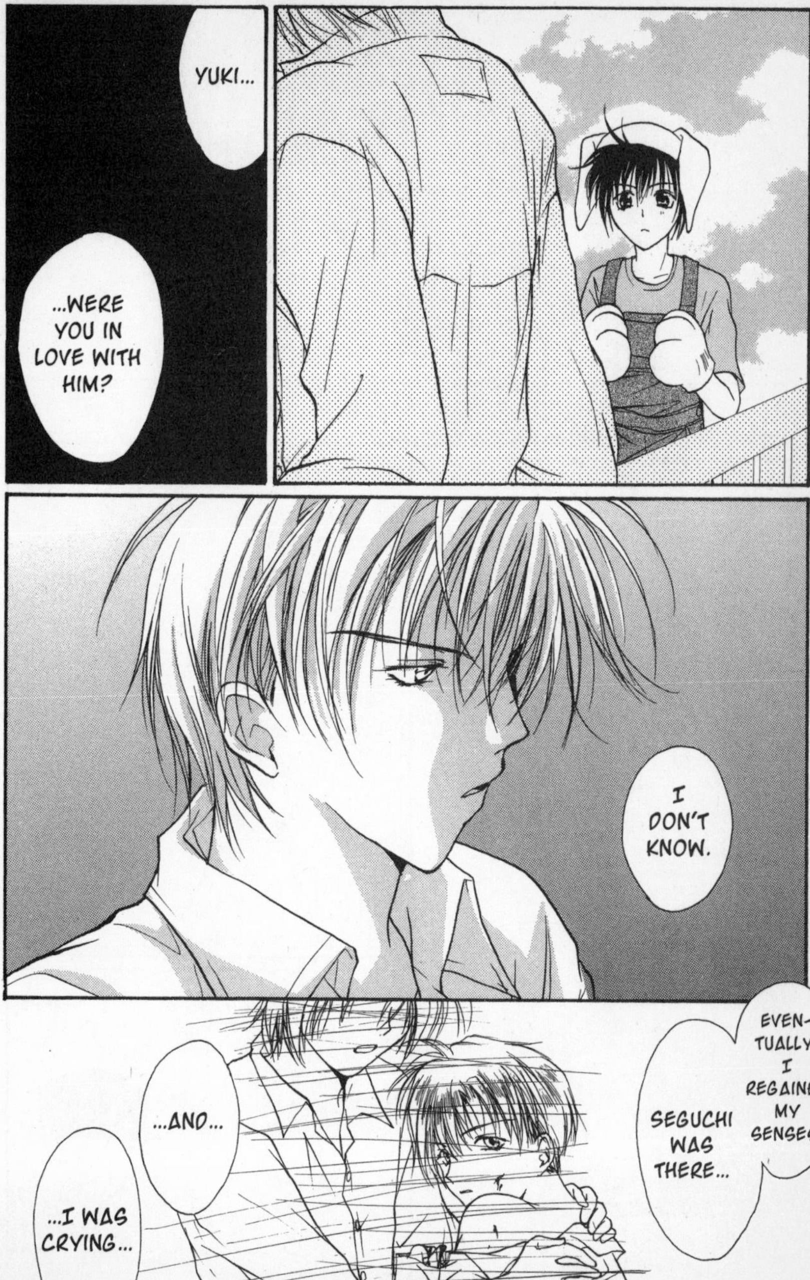
YUKI...
...WERE YOU IN LOVE WITH HIM?
I DON'T KNOW.
EVEN-TUALLY... I REGAINED MY SENSES.
SEGUCHI WAS THERE...
...AND...
...I WAS CRYING...

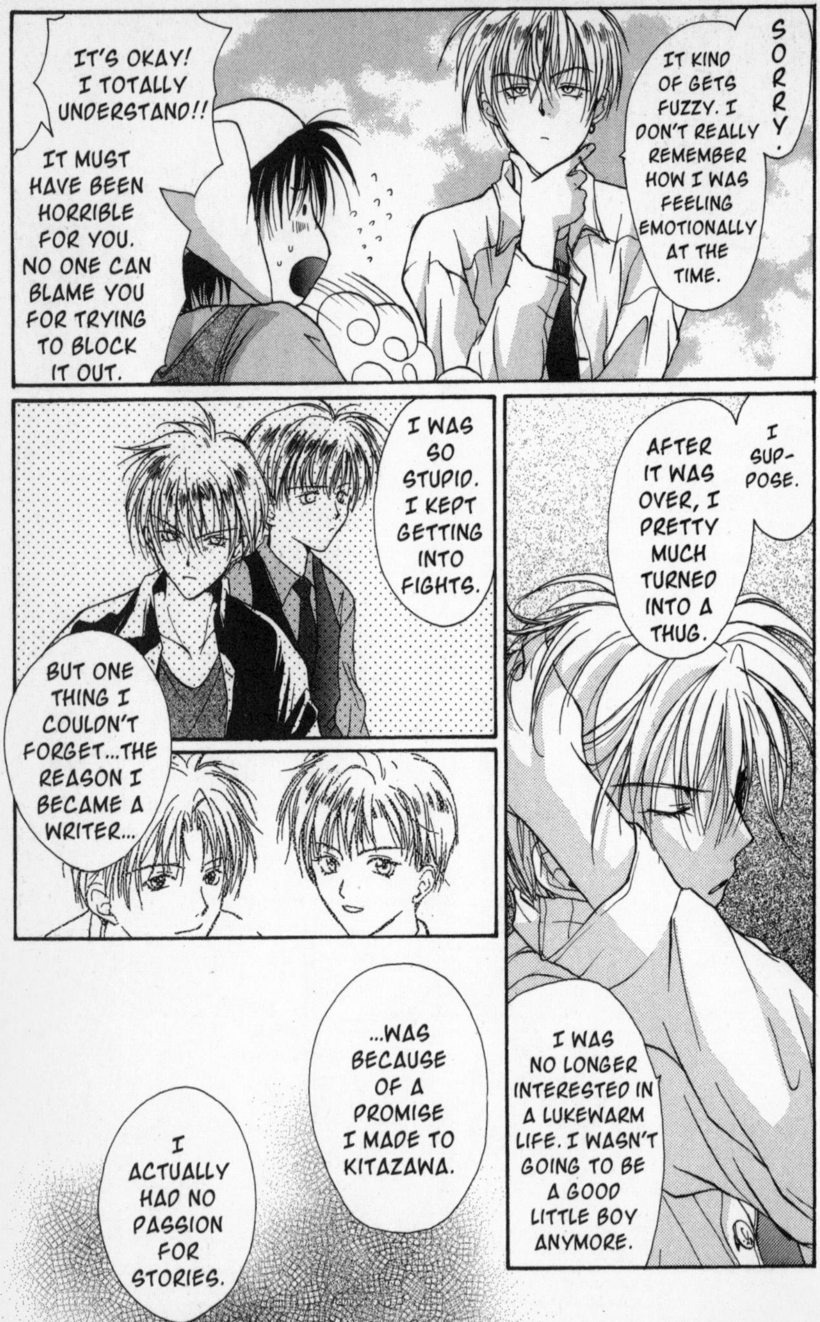
SORRY.
IT KIND OF GETS FUZZY. I DON'T REALLY REMEMBER HOW I WAS FEELING EMOTIONALLY AT THE TIME.
IT'S OKAY! I TOTALLY UNDERSTAND!!
IT MUST HAVE BEEN HORRIBLE FOR YOU. NO ONE CAN BLAME YOU FOR TRYING TO BLOCK IT OUT.
I SUP-POSE.
AFTER IT WAS OVER, I PRETTY MUCH TURNED INTO A THUG.
I WAS NO LONGER INTERESTED IN A LUKEWARM LIFE. I WASN'T GOING TO BE A GOOD LITTLE BOY ANYMORE.
I WAS SO STUPID. I KEPT GETTING INTO FIGHTS.
BUT ONE THING I COULDN'T FORGET...THE REASON I BECAME A WRITER...
...WAS BECAUSE OF A PROMISE I MADE TO KITAZAWA.
I ACTUALLY HAD NO PASSION FOR STORIES.

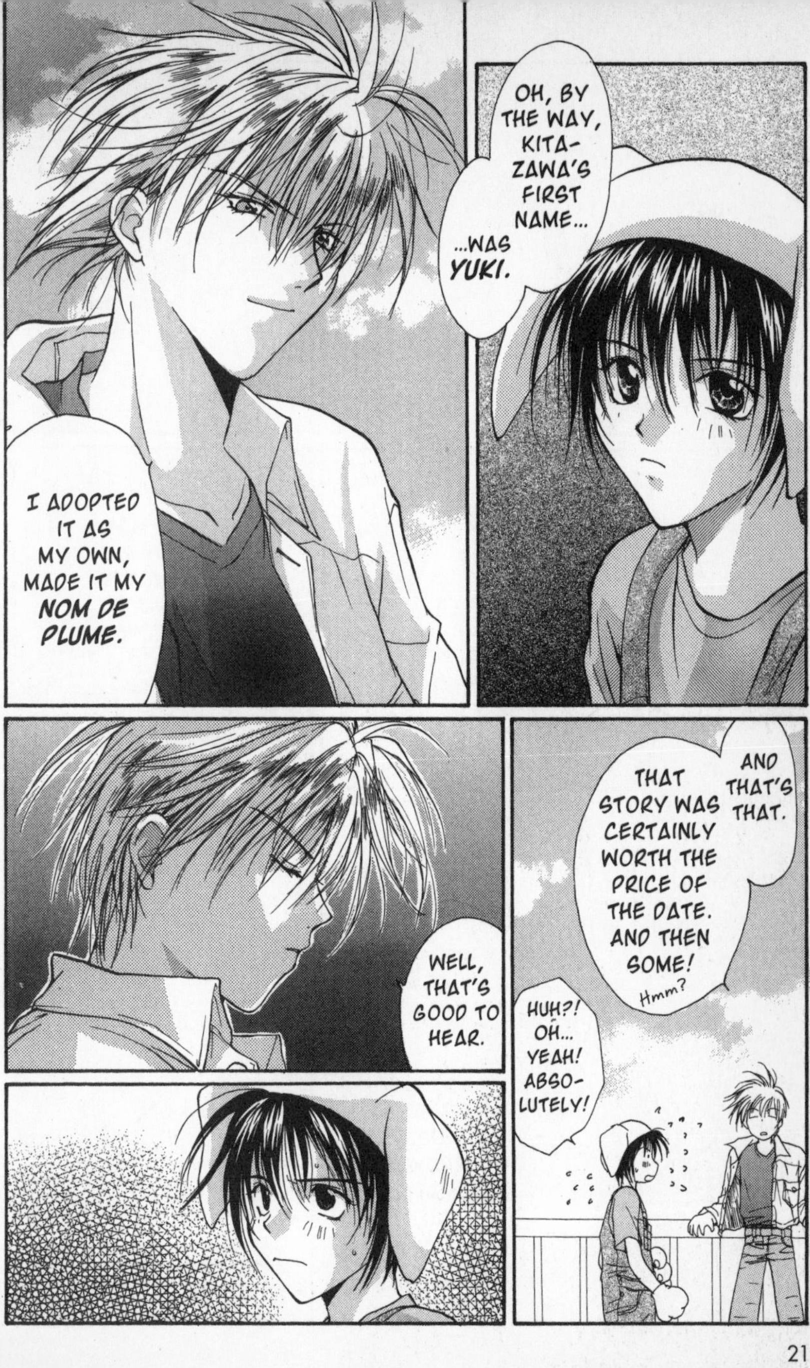
OH, BY THE WAY, KITA-ZAWA'S FIRST NAME...
...WAS YUKI.
I ADOPTED IT AS MY OWN, MADE IT MY NOM DE PLUME.
AND THAT'S THAT.
THAT STORY WAS CERTAINLY WORTH THE PRICE OF THE DATE. AND THEN SOME!
Hmm?
HUH?! OH... YEAH! ABSOLUTELY!
WELL, THAT'S GOOD TO HEAR.

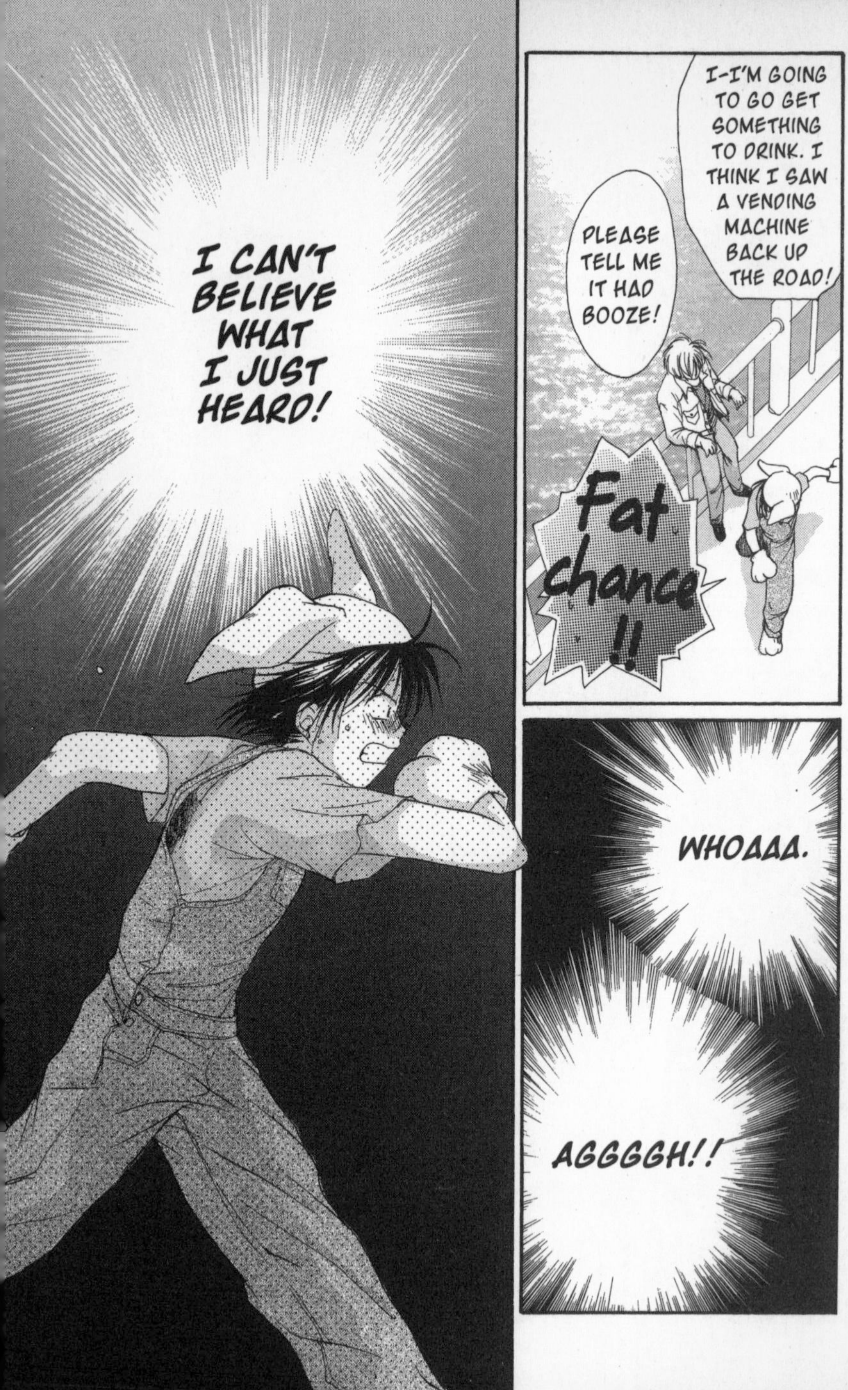
I-I'M GOING TO GO GET SOMETHING TO DRINK. I THINK I SAW A VENDING MACHINE BACK UP THE ROAD!
PLEASE TELL ME IT HAD BOOZE!
Fat chance!!
WHOAAA.
AGGGGH!!
I CAN'T BELIEVE WHAT I JUST HEARD!

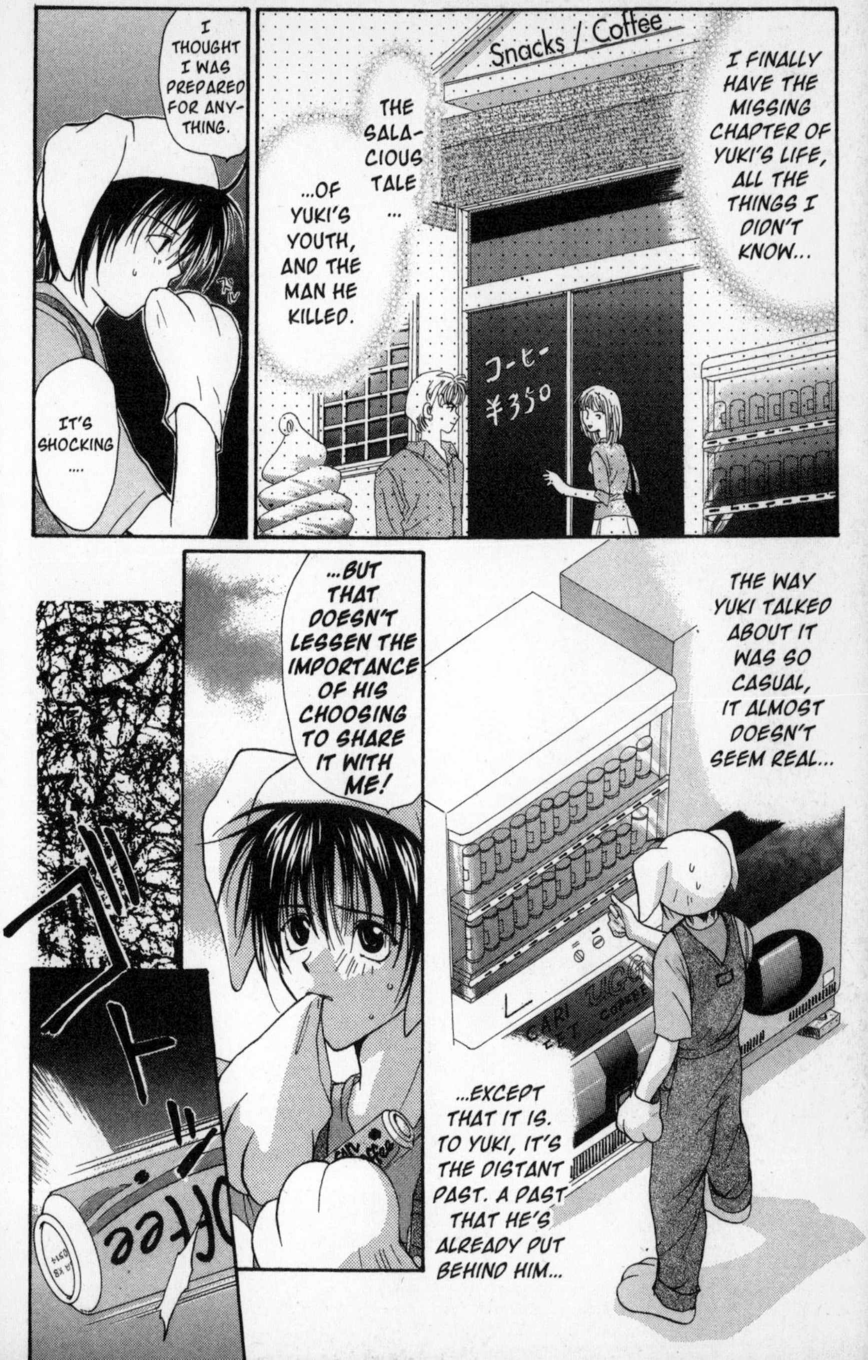
Snacks / Coffee
I FINALLY HAVE THE MISSING CHAPTER OF YUKI'S LIFE, ALL THE THINGS I DIDN'T KNOW...
THE SALACIOUS TALE...
...OF YUKI'S YOUTH, AND THE MAN HE KILLED.
コーヒー ¥350
I THOUGHT I WAS PREPARED FOR ANYTHING.
IT'S SHOCKING....
THE WAY YUKI TALKED ABOUT IT WAS SO CASUAL, IT ALMOST DOESN'T SEEM REAL...
...EXCEPT THAT IT IS. TO YUKI, IT'S THE DISTANT PAST. A PAST THAT HE'S ALREADY PUT BEHIND HIM...
...BUT THAT DOESN'T LESSEN THE IMPORTANCE OF HIS CHOOSING TO SHARE IT WITH ME!

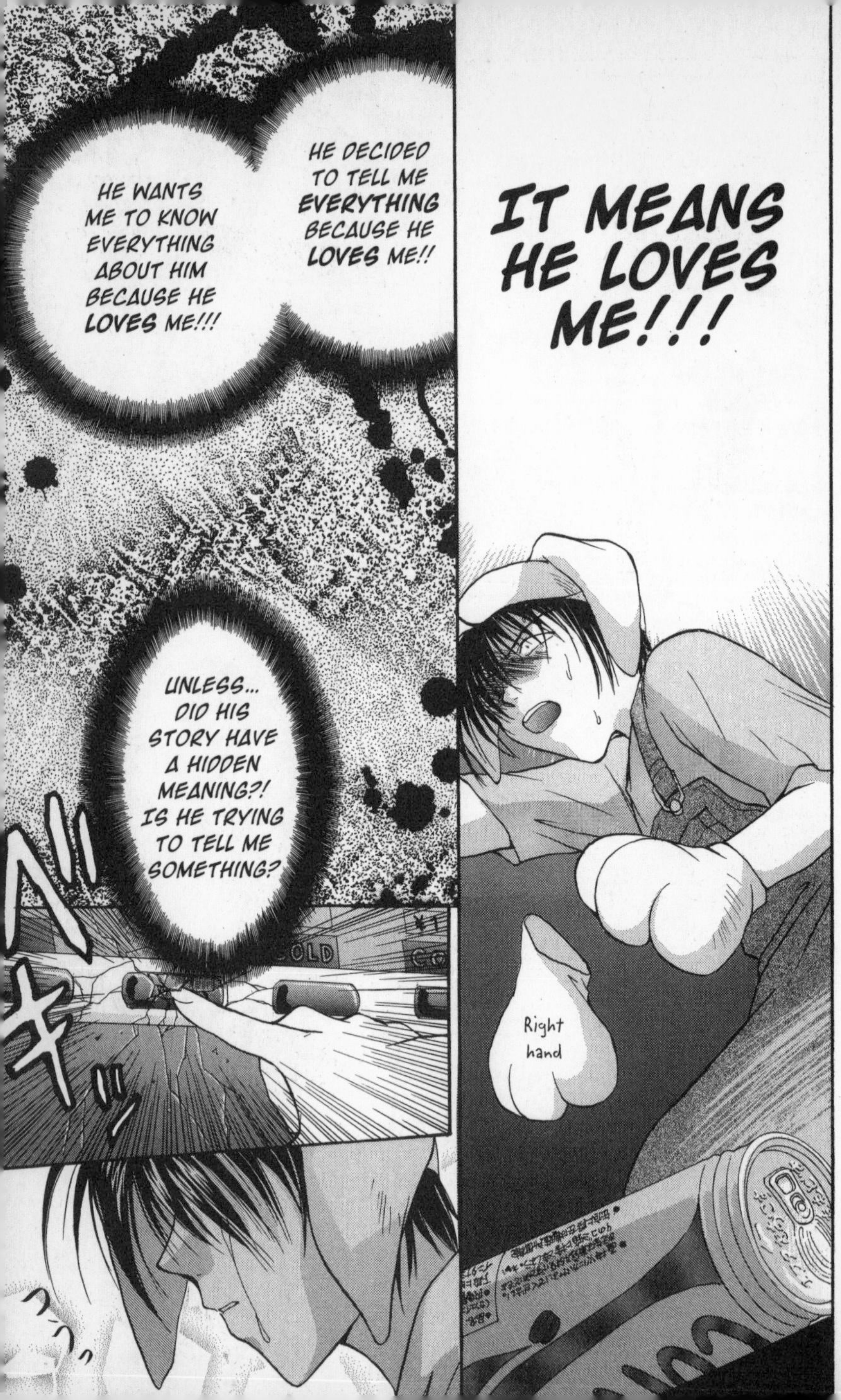
IT MEANS HE LOVES ME!!!
Right hand
HE DECIDED TO TELL ME EVERYTHING BECAUSE HE LOVES ME!!
HE WANTS ME TO KNOW EVERYTHING ABOUT HIM BECAUSE HE LOVES ME!!!
UNLESS... DID HIS STORY HAVE A HIDDEN MEANING?! IS HE TRYING TO TELL ME SOMETHING?
COLD

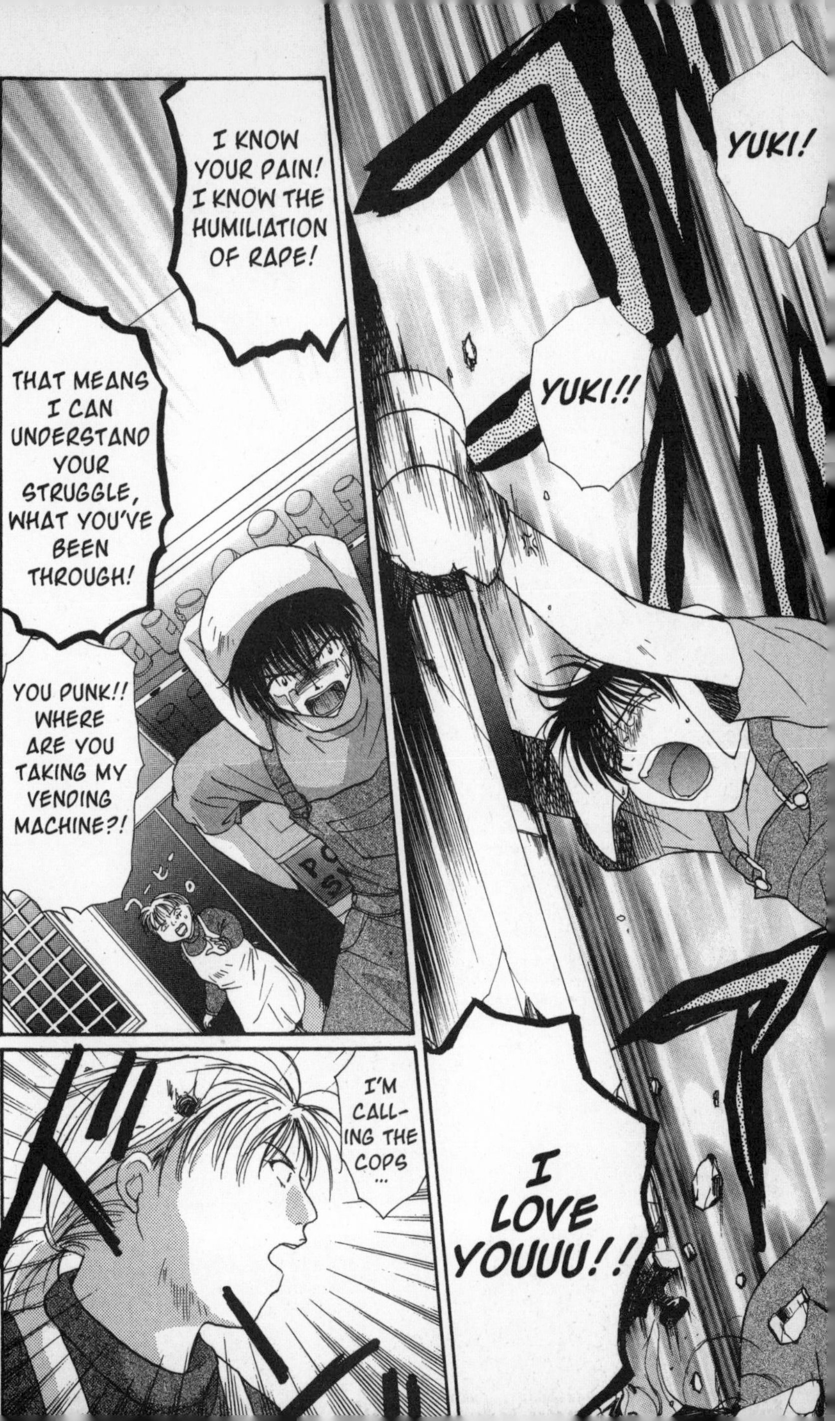
YUKI!
YUKI!!
I LOVE YOUUU!!
I KNOW YOUR PAIN! I KNOW THE HUMILIATION OF RAPE!
THAT MEANS I CAN UNDERSTAND YOUR STRUGGLE, WHAT YOU'VE BEEN THROUGH!
YOU PUNK!! WHERE ARE YOU TAKING MY VENDING MACHINE?!
I'M CALLING THE COPS ...

* drag drag drag drag drag

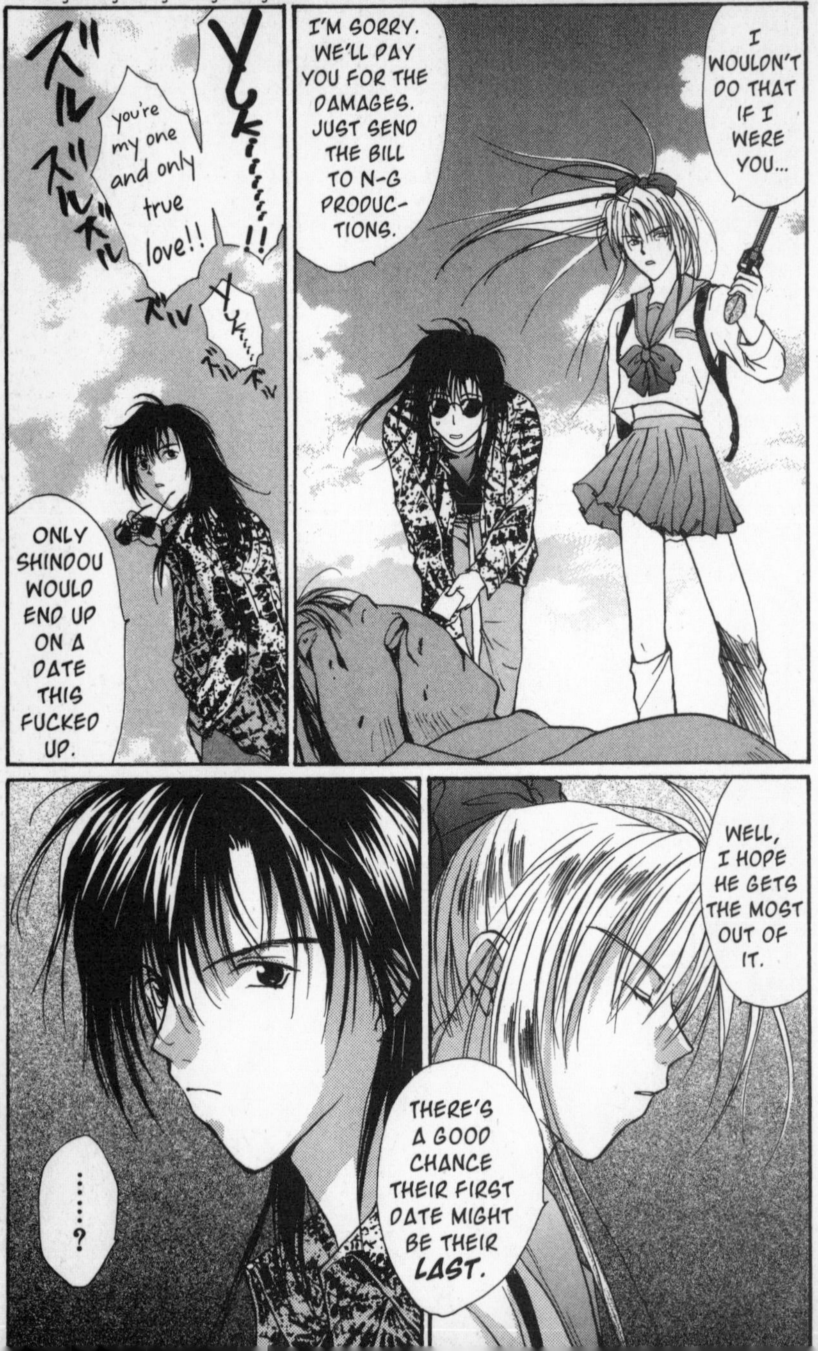
I WOULDN'T DO THAT IF I WERE YOU...
I'M SORRY. WE'LL PAY YOU FOR THE DAMAGES. JUST SEND THE BILL TO N-G PRODUCTIONS.
Yukiiiiii!!
you're my one and only true love!!
Yuki...
ONLY SHINDOU WOULD END UP ON A DATE THIS FUCKED UP.
WELL, I HOPE HE GETS THE MOST OUT OF IT.
THERE'S A GOOD CHANCE THEIR FIRST DATE MIGHT BE THEIR **LAST**.
......?

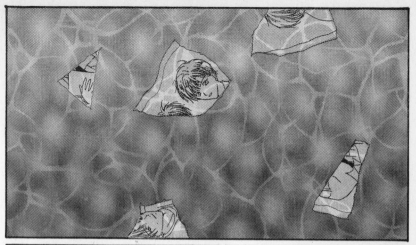

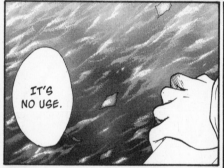

IT'S
NO USE.

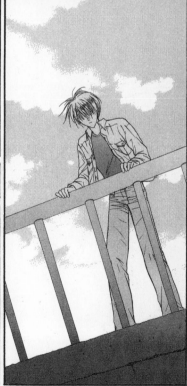

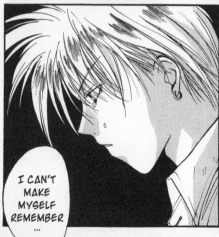

I CAN'T
MAKE
MYSELF
REMEMBER
...

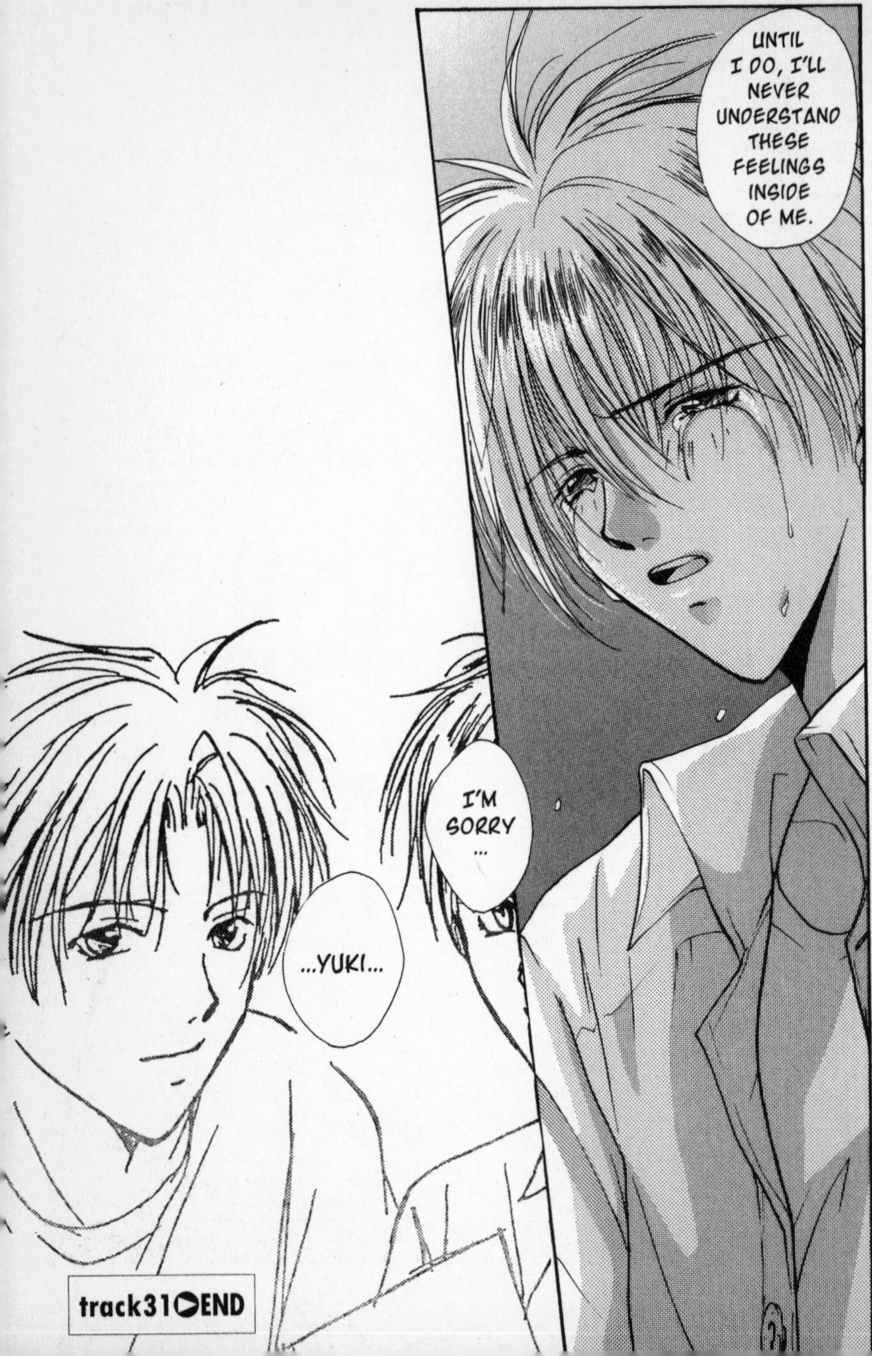
UNTIL I DO, I'LL NEVER UNDERSTAND THESE FEELINGS INSIDE OF ME.
I'M SORRY ...
...YUKI...
track31 END

Hello. For all of you out there who are starting to lose track of this convoluted story, I want to remind you that I am a member of Bad Luck.

Remember me now? I know I don't have much presence, but I don't want to ever hear you guys asking, "Hey, who's Suguru?" Come on, you can remember I'm the third member of Bad Luck, right?

Oh, forget it...

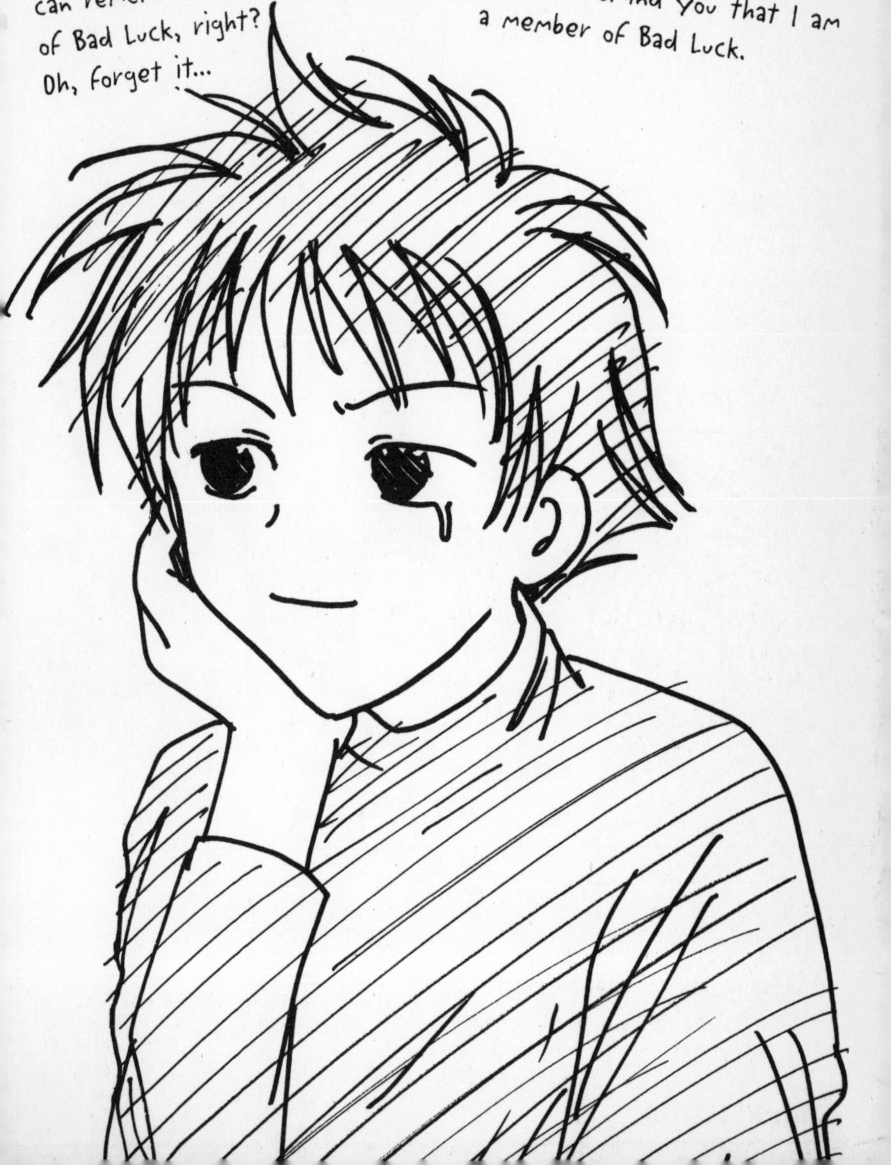

Does anybody remember me?

It's me, Taki. From that other band, ASK...

But at least I'm better off than K-chan... He could be in a lot of trouble!

Well, at least you're not me...

I probably won't be making any more appearances for the rest of my life...

What meaning does my existence even have anymore?

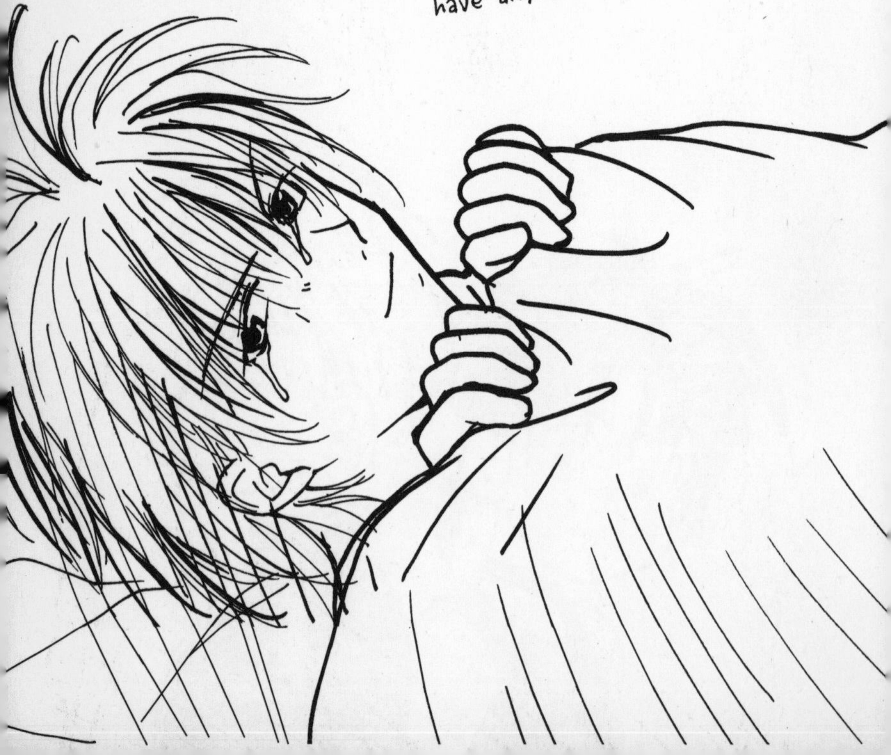

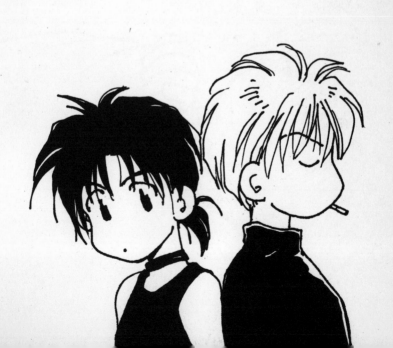

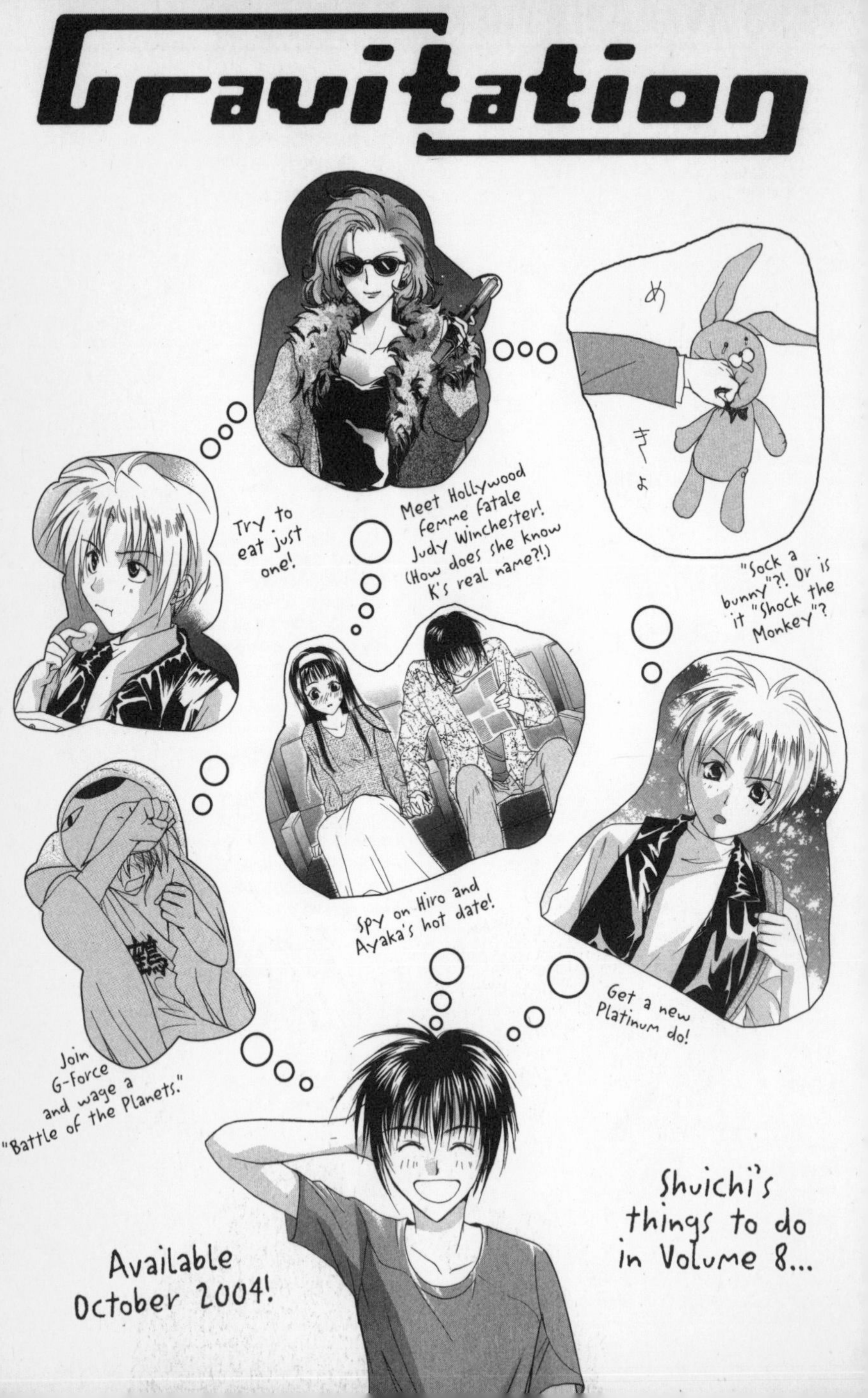

Gravitation
めきょ
Meet Hollywood femme fatale Judy Winchester! (How does she know K's real name?!)
Try to eat just one!
"Sock a bunny"?! Or is it "Shock the Monkey"?
Spy on Hiro and Ayaka's hot date!
Get a new Platinum do!
Join G-Force and wage a "Battle of the Planets."
Shuichi's things to do in Volume 8...
Available October 2004!

ALSO AVAILABLE FROM TOKYOPOP®

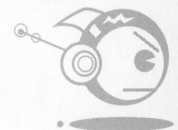

**You want it? We got it!
A full range of TOKYOPOP
products are available now at:
www.TOKYOPOP.com/shop**

05.26.04T

ALSO AVAILABLE FROM 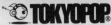 TOKYOPOP®

05.26.04T

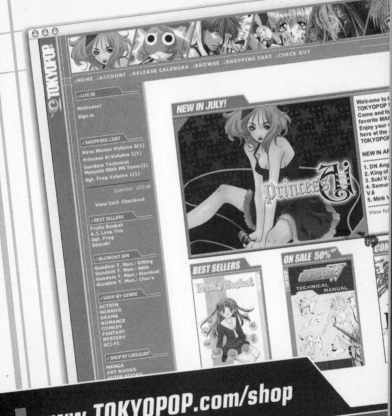

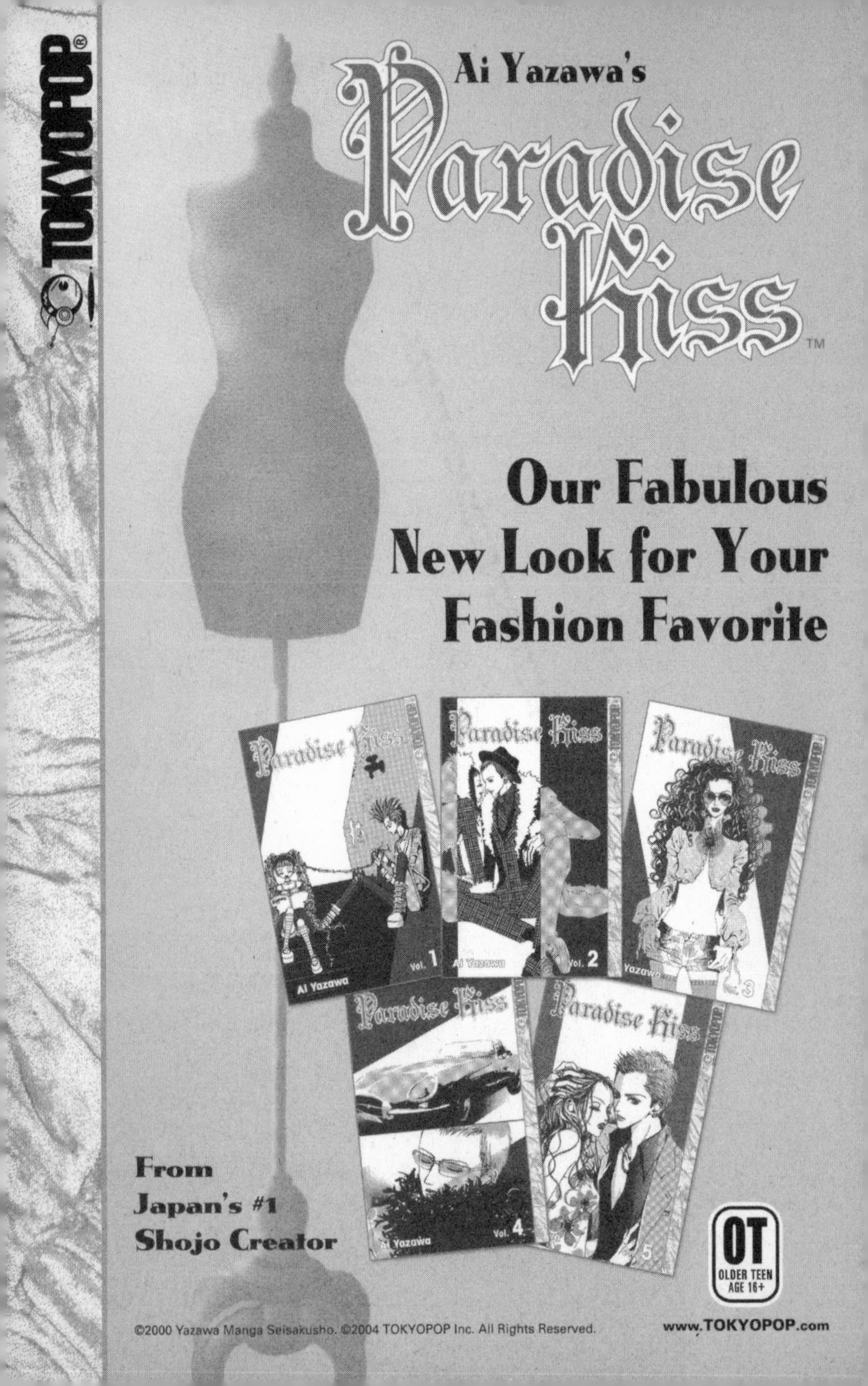
TOKYOPOP®
Ai Yazawa's
Paradise Kiss™
Our Fabulous New Look for Your Fashion Favorite
From Japan's #1 Shojo Creator
OT OLDER TEEN AGE 16+
©2000 Yazawa Manga Seisakusho. ©2004 TOKYOPOP Inc. All Rights Reserved.
www.TOKYOPOP.com

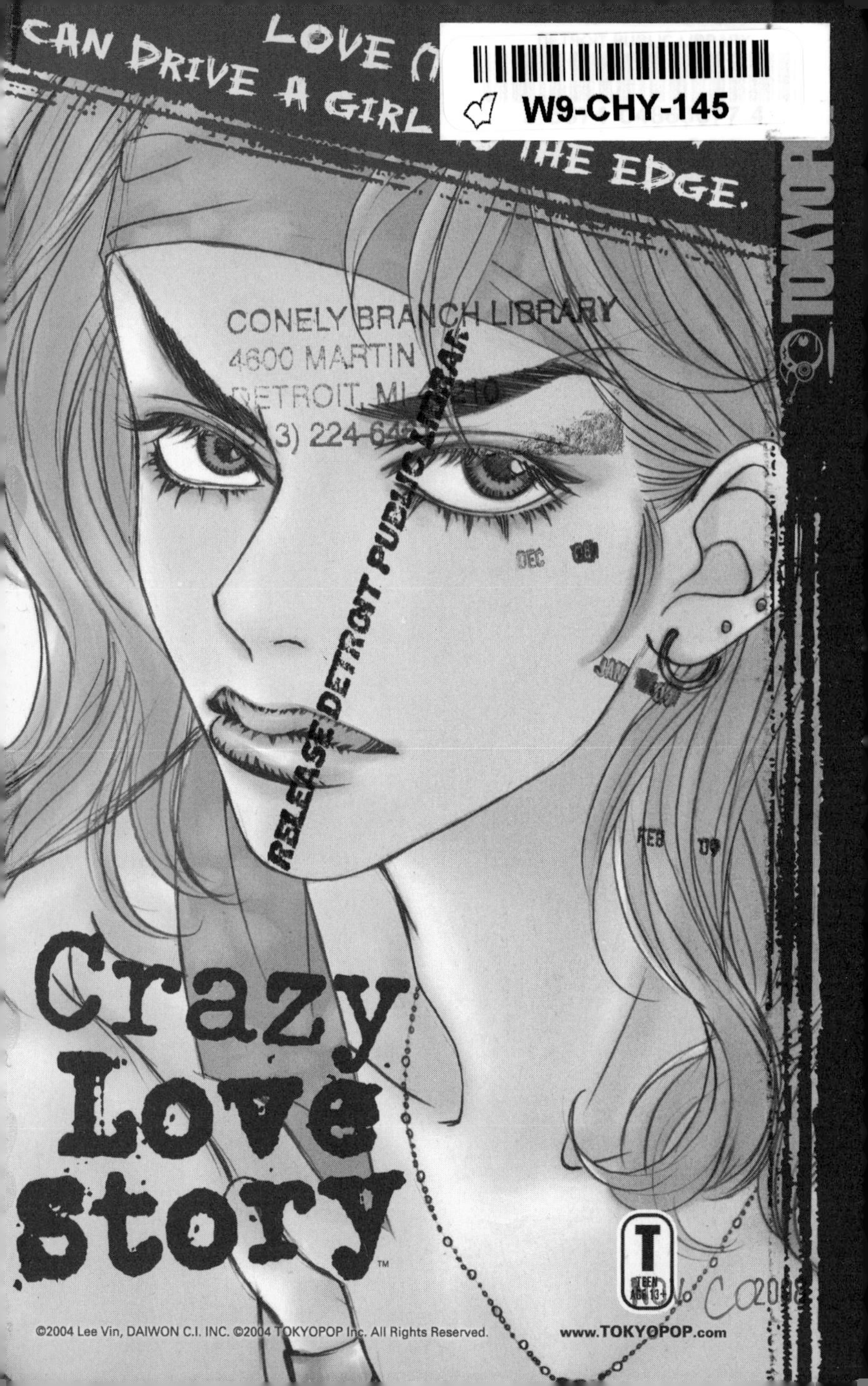
LOVE
CAN DRIVE A GIRL
THE EDGE.
TOKYOPOP
Crazy Love Story™
T TEEN AGE 13+

www.TOKYOPOP.com